QUEEN BY RIGHT

Anne Easter Smith

A Touchstone Book

PUBLISHED BY SIMON & SCHUSTER

NEW YORK   LONDON   TORONTO   SYDNEY

Touchstone
A Division of Simon & Schuster, Inc.
1230 Avenue of the Americas
New York, NY 10020

First Touchstone trade paperback edition May 2011

TOUCHSTONE and colophon are registered trademarks of Simon & Schuster, Inc.

For information about special discounts for bulk purchases, please contact Simon & Schuster Special Sales at 1-866-506-1949 or business@simonandschuster.com.

The Simon & Schuster Speakers Bureau can bring authors to your live event. For more information or to book an event contact the Simon & Schuster Speakers Bureau at 1-866-248-3049 or visit our website at www.simonspeakers.com.

Designed by Renata Di Biase

Manufactured in the United States of America

10 9 8 7 6 5 4 3 2 1

Library of Congress Cataloging-in-Publication Data

Easter Smith, Anne.
  Queen by right / Anne Easter Smith.
    p. cm.
  Includes bibliographical references.
    1. York, Cecily, Duchess of, 1415–1495—Fiction. 2. Richard, Duke of York, 1411–1460—Fiction. 3. York, House of—Fiction. 4. Great Britain—History—Lancaster and York, 1399–1485—Fiction. 5. Great Britain—History—Wars of the Roses, 1455–1485—Fiction. 6. Great Britain—History—House of York, 1461–1485—Fiction. I. Title.
PS3605.A84Q44 2011
813'.6—dc22

                                                                                    2011006027

ISBN 978-1-4165-5047-1
ISBN 978-1-4516-0822-9 (ebook)

For my sister Jill,
another courageous and fiercely loyal woman

Contents

Acknowledgments

Cecily's story from her childhood home, Raby Castle, to Westminster Abbey, where I take her at the end of this novel, could not have been told in such detail without the help of many people.

My thanks to Lord Barnard of Raby for his permission for a private tour of the castle by castle administrator Clare Owen and access to what is believed to have been Cecily's room in the keep. Clare also gave me copies of Neville genealogy charts, which were most helpful. Thanks also to Helen Duce, Ludlow Castle custodian, who pointed me to archival material that gave me further insight into the history of this beautiful ruin. Then, in Dublin, I was lucky enough to have the help of historian Jenny Papassotiriou at the castle. She not only showed me the remaining medieval parts of the castle but also gave me copies of maps surviving from the period. She told me that she was delighted to learn a part of the castle's history with which she had not been familiar before researching in the archives for my visit. Thanks, too, to Virginie Beaunier of the Bibliothèque Municipale de Rouen, who found me a medieval map of the city.

One of the delights of doing the research for this book was a reunion with one of my high school friends, Carol Rowntree, and her husband, Donald. My husband, Scott, and I spent several days at their home near Chester, and they drove us many a mile to Ludlow in Shropshire, to Snowdonia and Anglesey in North Wales. I cannot thank them enough, too, for sending me information from Fotheringhay, with the help of their grandson Benjamin, that I was unable to collect for myself. Another friend, Roxana Gendry, is owed love and gratitude for chauffeur duties in Yorkshire and Durham.

Once again I need to thank my friends with medical knowledge who never seem to mind obscure questions about childbirth: OB/gyn nurse practitioner Claire Denenberg, nurse midwife Maryann Long, and OB/gyn physician Jennifer Johnson.

I would be remiss not to again acknowledge my agent of nine years, Kirsten Manges, who believed in me from the start, and my editor, Trish Todd, who never fails to astound me with her insight and gentle patience. It can't be easy guiding this temperamental Brit!

To my husband, Scott—who *knows* it is not easy—all love and thanks.

The smartest thing I did during the writing of this book was to find an out-of-home office, for which I am in debt to my friend Mary Schaefer, who rented me a wonderfully bright, spacious room in her 1840s house two streets from my own. Finally, I must acknowledge my friend Cathy Thibedeau, who has dedicated so many hours of her precious retirement to being my "reader" throughout the writing process. A former chair of the English department at Hamilton-Wenham High School, MA, Cathy is used to deconstructing already written novels, so watching a novel take shape was a first for her—and a thrill, she told me, refusing all attempts to thank her profusely for her insights and corrections. Now my gratitude is in print for all to see!

Dramatis Personae

York family (see genealogy chart)

Richard Plantagenet, duke of York

Cecily Neville, duchess of York (see Neville family)

Anne, duchess of Exeter (Nan), *Richard and Cecily's oldest daughter*

Edward (Ned), earl of March, *Richard and Cecily's oldest son*

Edmund, earl of Rutland, *their second son*

Elizabeth (Bess), *their daughter*

Margaret (Meg), *their daughter*

George, duke of Clarence, *their son*

Richard (Dickon), later duke of Gloucester, *their son*

Isabel Plantagenet, countess of Essex and Eu, *Richard's older sister*

Henry Bourchier, earl of Essex and Eu, *Richard's brother-in-law*

Lancaster family (descended from John of Gaunt and Blanche of Lancaster)

Henry VI, *only child of Henry V* (see genealogy chart)

Catherine of Valois, *his mother*

Margaret of Anjou, *his wife*

Edouard of Lancaster, prince of Wales, *his only child*

John, duke of Bedford, *Henry's uncle and regent*

Anne of Burgundy, duchess of Bedford, *his first wife*

Jacquetta St. Pol, duchess of Bedford, *his second wife; later wife to* Richard Woodville

Humphrey, duke of Gloucester, *Henry's uncle, Bedford's brother and regent*

Jacqueline of Hainault, duchess of Gloucester, *Humphrey's first wife*

Eleanor Cobham, duchess of Gloucester, *Humphrey's second wife*

Henry Holland, duke of Exeter, *great-grandson of John of Gaunt, m. Anne of York*

Beaufort family **(descended from John of Gaunt and Katherine Swynford)**

Henry Beaufort, bishop of Winchester and cardinal of England, *their son* (see genealogy chart)

Joan Beaufort (see Neville), *their daughter*

John Beaufort, duke of Somerset, *their grandson*

Margaret Beaufort, *John's only child*

Edmund Beaufort, 2nd duke of Somerset, *John's brother*

Henry Beaufort, 3rd duke of Somerset, *Edmund's son*

Neville family **(see genealogy chart)**

Ralph Neville, earl of Westmorland, *Cecily's father*

Joan Beaufort, countess of Westmorland (see Beaufort), *Cecily's mother and Ralph's second wife*

Cecily Neville, duchess of York, *their youngest child*

Richard Neville, later earl of Salisbury, *Cecily's brother and oldest of the Beaufort Nevilles*

Alice Montagu, countess of Salisbury, *Richard Neville's wife*

Robert Neville, Bishop of Salisbury and Durham, *Cecily's brother*

William Neville, Lord Fauconberg, *Cecily's brother*

George Neville, Lord Latimer, *Cecily's brother*

Edward Neville, Lord Bergavenny, *Cecily's brother*

Katherine Neville, duchess of Norfolk, *Cecily's sister*

Anne Neville (Nan), countess of Stafford, *Cecily's sister*

Richard, earl of Warwick, *Salisbury's oldest son*

John, Lord Montagu, *Salisbury's third son*

George Neville, archbishop of York, chancellor of England, *Salisbury's fourth son*

Ralph Neville, 2nd earl of Westmorland, *grandson of Ralph's first marriage*

Woodville family

Richard Woodville, 1st Earl Rivers, *chamberlain to the duke of Bedford*

Jacquetta St. Pol (see **Lancaster**), *his wife*

Anthony Woodville, *his oldest son*

Elizabeth Woodville, *his oldest daughter*

Miscellaneous **(asterisk indicates fictional character)**

William de la Pole, duke of Suffolk, *councillor to Henry VI*

Humphrey Stafford, duke of Buckingham, *Anne Neville's husband and a king's councillor*

Anne of Caux, *the York family nursemaid*

*Rowena Gower, *Cecily's attendant*

*Constance LeMaitre, *Cecily's attendant and physician*

Gresilde Boyvile, *Cecily's attendant*

*Beatrice Metcalf, Cecily's *attendant and later Meg's*

*Piers Taggett, *Richard's falconer*

Sir William Oldhall, speaker of the House of Commons, *one of Richard of York's councillors*

Roger Ree, *one of Richard's ushers of the chamber*

Father Richard Lessey, *Richard's chaplain*

Sir Henry Heydon, *Cecily's steward*

John Tiptoft, earl of Worcester, *Henry VI's treasurer*

*Ann Herbert, *Meg's attendant*

Joan of Arc, *also known as Jeanne d'Arc, La Pucelle or The Maid*

Pierre Cauchon, bishop of Beauvais, *chief judge at the trial of Joan of Arc*

*Mathilda Draper, *midwife*

Plantagenet

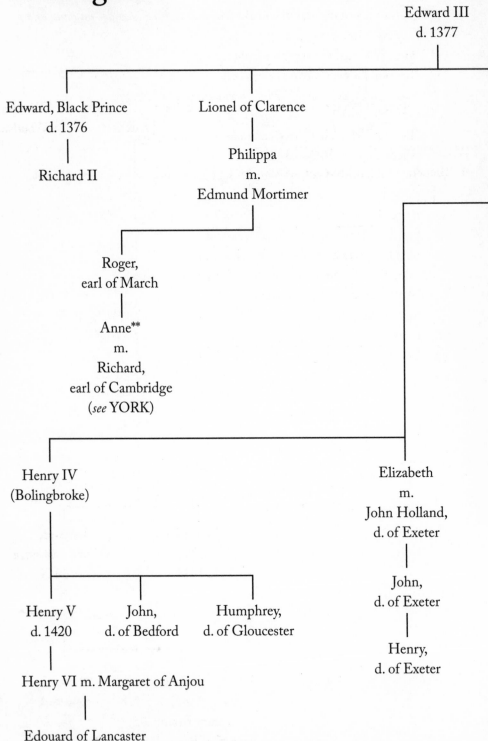

Edward III
d. 1377

Edward, Black Prince
d. 1376

Richard II

Lionel of Clarence

Philippa
m.
Edmund Mortimer

Roger,
earl of March

Anne**
m.
Richard,
earl of Cambridge
(*see* YORK)

Henry IV
(Bolingbroke)

Henry V
d. 1420

John,
d. of Bedford

Humphrey,
d. of Gloucester

Henry VI m. Margaret of Anjou

Edouard of Lancaster

Elizabeth
m.
John Holland,
d. of Exeter

John,
d. of Exeter

Henry,
d. of Exeter

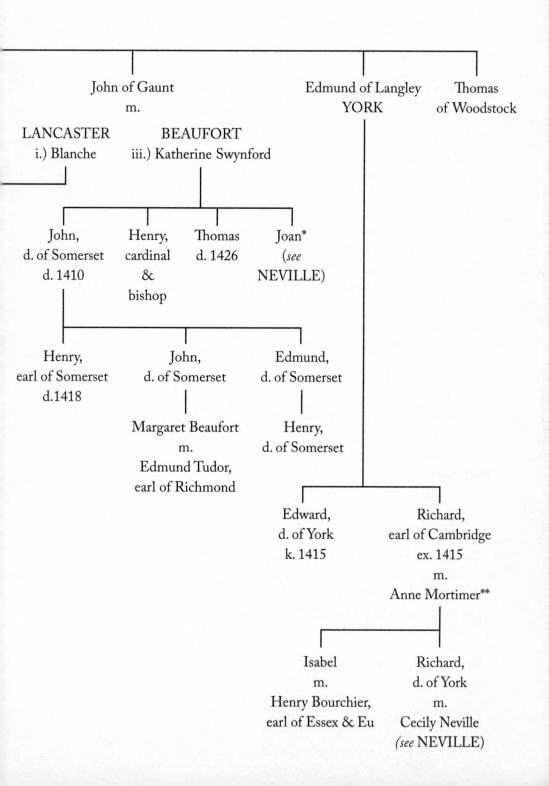

John of Gaunt
m.

Edmund of Langley
YORK

Thomas
of Woodstock

LANCASTER
i.) Blanche

BEAUFORT
iii.) Katherine Swynford

John,
d. of Somerset
d. 1410

Henry,
cardinal
&
bishop

Thomas
d. 1426

Joan*
(see
NEVILLE)

Henry,
earl of Somerset
d.1418

John,
d. of Somerset

Edmund,
d. of Somerset

Margaret Beaufort
m.
Edmund Tudor,
earl of Richmond

Henry,
d. of Somerset

Edward,
d. of York
k. 1415

Richard,
earl of Cambridge
ex. 1415
m.
Anne Mortimer**

Isabel
m.
Henry Bourchier,
earl of Essex & Eu

Richard,
d. of York
m.
Cecily Neville
(see NEVILLE)

Neville

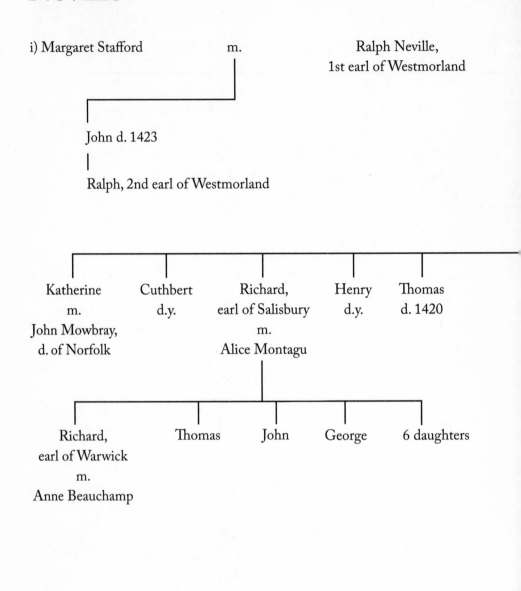

i) Margaret Stafford   m.   Ralph Neville,
1st earl of Westmorland

John d. 1423

Ralph, 2nd earl of Westmorland

Katherine	Cuthbert	Richard,	Henry	Thomas
m.	d.y.	earl of Salisbury	d.y.	d. 1420
John Mowbray,		m.		
d. of Norfolk		Alice Montagu		

Richard,	Thomas	John	George	6 daughters
earl of Warwick				
m.				
Anne Beauchamp				

Joan   Anne   Henry   Edward   Edmund   Elizabeth

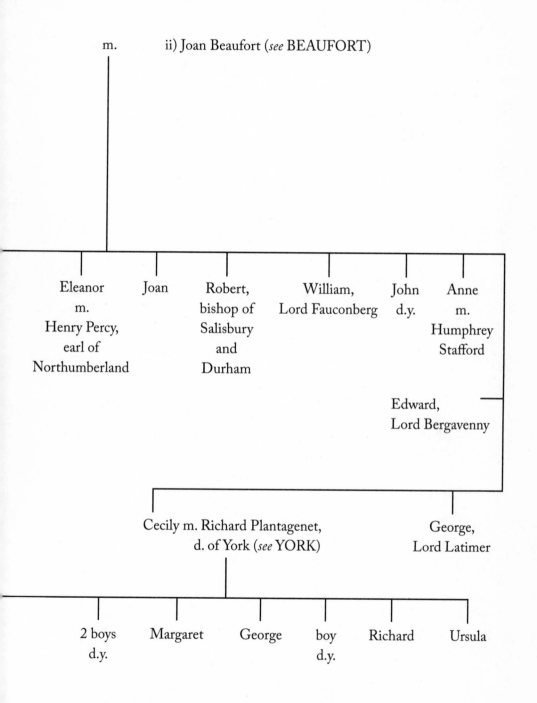

m.   ii) Joan Beaufort (*see* BEAUFORT)

| Eleanor m. Henry Percy, earl of Northumberland | Joan | Robert, bishop of Salisbury and Durham | William, Lord Fauconberg | John d.y. | Anne m. Humphrey Stafford |

Edward, Lord Bergavenny

Cecily m. Richard Plantagenet, d. of York (*see* YORK)   George, Lord Latimer

| 2 boys d.y. | Margaret | George | boy d.y. | Richard | Ursula |

d.y. = died young

North Sea

SCOTLAND

ENGLAND

WALES

IRELAND

Irish
Sea

Raby

Middleham

York

Wakefield

Chester

Beaumaris

Anglesey

Wigmore
Ludlow
Mortimer's
Cross

Shrewsbury

Leicester

Warwick

Worcester

Gloucester

Woodstock

Oxford

Windsor

Walsingham

Fotheringhay

Northampton

London

Greenwich

River Thames

Colchester

Canterbury

Drogheda

The
Pale

Dublin

A scream pierced Cecily's dreamless sleep. She came awake in an instant as every mother might upon hearing her child in distress.

"Margaret," she muttered into the gloom of her curtained comfort and then called to her attendant to light a taper. Her daughter's sobbing made Cecily bark a little more impatiently: "Hurry, Gresilde, Lady Margaret is having another of her nightmares." Hardly noticing the cold of the February night air, she pulled her velvet bedrobe around her, tucked her feet into matching slippers, and flung aside the heavy bed curtain. Dame Gresilde Boyvile held the taper aloft and lit her mistress's way along the draughty corridor to Margaret's chamber.

The servants shushing the distraught girl in the bed immediately fell to their knees in obeisance to the duchess of York as she swept in, her long sleeves trailing across the Turkey carpet.

"Margaret, my dearest child," Cecily clucked, seating herself on the feather mattress and gathering her fourteen-year-old daughter into her arms. "'Twas but a dream. Calm yourself, I beg of you." She thanked the ladies for their solicitation before drawing the curtains around her and Margaret.

"I dreamed of Micklegate again!" Margaret sobbed. "A terrible, ghastly dream. Why does it not go away?"

Margaret did not have to describe her nightmare. Her mother knew exactly what grisly scene the girl had conjured up.

Cecily's husband, Richard, and her sweet son, Edmund, had met their death five weeks ago at Wakefield, not far from Sandal Castle, where they and the Yorkist army were keeping Christmas. They had not expected the king's forces to come so soon nor to attack in the holy season, but it seems they were surprised, outnumbered, and Richard lost his life on the battlefield. Edmund, poor seventeen-year-old Edmund, Cecily grieved, was cut down in cold blood while attempting to flee the field. Lord Clifford had found him hiding under a bridge and, crying vengeance for his own father's death at St. Albans, had slit the lad's throat while his soldiers held him down. Her gentle, second-oldest son—a tall, good-looking charmer like his elder brother Edward—was no more, and his head, together with those of Richard and her favorite brother, the earl of Salisbury, were set atop the city of York's Micklegate on the orders of Queen Margaret. It was that hideous image that haunted young Meg night after night.

"Oh, why did they have to die?" Margaret sobbed.

Cecily tightened her hold on Margaret, inhaled the rosemary sweetness of the girl's long, fair hair, and squeezed her eyes tightly shut. She had not wanted to believe the messenger's tale of disaster. It had all happened so far away and, without physical proof, she could not grasp the reality of it. Her Richard beaten, killed, beheaded? Impossible. He had been part of her life since she was eight, and she could not imagine life without him.

"Oh, my dearest love . . ." she murmured.

She was unaware that she had spoken aloud until she felt Margaret gently pull away to study her. Cecily held herself erect, her face resuming the inscrutable expression she had learned to affect when in the public eye. But it was harder now after Wakefield.

"I am truly sorry, Mother," Margaret whispered. "I was only thinking of my own anguish." Her intelligent gray eyes searched her mother's still lovely face for forgiveness and some uncharacteristic show of emotion.

Cecily was moved and tears threatened. Don't cry, Cis, she told herself. This is not the time to cry. You must be strong for the children and strong for all the others who have given their service—and now their lives—to Richard's cause.

"You thought I had a heart of stone? Nay! I must tell you that my loss is so great I feel my heart is shattered in shards that pierce my skin and make me want to scream in agony." She pressed her hand to her heart and groaned. Then she raised her sad eyes to Margaret's face and took the girl's trembling chin between her fingers. "You know why your father and your brother died, my child. They died to right a wrong done to our house, and your father knew full well the price we all might have to pay. 'Tis the price all those born of royal blood are in danger of paying. You too must learn to sacrifice for your family whether it be the house of York or that of the man you wed. I will tell you now, Margaret, that as a woman born to a noble house, you may have your share of happiness, but you will also know great heartache, for we are at the mercy of our menfolk. We must accept God's will and bear it with dignity worthy of our name. Learn this now and well. You must learn how to bridle those feelings I see welling up in you every day. 'Tis what I have done these thirty years as duchess of York." She bent and kissed Margaret's face, smiling at her daughter's astonishment. "Aye, Meg, I have as passionate a nature as you"—she tapped her breast—"but I have kept it to myself in here . . . except when I was with your father." She chuckled. "I confess I was a handful when I was your age."

Meg smiled, and Cecily pulled her into her arms again. "You will always have solace in prayer, my dear. Our Blessed Mary, saint of all women, is always there to listen." The two women clung to each other for a few moments before they slid to their knees on the floor and made their supplications to the Virgin. Then Cecily tucked Meg into bed and padded wearily back to her own chamber.

Gresilde had thoughtfully placed a hot stone in the bed, and Cecily hugged its smooth warmth to her, curling herself into a ball and willing herself to sleep. Instead, the effort she had made for Margaret and the familiar position of childhood released all her pent-up despair, and her tears soon soaked her pillow. She put out her hand and felt the cold, empty place between the sheets where her husband should have been lying, and the ache in her heart became a violent pain. For a month she had maintained the demeanor of a noblewoman whose nickname—Proud Cis—had been well earned in the past few tumultuous years, but at that moment with her defenses finally breached, she allowed the flood of tears to spill unheeded and her thoughts to return to that golden autumn when Richard had come riding into her life.

She managed to smile then through her sniffling: Nay, she corrected herself, 'twas I who rode into his.

PART ONE

"A gracious lady!
What is her name, I thee pray tell me?"
"Dame Cecille, sir."
"Whose daughter was she?"
"Of the Earl of Westmorland, I trowe the youngest,
And yet grace fortuned her to be the highest."

FROM A FIFTEENTH-CENTURY BALLAD,
ANONYMOUS

1

Raby, Durham, 1423

"Faster, Father!" Cecily called to the rider on a handsome roan courser beside her. Her bright green liripipe streamed out behind her as father and daughter cantered across the parkland that surrounded Raby Castle and made for the forest beyond. A falconer and two grooms accompanied them along with several eager hunting dogs, held firmly in control by fewterers.

Ralph Neville, earl of Westmorland and sixth Baron Raby, grinned as he watched his youngest daughter lean over her horse's neck and urge the beast into a full gallop. The sight of her in the saddle never failed to give him pride; she was only eight years old and yet she could ride better than either of his younger sons, perhaps because he had taken it upon himself to teach her. "Spare the birch and spoil the child," his wife, Joan Beaufort, had recently chided him, but Ralph had merely chuckled, twitched his drooping moustache and told her: "My dear lady, I have sired more than a score of children in my sixty years, and my hair has been rendered gray by many of them. I beg you to allow me in my dotage to indulge myself as a father with this enchanting child of ours. I fear you will bear me no more, and so I shall do as I please with Cecily." And with that, he had bent over and given her such a smacking kiss on her upturned mouth that Joan did not have the heart to press the matter further.

Instead, she stroked his weathered cheek, saying, "You are incorrigible, my lord," and then straightened her cumbersome headdress.

Digging her heels into the horse's flanks and letting it have its head, Cecily willed her mount to cover the ground as if being chased by a demon. Ralph had taught her to ride like a man, defying all convention and amusing the many grooms who peopled the earl's ample stables. The first time Cecily had appeared in what looked like peasant braies, Joan, the youngest child of the great prince John of Gaunt, had thrown up her hands in horror and quoted:

" 'A woman shall not wear that which pertaineth unto a man, neither shall a man put on a woman's garment: for all that do so are abomination unto the Lord thy God.' Do you not remember your scriptures, my lord? Have you no fear for Cecily's immortal soul?"

Cecily had looked from one parent to the other, dismay written on her face, but Ralph had dismissed his wife's objection, claiming that the verse did not apply to children. He picked up his daughter and carried her through the vaulted passageway to the stables hard by the Clifford Tower. Trusting her father in everything, Cecily had pushed a tiny fear to the back of her mind, but she had asked God's forgiveness that night—and every time she rode out in her braies—nonetheless.

The day was crisp, and the leaves had turned russet and gold on the huge oaks, ash, and elms that dotted the park and canopied the forest. Just before crossing the Staindrop road to continue into the woods, they saw a small group of riders trotting up from the village toward them. Ralph reined in his horse when he recognized the falcon and fetterlock badge of the lead outrider and called out a warning to Cecily that he was stopping. But her horse had other ideas, and instead of obeying her tug at the reins, it wheeled around and began to head for the horsemen. Using all her strength, she finally succeeded in reining it in but not before it reared up, pawed the air, and came to a standstill a bare three feet from a youth astride a palfrey.

"Whoa, Tansy!" Cecily cried sternly enough, but then reached down to stroke and soothe the horse's neck. "Forgive me, sir," she addressed the astonished boy with the confidence of one who knew her place as an earl's daughter. "Something must have alarmed her. I trust she did not frighten you."

"Cecily, apologize to our guests at once!" Ralph's admonition as he rode up to join them made her hang her head. "This is not the most comfortable of meetings, my lord duke," he said, addressing the youth with a slight bow, and, leaning out of his saddle, he took hold of Cecily's rein. "I must beg your indulgence. This is my youngest unmarried, the lady Cecily Neville, who is usually in more control of her mount. You must think we are naught but ill-mannered clodhoppers hereabouts." He grinned down at the young man from his large roan.

But twelve-year-old Richard Plantagenet had forgotten about manners for a second, and he stared at the small figure he had taken for a boy. Cecily stared right back. When Ralph chuckled, Richard made a hasty bow. "My lord of Westmorland, I am at your service."

Ralph turned to the older man in charge of the party. "Sir Robert, you are right welcome to Raby." He maneuvered his horse so that he was beside Waterton, leaving Richard and Cecily to fall in behind them. "You have made good time."

"Lady Cecily, I give you God's greeting," Richard murmured politely by way of an introduction, and then he remembered to answer her. "I was not afraid just now, in truth. You ride well—for your age." He almost said "for a girl" but something in the toss of her head made him think better of it. She rode up to join her father.

"Shall we not hunt today, Father?" she asked quietly, so that Waterton could not hear her. "You promised."

Ralph's eyebrows snapped together. "Certes, we shall not hunt, Daughter. We have guests. Sir Robert Waterton and I have business to attend to in the matter of my wardship of Lord Richard."

"Wardship? Another one! Why have you not told me of this, Father?" a disappointed Cecily muttered to him, as the little cavalcade trotted back toward the castle. "Are we all to share you and Mother with him as well as the others?"

"Your mother will explain, Cecily. But for now, I pray you, be charitable," he said sternly. "'Tis certain your brothers will make Lord Richard more welcome, at least. He was orphaned by the time he was four and has no family to speak of, except for a sister."

"Oh," Cecily murmured. Turning around, she looked with pity at the slight rider, his over-large bonnet almost covering his slate-gray eyes. "How sad." With nine brothers and sisters and several half siblings, she could not conceive of being so alone. She wondered where his sister had been sent and murmured a prayer heavenward for the girl to be as fortunate as Richard in her enforced placement at a stranger's hearth.

Cecily saw that Richard was impressed by the many crenellated towers that graced Raby Castle. The towering stone barbican's portcullis was unneeded in this peaceful corner of England. Raby was not on the major road to the border with Scotland, unlike the earl's principal seat of Brancepeth a dozen miles away.

Cecily was too young to remember the only armed men to be seen at Raby during her lifetime—other than her father's guard—those who had left the castle to fight with Henry of Monmouth in France. She had been born just before that young king's thrilling victory at Agincourt. Who could have guessed that only seven years later, in his mid-thirties, the fifth King

Henry—affectionately dubbed Good King Harry by his subjects—would be dead of the bloody flux? He had only just done his duty by his royal French bride, Catherine. He had sired an heir nine months before his death, which had "set the cat among the pigeons," Cecily had heard her father say. A child king would mean a regent and in-fighting, Ralph had explained, "and who will now maintain our renewed hold on France?"

"Do you always dress that way?" Richard said to Cecily, catching up with her as they rode through the gatehouse and into the busy outer bailey. "I thought you were a boy. I have not seen a girl in man's garb before." Cecily bristled as he continued, "I thought 'twas against God's laws." He did not wait for an answer but threaded his way deftly through the throng of yeomen, stewards, grooms, and squires going about their tasks and then dismounted with practiced ease.

Cecily frowned, reminded of her mother's remark. But she loved the freedom the braies gave her, and she had often secretly wished she had been born a boy. She called out in defiance to the young duke, "Have no fear, my lord. You will see me in a gown within the hour." As if he were still in doubt, she removed her chaperon to show off her golden hair. Once freed, it spilled over her shoulders and down her back. The transformation made him smile for the first time, and Cecily liked the way his eyes crinkled up. She decided she might make friends with him after all.

"Shall I see you at supper, my lord?" Cecily asked, and seeing Richard nod, she skipped off up the newel stair to her own chamber high in the keep.

CECILY DID NOT see Richard again for a week, and when she did bump into him on her way to the stables, he was engaged in swordplay with her thirteen-year-old brother, George. Judging from the laughter and good-natured bantering from the other young would-be squires in the care of the experienced master of henchmen, John Beckwith, Richard was fitting in without difficulty. George was a formidable opponent, but it was clear that Richard had already received good instruction in the use of the small stick sword and was gaining ground despite his slighter stature. Cecily waved as Richard sprang out of the way of George's lunge, and he was momentarily distracted, allowing George to thrust his wooden weapon right at the heart.

"Aha!" George mocked, encouraging the others to tease the embarrassed Richard. "I see you already have an eye for a pretty girl, Dickon!" He swung around to face his sister. "Have a care, Cis. Doing what you did could be the death of a man one day," he admonished her.

Cecily's smile faded into a pout. She hated George scolding her, which wasn't very often, as he had adored his baby sister from the day she was born. He was her favorite brother, and she strove to win his approval.

"A pox on you, George!" she retorted, close to tears. Avoiding Richard's gaze, she turned toward the passageway that led to the stable yard.

Feeling sorry for her, Richard said loudly, "I should thank your sister if I were you, George. She saved you from a certain drubbing!" The other youths roared with laughter, and it was George's turn to redden.

Cecily's heart warmed to this newcomer, and she walked off with her head held high.

SEATED ON A footstool near her mother, Cecily watched intently as Joan showed her an intricate embroidery stitch on a piece of linen covered with Cecily's previous attempts to learn the skill. She was proud that her mother thought she was old enough to move from the basic and boring chain stitch into making knots and loops that would one day form intricate designs.

On the other side of Joan sat Cecily's twelve-year-old sister Anne, her pale blue eyes alternately lowered to her sewing and watching Cecily receive all the attention from their mother. She appeared to be a model child—never speaking out of turn, never causing her nurse or tutor trouble, and always seeking the approbation of her elders—but once out of adult view, Anne guarded a jealous heart and a spiteful tongue, and she resented her father's favoring of Cecily. When Cecily found a toad in their shared bed a few years ago, she knew it was Anne who had put it there; when her favorite bonnet went missing, she knew Anne was responsible but said nothing—not even when Anne pretended to come upon it unawares folded inside Cecily's second-best gown and was praised for her diligence. The two sisters dutifully said their nightly prayers side by side, but when the nurse had tucked them in and snuffed out the candle, there were no shared giggles or secrets. Each turned on her side and went to sleep.

Earlier that summer, when Anne was contracted in marriage by proxy to Humphrey, earl of Stafford, Cecily wanted to ply her sister with questions, but Anne had returned from the civil ceremony in her father's privy chamber and snapped at her sister, "I am married, 'tis all, Cis. Nothing has changed. All I know of him is that he is twenty-one and has been an earl since he was one. I do not even know what he looks like." To hide her bitterness, the older girl had knelt down to fondle a little Italian greyhound.

The countess finished instructing Cecily in the intricacies of a blanket stitch and, turning to Anne, asked her to demonstrate her progress on the psaltery. Anne gladly relinquished her embroidery and ran across the room to where one of Joan's ladies was quietly plucking the instrument. Making certain her mother was watching her, Anne pushed her floor-length sleeves out of the way, steadied the boxlike instrument on her knees, and began to play. Joan smiled encouragingly as Anne painstakingly struggled through the song.

Joan waited until her daughter was well along before nodding to her ladies to continue their quiet conversation and then turned back to Cecily. The maternal gesture was not lost on Cecily, and she marveled at how her mother made each one of her children feel special. And there are so many of us, Cecily grinned to herself. 'Tis a miracle she even remembers all our names. I shall have but two children, she decided then and there. A boy first, who will be a big brother to my little girl—just like George and me.

"Are you listening to me, Cecily?" Joan's voice interrupted her thoughts. She blinked up at her mother. With a heart-shaped face and complexion of a pink-tipped briar rose, a generous mouth, and a pair of blue eyes that could melt the stoniest of hearts, it did not surprise Joan that the villagers in Staindrop had begun calling Cecily their Rose of Raby. Ralph said his daughter's eyes reminded him of cornflowers. Bishop Henry Beaufort, Joan's brother, thought of a jay's feather. But Joan knew they were the color of her own father's eyes—of the sky above his beloved Aquitaine—and she smiled now as Cecily lowered her head.

"Aye, my lady," Cecily acquiesced sheepishly, "I am now."

"Your father wishes me to talk to you of your future, of marriage, my dear," Joan began, and then sighed. All her daughters were either promised in marriage already or were even in a second one, but that was what was expected of girls of noble rank. Having been born a bastard, Joan had escaped early wedlock and had been respectably married to a knight at the grand old age of seventeen. But by the time he died, her royal father's liaison with his mistress, Katherine Swynford, had been solemnized in marriage and his Beaufort bastards decreed legitimate. Then Joan was fit for an earl, and a year later she was married to Ralph, widower of Margaret Stafford and already the father of several children.

"Marriage?" Cecily repeated abruptly and searched her mother's lined face. "But I thought I must be twelve before I am married. Anne said . . ."

"Anne is quite right, Cecily. Twelve is the legal age for marriage, but you can be promised at any age," Joan told her.

"How old were you when you were betrothed, Mother? Older than eight, I'll be bound!" Cecily immediately regretted her outburst. The countess's expression hardened, and she gave a quick look around the room to make sure no one else had heard her daughter's insolent remark.

"You forget yourself, Cecily," Joan scolded quietly. "Your father may indulge you, but it is left to me to teach you manners, and not even he will tolerate disrespect, I assure you. Apologize at once and interrupt me no further." She chose not to inform her wayward daughter that in fact she had been twelve when her father had given her in marriage to Sir Robert Ferrers.

A tear rolled down Cecily's cheek, but she swiftly wiped it away and whispered an apology. In moments like these, it was not hard to remember that Joan was one of the children, surnamed Beaufort, of John of Gaunt and thus half sister to King Henry the Fourth. As mistress of the one hundred and fifty members of the Raby household, she was revered for her royal blood and equally regal bearing, but it was the care and concern she showed her servants that made them more devoted. Joan had learned this from her mother, who had begun in Gaunt's household as a servant—governess to his earlier children. Woe betide, however, anyone who forgot his place at Raby; it was said Joan Beaufort could wither with a look as well as her father ever had.

Seeing Cecily so contrite, Joan reached out and patted her hand. "There is hope, Cecily. I do not think you will be displeased with your father's choice, and aye, you must wait until you are twelve before you are officially wed."

Forgetting her dismay, Cecily's curiosity was piqued enough for her to ask, "Who is he, Mother?"

"A young man with whom you are already acquainted. And this young man will make you, as his wife, the noblest lady in the kingdom—after her grace, the King's mother." Joan's eyes twinkled at Cecily's open-mouthed stare. "Can you guess?"

But eight-year-old Cecily was not yet well versed in England's nobility, other than understanding how grand her eldest sister, Katherine, was as duchess of Norfolk. All she knew was that her mother and father were the king and queen of her little world at Raby. She shook her head. "Nay, Mother, I cannot guess."

"His grace, the duke of York, Richard Plantagenet, your father's ward," Joan told her triumphantly. "'Tis a high honor indeed, and one day you will outrank us all, Cecily. Now, what do you have to say for yourself?"

Richard's gray eyes, wiry body, and lopsided smile leaped into Cecily's mind, and she giggled. "But he's not a man! He's not a husband," she said, putting her hand over her mouth to hide her merriment. "He's just a boy. How can he be a duke? I thought dukes went off to France to fight."

Joan had to laugh. At least the child was not upset. Joan had been elated by Ralph's plan to secure Richard's marriage contract from the Crown along with the wardship, and the king's council had agreed. "As the others of my daughters are already pledged, Richard is the perfect match for my sweet Cecily," Ralph had told Joan. "There are only four years between them, and I do believe they like each other already." Joan had agreed and sent a prayer of thanks to St. Monica for her intercession in this affair. "Richard will be with us for several more years, ample time for them even to grow to love each other. They are fortunate."

"Is he not too young to be a duke?" Cecily was asking her now, and Joan brought her focus back to her daughter. "What happened to his father?"

Joan explained that Richard's father had rebelled against the late King Harry just before Agincourt and the king had executed him for treason. "This made our Richard earl of Cambridge. And, God is merciful, the king did not attaint him with his father, because he was only a boy," Joan said. "And when Richard's uncle, the childless duke of York, was killed a few weeks later at Agincourt, Richard inherited that title too. Are you following me?"

Cecily nodded, though Joan had lost her at the execution of Richard's father. She understood that to have been executed by the king, the man must have plotted against him. Her father had told her that the word for a person who did that was "traitor." And then the word "attainted" would be whispered every time the traitor was mentioned. As yet, Cecily had not grasped the significance of that second word, but as it sounded as though it meant rotten or having a bad smell, she would wrinkle her nose every time she heard it. How humiliating for poor Richard, she thought. 'Twas a wonder he could hold his head high or even sleep at night, knowing his father had been such a bad man.

A new question occurred to Cecily. Sensing her mother was in a talkative mood, she made bold to ask, "Does Richard know we are to be married? It will make a difference how I speak to him the next time I see him, I suppose. Do I call him 'dearest lord,' as you call Father?"

Joan smiled, wondering what else the little minx had observed about her relationship with Ralph. "Nay, Cecily. You must truly be wedded and . . ." She was about to say "bedded" when she remembered to whom she was speaking.

"And know your husband well before you may call him anything but my lord, my lord husband, or even your grace, the last because Richard is a duke."

"How silly!" Cecily exclaimed. "I cannot even call him by his first name? Or as George does, Dickon?"

Joan sighed, suddenly weary of Cecily's questions. Mercifully, Anne's one-tune repertoire had ended, and she was seeking Joan's praise. Joan put her finger to Cecily's lips and frowned a halt to the child's inquisitiveness.

"That was well done, Anne," Joan called across the room. "Do you not agree, ladies?" And she led them all in polite applause.

"YOUR GRACE," CECILY intoned solemnly, curtseying, when Richard approached her with his hand outstretched, asking for a dance. His straight eyebrows shot up, almost disappearing into his fringe. Richard wore his dark-chestnut hair in the old way, the way his first guardian, Sir Robert, did. It looked as though a bowl had been placed on his head and all hair visible below it had been shaved off. Cecily did not care for it and was glad to hear one of her mother's ladies say that it was unfashionable; she made up her mind that as soon as they were married, she would demand that he grow it.

"Your grace?" Richard quizzed, taking her hand and leading her out onto the floor for a carol dance. Several couples waiting for a full complement of dancers stood in a circle, tapping their feet to the jaunty tune played by the musicians in the gallery. "Why so formal? Have I done something to displease you, *Lady* Cecily."

Cecily tossed her head, happy that her heart-shaped headdress with its scalloped veil had been anchored so well, and she tried to sound grown up. "'Tis customary for a wife to call her husband 'your grace' if he be a duke," she said. "My lady mother told me so."

Richard grinned. "But we are not yet married, Cis. I pray you, call me Dickon like everyone else."

"As you will," Cecily answered merrily. "A pox on 'your grace.'"

"I would not say that in front of your mother," Richard teased. "'Tis not ladylike." More earnestly, he added, "So you know the way of things between us. What think you of the arrangement? I am well disposed to it. Are you?"

"Aye, I suppose I am. I like you, in truth. But it will not happen for a long, long time, will it?" Now that she was face to face with him, the thought that she would spend her whole life with this person suddenly alarmed her. Her fingers trembled in his, and he squeezed them to give her courage.

"Aye, we shall not be wed for a long time to come, sweet Cecily. Never fear."

Cecily, trying to show nonchalance, shrugged and lowered her eyes, as was customary. "I am not afraid," she murmured to her embroidered silk slippers, and as if to prove it, she suddenly said, "I am sorry about your father."

She felt Richard's fingers tense for a second. His tone was icy as he told her, "I do not remember him. He was a traitor to our great King Harry and thus deserved to die."

Cecily gasped. "But he was your father . . ." she trailed off, not understanding this coldness. Surely everyone loves their parents, she thought.

They began to dance, Cecily's dagged satin sleeves reaching the floor even when her arms were lifted, and while Richard spent most of the carol trying not to trip on them, Cecily avoided stepping on his long, pointed shoes. He glanced at her from time to time, trying to imagine what she might look like as a woman. She was taller than most boys of her age, not much smaller than he was, but he knew he had many years of growing yet to do. He looked forward to the time when his voice would deepen and he would be scraping his face.

He thought she was pretty but in a childlike way. George had told him that Katherine, the eldest, was the most beautiful of the sisters. "Eleanor is fair, too, but short and plump—a bit like Mother," he had whispered behind his hand. Somewhere in the middle of the siblings was Joan, a novice at an abbey, who had the unkind nickname Plain Jane. And then there was solemn Anne, who unnerved him with her stares. In truth, Richard was contented with the choice Lord Ralph had made, though Cecily was a little more forward a female than he was used to.

Richard's short, fur-trimmed tunic brushed Cecily's swirling blue and white skirts as they lightly touched hands to turn in a series of circles. Even though Cecily's eyes were firmly glued to the floor, as were the eyes of all the dancing ladies, she sensed the spectators were watching them. Usually she would have basked in the attention, but this time she found it disconcerting. She wondered what life with Richard would bring her—a fine stable and splendid wardrobe, she expected, and prayed she would not have to give up her beloved hunting. But she also resolved to pay more heed to her mother's daily routine so that she would be ready to be a duchess when the time came.

"A penny for your thoughts, Cis," Richard murmured, when a movement allowed them a few words. "You are looking very serious."

"I was just wondering what time Father was going hunting tomorrow, 'tis all," Cecily lied, hoping her hot cheeks were well hidden by her lowered head. "He has promised I can go with you all to hunt the white hind Master Laidlaw claims runs with a herd at the foot of Cockfield Fell."

"Aye, George and I are determined to be the ones to find it," Richard enthused, "although Lord Ralph fears it is naught but a mystical beast dreamed up by Laidlaw after too much wine. He seems to be the only one to have seen it."

The hornpipe and tabor players ended the carol with a slow crescendo, and the dancers saluted their partners with reverences as the last droned note of the symphonie faded away. But before they were able to leave the floor, they were caught up in a whirlwind of cartwheeling tumblers. They preceded a troupe of mummers enthusiastically shaking bellsticks and shooing the company back to their benches to watch an enactment of the story of St. George and the dragon.

Soon Cecily's eyelids began to droop, and the ever-watchful Joan sent the girls' attendants to escort them up to bed. For once Cecily was too tired to protest. She merely curtsied to her parents on the dais and then climbed to her quarters at the top of the keep. The girls were shivering by the time they reached the room, but a servant stoked the fire, and the red-and-green-painted chamber was soon warm enough for them to be undressed and readied for bed by Nurse Margery and Rowena Gower, a fourteen-year-old gently born local girl.

"Will you hunt with us tomorrow, Nan?" Cecily asked, although she knew full well what Anne would reply. "Dickon and George are determined to find the white hind, but I hope Father finds it first—or me. I want to find it."

Anne made a face and unpinned her long, mouse-brown hair. "How many times must I tell you how much I dislike hunting, Cis? Besides, 'tis likely to snow tomorrow, and I shall stay in where it is warm."

Cecily sighed and climbed into bed, watching her sister put on her nightcap.

"Now, then, my ladies, go to sleep, and God give you a good night," Margery said sternly as she drew the tester curtains around the bed, leaving the sisters in the dark.

"How do you like Richard, Cis?" Anne whispered to the drowsy Cecily, whose eyes then opened at the unaccustomed overture. "I confess I like him very much, and I wish 'twas I he must wed."

Cecily was now wide-eyed. "You do?" she exclaimed, and turned to her sister. "Why?"

"I think he is handsome, and he is a great deal richer than Humphrey,"

Anne answered. "If only Father had waited a few months before betrothing me, then I might have been the daughter he chose for Richard."

"Oh, Anne," Cecily whispered, patting the shoulder that was turned from her. "I am sorry for you if you are unhappy. How do you know that Humphrey isn't twice as handsome as Dickon? And he is a Stafford, after all, and he must be rich, too."

"Dickon likes me, I know he does," came Anne's petulant voice. "And besides, he is the duke of York. Humphrey is but an earl." She squeezed out a tear and sniffed. "You are naught but a child to him."

Irritated, Cecily withdrew her hand: "I am not a child! Besides, we have already talked about being wed. He likes me, too, you know."

"Aye, but, in truth, I think he *loves* me," Anne replied miserably.

"Like? Love? What is the difference?" Cecily shrugged. "You are pledged, you are wed, you have children, and you have a pleasant time together. What more is there to marriage, pray?"

Anne could not suppress a giggle. "You are only eight, Cis, and not near to being a woman, as I am. Love is when your heart aches for someone so much that you think you will swoon. Love is when you want to be with him, when you dream about him night and day. Can you not see?"

Cecily did not see, but she was not about to admit it. "I love Mother and Father—and I love George—but I do not dream about them night and day," she reasoned. "Perhaps you are ailing and need a physic." She was disconcerted to hear another sniff and snuggled into Anne's back. "What can I do, Nan? We must both do what Father tells us—and you are already betrothed. We cannot exchange husbands—or can we?"

"Oh, go to sleep. You just don't understand," the unhappy Anne complained, leaving Cecily more puzzled than before.

ANNE HAD BEEN right about the weather. When the cock crowed the next day and the pale Christmas sun crept over Keverstone Bank, it sparkled on the light covering of snow that had turned the frozen, furrowed fields into a completely new and tranquil landscape. After breaking their fast and attending Mass, the hunters hurried down the stairs from the different towers of the castle and converged on the marshalsea, where horses and dogs were snorting clouds of hot breath into the cold air.

Cecily loved days like this. It was as though God wanted to cover the drabness of brown November by dazzling His people with an immaculate, magical mantle in December. She was glad of her two pairs of stockings under her warmest gown today, and she called for a groom to help her onto Tansy's back and keep her leather ankle boots from getting too wet. For once she was content to be riding sidesaddle along with the other ladies in the party, with her heavy woolen gown tucked cozily around her legs. Her hooded, fur-lined cloak warmed her upper body and head, so that when the group trotted through the gatehouse and north toward Cockfield, she forgot about the frigid air and instead reveled in the excitement of the hunt: the running hounds yelping in the distance, picking up the scent of their prey, and the colorful cavalcade of riders jostling for position to ride in hot pursuit.

George called to her from a courser in the midst of his fellow henchmen, and she waved back gaily. Richard was there too, his chin jutting forward in concentration as he kept his mount in check. Cecily knew that she would have to hold back and ride like a lady today—a thought that chafed her—but when her mother chose to ride beside her, Cecily's heart sang. 'Twas an honor indeed to hunt with the countess, she knew, and so she sat her horse proudly.

There were more than forty riders that day, and some of the fewterers were having difficulty restraining their greyhound charges from slipping the leash. When a horn sounded in the middle of the forest ahead, Earl Ralph gave a whoop and a tally-ho and urged his horse into a fast canter. As she watched all the males in the group follow suit, it was all Cecily could do not to dig her heels into Tansy's flanks and join them.

Joan eyed her with amusement. "Good girl, Cecily," she said, taking a hand from her fur muff, pushing a graying curl out of her eyes, and tucking it back under her felt chaperon. "You must learn when you may let down your hair and when you may not. 'Tis not easy being a lady, my dear, and I fear that you, of all my daughters, may have the most trouble with it. Kat was ungovernable when she was a child, but she grew out of it quickly. Your father, I am afraid, encourages you." She watched her husband's saffron cloak float out behind him as he entered the forest, and she smiled. "He is sixty-one, and yet still he rides like a young knight," she said half to herself. "He swears 'tis the fresh, cold air of the north that keeps him healthy." Seeing that Cecily was still listening, she added: "For my part, I prefer the warmer London air—though the smell of that city can be more than unpleasant, in truth."

"When shall I go to London, Mother?" Cecily asked, enjoying the unexpected intimacy with Joan. "I should dearly love to see London Bridge. Rob told me that there are houses and shops on it. Is it true?"

"Aye, 'tis true. Your brother is a man of the cloth and so would not lie to you, Cecily," Joan told her. "You will go to London all in good time, but first we must arrange your formal betrothal to York sometime in the summer before Anne goes away."

Cecily gasped. "Anne going away? Where? Why? She did not tell me," she cried, slowing Tansy to a walk to keep pace with her mother's plodding rouncy. She forgot her disappointment in not riding with the men, for this news was more important. Her life was about to change.

"I have explained to you before, child," Joan said, a little testily. She was tired these days, and after bearing thirteen children, she was eager to put motherhood aside and enjoy her late middle age, knowing that each of her ten surviving children was well provided for. "Young women of noble birth must devote themselves to becoming wives, which oft-times means leaving their own home and joining another great house. 'Tis where we learn to become loyal to our husband's family and devote our life to our children and support our husband's ambitions. And thus Nan will go to Brecon and be under the protection of my cousin Anne, Humphrey's widowed mother. I expect Nan and Humphrey will be properly married inside the next two years."

Cecily digested this and stared ahead in silence. Despite the awkwardness between the sisters, Cecily drew comfort from having a sister close to her age share in her daily routine. Her three other sisters were long gone: Katherine to Framlingham Castle in Suffolk, seat of the Mowbrays, dukes of Norfolk; Eleanor to Alnwick Castle, where her husband, Henry Percy, earl of Northumberland, guarded the northeastern border from the Scots; and Joan, still a novice but soon to be veiled, to Barking Abbey near London. And now Nan was to leave and be out of reach in the wilds of Wales.

"Dear Virgin Mary," she prayed, "do not desert me too. Nan is not the best of companions, but she is always here. Please stay with me when she goes."

It then occurred to her that her turn would come one day, and her stomach lurched. But another blast on a hunting horn, much closer now, banished her morose thoughts, and the baying dogs told her that an animal was cornered.

This time she made up her mind not to be left behind, and before Joan could command her to stay, Cecily had urged Tansy into a canter, and horse and rider expertly wended their way through the woods toward the source of the commotion.

Then, as she drew closer and slowed to a trot, her eye caught a movement to her left. Every muscle in her body tensed.

"It could be robbers," she thought, knowing that they were common in the forests of lawless England.

She was just regretting striking out on her own when she gasped in wonder. Slipping between two white birch trees and perfectly camouflaged against the snow was an ethereal, almost mystical beast.

"The white deer," Cecily whispered, transfixed.

Suddenly the hind saw her, and for a second the delicate creature and the lovely girl stared at each other. Cecily held her breath. And then it was gone, springing over the snowy ground and disappearing behind a copse of hazel. Cecily exhaled in awe. Taught to believe in holy signs, she was convinced the Virgin had visited her, and she crossed herself reverently.

"You will be with me always, will you not, Holy Mother," she whispered. "I know that now." And so she vowed never to tell anyone about the hind. The idea of such a gift from God being felled by hunters and dogs horrified her.

Kicking Tansy into a fast trot, she headed for the huntsmen and their victim—an enormous stag, its summer-red fur turned winter gray, with a magnificent rack of antlers that Cecily knew would join others on the walls of Raby's great hall. The skilled huntsmen were making short work of the still warm animal, and after it was gutted, the dogs were given their grisly reward. Cecily hated this part of the hunt and looked away from the glassy eyes and lolling tongue as the stag's lifeblood oozed onto the snow. She was aware of a rider sidling close to her and recognized Richard's voice—half boy, half man, asking if she would like to leave the scene.

Cecily held her head high and shook it vigorously. "Nay, Dickon. One cannot join in the hunt and then not stay to respect the death of such a noble beast," she said, quoting her father word for word. "I cannot help but feel sorry for him, 'tis all," she murmured. With a brave smile, she asked who had found the stag's heart with his arrow.

"It was your father, Cecily. He felled the stag with one shot."

"And you and George? Did you loose your arrows?" Cecily inquired, one eyebrow raised.

"Aye, both of us did—and missed by a bow's length." Richard grinned back. "Master Beckwith will surely berate us for our lack of markmanship."

By now the ladies had joined the group. Standing by the stag, Ralph proudly lifted its head by the tines to show Joan.

"I won the day, my lady!" he cried. "We shall have venison to spare for the Twelfth Night feast." Joan smiled and waved, but she was cold and, calling to

Cecily to rejoin her, she and her ladies turned their horses and made their way back through the trees to Raby.

"When we are wed, Dickon," Cecily told him in confidence, "we shall have our own hunts and shoot our own deer, shall we not? I would dearly love my own hawk when I am bigger. Might it be possible?"

Her childlike earnestness touched Richard, and he leaned across his saddle and kissed her quickly upon the cheek. "Certes, it might, Cis," he said. "We shall have a merry time together, I promise."

Cecily's heart sang. "Nan cannot be right," she thought. "It seems he likes me just as well as her."

Though, if the truth were told, she did not feel the ache in her heart that Anne had described, nor did she feel a bit like swooning—whatever that meant. She shrugged, wheeled Tansy around, and trotted after her mother.

That night she dreamed she rode from Raby upon the white deer and, turning her head back to the square Bulmer Tower, she saw her father's haggard gray face gazing at her from its parapet, his heart shot through with an arrow.

THE HARSH NORTHERN winter turned finally into a breathtaking spring complete with the native gentians carpeting the grassy limestone banks with their vivid blue flowers. On Cecily's ninth birthday, the third of May, Anne was sent to her new family in Wales. Cecily was disappointed that Anne would not see her betrothal to Richard, but the Stafford family was impatient to welcome the young Neville bride.

Unable to stop herself crying, Cecily was puzzled by Anne's calm demeanor when she first made obeisance to her father and mother and then allowed herself to be embraced by both. Cecily was accustomed to Joan's lack of emotion and was not surprised by the countess's stoic "God be with you on your journey, Daughter." But she could not understand how Anne could resist throwing herself into her father's arms, as she would have done. Instead, her sister accepted his gruff kiss and admonition to be a good girl and walked to her brothers for their farewells. Something in Anne's serenity prevented her usually rambunctious siblings from teasing or hugging her. When she came to Richard, who stood quietly at the end of the line, she lowered her eyes and blushed.

"Farewell, Anne," Dickon said amiably. "I am certain Cecily will miss you."

Anne lifted her head and pouted. "And you will not, Dickon?"

Richard was taken aback, though he nodded an affirmative. "Forgive me. We shall all miss you. And I wish you all happiness with Humphrey Stafford."

Anne sniffed, turned on her heel, and stalked toward her waiting escort. This was too much for Cecily. Believing her sister had forgotten her, she ran after Anne and caught her arm.

"Nan, do you have no words of farewell for me? You forgot about *me!*" she cried, her tears wetting Anne's hand as she lifted it to her cheek. "Will you at least write to me when you get to Brecon? I promise I shall write back."

Anne's face softened for a moment, but, determined to show she was her mother's daughter and soon to be a countess, she gently pulled her hand away, and kissed Cecily's cheek lightly. "Aye, I promise I shall write, Cis. Now, I pray you, stop crying like a baby. It is not the way a duchess behaves."

Cecily stared in dismay as Anne left the hall, her brown velvet cloak billowing behind her. Then, seeking the comfort of her father's loving arms, she did not see the wayward tear that trickled down her mother's plump cheek.

Perhaps 'twas as well Nan would not be here to see my betrothal, Cecily thought uncharitably. Why, her sour face might spoil the whole day.

IT HAD TAKEN a bevy of tiring women to dress Cecily for her first public occasion. First they slipped a new shift of finest silk over her golden head and tied it at the back of the neck. Then they helped her into an underdress of crimson sarcenet and fastened it down her back, its tight sleeves coming to a point over her wrists. When she had been measured for the gown, Cecily had idly wondered when her breasts might start growing, and she was torn between wanting to retain her boy's riding garb and filling out a beautiful gown. Now she wished she was already a grown woman as she admired the exquisitely embroidered wide-sleeved houpeland draped like a coat over the sarcenet and belted above the waist, causing the satin fabric to flow in an avalanche of white around her lithe young body. The garnets that were sewn in the center of the large embroidered roses mirrored the red underdress, thus effecting a mingling of the white rose of York with the red and white Neville colors.

Joan bustled in to supervise the last details. She presented her daughter with a piece of her own jewelry: a heavy gold necklace from which hung a sapphire the color of Cecily's eyes. Joan's gray eyes reflected her satisfaction with her child's appearance. She commanded one of the women to brush Cecily's yellow mane twenty more strokes before proclaiming it ready to receive the simple coronet of white roses.

The women stood back in admiration, and Cecily grinned back at them.

Then she scrutinized her mother's critical gaze. "Do I look like a duchess, my lady?" she asked with a hint of concern, and then an urgent, "Mam, will I do?"

"Aye, Daughter, you'll do," Joan said, breaking into a smile. "Richard of York is a fortunate young man." The women looked relieved. Adding their compliments, they gave the gown a few last-minute adjustments and wished her well.

Rowena Gower had the honor of holding Cecily's train as the women processed carefully down the newel stair to the courtyard, where Ralph, the sun shining on his white hair, waited patiently with his entourage. He was joking with two of his squires. Standing a little apart, conversing with the Neville brothers, Richard nervously fingered the jeweled hilt of his dagger. When Cecily emerged from the shadow of the staircase, the men fell silent as one.

"Cecily?" Ralph mouthed in astonishment before he found his voice and his legs and strode toward her. "Lady Cecily Neville, you do our house proud!" he cried. Reaching out his arms, he would have crushed her to him had Joan not stopped him with a warning, "My lord, the gown!" Ralph took Cecily's hands instead and held her at arm's length to admire the transformation. Cecily found herself uncharacteristically blushing as her father inspected her from top to toe. "Magnificent!" he declared and called to Richard to come and claim his betrothed. "Certes, the house of York has never seen a fairer addition, do you not agree, your grace?" He presented Cecily to Richard and bowed. Cecily curtsied to them both, smiling happily.

"In truth, my lord, none fairer." Richard's thirteen-year-old voice betrayed him, breaking on the last syllable. Furious with himself, he colored.

Ralph chortled. "I have heard of a blushing bride, my dear wife, but never a blushing bridegroom," he said, as he took Joan's arm and led the company through the passageway to the outer bailey and the waiting litters. Joan slapped his hand playfully.

"Hush, my lord, 'tis ordeal enough for the young people without your teasing them," she chided, and glancing back, gave Richard a smile of encouragement.

St. Gregory's church was decorated to the rafters with bunches of the white wildflowers of June tied with red and white ribbons: scented meadowsweet, delicate cow parsley, dog daisies, yarrow, and Cecily's namesake, sweet cicely. In among these flowers of the Staindrop woods and hedgerows were white roses, emblem of the house of York.

Those local gentry invited to witness the betrothal of Earl Ralph's youngest daughter and the duke of York were already kneeling on tapestry cushions when the procession of chanting monks filed in. No one could deny that St. Gregory's was a substantial church for a small village, and this was due in part to the patronage of the lords of Raby. Its round Norman arches led to aisles on either side of the wide nave crowded with villagers eager for a glimpse of their own Rose and her young duke. And today the monks, now installed in the choir behind an elegant rood screen, were glad to offer their mellifluous voices to celebrate the betrothal of their founder's daughter. Indeed, the music made the congregation's long wait on its knees more bearable.

Finally the earl's party could be heard approaching, and as the organist began a reedy Introit, the congregation rose to its feet to greet the lord of Raby. First to enter behind the tonsured brother carrying a large silver crucifix were members of Ralph's first family by Margaret Stafford, who now rested beneath her painted alabaster tomb just inside the church door. They had ridden over earlier from Brancepeth, the seat of the Westmorlands, headed by the heir to the earldom, Ralph's nineteen-year-old grandson, who had lost his father on campaign in France two years earlier.

Young Ralph's self-importance was written all over his long, thin face as his pale blue eyes scanned the crowd for friends and passed haughtily over the awed yeomen of Staindrop. He was followed by his uncle, yet another Ralph, and three of his seven aunts and their husbands.

But Robert alone represented Earl Ralph's adult sons by Joan, and he now passed through the portal into the church escorting his mother. The three youngest boys, William, George, and Edward, marched down the nave behind them, very aware of their new finery and enjoying admiring looks from the members of the local gentry. Only one of Cecily's sisters was able to be present at this important family gathering. Eleanor, countess of Northumberland, had traveled from Alnwick Castle close by the Scottish border with an impressive escort and two of her children. Also missing was Ralph and Joan's eldest son, Richard Neville, who was occupied during these summer months as warden of the West March of Scotland.

When the music stopped, an expectant hush silenced the whisperings as heads swiveled to watch Richard walk slowly through the people and pass under the chancel arch to the altar.

"Why not just get married?" one ruddy-faced villager asked his neighbor. "It be what their ilk do, no mind the poor girl's age."

His friend nodded. "Aye, there be enough churchmen here to marry all of us," he said with a chuckle.

Two trumpeters, precariously poised on stools near the font, sounded a fanfare for the entrance of the lord of Raby and the Lady Cecily. Murmurs of approval rippled around the church as the radiant girl, clinging to Ralph's steadying arm, appeared on the threshold. She tried not to notice her father's effigy to her left as they began the long walk to join Richard. She knew it was customary for people of rank to have their likeness made long before their death, but when she saw her beloved father's familiar face staring hollow-eyed at the ceiling, it never failed to give her a shudder. Joan's effigy lay on the other side of him from Margaret Stafford. Cecily had always wondered what the first wife would have said had she known that she was not going to lie alone with Ralph for all eternity.

She dismissed this train of thought as she concentrated on not tripping over her heavy gown before she reached Richard, who was waiting for her with his pleasant face wreathed in a grin. Once again she liked the way his smile reached his gray eyes and made them crinkle, and she smiled back, forgetting the hundred people watching.

The ceremony of betrothal was so quick that it hardly seemed worth all the fuss, Cecily thought, after it was over and Mass was being said. For the most part, it was signing documents between Richard and her father, and in truth, she need not have been there, except for the moment when Richard kissed her on the lips in front of everyone. She had waited to swoon away, now that Rowena had explained the word, but nothing had happened. Ah, well, she mused, perhaps 'tis only ninnies like Anne who swoon.

But when they returned down the aisle and out into the sunshine, she knew something very significant had occurred that day. She now truly belonged to Richard, duke of York, and her life would be forever changed.

2

Raby, Durham, 1424 to 1425

*S*he was wrong—for a time.

Cecily still spent her days either in her room in the keep or in her mother's solar under the eye of Joan and her ladies. She would lean as far out of her chamber window as she dared to catch a glimpse of her betrothed when he crossed the courtyard. It was a good day when he remembered to look up and give her a cheerful wave, but when he forgot, Cecily merely turned away from the window embrasure, muttering "A pox on all dukes" or some other petulant remark.

"How I hate being cooped up in here. I am not a child, I am betrothed," she declared, not knowing why Rowena hid a smile.

"To be sure you are, my lady," Rowena reassured her, "but your lady mother knows best."

Cecily sniffed and pointed to the brightly colored bird sidestepping on its perch. "Pah! That popinjay is freer than I am," she grumbled. "Mother tells me 'tis important that Dickon and I get to know each other better. How can we do that when I am imprisoned up here?"

Joan reiterated her advice one hot day several weeks after the betrothal and elaborated on it. "You may talk about the weather, the hunt at hand, or even a passage you may have read at your lessons. But that is all, do you understand? When you are wed and have children, then your conversations will be about household matters and your ambitions for your little ones. You must listen and support your husband in all things. Men do not approve of women who appear too learned. 'Tis unsettling for them."

Cecily nodded dutifully, but the eyes she cast down at her embroidery were full of scorn. I am much cleverer than Edward at Latin and French, she thought. Must I hide behind a silly smile and pretend I am not? But for now she stored away Joan's many lessons, which she knew would prove invaluable to her as wife, housekeeper, and mother. She was beginning to believe being a duchess might even be hard work. She winced when she pricked herself with her needle and sucked her bleeding finger.

With the uncanny sense only dogs seem to possess, one of the huge wolf-hounds keeping the ladies company that day suddenly lifted its head and began to thump its tail, causing a whirlwind of freshly laid rushes and dust to rise into the air. Joan looked up with a smile, expecting to see Ralph come striding in, but instead she gave an uncharacteristic squeal of pleasure when her eldest son threw open the solar door and gave his mother greeting.

"Richard!" Joan cried, pushing aside the tapestry frame upon which she was working. Out of vanity, she removed her spectacles before holding out her arms to him. "What a delightful surprise!"

Richard Neville was a younger version of his father and had always been his mother's favorite. George had once told Cecily that being in the middle of the family did not count for anything. "Only the youngest and the oldest matter, in truth," he had complained. "Father dotes on you and Mother on Richard. It is just not fair."

After giving his mother reverence and an affectionate peck on the cheek, her eldest son turned his blue eyes on Cecily, who was looking shyly up at him from her stool next to Joan. She noticed that he, like Dickon, favored the ugly short hairstyle, and his thick yellow hair stood out from his forehead like a thatched roof on a cottage. He chucked his sister under the chin and gave an approving nod.

"How now, young Cecily, you are growing up, I see. How old are you now? Nine? Not yet old enough to be wed, although I regret missing your betrothal Mass," he said. "Were you prevailed upon to wear a gown for the occasion?" he teased her.

Cecily giggled as Joan clucked her disapproval, but she proceeded to mollify her mother by gushing over the ceremony, her wardrobe, the flowers in the church, and the number of guests who attended. "There were even two trumpeters," she finished proudly, grinning at Richard. "Father wanted to show Dickon that the Nevilles are not living in a backwater."

"Cecily!" Joan exclaimed, exasperated, as Richard covered a laugh with a cough. "I pray you guard your tongue. Where did you learn such an expression?"

Cecily's smile faded and she lowered her eyes to the floor. "I heard Father tell Rob before we went into St. Gregory's," she muttered.

Richard took the cup of wine offered by a page and gratefully slaked his thirst. He still wore his dusty riding boots, their thigh-high cuffs stained with his horse's sweat. He smelled rather rank, Cecily thought, wondering why Joan did not admonish him to go and wash before presenting himself to ladies. Cecily could not remember the last time she had seen him, but she knew it was many months before Dickon's arrival at Raby.

"I suppose I shall have to reverence you, little Cis, when you become her grace of York," he said. "An outstanding match, madam, is it not?" he murmured to Joan. "Even though he is a Mortimer," he added with chilly emphasis. "Does young Dickon know that as a descendant of Lionel of Clarence he has as good a claim or better to the throne than little Henry?"

Joan drew a sharp breath and glanced about them. "Hush, my son," she snapped. "That is treasonous talk! I believe the boy is merely glad to have a roof over his head and a good family to help him grow up. Do not put foolish fancies into his head, will you? We are Beauforts, Richard, and our Lancaster blood is as good as any of the Yorks'. Henry is our king—and our kin. Do not forget he is my grandnephew."

"*Half* grandnephew, my lady, if we must be precise. But your bishop brother is now chancellor of England," he said, twirling the stem of his cup and watching the red contents carefully. "'Tis as well he swore to refuse the cardinal's hat."

Joan shrugged. She knew her brother had stained his reputation in an attempt to buy the coveted cardinal's hat, but his charm, cleverness, and wealth—the last most welcome to the fund-strapped Crown—had put him back into favor at court and had even named him little Henry's godfather, making him a formidable player in the game to control the boy king. Joan reached over and patted her son's arm, signaling the end of the political discussion. If the truth were told, she was much happier talking about more mundane matters.

"What news of your Alice, Richard? Will you ever leave the borderlands and get the lady with child?"

Richard's expression softened. He had married Alice Montagu when she was fourteen, several years before. Her father, the earl of Salisbury, one of England's finest commanders in France, doted on his only child.

"It is my dearest wish, madam, but my duties keep me in the north, and as Salisbury requested that Alice keep her mother company in his absence, 'tis in God's hands."

He finished his wine and rose. "I must find Father before he is offended because I came to you first," he said, smiling down at Joan. She was growing old, he thought, noting the deep lines at the corners of her mouth and on her brow. Several of her teeth were missing, her energy was much diminished, and she had a slight tremor in her right hand. At forty-five, and after birthing fourteen children, she had a right to slow down, he mused. He picked up her hand and kissed it reverently. "Until later, my dear lady. You, too, Cecily. I want to meet this Dickon of yours."

Cecily started at the remark. She had been dismayed by her brother's cold tone when he had spoken of Richard earlier, and she resolved to ask Nurse Margery who the Mortimers and Lionel of Clarence were.

"Oh, you will like him, sir," she stated firmly. "Will he not, Mother? Everyone likes Dickon."

BUT THE TWO Richards were not certain of each other when they met. Richard of York knew exactly why Richard Neville looked at him askance. He knew it had to do with his lineage and his father's treason.

Dickon's former guardian, Sir Robert Waterton, had given him a long tutoring about his family history, and York was fully aware that, through his maternal blood line from the great King Edward, he was nearer to the crown than his Lancaster cousin, the present king. Henry of Bolingbroke had conveniently ignored that closer line when he had usurped the crown at the end of the last century. But Waterton had assured the boy, "You have royal blood from both your parents, Dickon. Your York grandfather was King Edward's fourth son."

At the time, the small boy did not believe he would ever understand or care where he came from. All he knew was that he missed his sister and disliked the damp manor house that Waterton owned. But at a later time, when Dickon came to appreciate his delicate position, he had told his guardian, "If I understand rightly, Sir Robert, I must tread very carefully."

Sir Robert had let out a low whistle of admiration. "Aye, Dickon, you have the measure of it. I would counsel you to keep this close and be contented with the fact that you were not attainted along with your father. Swear fealty to Lancaster and do not become too ambitious. I have known many men lose their life for ambition."

Now standing in front of him in Raby's great hall, Richard Neville saw an unprepossessing fourteen-year-old, with a pleasant face, intelligent eyes, and athletic build. If he was expecting arrogance, he found none. Dickon gave him a practiced bow, and Neville returned it with the customary, "God's greeting to you, your grace." Considering the wealth York was inheriting, it was surprising that the young duke was dressed so modestly, Neville thought. Not a bad thing at his age, he surmised, although he was certain the lad would learn soon enough that one's wealth—and so power—was always more evident if one wore it.

The ornate silver saltcellar was the last thing to be placed on the long table that ran from the raised high table and down the length of the hall. Richard Neville presided over the household dinner in place of his father, who was at Brancepeth. Joan resented the time Ralph spent there with his other family, and as she had never pretended to care for her stepchildren nor they for her, she kept away from the massive twelfth-century castle.

Tonight she sat proudly at Richard Neville's right hand, and in a gesture of deference, York was given the honor of sitting at Neville's other side with the three younger Neville brothers next to him. Cecily sat to Joan's right. The rest of the household knew their stations below the salt, and the meal was a lively affair, especially after the prodigal Neville had consumed several cups of wine and feasted on Raby's finest pheasants, quails, and haunches of venison. He conversed amicably with Dickon at first, describing a rout of some Scots marauders who had boldly crossed the border and met with Neville resistance. The young duke plied him with questions about the Scottish King James and a truce, and Neville was impressed by the young man's political knowledge.

Cecily half listened to the details of fighting the Scots, and as there was no one sitting at her other side, she had leisure to watch the servants hand out baskets of bread and jugs of ale. Those at the bottom of the table received the coarsest brown rye bread. Further up the table, round white cocket was served. Ralph's officers and squires enjoyed good wheat wastele. She broke a piece of her own *pain demain*, made with the finest white flour, and wondered how different it was from the others.

Cecily heard the adults discussing the politics at court. She recognized the names of the king's uncles—John of Bedford and Humphrey of Gloucester—but why anyone cared about their wives she could not fathom. She deduced that the elder uncle, Duke John, had pleased everyone with his wife from Burgundy, but Duke Humphrey had angered the King's council with his choice. She stifled a yawn, focused on the delicate flavor of the swan's meat she was nibbling, and wondered if her mother's monstrous, heart-shaped headdress would fall off her nodding and shaking head.

"Humphrey seeks his own piece of Europe through his wife, 'tis all. He has never been content with the role of mere Protector. He wanted to be Regent with Bedford and was slighted when King Harry chose Bedford alone to control his son," Richard told his mother. He then called for more wine.

"May we have music, please?" Cecily asked her big brother during a pause. "I would dearly love to show you what my dancing master taught us all recently. We have not had music since the betrothal feast. May we, Richard? Mother?" she pleaded.

Richard deferred to his mother, who nodded to the steward and asked him to prepare the room for dancing. Four musicians appeared in the minstrels' gallery, and Cecily sent instructions for them to strike up a *saltarello*. The timbrel player started the rhythm of the lively Italian dance, and the others joined with the melody. Cecily looked down the line and tried to catch Dickon's eye, hoping that he would invite her to dance. They had learned the steps together, and he was a fair enough dancer, she had concluded. Instead, Richard Neville rose and bowed over her hand, a twinkle in his blue eyes.

"Will you do me the honor, Lady Cecily," he murmured. "His grace of York can lead our lady mother out, *n'est-ce pas*, York?"

Dickon almost fell off the bench. Hating to be the center of attention, he had been relieved when Neville had offered to dance with Cecily, and with Nan gone, he preferred to sit back and watch. Joan observed with amusement the different expressions flit across the young man's face as he climbed awkwardly over the back of the bench, trying not to stand on the long toes of his hose-shoes. Finally he managed a graceful bow and offered her his arm.

"Have no fear, your grace," she assured him. "You will not have to lift me. I am too old to perform the leaps of this dance, so we shall be more sedate, you and I."

The rest of the household stood on either side of the hall as the oldest and the youngest of the Beaufort Nevilles demonstrated their prowess in the dance. Cecily was exuberant in her little leaps on the first beat of every bar, but her brother was more circumspect with his and simply enjoyed this unaccustomed entertainment after months of soldiering on the Marches. He tried to picture the earnest Dickon and his impetuous sister as husband and wife, and had to smile. "Perhaps these two will make a match of it," he thought, "they are so young yet."

And then he prayed, for his little sister's sake, that York would never attempt to assert his Mortimer right to the throne and put Cecily in any danger.

It was Friday, the only day of the week Cecily looked forward to during those months when summer turned to autumn. On that day each week, Ralph took her hunting with his sons, and Dickon usually rode along. She was learning that at this time of year, when the male deer began the rut, the archer's task was much easier than usual.

"They have only one thing on their minds," her father told her on a recent outing, pointing to a stag in the distance that was rubbing its hardened antlers against a tree to mark it. "To find a willing doe."

Cecily's blank look tickled her father's sense of humor, and he roared with laughter. "'Tis the time to get her with child—just as all males in the animal kingdom feel the urge to do, including us—and not just at rutting time!" he told her, pointing to a lurcher trying to mount a bitch and getting its leg nipped for its pains. At once he remembered that it was his daughter and not a son he was talking to and covered his clumsy explanation with an embarrassed cough. "Ask your mother. She will tell you all you need to know," were his parting words. But Cecily never dared approach her mother with the topic and so remained in ignorance—and gratefully so.

Today Ralph was planning to hunt near Brancepeth, where it was rumored that a pair of wild boars had been seen. The party that set out was larger than usual, and Cecily maneuvered herself next to Richard, who was among a group of henchmen that did not include her brothers. With George and Edward now riding with Ralph, Cecily saw her chance to have a quiet conversation with her betrothed, as her mother had sanctioned. The other young hunters fell away, and Cecily and Richard trotted side by side up the road to Brancepeth.

"What do you think of your Brancepeth family, Cecily?" Dickon asked. "It seemed to me on the day of our betrothal that your father's heir is somewhat vainglorious. Am I mistaken?"

"Vainglorious? I confess 'tis not a word I know. But if it means conceited, high and mighty, or a bore, you are being kind, Dickon. Why, he can barely give any of us Beaufort Nevilles a 'Good day,' and his nose would scrape the tree branches if he held it any higher. He is naught but a swollen-headed peacock, and I hate him!"

"God's body, Cecily," Dickon said on a laugh. "Why do you not simply speak your mind?"

Unused to sarcasm, Cecily replied, "But I did. 'Tis what I think." Then she giggled. "Heavens, I was only supposed to talk to you about the weather—or perhaps you would like me to recite a few of Master Chaucer's lines?"

Dickon made a face. "I detest verse," he declared. "Nay, I would much prefer we speak about the rest of your family. But we can tell your mother we spoke of the weather, if you don't mind a small untruth." He raised his eyebrow, and seeing her grin, he put his finger to his lips to keep their secret. "What more can you tell me of your sisters and brothers?"

Cecily was ecstatic. She felt so grown up, chatting with her intended about her family. Not only was she having private time with Dickon, but he did not mind conversing about things other than the weather. I think I shall like being married to him, she decided.

"I was happy when our Joan went off to the convent," she confided. "Nay, not happy she went, but happy it was not *me*. I think being a nun must be the dullest thing in all the world."

"What do you hope for in your life, Cis? Besides being my duchess, of course."

"What else is there, Dickon?" Then she dimpled. "If you promise not to tell anyone, I sometimes dream about being a queen. I think I would make a good queen." She looked at him from under her lashes, afraid he would laugh at her, but his face was perfectly serious.

"I dream about being a soldier—nay, commander of an army—and winning lots of battles," he said. He smiled at her as they crossed a clearing, following the sound of faraway horns. "I think my dream is more likely to come true, but I promise I will not tell a soul about yours."

Cecily's eyes shone. "A secret! I love secrets."

A pair of magpies flew over them, and the two young people looked up at once. Cecily was enchanted.

"One for sorrow, two for joy,

"Three for a girl and four for a boy,

"Five for silver, six for gold,

"Seven for a secret never to be told," she chanted. "Let's imagine there are five more birds coming to join them, Dickon!"

Richard was moved to laugh out loud, and Cecily stared at him in surprise. His face had lost its grave expression, she noticed, and what erupted from him sounded more like a horse's neigh than a man's laugh. But it made her want to laugh as well, because she had always thought that he was altogether too serious. So she joined in, happy that she was pleasing him.

"Ay, I shall like being his wife," she repeated to herself.

And unbeknownst to Cecily, Richard's thoughts were running along the same line as he caught his betrothed's hand and took it to his lips.

"We should catch up with the others," he said, and clicked his tongue to make his palfrey quicken its pace. "We have fallen a long way behind."

They urged their horses into a canter and followed a path that Cecily knew led into the forest, a dark place where the shade of the famous oaks was like night and raised the hairs on the neck of even the most stalwart huntsman. Cecily was used to it, and Richard admired her fearlessness as she wended her way through the trees and found Stockley Beck, a spring-fed stream teaming with salmon. The main hunting party was waiting for the stragglers on the other side of the beck, and George and Edward began chiding Dickon for leading their sister astray. Cecily was furious, but Dickon merely smiled and shrugged his shoulders.

"Your sister is often better company than you are, George," he said, pulling a heavy glove from his saddlebag and preparing to receive his lanner from one of the falconers. This compliment made Cecily cock a snook at her favorite brother behind Ralph's back.

That night, snuggled in bed next to a gently snoring Rowena, Cecily thanked the Blessed Virgin and St. Sybellina, protectress of all orphans, for sending Dickon to her at Raby.

"HUMPHREY STAFFORD AND *I were wed last week,*" Anne wrote in October, "*and so now I am a countess.*"

Cecily was basking in the late autumn sun on an exedra in Raby's neat herb garden, where she had gone to read her sister's first letter to her since leaving Raby in the spring. Cecily peered at the untidy script, wondering why Anne's impeccably neat embroidery efforts did not translate onto paper. "*For the wedding day, the dowager countess gave me red cloth of gold for a new gown, and a hundred guests came for the feast. I have never tasted anything as delicious as the roasted fawn that was taken in the hunt the day before. The eels from the river here are the largest and best I have seen or eaten. And much to my wonder, I saw a pie placed before us that, when cut open, ten blackbirds flew out—alive and singing. The master cook would not tell me how, saying it is a secret recipe. But I will know!*"

Cecily was impressed, and she vowed to ask Raby's master cook if he could attempt such magic.

"As I am certain Father has told you," Anne continued, *"Humphrey now sits in the regency council with him, and he is one of the most important people at court."*

Nay, Nan, Cecily thought, you are mistaken. Father has not thought to mention it.

"I miss the gentle countryside at Raby. Here there is naught but wild high hills, good for nothing but sheep, and many rivers, the biggest of which flows below the castle and town. Humphrey likes to fish all the time."

Cecily paused and gazed at a thrush singing blithely on a brick wall. Aye, poor Nan must be most unhappy if she needed to tell me that. She pictured her sister at her window high up in the castle above a sheer drop into a swiftly flowing river, watching her new husband, equipped with rod and creel, ride off with his squires. *"But when he is here, he is all duty to me and denies me nothing, although, in truth, he looks on me as though I were a child, even though I am now his wife in all ways."*

Cecily's mouth dropped open at Anne's insinuation. She wished she could talk to her sister about such matters. What does happen in bed, she started to ponder. Then she heard her father's stentorian voice calling her from the gatehouse.

Cecily folded the letter, stuffed it into a pocket, and flew along the paths to the iron gate that led out to the park. She saw her father waving impatiently.

"What is it, Father?" she asked when she reached him. "Is something amiss?"

Then she saw that Ralph was in his traveling clothes and his horse laden with double saddlebags. George and Edward waited beside Brown Baldric to bid their father good-bye and help him onto the huge horse's back.

"Where are you going?" Cecily asked, her blue eyes filling with tears as she noted that several of his gentlemen had already mounted. Ralph had not left Raby all summer long, and she had forgotten that as one of the regency councillors he must return to court from time to time. "Is it London this time? And why will you not take Mother and me with you?"

"Only a few hours ago, I received a summons from your Uncle Beaufort, and I must go to the council at once," Ralph explained, pulling on a pair of tooled leather gloves. "Duke Humphrey of Gloucester has gone abroad, which means that we must convene and govern in his absence, my child. With Bedford in France as well, we councillors must try to hold the throne safe for the young king. Do not look so downhearted, Cecily. You shall go to London soon, I promise." He tipped up her trembling chin and kissed her forehead. "George and Edward will take you hunting, have no fear. They have their instructions."

"What about Dickon?" Cecily said anxiously. "Can he come with us too?"

Ralph looked sheepish. "I forgot to mention that he comes with me to London. 'Tis time he was formally presented to the council and the king. He is fourteen now and cannot while away much more of his time up here with us." He wiped a tear from her cheek with his thumb. "Tears for Dickon, and you are not even wed yet? 'Tis very touching, but you must become accustomed to a husband's frequent absences, my sweet girl."

Cecily pouted. "I shall go with him wherever he goes, you see if I don't," she grumbled.

"Ah, there you are, York," Ralph called to Dickon, who was hurrying toward the stables with a servant tagging along with his saddlebags. Dickon's elaborate chaperon fitted him better these days, Cecily noted absently, but seeing him preparing to mount, she forgot about his hat and ran to him. She grasped his hand.

"Sweet Jesu, Cis," he said, amused. "You almost bowled me over." He carried her hand to his cheek. "Never fear, I shall write to you, and you will promise to write to me, will you not? I shall be back before you know it, I promise. Now farewell, and God keep you."

Miserably Cecily watched as he was helped into his saddle while his servant mounted a sturdy rouncy and settled the baggage.

Ralph gave the signal to walk off. Cecily darted past the kitchen tower and along the length of the low curtain wall to see the meinie trot down the road to Staindrop. Infuriatingly, the men failed to notice her as she frantically brandished her colored kerchief, but she dared not cry out like a peasant to attract the attention of the two men she loved most in all the world lest Joan be watching. She kept on running and waving. Then just before the party disappeared down the hill and over the stream, she tripped on a large stone in her path, and the next thing she knew she was flat on her face in the coarse grass under the wall.

"Cock's bones!" she exclaimed, much to the amusement of a mason nearby, who was patching a hole in the Bulmer tower. Her tears now unchecked—whether because her hands were grazed or because of frustration that Dickon had not seen her—she thumped the ground with her fist. "I wish I were a boy!" she complained. "I am left out of everything!"

3

Raby, Durham, 1425

The weeks came and went, and Yuletide was a less festive affair in the absence of the lord of the castle. On a snowy day during Advent, Cecily, George, and Edward accompanied some of the gardeners and woodsmen into the park to gather holly, ivy, and the mystical mistletoe and to cut down a tree for the traditional Yule log. Their horses slowed by the drifts to a walk, they made for the woods, and the servants, pulling sleds, tramped through the ankle-deep snow, trying to keep up. Bunches of mistletoe clung to the oaks' bare brown branches, the poisonous white berries glistening among the yellow-green leaves. By standing in his stirrups, George was able to reach and cut down several sprigs of it.

"Have a care not to drop any, George!" Cecily cried anxiously. "'Twill bring bad luck to our house if it touches the ground before Candlemas."

"Pah!" retorted George. "'Tis naught but an old wives' tale," he told her. Nevertheless he crossed himself for good measure. "For my part, I intend to hang some close by the buttery. There is a dairymaid . . ."

Edward moved forward and gave his brother a swift kick, making George's horse skitter and George drop some of the mistletoe. Cecily gasped in horror, and all three siblings stared at the unmistakable green lodged in the snow. A nimble woodsman snatched up the sprig and added it to the boughs of pine on his sled before others saw.

Cecily gave George a withering look. "How foolish of you, brother," she snapped. "I think I shall return to the castle, for now I am certain we shall have ill luck for the next twelvemonth. You see if we don't."

George leaned over and patted her hand. "Dearest Cis, I am heartily sorry for spoiling the day for you, but 'twas I who dropped the plant, and I shall be the only one to pay, in truth. Now, I pray you, let me see a smile again on that sour face."

Cecily sat unmoved, but George could always coax her out of a mood, he knew, and when he lifted her hand to his lips and winked at her, he was rewarded with the ghost of a smile.

"I will make it up to you if aught ill befalls the family," he promised. "Now, come with us. We have yet to find a suitable Yule log."

BEFORE THE END of January and a few days before Candlemas, it seemed that Cecily's superstitious fears were unfounded. News came that Richard Neville had been made constable of Pontefract Castle, one of the crown's important northern strongholds. And, more relevant to Cecily, word was sent to Raby that Dickon's maternal uncle, Edmund Mortimer, earl of March and descendant of Lionel of Clarence, had died of plague in Ireland, leaving no children and thus bequeathing to the young duke of York vast tracts of land in England, Ireland, and Wales, as well as the Mortimer claim to the throne.

"This is excellent news, Cecily. Your betrothed will be one of the wealthiest men in England when he comes of age," Joan exulted. "But for now, Duke Humphrey of Gloucester and my brother John have charge of his estates."

Cecily tried to look pleased, but then she asked, "When will Dickon and my lord father come back to Raby?"

"While Duke Humphrey is selfishly blundering into his wife's disputed lands in Burgundy and Bedford is succeeding in holding France for England, the regency council must keep close watch on King Henry's interests. My two brothers and your father are well placed to guide and govern. Be patient with a noble's obligations, Daughter, and proud of your family always."

Joan saw Cecily stifle a yawn and paused. Aye, she is still only a girl of ten, despite her intelligence, Joan thought. She will have to learn the intricacies of politics soon enough. Why not let her enjoy this quiet life for a little longer? And in an uncharacteristic gesture of affection, she pulled Cecily into her arms and stroked the lovely blond head, just as she remembered her mother doing with her so many years ago.

Joan sighed. "The year has begun well for the house of Neville, my dear," she murmured. "Be proud and pray for it to last."

* * *

CECILY'S HEART NEARLY stopped when she first saw her father again several months later. She came into her mother's solar, situated on the second floor of Joan's new tower, just as Ralph was being helped into a high-backed chair by two sturdy squires. She flew to his side and knelt before him, her eyes anxiously taking in the pasty face and dark circles under his eyes.

"My lord father," she began. "Are you unwell?"

"Certes he is unwell, Cecily," Joan snapped, as worried as her daughter. "You do not need to remind him with your tactless question. Now fetch a stool, sit down, and hold that runaway tongue of yours." Her tone softened as she regarded her husband. "Would you prefer wine or ale, my dear lord?"

"Hell's bells, ladies!" Ralph exclaimed. "I am not at death's door. The heat and the journey have wearied me, 'tis all, and the many hours of wrangling at the council table. I am, after all, more than sixty years of age. My body may be weak, but my mind is still strong. Cease your fussing, I beg of you! Or I shall return to plague-ridden London."

"Nay, you jest, husband." Joan smiled and caressed his hand. "You would not return home carrying a pestilence. In truth, we are impatient to hear the news from London, but only when you are rested."

Ralph regarded his wife with affection. "I have much to thank God for, my lady," he said. "But most of all I thank Him every day for bringing you into my life. Never was a man more pleased with his wife." Catching a glimpse of Cecily's upturned face at his knee, he hastily added, "And his daughter. I trust you have been a good companion to your mother while I have been away."

Cecily nodded vigorously. "I have done my best, truly I have," she replied, looking to her mother for assurance, but Joan chose the moment to fetch ale for her husband. She did not believe in swelling a child's head with praise. "I pray you, my lord, what word of Dickon?" Cecily asked.

"Has that boy not written to you, child? He swore to me that he had," he growled, lowering his eyebrows again. "He is well and makes an impression at court with his courtesy and intelligence, but he is no popinjay, nor does he prate or swagger like some of the young lords." He leaned over to Cecily and whispered, "Like Anne's Humphrey Stafford." Cecily giggled, reveling in her father's closeness and his conspiratorial tone.

Joan handed her husband a cup of ale and sat down again. "How is the little king faring, husband? Do you see him at all, or does he spend all his time in the nursery?"

Ralph harrumphed. "As a result of the bad blood between your brother

Bishop Henry and Duke Humphrey, the council saw fit to insist the infant be present at all council meetings and even to set the Great Seal between his knees. In truth, I thought 'twas ridiculous. What did they expect? That the king would give his opinion on matters of state? He gave his opinion often, but it was more in the fashion of a loud yawn of boredom or, worse, a nap!"

Joan shook her head in disbelief. "What were they thinking? The boy is only four. And my brother sanctioned this addle-pated nonsense?"

"Aye. Bishop Beaufort is Chancellor—for now—my dear. Because Duke Humphrey, the derelict Regent, has returned ruined both in body and in purse from his reckless campaigning on behalf of his foreign wife, and we, the other councillors, have forbidden him to fight more with Burgundy." He sighed. "How I wish Bedford could leave France. He is the only one to help us steer this difficult regency. He is the best of us. When I left, things were coming to a head between your brother and Humphrey. I was glad this little bout of sickness allowed me to come home." He leaned back in his chair and closed his eyes. "Cecily, my child, I am weary. Pray leave your mother and me for now. Be a good girl and summon my valet in my office. You will find something there for you I carried with me from London."

Cecily jumped up and clapped her hands, earning a disapproving frown from her mother. She hurriedly curtseyed to them both. "Thank you, my lord," she murmured, scurrying away before she could receive another rebuke.

"She is impossible," she heard Joan say wearily.

"She will keep us young, Joanie," Ralph replied. "Cecily is a clever girl, and your fine example will hold her steady throughout her life, I have no doubt."

Elated, Cecily ran along the dark passageway to her father's office. Knocking, she pushed open the door and then stopped short on the threshold. Seated at the tapestry-covered table, his head bent over a quill and parchment, was Richard.

"Dickon!" she cried. As soon as he saw her at the door, Richard pushed himself back from the table and hurried forward, his hands outstretched, and Cecily suddenly felt shy. He had grown an inch or so in the nine months he had been gone, and his fashionable blue-pleated tunic and hat with its up-turned brim all served to give him a maturity she was not prepared for.

"My dear Cecily," he said, looking her up and down and grinning. "I do believe you are prettier than ever."

Much to her annoyance, she blushed. She had always sworn she would never be like Anne, who had reddened every time Richard had glanced her way. And now she could feel her skin on fire as he held her hands. She dropped a little curtsey, hoping to recover her composure in that simple, reassuring act, but she did not have the chance, for he picked her up and swung her around before planting a kiss on her open mouth.

"Aye, very pretty indeed," he reiterated sincerely. "Those simpering ladies in London will be put to shame when the Rose of Raby is finally presented there. What? Has the cat pounced on your tongue? Or were you expecting me to talk only about the weather?"

Cecily finally closed her mouth and fixed her eyes upon her betrothed. "But Father never said you were with him. He told me to come and find the gift he had brought me from London. I never thought 'twould be you, Dickon. 'Tis the best present I have ever had. Welcome home, my lord," she said grandly and swept him a deep reverence. "It seems the saints do listen to my prayers," she added, with a smug smile. "Only last night I asked St. Jude for news of you."

Richard was amused. "Ah, you believe I am a lost cause?"

"Aye," Cecily retorted. "Two letters in nine months. And those were about the weather and your new horse. 'Twas unkind, my lord."

Richard was contrite at once, stammering an excuse about not knowing what to tell her and that London had really been quite dull.

"Pah!" Cecily muttered. "You just forgot us here in the wilderness—forgot *me.*"

Richard turned away and went to the window. Had word reached Raby about his flirtation with the Lady Agnes, one of Queen Catherine's ladies? A few years older than he, she had given him his first taste of the delights of the bedchamber, but he had admitted his lust in the confessional after each encounter, and eventually the young lady had tired of his clumsy attempts at wooing and reminded him of his betrothed far away in the north. Now Richard felt an uncomfortable prickling around the neck of his chemise and attempted to loosen it with nervous fingers.

"How could I forget you, Cecily? You wrote to me every week," he told her, hoping his guilty conscience was not obvious. "I confess your letters kept me laughing. You write well, sweet lady." He turned when he felt her close behind him and gently took her in his arms. "Truly, I missed you. I promise I shall be better when we return to court, *ma mie.*" She is only ten years old, he told himself again, and yet it is as though my body knows hers already.

Cecily plucked at a loose thread in his sleeve and sighed happily. "I hope that will not be for a long, long time, Dickon. I am all alone now that George has his lordship of Latimer and Edward has been made Lord Bergavenny. They have been sent to other houses, and I miss them."

"Then let us make the best of these days, dearest Cis. Shall we hunt on the morrow?"

RALPH SPENT MOST of his waking hours either reclining on a settle in Joan's solar, listening to her read to him, or walking in the park, leaning heavily on a stick, with Cecily skipping beside him, chattering away and amusing him. Joan was most concerned that he showed no desire to sit his horse and ride to the hunt, which was, in his healthier years, his dearest occupation. He groaned when he stood, even louder when he sat down, and he could barely walk without a shoulder or a stick to lean on.

One day late in October, Joan read a passage from the tale of Sir Gawain and the Green Knight to Ralph and Cecily: "Then came together all the noblest knights, Ywain and Erec, and many another. Sir Dodinel le Sauvage, the duke of Clarence, Launcelot and Lionel, and Lucan the Good, Sir Bors and Sir Bedivere—"

Ralph held up his hand for her to pause, muttering, "Lionel and Clarence— that reminds me . . ." He lifted his head and spoke to his daughter. "Cecily, have a page fetch York here, I beg of you," he said without explanation, giving her a weary smile. "He should be at the butts at this hour." He watched her hurry to the door. "I beg your pardon, my dear Joan. Please continue."

When Dickon knocked and entered fifteen minutes later, Cecily was with him, and Ralph motioned for both to approach the cushioned settle. Joan rose and excused herself, knowing with sorrow why Ralph wanted to speak to the young couple.

His thin gray hair had been combed carefully by Joan, and he had made an effort to prop himself up on several velvet cushions. Cecily took Joan's seat. Dickon stood beside her, his hand on her shoulder. Ralph smiled at the picture they made, the dark-haired, gray-eyed young lord and his own beautiful fair-haired daughter.

"I expect you to have handsome, intelligent children," he began, amused by Dickon's nervous, lopsided smile. "But that is not why I summoned you here." He paused, turning a large gold ring on his thumb, unsure of his next words. "It seems I have little time left here on earth. Nay, sweet child, I am at peace with it," he soothed Cecily when her sharp intake of breath interrupted him.

"The physician has turned up his hands and has no more knowledge of what ails me or how to treat me. If God in his mercy sees fit to take me on the morrow, I am ready." Cecily leaned forward and took his big hand in hers, covering it with kisses. "I would be even happier to know that I leave you contented with each other. York, you must have noticed that this willful child is the apple of my eye. I cannot go to my Maker without her assurance that she is pleased with my choice for her and that you will cherish her even more than I have."

Cecily's tears dripped on her wool gown, leaving dark spots in the green fabric. "Cer—certes, I am contented with D—Dickon, my lord," she faltered. "But I refuse to believe that you are . . . you are dying. You are merely weary, 'tis all. Mother and I shall soon have you up and well again, trust me." She sniffed and wiped her nose with the back of her sleeve.

"Most unbecoming, young lady," Ralph said, chuckling, and then he began to wheeze and gasp for breath. He waved his hands, signifying the fit would pass, which it did, and he pushed himself up further into a sitting position. "That's better. At times it feels as though I am drowning," he said, patting his chest. "Now where was I?"

"You asked if Cecily and I were contented with each other, my lord," Dickon prompted. He reached down and took Cecily's hand. "I cannot imagine a more suitable bride, and I shall be proud to have her to wife."

"Swear to me you will never betray her trust in you," Ralph commanded. "She is a loyal, good girl."

Dickon squeezed Cecily's hand, his gaze never wavering from Ralph's face. "I owe you all duty for your kindness to me these past two years, my lord, and I swear to you on my mother's grave I shall not betray your daughter—or your trust in me," he said. "You need not fear. I shall care for her all the days of our lives together and"—he paused and smiled over Cecily's head at his father-in-law—"if I can curb her importunity, then our union may well be close to perfect." He was rewarded by a laugh, albeit feeble, from the earl.

Cecily's eyes widened, and she tilted her head to look up at Dickon. "What is importunity, Dickon?"

"It means you do not always behave the way your mother has taught you," Ralph answered before Dickon could find a simpler word. "I fear I have overindulged you, and now that you are ten, you must change your childish ways and behave as befits the consort of a duke." His voice was tiring, and he stopped to catch his breath.

"Mind your mother, Cecily," he admonished her when he continued. "She is a great lady, and one day you will have to teach your own children what she is teaching you now." He fixed his eyes on Dickon. "Be not hasty to have the child to wife, your grace." He paused, watching closely for a reaction. When he saw genuine concern and agreement, he continued, "Countess Joan will have need of Cecily after I am gone, and I pray you allow Cecily to remain close to her mother until such time as you are both ready to take on the responsibilities of your office—and of a family."

Dickon gave Ralph a brief nod of acknowledgment. "Aye, my lord."

Seeing the earl close his eyes, Dickon drew Cecily toward the door.

Ralph suddenly said, "Before you go, I must confess something to you, Daughter." Cecily ran back to her father's side. "Your mother was right to chastise me for allowing you to ride in boys' breeches. I pray my hardheadedness has not imperiled your immortal soul." Cecily gulped and involuntarily crossed herself as Ralph continued, "Swear to me you will never again wear them, as it offends the Lord our God."

"Imperil my soul?" Cecily whispered, her eyes darting around looking for the Devil himself. "By wearing braies?"

Richard stepped in. "Aye, Cecily. Remember that when we first met, I told you then I believed 'twas so."

Cecily knelt by her father's head, her eyes brimming.

"Swear to me, Daughter," Ralph commanded. "I have confessed my sin, as must you."

Cecily whispered, "I swear, my lord." Then she laid her head on his chest, her tears spilling onto his nightshirt.

Ralph closed his eyes and stroked her hair. "I thought because you were a child . . ."

"Oh, Father, dearest Father, do not fret," Cecily implored, lifting her head and gazing at his dear, familiar face and seeing his tears on it for the first time in her life. "God will forgive us, I know He will."

"Come, Cecily," Richard coaxed and gentled her to her feet. "Your lord father needs to rest."

Obediently Cecily allowed herself to be led to the door.

"By all that is holy," Ralph muttered as he watched them go, "no man has ever been so fortunate in a child."

ON THE TWENTY-FIRST day of October, Dickon's fourteenth birthday and four days before the tenth anniversary of Agincourt, Ralph Neville, earl of

Westmorland, lay dying in his imposing canopied bed. As many Nevilles as could fit crowded into his chamber, the attending physicians and clerics swelling their ranks. Ralph's heir and two of his Stafford daughters and their husbands had arrived the night before from Brancepeth. Joan had sent for all her children in time for them to pay their respects to their father. Only his daughter Sister Joan had been unable to come from the convent.

Despite his loss of weight, Ralph was still an imposing figure as he lay between the white linen sheets, his torso propped up on feather pillows, a crucifix between his hands. Cecily knelt at the foot of the bed with Anne, who had not long since given birth to a daughter, and Eleanor from Northumberland. Their mother knelt at one side of the bed and young Ralph on the other. The room was stuffy. Open windows might let in the Devil, who could steal away with a dying man's soul, and so they had been shut against the summer breezes. A priest swinging the censer, a group of chanting monks, and Father John from Staindrop were all ranged behind Ralph. The churchmen had taken over the vigil from the tired physicians, who were now relegated to the doorway.

Somewhere behind her stood Dickon, Cecily knew, and her father's words came back to her then. Dickon would be her protector now, but as much as she cared for him, she could not envision him ever replacing her beloved father in her heart. All Ralph's children had gone one by one to receive his blessing a few hours before, and as last and youngest of the siblings, Cecily's few words from her father were then barely audible.

"Pray for me, my child. I shall be watching over you when I am taken into the kingdom of heaven. Never forget your faith and your family, Cecily. They will sustain you even unto death." Then he beckoned for her to bend close. She heard Joan's sharp intake of breath and knew her mother disapproved of this mark of favoritism. "Kiss me, Cecily, for I have loved you above any of my children."

Cecily had let her tears bathe his ashen face as she kissed his clammy forehead. "And I love you best, too, Father."

Then Anne found Cecily's hand and clutched it in the folds of their black gowns. Cecily stared miserably around at her family, some weeping, some telling their rosary, and others with eyes fixed on their father. Her knees were aching, and she felt as though she had no tears left inside her to shed. Hardly masked by the sweet frankincense, an unpleasant smell lingered around the bed, which she would later learn was the usual harbinger of death. The incense and the monks' voices lulled her into a half-meditative state, but when Ralph's breathing became more labored and she heard the ominous words of the priest reciting, *"Per istam sanctam unctionem et suam pissimam misericordiam, indulgeat tibi Dominus . . . ,"* something snapped inside her. Scrambling to her feet, she tried to climb onto the bed and stop the priest from dropping holy oil on her father.

"Nay, nay, he cannot die, he shall not die!" she cried. "Father, I shall not let them take you!" She caught sight of the stricken George, and the memory of their snowy adventure to fetch the Yule log flooded back. She pointed an accusing finger at him. "'Tis your fault. You dropped the mistletoe," she wailed, and she threw her arms around her father's blanketed legs.

In the moment of shocked silence that followed, Dickon alone moved to her and removed her from the inert figure, cradling her to him. Ralph's eyes fluttered open once more, and seeing Cecily in Dickon's arms, he smiled. "My precious child," he whispered, and then, turning his head to the priest to indicate he was now ready to meet his Maker, he rasped in his last breath, *"In Tuas manus . . ."* A strange rattling noise prevented more speech, his eyes glazed over, and he moved no more.

Joan took his hand to her cheek, moaning his name. His grandson Ralph was the first to rise. He crossed himself and with his usual hauteur left the room with his new title, Brancepeth and Raby castles but very little else. Most of the largest Westmorland estates were to be left to Joan's family.

The eldest of that family, Richard Neville, now kissed his father's bloodless lips and gently closed his eyes. One by one the Beaufort boys, as Ralph used to call them, followed Richard in showing the love they had for their father, and Robert, when his turn came, made the sign of the cross on his father's forehead with his thumb, tears streaming down his face.

Dickon had carried Cecily from the room as soon as he heard the death rattle, wanting her to hold in her heart the memory of her father alive and not the wasted flesh and bones of the corpse whose spirit had flown. Putting her down gently in the passage, he led her to a chair in Joan's solar and poured her a cup of wine.

Cecily sat slumped in the chair, her hand trembling as she raised the cup to her lips and slowly drank the tawny contents. She turned her rueful gaze on Richard and murmured, "I behaved badly in there, did I not? And after I promised Father . . ." She broke off, ashamed.

Richard shook his head. "No one will blame you, in truth, though a kind word to George might be in order." Cecily nodded sorrowfully. "I pray this is the worst pain we shall ever have to bear together, Cecily, but at least we have each other to lean on. Both of us will carry loving thoughts of Earl Ralph, I have no doubt. He was the father I never knew," Richard told her, a lump in his throat. He had never spoken to anyone of his own father's attainder and execution until a few weeks ago, when Ralph had mentioned it and had seen the boy's cheeks flush and his eyes turn darkly inward.

"No one faults you for your father's treason, Richard," the kindly earl had said. "But 'tis best soon forgotten. You have your own life to lead."

Richard sighed and addressed Cecily again. "Your father will always be in your heart, Cecily. He will always be with you. He was a good man. Praise God, he suffers no more."

Suddenly a bird flew in through the open window, startling the two young people. Bewildered, it fluttered frantically around the room, searching for an exit.

Cecily smiled then, believing the snowy dove was another sign from the Blessed Virgin, and she got down on her knees, lifting her eyes heavenward. "Holy Mother, I pray you be with my father as you were with me that day with the white hind in the forest. Take his soul now and ask your Son to welcome him into Paradise," she whispered, as the bird finally found its escape.

Cecily knew with certainty then that her father's soul had flown to Heaven, and she felt at peace.

4

London, 1426

*I*n his will, Earl Ralph had made his wife Richard's guardian, an unusual move but one that pleased the young duke greatly. He had learned to respect Joan Beaufort, and as Cecily would also be in her mother's care until she was at the legal age to marry, the two of them would remain in the same household. However, three months after Ralph's death, that household was leaving Raby.

"We are going to London!" Cecily exclaimed when she spotted Richard at the well in the central courtyard. Richard was now only one of three young knights in training left at Raby, and there was no doubt who among them was the leader. Richard's rank gave him precedence, it was true, but ever since the two Beaufort-Neville boys, George and Edward, had gone to other households, Richard had gained confidence. And when Ralph had died, many of the earl's officers looked to the young duke of York for leadership. He was well liked, Joan told Cecily one day after a particularly trying morning with Raby's steward, because the young duke put on no airs but had a serious, quiet way of listening and responding to problems.

"Servants respect those qualities in a master," she told Cecily. "'Tis unnecessary to wear rank upon your sleeve if you treat all comers with fairness, and Dickon does this. Just as our servants have a duty to us, so we have a duty to support and protect them. Never neglect them, Cecily. Dickon reminds me of Thomas," Joan continued, putting her hand on Cecily's arm. "To be sure, you cannot remember your brother, can you? You were only four when he died. Ah, Cecily, losing a child is the hardest thing a mother can bear, and I have lost four sons, God have mercy on their souls."

Cecily hung her head, ashamed because she did not feel any sorrow for her dead brothers. Then she brightened. "Aye, but all your daughters are alive and well, God be praised," she declared. "My lord father taught me that behind every cloud a ray of sunshine awaits."

Joan turned her face away at the mention of Ralph. She was finding widowhood hard, because she had truly loved her second husband.

When the summons had come for the countess of Westmorland and her daughter to join the king's household, Joan was relieved. Young Earl Ralph had begun to take an interest in the Raby property, and as Joan knew that she did not have the right to remain, she was contemplating removing to her inherited estate at Middleham in the Yorkshire dales and away from the bitter, haughty young man. So when the invitation from the king had come, the idea of being in a more temperate climate after a cold winter in the north appealed to her. It had been some time since she had gone south and seen Shene, Windsor, and Westminster, or watched the watermen on the Thames from the parapets of the Tower. Aye, it would be invigorating and warmer, she decided, and it would keep her from melancholy. She threw herself into the arrangements with an energy the household had not seen since Ralph's death.

"London!" Cecily cried when Richard extricated himself from his fellows and came over to her. "'Tis my first time."

Richard grinned at her enthusiasm. "When shall we go?" He paused. "I assume I am to go too."

Cecily nodded, her fur-lined hood swallowing up her answer. "I am sure you are."

A week later, the countess of Westmorland bade farewell to her home of many years with a stoicism she wished her daughter might emulate. In another of Joan's interminable lessons, Cecily had been admonished, "Curb your emotions, especially in front of the household. Showing our feelings makes us appear weak. Remaining strong and in command of ourselves and others is what sets us apart from the common folk. Hide what you feel somewhere inside you and only allow yourself to go there in private or in God's presence. Trust me, my child, prayer will see you through the worst of tragedies."

But despite her eager anticipation of London, Cecily found her sorrow at leaving Raby hard to bear. It was the only home she had known. She clung to her Nurse Margery, who was to return to her family in Durham, and even kissed the grizzled marshal of the stables on the cheek. He turned away so that his grooms would not see the tear that slipped down his face.

"The Rose of Raby will be sore missed by all at the castle and in the village, my lady," he told her. "I pray you, do not be forgetting us up north, and come back soon."

"Oh, I shall!" Cecily cried, as she hurried back to the curtained carriage, where Joan and two attendants waited. Cecily was very pleased when her mother had chosen Rowena to accompany them. Cecily had already found her a trustworthy and knowledgeable confidante.

Then began the long, arduous journey to the capital. Joan's carriage was sturdily built, and only once did the company lose half a day while a wheel was mended. Cecily reveled in the vehicle's luxurious cushioned interior. She spent many an hour wrapped in fur blankets, gazing out at the unfamiliar landscape along Ermine Street, the main road from York to the south, through a flap in the canvas side, with Joan's small spaniel Jessamine curled up beside her. As they traveled south, they seemed to leave the brown winter behind and watch spring arrive miraculously in a matter of days, not weeks. The trees and bushes began to leaf, and thrushes, robins, and wrens sang merrily in the branches. Golden daffodils nodded beside ponds and streams, and, sheltered in the woods, snowdrops and violets had pushed up through the cold ground to welcome a weak March sun.

On the sixth day, as they left the town of St. Albans and climbed the hill to Barnet, the traffic on the Great North Road to London swelled and slowed them down. Peasants and farmers, peddlers and priests stood to the side to let the noble party pass with its carriages, twenty-man escort, and several carts piled high with the countess's household belongings. More than once a carter had to lead his ox-drawn wagon off the road to make room for the entourage. In the abbeys where Joan directed her captain to find lodgings en route, and where Ralph had been a frequent guest, the countess was given a warm welcome.

The final morning dawned gray but dry. Cecily scrambled out of bed to dress, donning her riding gown and cloak and hoping her mother remembered her promise.

"If you are a good girl, I will allow you to ride pillion with Dickon into London on the last day," Joan had told her. "The view from the carriage will not be as magnificent, I grant you. But I cannot allow you to ride alone for fear you may fall foul of cutpurses or some drunken lecher. Do you understand?" Joan spoke sternly. Cecily was a trifle disappointed but submitted, muttering, "Aye, my lady."

Once in the inn's stable yard, Richard led her to his horse. "God give you a good morning, Cis," he said. "I am sorry I could not provide sunshine for your first look at London, but 'twill be impressive enough without it."

He marveled again at the color of her eyes, now alive with the anticipation of seeing the spires and roofs of England's largest city. He was impatient for her to grow into womanhood and for those eyes to notice him alone; she was still young enough to direct that look of joy at a puppy, a nosegay of flowers, or a new gown. Whereas he had stirrings of love and passion, as yet she appeared blissfully innocent. Reminded of his own fleeting dalliance the previous summer, he worried briefly that she might find someone else more attractive and worthy when confronted by so many young noblemen at court. But her attachment to him led him to dismiss the idea. Nay, they were made for each other, he truly believed, and he was moved to pick up her gloved hand and kiss it.

"What was that for, Dickon?" Cecily said, tilting her head to one side. "I pray you help me up."

And so, cupping his hands and receiving her dainty foot, he did as he was bidden.

Not long after they climbed the three-hundred-foot Highgate Hill, the ground suddenly dropped away and London spread out before them. Richard pointed out the tall spire of St. Paul's, which towered above those of other churches, and the thatched and tiled roofs of hundreds of houses, inns, and taverns. All were encircled by a high wall that meandered around the north, east, and west of the city like a heavy white girdle. And along the southern edge flowed the gray ribbon of the Thames.

Cecily drew in a breath. "'Tis beautiful," she said, craning her neck to see over his shoulders. "But also frightening. It is so big, I am sure to get lost. I wonder how people know where anything is. Do they even know their neighbor?"

They lingered a few more minutes, waiting for the heavy carriage to reach the top of the hill, which it did with the help of ten burly men pushing from behind. And then it was downhill the rest of the way to the city wall. Just before going through the Aldersgate, Cecily had to pinch her nose as they passed over the city ditch, the ordure in it steaming from a recently dumped cartload.

"The city is as safe with that cesspit around it as it would be with a moat, I wager," she told Richard, but her words were lost in the din of scores of people on foot, on horseback, and in wagons trundling through the narrow fortified gate into London. She was grateful for the escorts, who sandwiched Richard's horse between them until they emerged into busy St. Martin's Lane, at the end of which, rising into the sky, was St. Paul's. Cecily gazed in wonder at the spire reputed to be the highest in all of Christendom, and as if to accentuate its glory, the bells began to ring for Sext. Soon other churches in London echoed the call to prayer, and Cecily had to put her fingers in her ears against the deafening peals. The citizenry, in contrast, either hurried off to worship or went about their business, seemingly oblivious to the noise.

When the party turned into the Chepe, Cecily gasped at the wide cobblestoned street, mercers' shops lining both sides displaying rich damasks, silks, and satins, and scores of people bustling about, crossing the street, or calling to friends at upstairs windows.

A cookboy carrying hot meat pies on a wooden board on his head shouted his wares, several ragamuffins ran forward begging for alms, and a butcher in the pillory was being pelted with rotten vegetables by several victims of his cheating. Several dirty urchins were keeping warm by kicking around a ball made of straw and cloth, making the riders' progress difficult. Joan's armed guard shooed them out of the way, and Cecily was astonished to see one stick his tongue out at the man while the others laughed and cocked a snoot. Staindrop children would have cowered and run to hide, she thought.

Eventually, the Raby party entered the walled courtyard of the Erber, the Nevilles' London townhouse by Dowgate, and Cecily was delighted by its size and grandeur. She had imagined a townhouse would resemble the wool merchant's house her father had taken her to in York, which he had described as a townhouse. The Erber was three stories high. Sections of the rambling building were of ivy-covered stone with a central tower, and others were of wattle and daub between heavy black beams. Joan exclaimed at the ample light that filtered into the solar through the new and thinnest of horn panes. She spent a pleasant hour going from room to room admiring the changes Ralph had made.

"My lady, Sir Richard Neville is anxious to see you," Ralph's London steward announced from the doorway of the solar once Joan was seated by a newly laid fire.

"My son is here in London?" Joan was surprised and elated. "Does he stay here, Sir Edward?"

"Aye, madam. He lodges in the west wing, but he is this minute come from the king's business at the Tower," the steward replied. "The lady Alice is with him."

Cecily clapped her hands, frightening Jessamine, who was sniffing every corner of the new room. "Alice is here? She is with child, is she not? I wonder if little Joan is here, too? Oh, do send for them," she begged.

A look of annoyance flitted over Joan's face, but she gave her assent to the steward and asked that he arrange for refreshment. Bowing, he disappeared.

"When will you learn to curb your tongue in public, Cecily?" Joan scolded her. "One does not mention Alice's delicate condition in front of a servant."

"Aye, Mother," she answered, nodding gravely. "I should know better. I beg your pardon."

Joan looked askance at her daughter. This was not the first time that she had noticed Cecily's more circumspect attitude toward her admonishments and wondered what had changed her, not being present for the promise Cecily had made her dying father. She grunted, a pleased half smile curling her mouth. Perhaps the child is finally growing up, she thought.

Richard Neville was ushered into the solar accompanied by—except for her enormous waist—the tiniest woman Cecily had ever known. Childbearing was still a mystery to Cecily, but she noticed a radiance about Alice's birdlike features that had not been present the last time she had seen her sister-in-law. Alice curtsied demurely to Joan and greeted her as "my dearest lady mother," and her husband gave his mother a smacking kiss on her cheek.

"I am astonished to see you here, my lady," he said. "I thought you would join the king's household in Leicester."

"Leicester!" Joan groaned, sagging back in her seat. "How could we know? Your father always preferred the road through Lincoln, and so we never passed through Leicester. Sweet Jesu, I do not believe I could spend one more day on those lumpy cushions."

Neville hurriedly reassured her that he would ride himself to make her excuses to the council. "'Tis propitious you should come, I have to confess," he said, grinning. "The physicians did not want Alice to travel until her time, and I was languishing in London attending to minor matters on behalf of the crown while we waited—such as seeing that Monsieur le duc d'Orléans behaves himself in the Tower. Aye," he nodded, "he is still England's prisoner. There is no doubt you will be excused from attending the king if you are overseeing your daughter-in-law's lying-in. What say you?"

Joan's face was a picture of relief, and Neville laughed. "That is easily settled, then. For certain dear Alice is missing her own mother at this time, are you not, my love?" he said. Eleanor Holland had died two years ago and Alice had been heartbroken.

"Aye, my lord, I am right glad to see your mother here—and young Cecily."
Alice held her hands out to Cecily, who, afraid to hurt the baby, gingerly put
her arms around her sister-in-law's neck and pecked her cheek. "God's greeting, my lady," Cecily said shyly.

Alice held Cecily's face between her hands and gave her a smacking kiss.
"'Tis 'Alice,' not 'my lady' when we are together, Cecily. And may I say how
pretty you have become in the two years since I saw you? Quite the young
lady. Being betrothed suits you."

Cecily giggled. "Pish! 'Tis only a piece of paper that says I am betrothed.
Dickon and I must wait a few years, I suppose, until . . ." She eyed the belly in
front of her and did not finish the thought. It was too terrifying to contemplate. Alice laughed and led her to a window seat that looked out onto a pleasant garden brightened by dancing daffodils.

"What news of the king? Of Bedford and Humphrey of Gloucester?" Joan
asked her son, patting the chair next to her.

Richard Neville eased himself into it and put his feet up on a footstool. Instantly Jessamine spotted a new lap and leapt onto it in a flash. She was not disappointed. Neville fondled her ears and head exactly as she had hoped he would.

"One of the reasons I will be glad to ride to Leicester is to witness a reconciliation between Uncle Henry Beaufort and Duke Humphrey," he said. "After
Humphrey and his wife were beaten by Burgundy in January, they returned
and begged for more aid from the council. Beaufort refused, and the tension
between the two men caused Parliament to beg Bedford to come home from
France and mend their fences. He did, and his presence is greatly respected by
all. However, he will no doubt need to stay a goodly while to see this through."

Joan shook her head. "I am sure King Harry is turning over in his grave.
Thinking he had done the right thing by his infant son, he could not have
foreseen the turmoil the kingdom would be in less than five years later." She
paused. "And how is the little king? Is he healthy? Handsome? Does he have
his father's fiery temperament or his gift for leadership?"

Neville laughed. "He is somewhat young to show leadership, madam. But
he is healthy and has a pleasing enough countenance." He paused, steepling
his fingers and staring at the fire. "But he shows no hint of his father's spirit.
He merely sits there and watches, with large, passive blue eyes. I grant you,
he is only five years old, but in my experience most boys want to run, throw a
ball, or play soldier at that age. Sadly, he has no playmates, mostly because of
his mother, who clings to him yet, not letting him out of her sight except in

council meetings, when she must. She is withdrawn and still has not mastered the language." He looked over at his wife and Cecily, happily conversing in their nook, and suddenly snapped his fingers. "Od's pitikins," he remarked, remembering to soften his oath in front of his mother, "I forgot to mention. Cecily, are you listening?" he called. "York is to be knighted with the king in May. Does he know?"

Cecily at once asked leave to tell Richard, and Joan waved her off, instructing her to find the steward and see to the long-awaited supper. As her daughter made a reverence to both her and Neville, Joan said under her breath, "The child has finally learned some manners, thanks be to Our Lady. In truth, 'twas beginning to worry me."

Cecily knew she would find Richard either in the great hall or seeing to his horse. She wagered on the horse, and she was right. After finding her way to the stables, she passed several grooms, who touched their foreheads or snatched off their hats as she skipped in. She spotted Richard, currying his own horse.

"Why do you not leave that work for the grooms? 'Tis servants' work," she suggested, sitting on a three-legged stool and watching him. "I have some important news to give you, but it smells in here, and I'd rather be in the garden."

Richard stopped and stared at her, puzzled. "Since when have you become so high and mighty, Cis? You have always loved horses and the stables—at least you did at Raby."

Cecily lowered her eyes to the straw. "'Tis hard keeping my promise to my father, Dickon. But he wanted me to stop being so childish and be a lady, and I am trying."

"Ah, I see," Richard responded, relieved. "I thought I was losing the friend I have known these three years. I applaud your efforts, but I like you the way you are."

Cecily jumped to her feet. "Do you, Dickon? Then for you I shall never change! For Mother and my brother and—" She clapped her hand over her mouth as Neville's face flashed into her mind. "Brother Richard! Sweet Jesu, I am forgetting why I came." She snatched the currycomb out of his hand, set it on a stool, and pulled him to the door. "Hurry up, this is important."

"Soft, little one," he said, laughing at her. "Whatever it is, it can wait until I have washed my hands."

He went to the pump, rubbed his hands under the frigid water, and then wiped them on his tunic.

"You are going to be knighted with the king!" Cecily cried, without waiting another moment. "Do you think I can be there to watch?"

Richard stood stock-still, his eyes wide. "Are you sure? To be thus honored is beyond words. Perhaps I was more noticeable during my months at court than I thought."

"Pish, Dickon. You are the duke of York, and from what I have heard, you are just as close to the crown as any man in England."

Richard clamped his hand over her mouth and looked around the stable yard. "Where is the garden, you silly goose? You cannot say such things in the middle of London or you will bring trouble for both of us," he said gruffly. But upon seeing her chastened eyes, he sought to soothe her. "Forgive me, Cis, but you must learn to guard your tongue. I know who I am, but Henry is the Lord's anointed and I am the king's sworn servant—as are you. We must never forget our place. I learned from Sir Robert Waterton that ambition can undo a man and bring him naught but ill, and I have no need of it." He let go of her, and they followed the path around the house to the garden, now dusk-dark.

"I am tr-truly s-sorry," Cecily stammered. "God's bones, but why must I watch my tongue when I speak only the truth? You have more right than Henry to be king, do you not?"

"Hush, Cecily!" Richard rounded on her. "Never say so. Who told you that?"

Looking sheepish, she admitted she had overheard her uncle Beaufort telling Joan. "There I am prattling on again. God's bones!"

"Cecily!" Richard expostulated. "Where did you learn that? 'Tis not the language of a lady."

Proudly Cecily told him her father had used it in her presence on several occasions. "He said a lot of things that he ought not when we went hunting." She giggled. "He even tried to tell me about . . . um . . . well . . . where . . . how . . . babes are made," she finished, using the knife from her belt to cut a daffodil to give to him. "He did not succeed," she admitted, "and so I still do not know."

Richard was now embarrassed. "By my troth, *I* shall not tell you. 'Tis for the countess to inform you. Or you could ask Rowena—she seems nice." Hurrying her back to the door that led into the hall, he abruptly dropped the subject.

Not wanting to let him off the hook that easily, Cecily plucked up her courage and asked, "Do you know, Dickon?"

She was rewarded with a young duke's open-mouthed and reddened face, and she laughed delightedly at him. "Nay, you do not, do you?"

Richard hastily hailed a comrade looking for a seat and quickly invited him to join them, thus ending the awkward topic. The very next day, he and Richard Neville left London for Leicester, gratefully relinquishing the business of birthing to the women.

IT WAS ALICE, not her mother or Rowena, who instructed Cecily about carnal knowledge. For the three weeks leading up to the birth of her second child, Alice was sequestered in her shuttered room, as was customary. The young woman, who was as industrious as she was intelligent, chafed at her lying-in, and her favorite companion became the inquisitive Cecily. Merry laughter and confidential whisperings marked Cecily's long visits to the wood-paneled chamber in the west wing of the house.

After a visit from the nursery by the Nevilles' first-born—named Joan for her grandmother and nicknamed Jane—the two would snuggle up together to read Geoffrey Chaucer's *Canterbury Tales,* a book Cecily had smuggled in to Alice at the older girl's request.

Cecily's eyes widened as Alice, reciting with relish, came to the advice of the Wife of Bath on marriage:

> *Tell me to what conclusion or in aid*
> *Of what were generative organs made?*
> *And for what profit were those creatures wrought?*
> *Trust me, they cannot have been made for naught.*
> *Argue as you will and plead the explanation*
> *That they were only made for the purgation*
> *Of urine, little things of no avail*
> *Except to know a female from a male,*
> *And nothing else. Did somebody say no?*
> *Experience knows well it isn't so.*
> *The learned may rebuke me, or be loath*
> *To think it so, but they were made for both,*
> *That is to say both use and pleasure in*
> *Engendering, except in case of sin—*

Before she could finish, the curtains were flung aside by Joan, who snatched the book away, with several stern admonishments to the elder girl about immorality and being a bad influence. "He may have been my uncle by marriage and your step-grandfather," Joan had exclaimed, "but that does not mean I must approve of Master Chaucer's words."

Alice and Cecily had collapsed into quiet laughter after Joan left the room, and Alice whispered, "I wonder if Countess Joan has read his *Troilus and Criseyde*? Now *there* is a piquant piece about love."

An only child lacking companionship, Alice now loved having a sister, despite Cecily's youth. Cecily's lack of shyness and brimming confidence made her seem far older than her years, Alice thought, and she soon was treating the younger girl as a peer. And after closing the bed curtains, Alice decided to educate the curious Cecily as to what happens when a man takes a woman between the sheets. Cecily, rendered speechless for several seconds when her sister-in-law had finished, soon let fly with questions.

"Do you enjoy the act?" she demanded in an urgent whisper. Rowena Gower and Alice's tiring women were always present in the room, but Cecily hoped that as they had their own conversation to accompany the never-ending embroidery, they would pay no heed to what went on behind the velvet bed hangings.

In the light of a candle set in a sconce upon the bedpost, Alice reddened. "I confess I like Richard's hands on me," she said haltingly, but she did not confide any more.

Cecily screwed up her face. "Ugh! I do not want to think of my brother—or indeed any of my brothers—naked and . . . and . . ." She frowned. "What did you call it?—fornicating?—riding you like a stallion. 'Tis too disgusting to contemplate."

"But Dickon?" Alice asked. "What about with Dickon?" And she laughed, a rather loud laugh for such a tiny person, Cecily thought, but the sound always wanted to make her laugh too.

This time, however, Alice's face suddenly tightened and the laugh turned into a groan of pain. She clutched her stomach and raised frightened brown eyes to Cecily.

"The babe!" she whispered. "Sweet Jesu, I think the babe is coming."

Catching her foot in one of her long, dangling sleeves as she uncrossed her legs, Cecily almost toppled off the bed in her haste to fetch help.

"Quick, Rowena, call for the midwife. Lady Alice is having her baby!" she cried, pulling on her soft leather shoes. "I shall find my mother."

She ran down the corridor to her mother's solar, where Joan was taking her usual afternoon nap. Not stopping to knock—and hoping she would not be upbraided for it—she hurried to the bed to shake Joan awake before the attendants could stop her.

"Oh, do wake up, Mother," Cecily pleaded, bending over the snoring woman. "Alice needs you. The babe is almost here."

Joan's eyes flew open and a slight frown creased her forehead when she saw Cecily's unkempt hair falling around her face. She reached up and pushed an offending tress back behind Cecily's ear and muttered, "'Tis time you began wearing a headdress, Daughter." Then she sat up as Cecily's announcement sank in. "The babe is almost here? How long has Alice been laboring, and why did someone not fetch me before?"

Cecily knelt and put slippers on her mother's feet. "She had a pain a few minutes ago and told me the baby was coming. Hurry, Mother, or we shall be too late."

Joan winked at her ladies, and they all laughed, irritating Cecily, who stood anxiously glaring at them. "Why do you laugh at me, pray? Should I not be respected as the countess's daughter? My lady, tell them," she demanded, wheeling round to Joan. "Tell them I am no longer a child to be mocked."

Joan clicked her tongue and stood sternly in front of her, shooing the ladies away. "Know when to keep your pride in check, Cecily. You must not act so impulsively and you must learn when to assert your rank. You are still a child and, in front of my ladies, who at least deserve the respect due their age, you will never use such language or tone again, do you understand?" Joan held her youngest's mutinous expression with her own unflinching gaze and waited.

"I am truly sorry, my lady," Cecily said after a pause, "but one day you tell me to be proud of who I am and the next you scold me for it. Oh, it is too confusing. How can I ever please you?"

Joan softened. "It is a fine line, I grant you, but you will learn to walk it, I know you will. Now let us hurry to Alice."

"My brown worsted cote, Mary," she told the oldest woman, while the others busied themselves around their mistress, tying the neck of her chemise and slipping on the overdress.

"We were laughing, Cecily, because the likelihood of a child slipping into this world in five minutes after the first pain is one in a million. We all know how long it takes to birth a first or second child—oft-times a whole day—because we have either experienced it ourselves or been in attendance." She gave a short laugh. "Although you, my dear, as the fourteenth, did catch us all napping. You were here within the hour!" she recalled. "But today you will watch and learn what happens so that you will not be surprised when your turn comes." She held up her arms for the braided belt to be tied at her waist. "And a simple cap today, I think, ladies, and then we must go."

Cecily tugged at her mother's skirt as the little procession made its way back to the west wing. "If 'tis something you can laugh at, then why was Alice so afraid?"

"Poor child. I heard her first lying-in took more than a day and a night. You forget that she did not have the advantage of a mother or sisters to teach her. Now cease your questions for once. Just watch and listen."

Alice's chamber was a hive of activity when the countess arrived. Joan nodded approvingly as pipkins of water were boiled over the roaring fire and Alice's two attendants tore strips of linen for swaddling bands and washing their mistress. Cecily was the last into the chamber. As she was about to close the door, Rowena stayed her. "Nay, Lady Cecily, leave the door ajar to ease the birthing pains and let the Devil slip out." Cecily did as she was told, noting but not questioning the custom.

A moan from the bed announced another spasm. Cecily saw her sister-in-law propped up on pillows, the blankets thrown aside and only a sheet covering her bent knees. Joan and the midwife each held one of Alice's hands and conferred over the swollen body.

"It be a mite early, my lady," the elderly midwife murmured, "but Lady Alice be strong and the babe's stars be in a good place, so the soothsayer told me when I arrived. It'd be better for the child if he got his own mother's milk, if I may be so bold to say, my lady. But the wet nurse be waiting, in case."

Joan pursed her lips and nodded. She did not approve of ladies of rank nursing their own children. Breast-feeding kept a woman from conceiving, she knew, and it spoiled the look of her paps more rapidly, but she respected the wise woman's ancient knowledge and did not gainsay her. After all, the woman had seen three of Joan's children into the world, including this child's father.

"So be it," Joan replied, gripping Alice's hand as the young woman writhed in pain again. "Although for a short time only."

The midwife raised the sheet to better examine her charge's progress. Her gnarled fingers probed and prodded as she clucked and muttered to herself. Cecily stood as far away as she could from the horrifying scene and winced as Alice shrieked with more frequency, calling out to God, the Virgin, St. Monica, and even the Devil as she flailed about, trying to expel her child. This fearful scene lasted for a full six hours before the midwife called for the birthing chair and Alice was helped onto it. Cecily watched with worried fascination as Alice grunted like a wild beast, and finally, with the midwife's ceaseless encouragements, released a foam-flecked head.

"'Tis almost here, Alice!" Cecily heard herself announce. Tears of joy ran down her cheeks as the rest of the slippery body was deftly extracted from the birthing passage by the midwife's gentle hands. Exhausted, Alice slumped against the sloping back of the chair, and Cecily thought she seemed removed from the extraordinary miracle her body had been witness to.

"You have a daughter, my lady," the midwife said, as though she were commenting on the weather and, to Cecily's horror, she turned the baby upside down and spanked its slimy rump. A delicate objection to this indelicate treatment came from the tiny pink creature, making Joan laugh. "In truth, 'tis a young lady you have birthed, my dear."

Upon hearing her daughter's cry, Alice thrust out her hands to take the child and caught sight of Cecily gazing open-mouthed from across the room. "Then she shall be called Cecily, after her ladylike aunt. How should you like to be her godmother?" Alice asked, smiling through her exhaustion. "What say you, Cecily?"

Cecily clasped her hands to her chest and cried, "Are you sure? Oh, I should be so proud, Alice."

Once the midwife had settled the young mother back into a freshly made bed, little Cecily, now wrapped in fresh linen, was put into her namesake's arms. Cecily was awed with the perfection of God's creation. "Praise be to Him, who has wrought this miracle," she murmured to the screwed-up little face under hers. "But by the sweet Virgin, I hope you grow up prettier than you are now."

When Alice was finally left in the care of the nurse and two attendants, Cecily followed her mother out of the room with Rowena a step behind.

"I tell you this, Rowena," Cecily confided in a whisper. "I think I shall avoid having children. Or perhaps one, so I will know what 'tis like to hold my own babe. But how mother had so many after seeing what Alice has been through, I shall never know."

Rowena was shocked by Cecily's candor, frowned a warning, and jerked her head at Joan's stiff back. "I believe his grace of York will be the one to determine that, my lady," she whispered back. "He may have a dynasty in mind for the two of you."

"Then he may have to do it all by himself!" Cecily retorted.

5

Leicester, Summer 1426

With Alice recovered and the Erber running smoothly, Joan decided it was time she and Cecily went north, this time to Leicester to join the king. Baby Cecily was a noisy child, demanding to be fed at all times of the day and night, but she was thriving, and after the first two anxious weeks, she was given to the wet nurse. Alice endured a few days of unpleasant consequences due to halting the suckling, but she assured her mother-in-law that she could manage by herself until her husband was able to take them all to Bisham Manor in Berkshire, seat of the earls of Salisbury. She wanted to spend the summer with her two children in quiet tranquility under the beeches at that childhood home on the banks of the Thames.

On the first day of May, the small retinue set out from the Erber's high-walled courtyard into Carter Lane and Dowgate. Encountering throngs of young people with garlands and flowers making their way to Chepeside and the maypole, the captain of Joan's escort cursed himself for agreeing to leave on this the merriest of holidays and led the way toward Aldersgate along quieter lanes that could only just accommodate the large carriage. Cecily peeked through the curtain with longing at the exuberant young faces singing and laughing on the route, and resolved that she too would participate in the very first May Day after she was wed.

Joan had no time for such foolishness, telling her ladies, "'Tis a pagan holiday and leads to immorality among the young. I am surprised that the bishops do not put a stop to it," she declared. "If my brother ever becomes a cardinal, I shall suggest he ban the festivities."

Cecily rolled her eyes at Rowena, who pretended not to notice but covered her mouth to hide a smile.

"What is so bad about dancing around the maypole, my lady?" Cecily asked.

Joan pursed her lips. "'Tis a pagan festival of fertility. It leads to lust and wanton dalliance," she retorted. "And I have kept my daughters from it for that reason."

"Aye, well we know," muttered Cecily, stroking Jessamine's silky back, pleased she now understood something about men's lust. *Why is Mother so opposed to babymaking when 'tis certain she has engaged in it at least fourteen times?*

CECILY HAD NEVER seen anything as magnificent as the great hall of Leicester Castle, even at Raby, she decided. She stared about her as the brilliantly clothed courtiers milled about, laughing and talking. Looking down the hall to where the noonday sun was streaming through two lofty stained-glass windows, Cecily was unaware of the attention she was attracting. While in London, Joan had brought her own and Cecily's wardrobes up to date, including the obligatory mourning gowns. Cecily liked the purple silk dress that floated around her from the wide belt above her girlish waist. She thought it made her look older, especially as Joan had insisted on hiding Cecily's mass of golden hair under two horned templettes of stiffened fabric fastened to the sides of her head and decorated with gold filigree netting. Draped over the horns—thus creating a heart shape for her face—a piece of white silk with dagged edges floated down her back. Around her neck hung her sapphire, and Richard's gold-and-ruby betrothal ring weighted her index finger. Joan was gratified to see more than one admiring woman murmur to her neighbor and nod toward Cecily.

And then Cecily saw Richard coming toward her, a welcoming crooked grin on his face. After watching him make a reverence to the countess, Cecily held out her hand for him to kiss, which he did with enthusiasm, taking both hands and raising them to his lips.

"I hardly recognized you, Cis," he told her, sliding her arm through his. "You outshine even the beautiful Eleanor Cobham."

"Who?" Cecily asked, her cheeks pink with the pleasure of seeing him again and satisfaction from his graceful compliment. "Is she here?"

"*Oui, ma belle,*" he said, showing off his newly acquired courtly skills. "She is the woman in green and gold silk over there," he said, nodding in the woman's direction. He had forgotten about Joan, who was searching for Richard Neville among the courtiers but whose sharp ears never missed a piece of interesting information.

"So that's the common-kissing wagtail that has so beguiled Gloucester," she murmured, discreetly examining Eleanor from under her lashes. "Compared with his whey-faced wife Jacqueline, I suppose I can see why."

Unused to hearing such vulgar words from the countess, who looked as prim as a nun in her widow's wimple, Richard glanced nervously at Cecily. To be sure, she was too young to understand what a wagtail was, he decided, and diverted her attention to the musicians' gallery, where four trumpeters prepared to welcome the king to the hall with a fanfare.

Once the long notes died away and the small procession entered from the king's apartments, Richard pointed out the main characters. "Humphrey of Gloucester," he said, indicating a stocky man with wide-set eyes and a sensuous mouth in a handsome face who wore a knee-length purple gown. He chuckled. "I doubt he is pleased to have to walk side by side with Bishop Beaufort. They were made to reconcile in February, but 'tis not evident in their posture today."

Cecily had recognized her Uncle Henry, his tall, lanky body dwarfing his companion, his wealth apparent in the dazzling gold and jewels he was wearing. She knew her clever uncle had amassed a fortune second to none. He had even made loans to the king, Joan had told her proudly. But Cecily did not know what Richard meant by "made to reconcile" and determined to ask him later.

"There is my lord of Bedford," Richard whispered, "and his lady, Anne of Burgundy. She has impressed everyone with her grace and kindness, and indeed she has even sought me out particularly to ask after my well-being."

Cecily looked with interest at the tiny, thin young woman with the elaborately rolled and wrapped headdress that was almost as big as she was. Her lively brown eyes, the most attractive feature of her rather plain countenance, were scanning the courtiers near her for familiar faces, which were now bowed reverently over bended knees or in graceful curtseys. Cecily was more curious, though, to see John, duke of Bedford, for the first time. Henry the Fifth's most trusted brother and now regent, Bedford was a broad-shouldered, brown-haired man, with finely arched brows over steely blue eyes and an aquiline nose. As if he knew she was staring at him from across the room, Bedford turned to look in her direction, and Cecily was relieved to find warmth in his gaze. She smiled shyly at him, and he, not knowing who she was, merely inclined his head politely. Then he escorted his wife to her place with the other ladies near the raised platform and mounted the steps to his own position behind the throne, piled high with cushions.

"Duke John has taken a liking to me as well, Cis," Richard murmured, and Cecily heard excitement in his voice. "It may be that I go with him to France when he returns."

Cecily stiffened, her hand gripping his arm tightly enough to make Richard frown. "France? Why would you go to France?" she whispered. "Your place is here in England—and, when we are married, with me."

Richard grinned. "I will join the army in Normandy, I hope, if your mother gives me leave. I want to be part of the victories that I am certain will rid the English territories of the French once and for all. Bedford is a great commander and I will learn much."

Cecily stared at him. "You *want* to go and fight?" she asked. "Why? Now that we can be together." And then she remembered the day of the hunt when they had shared their hopes and dreams. "You still wish to be a commander, is that it?"

She did not get an answer. The trumpeters blew again in earnest to announce the entrance of the king and his mother. Standing on tiptoe, she caught a glimpse of the boy wearing a gold crown and a purple mantle trimmed with ermine. She was transfixed by being in the presence of the king for the first time in her life.

On his knees, Richard tugged on her skirts. She was now the only one in the room standing. Five-year-old Henry caught sight of her, and his big blue eyes registered her face before he continued slowly past his kneeling courtiers, an earl holding up his heavy mantle. The crown, too, weighted the boy down, Cecily could see, and she was sure he must want to throw it off. Twenty-five-year-old Queen Catherine held her son's hand, giving him strength, and when he would have stumbled on the first step of the dais, she bore him up with a kind word and lovely smile of encouragement. Cecily recognized the same maternal strength that she was lucky enough to enjoy in her own mother. Although a widow's wimple accentuated Catherine's hollow-eyed sadness, the Valois princess was very beautiful, Cecily decided, sinking to her knees.

"Your mother will present you to the king," Richard told her, when they were allowed to stand again. "I can be with you or not, Cis. As I have met him on more than one occasion, it matters not to me."

Cecily looked at him askance. "Dickon, it would seem to me that the more you are seen by the king, the more you will be in favor when he is grown. Am

I not right? Certes, you must go with me. I shall want to be presented as your future duchess so that he does not forget me either."

Richard was taken aback by her fledgling grasp of court politics, but before he could properly acknowledge it, a chamberlain reached Joan and begged her to follow him to the dais. The countess twitched Cecily's veil in place, centered the sapphire on her daughter's flat chest, and led the way behind the officer.

"The lady Joan Neville, countess of Westmorland, and her daughter, the lady Cecily Neville, your grace," the chamberlain called for all to hear. He leaned forward to catch Richard's name, but he was superseded by the little king.

"'Tis my cousin Richard, duke of York," Henry cried without waiting and, turning to his mother, he asked in his high, childish voice, *"C'est juste, maman?"* Catherine nodded and smiled, and Henry was pleased with himself for remembering yet another title. "You are right welcome at our court, ladies." He rattled off the rote greeting he had been taught. "And you too, my lord duke." Catherine bent and whispered something, and the little king was quick to add, "My mother, the queen, and I wish to offer cond . . . con . . ." He turned to his mother for help.

"Condolences, Lady Joan, upon the death of my son's much respected councillor, your husband Earl Ralph," Catherine finished for him. *"N'est-ce pas, Henri?"* and Henry nodded gratefully.

Cecily and Joan were still in deep obeisance, but Cecily looked up and caught the boy's eye.

"Oh," Henry said pointing at her. "You were the one standing just now when everyone else was on the ground." A few anxious intakes of breath were heard from those close to the Neville women.

Joan was mortified. "'Tis her first time at court, your grace," she told him, drawing herself up and attempting to hide Cecily with her wide sleeves. "And she misses her father's influence. Believe me, she will be punished later," she said, venturing an apologetic smile at Catherine. "I can assure your grace my punishment will be far more severe than your displeasure."

Henry's eyes spoke apologetically to Cecily's crestfallen face, cheering the chastised Cecily in a moment of understanding between children.

Catherine laughed and her face lost its haunted look. *"Tiens, Henri, mon fils,"* she murmured to him, patting his hand. *"Madame la Comtesse,* she is a very good mother, I think," she said in her accented English. She looked at

Cecily and stretched out her hand. "*Ma chère fille,* think no more about it. We are not offended, are we, *monseigneur?*" she asked Henry, who shook his head. "*Voilà, comtesse,* there is no need to punish her." Joan could do nothing but incline her head in assent.

"*Viens là,* milady Cecille," the queen continued. "You are soon to marry milord of York, *non?*" she asked, as Cecily mounted the four steps to the throne and knelt again. Joan held her breath and prayed to St. Nicholas to guide her child in courtly manners. She caught the eye of her brother, who was standing a few paces behind the throne, arching a brow. Henry Beaufort was known for his brilliant legal mind, not for his sense of humor.

Cecily knew she must beg the king's pardon, and taking advantage of Henry's empathy a few minutes earlier, she kissed his small hand with a pleading look. "Forgive me, your grace, I did not mean to offend, but I was so captivated by your majesty that, like Lot's wife, I was turned to a block of salt."

Joan almost fell sideways off the step. She heard Richard choke on a laugh behind her, and a smothered guffaw came from one of the councillors ranged behind the king.

But five-year-old Henry was puzzled by this explanation. "Lot's wife, Lady Cecily? Who is she? *Maman,* do you know?"

Queen Catherine was not fooled by Cecily's pretty speech, but she was amused by the young girl's gall. She told Henry that it was a story in the Scriptures that he would learn one day and then brought the subject back to Cecily's impending marriage.

"Aye, your grace," Cecily answered, relieved that her wild apology had been accepted. "I am betrothed to my lord of York, but we cannot wed until I am twelve—which will be in May of next year," she added for their edification. "I am counting the days, in truth. My dear father, Earl Ralph—God rest his soul—told me Duke Richard is a perfect match for me, and I believe he was right." Again, a smothered guffaw, but this time Joan realized it was from her half brother, John of Bedford.

"I think milord of York is fortunate to have you, milady," the queen commented evenly. "I can see you will be much help for him." Then she leaned forward and whispered so that only Cecily could hear. "A *soupçon* of advice. It is better to use your cleverness in private, *ma chère fille.* Men only care for ladies with wool in the head, you understand?" Cecily nodded, thinking that if the queen believes this too, then Mother must be right.

Queen Catherine gave Cecily her hand to kiss, signaling that the audience was ended. As Cecily again made a reverence to the little king, who was yawning and absently kicking his leg against the chair, the queen told Joan: "You have a beautiful daughter, madame. I anticipate to see her at court *souvent*— often."

Joan was so grateful for Catherine's graciousness in the face of Cecily's outspokenness that she backed out of the royal presence, bowing all the way, to the middle of the hall. Cecily copied her, a picture of proud contentment. The queen had singled her out, and she was sure Henry would remember her—and thus Richard. Aye, her first audience had been a success, she thought—until later in their chambers, when Joan unleashed her displeasure on her daughter.

"I thought you had turned a corner. I thought I could trust you to behave like a duchess, and a duchess should be stately and silent. Sweet Mother of God, I despair of you," she groaned, wringing her hands. "I only hope you did not offend the king with your foolish chatter. Lot's wife, indeed! Her grace was kindness itself, and 'twas as well the king did not understand you. Sweet Jesu, where do you learn to prattle so?" She sank down in her chair and shook her head.

Cecily's eyes filled with tears, and she ran to Joan's side. "I do not mean to be bad, Mother, truly I do not."

Her contrition was so sincere that Joan relented, stroking the now unbound hair. In truth, Joan believed the girl had tried to say the right thing, but nevertheless a boundary had been crossed that was hard to explain to her daughter. Perhaps Cecily was too young to have been presented, Joan mused, but she could not undo what had been done.

She sighed, blaming Ralph for the thousandth time for spoiling the child. "The sooner you marry York, the better," she muttered instead. "Then you will have to answer to him and not to me."

Joan did not really mean to be so harsh. Cecily was all the comfort she had at this lonely time in her life. But she was tired of raising children. While an element of truth was in her words, she regretted having to chastise this innocent child.

HENRY BEAUFORT, BISHOP of Winchester, sat stiffly on Ralph's old chair opposite Joan in the countess's wood-paneled chamber in a wing of Leicester Castle.

"I am this close to a red hat, Joan," Beaufort told his sister quietly, pinching his thumb and index finger together. "But I dare not hope that the pope will be any more successful this time than last, if Gloucester has ought to say in the matter. The man hates me, that much is certain."

Joan glanced across the room at her ladies, Cecily among them, and knew their loyalty to her was strong, but she kept her voice low. "Why, Henry?"

"Upon Christ's Cross, he is a menace!" Beaufort hissed, and Joan blanched at her bishop brother's blasphemy. "The truth is that he is as popular in London as I am unpopular. I have oft-times felt myself in danger, and indeed a threat came to my ear that the commoners were ready to drown me in the Thames."

Joan's barely perceptible eyebrows shot up. "Surely not," she exclaimed. He nodded, flicking a flea from his scarlet gown.

Beaufort swilled his wine and swallowed a mouthful. "Humphrey is not fit to govern, that is certain. He is rash and favors conflict."

Cecily found her uncle's permanent sneer and piercing eyes frightening at the best of times, but now that he was scowling, his eyebrows meeting in the middle over his long, hooked nose, she hoped that she would never be the cause of his ire.

Joan shook her head sympathetically. "I shall pray you receive your red hat, Henry. You deserve it above all men."

Beaufort's intense gaze now turned on Cecily. She carelessly pricked herself with her needle and winced. Pretending to concentrate on her sewing, she kept listening. This is how one learns what is happening in the outside world, she told herself. I need to know things like this when I am Dickon's wife. Then, in a panic, she realized that her uncle was now speaking of her, and she prayed that her heated skin did not mean that she was blushing.

"The child understands the stakes in all of this, does she not, sister?" he said to Joan, his eyes never leaving Cecily. "We cannot have York believing he has a right to the throne, and she must discourage him when they are wed. We must make sure the crown stays with Lancaster."

"Certes, she knows her place in our family and that Lancaster must endure. She is as sharp as flint, that one," Joan murmured, as Cecily strained to hear. "I shall keep her close and impress upon her where her loyalties lie. And 'tis my belief York is fond of her already, so she is likely to have influence with him." She grunted. "God knows, she asserts her will . . ."

Cecily was perplexed yet again. Had Joan not insisted that a wife must be loyal to her husband's house and to his ambitions above all? Dear God, will I ever learn to be a duchess?

A FEW DAYS later the castle was abuzz with the news that Beaufort had been nominated cardinal-priest by the pope. Richard told Cecily that speculation was the council might refuse him the right to accept it again. When Cecily looked confused, he enlightened her.

"He will be the pope's puppet here in England, some say. Englishmen have been suspicious of the pope's influence ever since Thomas Becket's time. Trust me, 'twill make the bishop more unpopular here at home if he wears the red hat. 'Tis no wonder he wants to leave on a lengthy pilgrimage," Richard explained.

Cecily leveled her blue eyes at him. "You do not like my uncle, do you, Dickon?"

Richard shrugged. "What I feel is of no import, Cis. I have no influence with anyone, young as I am. But I am learning that what the people of England think of you is very important—especially when our sovereign lord is only six years old." He pulled her arm through his and led her into the great hall for the noonday dinner. "And that is why I would like to go France and make my name as a soldier, as my lord of Bedford has done. Victories in France win Englishmen's hearts."

"But you have influence with me, Dickon. Does that count for naught? What will I do without you when you are gone to Normandy? Besides, I want to share in your victories. Can I not go with you as soon as we are married?"

Richard shook his head. "I will have been and come back long before we are married. Also we should not forget your father's wish that you be patient and see reason. Nay, do not turn down your mouth like that," he said, chuckling. "Never fear, I shall be back to wed you properly when the time is right, my rose of Raby."

"Then I may not be waiting, my lord. I may take the veil instead," Cecily retorted, and left him braying with laughter.

CECILY WAS IN another sulk when she learned that ladies were not permitted to witness knighting ceremonies, and Joan became impatient.

"I blame your father for ever putting you in boy's braies," she complained and crossed herself for mentioning it. "I suppose you will learn the hard way that women will never be a man's equal in this world. We may lend an ear, we may even counsel our husbands when asked, but we are a man's property from one end of our lives to the other. First 'tis our fathers who own and use us to profit from a marriage contract, and then we must honor and obey any husband thrust upon us. You would be well advised to learn obedience to your husband's wishes, Cecily, for to disobey is unforgivable in a wife and is a reminder of Eve and her first sin: that of listening to Satan."

Joan paused, hearing herself preach. Cecily needed sermons if Joan was ever going to teach her headstrong daughter the ways of good Christian women. "And you will obey your husband, Daughter," she added with finality.

Cecily sighed and stroked Jessamine's silky coat. "I know you are right, Mother, but it does not seem fair, 'tis all. But"—she brightened—"I am not yet married and my father is dead, thus I have no man to obey." She saw her mother cover a smile and forged on. "How I long to witness Dickon's knighting, Mam, and I do not see why ladies must be excluded. Why? Do men have to take off all their clothes?" This made Joan chuckle, and Cecily was moved to laugh, too. "Nay, I don't suppose they do."

Joan leaned into her on the window seat, where they were enjoying some fresh air. "Mayhap I can find a way to smuggle you into the old anchorite's cell behind the chapel, where you can use the squint. Let me see what I can do."

Cecily jumped up, sending the dog flying, and clapped her hands with delight. "Thanks be to St. Jude! And thanks be to you, dearest Mother. I promise to be as quiet as a mouse—a church mouse," she cried, pleased with her wit, and they both laughed. It was the first time Cecily had heard her mother laugh out loud since Ralph had died, and her heart was lifted too by the unexpected joy of it.

CECILY TRIED TO get comfortable in the cramped, dark space behind the west wall of St. Mary de Castro church, where the squint had given a long-ago anchorite access to the Mass from his cell. Rowena had procured a plain woolen gown for her, so she had been unremarked as she had slipped into the windowless room, clutching a tinderbox and candle.

Terrified she might be attacked by a rat, she sat down on an upturned barrel and drew up her legs as high off the dirt floor as she could. She lit the candle and settled down to wait, pulling a book from its protective pouch at her waist. When she recognized that it was the musings of her mother's favorite saint, Brigid of Sweden, she groaned. And Joan had even marked a particular passage she meant her daughter to read.

Her Latin was rudimentary at best, Cecily admitted to herself, but she applied herself to the text partly in gratitude for her mother's clever plan and partly to ward off boredom. She sighed and began a rough translation.

"I saw a throne in heaven on which sat the Lord Jesus Christ as Judge. At his feet sat the Virgin Mary. Surrounding the throne was a host of angels and a countless multitude of saints."

Cecily yawned and skipped down to St. Brigid's first question.

"O Judge, I ask you: You gave me a mouth. May I not say what I please?"

Aye, Mother. Cecily smiled into the gloom. I now know exactly why you chose this text. She read the answer aloud in an imitation of her uncle the bishop: *"Friend, I gave you a mouth in order rationally to speak words beneficial to your soul and body as well as words for my glory."*

"God's bones!" she expostulated and threw the book down. "I need read no more."

Just then she heard the fanfare, and she swiveled around to peer through the squint. Soon three dozen chosen young men processed up the aisle in pairs. Each wore a tunic of chain mail over a short white robe, with an empty scabbard by his side. They carried their sword upright by the point, their new golden spurs hanging from the hilt.

When the candidates for knighthood were ranged in two columns facing each other, Cecily heard a rousing "God save the king" from outside the church, and upon another fanfare, young Henry, under his royal canopy, passed by the others and to the choir. How small he looks, she thought, as he received his spurs. Bedford grasped the boy's sword and cried, *"Avaunces!"* Henry knelt and was dubbed knight by his uncle. "Arise, sir knight. *Soit chevalier,*" the duke cried.

Poor Henry, Cecily thought, watching the skinny boy rise and grasp the heavy sword offered by his uncle. It seemed that it was now his duty to dub the rest of the lads with it, but by the time the fifth boy was told to rise and receive his spurs, Henry was so tired that he relinquished his duty to Bedford, and Cecily was barely able to hear the rest of the names the king then called. She began to feel sorry for him.

But then it was Richard's turn. As he stepped forward, his head held high and his eyes shining with pride, something strange was happening to Cecily as she gazed at her betrothed, and she pulled back her head in surprise. A tingling, which had begun in her heart, she surmised, was now traveling to her lower belly, making her breathless for a few seconds. She thought she would faint. What is it? she wondered, hoping she was not ill. She returned to the squint in time to see Richard walk toward her back to his place, his face radiant, and she felt the warm sensation all over again. Can this be what Rowena meant by swooning? Could I possibly be in love? And she hugged herself.

The ceremony moved into the Mass. Cecily thought she had better return to dress for the banquet. Retrieving St. Brigid's writings, she snuffed the candle and slipped out of the cell, pondering the odd sensation she had felt.

Later, upon entering the great hall, the first person she encountered was her sister, Anne. Glad to see someone she knew at last, Cecily went forward eagerly to greet her. Nan reacted to her name being called from halfway across the room with a disdainful frown that stopped Cecily in her tracks.

"Really, Cecily," Anne murmured, casting a critical look at Cecily's clothes, "have you still not learned to behave like a lady?"

"I am happy to see you too, Nan," Cecily retorted, and went to find her place at one of the long tables.

Course after delectable course was brought out for the hundreds of richly garbed guests. The little king presided over the feast, his golden spurs on a red satin cushion by his side. The noonday sun streamed through the stained-glass windows, the dust from all the comings and goings on the rush-strewn floor making heavenly pathways in its rays.

After Nan's chilly reception, Cecily looked around for Richard to cheer her. Hearing his unmistakable laugh ringing out from a group across the hall, her heart lifted and the infectious sound made her laugh too.

ecily realized she was laughing out loud behind her heavy tester curtains and hoped she had not awakened her attendants. Dear Richard, I did so love your laugh, she thought.

Now the rest of the evening at Leicester came flooding back to her, a celebration of the knighting of their king. What promise the boy held then with his good looks, model behavior, and mingled blood of the great Henry the Fifth and the French princess Catherine of Valois.

Cecily harrumphed as she lay contemplating the weakling who still sat on the throne. How wrong we all were. It is not that he is a bad man, she thought, because in fact he is too good, too kind, but out of the goodness and piety has emerged an ineffectual king. She began to wonder what was it that made a good king, one like Henry's warrior father? Was it only power and prowess in battle? She dismissed the thought, knowing, after many conversations with Richard, that good governance of the people was the key, which meant taking and holding the reins. Shaking her head, she had to admit that this Henry had never had a chance to take them, surrounding himself as he had with unscrupulous sycophants. Poor Henry. He had inherited the crown as a babe simply through his right as a first-born son, and from that moment he had been manipulated by stronger men.

Aye, there is no doubt, she admitted, Henry is a weak man. But is his weakness the fault of his piety and goodness or is it because he has a weak mind? She could not decide. However, this jumble of musings about Henry and kingship led Cecily back to the knighthood feast in Leicester and to the first time she noticed any odd behavior in the king.

Henry had been seated under a canopy that night, his oversized sword by his side, and the poor boy did his best not to fall asleep as dish after dish of rich food was placed before him. Cecily remembered that Richard was one of the new knights honored to be chosen to serve the king on their knees. It was after several courses had been consumed greedily that Cecily had chanced to look up at the king, curious to know if he was enjoying himself. It was as though he had been in a trance or as if Jack Frost had run icy fingers over him and frozen him in place, she thought now. Henry's light eyes stared into space, his hand poised halfway between his platter and his mouth. What was wrong with the boy, she had wondered, and why was no one else noticing? But Henry just went on staring until Uncle Beaufort sidled up to him and gently moved the king's hand back to his plate. Henry had started, and it was clear that he was puzzled by the bishop's intervention. Cecily remembered looking around at her neighbors and wondering if others had pretended not to notice.

She stared into the darkness of her curtained bed, seeing again the magnificent hall and reliving that special day in her life. All her senses were satiated that night by the delicious taste of delicate dishes, the pungent aromas of roasted meat mingled with the heavy scents liberally applied to the throats and wrists of the ladies, the myriad colors of silks, satins, damasks, and velvets adorned with every precious gem known to man, the sweet sounds of gemshorns, viols, lutes, and recorders. And then there was the touch of Richard's hand as he led her out to dance.

Cecily gave a smothered snort of laughter as she recalled the other memorable event that night: her first stab of jealousy. Aye, Cis, you can laugh now, but at the time you believed the heavens had fallen about you.

It was after the tables were cleared and the dancing began that she tried to find Richard in the melee, she recalled. As she made her way to him, eager to share her secret viewing of the knighting, she had almost tripped over a small dog camouflaged in the rushes, trodden on the long points of several shoes, and felt a flea take a bite out of her ankle. She could not quite remember what oath she had uttered, but she would never forget the shock on the face of the man near her.

But then she spotted Richard and started to go to him but stopped short when she had seen *her*, Cecily recalled, conjuring up the voluptuous young woman whose face was turned from her. I suppose that if I had not felt that first flutter of love in the hermit's cell earlier, I might have ignored her, Cecily told herself. But, oh, how jealous I was to see a strange young woman with her hand on Richard's arm. Such boldness had rendered me speechless with disgust, Cecily admitted.

But if she remembered aright, Richard did not appear to be at all offended by such intimacy, and she was determined to confront them both if she could only stop her legs from trembling. However, by the time the large man blocking her path had moved out of her field of vision and she had taken a first step, the lady was gone.

When Cecily approached Richard, he was stunned by her indignation and pretended Lady Agnes meant nothing to him. She was Queen Catherine's attendant. He claimed that he had not even noticed the lady's hand on his arm.

Chuckling now, Cecily mentally wagged her finger at Richard. Ah, my sweet husband, she thought ruefully, I am certain that was not the only lie you ever told me in our lives together, but in the matter of Lady Agnes, they have all been long since forgiven. She had regretted not dropping the topic then and there and winced now at the memory of her prim retort. "I cannot think this . . . whatever her name is . . . is a lady. She had her hand on your arm in a most familiar way."

Richard had not cared for that remark, Cecily recalled sheepishly, and so had retorted, "You are too young to understand, Cecily. I swear to you, 'twas of no importance. It *is* of no importance."

Cecily sat up in bed suddenly, a piece of a puzzle slipping into place. I do believe she had to have been important to you, Richard, she reasoned, for it was only a few days later that you presented me with a gift that was likely to assuage your guilt in the matter of Lady Agnes.

She plumped the pillow and tried to straighten out the rumpled bed sheets before settling down to remember the details of that wonderful day when Nimuë had come into her life.

PART TWO

That you may be a lover tried and true,
My wish and will are that your heart be fixed
In one sole place whence it can not depart
But whole and undivided there remain;
For no halfhearted service pleases me.
He who in many a place bestows his heart
Has but a little part to leave in each;
But of that man I never have a doubt
Who his whole heart deposits in one place.

ROMAN DE LA ROSE

6

Leicester, Summer 1426

The summer passed pleasantly enough in the midlands city, though Richard spent much of his time in the duke of Bedford's train, with his guardian's blessing. "You are better off traveling with my learned nephew than wasting your time dancing attendance on me," Joan said. "My husband had great respect for John, and he would have approved, I have no doubt. But I beg of you, do not forsake Cecily for too long. She needs your guidance, and I confess I weary of her robust health and unflagging curiosity."

"Whereas I, my lady Westmorland, find it enchanting."

Richard's earnest response amused the older woman, and she arched one eyebrow. "I hope you are not dissembling, Richard. Cecily can be a trial when you are with her morning, noon, and night."

She dismissed him when she saw that she could not move him. "You will see, mark my words, my daughter is as busy as a bee."

Richard bowed and left the room in search of the subject of their conversation. He had a gift for her, and he was looking forward to witnessing her delight in it. After the incident with Lady Agnes, Richard was eager to make amends. Two days after the knighting, Queen Catherine had been advised by the council to sever the king's leading strings and leave him to its governance. He had watched the sorrowful queen and her party disappear through the castle gate and into Church Lane and noted that Agnes had not cast a backward glance. He sighed with relief and thanked God for his escape from an embarrassing situation with Cecily. He made up his mind that he would never again dally with a woman, wanton or no, unless she was his wife.

His mood now was greatly lightened by his talk with Joan and the increased certainty of going to France with Bedford, and he set off to find his betrothed. On such a fine afternoon, he was certain she would be outside somewhere, picking flowers or reading in the shade of a willow. He hoped she was not out riding, for he was impatient to give her his love token. Instead, he found her with a squire having a fishing lesson, and she was obviously enjoying herself, judging by the laughter and the mud on her face. When she turned upon hearing his call, he felt his heart leap in his chest and an ache in his loins. The warmth of her eyes and voice when she said his name told him she must have similar feelings for him, and he hurried forward to kiss her dirty hands.

"Will, I thank you for entertaining my lady. How is she as a fishwife? I can see she has baited her own hook."

"Pish, Dickon!" Cecily answered and laughed at him. "I am not such a ninny as to be afraid of a worm. And I thought a fishwife was someone who sells fish, not catches them."

Richard gently pried her fingers from the pole she was holding. Giving Will a friendly slap on the back, he excused himself for stealing Cecily away and led her back to the castle's outer bailey.

"I have a surprise for you, Cis, but first you must wash your hands. They smell awful," he told her, shutting the back gate and making for the well in the castle yard.

"A surprise for me?" Cecily said, her eyes shining. No one had given her a gift since her father had died. An exchange of new year's tokens during the mourning period would not have been seemly. She looked expectantly at the three-cornered metal bag at his waist. "Is it in there?"

Richard drew a bucket from the well, and she let him pour the cold water over her hands while she scrubbed them with the harsh potash soap. Drying them on her apron, she pointed at the bag and repeated, "Well, is it?"

"Nay, it is not. And you shall not make me tell you. 'Tis a surprise, after all," he admonished her. "Follow me."

They skirted the stables, drawing curious looks from the grooms. Passing the smithy, they came to the dog kennels, a long, low shed built against the castle wall. Cecily clapped her hands with excitement, setting up a cacophony of yelping and yowling.

"A puppy, you are giving me a dog of my own," she cried, but upon seeing Richard shake his head, her face fell. "No?"

"Nay," Richard teased her, "'tis better than a dog." He continued past the noisy kennel to a shed with a thatched roof. One of the king's falconers was mending a heavy leather glove when he saw them coming toward him. He jumped to his feet and executed a low bow. "My lord of York, God's greeting to you. My lady," he bowed again to Cecily, impressed by the comely young girl at Richard's side. "Wat Percival at your service. Would you like me to bring out Phoenix to you or your new hawk, your grace? She is a game one, faster than most in this mews."

"Then he will suit Lady Cecily very well, Master Percival, very well indeed, as it is a belated betrothal gift. I pray you, fetch her out." Richard turned to the delighted Cecily. "I hope you will accept the token and not pine too heavily for a pup. I am told this merlin came from Turkey."

"My own hawk? Oh, Dickon, how can I thank you enough?" Cecily cried, and forgetting herself, kissed his cheek. She felt Richard stiffen and too late realized she committed the same impropriety as Lady Agnes. "I am sorry," she whispered, looking behind her to where Richard's valet and Rowena stood at a discreet distance, "but I was quite overcome by your generosity."

"Do not fret, Cis." Richard tried to sound stern, but as the falconer returned, he whispered conspiratorially, "I shall not tell the countess; after all, we *are* betrothed. In truth, I rather enjoyed it."

Master Percival presented the handsome, hooded merlin for Cecily's inspection, while Richard beckoned to his valet to bring up the large bag he was carrying. Rowena sidled closer for a look at the magnificent bird perched immobile on Master Percival's wrist. Cecily stroked the shining brown feathers, and the bird responded by scooting along Percival's protected hand, making Cecily jump away.

"Easy, girl," the falconer soothed it, "Easy."

"Does she have a name?" Cecily asked the man, who shook his head.

"It'd be best for you to name her, m'lady. She must learn to obey only your voice and expect food only from you."

Cecily studied the creature, admiring its strength and beauty, and then allowed Richard to fit a cream-colored leather glove on her hand to which was attached a small metal ring.

"When your bird is properly trained, Lady Cecily, you will let it perch here with the leash around its leg. Now hold out your arm stiffly, please. Aye, that is good."

Master Percival untied the leather thong from the ring on his glove and gently transferred the bird to Cecily's wrist. She eyed the yellow talons gripping her hand with misgiving but confessed that she could not feel anything except the bird's weight through the finely tooled glove. Richard deftly attached the leg leash to the ring as the little bell on the bird's leg tinkled merrily.

"I know it is for me to know where she is in flight," Cecily said, sticking her arm out in an exaggerated pose. If truth be told, she was a little afraid of those claws and the powerful, hooked yellow beak. But Richard assured her that with the hood on, the bird was too afraid to move but a few inches from where it stood, and she had nothing to fear. Little by little, she brought her arm and the bird closer. She could not take her eyes off the glossy plumage, the black streaks on the breast, the deep brown wing feathers, and the buff-and-brown-barred tail.

"She is truly beautiful, Dickon," Cecily said, her eyes shining. "Is she not, Rowena?" Then a wistful look clouded her face. "Poor thing, I am certain she would love to fly free. I know I would, if I were a bird." She laughed off the thought and turned to her betrothed.

"When do I begin training?"

FOR THE REST of the summer, the duke of York and young Lady Cecily could be seen riding out of the West Gate and over the island to the countryside beyond, followed by a gentleman usher with Rowena riding pillion. Cecily had her merlin on her wrist and Richard his falcon. The two young people never tired of conversing and laughing together. Fields of corn were ripening in the August sun, and the hedgerows were full of twittering sparrows, chiffchaffs, whitethroats, wrens, and warblers flitting after winged insects or pecking at the ripening blackberries and hawthorns.

Richard was a good teacher and Cecily a ready pupil. She had watched her father and brothers hawk for many years in her childhood and understood the rudiments of the sport, but the finer points were now being taught her and she exulted when the merlin made her first kill. This raptor, easier for a lady to handle, was a hand-bird, a hawk that came back to its owner without a lure, and Cecily loved it when the bird returned to her hand. Richard noticed her fingers were nimbler than a man's as she hooded the bird and attached the leash, and he admired her ability to calm the bird so quickly. His respect for this half-child, half-woman was growing daily.

She named the bird Nimuë, "because she was the enchantress who cast a spell on Merlin," she explained to Richard, "and she has cast a spell on me." It had taken her days to find just the right name, and now she loved the way it rolled off her tongue. She had whispered it over and over to the hawk until she was convinced the bird would react with its *kee-kee-kee* cry when she approached the mews and called out, "Nimuë, my beauty."

Richard had been patient, telling her that training a bird was not the same as training a dog. "'Tis a wild thing, Cis, and it will as lief fly away as return to be shackled. But by rewarding it with kindness, a good deal of respect, and meat from your hand alone, it will learn to do your bidding—and only your bidding." He taught her how to put the hood upon the bird's head in one swift motion without getting pecked, how to whistle through her teeth to recall the bird to her glove and reward it. At first, Nimuë was attached to a leash and small birds were loosed for her to attack. After many short flights, kills, and returns on a longer and longer leash, the merlin was ready to hunt with her mistress.

Cecily had not been this happy since before her father died.

But on the fifteenth day of September, when Richard came to fetch Cecily for their daily expedition, she immediately noticed his anxiety.

"What is it, Dickon? Have I upset you? Your smile is not wrinkling your eyes as it usually does."

Richard frowned. "Not wrinkling my eyes? Whatever do you mean?"

She told him of her decision to trust him at their first meeting because of his crinkly eyes. He burst out laughing. Cecily decided not to tell him that she preferred his smile to the neighing laugh he could not control, so she merely nodded and continued, "My father once told me that you can trust a man whose smile reaches his eyes. I have seen so many instances when he was right." She looked right and left and then murmured, "Like my Uncle Beaufort. He smiles but his eyes do not. He frightens me."

Richard grimaced. "I suppose he is smiling now that he finally has his cardinal's hat," he said half to himself. "Pray put Henry Beaufort from your mind, Cis. I have some news that will affect us, and though 'tis everything I could have hoped for, I believe it may cause you distress."

Cecily drew in a breath and played with the long liripipe of her floppy felt hat. "You are going to France, are you not?" A simple question, plainly asked, and Richard could do nothing but nod. He stood by quietly, expecting a flood of tears, but instead Cecily held her head high and tried to sound grown up as she wished her betrothed God speed.

"'Tis what you wished for, Dickon, and I shall manage, I dare say. Mother needs me, and I promised Father I would stay with her. We are to return to London for the winter—or perhaps to Windsor to be with the king. Like as not, I shall be well amused."

Richard was astonished. He was certain his volatile Cecily would have begged him not to go or turned on her heel and walked off in a huff. He reached for her hands and fingered the ruby betrothal ring. "I promise I will be back to wed you, but for now I need to learn to be a soldier and I cannot do it hawking in Leicester, as much as I have enjoyed our afternoons." He looked at her impassive, lovely face and tried to read her expression, but she was giving nothing away. "We leave on the morrow," he finished. "Early."

After formal farewells the next day and Richard's pledge that he would be a better correspondent this time, Cecily tucked a silk kerchief in his tunic for luck and looked into his honest gray eyes. "I think I love you, Richard Plantagenet, if I understand what love is. I pray you, return to me safe and sound."

Before he could answer, and before the tears that were held back by sheer force of will overcame her, Cecily reverenced him and walked calmly away. Richard stared after her, part of him wanting to run and hold her, part of him lacking the courage.

"I think I love you, too, Cecily Neville," he whispered into thin air. "God keep you until we meet again."

7

Windsor, Winter to Summer 1429

*C*ecily sighed with frustration when drifting snow in the middle of January put a stop to her favorite activity. And so she whiled away the winter hours learning French and Latin with her tutor, working on a tapestry with Joan, learning to play the psaltery, or on her knees in the chapel at Windsor, where the king and his court had chosen to spend her thirteenth Christmas and Twelfth Night.

Not long after, Cecily was overjoyed to receive a letter from Richard, which she opened with trembling fingers.

Orléans, Yuletide 1428

Right well beloved Cecily,

It is with deep sadness that I send news of our great commander Salisbury's death on the third day of November last. May he rest in peace. It is said that he was struck by debris from a cannonball that flew through the window of a tower where he was surveying the scene across the river. He did not perish instantly but was transported to a small town nearby, where he died a week later.

I am writing from outside the walls of Orléans on the Loire, where we have been besieging the city since October. Upon learning of Salisbury's death, our brave English soldiers appeared to lose their confidence, and the new commander, William de la Pole, earl of Suffolk, chose to withdraw most of the troops from the walls, leaving only a small garrison to guard the tower guarding the bridge over the river and into the city. Many of us who have only minor appointments thought it was foolish, but what could we do? I am happy to say that

Lord Talbot, upon hearing of Suffolk's rash decision, immediately sent us all back again.

Do not concern yourself for my safety, Cis, because other than a few daily skirmishes here and there, most of our time is spent waiting for the city to surrender. I have become adept at chess, and before the snow came a week ago, I caught many a fish along this beautiful river. I often wondered what war was like, but I did not imagine this inaction. Other than one day when my little band was attacked for half an hour, I have not used my sword in service of the king once—but I killed a rat with it a week ago.

But now the cold keeps me and most of my fellow captains huddled in our tents, warming our hands over braziers, praying, swapping stories of our childhood, or writing letters. The poor billmen and archers have naught but their cloaks and open fires to keep them warm. I cannot believe the people inside the walls can survive much longer, and we pray daily for a command to breach the walls and finish the job or to see the French garrison commander send out a message of surrender. I think of you in your cozy apartments, fires blazing in the hearth, shutters and arras to keep out the winter wind, and good food warming your bellies. How I wish I could be there to celebrate Christ's birth with you and your mother.

I believe you will need to comfort your sister-in-law, Alice, in her loss. She was Salisbury's only child, I seem to remember. I expect she may have received word before this. Now the only consolation is that it will not be long before her husband has the Salisbury earldom awarded him through her. Your brother is a good man and will wear the rank nobly.

May the Blessed Virgin have you in her keeping each and every day. I shall count the days until I have news from you. Your letters brighten my days and oft-times make me laugh. Pray also remember me dutifully to your mother and my guardian, the countess.

Your devoted Richard.

Cecily refolded the letter tenderly and stared at the falcon and fetterlock seal of the house of York. She had sometimes been curious as to why an instrument of imprisonment had been chosen as a badge. The falcon was perched, wings open and ready for flight, and yet it was clearly manacled to the fetterlock. The meaning was lost on her.

Cecily shivered as she imagined Richard huddled in his tent, blinding snow whirling around outside and howling winds penetrating the canvas. She tucked up her feet under her warm velvet skirts and gazed into the bright flames of the fire in Joan's spacious solar. She liked Windsor, its round keep upon the motte high in the center of the extensive castle walls giving one a view of the Thames flowing through its wide valley on its way to London and the sea. True, the countryside here was also mantled by snow, but it was a peaceful, bucolic scene unlike that under the walls of a besieged city, where at any moment boiling oil, arrows, stones, and cannon balls might rain down upon the attackers.

"Mother, does Alice know her father is dead?" she asked Joan, who was peering at Christine de Pisan's book *City of Ladies* through her gold-rimmed spectacles.

"Aye, poor lamb," she said, sighing. "I thank God your brother was home from the borderlands when the news reached them at Bisham Manor. I did not think to mention it to you, Daughter. You did not know the man, but he was England's best general. God rest his soul. 'Tis said Suffolk took his place, but we have heard no more."

Cecily rose from her window seat and grandly gave her mother and the other ladies Richard's news, proud to be more informed than they. Joan was plainly astonished that Richard would entrust such important information to his young bride-to-be. Such indelicacy, she thought. She resolved to talk to him of it as soon as he returned to England. She entreated St. Brigid to return him soon from this dangerous adventure to which she had agreed far too readily. Cecily did not need to be widowed before she was even properly wed, Joan thought. If he came within the next few months, she would insist on the formalizing of the marriage, and she would ask Duke Humphrey of Gloucester to find a place at court for Richard that would preclude his running back to the French war. She well remembered consoling Cecily when the girl's twelfth birthday—the time when she might legally be wed—came and went without a sign from the young duke.

"I thought he would surely return as soon as it was legal for us to be married, Mother," Cecily wailed a month after her birthday while staying with Alice at Bisham. "He promised!"

"Hush, Daughter," Joan had snapped, turning her irritation at Richard's silence on Cecily. "There is naught you can do, so resign yourself and learn a little patience. Our lives as wives and mothers are all about waiting—waiting for our husbands to return from somewhere else, then awaiting their pleasure, or waiting for the next babe to come. You must learn how to fill your days so that you do not notice the waiting. 'Tis the best advice I can give you."

Joan smiled to herself now as she recalled Cecily's uncharacteristic acceptance of the little homily with a demure, "Aye, my lady." She wished for the thousandth time that Ralph could see how Cecily was growing—nay, blossoming—from cygnet to swan. She was tall for her almost fourteen years, and the gawkiness of pubescence was disappearing. Her waist was tiny and her breasts, although not yet fully formed, filled the bodice of her gown with a promise of the voluptuousness that was fashionable in this time of low-cut gowns, their generous collars plunging from the tips of the shoulders to a wide V at the cinched high waist. Perhaps her neck was a little too long, but the eye was quickly drawn to a perfectly oval face, cherubic mouth, and those glorious gentian-colored eyes. How fortunate that Cecily had inherited the shapely Neville nose and not the Beaufort beak, Joan mused. Aye, it was time York claimed his young bride or she would have trouble keeping her daughter's virginity intact, she chuckled to herself.

JOAN HAD CAUSE to worry, for Cecily had had several opportunities to explore her sensual side since feeling the first flutters in the hermit's cell at Leicester. There were many eligible young squires who made sheeps' eyes at the youngest Neville daughter, and Cecily was becoming increasingly aware of her own beauty and its effect on the opposite sex. She was attracting their attention. But her fear of betraying Richard's trust—not to mention her fear of being branded a harlot—had so far kept the young men at bay. Her height, regal posture, and direct gaze made Cecily's admirers afraid of approaching her. She was, however, never at a loss for a dance partner.

In truth, one seventeen-year-old tow-headed squire—the same Will who had taught her to fish—had appeared in some of Cecily's dreams of late and flustered her when he smiled across the room at her. She did not know quite how to respond to a lightly pressed hand, a murmured compliment, or overlong kiss on her fingers. Soon Richard's teasing nickname, proud Cis, was being bandied about the squires' hall and dormitory in quite another context, for all the young men were of the same mind: to break down her reserve and steal the first kiss.

As the winter turned to spring, Cecily practiced waiting. It was time to take Nimuë out of the mews to exercise her beautiful wings as well as to let

her jennet stretch his legs across the fields. The hours following Mass and before the main meal of the day were Cecily's favorites. Then she joined young
squires and other ladies in riding to the hunt, accompanied by fewterers han-
dling lithe greyhounds, and falconers. It was on these rides that those same
squires who so admired Cecily's beauty saw the young woman shed her aloof-
ness and handle a horse and hunt as well as any man.

One particularly successful late-May morning, Cecily murmured farewell
to her merlin, making sure that the bird had received the choicest of meat
tidbits from the two hares she had caught, and hurried back to her apartments
to change her habit for a more suitable gown for dinner. She arrived breathless
at the top of the spiral stair and stepped into her mother's solar just in time to
see Joan react to a piece of gossip that had been passed on by one of her ladies.

"Scandalous!" Countess Joan declared. "Sweet Jesu, but Queen Catherine
must indeed be her wanton mother's daughter. Such disregard for her rank, for
her son, and indeed all of us."

"What has the queen done, Mother?" Cecily cried, removing her green
felt bonnet and pushing a wayward strand of hair from her face. Jessamine
waddled toward her to be patted, and Cecily bent down to make a fuss over
the old dog.

"She has given birth to a bastard," Joan answered, fairly spitting out the
distasteful word. Cecily hid a quick smile in Jessie's brown and white fur. But
Mother, she wanted to say, you were a Beaufort bastard once. Instead, she lifted
her head, eyes wide with surprise. "A bastard? Do you know who the father is?"

Joan's companions all swiveled their heads from daughter to mother, agog
to know the answer. The gossipmonger had not been given that information.
Joan lowered her voice, and four necks craned to hear who might have sired a
child on the king's mother.

"I cannot know for certain, but before she left court," Joan told them, "it
was apparent that she was enamored of a servant of her late husband, King
Henry, one Owen ap Tudor—a Welshman and a most handsome gentleman,
but . . . a servant!" Two of the women nodded, snickering. "He became her
own keeper of the wardrobe, if you remember."

Cecily stood up and faced her mother. "I remember she was kind to me. I
feel sorry for her. She was so young when King Henry died, and then she was
sent from her little son's court. She must have been very unhappy, and I am
glad she has someone to love her."

The ladies sat stock-still and watched Joan's face harden. "It is not our place to love wherever we will, Daughter, and we in turn cannot expect to know romantic love. All of us are bound to do our duty according to our family's wishes. You find respect and love when you find a husband. Anything else is harlotry. Any more talk like that, young lady, and we shall remove you from court and keep you close until York comes calling for you."

Cecily's face fell at such a public upbraiding, and tears were close. But heeding the lesson to show no emotion, she curtsied to the countess, murmured an apology, and fled from the room as the bell rang for dinner. She flung herself on her bed and pounded the pillow with her fists. I hate being a woman, she thought vehemently. No one thinks ill of a man who takes his pleasure where he may. How dreadful to fall in love with someone you should not be with, she mused, turning over and lying on her back, imagining the queen with her servant-lover. As it often did, her daydreaming returned to Richard and what it might be like to have him touch her.

"Lady Cecily." Rowena's voice pierced her thoughts and she sat up with a guilty start. "You must ready yourself for dinner. The bell has sounded, and your lady mother will be angry with you again."

"Oh, Rowena! I pray you make my excuses. Say I have a headache, I beg of you. I cannot face my mother and her ladies now." She lay down on the feather bed and stared at the canopy above her. "Please go quickly and, if you can, bring us some food for, in truth, I am ravenous."

Rowena returned as quickly as she could after informing the countess of Cecily's headache, and then slipped down the great hall staircase to the kitchens below and wheedled food from a grumpy cook. The two young women set about devouring half a fish pie, two custards, some roasted rabbit, and a bowl of dried plums and nuts.

Cecily looked at Rowena curiously as the older girl bit into a filbert. "Why are you not married, Rowena? You are eighteen now, are you not?"

A sudden sadness suffused Rowena's broad face: "My father is unwell, my lady. He must first find good positions for my younger brothers, and as I am the last of three girls, I am less important. He was pleased when your lady mother took me in to attend you." She sighed. "I shall probably end up an old maid."

"Nonsense!" Cecily cried, moved by Rowena's plight. "I shall set about finding you a husband, never you fear." She chewed her bottom lip, a childhood habit that helped her think.

Rowena dropped a little curtsey. "You must not bother yourself on my account. I am perfectly content here with you. Look at how I am living," she said, spreading her arms and taking in the elegant tester bed with its heavy tapestried curtains, rich turkey carpets on the polished tiled floor, two huge chests, a finely carved high-back chair, and a small cushioned settle all gracing the large room.

Cecily wandered to the window, its horn panes almost transparent but not clear enough to give anything but a blurred impression of the crenellated roof of St. George's Hall on the other side of the small courtyard, where the king's household would be at table. Why am I fretting about Rowena's lack of a husband when my own betrothed has not even written to me for two months? She grimaced. 'Tis certain he has forgotten me, she thought, then immediately felt guilt for her unkindness, for word had come to the council that the English army was plagued by sickness and deserters and was sadly depleted, allowing new French soldiers and supplies to sneak into Orléans. But this news had not concerned Cecily. Perhaps Richard, God forbid, had been wounded or even worse, but Joan had assured her daughter that if such a noble as York had been killed, the king would have been apprised. But Cecily fretted. He could still be too ill to write.

Cecily sighed. Dear Mother of God, do not desert me now, she begged silently. I promise I have discouraged all those other young men and kept myself for Richard.

So deeply was she in thought on the window seat, watching a flock of starlings lift from the great hall roof, that she did not hear a knock on the door and turned only when a man's voice softly spoke her name.

"God's greeting, Cecily. I trust I find you well."

Leaping down from her perch, she squealed with joy and flung herself into Richard's arms. Rowena had taken up a discreet post by the door and watched the happy reunion with pleasure. Richard was unprepared for such a reception and, as gently as he could, extricated himself from his betrothed's embrace, using his left hand to protect his right bicep.

"Sweet Jesu, but you are grown even lovelier," he murmured, scrutinizing her for many seconds with his gray gaze. "Do I gather from your welcome that you are glad to see me, Cis? I feared a rebuke for my dismal lack of correspondence, but I do have an excuse." He tapped his arm gently.

"Oh, you are hurt, dearest Dickon. Forgive me. Were you wounded?" She hung her head. "I was just thinking how cross I am with you because you had not written. But be sure I am glad to see you. Is the siege over? Why are you here? Tell me what happened to your arm."

Richard had forgotten Cecily was capable of so many questions at once and chuckled. "An arrow found me as I hurried back to my tent one day with only my breastplate and helmet on." He fingered his arm gingerly. "'Twas my own fault, I confess, and I cursed my bad luck, and although the wound is healing, my lord of Suffolk decided I was of more use to him as an envoy and sent me home." His derisive inflection of the word *envoy* told Cecily that he felt himself demoted. "I had been giving the council the latest news until dinner was announced. When I did not see you in the hall, I came to find you. Are you unwell? Your mother's attendant mentioned a headache."

"Pish! I do not have a headache. Mother and I quarreled, 'tis all, and I did not feel like getting another homily at dinner." She hung her head sheepishly. "I fear I am still not the lady Mother would wish for. But no matter, tell me your news. Is the siege over? Did those Frenchmen surrender?"

Richard went quiet. He had been sequestered with the council for more than an hour, recounting the sorry story of the siege and answering endless questions. He was tired of the subject, but Cecily deserved a response to her eagerness to know the outcome of the siege, and he could spare her the details. Besides, he wanted time to drink in the beauty of her. Twisting the large signet ring on his first finger, he took a deep breath and began.

"You may be surprised to know that the French themselves raised the siege, Cis." He smiled at her slack-jawed face. "Aye, 'tis hard to conceive. They must have been starving in the city after the long winter. But in truth, something happened that will puzzle Englishmen for years to come, and only we who witnessed it could believe it." He shook his head and crossed himself.

Cecily held her breath for a second before blurting out, "What? What happened?"

"On the twenty-fifth of last month, Duke Philip ordered his men to leave Orléans, and that left only the English surrounding the city, our numbers much cut by sickness, death, and desertions. We were daily expecting the white flag of surrender—surely they could not hold out any longer. Four days later, we did see a white flag, but it was decorated with a portrait of Jesus and two angels and was carried by a youthful French soldier who seemed to have God on her side."

"*Her* side? You mean his side, my dear Dickon," Cecily teased.

But Richard was not joking. "Nay, I mean *her*," he said firmly. "Her name was Jeanne—Jeanne d'Arc," he told a now-rapt Cecily. "We heard that she had traveled from her village in eastern France at the command of heavenly voices to seek the Dauphin Charles and affirm that he was indeed the true French king." Cecily stared openmouthed and fascinated as Richard quietly continued: "It is said she journeyed to Chinon, where the dauphin was awaiting the fate of Orléans—and indeed of France. It seems that Charles's father, our king's grandfather, had so many bouts of insanity that people believed he could not have sired this young dauphin. Charles should have been proclaimed king as successor to his father, but he has never been crowned because the people believe he is a bastard. Anyway, we heard this Jeanne—she is naught but a peasant's daughter, mind you, and only seventeen—was able to have an audience with the dauphin—I mean king."

"Seventeen?" Cecily's imagination was afire. *She is but three years older than I*, she surmised, *a mere peasant girl, and she leads an army?* "How can this be, Dickon?"

"I swear I am telling the truth," Richard replied. "Do you want to hear more or not?"

Cecily nodded. "Forgive me, I am dumbfounded, 'tis all. But I wish you would hurry up and tell me how she became a soldier—you mean in armor and carrying a sword?"

Richard nodded. "Just so—and she was not afraid to wield it. I have not told you the most important part of the story, but if you would stop interrupting, I will."

Cecily glared at him. Gripping her hands together in her lap, she sat silent.

"That's better," he said, though it was all he could do not to laugh. "It is said Jeanne has been hearing heavenly voices—St. Michael, St. Catherine and St. Margaret, they say—telling her to find the dauphin and announce to the court that he is indeed his father's son and has every right to wear the crown." He paused. "To test her powers, Charles stood among his nobles to see if she would know him, a man she had never seen before."

"Sweet Jesu, she must have been brave," Cecily breathed, admiring the intrepid Jeanne more by the second. "And did she know him?"

"Without faltering, so we were told. She then asked to be allowed to join the army, which is what her voices told her she should do, and help free Orléans. It is hard to believe, but after the priests were satisfied that she was not a witch—and it was confirmed she was still a virgin—she was allowed to arm and go to the Orléanists' aid."

"Did you see her?" Cecily whispered, fascinated. She fancied she could see this maid upon a white horse, carrying the banner of Christ, her armor shining, her hair streaming out behind her, and a bright halo about her head. How I should love to have seen her, she thought enviously. Nay, how I would like to *be* her.

"Aye, Cis, I did see her. From afar, you understand, and not long afterward I was wounded and taken to the surgeon's tent. The common soldiers said they saw a light shine from her as she rallied the French during a sortie from the city, but we captains knew it for mere fanciful thinking. Our troops were on the verge of crushing the enemy when she raised her banner, and all those French-men who were starving and weary were miraculously revived and fought like crusaders again. It was too much for us, and we lost fortress after fortress as well as our nerve. It did seem to us that perhaps she had God on her side."

Both sat in silence for a spell, each with their own vision of Jeanne d'Arc.

"So, Orléans has fallen," Cecily murmured at last. "Whatever next?"

Richard shrugged. "I left to bring the news, but I fear for our other garri-sons along the Loire."

But Cecily's mind was still on Jeanne. "Even though I have no wish to go off and fight, I should dearly love to see myself in armor upon a caparisoned courser."

"Cecily!" Richard expostulated, rising. "'Tis unnatural, and many were shocked that she would dress as a man. As my wife . . ." He stopped, not need-ing to remind her of her father's long-ago flouting of the Scriptures.

Cecily lifted her chin defiantly and looked him squarely in the eye, unaware how desirable her indignation made her. "But I am *not* your wife, am I? I have waited and waited . . ."

Richard could not resist her. He pulled her to her feet with his one good arm and slowly and deliberately kissed her full on the mouth, tasting a hint of honey. He felt her breasts against him and realized with a jolt that she was indeed no longer a child.

Cecily was so taken off-guard that she was unable to savor the moment she had fantasized so often in her waking dreams. He let her go as quickly as he had taken her, which was just as well. Joan's voice floated to them from the corridor, and they jumped apart before she swept in.

"Ah, York, I see you have found the truant," she said, eyeing Cecily's flushed face with more than a hint of understanding. "I think it is best you do not stay to hear what I have to say to her. *A tout à l'heure, monseigneur.*" She put out her hand for Richard to kiss and watched him scurry through the doorway, a gleam of amusement in her eyes.

"Now, Daughter, what is all this about a headache?" she said, arranging her black skirts around her as she settled into the high-backed chair. "You seemed perfectly fine when you left my chamber in a huff before dinner and you seem perfectly fine now. Well?"

THE STORY OF the maid of Orléans preoccupied everyone for many days after Richard's return. Indeed, the court spent much of the month of June hearing about Jeanne d'Arc's military successes and inspirational effect on her countrymen. Cecily could not hear enough about her, and each reimagining of Jeanne's courage and faith intoxicated her further.

Only a year before, the English had dominated most of northern France down to the northern banks of the Loire. Philip, duke of Burgundy, controlled not only his duchy of Burgundy but also all the territories in the northeast as far north as Holland. Philip's alliance with England was hanging in the balance following his standoff at Orléans, but neither party wanted to cede any territory to the French crown. At least they were united in that goal. Humiliating though it was, Charles and his Armagnac party hung on in what was left of his lands from south of the Loire to the Mediterranean. Only after Jeanne affirmed his legitimacy in the eyes of God and prophesied that she would see him crowned and France rid of its enemies did this uninspiring prince find a modicum of courage. Jeanne went from strength to strength after Orléans, finally defeating the English on the Loire at Patay. And in another humiliating defeat, Lord Talbot, one of England's foremost commanders, was taken prisoner. The future of Henry's holdings in France looked black indeed.

The mood at Henry's court was grim. In four short months, this peasant girl from a tiny hamlet was threatening English dominance in France. At home in England, the king's council was divided between those who favored a peaceful pullout backed by Cardinal Beaufort and his ally in France, the earl of Suffolk, and those, like John of Bedford and Humphrey of Gloucester, who could not bear to see their French lands relinquished. And it did not help that the English people were tired of being taxed to fund the never-ending campaigns in France.

One evening after the little king had retired and some at the court were taking advantage of the long July evening to stroll around the gardens at Windsor, Humphrey of Gloucester and his new wife Eleanor fell into step beside Joan and Cecily and their attendants. Joan was surprised but gracious.

It was unusual for Gloucester to single her out for conversation, and she won-dered what his motive might be.

"Today I received news that the peasant girl has fulfilled another of her prophecies. Not a week ago she saw Charles anointed king at Reims, and she is now approaching Paris," Humphrey growled.

"Sweet Mother of God, do not say so," Joan exclaimed, her hand over her mouth. "But where is Bedford, my lord? Is he not defending Paris?"

Gloucester's rasping voice was hard to avoid. Walking a step behind, Cecily was able to indulge herself in eavesdropping. She had become obsessed with the story of Jeanne—la Pucelle, they were calling her, which Richard told her meant the Maid—and every time she heard the name, Cecily's ears pricked up.

She is only three years older than I, she thought for the hundredth time, and yet she has led an army, scaled a city wall, been wounded, and even crowned a king. What have I done? She could think of nothing important at all, and the notion disheartened her. She wasn't even married or could not even boast a title. She was now, however, firmly convinced that Jeanne must have heard saintly voices. Why, had not she, Cecily Neville, been visited by the Virgin herself twice in her life: once in the forest at Raby and then by the white dove? It was probable that Jeanne was also thus visited.

"Thanks be to God that your brother the cardinal agreed to allow the troops he had raised for his crusade in Bohemia to be put under Bedford's command, madam," Gloucester was telling Joan. "They will reinforce Paris, I have no doubt."

Then without even a pause, the duke came to the point of his walk with Joan. "By your leave, Lady Joan, I would know your opinion of your nephews, John and Edmund of Somerset. You must have watched them grow up."

It was asked almost flippantly, but Joan saw through Gloucester's guile and trod warily. In as flippant a tone, she gave an ambiguous response that told the man nothing.

"Oh, pish, Mother," Cecily broke in, unable to resist speaking her mind. "Edmund is a bully, and I have never cared for him. He swung a cat around by its tail at Raby once and Father gave him a whipping for it, remember?"

As soon as the words had left her mouth, Cecily regretted them, for Joan slapped her roundly for eavesdropping and interrupting a royal duke, but al-though smarting, Cecily noticed that Humphrey was looking curiously at her, as if her words had struck a chord.

* * *

RICHARD RAN UP the steps to the countess of Westmorland's apartments a week later and asked to be announced. He found Joan standing by the window of her solar and knelt to kiss her hand. "My lady, it is good of you to see me, and I shall not keep you long," he began, aware of others in the room but intent on speaking with the countess privately.

Joan smiled at the earnest young man and noted the broadening shoulders, wisp of a beard, and sharpening features. How old was he now, she mused, eighteen? He was a fine-looking man, if not the tallest or broadest of his fellows. He and Cecily would make beautiful children together, she thought. She glanced over his shoulder to where Cecily lay curled upon the bed, napping after the midday meal. Putting a finger to her lips, Joan nodded in Cecily's direction.

"You look so serious, Richard. What is it?" she murmured. "Do not tell me you are returning to France. It would break Cecily's heart." Despite the question, Joan already knew the answer. She had persuaded her nephew Humphrey of Gloucester to find the young duke a role at court, pointing out that it might be wise to bring Richard into the family sooner rather than later by sanctioning his marriage to Cecily. She knew she did not have to spell out why; Gloucester was well aware of the implications for Lancaster of Richard's Mortimer claim and had at once acquiesced. "But no fanfare, countess, in view of the dire news from France," he had said.

"Is this better?" Richard answered Joan's question, giving her his warmest smile. "Now that I have learned I will remain at court for the foreseeable future, I believe there is no reason to wait. I am here to ask you formally for permission to wed Cecily."

Neither had noticed that Cecily had awakened and was craning her neck to hear the conversation. When she heard the word "permission" and her name, she sprang off the bed but, remembering to control herself, she walked sedately to the pair by the window.

"Good afternoon, Dickon," she said as coolly as she could, hoping her expression did not reveal her racing pulse. "'Tis abominably hot, is it not? To what do we owe the honor of a visit?"

Richard turned abruptly when he heard her, and kneeling on the red-and-white-patterned tiles, he kissed her hand.

Joan arched a cynical eyebrow. She had not missed the flush of excitement on her daughter's neck or the quiver in her voice. Little minx, she must have overheard, her mother guessed.

"How now, Richard, will you answer her? Why did you come a-calling?" she teased the flustered man. Then she leaned forward and whispered, "You have my permission, my lord. Now put her out of her misery." She rose, snapped her fingers at the two attendants, and went to the door. "Come and find me in the rose arbor, Cecily. I have no doubt you will wish to talk. God bless you both."

Richard waited until the door clicked shut and then he clasped Cecily's fingers and looked up into her expectant face. "I came to seek your hand, my lady," he said simply. "I know we were promised those many years ago at Raby, but the time is . . ."

He got no further. Cecily went down on her knees to join him and took both his hands. "Then let us seal the bargain, my lord of York—with a kiss," she said grandly, and closing her eyes and pursing her lips, she waited. His neighing laugh startled her and broke the spell. Now she frowned. "What is so amusing, Dickon? This is no laughing matter. You are supposed to kiss me. It says so in *Roman de la Rose,* or so Alice told me."

She was about to get off her knees when Richard stayed her. "Forgive me, Cis, but you looked so comical with your puckered lips, I could not forbear to laugh," he explained. Then, looking deep into her eyes, he spoke the words he had practiced so often in his tent outside Orléans when he thought he might never see her again. "Cecily Neville, I love you with every breath that I take. From the first day I saw you, you have been in my heart. Even before your father decided that we should be man and wife, I knew 'twas what I wanted, too. Would you do me the great honor of becoming my wife, my duchess, and my companion for life?"

Tears of joy filled Cecily's eyes as she listened to the words she had been yearning to hear since his homecoming. The weeks of waiting melted away in the happiness she felt at this moment. "I will," she whispered, "with all my heart I will."

"Now you shall have your kiss, my dearest." Richard took her face in his hands and their lips met first in a kiss of promise, then deepened into one of desire and wonderment.

8

England, Autumn 1429

The small cavalcade meandered slowly along the towpath beside the Thames on its way to Bisham twelve miles upstream from Windsor. The road was pitted by dried hoofprints made by the huge carthorses and oxen that pulled the barges along the river, and Cecily was glad that she and Joan had chosen not to take the carriage.

"It would have been a bone-shattering ride," Joan said, traveling pillion behind Richard Neville on his bay horse. "We are so grateful to you for giving us your escort, my son. I have no doubt we would have found our way, but it gives me a chance to have you to myself."

Neville chuckled. "Alice was insistent I fetch you, Mother. She was convinced you would prefer to ride. How could I disappoint her after she gave me a thriving son and heir last year." He looked back at the rest of the group to make sure they were keeping up, and chuckled again. "I am astonished to see Cecily up behind Dickon. I do not believe I have ever seen her ride except on her own horse since she was in brai—I mean swaddling bands."

"Braies is what you were about to say," Joan finished for him. She sighed. "Sweet Jesu, how that father of yours spoiled her. But look at them, like a pair of moonstruck peasants. 'Tis unseemly how they kiss and coo."

"Let them be, Mother. I well remember Father taking you in his arms in front of us and covering your face with kisses."

Joan simpered like a young girl. "Aye, he had no sense of decorum whatsoever."

"And you loved it. Confess it, my lady!" he retorted, and his mother gave him a playful thwack.

Cecily had her arms around Richard's waist with her head resting on his back. It felt strong and hard beneath his worsted tabard. She breathed in his musky scent. She had requested to ride pillion just to be near him. Richard guided his horse with one hand on the reins; the other had Cecily's concealed in the folds of his tunic. He could not wipe the grin from his face, despite daily mockery from his comrades at dinner in the great hall.

In two days we shall be wed, Cecily said to herself, watching a kingfisher flash blue and orange into the water and use its daggerlike bill to spear a fish. Dear Mother of God, you will be there with me, will you not? Aye, I expect you are there for all young women at those important times in their lives. This will be my most important time, sweet Mary—except perhaps when I am giving birth. She gulped and lifted her head. In her happiness at knowing she and Richard would soon be united, she had forgotten the other part of marriage, the part that Alice had described during their secret talks at the Erber. Come now, Cecily, she told herself, be truthful. You have indeed thought of this often in the past few years. How many times have you looked at a couple and imagined them naked and fornicating? She shook her head. She did not want to imagine herself and Richard in that naked, tumbled state. She wanted him to entwine his fingers in hers, kiss her gently, and call her his love, and indeed he had done so several times since they had pledged themselves, but they had always been fully clothed.

"Is there something amiss, Cecily?" Richard asked, when he felt her move and pull away her hand. "Would you like to climb down and stretch your legs?"

Cecily thought it a very good idea, and so Richard called out to Neville to stop. Joan was pleased for the halt and after reaching the ground with her son's help, went off to find a convenient bush to take care of her need.

The respite on the riverbank cleared Cecily's mind of awkward thoughts, and soon the group was trotting eastward away from the river toward Bisham. It was almost dark when they arrived, but the old white stone of the centuries-old former priory, first built for two Knights Templar, glowed against the inky sky. Flambeaux and candles in the great hall welcomed the Neville party, and within a half-hour, plates of steaming pheasant pie, delicate trout, roasted capon, and goblets of good Bordeaux wine were replenishing growling bellies and soothing aching limbs.

Alice and Cecily tumbled into each other's arms as soon as the formal greetings were over. Alice could not wait to show her sister-in-law where she would be lodged in the comfortable, rambling house. "I have set aside my mother's favorite solar for you and Dickon," she whispered. "You will stay in it alone until your wedding night—" she broke off, looking at Cecily's hand gripping her arm and then up at Cecily's frightened face. "What is it, Cis? Surely you are not still afraid of . . . Ah, but I see that you are."

She pushed Cecily inside the solar, shooed Rowena away, and locked the door. Within a few minutes, Alice had calmed Cecily and reminded her of the beauty of intimacy with one's husband.

"Do we have to do it naked?" Cecily ventured. "I do not think I would like to see Dickon naked. I like him in his fine clothes."

Alice tittered, her huge brown eyes full of merriment. "You will like him without clothes, you will see. Why, 'tis plain as a pikestaff the two of you are head over heels in love. If you are so fearful of that first time, just ask him to blow out the candles. Believe me, you goose, he will feel just as anxious," Alice reassured her.

But Cecily was crying. Alice pulled her into her arms. "What is it, sweet Cis?"

"This will not be Richard's first time, I am certain of it. What if I do not please him as those court ladies did?" Her voice was muffled in Alice's damask gown as she wailed, "I fear he has already made a cuckold of me."

Alice shook her hard then, trying not to laugh. "First of all, you have to be a man to be a cuckold, silly, and second, you must never speak to him of this. My sweet simple Cecily, there is not a male worth his salt who has not poked his pestle where it does not belong before he is wed." She rose and put out her hand. "Now, dry your eyes, for I would take you to the nursery. You will not believe how your godson has grown."

Sir Richard Neville led the way across the broad meadow toward the woods south of the manor that was part of Windsor Great Forest. Cecily's wide skirts slapped against her horse's flanks and the liripipe of her felt chaperon streamed behind her. She skillfully maneuvered her horse out of the way of a bramble bush and urged it to soar over a small brook, which gave her the exhilarating sensation of flying. How she loved to ride! She felt a twinge of guilt as she glanced back over her shoulder to see Alice lagging by a furlong, but as her sister-in-law was accompanied by Neville's squire, Cecily chose to forge ahead and catch up with Dickon and her brother.

Zigzagging her way through the smaller trees at the edge of the wood, she was forced to slow her excited jennet down to dodge overhanging branches. She let the horse find its path while she kept a lookout for any leafy hazards at eye level, muttering oaths under her breath as the men pulled further ahead.

They think I am back there with Alice, she decided, or surely they would have waited for me.

Being alone in the forest always took her back to the scene with the white hind. A noise to her right made her look eagerly in that direction, too late to see the vagrant wielding a stave who stepped from behind a tree. She flung up her hands to protect her face and screamed before she felt the blow. A white light blinded her as she tumbled like a stone onto the mossy ground. The man only had a few moments to pull off her betrothal ring and cut the leather purse from her belt before he heard shouts of alarm from Alice and her escort. He clambered clumsily onto Cecily's horse and clung to its mane, urging it forward in a westerly direction. By the time Alice and the squire arrived on the scene, the thief had disappeared into the forest.

"Christ's nails! Is she dead?" the squire exclaimed, sliding from the saddle. Gingerly he picked up her hand to feel a pulse. "Lady Cecily, can you hear me?"

"Dear God, she cannot be dead," Alice cried. "I knew when I saw that lone magpie from my window this morning that something might go amiss. Get me down from here, Jack, I beg of you."

While the squire attended to Alice, two other gentlemen and their grooms cantered onto the scene and stared aghast at the limp young woman on the ground. A groom blew an alarm on his horn to alert the two Richards, and Jack, giving his friends instructions to stay with the ladies, leaped on his horse and rode after the vagrant.

Alice cradled Cecily's head in her lap, pulled off the restrictive headdress, and stroked her forehead, urging her to open her eyes. "She is breathing," she murmured. "Thanks be to St. Hubert."

"Who is St. Hubert?" Cecily's whisper startled Alice.

"Bye the rood, Cecily! You have frightened us half to death. Are you all right?" Alice turned her head on hearing hoofs, and relief spread over her face. "Thank heaven, here are Dickon and Richard. Oh, I am so happy you are alive, my dearest Cis."

"I am, too," muttered Cecily, putting up her hand to feel the enormous lump on her temple that was now oozing blood. "What happened?"

Alice motioned for Dickon to dismount. "I think you were struck by a lout with a stick, but we were too late, and he got away on your horse. My squire has gone after him."

Dickon was now on Cecily's other side and took her gently from Alice, his anxious gray eyes searching her face as questions tumbled from his lips. "What?" "How?" "Why were you alone?" and "Are you hurt anywhere else?"

Cecily smiled, reveling in his concern, and snuggled closer to him. "I thought I could catch you and Richard, and I foolishly left the others behind," she confessed. "Other than in my pride, I do not think I am badly hurt." When she lifted her hand to stroke his face she noticed the ring was missing and moaned. "My ring, Dickon, he took your ring. Is it an omen, do you think?" Could this be a sign from the Virgin? Surely not, she hoped, and crossed herself.

"An omen? Foolish girl, certes it is nothing more than an unfortunate robbery—all too common, I fear," he assured her, laying her head back onto the moss. "The ring is not important compared with your life, dear Cis. Some water, I pray you, Neville."

Richard Neville pulled a leather flask from his saddlebag and took it to Dickon. As Dickon held it to Cecily's lips, he pondered how many such violent encounters occurred in the forests of England these days, and in broad daylight, too. Englishmen were taxed to the hilt to raise money to defend the garrisons in France, and many men were forced to flee into the forests to forage for food or rob innocent travelers. The young duke had always privately thought that holding on to Normandy was worth the few extra pennies of tax each man must pay, but now reality had handed him a new perspective.

In his few weeks back at court and in council meetings Dickon had seen that even among the nobles there was dissension over which was the better path for England: keeping a stronghold in France at the expense of English manpower and crippling taxes or making a peaceful and conciliatory end to English rule in Normandy, Maine, and Anjou. Despite the disappointment of Orléans—his only foray into military life—Dickon's views had aligned more closely with those of Bedford and Gloucester in the name of a strong English France. However, having seen Cecily thus attacked, presumably by a disaffected peasant, and knowing she might have suffered far worse than a bump on the head, Dickon now wondered if he was right.

"Look! 'Tis Jack returned," Alice cried, jumping up and pointing to where the squire was threading his way through the trees, leading the robber upon Cecily's horse. A coarse brown hood concealed the man's face. "Thanks be to St. Hubert! He has caught the whey-faced measle."

Cecily's head pounded, her neck was stiff, and she still felt lightheaded, but she kept her eye on the outlaw as Jack pulled him from the saddle and threw him to the ground.

"Filthy thief!" Jack cried, giving the man an extra kick in the kidneys for good measure and laughing at his cry of pain. He took a leather thong from his belt and threatened the man with it. "Cowardly maggot! I should hang you here and now, but the sheriff will deal with you later. Now answer me. Where have you concealed your booty?"

The hood had fallen back from the face, revealing a terrified young man not much older than fifteen. Cecily drew in a sharp breath of surprise. "Sweet Jesu, he is but a boy," she murmured.

"Enough, Jack," Richard Neville commanded, stepping between the angry squire and his captive. "I thank you for your trouble and commend you for catching the varlet. Now, I pray you, take charge of Lady Cecily's horse and escort Lady Neville home." He turned to his wife. "My dear, I trust you will make ready for Cecily. We shall follow later."

"Can you stand, Cis?" Dickon asked. "I could take you up in front of me or I can stay with you while we await a litter."

"Pah! I do not ever want to be seen returning from the hunt on a litter. I can perfectly well sit pillion," Cecily retorted, struggling to her feet. Her legs wobbled, and she stumbled and would have fallen had Dickon not steadied her. She gave him a rueful grin. "Perhaps you are right. I suppose I shall have to be carried home like a child. How humiliating." She winced as she tried to turn her head.

Dickon chuckled. "Ah, proud Cis. For once, 'tis not a weakness to admit you need help."

"We must send for the sheriff," Neville called to them. "My groom can put the thief behind him and lock him up in the root cellar until Sheriff Gossage arrives." He bellowed at the prone figure on the ground, "What is your name, peasant? Your name?"

"P . . . Piers, m'lord. Piers T . . . Taggett," the lanky youth stammered, getting to his knees. He was unshaven, but his beard was soft and he had several pimples on his face typical of his age. "Have m . . . mercy on me, I b . . . beg in the name of the Blessed Virgin." He looked up at Neville's stern face, hoping for some sign of sympathy, but there was none. "Me mother and sisters have no food. Me dad went to France with m'lord Salisbury and never came back. I had to rob so's the family could eat," he jabbered. "I am sorry, my lord."

Neville held up his hand. "I am sorry for you, but you have done wrong and you must be punished. You almost killed my sister."

"I d . . . did not m . . . mean to harm her, sir, I swear. But I was d . . . desperate." Despite his size, Piers was trembling, and the boyish voice wrung Cecily's heart.

"Soft, Richard," she said, hobbling to her brother while holding fast to Dickon's arm. "If he gives me back my ring, can we not let him go to his family? I am not so badly hurt."

Neville's eyebrows shot heavenward. "What? Allow a thief to go unpunished? What would that serve, Cecily? 'Tis my belief he should hang not only for his act of thievery but for assaulting a noblewoman. This sort of conduct needs a lesson in English justice, and I intend this outlaw shall receive it. Now enough of your mawkish nonsense."

Dickon felt Cecily's hand grip his arm as she straightened herself to her not inconsiderable height and faced her eldest brother. "I am the person wronged here, my lord, not you," she said steadily, though her legs quaked. She had never asserted herself with her sibling before because of the fifteen-year difference between them—not to mention his gender. "You can see I am not badly hurt, except for this wound on my head." She fingered it tenderly. "How can you not be moved by the lad's story, Richard? And his father died for England under your father-in-law's banner. 'Tis not his fault he was too young to look after his mother and sisters and has resorted to crime in order to eat. 'Tis a cruel land we live in where we will not tend our own neighbors who have naught to live by." She held her chin high and stared Richard down. "Can you not have pity on him?"

She glanced now at Piers, who was looking in adoration at this angel of mercy with her porcelain skin, blue eyes, and sweet voice. The sun glinted through the leaves and into her waist-length fair hair, making her appear ethereal. He thought her a vision, for she was the way he had always pictured the Virgin Mary when he prayed to her each night. He crossed himself reverently.

"Mother of God, help me," he begged her. "They will brand me or even hang me."

Cecily touched the lad's tousled head. "God have mercy," she murmured. "Perhaps the Holy Mother will hear your plea." She was taken aback when he prostrated himself mumbling an *Ave Maria*. Staring at his quivering body, she was aware for the first time of her power, and it made her brave. Suddenly she imagined La Pucelle facing the Dauphin Charles and all his court, and she was inspired. She turned back to her brother and tried again. "Richard, I beg of you, have mercy and give him another chance."

Dickon could see tears in her eyes, and he wondered briefly if they were conjured up to soften her brother's heart or if they were genuine. Whichever way, he was impressed.

For a moment, Cecily thought her brother would not bend, but all of a sudden, his face softened and he chucked her under the chin. "Certes, Cis. How can I resist such a supplication?" He turned back to Piers and told him to rise. "You owe your freedom to the lady Cecily. I hope you will not make me search you for the treasure you took from her. Return it immediately before I change my mind."

Dickon was amazed at the change of heart in this stiff-necked knight. He was also struck by Cecily's charity for this sniveling peasant. It made him think.

Piers rummaged around in his tattered tunic and produced Cecily's small purse. "I be sorry m'lady. Truly sorry. This be what I took." He handed the booty to Cecily with an awkward little bow. "Pray for me, a sinner," he murmured and straightened up, looking at Richard Neville for dismissal.

Dickon was observing the boy, who was tall, obviously malnourished but with a promise of strength, and he suddenly spoke. "I need a man I can trust to care for my falcons and my lady's hawk. I have a mind to apprentice you to the king's own falconer. I will pay you when you are properly trained. What say you?"

Neville and Cecily stared open-mouthed at Dickon, but Piers was once more on his knees and kissing his savior's boot. "Grew up in these woods, so I did. Know something of hunting, m'lord," he said, sheepishly. "More than I should, mayhap."

Neville harrumphed. "Poaches as well as robs, no doubt," he said with a snort. "Dickon, have you taken leave of your senses?"

"Come to Bisham Manor on the morrow, after informing your family of your new employment," Dickon told the young man, ignoring Neville's derision. "Now get up and go and tell your mother the duke of York is grateful for your father's service."

Piers's eyes widened in shock. "The duke of York? God's truth!" he muttered, staggering to his feet.

Cecily's eyes were now shining with pride for her betrothed. "What a splendid idea," she cried, digging in the purse and pressing two angels into the hand of the astonished Piers. "This will help your family until you are able to send more. Tell your mother that the lady Cecily Neville is grateful to her for letting you leave." She could no longer ignore her throbbing head. She leaned into Richard as Piers bowed his way backward, turned, and raced through the wood. "I should like to go home now," she said.

As she dozed happily in Dickon's arms, rocking gently with the horse's gait, she remembered the ring. She took it from the pouch, slipped it back on her forefinger, and sent a prayer to the Virgin. You were with me today, Holy Mother, were you not? The poor man thought 'twas you and not me who saved him. She marveled at God's work; out of possible disaster had come triumph. If I had not been alone in the wood, she mused, events would not have taken the path they did to save a young man from a life of crime and a family from starvation. It was God's will, she believed with all her heart.

"Thank you for helping the boy, Dickon," she murmured. She held up her hand, the ruby glinting in its golden setting on her finger. Her father had once told her that to give was infinitely more rewarding than to take, and she hoped she would always remember the glow of satisfaction that filled her now. "This ring will always remind me of this day and how you and I saved a soul."

Dickon took her hand and kissed the ring. "Let us never forget in future to be more compassionate to those less fortunate." He chuckled. "Remember the day when I told you I wanted nothing more than to be a soldier and you, I believe, wanted to be a queen? Here we are again, in a forest, sharing another intention."

"I love you, Richard Plantagenet, and I would not care if you wanted to be naught but a gong farmer."

Richard Neville turned back to see what had caused the now familiar neigh of laughter.

JOAN TOLD HER daughter that she was not to leave her bed the next day. With her head still hurting and the effect of ground valerian root taking its time to wear off, Cecily had agreed to a postponement of the wedding for a spell. "I have waited for six years. I can wait a few more days," she told Alice. Alice was sponging Cecily's head wound. "I do not want to get married with a black eye," Cecily said, chuckling.

So for four more days, the men hunted or competed with bow and arrow at the butts, and Alice and Cecily played with the older children while baby Richard—at ten months already a force to be reckoned with—struggled with his swaddling bands and babbled nonsense.

From her window Cecily saw Piers Taggett arrive on foot from the nearby village of Marlow. His hair was cut and combed, and he walked with purpose toward the stables. Alice had been astonished when Cecily had described the scene in the woods. She had crossed herself upon hearing Cecily's belief that the Virgin herself had sent Piers to teach her a lesson in mercy.

"I should have known some joy would come from the incident," Alice said, clapping her hands. "On my way back to the manor I saw two magpies fly across our path."

"One for sorrow, two for joy," Cecily intoned, nodding. "Let us hope Piers rises to his reward."

THE WALLS OF the private chapel at Bisham reflected the silver and scarlet colors of the Salisbury coat of arms, with its green spread eagles decorating the door columns. Today a Neville and a York banner had been hung for the occasion of Cecily's marriage. The tiny space could accommodate only a dozen people, but as the event was private, all the guests of honor were able to kneel in comfort upon the tapestried cushions and watch the young bride wed her duke.

Cecily wore a gown of palest blue cloth of silver. Joan had commissioned it for this occasion more than a year ago, and the bodice was too tight when Cecily had tried it on at Windsor a month before. With much blushing she had allowed the seamstress to measure her chest. Several inches of white satin were inserted into the front of the bodice to allow for her blossoming. When the dress was finished and Cecily tried it on, Joan nodded in satisfaction, but Cecily had grimaced in the polished brass mirror.

"It has spoiled the line of the gown, in truth," she complained, and the seamstress rolled her eyes behind Cecily's back as she worked on the silver-sable hem. "The satin should have been put in at the sides or in the back. It will cry out that the gown is old and we had to alter it."

Joan had had enough. "Hold your tongue, young lady," she snapped. "Mistress Roberts has performed a miracle, and you should be thanking her instead of upbraiding her. Rowena, take the gown off your mistress, wrap it in linen, and lay it safely in the oaken chest. She does not deserve to wear it."

Joan smiled to herself now as she bent her head over her polished amber rosary and waited for Mass to begin. Cecily looked magnificent in the gown, her sapphire necklace a startling blue against the inserted white satin. Even Cecily had admitted that she was pleased with her wedding attire once she was dressed, and she had spun round and round, letting the yards of shimmering fabric billow out like a bellflower. Her hair was undressed, falling in straight rivers of gold down her back and over her shoulders, a simple circlet of flowers crowning its glory.

When Richard saw her enter the chapel on her eldest brother's arm, he felt his knees go weak. Steeped in the romance he had read of in books of chivalry, Richard desired Cecily, but he cherished her virtue first. They had been promised to each other for so long that he had almost forgotten a time when he had not known she would be his. She had become first his little sister and then his friend, but in the few months since his return from France, a tender love had grown. When he thought of Cecily, he had fleeting visions of her naked body next to his, but they seemed almost disrespectful, and he would chase them from his head. Last night he had chosen a verse from his favorite *Roman de la Rose* to read before he fell asleep, and now he remembered these few lines:

> *Her name was Gladness, she a singer gay*
> *Who since she was but seven summers old*
> *Had given him all her love. . . .*
> *Well did they suit each other. . . .*
> *Color of new-blown rose*
> *Glowed in her flesh so tender.*

Aye, my dearest Cecily, you are indeed the color of a new-blown rose, he thought, watching her now. He raised his left hand to shoulder level, his palm facing the priest. In his right hand he held the traditional garland of flowers through which the couple would kiss to seal their vows. He waited impatiently for Neville to relinquish Cecily to him and for her open hand to touch his in a sign that the couple came before God with open hands and hearts.

Cecily had never felt more vital in her life. When she saw Richard standing near the carved wooden altar, waiting for her with an expression of such awe on his dear face, she felt power surge through her veins. She was so eager to begin her life with him that she wanted to rush to his side, but at the sight of her mother's anxious face, she counted to five, assumed a pious expression, and slowly stepped down the aisle in time with her brother. Her eyes held Richard's unwavering gaze as she made her way slowly to his side, and she heard a tiny sigh of pleasure from him when they were side by side, her raised hand touching his.

"Cecily, here I take you as my wife, for better or worse, to have and to hold until the end of my life; and of this I give you my faith," Richard said, a slight tremor in his voice. Then it was Cecily's turn to repeat the words, and she found herself moved by the simple yet binding troth.

The chaplain made the sign of the cross over the gold ring before offering it to Richard and prompting him in the blessing. *"In nomine Patris,"* Richard repeated, slipping the ring briefly over Cecily's thumb, then the index finger, *"et Filii,"* and the middle, *"et Spiritus Sancti,"* and finally to the fourth, where it belonged.

"Amen," she and Richard murmured in unison. When she looked up again, her eye was drawn to the painted altarpiece upon which the radiant face of the fair-haired Virgin smiled down at the newborn baby on her lap. Bless us, I pray you Holy Mother, Cecily pleaded and closed her eyes tight as the priest signed over them and chanted, *"Benedicite."*

She could smell the sweet scent of the honeysuckle as she leaned forward for Richard's kiss through the garland, wanting to savor this moment for the rest of her life. He lingered on the kiss a little long for the pudgy priest's liking and only pulled away when he felt the man tugging at the fur trim on his tabard. It was time to kneel for the rest of the Mass.

Richard reluctantly let go of Cecily's hands as they sank onto their cushions. It was then he saw the first tear from his bride. He felt for her hand and squeezed it, envying for once a lady's license to cry with joy.

THE FEASTING LASTED for hours, six courses of tasty fare from the Salisburys' cook, employed these twenty years by Alice's father. He was known more for the heartiness of his dishes than their elegance, Joan had complained, suffering from indigestion after two days at Bisham Priory. Following a soup of ground almonds and milk, servants brought in a side of beef served with a spicy verjuice, a haunch of venison taken in the hunt by Richard the day before Cecily's accident, pheasants and partridges re-dressed in their colorful plumage, and a heron and dozens of snipe, all of which had been roasted to perfection all day in an open pit behind the house. The tantalizing aromas of ginger, cloves, and cinnamon mingled with the mouth-watering smells of the succulent meats, and the hungry guests fell upon their food as though it were their first meal in a week.

Cecily and Richard sat alone on a small dais, a spotless white linen cloth covering their table with Alice's family's finest silver upon it. Their hands touched often under the cloth, and once Richard leaned into Cecily, ran his finger along her thigh, and whispered, "I am counting the minutes until we are alone together, Cis."

Cecily suddenly found herself blushing furiously, a feminine trait she had disdainfully laid at simpering girls' feet but never her own. "My lord," she murmured demurely and she could have kicked herself. Tell him you can wait, you goose, she thought. Tell him you should not be bedded until you are at least sixteen, and maybe even twenty. Tell him . . . tell him anything. Oh, sweet Mother of God, don't let him see that I am terrified! Please let me find the words, she prayed.

"How do you like my gown, Dickon?" she asked brightly, taking both herself and Richard by surprise with this absurd non sequitur. Mother of God, did I really say that? she groaned inwardly, but she heard herself chatter on regardless. "Your tunic is one of the handsomest I have seen. Pray did you have it made for this occasion?" And she gave him an innocent smile that heightened rather than hid her anxiety as she bit into a filbert.

A neigh of laughter ricocheted off the rafters of the old great hall, abruptly halting conversation in the rest of the room. Alice caught Cecily's eye from the ladies' table and raised an eyebrow.

"Pray what is so amusing, York?" Richard Neville called, chuckling. He leaned to his neighbor and elbowed him with a guffaw. "I suspect the lad is lily-livered about bedding his lady. What say you?" he murmured. "And look at my sister; would you not describe her as a roe caught in the crosshairs." The two men roared, and Dickon saw an escape. He pushed back his chair, wiping his mouth with his napkin, and ran down the three steps to join them, slapping Neville on the back and leaving Cecily staring after him in dismay.

A fine way he has of showing me he cannot wait for us to be alone together, she thought miserably. I suppose it was my fault. That was a stupid remark I made. She sought out Alice's anxious face and sent her a silent plea for help.

Alice took charge of the situation at once and called for music. Then she marched over to Dickon, took him firmly by the arm, and led him away from her husband. "You had better invite your wife to dance immediately, Dickon, or you will be sleeping alone tonight," she hissed. "Do I make myself clear? Can you not see the poor little thing is afraid of what is to come later?" She clicked her tongue. "Certes, men have no sense at all, it seems to me." She almost pushed him back up the steps, and the startled Richard found himself on bended knee begging Cecily to dance.

"Cecily. My lady. My dear wife, I am sorry that I laughed at you," he murmured, genuinely contrite. "I do like your dress, truly I do. Come, will you not step out with me? Our guests are here to wish us joy, and here are you on the brink of tears. What must they think?"

"That you are unkind, in truth," Cecily replied, pouting. "Why did you laugh at me and leave me like that to join the men?" She lowered her voice, informing him, "'Twas humiliating, and I do not enjoy being humiliated." Then, noticing everyone looking at them, she raised her head, blinked back tears, and gave him—and the hall—a brilliant smile. "I should like nothing better than to dance with you, dearest lord," she said loudly. "Come, give me your hand."

She would have giggled at his slack-jawed face had she not wanted to show the world that Cecily Neville—nay, Cecily of York now—was fully in control of herself.

To the sound of rebecs, recorders, a gittern, and a tabor, Cecily and Richard glided effortlessly together on tiptoe in the slow, romantic steps of a *basse danse*. Others joined them on the floor and the hall resumed its gaiety. But running woefully through Cecily's head was the refrain of a ballad she had recently heard at court:

> *That unkindness hath killed me*
> *And put me to this pain.*
> *Alas! What remedy*
> *That I cannot refrain.*

I have looked forward to this day for so many years, she thought, and now Dickon has ruined the moment—or, she thought guiltily, perhaps 'tis I who have spoiled it.

"A pox on all dukes," she muttered under her breath, and Dickon cocked his head, asking what she had said. "Nothing," she replied. "'Twas naught but an idle thought."

THE PRIEST HAD blessed the bed, Cecily had been bathed and dressed in a yellow silk shift—a gift from Alice—and she sat waiting in the soft feather bed as one by one her family bade her good night. Earlier a maid had searched carefully for bedbugs before tucking a few sprigs of lavender between the sheets and into the goose-down pillow. Although it was only September, a fire had been lit to take the chill off the room.

Joan had attempted to warn her daughter about the initial pain of deflowering, as she called it, but had expressed herself in such evasive terms that she came to an abrupt halt with a lame "God bless you, my child," and merely kissed Cecily on the forehead. Joan had avoided this conversation with all her daughters, not having had the benefit of such a conversation herself. *Cecily will find her own way, just as I did,* Joan decided, *just as all women have through the ages.*

Cecily's sister-in-law made certain that she was the last to wish the bride well, and her heart went out to the exquisite young girl, whose face was as ivory as the bed pillow and whose long, delicate fingers plucked nervously at the damask coverlet.

"You will see, dearest Cecily, 'tis only as bad as grazing a knee or stubbing a toe," Alice whispered, stroking Cecily's arm. "It hurts for a second and then you can enjoy yourself. Perhaps not the first night, but soon you will count the hours until you are together again. Believe me, I know. As well, I have watched Dickon these few days here at Bisham, and I see a kindness that many young men lack. I promise you will learn to desire him just as much as I desire my lord every minute of every day."

Cecily giggled. "You do? Truly, Alice?"

Dimpling, Alice nodded. "Truly," she asserted. "Just you wait." She kissed Cecily's soft cheek and slipped away.

Cecily suddenly felt horribly alone. Sliding out of bed and onto her knees, she whispered a supplication to her friend the Virgin. "This is a time when I need you to be with me, Holy Mother." She paused for a second. It occurred to her only then that perhaps Mary was not the best person to be asking. The Holy Mother had not had to suffer through a night like this to conceive her Son. But Cecily was desperate, and did she not have a special bond with the Virgin? "Let me be everything my husband desires, if it please God."

A few lit candles had been left and Rowena had hurried in to make sure all was tidy when a tap on the door told them Richard was outside. Cecily jumped into bed and watched Rowena move to open the door. The attendant turned back to her mistress for permission to let the young duke in, her eyebrows raised in question.

Do not open it, Rowena, Cecily wanted to cry. *Leave him outside. Nay, tell him to go away and come back another day.* But desire for him overcame her nerves, and she called to the attendant with new-found courage, "Rowena, open the door and then leave us." She wanted to add, "However, do not go far," but she relented.

Richard entered wearing only his gipon, shirt, and hose and tiptoed to the side of the bed. "Am I welcome, Cis?" he asked simply, looking worried. "I feared I would not be welcome."

Cecily could not resist his hangdog expression. She held out her hands to him. "To be sure, you are welcome at my bedside tonight and always, Dickon." She patted the bed, and he sat down facing her on it and boyishly crossed his legs, grinning with relief.

"I have thought upon my words to you this evening," Cecily began, "and I believe 'twas I who wronged you, not the other way." She pulled up her knees and wrapped her arms around them. "I will try and explain," she began, "because I do not want to begin our marriage with deception or dissembling." She told him of her fear of this night and how her anxiety had affected her behavior earlier that evening. "But when you laughed at me, it hurt my feelings," she finished. "So I was angry."

"Ah, Cecily, I wish with all my heart I could take back that laughter now. You must believe that I did not mean to hurt you." He started to chuckle. "But, in truth, asking if I liked your dress was such a comical response to my intimate remark about being alone with you that I could not refrain from laughing." He was pleased to see her smile. "I was foolish not to realize you must be afraid, but you should know that in truth I am every whit as afraid as you are tonight, my love," he told her quietly. "We must be gentle with each other. You should know I desire nothing more than to make you happy."

"Ah, Dickon," Cecily breathed and reached out her arms to him. Her whole body yearned for him to touch her, look at her, love her. "Show me how it is done."

"First I must remove these unholy hose," he said. "You could help greatly, if you have a mind."

Perhaps because they knew they had a lifetime of such nights together, they were in no hurry now. Cecily carefully untied the silver-tipped points that attached the hose to his gipon and slipped off each stocking and dropped it on the floor with a flourish. Dickon's legs were very hairy, she noted. She touched his calf shyly as he unbuttoned his tightly fitting gipon and discarded it. The linen shirt underneath then modestly covered him down to his thighs. He pulled back the bedclothes, and they lay down together, his dark head and her fair one side by side on the pillow. Then raising himself on his elbow, Dickon gazed on her perfect profile, the sweep of her neck, and the tips of her young breasts outlined under the pale primrose silk of her shift, which almost matched her yellow hair.

"Dear God, but you are beautiful. Almost too beautiful to touch," he said, reverently, but he put out his hand anyway and slowly traced a course with his finger from the tip of her nose all the way to her breast and circled the nipple a few times, marveling at the way it hardened under his touch. Then he bent and kissed it through the silk.

Cecily gasped and felt a rush between her thighs, and when he took the tit gently between his teeth, she cried out in pleasure.

"Soft, my love," he teased. "Do you want the guard to come in?"

"Do not be so foolish, Dickon," Cecily retorted. "There is no guard." Then she turned her head to him. "Kiss me, I beg of you. I want you to finish what you started at the altar."

He did as she asked, but she was unprepared for his passion, his tongue probing deep into her mouth and his teeth gently pulling at her lips, the exquisite sensation overcoming her initial distaste of tongue touching tongue. After a long moment she thought she would suffocate and pushed him away with an embarrassed laugh. "Am I doing something wrong? I can't breathe."

"You will learn, little rose of Raby," he murmured in her ear, nibbling the lobe and letting his hand finger the hem of her gown. "Now will you allow me to see all of you? I dreamed of this each night during the long winter in France, and I want to see if you are as lovely as the woman of my dreams."

Cecily took a deep breath and nodded. "'Tis your right, I know," she said. "I pray I am worthy of that dream." She allowed him to lift the silk from her and gentle it over her head, her eyes squeezed shut in case his face gave away disappointment. She opened them quickly at the long-drawn, silent whistle of awe and saw his eyes admiring her. She had often witnessed such a look on her father's dog when he was made to wait for a bone, and at once she knew she was desirable.

"Nay, I am not worthy of such treasure," Dickon whispered and then quipped, "but as a priest told me today, in the eyes of God, you are all mine. So I shall accept my unworthiness gladly." Cecily could not help but chuckle.

Kneeling, he straddled her legs and caressed her breasts until she moaned her delight. But his intuition had told him that tonight he should not remove his chemise. He did not want to frighten such a lovely creature with his nakedness, especially as his prick was in need of a haven as fast as he could sensitively moor it. Gently he eased her thighs apart and entered her with a groan of satisfaction. A slight pressure told him he was about to take her virginity, and he whispered, "I am sorry if this hurts." He was taken aback when he felt her hands on his buttocks helping him achieve his goal, and a tiny cry was all he heard as he moved forward in her and climaxed almost immediately with a loud grunt.

Cecily lay still beneath him, stroking his hair. Richard knew she had not enjoyed the same ecstasy, and a momentary guilt dampened his pleasure, but he whispered his love to her and how she had pleased him, and her loving murmurs told him she was satisfied. How different it had been for him, he thought, with wild, sensual Agnes, who knew exactly how to satisfy herself. But together he and Cecily would learn, he had no doubt. He rolled off her and pulled the bedclothes over them both, snuggling her to him and kissing her warm mouth.

"Good night, Cecily—my wife, my duchess. May the angels send you pleasant dreams." Reaching over he snuffed out the candle.

"I love you, Dickon," Cecily said simply. "And thank you."

"Thank you for what, my dearest?"

"For gentling away all my fear."

WHEN WINDSOR CASTLE came into view, the recent Bisham residents were surprised to see the king's household belongings scattered the length of the wharf and being loaded onto several barges and shouts.

"'Twas my understanding that the court would stay at Windsor until Martinmas," Richard Neville told Dickon. "I hope nothing is amiss." Then he cantered along the river road and up the hill to the gate to discover what was afoot.

Later, when the Nevilles gathered in Joan's solar to hear Richard's news, they saw that the hangings and carpets had been folded and stacked in one corner, two carved wardrobe chests neatly packed with clothes, and the bed linens with Joan's silver wrapped securely in them locked in a coffer. The few chairs and stools stood forlornly about on the floor swept clean of rushes.

"We are to leave after matins," Neville told them, his voice echoing off the bare walls. "News has reached the council that after King Charles and La Pucelle unsuccessfully attacked Paris, Bedford and Phillip of Burgundy became reconciled to oppose them, with Bedford now ruling Normandy and Duke Phillip governing Paris and those provinces south and east of the

Seine. Bedford has strongly recommended that in order to maintain English rule over there and to counteract Charles's crowning at Reims, young Henry should be crowned in Paris. So . . ."

"I think Bedford is right," Dickon stated before Neville could finish. "But the king is still not of age. Who makes that decision?"

Neville was startled by Dickon's interruption. Used to being in charge on the Scottish marches, he did not often encounter anyone superior to him, but he inclined his head in York's direction, acknowledging the young man's higher rank. Cecily drew herself up and threw her husband a proud glance. *Husband.* How she loved the sound of it.

"The council will decide, and Gloucester will most certainly agree with his brother," Neville said. "I am of two minds about it. After all, the king has not been crowned on English soil as yet."

Dickon nodded and was about to respond when Joan's quiet voice intervened. "I doubt Humphrey of Gloucester is in any hurry to conclude that piece of business, my lords," she said. "It will mean the end of his protectorate."

"And not before time," her son growled. "The man is insatiably ambitious."

"Soft, Richard," Joan warned him, looking over her shoulder. "Humphrey can be dangerous."

In the end, Richard Neville got his wish. The council announced soon after the court's arrival at Westminster that Henry would be crowned on the sixth day of November in the adjacent abbey.

Although Cecily was now Richard's wife, she was still in attendance on her mother, and Joan insisted Cecily be housed in her mother's apartments for the time leading up to the coronation.

"The palace is full to bursting, and young couples cannot have the luxury of a bed to themselves," Joan snappishly admonished a disappointed Cecily. Despite the first two nights together at Bisham, the young Yorks had not had the pleasure of each other's company in bed since then. "'Tis not unusual, believe me," she said less harshly, regretting her abruptness.

Joan had sent Rowena away that night and was enjoying brushing her daughter's hair with the customary one hundred strokes. It gave her time to speak privately with Cecily. "Your father and I were not always together when we were in residence at another's castle, my dear. You will have many a lonely night, and that is when you will be glad of a sister's or Rowena's warm body next to you." She stopped brushing, struggling to find the right words.

"Besides, other than . . . than consummating the marriage, you are still too young to fully enjoy wedded . . . um, bliss." She resumed brushing a little too vigorously. Cecily winced. "I have prayed hard that you are not with child, Cecily. You are indeed too young and too fragile for an easy birth. You should wait a few years."

Cecily was only slightly embarrassed by her mother's uncharacteristic little intimacy. Indeed, she was emboldened by it. "No fear of that, Mother," she responded gaily. "I have not yet started my courses, and from what Alice tells me, I believe I must be bleeding before I can conceive."

Joan was shocked. "Why have you not told me this before?"

Cecily shrugged. "You did not ask me, Mother. I only found out that I was later than most girls when I talked to Alice at Bisham. She asked me if there was a chance of conceiving that first night, and I asked her how I would know such a thing." Cecily did not mention that she knew about the woman's curse only because she had been privy to Rowena going through days of bellyaches, eruptions upon her face, and bundles of soiled rags hurriedly disposed of down the garderobe chute, and Rowena had enlightened her.

"But you are fourteen, my child," Joan murmured, feeling guilty for having avoided talking to Cecily about womanly matters before now. "Perhaps I should have the surgeon attend you and make certain you are fertile, Cecily. You must not disappoint York."

Cecily's face fell. "Not fertile? How can they tell? Oh, how I wish I *were* like everyone else, Mother. I am told bleeding makes one a woman. How I long to join you all."

Joan was moved to chuckle. "Do not wish too hard, Cecily. 'Tis not named our curse for nothing."

Just as luck would have it, Cecily's wish was granted a few days before the coronation, and she was told she would be unable to attend. "Men believe we are unclean at this time, my lady," Rowena told her chagrined mistress. "They do not want us in their midst when we are bleeding. You must keep to your rooms."

By the time she had spent two days lying on the bed with hot stones on her throbbing belly to alleviate the dull ache or running to the garderobe, she could understand why cursed ladies preferred to keep to their quarters. And she did not want Richard to see the angry blemish that had suddenly appeared on her chin. But she was relieved to know that there was nothing wrong with her and trusted the Virgin Mary to watch over her.

It was galling, however, to hear the crowds roar outside her window in the square between Westminster Palace and the abbey the next day when eight-year-old Henry arrived. So this is what happens when I finally arrive at womanhood? I miss what must be the most splendid ceremony of the decade. 'Tis simply not fair, she grumbled, and vaguely wondered if she had asked too much of God and His Mother lately.

She was even more chagrined a few days later—when she was set free from her confinement and spent a cozy hour alone with Dickon in Joan's spacious solar—to know that she had been right about the splendor of the event.

"Henry was so mindful of the significance of the occasion that he behaved almost like a sad and wise old man," Dickon reported. "'Twas as though the crown was too heavy for his small shoulders to support. I hope it is not a portent of how he will support the office as a man."

"Pish, Dickon. He is but eight. You would find a big gold crown heavy on your head if you were only eight. Who set the crown on his head? Was it my uncle Beaufort?"

"Aye, and the cardinal sat on his right all the way through the ceremony. That place should have been Humphrey's, in truth, or Warwick's, who has been Henry's guardian all these years." Dickon frowned. "Sadly, while the magnificent festivities were much enjoyed by the citizens along Henry's route from the Tower, word came that several people had been crushed to death by others eager for a closer look."

Cecily's hand first flew to her mouth and then made the sign of the cross. "How dreadful. God rest their souls. I pray 'tis not an ill omen for his reign. A king's enemies should be killed, not his loyal subjects."

She sighed. "What else of note, Dickon? I am starved of news. Mother has been in attendance on the queen dowager, and I am called to her grace's apartments on the morrow."

Richard took her hands and kissed each finger tenderly. "I have no more news, in truth. But I miss you, Cis," he said simply, grinning at her. "I pray I shall soon share your bed again. I must leave court and see to my family's seat at Fotheringhay. Nay, do not look so downhearted. It will be your home, too, as will my castles of Ludlow and Wigmore on the Welsh marches, and I cannot wait to share them with you. But not until your mother gives us permission." Then his face resumed its quiet seriousness. "I have taken the liberty of choosing a gift for both of us that I am certain will enrich our lives."

Cecily's eyes shone. "What is it, Dickon? New horses? A carriage?"

Richard frowned. "Naught so mundane, Cecily. You shall have a carriage if you so desire, but my gift is far more lasting. I have received an indulgence from the pope for a portable altar. And he has seen fit to grant not only that but our own confessor to care for our spiritual needs."

Cecily did not know how to respond. Although she spent as much time on her knees as everyone else at court, her spiritual needs seemed basic. As long as she could call upon the saints and her special advocate, the Virgin, to help her through any hardships, and as long as she knew she satisfied a supplicant's daily rote of prayers, readings, and the occasional confession, she considered her duty done. She had not thought of Richard as particularly pious, but now she looked at him curiously. There was more to this husband of hers than met the eye, and her heart was filled with pride and love for him. That he should care so much for her immortal soul spoke truly of a great love.

"Then I am the most grateful of wives, my dear," she cried, smiling happily. "What a comfort to have something so precious always with us. I beg you to let me be part of choosing who will paint the scenes upon the altar panels, and I would ask that the Virgin be among the figures. I will trust you to find the confessor. But," she giggled, "one who will not be too hard on my sinful soul!"

9

Normandy, Spring 1430

*C*ecily could hardly contain her excitement as the king's train, like a multicolored caterpillar, inched its way along the north Downs, the grassy hillsides awash in the gold of broom, primroses, and cowslips, and into Dover, nestled between sheltering chalk cliffs and astride the River Dour. The harbor was filled with ships, but even so the carracks and cogs were not large, and Cecily wondered if the king's entourage of three hundred strong could be accommodated on them. Henry was going to France to be crowned again there for the benefit of his French subjects.

At Barham Down, a few miles from Dover, Richard had wheeled his horse away to join his own retinue, as did the other seven dukes and earls who were accompanying the little king to France. These lords' ships were anchored off Sandwich and would join the royal party at Calais. As she watched Dickon ride off, Cecily sank back on the cushions, remembering the few nights they had spent together before leaving for France, when their lovemaking had progressed to where, as Alice had promised, Cecily looked forward to their intimacy.

Pulled by a pair of oxen, the cumbersome carriage, its protective canvas wall rolled up on one side to let in the fresh air, creaked and groaned its way over the rutted road through the scrubby, chalky grassland, causing its passengers to become more than a little crabby.

"Your lord would appear to be very attentive, Sister," said Katherine, Duchess of Norfolk, with a chuckle. Together with her sisters Anne and Cecily, she was sharing Joan's carriage.

"Aye, like an unweaned pup," Anne muttered.

Cecily glared at her. "Dickon does not deserve your spite, Nan," she shot back. "'Tis only because your lout of a husband prefers baiting his hook to keeping you company. Confess you are jealous. You have never forgiven Dickon for not preferring you."

"Pah!" was all Nan could think to reply.

Katherine was amused. As Ralph's and Joan's eldest child, Katherine was eight years older than their next daughter and thus had not had to endure such sibling rivalry. Waiting until her mother's head drooped sideways in sleep against the side of the coach, she whispered to Cecily, "What is this about York and Nan? Do tell."

"If you do, Cecily, I shall never speak to you again," Nan's voice hissed from the other side. "I swear on His holy cross, I shall not."

Cecily felt Katherine's hand find hers under the blanket and give it a squeeze.

Cecily took a deep breath and was silent for a change. Certes, Nan must hate me, she thought, as the carriage began to descend to the town. It is not my fault that Father contracted me to Dickon, she reasoned. Could it be that she is envious of my title, now that I am a duchess and she only a countess?

After an uncomfortable night sharing a room as guests of one of Dover's prominent merchants, the Neville women went aboard their assigned vessel and settled themselves in the captain's quarters not long after dawn. Cecily leaned out of the porthole and watched the shoremen untying the massive lines and holding the ship fast until the signal was given to cast off. Joan was meting out galingale powders to Eleanor, Katherine, and her two attendants and then took some herself.

"Cecily, pull your head in before you get hurt. By all that is holy, you have a curiosity that would kill a cat. Come, take some of this powder. 'Tis said to ward off the *mal de mer*," she advised her youngest. But Cecily would have none of it and made a face. Joan shrugged. "Suit yourself, Daughter, but you may be sorry."

The day was crisply clear after a night of rain, and as the sun rose higher, the dark line that was France was visible on the horizon. Cecily gave a shiver of pleasure. She had never been anywhere but England, and other than the barges and boats on the Thames, never on a ship before. Her skirts and cloak billowed about her, and she clutched Katherine's arm as they made teetering progress around the ship, laughing at the ungainly gait caused by the pitching deck that had them taking several steps back to their few steps forward.

As France crept ever closer, the sisters remarked on how flat the land was compared with the cliffs they had left behind at Dover. Long sandy beaches hugged the low coastline for miles and miles, and the deep channel into the harbor was well marked by a breakwater wall that guided the flotilla into Calais on the mouth of the river. The walled town was an imposing bastion encircled by canals with a four-towered castle at its heart. Against the city wall, sheds and warehouses were packed with precious bundles of fleeces and other merchandise that were the lifeblood of this important English-ruled staple town, where English wool was the source of its wealth.

But the town was also a marshalling point for English armies venturing into France. Dominating the skyline and dwarfing the castle was the Lancaster Tower, the watchtower platform giving the English a view for miles both inland and out to sea. To be named Captain of Calais, Cecily knew, was an honor given only to royalty or the very noblest of commanders, and since 1427, John of Bedford had held the title.

The wharves were alive with sailors, stevedores, fishermen, and the party assembled to greet the king. A roar went up when nine-year-old King Henry stood up in the middle of the small barge that had been sent to fetch him and waved to those watching, the sun glinting off the circlet of gold. Cecily noticed that his light brown hair was cut in the new fashion. She thought he looked very dignified for one so young.

Just as Cecily and her fellow passengers disembarked, they heard a fanfare of shawms and trumpets that heralded the arrival of the king at the castle gate, and they all hurried up the cobbled street to catch up. The royal cavalcade passed through the fortified gatehouse and into the inner bailey, where John of Bedford and the aldermen of Calais waited to receive their sovereign lord.

CECILY'S FIFTEENTH BIRTHDAY on the third day of May had been marked by her family with special prayers after matins, but it wasn't until a few weeks later that Joan received word from Alice that upon that same day Sir Richard Neville had finally been granted his father-in-law's title of earl of Salisbury, and more prayers of thanks were offered. Alice's news also included the birth of twins.

"Richard appears to have inherited his father's virility," Joan chuckled, when she read the letter quietly to her daughters.

"And I hope to have your fruitfulness, dear Mother," murmured Nan, who had already produced three children. She cast down her eyes to her needlework to hide her delight in snubbing both her sisters; Katherine had only the one son, and six months of marriage had not yet resulted in a pregnancy for Cecily.

Cecily gritted her teeth and bit her tongue, but placid Katherine merely changed the subject. "When will we leave this rat-infested place and go to Paris?" she mused. "I wonder the king does not return to the comfort of Westminster."

As if on cue, a steward knocked on the countess's door and bade the ladies join their husbands and other members of the king's household in the great hall. In a rustling of silks and damasks and lighted by flambeaux the women processed in single file around three sides of the castle to the great hall.

"It must be safe to leave Calais," Cecily whispered to Rowena, who was following her mistress. "I pray I am right."

Richard stood in a place of prominence near Henry. Attendant upon the king and trusted associate of Bedford, he had not been able to spend much time with Cecily since their arrival. Cecily had treasured a letter he had sent a few days before in which he had spoken of his undying love and longing for her.

> *If only we were again at Raby, the woods and meadows stretching before us, our horses straining at the bit, the wind at our backs, and we without a care in the world. How I long to spend time with you alone, my sweet Cecily, take you in my arms, and share our love. Perhaps I should not tell you this for fear of swelling your head, but I am the envy of my fellow lords, who tell me you are the most beautiful of any lady in Calais. I thought disaster had befallen me and God had deserted me when I was left with an uncertain future as an orphan of a traitor. But then fortune smiled upon me and took me to Raby, and now I must be the happiest man in England. All the love I have in my heart is yours always. Your Dickon.*

Cecily now smiled across at Richard and touched her heart with her hand. Her husband bent his head slightly and smiled back. Warmth flooded her once again, and she was beginning to believe that it would be thus every time she saw him.

She took her place next to Joan, who had Anne of Bedford on her other side, and took note of the array of English nobles grouped around the throne. The lions of England and lilies of France decorated the canopy above the boy king. An energy emanated from the nobles that Cecily had not seen before in the month they had been entrenched at Calais. Certes, we will be leaving, she told herself, impatient for the good news.

"My lords, ladies, and gentlemen, in the name of our gracious sovereign, Henry, king of England and France, I am commanded to give you the report heard this day from our Burgundian ally, John of Luxembourg. At the city of Compiègne, situated between here and Paris and under siege by our allies, the heavens have smiled upon us and the peasant witch known as La Pucelle is finally captured."

"Thanks be to God!" the company cried as one, and neighbor nudged neighbor, smiling and whispering excitedly. Even Henry grinned. But Cecily could not be glad. Whatever will become of her now? she wondered.

Bedford held up his hand. "Aye, thanks be to God indeed. We believe King Charles's soldiers will lose heart without their champion and we will soon repair to Paris." Another cheer went up, and Bedford stepped back to allow the courtiers time to savor the English success.

"How now, wife." Richard appeared from nowhere and took Cecily's arm. "You look good enough to kiss in that ruby gown, and if your mother does not notice, I am leading you from here to somewhere quiet where we can be alone—for once."

Cecily gasped at his audacity. Jeanne was forgotten as she thrilled to his suggestion. She looked around for Joan, but her mother was safely making her way with Nan and Eleanor to Cardinal Beaufort's side, undoubtedly to hear more of the Maid's capture. Cecily clutched Richard's arm tightly as he negotiated their path to the stairs that led from the hall into the tower where he was housed. Richard pushed open the heavy oak door that led into a small chamber that he shared with Nan's husband, Humphrey Stafford. A wide, simple bedstead took up the bulk of the space; armor and weapons were stacked in a corner.

"My lord," Cecily whispered, her eyes darting around the room, "I should not be here in the gentlemen's quarters. What if we are discovered?"

"Can a man not lie with his wife, my dear?" Richard grinned at her. "God's bones, Cis, where is that fearless spirit I remember so well at Raby? Soon the bell will call us to a special service of thanksgiving, but that is not for another half-hour. We have time to dally, do we not? Besides, sweetheart, I have locked the door." He began untying the neck of her underdress and bent to kiss the hollow of her neck. Cecily sighed and stroked his dark hair, pulling him lower and giving in to her desire. Soon they stood naked facing each other, and Richard reverently ran his hands down her sides and over her narrow hips, marveling at the silken skin and curve of her.

Cecily shyly touched his erection. "The skin is as soft as silk," she murmured, fascinated. Then she looked up at him and dared to ask, "Can we come together standing, do you suppose?"

Aroused by his adventurous wife, Richard asked, "Is that what you would like?" And when he saw her mischievous dimple, he laughed and kissed her waiting mouth. Pulling her to the wall, he positioned himself against it so that he could gently guide her to him. Their coupling was so intense that their thrusts were almost desperate. Cecily was vaguely aware that they were both wet with perspiration. Suddenly an exquisite sensation flooded her and made her cry out in surprised ecstasy. Within seconds Richard gave in to his passion and clutched Cecily's buttocks hard against him as he grunted his own satisfaction. Slithering to the floor, they were speechless with wonder until Cecily leaned toward him, whispering, "I love you, Richard of York. I swear, I could never have dreamed of such pleasure." She kissed him, tasting the salt on his perspiring upper lip, and was gratified that he was still breathing heavily.

A slow smile spread over Richard's face and he flicked his tongue over her lips. "Such a hussy I have wed," he teased her, cradling her to him. "I warrant we must have made a child this day."

A WEEK LATER Cecily knew it was not so. Not only were her pains worse this month, but also her disappointment made her melancholy. She had prayed to St. Monica three times daily following the tryst in the tower room, to no avail. What use are saints, she groused to herself as she lounged hour after hour alone on her bed during her week of forced retirement. She did not know when her next chance of conceiving might come now that Richard had ridden off with his contingent to give aid to Bedford.

Cecily tried to read, but she could not focus on the words that afternoon and began to imagine the scene of Jeanne d'Arc's capture instead. Part of her had wanted to cry, "Nay, say 'tis not so!" when Bedford had made his pronouncement. Now that she was on French soil, she had fancied that she might witness for herself the young woman at the head of her troops, but she knew that was only in the realm of dreams. Her mother had relayed the manner of the capture later that day when she had sought out Cecily following the special Mass.

"The woman had led the army out of Compiègne to attack the Burgundians, but when her troops fled back there, she was now at their rear and easily caught."

"How brave she must be," Cecily interrupted, her eyes shining.

"Brave?" Joan retorted. "She was rash—nay, downright foolish—for she is lost to her countrymen and is now Philip of Burgundy's captive."

"What will they do to her, Mother?" Cecily asked.

"Let her rot in prison, for all I care," Nan had suddenly said from her perch on the window seat. "Humphrey says Bedford believes she is a witch and a heretic. They burn such people, do they not?"

Cecily gasped in horror. "Burn her? For trying to save her country? Certes, she is not a criminal. She should be treated the same as other prisoners of war."

"I am afraid she will not be," Joan answered. "'Tis said she heard the voices of saints who told her to dress like a man, crown the dauphin, and take France back from the English." She crossed herself. "If she speaks the truth, then she is a most holy woman. But if she gives false witness, then I have no sympathy."

"My lord is convinced she must be done away with," Katherine joined in. "He thinks that as long as she is alive, the French will believe she can work miracles."

The conversation ended with the bell for compline, but Cecily prayed for Jeanne locked away in her prison, even though she, as all good English people concerned for their own men, should have been glad of the Maid's capture.

IT WAS NOT until July that John of Bedford declared it safe for Henry and his entourage to venture out of Calais. But even then, the road to Paris was not cleared of danger from the French, and so the king was to move to Rouen, the largest city in Normandy and the seat of English governance, which was surrounded by a formidable wall with the Seine along one edge.

"Rouen will please you," Anne of Bedford told Joan. They had left the Lancaster Tower far behind and were traveling toward their first stop, St. Omer. She did not speak English, and Joan enjoyed revisiting the language of her childhood spent at Chateau Beaufort when she conversed with the duchess.

Cecily had willingly ceded her place in the carriage to the duchess, preferring to ride in the fresh air and take in her surroundings. Bedford's chamberlain had been selected to keep her company. Sir Richard Woodville was ten years Cecily's senior and the handsomest of knights, Cecily admitted. The chestnut hair framed his good looks with almost girlish curls, but there was nothing girlish about the six-foot athletic man who had been knighted for bravery after Agincourt. Cecily glanced sideways at the strong figure sitting his horse so naturally, and she wondered why he had not yet found a wife.

"May I be so bold as to point out the road to Agincourt, your grace," Woodville said, indicating a path leading off the main road to the left. He shook his head sadly. "So many Frenchmen dead in the sea of mud. The Lord God shone his light upon us that day, my lady. I remember it as though 'twere yesterday and not so many years ago."

"A splendid victory indeed, Sir Richard," Cecily replied, scanning the landscape and conjuring up battalions marching over the rise. "It must have been inspiring to be led by good King Harry."

Woodville nodded. "Aye, he was a very great commander, hard yet fair," he replied. "If his son has half his valor and leadership, we shall hold on here. It must be daunting for a boy to look upon this French land and know he rules it by right just as he does England."

Cecily murmured an assent, although her thoughts were not with Henry but with the poor, ragged peasants they passed in villages or along the road, foraging for food in a landscape that was so desolate Cecily felt like weeping. Many armies had tramped up and down the Normandy fields for nigh on a hundred years, and now nothing could or would grow in the lifeless furrows. Trees had been felled for firewood for so many camp fires that forests were naught but stumps. The once fertile Norman landscape was now a barren wasteland. She thought of the green English countryside, the rich farmland ripe with corn, and the lush hillsides feeding flocks of fat sheep or herds of cows, and she was almost ashamed. Was ruling France worth this cost? She wanted to turn back and gallop for Calais, the sea, and home.

She lapsed into silence and concentrated her gaze on the colorful cavalcade ahead of her to avoid the depressing scenes that flanked the road.

"I see you are contemplating the devastation, Lady Cecily," Woodville interrupted her reverie, and, as though he had read her thoughts, he continued, "Let me assure you, King Harry—and now his brother of Bedford—did not treat these lands or their people in the destructive ways of the French armies. 'Tis why I pride myself on being English and not French." He added with disdain, "The French are savages."

Although she murmured some response to him, Cecily could not help but think that were it not for the English here in France, there would be no need to ravish the land.

* * *

HER MOOD HAD lightened by the time they approached Rouen. Richard had joined her several times on the journey and fallen into conversation with Woodville, who either did not take the hint and leave the young couple to ride alone or had been given instructions not to leave Cecily's side. However, as he had lived in Rouen for some time, he was able to educate them about the city.

To welcome the king, the people of Rouen had been encouraged to line the streets that led to the Chateau Bouvreuil, an imposing castle set in the western city wall. Compared with the reception that the king had enjoyed from the Kentish folk throughout his progress to Dover, the mood here was more subdued, and Cecily noticed more than one citizen staring sullenly after the royal party, while English men and women, standing separate from the natives, cheered wildly and flung flowers.

Under the high walls of the castle, Cecily shivered. There was something sinister about the place, she decided, and resolved to escape from it when she could and explore the jumble of streets and squares with their half-timbered houses and pleasant greens. Anne of Bedford had proudly pointed out her three-story manor house named *Joyeux Repos* hard by the St. Hilaire Gate. It was surrounded by the tranquil, verdant estate of La Chantereine with its gardens and apple orchard. The manor was a welcome sight after the desolation on the road, and Cecily decided that she would visit her grace of Bedford often if she had permission.

The castle had been readied for the king, but workmen were still making hurried repairs to the two-hundred-year-old building, which had fallen into disuse because the English governor had preferred La Chantereine as a residence.

And so, as the matriarch of two duchesses and a countess, Joan was immediately welcomed at *Joyeux Repos* with her daughters instead. The overflow of the king's three-hundred-strong entourage had to find accommodation in the town.

WITHIN A FEW days, Cecily had explored the Chantereine property and found a favorite exedra to sit on and read, embroider, or simply enjoy listening to the birds. She was joined by her sisters on occasion, but mostly her companion became the twenty-six-year-old Duchess Anne. Cecily worked hard to improve her French, engendering merry laughter in the garden when she mispronounced a word. The summer days lingered long into the evening, and she had to remind herself that war was being waged not far from the peaceful manor. Richard was a frequent visitor, and if the squirrels had been able to talk, they could have told of surreptitious skirt rustling, rapturous kisses, and whisperings of love under the apple trees. But much of Richard's time was spent in attendance on the king or learning from Bedford how to govern and command.

"My respect for his grace the duke grows daily," Richard told Cecily during one of their meetings in the orchard, where the rosy apples were ripe for picking. "The king should be grateful for Bedford's wise governance. To be sure, Henry listens to that uncle, but he hangs far more on Cardinal Beaufort's opinions than I am comfortable with. I pray you, take no offense, Cis, I know he is your uncle, but I fear he hates his half nephew Gloucester, and I cannot blame him for that. The man is a hothead sometimes, but he and Bedford have always upheld the honor of their late brother King Harry and done their duty by him as regents to young Henry." He paused after this long and slightly awkward speech, stroking Cecily's hand and twisting the wedding band. "I do not find myself aligned with the cardinal's thinking, 'tis all, and fear that one day I may be tested where he is concerned. For no good reason he likes me not, although he outwardly shows civility. I have shown myself loyal to Henry, but I am wary."

"Perhaps you dwell too much upon which way the wind blows with my uncle," Cecily remarked. "As far as I can remember, he has said nothing untoward about you." She paused, suddenly reminded of the conversation she had overheard at Raby about Richard's lineage. Her mother and uncle had been concerned by his closeness to the throne, she remembered. But that had been years ago. "Aye, you are thinking on this too much, Richard," she continued, sounding older than her fifteen years. "What have you ever done to cause his dislike? Not a thing, I warrant. You discharged your duty well overseeing that duel last year, when you took the absent Bedford's place as constable. And you were wounded in the service of your king at Orléans. You are not puffed up like Nan's husband, Stafford, but are quiet, dignified, and not easily angered. Nay, my dearest, 'tis your imagination that betrays you."

"You may be right, Cis, but still . . ." He paused, searching her face, and then decided to trust her with what had lurked in a dark place in his heart since he was four. "I am the son of an attainted traitor," he began huskily. "I must live with that knowledge all my life. My father had his head hewn from his body for trying to win the crown he thought rightfully his family's. But his action was treasonous. Each time I walk into council meetings, into the great hall, into a room that at once goes silent, I believe I am being judged as his son. I believe they think I may repeat my father's folly." He put his head in his hands. "You are the first person I have ever confided in—although your father tried once to talk to me of it. Oft-times it consumes me so, I think I shall be swallowed up."

Cecily gently pulled his hands from his face and made him look at her. "Ah, Dickon. Such pain you have held inside you these fifteen years, 'tis no wonder it consumes you. Forgive me, my love, I childishly never thought of your suffering, of your fear. You always appear so sure, so strong, and yet so very amiable."

He smiled at her. "Is that how I am perceived? Then I have succeeded in my intent." He paused, weighing his words carefully, hoping she would not find them childish. "I made a pact with God many years ago that if I conducted myself with civility to all men, He would protect me from their suspicion. I confess it has been hard at times to hold my peace. There is another side of me that is aching to emerge."

Cecily frowned. "Another side? Do not tell me the Richard I love has treasonous thoughts?"

"Nay, I know my duty to my king. But I want to be recognized as being as high born as the king himself, even though I have no intention of challenging him for his crown. I am content to be his liegeman . . . *but* I am also his royal cousin. Do you understand, Cis?" He had paced away during this declaration and now swung around to face her, his anguish evident.

"With all my heart, Dickon," she replied, rising. Wrapping her arms around him, she snuggled into the soft folds of his worsted tunic, breathing in his familiar smell. "If there is anything I can do to help you achieve this balance, you know I will. Did we, too, not have a pact to share our dreams and aspirations?" She fingered the ruby ring. "Remember, your hopes and ambitions are mine, my love."

Richard squeezed her tightly, struck by his wife's sudden maturity. Somewhere along the road to Rouen, he thought, Cecily had left her childhood behind.

"I pray you will say nothing of this to your mother or your sisters. Especially the thoughts I have of your uncle the cardinal."

"Why would I?" Cecily replied, indignant. "I am your wife and confidante, and you can trust me with your secrets. Besides, I do not like my uncle Beaufort either."

Richard laughed then, his burden lighter, and he kissed her tenderly. "Never forget how to make me laugh, my dearest, and love me always as I shall love you."

He picked up his bonnet and crammed it on his head, the ostrich feather fluttering in the late-afternoon breeze. A look of tenderness suffused his face as he told her, "'Twas providence made me your father's ward. I cherish your devotion." Then he bent down to kiss her and whispered, "No sign of a child yet, Cis? Nay? Then we shall simply have to try harder." He kissed her again and made his way back to his horse, which was champing on the orchard grass, and rode off with a wave of his blue bonnet.

Cecily sank down on the grassy exedra, suddenly feeling tired. Taking on another's suffering was new to her, and she could hardly bear the weight of it. And yet there was a singing in her heart that her husband trusted her so completely.

She rose from the grassy seat pondering Richard's last question and resolved to visit the abbey church of St. Ouen the next day to ask the Virgin to intercede with her Son for the gift of a child. Perhaps fatherhood might ease Richard's troubled thoughts of his own father's betrayal.

"I WAS TOLD I could find the two most beautiful ladies in Rouen here." John of Bedford's voice startled Cecily and Duchess Anne not long after Martinmas. They made quite a picture, he mused: tiny French Anne with her creamy skin, dark hair and eyes, and the tall, lithe English rose whose fair beauty was the talk of Rouen. "What are you gossiping about today, your graces?" he teased as he kissed his wife's upturned face. It did not seem to matter to the duke that Anne had remained barren. The love he bore her was evident every time he looked at her.

"*Monseigneur, fais attention, je t'empris!* Do not creep up on us thus," Anne chastised him, petting the exuberant wolfhound that never left John's side. Then she fluttered her long lashes at him. "It may be one day you will hear something that does not flatter you."

"*Tiens,* Anne, you flatter him by even suggesting he was the subject of our conversation," Cecily ventured, her boldness surprising even herself: Duke John's presence often awed her. "Today it so happens that we were talking of Anne's wish to go hunting, *n'est-ce pas, madame?*"

Anne's eyes widened in surprise. "Were we, Cecily?" she said before she could stop herself. And then she smiled. "*Mais bien sûr,* that is what we were wishing. *Alors,* your grace," she cajoled her husband, "may we? You say the French are many leagues from us now, and La Pucelle is safe within the dungeon at Beaurevoir, the other side of Normandy. What danger is there for us to hunt near St. Catherine's Mount?" She turned to look toward the city wall where the high hill was just visible over the top. "'Tis the best place to hunt, and we can eat out in the fresh air. Can you not persuade the king to allow it? After all, the huntsmen go out often to put food on the king's table and have never been attacked."

Bedford's blue eyes twinkled over his high-bridged beak of a nose, and he nodded. He had easily seen through Cecily's dissembling but thought it harmless enough. "In truth, there is no danger and thus no reason why we should not have some sport. How can I resist two such charming ladies?"

Cecily beamed at him, and not for the first time did he envy young York his bride, although his *petite passereau* delighted him in every way.

"Merci, monseigneur," the little sparrow said, raising his hand to her cheek. "You work too hard and you look tired. You must take a day to think of nothing but the pleasures of the hunt. No talk of war or even La Pucelle, do you promise me?"

Bedford's expression darkened. "Forgive me, *ma mie,* but in the matter of the Maid, you may know that we are attempting to buy her from Burgundy."

Although intent upon gleaning any new snippet of information about Jeanne, Cecily could not help casting her mind back to a talk with Richard and how angry she had been when he had told her that the bishop of the Beaurevoir diocese, Pierre Cauchon, was negotiating the sale of the difficult prisoner to the English. Upon hearing that Jeanne was now chained to her bed for attempting an escape, Cecily had even declared, "His name should be *cochon,* not Cauchon, for he must be a pig to treat a poor girl thus."

"Tiens, milord. Her grace of York is distressed by the story. I beg of you, if it be your wish, may we not talk of other things?" Cecily looked up when she heard Anne mention her name.

John, duke of Bedford, eyed Cecily with interest, wondering what in the good news concerning Jeanne d'Arc had distressed her. He had grown to admire this spirited young duchess and was often torn between amusement and disapproval at her enthusiasm for entering into delicate political conversations, in which, he was convinced, women did not belong. His beloved Anne had marked well the words of the Goodman of Paris, whose written homily to his new young wife at the end of the last century had been copied for many high-born nobles to present to their own wives. Indeed, Bedford had given it to Anne at the time of their wedding, and he resolved to make young Richard of York aware of it—especially in the matter of a wife's duty.

> . . . that you shall be humble and obedient towards him that shall be your husband, the which article containeth in itself four particulars. The first particular saith that you shall be obedient to wit to him and to his commandments whatsoe'er they be, whether they be made in earnest or in jest, or whether they be orders to do strange things, or whether they be made concerning matters of small import or of great; for all things should be of great import to you, since he that shall be your husband hath bidden you to do them . . .

Aye, Cecily could use some advice in the matter of wifely obedience, he thought, even though he admitted he was taken with the comely young woman. Bedford was not to know that Anne had already pressed the book on Cecily, who, on one occasion while reading alone in her chamber, had pitched the leather-bound volume across the room in disgust.

The Goodman wrote:

> The fourth particular is that you be not arrogant and that you answer not back your husband that shall be, nor his words, nor contradict what he saith, above all before other people.

"A pox on the Goodman," Cecily had muttered. "He needs a good dose of the wise Wife of Bath." She had smiled to herself as she recalled the Wife's final prayer:

> And—Jesu hear my prayer!—cut short the lives
> Of those who won't be governed by their wives;
> And all old, angry niggards of their pence,
> God send them soon a very pestilence!

10

Normandy, Winter to Spring 1431

Ten thousand francs was what it took to transfer custody of Jeanne d'Arc to the English, and on Christmas Day in the tenth year of Henry's reign, the young peasant woman from Domrémy was finally brought in chains to Rouen and imprisoned in the high donjon of Bouvreuil Castle. While the English king's court made merry that Yuletide season, a few corridors away the hope of the French languished in a dank cell behind thick stone walls. There she awaited trial by those French clergy loyal to Henry.

Cecily had learned she was virtually alone among the nobles and their wives in her sympathy for the young woman. After a few months of living with Duke John, she began to see the truth of Queen Catherine's advice to her those few years ago. The ladies were not expected to show knowledge of the discussions that went on among the men. But Cecily noticed that many women eavesdropped, as she did. She wondered how many of them also talked to their lords in moments of intimacy, as she was wont to do with Richard. Their snatched time together, however, was so precious that much of it was taken with releasing pent-up passion.

Every now and again, she could cajole Richard into divulging what was happening with Jeanne. He had told her that the Maid had been moved from stronghold to stronghold once she was sold and that the English had indeed treated her more kindly than the Burgundians, which fact was a small comfort to Cecily. They had allowed her to attend Mass presided over by another French prisoner, a bishop, Richard had said. "But she still refuses to remove her men's clothing."

"Oh, pish," Cecily responded, and yet she was instantly transported back to the scene with her father before his death and refrained from saying more.

She was grateful Richard had not reminded her of it, though she was certain he was recalling the same event.

"Jeanne's sin is that she swears God made her do it," Richard went on, "which contradicts His word in the Bible. 'Tis a piece of evidence that will be used against her, can you not see? 'Tis heresy," he had ended.

Two weeks had gone by following that conversation with no word on the notable prisoner in the donjon, and so, on a snowy mid-January day, Cecily chose a sweet afternoon of lovemaking in Richard's fire-lit room at the castle to ask him for more information.

"Why are you so preoccupied with her?" he asked a touch resentfully, nuzzling the milky skin between her breasts. He rolled onto his side and propped himself up on his elbow while she playfully fingered new silky hairs on his chest. "How can you think of her at a time like this, Cis? In truth, it makes me wonder if your mind was on our lovemaking at all."

She wrinkled her nose at him. "How can you doubt that? I was pleasured as much as you, I dare say, and you know it. But now, Richard, I beg of you, indulge me."

Ever since their pivotal conversation in the Chantereine orchard, Cecily had ceased to call Richard by his nickname. It was as though they had moved from their first innocent love to a more mature relationship, and both were aware of a deepening of their affections.

Now, having so enjoyed his wife's attention that afternoon, Richard found he was unable to resist Cecily's thirst for information about Jeanne.

"Very well, my inquisitive wife, I will give in. I know she will be tried soon," he revealed, sitting up and stretching. "In fact Pierre Cauchon is here. It is said he will preside over the first tribunal in a few days. It seems he has temporarily assumed the title of bishop of Rouen since the old bishop moved on last year. This means he can conduct the trial here, which is a safer place for it than Paris."

Cecily frowned, cupping her hands behind her head on the pillow. "Cauchon? Why is Duke John not presiding? Why is the church involved at all? Is she not a prisoner of war?"

Richard gave a sigh. "I regret to tell you, my innocent, that were she simply a prisoner of war, she would not need to be tried at all. She could be ransomed or kept indefinitely—until the war ends, I suppose." He grunted then. "It has been the source of much talk in the council chamber. Why has the French king, who owes his crown and his recent successes to the Maid, not attempted to rescue or buy her? It seems he has abandoned her to her fate, and for that reason I have some sympathy for her. It is now a matter for an ecclesiastical court as," he lowered his voice, crossing himself, "she will be tried for heresy."

Cecily gasped and signed herself too. "So you are saying that Duke John wants her to be found guilty of something, no matter what, so he can dispose of her, and so heresy is the accusation?"

Richard nodded. "And due to the way the French courts work, 'tis almost certain she will be found guilty. In England one is innocent until found guilty. Do you see? It will look better for the English if she is tried by her own people. But make no mistake, Cis, Bedford will make an example of her. 'Tis the bishops and clergy—her own countrymen—who want to bring her down."

"You mean the Inquisition?" Cecily whispered, sitting up, her eyes wide with fear.

Richard nodded. "Aye, and Bedford, your Uncle Beaufort, and the king are happy to agree. Heresy or witchcraft, it matters not."

Cecily chewed on her lip, frowning. "What is the difference?"

"I confess 'tis a distinction that begs more learning that I have. But if I have it right, a witch may consort with evil spirits or Satan to perform magic, whereas a heretic defies the Word of God. Jeanne swears her holy voices instructed her to dress in men's garb and become a soldier. In so doing she offended God, so her enemies say, but 'twas in the name of God that she dressed in that way, became a soldier, and raised the siege of Orléans and then of Compiègne, not to mention crowning Charles. What is more, she predicted all these events exactly as they happened, and she claimed to have worked miracles. It is said she used secret charms to protect her soldiers and that she led common people to worship her. Some of it is heresy, some of it witchcraft. You choose."

Cecily contemplated the answer as she drew her chemise over her head and tied the neck ribbon. Then she ran her fingers through her tangle of yellow hair and began to braid it slowly. "Does she still dress like a man? In truth, that would be easy to change now that she is no longer a soldier. Would that not mollify Cauchon?"

"It would be a start," Richard replied, tired of the subject. "And now I must leave you."

He got out of bed, giving Cecily a full of view of his strong back, narrow hips, and muscular thighs. He was not tall like her father, but he was well made, and she could not help but admire him as he walked about the room.

"How did my hose find their way over here?"

He rescued one leg from one side of the room and the other from the bottom of the bed and sat down to pull them on. Looking over his shoulder, he saw a seductive smile on her lips. He grinned. "Are you going to help me with these confounded points, Cis, or do you want me to come back to bed? Nay, my love, I was jesting," he teased as she moved toward him. "I have been gone too long and must tend to my next office, more's the pity."

He caressed her head as she knelt at the edge of the bed to thread the silver points of the laces that tied the hose to his short gipon. "I regret I shall be in attendance on the king in the next days and unable to enjoy you for a while."

After tying the sides of his tunic, he suddenly slapped his forehead. "God's truth, I almost forgot. His grace has invited us to an audience with him in his private apartments the week following Shrove Tuesday. He has expressed a wish to know my new duchess better."

NINE-YEAR-OLD HENRY WAS gracious when the duke and duchess of York were ushered into his cavernous audience chamber in the castle. Neither the many wall hangings nor the roaring fire in a hearth that would accommodate four men shoulder to shoulder could ward off the draughts in the room, and Cecily was glad of her fur-lined velvet mantle. She was wearing a gold filament mesh that concealed her hair and over which was perched, in the latest fashion, a heart-shaped roll of fur. The blue of her velvet gown paled beside her eyes, which glowed sapphire in the firelight. No one would have guessed the agony of indecision she had gone through not two hours before about which gown and mantle to wear.

"York spoils you," Joan had muttered, tweaking the creamy underdress visible through the split front of the gown and standing back to study her daughter's magnificent appearance. "How can he pay for all this finery? He does not truly come into his inheritance until next year. Your father would say you are extravagant, my girl." She gave a snort of laughter. "Nay, he would not have uttered a word—never did where spoiling you was concerned. First your father and now your husband. It has taken all my resolve to turn you into a modest young lady, which I am gratified to see has been successful—most of the time. If I cannot curb the expenditure on your wardrobe, at least I can curb that tongue of yours. Now turn around, and let me see if you need a veil."

When Cecily was ready, Joan had nodded her approval and admonished her to speak only when she was spoken to and allow Richard to lead the conversation, "for he understands correct behavior with the king."

Cecily for once heeded her mother's advice and behaved like a lady during the audience, deferring to her husband and sitting quietly on a stool when invited by the king, while Richard remained standing. Richard was astonished and pleased with his beautiful, demure wife.

"Do you play an instrument, duchess?" Henry asked, turning his solemn gaze on her, his fine eyebrows slightly arched over a long but still childish nose.

"Not well enough to play for you, your grace," Cecily replied, smiling. "I am not a good pupil, so my lute teacher tells me."

Henry motioned to his bodyguard to bring a lute, and the strapping Sir Ralph Botiller hurried to the other end of the room to borrow one from the trio of musicians playing in the background. Cecily was discomforted by the admiring look Sir Ralph gave her as he put the delicate instrument into her hands. She held the lute to her chest and wished she had covered that exposed part of her with a plastron as Joan had suggested.

"I beg of you, your grace, let someone play who will do credit to this beautiful instrument," Cecily murmured, hoping Richard would intervene and save her from embarrassment. She had learned one melody on the lute, but at Raby she had often skipped practicing to go for a ride.

"I should like to hear you play, my lady," Richard remarked. "I cannot recall ever seeing you with a lute." He winked at Henry. "Usually, my wife is not one to hide her light under a bushel, your grace. I am surprised by her shyness."

Henry grinned and said, "I observed how she outshone every lady in the hunt last week, and in some cases, even the men. I was particularly impressed with how she managed to jump that hedge—wearing all those skirts as well."

Cecily began to resent being spoken about as though she were invisible and was gathering her thoughts in her defense when Henry fumbled his cup of ale and it fell to the floor, spilling its contents onto his white satin shoes.

"Forsooth!" he exclaimed, jumping up and staring at the spreading liquid in the rushes. "Forsooth and forsooth! Botiller, send in a servant, I pray you. Forgive me," he said to his guests, "how clumsy of me."

He looks like a little boy who expects to be chastised and not at all like a king, Cecily thought, feeling sorry for him. "Your grace, I have to thank you for your charming courtesy," she chirped, picking up the cup and handing it to Botiller. "You cannot think I did not recognize your gallant attempt at preventing me from making a fool of myself with this lute. 'Tis I who must beg *your* forgiveness for causing you to take such a measure."

Richard was too stunned to do anything but grin his appreciation, and his eyes shone with pride. Henry's jaw, however, did register his astonishment, but his eyes spoke their thanks with a genuine warmth. And Cecily put the lute aside with relief.

"Perhaps your grace would honor me with a game of chess," Richard said, shifting the king's focus. "I believe you are hard to beat, but I should like to try. I have quite a ruthless reputation among my fellows."

"Then prepare to meet your match, Lord Richard," Henry said with enthusiasm, his embarrassment deflected. He allowed Botiller to fit a clean pair of slippers on his feet and rubbed his hands together as two gentlemen ushers set up the ivory chessmen on the table. "Lady Cecily, forgive me while I concentrate on beating your husband. Perhaps you would keep Dame Alice company."

And so Cecily spent the next hour conversing with the king's governess, a motherly, intelligent woman who gave Cecily news of the queen mother. "The queen has another son," she told Cecily out of the king's hearing, "and has named him Edmund. I daily thank God for allowing her a little joy with Master Tudor. Such an unhappy life she lived with her family in France, and then to lose her beloved King Harry so soon after their marriage. He adored her, you know," she said, shifting her gaze from the attentive young duchess to her charge, who was deep in thought at the chess board. "A tragedy for her—and for England. And I thought it would break her heart when she was separated from her son, her only link to her husband. Gossips may say what they like, but I believe my dearest lady deserves this happiness."

Cecily murmured her agreement but could not forbear to ask, "Has Queen Catherine married Master Tudor, Dame Alice?"

"'Tis none of my affair, your grace, but it would surprise me if she has not," came the tempered response. Then, to change the subject, Alice nodded at Sir Ralph. "He is my son, did you know? A good boy, but"—she leaned in with a conspiratorial whisper—"he has a roving eye."

So I have noticed, Cecily wanted to say, but she inclined her head and mouthed "oh" instead.

A cry of glee came from the chess table. "Checkmate! See, Dame Alice, I have won," Henry exclaimed, reaching over to grasp Richard's outstretched hand. "It was a challenging game, was it not, my lord duke?"

Richard grinned and wiped his brow. "One of the hardest I can remember," he said, and Cecily knew he was not merely flattering this boy king but speaking the truth. "I have a boon to ask of you, your grace. May I have a rematch soon?"

"Bien sûr, monseigneur," Henry said in his perfect French. "I shall look forward to it. And now, forgive me, I feel a little tired. I thank you and Duchess Cecily for your company. It has been a pleasant change, has it not, Dame Alice?"

"Indeed it has, your grace, a most pleasant change." She and Cecily rose in unison as the older woman whispered, "He tells me he thinks you are the comeliest woman at court, madam," and gave Cecily a knowing wink.

Cecily and Richard knelt, heads bowed, in front of Henry. When he put his hand out for them to kiss, Cecily could not help noticing how cold the fingers were. Richard rose and was about to help Cecily up when Henry stayed him. Leaning over Cecily, the young king had one more thing to say to her. "I shall not forget your kindness this afternoon, your grace. If ever I can repay it, you have but to ask."

Cecily flushed with happiness. "You are gracious, my liege." Then she gave a conspiratorial smile. "Perhaps you might let Lord Richard win the next game of chess."

Catching them all off guard, Henry laughed. The forced, harsh laugh reminded Cecily of a poor madman she had heard once at Raby, and she stared at the floor to avoid showing her dismay. It was as though the boy had no control over the unpleasant sound and that it came from the throat of a much older person. It caused Dame Alice to hurry to him and pat his arm, which gesture the king shook off.

"Leave me be, madam," he snapped at the unfortunate governess. The others in the solar stiffened. "I am the king, and if I wish to laugh, I shall do so whenever I want." Dame Alice fell back and curtsied. Then, as if nothing had happened, his young face softened and he turned back to Cecily. "Forgive me, your grace. I am not certain I shall grant you that wish, because I do not know how to lose, but anything else in my power is yours for the asking."

The duke and duchess bowed their way from his presence. When the door closed behind them, Richard gripped Cecily's arm and hurried her down the staircase and out into the cold air. His face was tense when he told her, "I have seen him laugh like that once before, Cis. It is a devilish sound, and I fear for his mind."

Cecily crossed herself and then nodded slowly. "Yet in all other ways he appears to be an intelligent, caring boy, if a trifle grave." She gave a little smile. "Not unlike you, my love."

Richard ignored the last remark but said in a low voice, "I have heard his grandfather, Queen Catherine's father, was known by his own countrymen as *Charles le Fou*—the Mad. Do you think 'tis possible . . ."

"Pish, Dickon, your imagination runs amok. Now, let us think no more on it or it will spoil the memory of the afternoon and how I won a favor from the king."

"God's bones." Richard had to laugh. "I do believe you have bewitched the king as surely as you bewitched me."

THE YOUNG WOMAN sat on a stool in the middle of a stuffy chamber holding a lily, her shoulders drooped too low for her lank yellow hair to reach. Encircling her, their malicious black eyes staring and their whiskers twitching, a dozen black-hooded rats standing on their hind legs waited for her to speak.

"Confess!" the biggest rat snarled, stepping forward and pointing an accusing finger at the girl. "You bewitched the king?"

"God made me do it, I swear," the woman cried, raising her fearful eyes to him. The rats squeaked among themselves, shaking their heads and shuffling ever closer.

"Do you know the difference between witchcraft and heresy?" their leader shouted. "Well, do you?"

"Who do you think you are? The Inquisitor General?" asked the woman, a little more bravely. "How dare you treat me thus. I am a lady. I am a duchess. You are only a rat."

"I am your judge. I am Cochon," the rat replied, snorting for effect.

She stood and thrust the lily at him. "This is my symbol, my banner, my sword. God gave it to me because I am his messenger. Now let me go."

The room erupted in laughter, the harsh uncontrolled laughter of the insane that made the woman flinch, and the rats moved in closer and closer until she could not breathe.

"Help me!" she cried. "Save me, Dickon!"

"Your grace! Madam!" Rowena interrupted Cecily's dream, shaking her mistress awake. "You are safe, here in your bed. Here with me—Rowena."

Cecily started and opened her eyes. She could see nothing in the dark.

"The rats! Where are the rats?" she whimpered, still living her nightmare.

Rowena found the tinderbox and lit a taper, shielding it with her hand yet casting grotesque shadows on the wall behind her. Cecily cringed but gradually recognized her surroundings and was soothed by Rowena's assurances about the absence of rats.

"Sweet Jesu, but the dream seemed so real," she whispered, shivering. She took a cup of wine from Rowena's hand and sipped carefully, comforted by the warm sensation the liquid gave her as it slipped down her throat. "I was La Pucelle and the judges were all rats. 'Twas all so strange."

Rowena harrumphed. "You dreamed about the heretic, your grace? It must be the Devil's work that she enters your dreams."

"You believe that, Rowena? Why, she has not even been tried yet," Cecily said. "You are too quick to judge."

Rowena snorted her disapproval again.

Cecily shook her head, remembering the nightmare, and crossed herself. And then for good measure she pulled her amber rosary from under her pillow, climbed out of bed, and went to her little altar. "*Ave Maria, gratia plena* . . ." She murmured the soothing rote prayer to her benefactress, the Virgin, who smiled down at her from the delicate painting on the center panel. "Dear Mother of God, what can the dream mean?"

Rowena had crawled back under the bedclothes and had already fallen asleep. But Cecily pulled her bedrobe around her, went to the window embrasure, and pushed open the heavy wooden shutter. The sky was just lightening to the east, and silhouetted against it was the grim donjon where she knew Jeanne was held prisoner. Cecily strained to see any sign of life at the high window—perhaps Jeanne, too, could not sleep and was looking across the courtyard at her. But then she recalled Richard saying Jeanne did not have a window in her cell. "Only an arrow slit in case she thinks about jumping out again," he had said.

Cecily went back to the altar and leaned her head against the wooden prayer rail, pondering Jeanne's fate. I wish I could see her, she thought, but she could not imagine how this might be achieved. She quietly closed the shutter, slipped back under the covers, and finally went back to sleep.

"WOULD YOU ACCOMPANY me on my weekly mission of mercy at the castle prison, Cecille?" Anne of Bedford asked the young duchess of York the very next day.

Cecily could hardly contain her mounting excitement. "A mission of mercy, your grace? What does that entail?"

"I have been visiting the prisoners there—French soldiers for the most part—every week since we returned to Rouen, but"—she leaned over to whisper as far as her heavy headdress would allow—"this is the first time I shall be seeing La Pucelle. I am as curious as you to see her, and as I thought my husband would more likely allow two of us to offer a kind word and food, I asked if you might accompany me. To my surprise and delight he had no objection. She has been unwell, it seems, and my lord agreed she might be grateful for a little comfort from a woman. What say you, my dear friend, will you come?"

Cecily sent a fleeting word of thanks to the Virgin, for surely Mary had heard her prayer.

EVEN BEFORE THEIR escort opened the door to the guardroom the foul odor of human waste assailed Cecily's nostrils. She pulled out a kerchief doused in rosewater for this occasion and held it over her face. It seemed Duchess Anne was used to the stench, because she walked through the doorway with her attendant and into the outer of two cells where Jeanne was held without even wrinkling her nose.

Four guards lounging on stools and the floor were throwing dice. They hurriedly rose, touched their foreheads, and flattened themselves against the wall when they recognized Bedford's wife, and upon seeing the duchess of York as well, two of them elbowed each other, awed and hardly believing their eyes. A window set high in the wall let in enough light for them to see, and Cecily wondered if that was the window she had seen from her chamber on the night of her dream. The second room, separated from the guardroom by iron bars, had a low ceiling and only an arrow slit for a little air and light. In the gloom, Cecily could just make out a slight figure sitting still on a narrow bed attached to the wall. Two buckets of waste waiting to be emptied were ranged against the bars. Cecily's anger overcame her misgivings.

"Can you not see the jakes are full!" she cried at the cowering men. "You are not fit to be called Englishmen. One of you take them away at once!" They all stumbled over one another in an effort to do her bidding.

Anne nodded her approval. "Bien fait, well done, your grace," she murmured, and taking Cecily's arm, she moved up to the bars of Jeanne's cell, where Cecily could see the prisoner was cruelly chained to the poor excuse for a bed. Turning to the guard nearest the bunch of keys that hung by the door, Anne told him to unshackle the prisoner and to allow her to approach the bars. Eager to please, the guard worked quickly and then pushed Jeanne in the direction of the two women gazing in pity at the poor creature who slowly shuffled toward them. The man relocked the grille behind him and sauntered back to his mates, who were still gawping at the visitors.

Hoping for a moment of privacy with Jeanne, Cecily snapped, "Enough of your staring, sirrahs. Go back to your game of dice. We shall not be long." The men were happy to oblige and were soon absorbed in their sport.

"*Venez là,* demoiselle." Anne's gentle voice caught Jeanne off guard and Cecily saw her lip quiver. "We are here to bring you comfort and a little food. I am Anne, wife of the duke of Bedford, and this is her grace the duchess of York."

Jeanne stared through the bars at the two noblewomen with a mixture of fear and awe, rubbing her eyes as if she could not believe them. It had been some time since she had been among her own sex, let alone in the presence of women of such rank. For her part, Cecily could not help but stare back, surprised that Jeanne was nothing like the radiant, self-assured warrior of her imagination but a rather plain, frail peasant girl seemingly terrified of her and Anne.

Cecily took some bread and cheese from the basket on her arm. "Demoiselle Jeanne, do not be afraid. We are come as your friends to give you a little comfort," she said in her best French. Still awed, Jeanne shied away when Cecily attempted to pass the food through the bars.

"Do not be afraid," Cecily murmured. "I pray you, take the food." She was dismayed by the haunted look in the brown eyes and gave Jeanne a reassuring smile.

Anne nodded and smiled beside Cecily, and finally Jeanne reached out and took the bread. "*Je vous remercie,* madame la duchesse," she murmured in a deeper voice than Cecily had envisioned, and Cecily had to concentrate on the unfamiliar accent. The hand that held the bread was so small that Cecily wondered how the woman had been able to wield a sword. But it was also scratched and bruised and the nails black with dirt. There was no doubt Jeanne had not bathed for months, and Cecily longed to pull out her kerchief again but did not want to offend the quiet young woman. How had this simple peasant so galvanized one army and threatened another? Cecily pondered. Was it God's work or—she shivered slightly—was it the Devil's?

The visitors waited for Jeanne to take a bite from the bread and savor the good Norman cheese, and they were rewarded with a smile of pleasure. Cecily noticed Jeanne's coarsely woven hose woefully bagged around her thin thighs and pooled at her ankles, which were caked in blood from the open sores from the shackles. Cecily winced.

"Are you treated well, Jeanne?" Anne asked, after Jeanne had swallowed her mouthful.

Looking warily at the guards, who were paying the women no heed, she stepped closer to whisper. "The guards shout at me, madame, but I do not understand, as I cannot speak English. They beat me sometimes," she complained.

Anne clucked her tongue. "I shall speak to my lord about this, have no fear, demoiselle." She suddenly wanted to leave this place, and she took Cecily's arm. She did not know what she was expecting from this heroine of the French army, but she had not thought to be confronted with such an uninspiring person, and her disappointment showed in her voice. "We shall pray for you, demoiselle, that you may see the error of your ways."

Cecily was surprised by the dismissive tone and removed her arm from Anne's hold. "I will follow in a minute, your grace," she said, standing her ground and using her height to assert herself. "I should like to offer up a prayer with Jeanne before I leave, if it please you."

"Very well, my dear duchess." Anne inclined her head, surprised that Cecily did not feel the same desire to leave as soon as possible. "Have the guard escort you to the cell beneath us." She eyed Rowena standing by the door as she left. "Stay with your mistress." The attendant curtsied and murmured, "Have no fear I will, your grace."

Now that Cecily was alone with Jeanne, she did not know what to say. Jeanne was looking at her strangely, and so she crossed herself and looked at the ground for a clean spot to kneel upon. She pulled out her kerchief and sank down on it. Jeanne lowered herself painfully, but as the young peasant raised her eyes to heaven, her face was lit with a radiant smile.

"Oui, mon Seigneur," she suddenly cried, startling Cecily. "I will do as you bid me." As Cecily studied Jeanne's rapt face, she thought a window in the ceiling must have opened to let the sunlight stream in, because she sensed a glow all around her. She was awed. Jeanne was gazing up into the light as though she could see through it into heaven beyond. Cecily wondered that the guards and Rowena did not pròstrate themselves, but it appeared they were oblivious to this heavenly sight. She crossed herself and fingered her rosary, knotted as usual on her belt, and strained to hear Jeanne's voices as the Maid continued to address them.

Sweet Jesu, does she really hear the saints? she asked herself, a little afraid now in the bleak prison. She was just beginning to feel faint when the light faded and Jeanne turned to her, speaking in a low monotone.

"You are a good woman, madame, and I am told to thank you for your kindness. I beg of you, keep me in your prayers." She glanced through the bars at the slovenly guards still throwing dice and sighed. "But do not fear for me, my lady. I am promised by my voices that I shall be delivered. I know not when, but I trust in Him—as you must." She reached through the bars and touched Cecily's hand holding the rosary, and as she did so, the amber beads grew hot as if in a flame. Cecily heard Jeanne's words as though in a trance. "May God bless you, Cecily Neville, and your sons, who will one day wear the crown of England."

Cecily felt the hairs on her neck prickle and she was suddenly very warm in the chill, dank cell. She closed her eyes, swaying back and forth, aware she was swooning, but instead of the usual blackness, all was infused with white light. She felt Rowena gently raise her to her feet.

"Come, your grace, we should go now," the attendant said, glaring at Jeanne, who moved back from the bars. Rowena had been watching the exchange and was horrified when the heretic had dared to touch her mistress. "Guards, you may shackle your prisoner. Her grace is finished here."

Still in a trance, Cecily allowed herself to be led from the room. "May God watch over you, Jeanne d'Arc," she called over her shoulder. With deep sadness she knew that no one else would.

THAT NIGHT SHE lay next to her husband for the first time in a week. She would usually have been delighted to welcome him back to her bed, but her heart was still filled with the mystical incident in the prison cell. Richard had been interested to hear of the visit and asked a few perfunctory questions about the Maid's appearance and her behavior, but Cecily did not tell him— nor would she tell anyone yet—of her extraordinary experience that day. It would be for her, Jeanne, and God alone.

It seemed Richard was not able to discern that her mind was not on their lovemaking as he spent time with foreplay, and she aroused him to several brinks of climax with her new-learned skills. When he had finally had his fill of her, and she had masterfully pretended her own rapture, he slumped down onto the feather mattress breathing hard.

"I cannot imagine going through life a virgin," Cecily said, then chuckled.

"Whatever made you think of that?" Richard asked.

"La Pucelle," Cecily said simply. "She has given up all of that—and her freedom—for the love of God."

"Aye, and so do those who take holy orders, Cis. Only they take their vows and go quietly about their business. They do not ride into battle and consort with the Devil."

"How dare you say so," Cecily cried, sitting up and thumping the bed. "How do you know Jeanne does not hear holy voices? Just because God has not chosen you as His messenger—"

"God's bones, Cis, what did that little witch say to you today? I pray she has not cast her evil eye upon you. Can you not forget about her? I pray you, do not let this woman come between us," he cajoled, stroking her back. "It was good of you and Duchess Anne to visit her, but there is an end to it. If it affects you thus, I will forbid you to go on errands of mercy like this again."

Cecily took a deep breath. She knew Jeanne was not a subject Richard liked to discuss and she did not want a quarrel. "I have done nothing wrong, my love, and my only thought was to bring a little comfort to the poor woman. 'Tis our Christian duty to help our fellows, is it not? I pray you, turn to me. I would not have you cross with me. We have so few opportunities to be together like this, and I would feel your love for me, not your ire."

Richard acquiesced, and she snuggled into his warm body. He had yearned for her all evening as they supped with Duke John, his duchess, and Cecily's sisters. Joan had not been well of late, and she had spent all day in her chamber. Cecily had decided it was best not to upset her mother with the knowledge of her visit to Jeanne; she would tell Joan of it one day, she had no doubt.

Richard for his part hoped that now perhaps Cecily would forget her obsession with the Maid and would concentrate on her duty to him. But he had known Cecily long enough to recognize when her stubbornness might overrule common sense. He had long since agreed with Joan that Ralph had spoiled his daughter. Richard gave a little sigh. Aye, he loved her spirit, her intelligence, and her beauty, but not being an assertive man where women were concerned, he needed her wifely obedience. Was it not his right to expect that of her?

On her side of the bed, Cecily found her thoughts returning again and again to Jeanne's prophecy. How did she know my name was Cecily Neville? And what did she mean that my sons would be kings? Did she mean that Richard would one day wear the crown? How could that come to pass? Henry was on the throne, he was healthy and would bear sons. Besides, Bedford and Humphrey would come before Richard in the succession, would they not? It was too fearful to contemplate, she thought. The whole order of their lives would be turned upside down. Nay, Jeanne must have misheard those voices of hers.

"Cis, stop mumbling," Richard grumbled. "Are you not tired?"

"In truth, I am a little tired, Dickon."

"Then God's good night to you, *madame ma duchesse,*" he said, closing his eyes. "May you waken on the morrow a humble and obedient wife."

"Oh, Richard, is that what you really want?"

"Sometimes," he answered, yawning. "But not in bed."

11

Rouen, Spring 1431

On the twenty-first day of a dreary February, when the snowmelt and daily drizzle had made the streets of Rouen a sea of mud, John of Bedford and his attendants accompanied Bishop Cauchon on horseback from *Joyeux Repos* across the city to Château Bouvreuil to begin the trial of the Maid of Orléans.

From Countess Joan's solar window, Cecily and Katherine watched them go. Cecily's heart was heavy. She was thinking of the conversation at dinner the day before, after Bishop Cauchon had spent the morning in the duke's office going over the details of the first day of the tribunal.

"How long do you think the proceedings will last, my lord bishop?" Anne of Bedford had asked her guest. "And will they be held in public?"

All eyes turned to Cauchon. With his roly-poly physique and wobbling chins, he certainly fit her new name for him: *"Cochon."*

"I have no doubt we shall obtain a confession from La Pucelle within a few hours once the tiresome preliminaries are over," he said. "She has been summoned and will appear before us on the morrow. And aye, the session will be public, but I regret, madame, that ladies are not permitted." He beamed at Anne, his watery eyes disappearing into folds of larded cheek.

"She agreed to appear—and without conditions, my lord bishop?" Anne persisted. "From what I have heard"—she purposely avoided Cecily's eyes—"the Maid is not afraid to speak her mind. I am surprised to know she agreed to appear so meekly."

The smile faded from Cauchon's face, and he lifted his snowy napkin from his lap and wiped his entire face with it. Cecily noticed he was missing half an index finger on his right hand and irreverently wondered if he had bitten it off himself, mistaking it for a sausage. He avoided Anne's gaze on his left and stared ahead as he responded, "You are correct, *madame la duchesse*. The heretic had the audacity to demand to hear Mass before being tried. How could I, in all godliness, allow a heretic into His holy presence? You may rest assured I refused."

Cecily could not stifle her gasp in time to prevent Bishop Cauchon's accusing eyes from finding her among her sisters at the ladies' table. She pretended to choke a little and busied herself with her cup of wine, feeling the odious man's gaze on her.

"Certes, you refused," John of Bedford exclaimed. "Until she is proven innocent of heresy, she must be denied God's comfort."

Cauchon turned his attention to his host, inclining his head in acknowledgment. "Just so, your grace. And what sacrilege to stand before God's holy altar in those unwomanly garments. Indeed, the voices she hears must be from Satan, and if nothing else, that transgression will condemn her. Have no fear, Lady Anne, she shall be proven guilty—and by her own confession, I promise you."

"It seems to me, Bishop Cauchon, that you have already made up your mind that she is guilty." Anne's smile was sweet, but her husband on the other side of Cauchon frowned.

"My dear, you misunderstand our guest. Indeed, we all hope the Maid will confess her sins and recant. It behooves us to rid ourselves of such a dangerous threat to King Henry's kingdom here in Normandy, and it is the tribunal's task to accomplish that. If she recants, she will make her French followers ashamed they listened to her, and they will soon forget her." Bedford's tone was, as always when addressing his wife, courteous and kind, but it contained admonishment just the same.

Anne blushed and hung her head. "I beg your pardon, my lord bishop, if I spoke too boldly. All of us hope that Jeanne will recant and be allowed to return to her family."

Cauchon patted her hand. "I forgive you, my dear duchess." Then he turned and arched a brow at Bedford. "Will you send Jeanne home if she recants, *monseigneur?*"

John of Bedford's answer had been smothered by a mouthful of meat, and so no one heard his expostulated, "Nay!"

KATHERINE PROPELLED CECILY away from the window and back to their cushioned settle. Nan looked up from her embroidery, jealous of the friendship that had blossomed between her eldest and youngest sisters. She was, however, happier to be with the court than stifled in her Welsh castle and enjoyed her position as Humphrey Stafford's wife. Humphrey was now Bedford's lieutenant general in Normandy. A few months ago, when Humphrey had been created first count of Perche in Normandy for his loyal service on the king's council and in the province, Nan had not endeared herself to her sisters with her boasting.

"She is jealous because you and I are duchesses, 'tis all, Cis. Take no notice of her," sensible Katherine had told her passionate young sister and had chuckled at Cecily's characteristic "Pish!" in response.

"Humphrey says Cauchon will get a confession from La Pucelle and is wagering it will happen within a week," Nan now said loftily. "Humphrey says she does not have the intelligence to understand the inquisitor's questions." She paused, biting off a bright scarlet thread. "Humphrey says . . ."

"Humphrey says, Humphrey says," Cecily mimicked her in a childish voice. "Sweet Jesu, Nan, do you not have a thought of your own?"

"Hush, Cecily." Katherine stayed her with a finger to her lips. "You will wake Mother."

Nan stood up stiffly and made to leave. "I see you do not like my company, Cecily. Let me tell you, the feeling is mutual, and so I shall remove myself," she declared, and putting her sewing basket under her arm, she nodded to her attendant and they left the room.

"Good riddance," Cecily muttered after her. "Confess you do not care for her high and mighty ways either, Kat. Ah, but you are more sanguine than I and can see the good in all. I would I could be more like you." She sighed and took up a book of proverbs by Christine de Pisan that Anne of Bedford had lent her.

> *Willingly read fine books of tales*
> *Whenever you can, for it never fails*
> *That examples such books comprise*
> *Can help you to become more wise.*

How true, Cecily thought, turning the page to see what other words of wisdom the erudite Christine had written. She resolved to apologize to Nan before nightfall.

HUMPHREY STAFFORD WAS wrong; the trial was now in its third week, and it had moved from the public space of the castle's great hall to Bishop Cauchon's private house. Cauchon had subjected Jeanne to all manner of examinations and deprivations and still the young woman held to her original story. Her clever replies had even impressed Duke John. Now Cauchon had been reduced to employing a canon of Rouen, Nicholas Loiseleur, to be a false friend to Jeanne in the hope that she would confess her sin to him in private. He justified his action by quoting from the Inquisition's handbook, allowing "one or two faithful people to approach the accused and pretend pity, warning him of the fire that would be his lot if he did not confess his heresy." And so Loiseleur, dressed as an ordinary citizen, gained access to the Maid by pretending to be someone from her own region, and Cauchon hoped she would let down her guard.

Much of this information was kept from the residents of *Joyeux Repos*, but one day in mid-March, when Richard found time to leave his administrative duties with Duke John for an hour to visit Cecily, he found himself bombarded with questions by his curious wife.

"'Tis monstrous!" Cecily whispered to Richard as they stretched their legs up in a gallery at the manor house. It was raining again. Cecily noticed that Richard had given up his usually fastidious attention to neatness, judging by the mud that was spattered on his hose and tunic. "You say the man blocked Jeanne's view of the altar with his body in the royal chapel when she was passing because Cauchon forbade her to look inside? What madness is this? What harm in her wanting some comfort from the crucifix?"

"Soft, Cecily," Richard warned her, checking up and down the paneled gallery that overlooked the hall. "Remember she is believed to be a heretic and thus banned from seeking God's love—at least the succor one finds inside His holy house. Now, I pray you, leave the subject alone or you will make Duke John suspicious."

Cecily nodded glumly. "Aye, Dickon, I know you are right, and yet I cannot believe that she is full of sin. If only you could have seen her . . ."

"Enough!" Dickon almost spat, making her gasp. He sat her down brusquely on a bench and gripped her shoulders so tight he made her wince. A few inches from her face, he demanded, "Do you want to be brought up in front of the Inquisitor General? Did you know that a woman who spoke out on Jeanne's behalf last year in Paris was burned for a heretic? You must hold your tongue or I will find a way to send you home to England."

Cecily forced herself to demur. True, she was angered by Richard's treatment of her, but his words and concern for her finally broke down her resolve to defend Jeanne in public. Besides, Richard's vehemence frightened her. "I am sorry," she muttered.

He straightened and walked to the balcony rail and glanced over, making sure no one could have overheard their conversation. A few lackeys were sweeping the floor, talking among themselves, and he was satisfied. He turned back to the dejected Cecily and frowned. Was this Maid of Orléans driving a wedge between them? The witch was not worth one speck of dust upon the ground where Cecily walked.

He hurried back to her. "Forgive me if I hurt you, my dearest, but I do not believe you understand the danger you put yourself in. I implore you simply to listen when news of the trial is brought here and not betray yourself. If you will promise me that, I shall rest easy. Do you swear?"

Cecily nodded slowly, acknowledging the sense in his request and finally comprehending her peril. She bent and kissed his cheek, the late-day stubble of his heavy beard in need of a scrape. "Upon my honor, I will, Dickon."

Knowing Richard's anger was usually short-lived, she cocked her head, giving him a mischievous smile. "And to prove I know how to change a subject, husband, what say you to becoming a father?"

Dumbfounded, Richard stared at her, and then a grin suffused his face and he delighted her with those crinkling eyes. "By the Rood, Cis! Why did you not tell me at once? When did you know? How long has it been? When will the child be born?"

Cecily clapped her hands in delight. "So many questions, my lord. Where shall I begin?" She had not told anyone, though she was certain Rowena suspected, being responsible for preparing the monthly pile of clean rags. But when a seventh week without her courses went by, she was convinced she had conceived. "'Twas that day in your room at the castle, remember? By my reckoning, we should hold our first child close to your next birthday. I pray it is a boy for your sake, my love."

Richard was on his feet, hardly able to keep from shouting the news over the balcony to the servants below or to anyone in earshot. "I am going to be a father," he told Cecily with incredulity, as if she did not know. "God be praised!" he exclaimed, pulling her to him and covering her face with kisses. "He has been good to us, has He not?"

Cecily made a face. "In truth, Dickon, He has taken His time. I have prayed to so many saints, lit candles to St. Monica, and made all sorts of promises to the dear Virgin long before this, and my knees are worn out. But aye, I am grateful He has finally heard us. Let us go to St. Ouen and give thanks."

It was Richard's turn to grimace. "What, in this rain? We can go on the morrow. First let us go and tell your mother and sisters."

WORD WAS LEAKED that Jeanne was to hear the articles of accusation against her two days after Palm Sunday, and if she still denied her guilt, she would be threatened with excommunication and death.

"Seventy of them?" Cecily exclaimed, between meager mouthfuls of a steaming fish pie that she and Richard were sharing for supper. If truth be told, she had little appetite these days, but she also worried the Lenten diet was not sufficient for a woman with child. "They found seventy ways to accuse her?"

Richard nodded, pouring himself some more ale. "I have heard from my lord of Bedford that the Maid's answers to the hundreds of questions put to her by the forty judges and assessors were of astonishing intelligence, as though she were a theologian," Richard continued. "If Cauchon was hoping to entrap her into heretical statements easily, he has been thwarted."

Nay, Dickon, Cecily wanted to say, Jeanne answered not as a *man* of God but as an *angel* of God. Instead she shook her head in disbelief. "Day after day they have questioned her. That poor woman must be half-spent. In the prison conditions in which she is kept 'tis a wonder she has not fallen ill. Do you know if she has put off her men's garb?"

"I understand she was asked which she would prefer: to hear Mass in female dress or wear men's clothes and be deprived of the sacraments. She answered that if she were assured of Mass in a gown, then she would don one for it but put the breeches back on afterward immediately," Richard said, leaving the table to warm his back by the fire. "To be sure, Cauchon refused to accept that. It seems he is most offended by the men's clothes more than by all the other offenses."

Cecily hardly dared ask what the next step might be, but Richard took her hand and gently told her. "They could send her to the stake if she does not recant. If she does, I believe she will be imprisoned anyway. But they are determined to make her recant, Cis, even if it means torture. The English cannot allow her to become a martyr or her very name will inflame the French into chasing us from Normandy."

Dejected, Cecily stared at the fire. "I do not care for your choice of words, Richard."

Richard took her hand to his lips and kissed it gently. "I wish I could spare you all of this, my love, but trust me, it will soon be over." He did not voice how concerned he was about his wife's mien. She had lost the roses in her cheeks and, considering she was with child, she looked thinner than he could remember. He hoped the trial of a heretic who seemed to have so captivated her imagination was not an ill omen for this pregnancy, and he sent a silent prayer to St. Monica to protect mother and child and to his own special saint, the soldier-martyr Maurice, for a speedy end to the Maid's ordeal.

BUT IT SEEMED Cauchon was in no hurry, and the trial dragged on.

"The Maid was unwell lately, and the king sent his own physicians to care for her," Cecily's uncle Beaufort told Joan one day in early May. He had come to pay his respects to his sister, who was recovering slowly from her winter malady. He gave a short laugh. "My lord of Warwick and I advised the king on this, and he agreed 'twould be a waste to let her die of natural causes."

Cecily was pretending to read on the other side of her mother's bed. She bit her lip to stop herself from crying "foul."

"A waste, Henry?" Joan asked, searching her brother's round, deeply lined face. "Is not her death what you wish for? What we all wish for?"

Henry patted her fidgeting fingers. "Aye, sister, you have the measure of it. But the king bought her dear, remember, and she has been a canker in our efforts to hold on to France. 'Tis why we think she needs to feel the full force of English justice to pay for her meddling. We want her to die by justice and"— he paused, glancing at Cecily, who still had her nose in the book—"by fire."

Cecily could no longer feign indifference, and raised her startled eyes to him. "My lord uncle, do you believe in your heart that the Maid deserves to die at the stake?" she said, achieving an even tone with every ounce of self-control she could muster. She even gave him a small defiant smile as his gaze attempted to bore into her very soul.

It was too much for Joan, who suddenly sat up with far more vigor than a woman recovering from sickness. "If I were not in bed, I would box your ears. How dare you question his Eminence thus? Have you no fear for your immortal soul?" Her pale face was now blazing as she willed Cecily into submission. Beaufort had risen, scorn on his face. His sister had relieved him of an answer, for he was by no means certain of Jeanne d'Arc's heresy yet.

"Forgive her, Henry," Joan implored him. "Conception has addled her wits."

Beaufort harrumphed. "I do not believe your daughter's disposition has changed one whit since the first time I met her, my lady." He glared at Cecily, who continued to keep her head lowered. "Have a care, niece. If La Pucelle is proven guilty and she recants, the beliefs of those who supported her may also be questioned."

Joan gasped and crossed herself. "On your knees, Cecily," she commanded. "Beg your uncle's pardon and blessing before God and swear you have no such belief."

But Henry Beaufort had had enough of these silly women and wanted to return to the castle for news of the latest day's trial. "Nay, Joan, I will not force Cecily to her knees, but I would hope common sense would prevail and that my niece will put foolish notions about the Maid from her mind." He now addressed Cecily, who was on her knees in front of him. "I shall look for you at Mass on the morrow, niece, and hope you will be guided by prayer. God give you both a good day," he said, presenting his great bishop's ring for both women to kiss. He smoothed out his immaculately pleated scarlet robe and walked slowly from the room.

"I hate him!" Cecily muttered miserably. "They all want Jeanne dead one way or another." She bowed her head and wept.

Joan stared at her daughter in amazement. "What has come over you, child? Why the concern for a peasant who has caused such turmoil with her nonsense."

"But 'tis not nonsense, Mother," Cecily cried, and told Joan of her visit to the prison and the divine experience with Jeanne.

"Sweet Jesu, she has bewitched you," Joan moaned, struggling out of bed and taking Cecily in her arms. "Certes, can you not see now that she must employ demons to convert the innocent, like you, to her cause."

Through the bedgown Cecily could feel her mother's soft belly against her cheek and gave herself up to the childish urge to wrap her arms around Joan's waist. She did not realize she was weeping until Joan gently tipped up her face and wiped away her tears. Had she truly been bewitched? Cecily wondered, mulling Joan's words. Perhaps she should admit that she had, and then perhaps she could let go of her obsession with the Maid. Why, Jeanne's predicament had even clouded her happiness at carrying Richard's child. How cruel was that? Slowly her sobs diminished and she allowed Joan to take off her slippers and her filigree cap and ease her into her mother's bed.

"You must not think of that woman anymore, my dear child, for fear it will . . ." Joan paused, searching for the perfect phrase, "upset the balance of things inside you. Pray to St. Brigid to put her away from you. You owe that much to your husband and unborn child," Joan declared. She was tiptoeing to the door to summon Rowena and her own tiring woman, when she heard Cecily's whispered, "Thank you, Mother. God bless you."

Before Joan returned to the bed, Cecily had fallen asleep. For once, her daughter's dreams were not about the unfortunate woman chained in the castle cell but of her own childhood at Raby.

12

Rouen, May 1431

Within a fortnight, it seemed to all at *Joyeux Repos* that Cecily's humors were once again aligned and her appetite had returned. She had prayed hard to the Virgin—and St. Brigid, to appease her mother—to help her concentrate her energies on bearing a healthy child, and with Joan once again restored to the household, the sunny days of May passed pleasantly enough, including a small celebration for Cecily's sixteenth birthday. It was easier to forget the grim proceedings on the other side of the city in the pretty Chantereine gardens.

On the twenty-fourth day of the month, Cecily and Anne of Bedford were walking arm in arm along the grassy paths of the estate carpeted with violets, buttercups, celandines, and clover, when they saw a group of horsemen trot through the St. Hilaire Gate. Even from that distance Cecily recognized Edmund Beaufort, second son of the earl of Somerset, and she frowned.

"My cousin, your grace. I have no love for him, I regret to say. Not only did he mock me unmercifully for being my father's favorite, but he was cruel to animals, so my brother Edward told me. I wonder why he comes now."

Anne bent to pick a lily of the valley and inhale its honeyed scent. "My lord sent for him," she replied. "He has had some success in the field, John tells me. Only his first command, I believe."

Cecily noted the noble carriage of her tall cousin seated so naturally upon his horse and nodded. "Aye, I would expect him to be a forceful leader," she mused. "And arrogant. Like all Beauforts, an abundance of pride is never far from the surface."

Anne laughed, shooing away a spaniel who was wanting to play. "*Va-t-en,* Sami! Nay, I will not throw sticks today." She took Cecily's arm again, chuckling. "My dear Cecille, are you forgetting you too are a Beaufort?"

Cecily grinned. "I am not allowed to forget, your grace. My mother reminds me almost daily. But in my heart I am first and foremost a Neville," she said. "And now I have taken Dickon's name—Plantagenet. I am proud to bear it, in truth." She patted her stomach. "And our son will be too."

"Are you so sure you carry a boy?" Anne teased her.

Cecily sidled away, lifting her heavy hem off the dew-drenched grass, and twirled around and around, making Sami bark noisily. "As sure as I am Cecily Neville and Beaufort and Plantagenet," she cried. "Today I am just happy to be alive."

Anne hesitated but then chose her words carefully. "In that case, my dear, happy duchess, I do not think you should spoil your mood by accompanying me to St. Ouen this afternoon. It will likely dampen this new *joie de vivre* that we all rejoice to see."

Cecily stopped turning and returned, anxious, to Anne's side. "St. Ouen? What happens there today, Anne? You cannot now leave me guessing."

"La Pucelle will be sentenced in public, but this time the citizens are encouraged to attend. I was curious to see the event," Anne said. "But on second thoughts, I think I shall remain here with you."

There was no stopping Cecily once the cat was out of the bag, and the group who set out on foot to walk the mile from *Joyeux Repos* to the cemetery of the abbey church included Anne, Joan and her three daughters, and a small escort of squires.

"Humphrey says they chose the cemetery instead of inside the church so that more people could bear witness," Nan remarked, her pale blue eyes scanning the crowd for her husband. "There is my lord Buckingham on that platform," she cried, pointing.

"I believe 'twas because the transept is still under construction," Anne whispered to Cecily, "but a cemetery seems a macabre choice, in truth. Perhaps Nan is right, however, look how many are here."

The townsfolk stood aside to let the English noblewomen pass to the front of them, although all were eager to catch a glimpse of the Maid, who had been the subject of conversation in many a citizen's home these past three months.

"There she is!" a woman cried from the middle of the crowd as a wagon pulled by a cart horse neared one of two platforms erected for the event. The stands on the larger platform, where Nan had spotted Humphrey, were filled with other English lords, the trial assessors, and various clergy, including

Cecily's uncle and two of Normandy's preeminent abbots. In the middle of the front row, Cecily saw Cauchon, today dressed crowlike, all in black. She craned her neck to see Richard, but as he was not as tall as Humphrey or Edmund Beaufort, she could not find him among the many-colored gowns, mantles, and chaperons clustered in the confined space. The earl of Warwick, the king's guardian, resplendent on his caparisoned courser, patrolled the space between the platforms, while English captains and soldiers kept the throng quiet. Cecily was somewhat mollified to note the crowd was expectant but respectful. Perhaps they believed, as she did, that Jeanne would be found not guilty and would simply be taken back to the English prison for the duration of the war.

But she changed her mind when Jeanne was roughly pulled from the cart and thrust upon the empty platform, her guards pinning her between them. Where did they think she could go? Cecily asked herself, grimacing and pitying the slight figure. The crowd egged the guards on, and a young man launched a clod of earth at Jeanne. One sharp bark from Warwick intimidated the culprit, who looked up sullenly at the earl.

She is still in men's garb, Cecily noted sadly. Ah, Jeanne, where are your voices now? How ill they have advised you!

A short, fat priest ascended the steps to Jeanne's platform. Standing a few feet from her, he held up his hand for quiet and then proceeded to bless all present.

"'Tis the preacher of the abbey church, Guillaume Erard," Anne told Cecily.

For thirty minutes Erard enumerated Jeanne's crimes, exhorting her to recant, repent, and be saved from excommunication. Much of the abusive sermon shocked Cecily, but Jeanne appeared impervious to his accusations and slanders. The only point she vehemently spoke out to deny was not one against herself but a condemnation of King Charles. Erard, infuriated by her interruption, cried, "Silence!"

Then he instructed Jeanne that if she did not abide by the laws of mother church she would be condemned. The crowd hushed as they waited for her answer, and Jeanne lifted her eyes to heaven as if to beg for help.

"If you do not submit, Jeanne d'Arc," Erard told her again, pointing to a man in a black hood, "your executioner awaits to take you to the stake—now!"

"Oh, Jeanne," Cecily whispered to herself. "Save yourself, I beg of you. Sweet Mother of God, save her."

Some of the other priests, including Cauchon, were now clambering upon

Jeanne's platform, pressing around her and threatening her. She looked into the crowd as if to find her answer and then she saw Cecily, whose eyes implored her to save herself. A sweet smile suffused her face for a second, and Cecily gasped, her legs buckling. Anne sensed her trembling and put an arm around her friend for support.

"She will recant, Cecille," she murmured. "You will see. The fear of fire is too great, even for a brave woman like Jeanne."

Cauchon then gave Jeanne yet another warning. "Do as you are told! Do you want to die by fire? Change your dress and do as you are told, and you will be put under the protection of the church." Then he pushed a piece of paper toward her and told her to sign it. But Jeanne still hesitated. Many bystanders were angry by now and hurled a few stones, missing Jeanne but causing the soldiers to push the crowd back.

"But she cannot read!" Cecily murmured indignantly. "They must know she cannot read. 'Tis unfair."

"Hush, Cecille. People are watching us," Anne whispered as Cauchon stepped to the edge of the platform and began slowly and deliberately to read the sentence in Jeanne's native tongue that would give her up to her secular judges and certain death.

But the Maid herself interrupted him, muttering something only those closest could hear, and Cauchon cried out in triumph, "She has submitted! I heard her submit." He pulled Jeanne from between her guards. "Now, sign!" he screamed, thrusting the parchment in front of her, whereby Jeanne reluctantly took the pen and made a trembling mark upon it.

The distraught young woman would have fallen had she not been supported again by her guards and surrounded by churchmen eager to keep her standing to hear her sentence. Cauchon, knowing full well Jeanne would not understand one word he would say, used Latin to enumerate her crimes against mother church and against God. Then he announced in French that as she had recanted, she would be released from excommunication. A roar of approval drowned out several gasps of disappointment from Jeanne's sympathizers, who had fervently believed in her holy mission.

"Her crimes were great. She is sentenced to a life of imprisonment with only bread and water to nourish her, but she must repent of her sins every moment of every day and never sin again," Cauchon pronounced.

"What prison is that, my lord bishop?" Jeanne's voice was barely audible. "I pray you put me in the church's prison."

Several of the assessors and priests on the other platform nodded their assent, but Cauchon knew who his masters were. King Henry and his council wanted Jeanne kept close, and as he could not pronounce the sentence of death on her, then he knew what must be done.

"Take her back from whence she came," he commanded, turning his back on her. The guards then dragged her down the steps and into the wagon, where the young woman, tied to the rail, had to endure taunts and insults in silence. Cecily watched in pity.

"I did not know you were coming, Cis." Richard's quiet voice behind her interrupted a prayer of thanks for Jeanne's deliverance. She closed her eyes and with a sigh of gratitude leaned back against his strength. "For all it was spectacle, you must be glad of the outcome."

Cecily nodded, unaware of the disappointment her husband and the other English lords were experiencing. She would learn much later that they felt betrayed by Cauchon, who had promised the council the stake, whereas Jeanne alive and in prison could still be a powerful symbol and rallying point for the French. The death sentence was the only way to rid themselves of a nuisance and mollify the thousands of troops angered by the Maid's military exploits. But Richard suspected the fat Cauchon was not about to imperil his immortal soul by burning a repentant heretic. Imprisoning her to repent at her leisure for the rest of her life was a suitable punishment from the church, and Cauchon was relieved to choose it, Richard told Cecily. Only an about-face on the part of Jeanne could result in a sentence of death. This day had provided a blow to the English, and Richard felt it as keenly as the others on the council.

He cradled Cecily's weight against him, pondering all he had witnessed and understanding one thing clearly. Cecily must not know how he felt at this moment, he decided, and certainly not while she was carrying their child. This affair of the Maid was the first dissension they had had in their young marriage, and he hoped Jeanne would disappear from their lives and Cecily's thoughts as quickly as possible

"Aye, Richard, I am thankful she repented," Cecily said eventually, turning and resting her cheek in the folds of his soft gown. "She does not deserve to be burned, although going back to that terrible prison will be enough of a hell for her. May God now keep her safe from those vile guards for, in truth, they will not be kind."

Richard said nothing; he knew she was right.

* * *

"How DID IT come to this?" Cecily murmured to Anne as they sat side by side among the other dignitaries summoned to witness the execution of La Pucelle on a hastily built stand in the old market square. Not a week had gone by since Jeanne's repentance at St. Ouen, and today she would be put to death as a relapsed heretic.

According to Anne's instructions, Cecily had been assigned the last seat in the row, which was a few paces from the makeshift staircase, in case she felt unwell and needed to depart quickly. Rowena was positioned close by, ready to help her mistress. Cecily had pooh-poohed the notion, but as she had slept ill and the morning sickness had been especially violent that day, she was grateful that Anne had taken pains to provide for her well-being. Despite a cushion, the hard wooden bench was certainly not comfortable, but after a few unusually hot days, the thirtieth day of May had mercifully dawned pleasantly mild and had caused Katherine to remark earlier, "At least we shall not be overcome by the heat." Almost immediately, she had clapped her hand over her mouth for her lack of tact.

"If my brother of Burgundy were only here," Anne said in a hushed voice, "perhaps he could persuade John to spare her." She sighed. "Indeed, I could not."

"I, too, entreated Richard to reason with the duke, but I fear those pleas fell on deaf ears." Cecily gritted her teeth, remembering that morning when she had gone down on her knees to ask her husband to save Jeanne. But he had remonstrated harshly with her for being disloyal to the English cause and had flatly refused. For the first time, Cecily's unwavering faith in him had faltered. She had left the room with her head held high but her heart aching. Why could he not feel as I do, she asked herself. We have always agreed before.

On his way to his seat on the platform now, Richard bent to her to make sure she was well enough to endure such a hideous spectacle. "I beg of you to leave the second you cannot," he urged, and she nodded stiffly, sending him away.

Cecily sighed. "Once Jeanne threw off the woman's gown she had agreed to wear and donned men's clothes once more, she was doomed," she said, squeezing the duchess of Bedford's small hand. "What made her change her mind, I wonder?" She watched the king's council mount the stairs and take their seats in front of the women. "Something must have happened to make her put them on again."

Anne was cautious with her response and glanced around before whispering, "If I tell you, you must swear not to repeat it. 'Twill upset you, Cecille, as it did me, but"—she gave a Gallic shrug—"what can we women do? John told me 'twas Cauchon's idea. He was not convinced of Jeanne's abjuration, and he suggested that if the guards were to . . . to use her as they would any other woman they disrespected, that she might want to throw off the gown and resume wearing the men's tunic and leggings."

Cecily's horror was about to manifest itself in a cry of disbelief when she saw Anne's warning frown and controlled herself. "And I presume the guards made sure the men's clothes were close at hand," she seethed, and when she saw Anne's nod, added, "That pig Cauchon. May he rot in hell!"

"Once Jeanne relapsed, the churchmen were free to condemn her to die," Anne concluded.

"Thus putting her fate into our hands," Cecily murmured, her eyes sweeping the front ranks of English lords. "Just like our Savior's priests." She shook her head, her heart so heavy that it made her slump forward in her seat. What a tragic end, she thought bitterly, aware of a hush settling over the swelling crowd of citizens both English and French.

As the rays of the morning sun glinted off his crown, young King Henry mounted the stairs and passed close enough to Cecily for his purple robe embroidered with the lilies of France to brush her skirts. However, she did not see the dismay in his round blue eyes when he caught sight of the stake anchored in the middle of the square, a wall of faggots piled at eye level in a circle around it. At least, he had been told, this burning would be mercifully quick, as the smoke from the wall of wood would suffocate the Maid long before the flames consumed her flesh.

A second platform near the market church of St. Sauveur was filling up with the many members of the clergy in black or scarlet robes who had presided over the trial. They formed a semicircle—like vultures circling for the kill, Cecily thought, and she shuddered. A simple stool was placed in front of them. Her uncle Beaufort sat next to Cauchon, and they seemed to be sharing a joke. The bile rose again in her throat.

Her eyes roamed around the square, usually so lively with farmers and their animals, carts full of vegetables, pie-men hawking their fare, and peddlers enticing shoppers to buy their ribbons and geegaws. Instead she observed the same noisy men and women jostling for position and glad of a day off. She tried not to stare at the gruesome woodpile with the sturdy stake standing sentinel, iron rings ready to accept the prisoner's chains. Poor Jeanne, how can she escape now?

"Elle arrive!" A shout rose from the back of the thousand-strong crowd, many of whom had traveled for hours to be here, for word of the execution had been sent to towns and villages two days ago as soon as the Inquisitor had finished his job. At first the voices were loud and insulting, but as the prisoner was brought among them, barefoot, clad in a penitent robe of black, and her lank hair now grown into a more feminine length, the spectators fell silent.

Two black-robed friars walked behind her, mouthing prayers, and stayed below as she was hauled up onto the second platform and told to sit upon a stool facing her judges. Cecily suddenly felt faint as she remembered her dream of the circle of rats in their black robes accusing her as she sat, just like Jeanne, on a stool before them. Anne, frowning her concern, nudged her friend, and at once the ugly vision faded. Cecily whispered her thanks and said that she was quite well.

As the nine o'clock hour tolled, the canon of Rouen, Nicholas Midi, rose from among the clergy and began a sermon that droned on for almost an hour. Jeanne sat rigidly on her stool, her eyes raised to heaven and her lips moving in prayer for the duration of the homily. Then Cauchon rose awkwardly to his feet, his short legs taxed by the overweight body, and stepped in front of Jeanne.

"What now?" Cecily murmured. "Dear God, has she not endured enough?"

"Because you have been found guilty of heresy, idolatry, and sorcery," Cauchon shouted, "it is meet that you, as a limb of Satan, shall be excommunicated from the church and your body burned, so nothing remains with which to taint the living!" Then, in one terrifying gesture of unity, Cauchon and all the priests grasped the ends of their crucifixes, held them out to Jeanne, and turned them upside down. A gasp of horror rose from the crowd, knowing Jeanne could now never enter the kingdom of heaven. "We now commit you to the bailiff, who will deliver you into the hands of the executioner!" Cauchon announced.

"May God have mercy on my soul!" Jeanne cried, standing boldly to face the crowd. "Rouen, I fear you will pay a costly price for this day."

This ominous prediction for their city sat ill with its citizens, and they began to shake their fists and jeer at the young woman, who was now being jostled down the steps. Two Dominican friars continued their prayers as the bailiff and a guard led her to the wall of wood. Cecily saw Jeanne stumble. Her ankles were raw from the shackles and there was blood on her feet, and instinctively Cecily reached out her hand as though she could help Jeanne. The desperate young woman implored those nearest her to give her a cross, and one grizzled English soldier tied two sticks together and thrust it into her hands as a joke. But then, transfixed by Jeanne's radiant smile of thanks and her kissing the makeshift cross with passion, he signed himself, chastened by her piety.

A black-hooded giant of a man with a heavy chain wound about his arm took hold of Jeanne and led her through a gap in the faggots to the stake. Only those on the platform and those spectators hanging out of upstairs windows could now see the prisoner over the wall of wood as she was shackled to the stake.

Cecily tried to look away as her tears blurred the hideous scene, but she could not. Jeanne begged the friars standing near her to fetch a proper crucifix. One turned his back, but the other, compassion finally overcoming him, called over the woodpile for someone to fetch the crucifix from the church. While the executioner made a drama of thrusting the tallow-soaked torch into the brazier and holding it aloft to rouse the crowd, Brother Isambard held the delivered cross for Jeanne to kiss.

Time had run out for Jeanne. There was no last-minute rescue by a grateful King Charles, no thunderbolt from God to strike them all down, no heavenly voices to stay the executioner, and no reprieve from the priests on the platform or from the boy king of England.

Cecily lifted her eyes to the sky. "Where are you, Mother of God? I beg of you show me a sign that you are watching over her as you watch over me," she whispered. But she saw nothing but the first fingers of black smoke curling from within the pile, and her heart sank.

The kindling around the base of the woodpile crackled and popped, orange flames licked upward searching for more wood to feed their hungry tongues, and within minutes thick smoke enveloped the air, some wafting toward the lords' platform. From within the inferno, Jeanne's voice could be heard, crying, "*Jésu . . . Jésu . . . Jésu*," and as the pitiful sound gradually died away, the crowd was silent.

When the first whiff of burning flesh reached Cecily, she struggled to fight down the vomit that surged, and she began to heave. "I cannot stay, Anne," she gasped. "I beg of you, find Richard." Anne tried to restrain her from standing while at the same time frantically calling York's name. Further down the row Katherine heard the cry and shouted more loudly for him. But Cecily had shaken off Anne's hold and was wavering at the top of the staircase, her tears still blinding her as she felt for the first step. She missed her footing and, with a terrified scream, tumbled headlong down the flight of stairs, landing face first on the unyielding cobblestones. A searing pain in her belly was the last thing she remembered before the world went black.

"Y̶our grace!" Dame Boyvile's urgent whisper intruded on Cecily's reverie, and she sat bolt upright in the bed, clutching her belly. The vivid
memories of Jeanne d'Arc's burning and her own disastrous fall were slow to
dissipate, but she realized she must have been finally falling asleep and was
annoyed with Gresilde for disturbing her. Sleep would have been a blessed
release, she thought.

"When I heard your cry, I thought perhaps you needed me, madam," the
kindly attendant said, holding the candle aloft. "You sounded as though you
were in pain."

"Did I?" Cecily sighed. "Forgive me for waking you, but I am well, thank
you. It must have been a bad dream. How long since we left Margaret?"

"The watch just called two of the clock, your grace. Margaret's nightmare
was before the midnight hour." Gresilde fixed the candle into its sconce on
the bedpost and busied herself straightening out the bedclothes, hiding a
yawn. She had immediately recognized the red nose and swollen eyelids of
someone who had been crying for a time but knew her proud mistress would
be ashamed to appear weak in front of a servant and so said nothing. Besides,
being awakened twice in one night did not make her talkative.

"Is Margaret sleeping?" Cecily asked, hoping her daughter had been more
fortunate than she. Cecily had not slept well since hearing of Richard's death
five weeks ago.

"Aye, and so sweetly," Gresilde assured her mistress. "I told Beatrice to stay
with her, madam. She knows Lady Margaret better than all of us and will be
of comfort should the child awake."

"'Tis a long night, Gresilde," Cecily remarked, yawning and straightening
her cap. "I know not why, but I cannot sleep." Her forty-five-year-old face
would show the telltale signs of a restless night on the morrow, she supposed.

"Perhaps you would fetch me a cup of wine, and then you may return to your own bed."

"I would be happy to fetch the rest of Lady Margaret's infusion of valerian, your grace," Gresilde said over her shoulder as she went for the wine, though going back to bed was all she yearned for.

"The wine will suffice, thank you," Cecily told her, cupping the silver hanap in her hands and taking a sip. "You may blow out the candle, and draw the curtains close, if you will. God give you a better night than mine."

She drained the cup and settled down on the bolster again, pretending to close her eyes, as Gresilde finished her tasks.

Once more in the dark, but now wide awake, Cecily dreaded returning to that month of May in 'Thirty-one at Rouen, but blessedly, she found much of the rest of the year blocked from her memory. Aye, she had sadly lost the child, for which she had cried bitter tears, and for two months she had lain in bed while plans were made for the king's coronation in Paris. For a time she had felt betrayed by God and all his saints because they had not saved Jeanne.

Richard had visited her every day and begged her not to fret over the loss of this first child. She was only sixteen and they would have many other children. Even Nan had been impressed by Richard's solicitous treatment of his wife, and with the loving care of her mother, sisters, and Duchess Anne, Cecily recovered slowly in body and spirit. No one ever mentioned the Maid in Cecily's presence for fear it might bring on a relapse, but Cecily herself prayed nightly for the repose of Jeanne's soul, so convinced was she that the woman was more godly than a hundred Pierre Cauchons or Henry Beauforts. She knew the months had passed somehow, but she could not say now what had occupied her time.

Henry and the court were eventually able to move safely to the capital, and on the sixteenth day of December, he was crowned in front of his French subjects at Nôtre Dame. The mood in the city had been less than welcoming, and considering the unsecured environs, it was thought best the young king return to England as soon as was diplomatically possible. It had not helped the English cause that Burgundy and France had signed a truce then, which had lessened the importance of the coronation in France as well as weakened the Lancastrian hold on English France.

Cecily remembered refusing to look over the stern of the vessel to watch the French coast slip into the fog on that late January day eight months after the execution, hoping she might never return to the place where she had lost her first child.

She was saddened again to conjure up the scene of farewell with Anne of Bedford. They had shed tears at parting. "You will return, Cecille, I know," Anne had said. "We are such good friends, you and I, and my lord husband is fond of your Richard. We shall grow old and enjoy our children together, I promise," she predicted cheerfully, despite not having conceived once in her nine-year marriage. Ah, *ma chère* Anne, Cecily mused sadly, if only you had been right. A letter from Anne had arrived at the Erber in the spring of that year, 1432, with the happy news that she was with child at last and that Duke John was crowing like a rooster. But things went terribly wrong in November, and Bedford's beloved consort died in childbirth at the age of twenty-eight along with the babe. Cecily had been inconsolable for days. Except for Alice, Anne had been the closest friend she had ever had.

That news had come hard on the heels of Cecily's eldest sister Katherine's widowhood, but no one had had time to mourn with her for long, for Kat was happily remarried within the year to Thomas Strangways, a knight from an important Yorkshire family, and she moved back to the north. She was now styled dowager duchess of Norfolk, not losing her title because of remarriage.

Cecily turned onto her side, hoping the change in position would induce sleep, but it only served to remind her of her missing husband's warm body cradling her as he always had. Nay, I will not cry more, she admonished herself, and instead turned her mind to the political upheaval that had begun to turn England's wheel of fortune during those next years.

At twenty-one, Richard attained his majority and had come into his inheritance. He had left Cecily in London for several months to visit all his new estates and to hire overseers, bailiffs, chamberlains, and wardens and make himself known to his retainers. His holdings stretched from the Welsh marches to East Anglia and from Yorkshire to the south coast and even included the Mortimer estates in Ireland. And when the old countess of March died that year, giving him possession of that earldom as well, it was murmured that the young duke of York was now one of the greatest landowners in the kingdom.

Pish, Cecily thought now, we had no idea at what a cost those lands came, for most were entailed and a mountain of debt faced us upon their livery.

Then sadly Richard's mentor, Duke John, thwarted over and over again in his attempt to save English France, went into a decline. However, it was not before he found himself another bride, Cecily grunted now. Who could have replaced Anne? The court, at Windsor in June of 1433, soon found out.

"How could he?" Cecily had lamented to her mother the next April, when news of Bedford's marriage to a nineteen-year-old beauty, Jacquetta of Luxembourg, was announced. "Dear Anne is not yet dead six months."

Jacquetta St. Pol was a political pawn, Joan had told her daughter, just as Anne of Burgundy had been before her. Joan chuckled. "My dear Cecily, surely you have noticed that marriages among our rank are of convenience. It appears that Duke John and his Anne fell in love, and"—Joan's expression softened—"your father and I shared deep affection. It happened that you and Richard were able to grow to love each other slowly as children. We are the fortunate ones. You do not think Kat loved her Mowbray, do you? He was a bore, frankly. No wonder she fell in love with Strangways."

Cecily gave a little laugh now as she thought of her mother's remark, but her thoughts turned to Jacquetta of Bedford. Aye, now there is a woman who knows about passion. Within two years of Bedford's death, she had married in secret and produced a daughter with the handsome Sir Richard Woodville, Bedford's chamberlain and Cecily's escort on the road to Rouen in 1431.

As the sleepless night dragged on, she wondered where Richard had been in 1433. Ah, yes, his first appointment as lieutenant of Normandy. It had come as a complete surprise, she remembered, as he had spent but a few months in Rouen before the coronation, but as a royal duke, he had been an appropriate choice. She remembered his arrival in Harfleur in June had come inauspiciously upon the heels of the English loss of Paris, but that had hardly been Richard's fault.

In 1434, during a meeting in Calais, the rivalry between Duke John and his brother Gloucester had come to a head over the future of the war in France. Knowing that he and his policies were unwelcome in England, Bedford and Jacquetta returned to Rouen. But the life had gone out of him by then, as more and more French gains began to whittle away the work he had done to secure England's claim upon France, and on the fourteenth day of September, John, duke of Bedford, brother of the great King Harry, died and was entombed in Rouen Cathedral. The death left Humphrey, duke of Gloucester, sole protector of the king.

As if the feud between the brothers had not been bad enough, Cecily grimaced now, another still raged between Gloucester and Cardinal Beaufort, the two most powerful men on Henry's council. Gloucester's abrasiveness did not endear him to the maturing king, and Henry angered his uncle by turning more and more to the cardinal for counsel. Nobles began to take sides, and Cecily remembered trying to keep up with the political in-fighting.

But what she recalled now was how nobly Richard had comported himself during this divisive time. He had been determined to remain neutral. He wanted to be known simply as the king's loyal subject. But even so, a schism was opening between Lancaster and York, not aided by the growing mutual distrust between Richard and the Beauforts. On the positive side, she thought, it had helped that the young king liked Richard, and indeed she also had enjoyed high favor with Henry back then. So what had gone so terribly wrong? she mused. What had led to the fateful day only a month ago that had taken away her beloved husband, her cherished brother, and her favorite son?

"Edmund, my son!" she moaned, remembering his loss anew with a sharp pang of grief. She turned her face into the pillow so as not to disturb Gresilde. "My beautiful boy! You were only seventeen and much too young to die." She saw again his bright blue eyes, the mirror of her own, and his cheeky grin. He had been the most hale of her baby boys and the most endearing. She discovered a few more unshed tears in what she thought had been a dry well, but then forced herself to put aside the grisly vision of Edmund's handsome head impaled upon York's Micklegate and think of a happier time.

Cecily turned her mind to the joys that motherhood had finally brought to her life, despite seven long years of barrenness after her violent miscarriage. Richard had been absent for weeks and sometimes months on estate business and that first lieutenancy in France, and it had taken her body a long time to recuperate from her fall.

But then one happy day in spring of 1438, she learned they had finally succeeded, and she remembered the day as if it were yesterday.

PART THREE

*The kind and loving mother who knows and sees the need of
her child guards it very tenderly, as the nature and condition
of motherhood will have. And always as the child grows in
age and in stature, she acts differently, but she does not change
her love. . . .*

*The mother may sometimes suffer the child to fall and to
be distressed in various ways, for its own benefit, but she can
never suffer any kind of peril to come to her child, because of
her love.*

JULIAN OF NORWICH,
A BOOK OF SHOWINGS

13

Fotheringhay, 1438

"Are you certain, Constance?" Cecily asked her personal physician in French, her voice trembling with anticipation. "We have been disappointed so many times."

Constance, a woman of few words, nodded, the look in her keen brown eyes telling Cecily what she wanted to hear. "Six or seven weeks, your grace," the doctor answered, rearranging Cecily's skirts over her legs after the examination.

I must have conceived the child on the night of the Epiphany, Cecily mused, returning to the evening of merriment that had culminated in Richard's carrying her up the stairs to her chamber, nuzzling her ear, and whispering of his plans for the rest of their evening. She smiled and told herself this child must surely be a happy soul born of a night of much joy and laughter.

She watched Constance carefully wash her hands in hot water poured into the pewter bowl from the pot hanging over the fire. How many prayers of thanks had she sent to the Virgin for the gift of this wise woman, Cecily thought, standing up and smoothing out the many folds of the russet velvet of her gown. The doctor's serene, gentle manner belied the wealth of knowledge hidden in her head. In truth, Cecily had been startled when Anne of Bedford had first suggested that thirty-year-old Constance might nurse her friend those first dark days after losing the child, as doctoring was a male bastion, and women practicing medicine were few and often vilified. But not long afterward, Cecily would have no other physician attend her and was not content until Richard had agreed to employ the woman as her personal physician, even though his traditional beliefs made him more than a little skeptical.

"It goes against all the laws of God for a woman to take on such a role, does it not?" Richard had asked Duke John, who had stopped in to visit the patient.

"How can a woman know as much as a man of medical matters? 'Tis well known their brains are smaller."

Cecily stopped herself retorting that she was every bit as clever as he—indeed, had he not said so many times? Instead, she chewed on her lip.

"My dear York, I must tell you that your wife is in good company. Not only does Anne prefer Constance to my own learned doctor, but you may be interested to know that my great-grandmother, Queen Philippa, was attended by a female physician."

Joan looked up from her embroidery. "My nephew is quite correct, Dickon. Cecilia of Oxford was a court surgeon and much respected, so my mother told me. I see nothing wrong with Constance attending Cecily. Do you?"

Richard had hurriedly backed down when his mother-in-law had lowered her finely plucked eyebrows at him, and within a few weeks he had begged Anne of Bedford to make arrangements for the brilliant young woman to join his household.

Constance had been born in Rouen, the only child of a member of the University of Paris medical faculty, who had taken his wife with him when he entered the university. When her mother had died in childbirth and Constance was ten, she had been educated by her widower father and encouraged to seek work as a physician. He had even sent her to Salerno, the acknowledged center of medical learning at that time. And then had come the summons from the duchess of Bedford, and now from her grace, the duchess of York.

If Constance was surprised by this new turn in her fortune, no one would have guessed it. Being a pragmatic soul, she took the exchange of one noble patron for another with equanimity. After all, she had no family to speak of. "Therefore, dear Constance," Cecily had said, "you are free to go wherever fate takes you, are you not? Why not go with me?"

Constance had inclined her head, but if Cecily had pushed her, she would have admitted she was not anxious to experience the famously cold English winters, that she respected Anne of Bedford immensely, or that she was loath to leave Normandy. But the young duchess of York had a way with her, Constance had noticed, and as Anne had proved to be barren all these years with Duke John, her physician's curiosity saw the potential of using her considerable childbirthing skills for Cecily. And so she accepted gratefully. Cecily had been ecstatic, though when she heard of Anne's death in childbirth a little more than a year later, she felt a pang of remorse.

Watching Constance dry her large, capable hands now, Cecily longed to take this intelligent woman into her confidence. How could Constance possibly know how lonely I am too most of the time? She must see me as the head of a large household—indeed, I now have more than forty servants; the wife of an adoring husband; a woman with a busy daily routine that includes an hour to dress, then discussions with the chamberlain, the steward, the cook, and the pantler; a devout woman who attends Mass as well as my own devotions at my beautiful little altar for which Richard received the indulgence; the judge who hears petitions from servants and villagers; and the woman who also finds time to ride, play her psaltery, ply her needle, or read. No, my loneliness would not be obvious to Constance.

The doctor turned back to Cecily and advised her mistress, "Take as much rest as you can in the coming weeks. I shall not forbid you to ride, as I am certain you will disobey me." She arched an eyebrow, a small smile twitching her lips. She had a deep, resonant voice that matched her somewhat masculine features. Constance was no beauty, but her serenity made her beautiful to Cecily. "I will allow you to ride to the hunt but *only* in the usual manner of ladies."

Constance's confirmation of her being with child had made Cecily so happy that she acquiesced without a murmur and, thanking her physician, hurried off to find Richard.

Fotheringhay was a large motte and bailey castle on the edge of the fenlands and had been the York family seat from the time it was given to Edmund of Langley, first duke of York and Richard's grandfather, who had designed the imposing keep in the shape of the family's fetterlock emblem. Round towers punctuated the corners of the outer crenellated walls, which enclosed the keep, ducal apartments, great hall, kitchens, household lodgings, and a central courtyard.

Since leaving Raby, Cecily had felt more at home there than anywhere else and loved watching the changing seasons along the riverbanks and across the flat fenlands to the distant hills. Sometimes Cecily would climb the spiral staircase to the ramparts of the keep and wait for Richard to return from the king's business in London or from one of his other vast estates. She could watch her husband and his retinue, their murrey and blue tabards standing out against the bright green grasslands, crossing the wooden causeway that spanned the floodplain and bridged the Nene. She would then see him disappear through the adjoining college buildings and into the large collegiate church of St. Mary, with its two-tiered tower and delicate flying buttresses, where he would kneel for a moment to give thanks for his return. Duke

Edmund was entombed in the choir of the church, and Richard had told Cecily that there, they too, would one day rest in peace. Cecily had been elated to learn the church was dedicated to the Virgin Mary, and she had spent many hours on her knees in a private chapel near the tower, begging the saint to protect her unborn child.

After visiting St. Mary's, Richard would remount and lead his men to the castle. Once inside the castle yard, Richard could see Cecily waving to him from her perch, and he would canter alone over the inner moat bridge and through the fortified gatehouse to the steps of the great hall. By then she would have flown down the stone stairs through the armory and into the courtyard in time to be swept up in Richard's embrace. It had become a ritual they both looked forward to. "I am almost glad when you are away, my dearest, for our reunion gives me the sweetest pleasure," she told him once.

Today she was not surprised when she found Richard ensconced in his privy chamber with his new councillor, Sir William Oldhall, a portly middle-aged man with a red face and crown of wispy white hair. Since his unexpected return from France the previous summer, Richard was often found in the company of this experienced soldier, a trusted former member of Bedford's staff in France. Originally appointed for one year as lieutenant governor and Bedford's successor, Richard had agreed to serve provided he and his retinue were paid in advance. When the money had not appeared after a year in Normandy, Richard asked to be recalled. All the council could offer him was payment for his own pawned jewels, and Richard, infuriated, had stormed back to Fotheringhay. Cecily, however, had been delighted as, against her will, she had been left behind in England.

"Aye, Gloucester's power is much abated with the council, your grace," Oldhall was saying as Cecily motioned to the servant outside the room to announce her. "He alone seeks to prolong the war with France, it seems, while the Beaufort band works for peace and the surrender of our lands there." Oldhall's bitterness toward the peace-brokers was evident in his voice, Cecily noted. However, she understood how the loyal fifty-year-old veteran of so many French battles must loathe those at home who merely sought to line their pockets by eliminating the expensive war-chest. Humphrey of Gloucester, for all his bull-headedness and thirst for power, was indeed the only strong voice left for fighting off the French.

"Gloucester knows I am somewhere in the middle, I presume," Richard remarked quietly as Cecily was announced.

He at once went to Cecily, taking her hand to his lips, while Oldhall got painfully to his feet and bowed.

"My dear, to what do we owe the pleasure of this visit? Will you not take my chair and join us in some wine?"

"If it please you, my lord—and I trust I do not interrupt," Cecily replied, hoping Sir William would take the hint, "but this news cannot wait."

"News!" Richard exclaimed. "What news, my lady? Tell us quickly, I beg of you. Is that cousin of yours, Edmund Beaufort, struck down? Or better still, your uncle the cardinal gone off on a pilgrimage to Rome?" He winked at Oldhall, who smirked.

Cecily tugged at his arm, too excited to be peeved by these slights to her family. "'Tis of a private nature, my lord," she murmured, and Richard at once nodded to Oldhall, who acquiesced and shuffled out painfully on his gouty leg.

"We shall welcome a child at the end of the year, my love!" Cecily exclaimed, as soon as she heard the latch click shut. "Constance has examined me and confirms my suspicion."

"God be praised, Cis, I am indeed glad to hear it," Richard cried, picking her up and swinging her around, almost knocking over a pile of new parchments and an inkhorn in his exuberance. "After all these years a child will complete our happiness, in truth. My prayers to St. Monica at Ely last month must have borne fruit." He kissed her laughing mouth, and her carefully pinned headdress fell to the floor.

"No more nightmares?" he asked, his gray eyes searching her face anxiously. Cecily had written to him often in France of the dreams she had concerning the accident in Rouen: terrible scenes of flames, rats, a staircase to Hell, and a bloodied, accusing infant. She had never told him of the visions of Jeanne she had had and that the martyred woman's face often penetrated her quiet moments at prayer. Her attendants knew that merely hearing Jeanne's name would distress their mistress in the first years following the execution and were careful to avoid the subject.

Cecily shook her head as he put her back on her feet. "I have not dreamed of Rouen since your return. 'Tis only when you are not with me that I am afraid of the dark and my dreams. I never want to be separated from you again, except, certes, when military affairs interfere. I feel like half a person when you are gone. Promise me from now on you will take me with you."

Her arms were around his waist, her face a few inches from his, and her eyes pleading. He could smell the rosemary oil in her hair, feel her breathing against his chest, and already he sensed the fullness of her maternity, all of which made him pull her closer, kissing her eyelids, her cheeks, her nose, and finally her mouth, his desire mounting.

"Richard!" Cecily wriggled from his embrace, giggling. "Sir William is just outside the door. We cannot do anything now—in here." Then she laughed at Richard's disappointment. "Later, my lord, later," she promised with a seductive smile.

Retrieving her headdress and brushing off some dust, she handed it to him to reposition. "Besides which, my dearest husband, you have avoided answering my question."

"Aye, you wanton woman, I promise to take you with me wherever I have to go—provided there is no danger," he told her while replacing the headdress. He stood back to study his handiwork and chuckled. "I think it is on backwards, but as 'tis a truly ridiculous piece of fashion, I do not think anyone will notice."

"Richard!" admonished his vain wife, anxiously putting up her hand to feel the heart-shaped roll. "Can I be seen or not?"

"Aye, you'll do. Now get you gone and leave us men to our work." He grinned and went to hold the door for her. "Did I tell you how happy I am you are with child? I cannot remember, but if I did, I tell you again—with all my heart I am."

A SUMMER WITHOUT riding hard to the hunt was torture for Cecily, but she kept her word to Constance and instead rode sidesaddle sedately around the gentle Northamptonshire countryside with her attendants and Piers Taggett, who had spent the two years Cecily had been in Rouen learning to care for the York falcons and who was proving a good student and loyal servant. It amused Richard that Piers still worshipped any ground that Cecily's hem brushed, but he had the peace of mind that no harm would befall his wife while Piers escorted her. He had left the man behind at Fotheringhay during his second foray into France, and it seemed Cecily's hawking had improved even further with Piers's newly learned skills.

It had not been a good harvest, as England had undergone one of the worst droughts in memory that summer, but nevertheless, Richard believed the inhabitants of Fotheringhay should give thanks at Michaelmas as usual.

"We can be grateful we do not have to live in London, my dear. It is said many have starved there this summer," Richard told her. "There have even been riots."

And so he, with Cecily in an open litter, processed slowly from the castle to St. Mary's, with the merchants, farmers, yeomen and elders of the village greeting their lord along the short route. As many as could do so crammed into the church, which was decorated with sheaves of wheat, baskets of apples, nuts and berries, vegetables, and bunches of autumnal wildflowers. Heavily pregnant, Cecily had bloomed like a late summer rose, and her shimmering pink gown of silk damask, embroidered with white roses, trailed behind her in graceful folds. Richard helped her to a seat in the choir in the larger part of the church, which was usually reserved for the collegiate body. This chancel was separated from the parishioners by a filigreed stone screen, so that all might hear the Mass and give thanks for God's bounty, meager though it was that year.

Later, as guests of the duke and duchess, the villagers feasted and danced on the grounds of the castle farm. Cecily was given the seat of honor on a throne woven of rushes, its legs studded with apples, and a canopy of blue Michaelmas daisies above her. The young girls of the village had made her a crown of sweet honeysuckle. Glowing from the affection shown her in her full pregnancy, Cecily nearly rivaled Mother Nature that day.

Richard's face shone with pride for his lovely wife. He caught her eye several times and grinned as yeomen and their wives curtseyed to her as they presented gifts of honey, fruit, and nuts. How he wished Cecily's mother might see her now as she graciously accepted the presents and bestowed a kind word on everyone, even knowing many by name. She had never failed to send a small token at the birth of a child, an infusion or a salve upon hearing of sickness or hurt among the servants, and Richard could see that his people loved her. He marveled that in only a few years she had changed from the impetuous, outspoken, and spoiled daughter he had first met to a dignified, dutiful duchess—although, he had to admit, he was secretly pleased that she had never lost her adventurous spirit, especially in the bedchamber. He had felt relieved and grateful when, after all this time, she had conceived again, afraid that her fall down the stairs at Rouen might have left her barren.

Richard watched Cecily on her rush throne with concern as the afternoon wore on. He needed an heir—he was the last male York descendant of the Plantagenet line—and Cecily was well aware of it. He did not want her to become overtired, he told her while accompanying her litter back to the castle. Cecily laughed at him and scoffed at his worried frown, and he took heart.

But one night when Richard was away, Cecily awakened drenched in sweat. The flames had enveloped her once more, she whispered to Rowena, and she was much afraid. Constance came as soon as Rowena sent for her, and with her calm voice and sensible explanations soon alleviated Cecily's fear of devils ready to set her on fire from under the bed. Sending Rowena back to her truckle, Constance drew the tester curtains around her mistress and fixed the candle in its sconce on the bedpost. Then she knelt beside the bed and took Cecily's hand, anxiously noting her pallor.

"Are you well now, your grace?" She saw Cecily nod and continued, "Do you have any pains in your belly? Any bleeding?"

"Nay, Constance, all is well." Cecily eased herself up on her pillow and patted the murrey and blue tapestry counterpane. "I pray you, sit up here with me. I would ask you something."

Unaccustomed to any such intimacy with her mistress, Constance perched herself as far to the edge of the bed as was comfortable. She worried that should Richard suddenly appear, her position in the household could be in jeopardy. After all, she was merely a servant in the ducal house and a foreign one at that. Duke Richard's own physician, an elderly Englishman with, in Constance's opinion, decidedly outdated ideas, avoided her. She had been dismissed as a charlatan on several occasions and had learned quickly that men did not believe women had intelligence to match theirs. Thus, during her training, she had set about proving she was better than any of them. Rowena was in awe of her, and the language barrier kept them distant.

"It has not gone unnoticed that you are isolated here, Demoiselle Constance," Cecily began, "and I am grateful to you for your considerable skill both in helping me and my mother, who asks after you in every letter she writes. Aye, I do not dissemble," she assured Constance when she saw disbelief in the physician's eyes. "She does."

Constance was moved. "I pray you, thank the countess on my behalf, your grace."

"Certes," Cecily murmured, but her mind had moved past the preliminaries and was trying to find the right words to bring Constance into her confidence.

When her mother had left, she had no one to talk to. How she wished she lived closer to her sister-in-law, Alice, with whom she kept up a sporadic correspondence but who was busy producing more little Salisbury babes—indeed, she was carrying the seventh at the time Cecily awaited her first. Even her sister Kat, whom she grew close to in Rouen, was too far away in Suffolk for frequent visits. Aye, I am lacking female companionship, she recognized, even though she had Rowena and two other ladies to attend her. It did not help that in a household such as hers, all the servants but a laundress or two and a dairymaid were men. Aye, a castle was a lonely place for a woman, she mused, and then realized Constance was waiting patiently for her to speak. Perhaps now is the right moment for a confidence, she thought, and took a deep breath.

"I may not have told you enough how much I respect your knowledge and skill, Constance. Not a day goes by that I am not grateful for your service. But I have need of you in another way," she said, hesitating when she saw the doctor stiffen slightly. Cecily gave her a bright smile and hoped to allay Constance's worry. "Nay, I am not asking that you lay down your life for me, but only that you be my friend. You see, I have no one to talk to."

Constance gazed at her mistress in amazement for a moment, and then a slow, gentle smile softened her face into a semblance of beauty.

"I would not presume to be your friend, madame. But perhaps confidante would be more suitable? 'Twould be an honor and a pleasure, your grace," she murmured, nodding. "I believe your mother trusted me, and I promise you too may put your trust in me." Her heart sang. Now she might not be so miserable in this damp, dreary land, she decided.

"Then I shall trust you with the reason for my dream, Constance, for I must tell someone." Constance cocked her head, her eyes encouraging Cecily to continue.

"You remember La Pucelle?"

The name from the past surprised Constance into crossing herself. She nodded, "*Bien sûr,* madame."

Cecily met her steady gaze. "I met her, you know. Aye, I was fortunate enough to speak to her in her prison cell before the trial. Before Cauchon began his witch hunt. My mother and Duke Richard knew of it at the time, but I have not talked about this meeting to anyone—except God—since that dreadful day in the marketplace," Cecily said, watching the doctor's face. "Were you there, Constance?" she said warily.

"Nay, I was not, my lady, I was praying at St. Ouen that the woman would recant." Constance had been in residence at the abbey while serving Anne of

Bedford, and the nuns had convinced her Jeanne was a witch. To be sure, the English believed it too or they would never have burned her, she reasoned.

"You think she was a heretic?" Cecily demanded. "After all she suffered? Her last words"—she paused, remembering vividly the ghastly choked sounds—"were *Jésu, Jésu.'* Did the holy sisters tell you that?"

Constance hurriedly crossed herself. "I had only the small pieces of gossip that came from the trial, madame. The abbess told us what little she knew, and it did seem to me and the sisters that Jeanne d'Arc was hearing the Devil's messages."

Now it was Cecily's turn to make the sign of the cross, and she weighed her next words carefully. "I will try to convince you otherwise, if you will hear me out. I believe with all my heart that Jeanne had true faith in God. I have no doubt she was touched by the Holy Spirit and that she truly heard the voices of St. Catherine and St. Michael. I saw a light around her head when she went down on her knees in that filthy prison and spoke into the thin air. 'Twas a white light. It appeared from nowhere in that windowless cell. No candle or lantern could have made it, and it seemed she was conversing earnestly with an invisible being." Cecily took a breath after releasing these memories aloud for the first time since Jeanne's execution. Constance, in her turn, was holding hers. "Then she took my hand, and 'twas—I cannot describe it truly—'twas like a fire that did not burn. I believe God's hand touched me that day, I am certain of it, and I all but swooned. And I swear on this rosary I did not dream it."

Constance felt the hairs on her arms prickle, but she did not move a muscle. She knew there were good reasons why Cecily might have felt faint in the prison—too long on her knees, early pregnancy, lack of air in the cell, or the beginnings of a fever perhaps. But listening to the duchess's revelation stirred her inborn belief in the mystical power of God, and she was awed by Cecily's description.

"You truly think she was God's messenger, madame?" she said, weighing the possibility. "I can see why you would," she murmured.

"It has been on my conscience all these years that I was not able to save her from the fire, Constance. I know 'tis why I have nightmares about flames, and it is certain I will never forget her sacrifice."

"You have done me a great honor to tell me of it. I swear on my dear father's soul no one shall ever hear of this great mystery from my lips." She could see the relief this revelation had given Cecily as she helped her mistress settle onto the pillow.

Cecily smiled, finally ready for sleep, and once again Constance was struck by the twenty-four-year-old duchess's beauty. "I thank you for your confidence, Constance," Cecily said sleepily. "May the grace of God go with you this night."

"And with you, duchess. Your story is most persuasive, and I promise I shall search my conscience tonight and ask God for guidance in the matter of Jeanne d'Arc's innocence."

"She was innocent, I am certain of it," was Cecily's sleepy insistence. "Why else would she haunt my dreams thus."

Cecily decided before she fell fast asleep that should her babe be a girl, she would name her Jeanne—nay, the English Joan, of course. After all, surely Richard would not prevent her naming their first daughter after her beloved mother.

BABY JOAN TOOK her time coming into this world. Cecily thought her body would not tolerate one more spasm when Constance gave her permission to push. As soon as word was put about that her grace was in labor, servants had run throughout the castle opening the doors, cupboards, chests, and anything else with a lid to ease the pains and allow the evil spirits to creep out. They hung bunches of dried rue to ward off those same spirits, who might snatch the newborn before it could be baptized. Cecily attempted to keep her groans to a minimum, but as the birth canal stretched wide for the first time, the pain racked her to its breaking point and she screamed.

"Give me something to bite down on," she begged her mother, who had arrived at Fotheringhay a week before. "I would not have the servants hear my cries. By God's bones, Constance," she swore, using her father's favorite expression, "you did not warn me how much pain there would be, only that there would be some."

Joan chose not to chastise her daughter for her blasphemy but smiled at her forbearance as she placed a rolled-up cloth between her teeth. "Aye, Daughter, I have heard you are known as proud Cis now that you are a duchess, and I can see why."

Cecily tried to laugh through the cloth, but then her eyes glazed over again and her body arched anew.

"Move the jasper stone up higher and give her some more of my tincture," Constance ordered the midwife from Fotheringhay village, who had been none too pleased to learn that she would be supplanted in the birthing chamber by this foreign female.

Doctor, my eye, Mathilda Draper had thought when she had first seen Constance. And the woman can't even speak English. Hadn't she birthed three score babies in her time? All this Matty had bottled up over the hours of Cecily's labor and now, instead of applying her skills to the duchess, she was being ordered to merely administer a potion.

"She 'as 'ad enough medicine, madam. She needs to get on the birthing stool right quick, if you ask me," Matty snapped in her country dialect, causing Constance to raise an eyebrow at Joan.

"Qu'est qu'elle a dit, madame?" she asked.

"She is not happy she is not in charge, doctor," Joan replied in French, smiling sweetly at the irritated midwife as she did. "In truth, she believes 'tis time Cecily was put on the birthing chair."

Cecily snatched the roll from her mouth and retorted in English, "By all that is holy, one of you make up your mind. I need to pu—" She got no further. Another labor pain reached a crescendo and she pushed the cloth back into her mouth.

Constance nodded to Matty and acquiesced. "You are correct, Mathilde, we go to chair."

Five minutes later, a scrawny, slimy girl child slipped into Matty Draper's capable hands, and the midwife gave Constance a reluctant smile of gratitude. As the doctor and Joan supported the exhausted Cecily on the chair, Matty turned little Joan upside down and slapped her tiny buttocks. A cry of protest told the midwife that this child was hale and, but for a purple birthmark upon her left shoulder, perfectly formed. All four women stared at the mark, none wanting to voice the superstition that the child was touched by the Devil, but then Cecily put her hands out, gently took the babe, and cradled her to her breast.

"'Tis an old wives' tale, in truth," Joan said with finality. "It will probably disappear in a few days, mark my words. Come, Cecily, give me the child while these women finish their work."

"Otherwise she is beautiful, is she not, Mother?" Cecily murmured, suffering but minimally as Matty helped her expel the afterbirth. "God be thanked. I have a healthy daughter."

Joan and Constance smiled and nodded, while Joan washed the infant and then rubbed the pink skin all over with salt, causing the little mite to fuss and wriggle until a spotless linen cloth was wrapped around her to keep her from the autumn chill.

"Joan, my sweet Joan. How you have filled me with joy," Cecily whispered, marveling at the tiny hands waving helplessly at her chemise, the mouth pursing and unpursing as the child sought her mother's milk. Constance was in favor of Cecily suckling for two days but no longer. According to the tradition of the nobility, a wet-nurse would feed the babe for the first year of her life. A large young farmer's wife who had just given birth two months before had been chosen, and baby Joan would reside with her until a routine could be established.

Countess Joan bent toward the bed when she heard the child's name. "You have Richard's consent?" she asked, brimming with pleasure. "You and Dickon honor me, truly." Certes, this was not the first grandchild to be named after her, but because of the special bond she had formed with her youngest daughter, she was touched beyond measure.

"Aye, Richard knows, Mother," Cecily said, purposely looking down at the greedily sucking child and avoiding her mother's eyes. "It was my choice, and I am pleased you approve. Now perhaps you might go and tell my husband his daughter would like to meet him."

She briefly wondered if Richard would be disappointed it was not a boy, but when he arrived breathless a short time later, had kissed her ardently and swept the tiny bundle into his embrace, she knew her answer.

WATCHING FROM HER window as her child was carted away two days later almost broke Cecily's resolve to be brave. At first she stood there quietly when the farmer helped Rowena into the back of the cart and Richard placed the precious basket next to her. But then she opened the casement wide and cried out for her child, and all turned to look up at the duchess, secluded from public view as was customary. She quickly pulled in her head and turned into Constance's comforting arms. Constance shielded her mistress from seeing the farmer flick his whip over the placid ox's haunches and the cart rumbling slowly away.

"How did you do it, Mother?" Cecily asked Joan later, and her mother shrugged. "It gets easier each time, Cecily. But 'tis for their and your own good."

Cecily was not in the mood for a lecture and remained unusually silent during their shared supper. After Joan left and Cecily had been readied for bed, she dismissed her attendants quickly, buried her face in the pillow, and wept.

"A FEVER?" CECILY felt cold fingers of fear grip her heart as her steward, Sir Henry Heydon, brought in the news a few weeks later that little Joan was ill. One afternoon, one of the farmer's children returning from helping his father plough their field complained of an aching head and chills and had been put to bed. Because all the farmer's children, excepting the two infants, slept on one straw mattress, the illness had spread.

Cecily sent the steward to alert the head groom that she needed a palfrey saddled with a pillion seat and a groom to accompany them to the village. In the name of God, Dickon, why are you always gone when I need you, she thought. He was at Wigmore for the week, hearing a petition in a land dispute, and had waved gaily to her as she stood on the keep's roof, watching him leave, her marten-lined hood protecting her from the steady drizzle.

"Find Constance at once and tell her to prepare her traveling bag of medicines," Cecily told Rowena. "Then fetch my cloak and meet me in the courtyard."

Within half an hour, Cecily, with Constance behind her clutching her precious potions and accompanied by Piers Taggett, trotted over the drawbridge and then cantered along the Nene Way past the inn and the marketplace to a turn in the road heading north. Soon they saw the reed roof of the Woodsons' farmhouse above the untidy hawthorn hedge.

Goodwife Woodson greeted the trio from the castle with tears and apologies. She flung herself at Cecily's feet, her cap falling off revealing curly carrot-red hair.

"Raise yourself up, goody, I beg of you," Cecily told her with great control. The woman's hysterics terrified her. "Conduct me and my physician to my child at once. Cease that noise forthwith, and tell Doctor LeMaitre here how Joan is faring."

Cecily's calm but assertive voice had an immediate effect on the distraught woman. Wiping her nose with the back of her hand, she bobbed a curtsey and, chattering nervously to Constance, hurried them into the house. The yeoman's wife readily accepted that the duchess's physician was a woman; most common folk in a village relied on the wise woman for cures and remedies.

The small house was clean enough, Cecily noted approvingly, the hard-baked earthen floor freshly swept and the scrubbed oak table neatly laid with six wooden trenchers, a seventh piled high with rosy apples. A pair of pale blue eyes gazed at the duchess from one of the benches against the wall, and Cecily acknowledged a young girl with a quick smile, glad to see her face was washed and clothes well tended. The farmer's wife kept an orderly house, Cecily thought, and she breathed more easily. Richard's steward had made the wet-nursing arrangements with the Woodsons and had told Cecily that the Woodsons were a quiet, hard-working family and that Joan would be in good hands.

Cecily and Constance followed the goodwife up an open stair to the loft. A wooden bedstead took up one end. Two cradles were placed side by side next to it. Along the opposite wall, warmed by the chimney stack, lay a straw pal-liasse occupied by three other children, one coughing helplessly and the other two fretful, all gawping at the visitors. Constance bent down to touch the forehead of one and shook her head.

"La fièvre, madame," she murmured to Cecily. *"C'est évident."*

With great care Goodwife Woodson lifted Joan from the sturdier of the two cradles and offered her to Cecily. Then the woman beat as hasty a retreat as she could, stopping to pick up an empty cup and fuss with one child's shift, before disappearing downstairs.

Cecily sat down gingerly on the rope-strung bed and held Joan in the crook of her arm. She marveled how quickly the child had grown but then puckered her brow at the waxy white of the baby's skin. Joan's eyes fluttered open and she let out a small cry, which was stifled by wheezing as the child fought for breath. Even through the swaddling bands Cecily could feel the heat emanat-ing from the babe. Cecily sought Constance's sympathetic eyes as she held the infant out to the doctor to examine. When Joan whimpered again, Cecily felt a tugging in her breasts, and she was vaguely aware the urge to feed her child was still very much alive.

With infinite care Constance unwrapped the confining bands, concerned that the child's humor was still so hot and dry. The doctor pondered bleeding her but did not think Cecily would sanction it. She is but five weeks, Con-stance calculated, indeed she is very young. She decided against the fleeming.

Cecily was now crying. She had waited so long for this child and had been convinced the Virgin had protected her through the months of pregnancy and through the birth of such a healthy little girl. Do not abandon my child now, sweet Mary, she pleaded before asking Constance, "What will you do, doctor? Will she live?"

Constance very much doubted the child would survive. The fever had been on her for two days, according to Goody Woodson, and unless it broke soon, she believed the heat would cause the tiny heart to explode. She took a deep breath and lied, "*Bien sûr, madame,* she will live. But we should take her away from the other children to where I can tend to her day and night." She frowned as Joan wheezed again. "It will be dangerous to let her breathe the cold air on the way back, but I will tuck her inside my cloak, and with the saints on our side, we shall make her well again."

Cecily nodded and busied herself rewrapping the child in the linen bands while Constance descended the stairs and informed the waiting goodwife of their intentions. Taking a vial from her leather medicine box, Constance gave instructions for administering it to the other sick children. The woman babbled her thanks, all the time casting anxious eyes at the loft, where Cecily had paused to say a few words of encouragement to the Woodson children.

Cecily was gracious upon taking her leave and pressed a shilling into the astonished goodwife's hand. "When is Joan's next feeding, goody?"

The woman hesitated and finally admitted that Joan had not nursed for more than a day, and it was that fact as well as the fever that had caused her to send a message. Cecily paled, but then told the woman to come to the castle at whatever time, day or night, she was summoned. Nodding vigorously and with an awkward bob, she followed the two women out into the farmyard, shooing chickens from Cecily's path.

Dear Mother of God, Cecily prayed as her horse picked its way along the rough path, do not let this innocent child die.

As soon as Cecily arrived back at the castle, she dictated a letter to Richard. She signed off herself, writing, "*All I wish for now is your swift return. Your loving wife, Cecily.*" She pressed down on the hot wax with her falcon seal.

Then she returned to her solar, where a roaring fire greeted her. Constance had already sent a servant for the cradle and a large copper pan of cold water. Rowena and a tiring woman were laying a simple meal upon the green felt cloth on the table, and Rowena urged Cecily to take some nourishment in case the night was a long one. But Cecily could only nibble at some cheese and a slice of apple, anxiously watching Constance.

"You do not intend to bathe her in that, do you?" Cecily demanded, rising and removing Joan from the cradle. "The water is cold, doctor. It will almost certainly kill her."

Constance put down her bottle of cherry-bark syrup, which she was diluting with rosewater. Although Joan's glazed unblinking eyes frightened her, Constance was more concerned with reducing the high fever in the child. In Paris, she had learned that the idea of immersing a feverish body in icy water had proved effective for a fully grown man, but she was reluctant to try it on a babe, especially with Cecily hovering. But Constance persisted.

"I swear to you it will not kill her, your grace." Her brown eyes courageously held Cecily's terrified blue ones. She dared to murmur, "Do you truly believe I would wish to harm the child? Trust me in this, as you did the night of your dream."

Cecily dropped her gaze to the feverish child in her arms. "Certes, I know you for a good woman, Constance," she said. She hesitated for a brief moment before deciding. "Very well, if I let you dip her in the water for a moment, will you also try another infusion? What else could help?"

"I have an old remedy given to me by a doctor in Salerno, madame, but I do not know if a child should be submitted to it," she replied, biting her lip. She did not stand by some of the old medicines, including the one that Cecily wanted. It called for ground horn of unicorn and dried mare's blood. But the doctor desperately wanted to try the cold-water method of reducing a fever and hoped the panacea might help the infant and pacify the desperate duchess.

Cecily nodded vigorously and began to undress Joan, while Constance mixed her potion and coaxed a few drops of the medicine between the child's cracked lips. The child's blocked windpipe caused her to gag and struggle for breath, and Constance grimaced, wiping away the expelled elixir.

"Try again," Cecily urged. This time Constance dipped her finger in the mixture and gentled it into the baby's mouth with more success. Cecily smiled, stroking the child's cheek. Constance opened her hands for the baby, and Cecily sighed and nodded again. "Aye, now you may try the water—but only for a second, mind you."

Knowing it took more than a quick dip to produce results, Constance reluctantly obeyed her mistress, sensing that Cecily would not tolerate more dissent. The child spluttered and seemed to revive as soon as she felt the cold water upon her fiery skin, and Constance was cheered. But Cecily cried out, "Enough!" and the doctor withdrew the whimpering Joan. But there was no miracle, and the fever persisted.

"Your grace, I know not what else to do," the doctor finally said as Joan's breath became shallower. "I believe we all need to ask for God's guidance and perhaps"—she hesitated—"send for the chaplain."

Cecily's wail sent Rowena to her knees, wringing her hands and reciting the paternoster. Constance was by Cecily's side in an instant and, without thinking of her station, took Cecily in her arms and rocked her.

Father Lessey was summoned to the duchess's apartments a few minutes before the church bell was rung for vespers. He took in the scene at a glance: the child lying unnaturally still, her eyes staring unseeing at the colorfully painted beams; the duchess kneeling by her daughter's cradle, tears running down her face; the Frenchwoman discreetly kneeling in a darkened corner; and the two attendants telling their rosaries in unison.

"*In nomine patris, et filius, et spiritus sancti,*" he began quietly, joining Cecily at the cradle. Reaching into his robe, he brought out the holy oil. Dipping his finger into it, he performed extreme unction by making a sign of the cross on the baby's burning forehead. After intoning the ritual deathbed prayers, he blessed the kneeling women and quietly left the room. He had never seen Cecily Neville cry before, and indeed he had not thought her capable until now.

Constance got to her feet and approached Cecily, who had not moved since the chaplain's arrival. Her tone was anxious. "Madame, can I do anything for you? Would you prefer to be alone or shall we stay and keep you company?"

"Go! All of you," Cecily commanded, not looking up. "I must watch over her alone tonight." She lifted her eyes to the heavens and cried in a loud voice, "Perhaps You will be merciful this time, Father. You alone can help Jeanne now. She is burning alive!"

Constance had never heard Cecily use the French name for her child before. She was at first startled by the description of the fever-racked Joan but then understood the parallel. Dear God, she thought with alarm and awe, the duchess must be thinking of La Pucelle, and she crossed herself, whispering an *ave*. She was watching from the doorway and wondered if she should stay. But then she thought better of it and left to join the others in prayer.

Cecily was unaware she was now alone. She could not take her eyes from her precious daughter's face, but the face she was seeing was not Joan's but Jeanne's just before the faggots leaped into flame.

"I should have stopped them, Jeanne," she whispered to the dying child. "Maybe I could have saved you. Is this my punishment? That He must take your namesake? Ah, Jeanne, Jeanne, have mercy on me. I lost one child that day. Do not let me lose another. Sweet Virgin, Mother of our Lord Jesus Christ, have mercy on this wretched mother."

But as soon as Jeanne's face dissolved into the lifeless one of her child she knew her prayer had not been heard, and picking Joan up, she carried her to the tester bed. Drawing the curtains around them both, she curled up with the tiny limp form whose soul had flown to heaven, and she grieved well into the night.

RICHARD'S SPEEDY ARRIVAL astonished even Sir William Oldhall, who had seen his patron cover dozens of miles in half the time taken by other men during the duke's governorship in France. He had often observed the duke and duchess of an afternoon riding out together at a sedate trot along the outer moat path to the east gate bridge, gardeners and other yeomen doffing their caps as they passed, only to see them break into a full gallop across a field and into the castle's great park, each trying to outdo the other in horsemanship. Richard's distinctive laugh would often float back to Oldhall at his third-story window in one of the towers.

Two pages were loitering by the marshalsea when their master and his small retinue clattered into the cobblestoned stableyard three days after little Joan had died and the castle had been plunged into mourning. Richard dismounted before his horse had even stopped. He flew up the stairs of the duchess's apartments, along a dark passageway, and to the door of her solar. A guard jumped to his feet, but before he could put his hand on the latch, Richard had already thrown the heavy door open without an announcement.

"Richard!" Cecily cried when she saw her husband come striding into the room and, not caring for decorum in front of her ladies and Father Lessey, she fell into his arms. "Oh, my lord, you are come at last! I did not know how I could go on another day without you." She was weeping now. Richard, behind her back, motioned for everyone to leave.

"My dearest, I came as fast as I could. I shall never forgive myself for not being here with you for this terrible ordeal. I pray that you will forgive me," he said, gently holding her and noting with dismay how gaunt her face looked and how haunted were those lovely eyes. "Come, let us kneel together and say a prayer for our dear little Joan." He knew the act of kneeling and praying would calm her. He led her to their exquisite altar, and they both gazed in awe at the perfect face of Jan van Eyck's heavily pregnant Virgin with the light of the Holy Ghost upon her.

"Even she did not help Joan," Cecily whispered, sniffling. "The Blessed Mother, my own benefactress." Richard squeezed her hand and turned the pages of the book of hours on the lectern to recite a prayer for the departed.

"Deus veniae largitor et humanae salutis amator," he began, and the Latin in his rich baritone resonated with Cecily, stemming her tears. She peered at the words with him and they prayed in unison. "We beseech thy clemency: that thou grant the brethren of our congregation, kinsfolk, and benefactors, and especially our beloved daughter, Joan, which are departed out of this world, blessed Mary ever virgin making intercession with all the saints, to come to the fellowship of eternal blessedness."

Then without another word Richard led her to the bed, helped her off with her soft velvet shoes, and lay down beside her, curling her into him as he always did. In less than a minute he knew that she was sleeping and then, unabashedly, he shed his own tears.

> *"THE BOAR'S HEAD in hand bear I,*
> *Bedecked in bays and rosemary.*
> *And I pray you, my masters, be merry*
> Quot estis in convivio . . ."

So sang the college choristers from the minstrel gallery of Fotheringhay's great hall on Christmas Day, their mellifluous voices rising to the blue and gold star-studded roof. The song always gave Cecily gooseflesh, and when the cooks and kitchen boys brought in the platters piled high with food, led by the duke's master cook, who presented the roasted boar's head to Richard and Cecily, it seemed that the black mist that had enveloped her since Joan's death began to lift. She found herself taking pleasure in the music and the traditions of the season and beamed at the cook as he sliced her a sample of the delicate cheek meat from the ferocious-looking head of the boar.

Richard had watched with relief in the weeks that led up to Yuletide as his wife's face regained its bloom, the dark circles under her eyes disappeared, and her trill of laughter reemerged. Infant Joan had been laid to rest in a niche in the tiny chapel of the castle, where Cecily was now wont to go daily rather than to St. Mary's. "She is too little to be buried all alone in that vast choir," she told Richard. "Indulge me in this, I beg of you. No one but us will remember her, and I can keep her company by her little tomb so much more easily in the chapel." How could Richard refuse such a simple request? And as the child had been baptized there, it seemed fitting.

He was feeling the effects of the tun of wine he had had sent from Gascony for this Christmas season, and he had difficulty in controlling the urge to caress Cecily's thigh as they sat side by side, very visible on the dais. Her dress of rose damask embroidered with pearls was trimmed with ermine, the mark of royalty, and with her gold filigree headdress sparkling with jewels framing her oval face, she looked a queen tonight, he thought. She turned to him and offered to feed him the second slice of meat from her fork, which he gently slid off with his teeth and relished with his tongue, their eyes never leaving the other's face. It was then Richard knew Cecily was ready to be seduced again.

With more passion than both knew they possessed, husband and wife made love for many hours that night after the mummery, music, and merriment were over. The Lord of Misrule presided over the rest of the revelries, allowing the duke and duchess to escape to their private chamber and revel in each other. A very few weeks into the new year, Cecily knew she had conceived again, and this time took no chances. She lit a candle in the chapel daily to the Virgin, St. Monica, and St. Anne, and prayed fervently for an heir to the dukedom of York.

14

England and Normandy, 1441

nne, namesake of Richard's mother Anne Mortimer, was a year and a half when Cecily finally gave the duchy of York its heir one snowy February day in 1441. Overjoyed with their son with his almost white hair and dark blue eyes, the proud parents named the baby Henry in deference to their sovereign lord.

Cecily was so disappointed when the second child turned out to be another girl that she could not find it in herself to love Anne as she had her beloved Joan. Thus, with a boy in the cradle now, the little girl had to find comfort in her adoring nursemaids. A quiet, pretty child with Richard's dark hair, fortunately Anne was too young to recognize the difference between her mother's affection for her and her new baby brother.

Cecily's disregard for her daughter did not abate after a messenger arrived suddenly from Howden Manor in Yorkshire with the sad news of her mother's death following a lengthy illness. Cecily had collapsed in a dispirited heap, blaming herself for not traveling with Constance to be at Countess Joan's bedside in time. Unbeknownst to Cecily, Constance had learned Joan had a canker in her breast when the countess had come for little Joan's birth, but she had begged Constance not to tell Cecily for fear of compromising the impending delivery. The doctor had held her peace for almost a year until Cecily had received a letter from her mother following Anne's birth.

> *My dearest daughter, I greet you well and I trust you are recovered
> from the birth of your second child, which news brought me great joy.
> It is fitting you should name her for Dickon's mother, as I was already
> honored with little Joan, God rest her soul.*
> *Forgive me for not being present this time, but I am not quite myself*

these days. My physician tells me I have a canker growing in my breast
that leaves me without my usual vigor, and thus I am not strong enough
to travel. I pray that when baby Anne is past the first stage of life, you
will ride to Howden Manor so I may know her. It is a pleasant place, and
I am fortunate your brother, the bishop, allows me to make it my home.

Richard had relayed news to Cecily the previous year that Robert Neville
had been elevated to the bishopric of Durham, and Howden was now part of
his estates.

I found Middleham too large on my own, despite many visits from
Richard and Alice, and this small cozy manor suits me well.

Not long after discovering she had conceived Henry, Cecily had indeed visited the countess with the infant Anne. The sixty-year-old Joan had lavished
affection on the child, who was at the standing stage and who seemed to prefer her grandmother's lap to her mother's.

"You are distant with your child, Cecily. Are you afraid of loving her too
much and losing her?" Joan asked one day with Anne perched on her knees,
and as though she knew she was being talked about, Anne jerked onto her
little legs, her strength surprising Joan. The delighted child bounced, gurgled,
and flailed her arms like a windmill.

"I pity you for losing your first-born, but when one is a mother, each child
must be loved for who she is and not for who she is not," Joan told Cecily
gently. "I lost my share of babes, my dear, and there is not a day goes by when I
do not grieve for the little mites. But not at the expense of the living children,
who need our love and help to grow into good Christian men and women
until they are sent away—which is another grief we mothers must bear." She
leaned forward and patted Cecily's hand. "You must not deprive this poor
child of a mother's love because she is not Joan."

Cecily had broken down and wept then, recognizing the truth in her mother's words. But try as she might, her heart would not open wide for this little
girl. And now her wise mother was gone, the last friendly Beaufort link to her
and Richard.

Not only were Joan's siblings and their progeny beginning to alienate Richard at the council, but the countess's death had caused a serious rift between
the two Neville branches of Ralph's family.

Perhaps her mother's famous wisdom was faulty when she chose not to leave a little more of her inheritance from Ralph to the Nevilles born of his first wife. Granted, Joan had never been accepted by them, but Cecily could well understand how her half brother, the second Earl Ralph, may have felt slighted by his grandfather's will in favor of the second wife.

Was it because Joan could not bear to think of the Staffords casting aspersions upon her bones that she chose to be buried alongside her beloved mother Katherine Swynford at Lincoln? Cecily wondered. She well remembered Ralph's tomb and the effigies of both his wives at Staindrop, but he now lay with Margaret Stafford alone. Cecily was saddened when she discovered her mother's wish, because she had witnessed the great love her parents had enjoyed. Family feuding is accursed, she thought, especially in ours.

And now Alice had written that young Ralph and his siblings were making life difficult for the Beaufort Nevilles. A feud had begun with Richard Neville and Alice that had spread to include Cecily's other brothers, George, William, and Edward.

Even the king had ordered both sides to stop squabbling, but things were still no better. What good was a title, young Ralph complained, without estates to accompany it? He demanded that Richard Neville, now earl of Salisbury and thus enriched with all the lands that came with the title, give up Middleham—by far the largest of the Westmorland estates—and Sheriff Hutton Castle, but Salisbury had refused.

Cecily had gleaned from conversations with Sir William Oldhall that from the time King Henry had taken the reins of government into his own hands at his majority three years before, the lawlessness of his early years had continued unabated due to his ineffectual governing. The Neville in-fighting that went unchecked was just one more example of that unrest. The solemn little boy king had grown into an indecisive, pious young man—or at least so Sir William believed. Henry was easily swayed by forceful personalities on his council. The elderly Cardinal Beaufort's influence was gradually being superseded by that of his two nephews, John of Somerset and Edmund Beaufort, and, more significantly, the old councillor told Cecily, "by William de la Pole, earl of Suffolk."

"And where does my husband stand with the king?" Cecily asked, her wide eyes and innocent expression not fooling the wily Sir William for a second. He had long since recognized the duchess's intellectual capabilities. "A magnificent consort," was how he had described her to another of Richard's loyal councillors. "'Tis said her father gave her her head when she was a girl, and I swear I have yet to meet a more spirited lady. She may have been named the Rose of Raby then, but this rose has grown thorns," he had said, enjoying his own wit.

"Your husband remains a faithful servant of the king, your grace," Oldhall answered her. "He is viewed by the Beaufort band as a possible spoiler in their power game. They can never forget that when Gloucester dies, and it does not seem likely that Eleanor will bear him a child now, his grace of York is closer to the throne than any of them, save perhaps Exeter. Duke Richard is wise to keep his own counsel and simply serve the king."

Cecily nodded. "Ah, aye, Exeter. I had forgotten about Exeter. But if Exeter can claim he is next in line after Gloucester through *his* female ancestor, then is it not true that my husband's similar claim from Lionel of Clarence would supersede any of John of Gaunt's descendants? He was younger than Lionel."

Sir William glanced over her shoulder at the closed door and put a gnarled finger to his lips. "I beg of you, your grace, do not say such a thing to anyone else. 'Tis treason, you see, and why Duke Richard's father was executed and attainted."

Cecily murmured, "I know," and she too glanced back at the door. "I quite understand." Then, in a loud, cheerful voice, she brought the conversation to a close. "I thank you for your patience, Sir William. I fear I take too much of your time with idle questions, and I beg your pardon." Cecily wondered if she had actually seen the look of admiration in his eyes or if it had merely been a trick of the light.

But the information she had gleaned had made her even more determined to bear York a son.

HENRY'S BIRTH HAD been easier than the other two, Cecily admitted three days afterward, which allowed her to enjoy the triumph of giving Richard an heir.

She lay quietly in the early morning watching Rowena tie up the shabby bed curtains, letting in the light. She missed the luxury of Fotheringhay here at Hunsdon, another of Richard's many properties, but one that had been sadly neglected. He had promised that he would carry out renovations to the lodgings as soon as he was reimbursed for the money he had had to spend on the crown's behalf in France.

"I am only keeping my promise to you, Cis," he told her, grinning at her disdain. "You said you wanted always to be close to me, and this is only an hour or two away from London. The Erber is no longer at your disposal now that Salisbury has inherited your mother's estates, so until I find us a suitable town house, this is where we can be together."

Cecily sighed as she looked around at the dingy walls, the horn-paned windows without shutters, the faded arras covering a hole in the wall facing her rickety bed, and the poor excuse for a garderobe. Little Henry had yet to see his father, and Cecily wondered what could be keeping Richard. It must have something to do with his new appointment, and she grimaced, as she did whenever she thought of it. Surely whatever it was Parliament needed from him could wait so the duke of York could greet his heir? After all, what could be more important? But she had given up trying to understand the ways of men.

Her eyes went to the fireplace, where Rowena and Mistress Lawler, Henry's nurse, were bent over an elegantly carved cradle, cooing at the baby, who was whimpering for a feeding, and her frown turned to a smile.

"Bring him to me, Nurse, and pray send for the wet-nurse," she said, holding out her arms. "Who is a greedy boy?" she teased, as the baby's eyes turned to the window, seeking the source of light. He recognized her voice and began a sucking reflex, making Cecily's breasts ache for him through the tight bands about her chest. "So you know me already, do you, my sweeting? Aye," she whispered, stroking the barely visible wisps of snowy hair. She inhaled the sweet baby scent of him and knew she would never tire of it. "I am your mother and so love you the most dearly, no matter what your nurse may tell you."

When the wet-nurse arrived and took charge of the now-wailing infant, Cecily lay back on her goose down pillow, a favorite household item without which she refused to travel, and absentmindedly wound a strand of her yellow hair around her finger. Richard had ridden off a week before after being summoned to report to the council. Again she scowled at the thought of his appointment and recalled the day he had ridden hard to Fotheringhay the previous summer to tell her of it.

"I have been appointed to succeed Warwick as governor of France for a term of five years," he had exulted, as he took her in his arms in the privacy of their chamber after their ritual reunion on the great hall steps. "They almost begged me to go, after the mess John of Somerset is making of it over there as temporary governor. And this time, my love, you shall go with me. What say you? We shall hold our own court in Rouen just as Bedford and his duchess did."

He was unprepared for Cecily's reaction. Her body sagged against him as she muttered, "Oh, no, not Rouen."

"By Christ! I am the right man for the post, my lady," he cried, pushing her away. Cecily cringed at his harsh tone. "I have the experience. I am a good commander. And I have royal blood. I am the natural choice. With all my heart I told them Aye, I am your man! I thought you would be pleased. It means I have been noticed. Tell me, madam, why would you not wish me to go?"

Cecily lifted her head and glared at him: She hated him calling her "madam"—such a cold, unfeeling word from a husband and lover. "In case you have forgotten, sirrah"—she rolled the r's for emphasis—"I lost our first child in Rouen in the most tragic of circumstances. 'Tis a scene that haunts my dreams even today, and I thought never to return," she said, turning away so he could not see her tears.

At once he was contrite, gentling her back to him and taking her face in his hands. "Ah, sweet Cecily," he said, "no tears, I beg of you. I cannot bear it when you cry. Where is my fierce Cis?" he cajoled, kissing her downturned mouth. "Is she there?"

He felt her lips curve into a wobbly smile, and he sighed with relief. "Forgive me, my love," he murmured, drawing her to the windowseat. "I confess I was only thinking of my own selfish pride at being selected for this duty. It is a singular honor, you understand, and a dream come true. As I wanted to share it with you so dearly, I rode here in all haste. How foolish of me to forget the dark time you had there all those years ago."

"Nine years and one month ago, Dickon," Cecily whispered, holding tightly to his hand. "Sometimes it seems like yesterday." Then she straightened and tried to put the memory from her mind. "But let not my ill humor spoil your important news, my love. Felicitations on the appointment! I am so proud of you. Aye, your dream of being a general is coming to pass." She smiled at him from under her lashes. "Come, kiss me, Dickon."

"Why Cecily Neville, I do believe you are flirting with me," he exclaimed, his eyes twinkling, but he obeyed without hestitation. She answered by fumbling in the folds of his short worsted gown for a sign he was ready to pleasure her. Despite the efforts of a thrush trilling outside the window of her solar and the sounds of a castle thrumming with activity floating upward on the summer breeze, the two lovers remained intent upon their pleasurable path of passion.

* * *

"AH, HENRY," CECILY murmured, smiling now at the memory of Henry's conception as she watched the wet-nurse tie up her bodice and Mistress Lawler take the sleeping child to change his swaddling bands. "You were indeed born of love that day and . . ."

She got no further, for suddenly the door flew wide and Richard strode in, his face creased in a grin. "Where is he?" he demanded, and seeing the astonished Mistress Lawler tying the final bands about Henry, he whisked his son from her grasp and held him aloft as a champion might hold a trophy. Not heeding the tut-tutting from the nursemaid, he took the child to Cecily, who held out her arms to him. After he gentled the baby into them, he embraced them both.

"You have made me the happiest man in the kingdom, Cis," he whispered, as both now looked down on the still-sleeping infant. "We must christen him at once. What shall we call him, do you think?"

Cecily looked at him meaningfully. "I think we should call him Henry."

NOT LONG AFTER Henry's simple baptism at Hunsdon, the Yorks returned to Fotheringhay to prepare for the long sojourn in France. After an exhausting day of making sure every piece of furniture, arras, carpet, and bed linen had been inspected and accepted or rejected and listed on the household roll, Cecily confided to Constance that the move was proving to be her most daunting task to date as duchess. Three times she and Steward Heydon had gone over the roster of servants who would be traveling with the duke and duchess and those who would be left behind to maintain the castle. Richard had ridden all over the country, ordering men from his estates to muster at Portsmouth, Southampton, and Poole and await the ships to take them to Normandy. The council chafed at this lengthy process and grumbled that Richard was dallying.

Richard harrumphed when he had received an impatient letter from the earl of Suffolk and the council, who were expecting York to set sail with his family at the end of April.

"Have they forgotten that I have estates in eighteen counties, and so it takes time to muster troops from so many places? They will simply have to wait until I am ready." Then he had chuckled. "Perhaps, also, they do not know how long it takes to pack up my wife's vast wardrobe and furnishings for a sojourn abroad." Before Cecily had had time to retort, he took her in his arms and kissed her tenderly. "Let me finish, my dearest. I would remind the council that any delay is worth enduring for England to be so regally represented in Rouen by its beautiful duchess of York."

* * *

AFTER A WEEK on the old Roman road, the ducal party reached London, and Cecily asked to rest. There she took leave of her brother Richard and her dear sister-in-law, Alice, who felt guilty showing Cecily her four youngest children, two boys and two girls. Cecily hardly recognized her godson, another Richard, who was now a strapping lad of twelve, boasting his father's yellow hair and his mother's intelligent eyes and sharp features. Alice had delayed her departure for Middleham to see her sister-in-law and meet Anne and baby Henry.

"Middleham is so far away, and I confess I find it too vast to be a cozy home," Alice confided. "But Richard is afraid to leave the castle for too long for fear Earl Ralph will take it into his head to try and capture it. He still believes all of Westmorland's estates should be his, despite your father's will. 'Tis not a pleasant state of affairs. And when your brother William returned from France in 'thirty-seven, he and some of Ralph's followers came to blows. You must know that Dickon asked Richard to go to France with him, but my Richard understandably declined."

"More's the pity, dearest Alice," Cecily replied. "What a delight it would have been to have you in Rouen." She glanced around to make sure they were not being overheard. "It will be interesting to meet Jacquetta Woodville, Bedford's young widow, remember? Dickon tells me she will be accompanying her new husband to France with us. The king must hold Woodville in high regard to have forgiven the couple their secret marriage. Aye, I heard they were levied a hefty fine for not asking permission to wed, but Dickon tells me they are so much in love that they paid without a murmur. 'Tis also said Jacquetta dabbles in witchcraft," Cecily whispered. They both quickly crossed themselves and then giggled like girls. "She boasts she is descended from the water-witch Melusine, the half-woman half-fish who seduced Raymond of Poitiers. Certes, I would not claim it even if it were true. I have seen what they do to witches," she murmured, thinking of Jeanne. "I have heard she is very beautiful, but I confess I cannot like anyone who has taken sweet Anne of Bedford's place."

Cecily thought back fondly to her few days with Alice as she and her retinue crossed over London Bridge into Surrey. At every stop the duchess and her immediate household were housed in tents, while the rest found hedges to sleep under. They built fires in the fields during the chilly spring evenings. Barrels of salt pork fed everyone, though enterprising young pages would trap rabbits and shoot fowl. Along the route, yeomen and their families would peddle cheeses, bread, and vegetables. Richard had spent a few days riding along at first, but then he went back to London to argue over the finances for his five-year appointment. He was still stinging from the lack of payment for his first term in France, but this time, the council assured him, money and supplies would be forthcoming regularly to pay his entourage.

And so the ducal cavalcade of packhorses, carts piled with furnishings and pulled by long-horned oxen, coffers of silverware, chests of clothes, and two wagonloads of servants followed Duchess Cecily's personal retinue, escorted by two dozen men-at-arms, along the road, which still boasted flint paving from Roman times. At Dorking, a small but thriving market town on the River Mole, the steward called a halt to the procession to set up the overnight quarters for the duchess and her ladies in a field.

Cecily was struck by the beauty of a high chalky hill above the town and called for Piers to bring her horse so that she could ride up to the top and admire the view. Rowena pursed her lips in disapproval when she realized Cecily would go alone with Master Taggett, but he was so often in Cecily's company that she presumed none of the other retainers would find anything untoward in it.

"'Tis as well your mother is not here to see you, your grace," she admonished her, as she helped her mistress into her split riding skirt. She never understood why the duchess could not simply ride sidesaddle, as other ladies did, and save her the tedious work of changing Cecily's clothes. "If the duke is displeased, I hope you will have the grace to tell him I did try to stop you."

This made Cecily laugh, though she suffered a little pang of remorse at the mention of Joan. "No doubt all will be able to see me up there, so pray stop being a killjoy. I deserve some time to myself after this nightmarish month, do you not think?" It is true, Rowena thought. My lady has not stopped to breathe since giving birth to little Henry. "My son is in good hands," Cecily added, turning and smiling at Constance. "I will be back before he even wakes."

After helping Cecily into the saddle, Piers leaped on his mount, and they trotted off through beech, birch, and oak trees, with carpets of bluebells on either side of them, until the trees gave way to coarse grassland upon the steep chalk slope.

"You are happy in our service, are you not, Piers?" Cecily asked him. "His grace, the duke, is pleased with your work at the mews."

Piers blushed a delightful pink at this praise, and Cecily hid a smile. "Aye, your grace, I be content. Who could not be?" he said earnestly. "I did never dream of such a life as this."

"Do you still think I am the Virgin Mary?" Cecily teased him. "Nay, that is unkind of me, Piers, for certes, you have grown out of such a childish notion." She chuckled at his chagrin as she urged her horse upward. "Come now, who will reach the top of this hill first, do you think?"

Piers grinned and replied without losing a beat, "You, my lady."

They allowed the horses to rest once they reached the summit. Cecily sat on an outcropping to contemplate the valley and the Surrey hills spread before them in their early May glory—yellow broom, cowslips, and primroses, pink and white hawthorn—and she felt a pang of regret that she would not see an English spring again for several years. She wondered whether Normandy had had time to recover from so much devastation, remembering well the scenes from her first time there. Her ruminations led her to wonder where Richard was at this very moment. He had promised to catch up with her as soon as he could, but she knew he had much on his mind. In only a few more days, the long procession would arrive at Portsmouth, and surely Richard would be escorting them upon the final leg. So far, they had not been attacked by any bands of vagrants, and for that Cecily was grateful to Richard for the thirty-man armed escort that he had provided.

Little Henry seemed to be enduring well the long, tedious journey, she thought tenderly, though she had complained to Richard before he left Fotheringhay that the child was rather young for such travel.

"Look at him," Richard had answered, watching his son cry lustily and kick the end of his cradle with sturdy little legs. "He is only six weeks, Cis, but he is as strong as an ox." And Cecily had inclined her head proudly in agreement and accepted the decision.

After swallowing a few mouthfuls of water from a leathern flask, she bent and snapped off a yellow sprig of broom to put in her green felt chaperon.

"Did you know how my ancestor, Geoffrey of Anjou, came to give the name Plantagenet to the royal dynasty, Piers?" Observing the blank look in the young falconer's eyes, Cecily educated him. "He was often seen with just such a stalk of broom in his hat and took it for his badge. As the Latin name for the bush is *planta genista*, he was nicknamed Geoffrey Plantagenet. When he married the daughter of our first King Henry, their son—called Curtmantle—took the name, and then his son, and thus and so on until our present sovereign lord. No doubt English kings will carry the name forever." She saw with amusement that this was more than he wanted to know and pointed to where her horse was grazing. "Here endeth your history lesson for today, Master Taggett. See to the horses, if you please. I will join you anon."

She walked along the edge of the escarpment and looked down on the encampment below at some servants fetching water from the river, her guards lolling on the grass, and the carters leading their oxen to drink. They look like so many insects from this height, she mused. This is what we must look like to God. How can He know each and every one of us and what we do and think? And yet we believe He watches over us all. Why, Cis, she chastised herself, are you questioning the church's teachings? She crossed herself for good measure and idly watched the scene below.

There were few females in her train, and so when two women ran out of her murrey and blue striped tent, one carrying something—Anne perhaps—and the other waving her arms, Cecily noticed them at once. She recognized Rowena's bright blue dress and assumed she was playing a game with little Anne. Or perhaps Henry had awakened early and was demanding his food and the wet-nurse had wandered away. She smiled when she imagined his bright red face and wide-open mouth in full voice. He was a lusty one, indeed, and even the king had complimented her on his namesake during the brief audience she had when she had stopped in London the week before.

At that meeting, she had also noticed the swarthy-faced earl of Suffolk's false smile as he bowed to her and chucked the baby under the chin, immediately setting him to whimpering. "So his grace of York has an heir," he had murmured to his companion as he walked away, thinking Cecily was preoccupied with paying attention to the crying child. "We must make sure the duke stays loyal to the crown." Her ears had pricked up, and she stored the remark for a future discussion with Sir William.

'Tis no wonder your badge is the ape's clog, Sir. You are as clumsy with your words as if you were wearing one, she mused now, kicking a stone and watching it roll down the hillside. Aye, my lord Suffolk, York does in truth have an heir, and I hope you will not forget it as you fawn on the king and whisper to my Beaufort cousins. Do not imagine I am ignorant of your power on the council. Sir William has told me of your rising star now that Uncle Beaufort is aging. She grimaced as she recalled that Suffolk was now the king's steward but her husband was nowhere in the king's immediate circle. And then it occurred to her that in Normandy he would be even further from the king, and she wondered if that had been Suffolk's intent.

She sighed and made her way back to Piers. "Come, Master Taggett, let us rejoin our fellow travelers," she said.

Wheeling her palfrey around, Cecily loosened the reins to allow the horse to extend his neck for balance and carefully controlled the descent on the crumbling hill until she reached the footpath, where she cantered along its length, loving the wind in her face, the birdsong heralding spring, and the overpowering smell of bluebells. A country girl at heart, she often chafed when confined by narrow, overcrowded streets of cities.

As they approached the camp, she was surprised to see Rowena running headlong on the path toward her, cap askew and tripping on the hem of her muddied blue gown. Cecily spurred her horse faster and reined him in so sharply that he reared up in front of Rowena, causing her to fall flat on her back on the soft ground.

"Whoa, boy!" Cecily quieted the animal and asked if Rowena was hurt.

"N-nay, your grace, only a little afraid," she answered quickly, righting herself and straightening her clothes. "But you m-must hurry back. 'Tis the b-babe . . ."

Cecily paled. "Henry? What of him? Is he ill? Answer me, madam!" She heard her own shrill command and was immediately sorry, for it made Rowena stammer all the more.

"A—a—bee or a w-w-wasp, your gr-grace," she managed. "His f—f—face swells like . . ." And she puffed her cheeks out to demonstrate.

Cecily did not wait to hear more but took off at a gallop, leaving Rowena staring miserably after her. Piers swung the unfortunate attendant up behind him and followed at a slower pace.

The small crowd around the ducal tent told her where Henry was, and as a groom ran to hold her horse, she slid down by herself and was at his side in an instant. The baby's face was horribly bloated and, snatching away the blanket, she saw someone had unwound his bands, revealing the puffy arms and legs of a devastating reaction to the sting. Constance had thrown open the tent sides to let in as much light and air as possible, and she was searching among her herbs and potions for a remedy. Cecily stared in horror at the swollen, naked child struggling for every inhalation of shallow breath. Henry's dark blue eyes conveyed desperation. She smothered a groan of anguish. Blessed Mother of God, she prayed, I beg of you, not again.

"Do something, Constance!" Cecily's ashen face turned to find the doctor.

"I find ze barb, *madame la duchesse*," Constance began calmly enough, though Cecily noticed beads of sweat on her upper lip. Seeing Cecily's impatient frown, she hurried on in her native tongue: "Some bees sting only once and then they die because they leave the barb behind. 'Tis necessary to remove it, but . . ." She hesitated and looked down at her bag.

"But what?" Cecily snapped from beside the wheezing child, a rising panic clutching at her throat as she stroked his hot little head.

"I was unable to remove it all," Constance apologized, joining Cecily at the bedside. "You can see it there," and she pointed to the minuscule remains of the dart at the center of a red welt on the baby's leg.

Cecily shook her head in disbelief. "How could a bee sting him through the binding cloths, doctor?"

"We had taken them off after he soiled himself, your grace, and the nurse was preparing a clean set," Constance replied. "We saw the bee fly in, and Rowena tried to chase it away, but it became angry, and we were all trying to kill it when it landed on Lord Henry and stung him. 'Twas nobody's fault, madame, truly it was not."

Cecily nodded helplessly, picking up the child and kissing his downy head. "And what will happen now, Constance? What can you give him to ease his suffering?"

Constance hung her head. She could not bear to see her mistress endure the loss of another child and was silently cursing her Maker for this extraordinary misfortune. She knew only a miracle could save the little boy now.

"I have used the juice of an onion, but it only stops the stinging. I will try applying honey, but I know not what that will serve, as it too only eases the pain. I fear Henry's body cannot tolerate this bee's poison, and I have no remedy for that. I cannot lie to you, *madame*, 'tis in God's hands now," she murmured, desolate. Once again, she was convinced that immersing him in the icy river might reduce the swelling, but she did not dare to suggest it. The duchess had never accused her of causing Joan's death with the cold-water bath. Cecily had acknowledged that they could never be certain whether it was the fever, the cold bath, or the unicorn elixir that had been the culprit.

"In God's hands? In God's hands?" Cecily cried, impatient with the doctor's outward display of calm. "'Twas what you said at Joan's deathbed. Sweet Jesu, you are the doctor—you *must* know what to do. Please, Constance, please! We cannot let him die. He is York's heir. He is everything to us." She laid Henry back in his bed and brushed tears from her eyes.

Constance had drawn the tent curtains closed, shooing away the gawking servants, knowing Cecily would be mortified that they should see her cry. Then she led Cecily to the traveling bed and made her lie down. "Conserve your strength, your grace. I will instruct Sir William to lead the company in prayer for Henry's life. And I will search my receipts for any remedies I may have missed. Have no fear, Henry will rally, for he is a strong little boy."

Cecily sighed. "Aye, mayhap if everyone prays for his recovery, God will listen."

Cecily spent hours on her knees with her dying child clutched in her arms in Dorking's tiny parish church hard by the camp. At midnight, in front of a rough-hewn statue of the Holy Mother and as one by one her eight candles guttered and went out—one for each week of Henry's life—she heard the breath leave her infant son for the last time in a slow labored sigh and felt the swollen body go limp.

"Henry!" she screamed, shaking him. "Wake up! Wake up in the name of Christ Jesu, our Savior. Nay, nay, do not take him, Lord. 'Twas only a bee sting! Dear God, what have I done that you have forsaken me?" Then, addressing the wide-eyed statue, tears streaming down her face, she cried, "Ah, sweet Virgin, I must truly be cursed. Two babes have been taken—nay, three, if you count Rouen. Truly, 'tis more than I can bear! Am I such a great sinner? Is Richard? Speak to me, Holy Mother, I beg of you, tell me how I have sinned!"

She was aware of a robed figure gently prying her son from her trembling fingers so that he could bless him with holy oil. "*In nomine Patri . . .*" the priest intoned, expressing compassion for this tragic woman in his gentle voice, while his thumb made the sign of the cross on the baby's forehead.

"Richard!" Cecily moaned into the gloom, falling prostrate onto the cold flagstones and feeling her bile rising. "Why are you not here with me—again?" As she wept, she pounded the ground with her fists, astonishing the priest with the furious tirade that tumbled from her mouth. She railed against her husband, at God and at the Virgin in particular, spewing blasphemies—like any heretic, the shocked priest thought. He considered stopping her and reminding her where she was, but she was a duchess, he knew. Instead, taking one of the white linen napkins from the altar, he gently placed the dead baby upon it beneath the crucifix and quietly left Cecily to her misery.

In the darkened unfamiliar church, her body spent and racked with grief, Cecily's faith in God and her husband faltered for the second time.

* * *

AFTER A CONSULTATION with Constance, Sir Henry Heydon elected to delay the departure of the duchess's retinue for a few days, and Piers was once again dispatched with a message to Richard, though the duke's whereabouts was a matter of conjecture. On Constance's advice, a second messenger was sent east to Reigate Priory to request a temporary lodging for her grace the duchess of York, who was indisposed. The prior of the Austin Friars would no doubt rub his hands with glee in the hope of an ample reward for his hospitality, Sir Henry whispered to his clerk as he sealed the letter.

Little Henry Plantagenet was placed in a lead coffin and escorted away in all haste to be buried at Fotheringhay. In a daze Cecily had agreed to the plan, though she was distraught as she watched the somber little party leave the camp, believing she ought to be with them. But not only was she too exhausted to travel; she knew in her more lucid moments that the king's business would not stop for tragic events such as this, and that Richard's timely departure for France must take precedence over the death of a child. In her heart, however, she protested such an unnatural course, and her anger grew.

She allowed herself, therefore, to be drawn in a litter the six miles to the priory, which was nestled under a hill with a splendid view of the distant South Downs. Cecily was given the prior's house for her use, and Constance and Rowena set about making the rather drab surroundings into a haven for the mourning mother.

In the meantime, the rest of the duchess's household continued west toward Guildford before turning south.

CECILY SAT BY the open casement of her chamber and watched Rowena pick daisies with Anne on the grassy slope beneath her. Her tears were spent, but her heart was still heavy after a week at the priory. Every day that passed without word from Richard found her deeper in a hole of self-pity and resentment. Worse, she could not even bear to have Anne in her presence, and so Rowena smothered the little girl with love to make up for her mother's lack.

For the first time in Cecily's service, Rowena was heard criticizing her mistress in front of the other attendants, and Constance gently tried to talk to her about the imprudence of this. But Rowena was stung that Cecily sought Constance's presence over hers, and she bristled at the doctor's homily. She began to prattle about the doctor behind her back, and soon it was whispered that Constance had been the cause of baby Henry's death. Only one word remained unspoken: witchcraft. Rowena knew that if Cecily ever suspected her of spreading the rumor out of wounded pride, she would lose her position.

Seated by the window, Cecily gazed out with indifferent eyes at her only child, who was dutifully holding Rowena's hand and stopping to pick a flower to add to her posy. Why could it not have been Anne whom the bee chose to sting? Cecily's question came from the darkest part of her heart, and she gasped at the wickedness of it. Nay, you do not mean it, her goodness whispered back. Anne is a beautiful child, so like Richard with her dark curls and solemn eyes. I should be grateful I have one healthy child, she mused, but the thought gave her no comfort. She glanced back into the room and watched Constance quietly measuring more poppy juice into a vial. The medicine had given Cecily some respite from sleeplessness. Dear Constance. Their friendship had grown through the years, and Cecily cherished it daily. How could she blame Constance for the death of her babes? In her heart, she knew the doctor had done all she could do, given Cecily's sometimes unreasonable conditions.

All at once, the clatter of hooves on the stone path broke upon the quiet afternoon, and Cecily leaned out to see who the visitors were. She saw the falcon and the fetterlock badge on the three men-at-arms and then recognized Richard's oversized murrey and blue chaperon and his black courser, Geraint. She wanted to call out to him but instead his name stuck in her throat. A rush of unexpected emotions overcame her: fear, sorrow, shame, anger, and self-pity. But where was love? She sat down on her stool with her hand over her mouth, tasting bile. So she did not see him spring down from his saddle and scoop the excited Anne into his arms and cover the little girl's face with kisses. Instead, she sat fighting an urge to hide so that she need not face him.

She had willed him to come to her every waking moment since watching Henry's coffin disappear from view. She had thought she could not suffer this loss without Richard's strength to support her. She thought his arms about her would take the grief away. But for a week she had grieved alone, and so she had realized she did not need Richard to help her survive a tragedy. This had been a sobering discovery at first, and she had never felt so alone. In their whole life together she had never questioned her love or need for him until now.

All this she had confided earlier to Constance, who had sat quietly and listened before offering her advice. "I pray you, forgive me for being blunt, but I would tell you the truth. I am not married, madame, and neither have I ever loved a man. But in watching you and the duke, I have regretted that such love may never be mine. It is a gift from God when two people who are forced, as you are, to spend their lives as husband and wife can find such a meeting of the heart and soul. There is not a person in this household who does not see the duke's desire for you, and I see the same desire in your eyes whenever you look at him. Certes, you are angry with him for what you perceive is his abandonment of you at a tragic time, but I assure you, anger will fade while love will endure, as our Savior taught us."

Cecily had wept when Constance left the room, asking herself over and over why God had forsaken her. Had she been too consumed by her love for Richard, she asked herself, craving his touch, aching for him to bring her to ecstasy? She thought of the wild nights of lovemaking, the passionate kisses, the pleasurable positions they had devised, and she guiltily wondered if they had sinned.

As she pondered how to greet her husband, turning her ruby betrothal ring on her finger, Cecily thought on Constance's words, and they calmed her. It would not be like the joyous reunions of old, she resolved. She needed to find the part of her heart that loved him, and she must also give Richard time to express his grief.

"Pull the veil over my face, I pray you, Constance," she said, rising and smoothing her skirts. "My husband has arrived, and I must greet him, but I would not have him see me like this."

Richard stopped in the doorway when he saw Cecily, framed by the window casement and veiled. "Cecily? My love, my dearest wife." His voice was hoarse and his eyes full of compassion. "Why the veil, Cis?"

Cecily gazed at him through the translucent fabric as though she were seeing him for the first time. He had been wearing his hair in the longer fashion since returning from France, but he was now sprouting a curly beard. His face was tanned from so much time on horseback, and he had lost weight, which he could ill afford. Was this the man she had loved for so long? The man she had given her heart and her body to? She no longer knew.

He approached her with his hands outstretched, but she took a step back, and for the first time in their lives together he felt rebuffed. He took in a sharp breath and spoke again, this time with authority. "What is this manner of greeting, my lady? What have I done to deserve your distance—your coldness?"

Cecily stiffened. "Coldness?" she echoed scornfully. "Nay, my lord, 'tis grief that consumes me, and I am dismayed you do not recognize it. But perhaps you do not because you have not known it." Her voice did not seem to belong to her but to some hard-hearted harpy. "I have had to suffer it alone while I waited here at your convenience."

Richard snorted his disbelief, and Cecily flinched. "At my convenience? At *my* convenience?" he snapped. "Christ's nails, Cis, I am at the king's convenience. Believe me when I say I came as soon as I could—"

"Not even a letter, not even one word," she interrupted, her voice cracking. "I felt abandoned. Your heir is dead—our little son—and I feared from your silence you blamed me." She was faltering now. "I thought you'd stopped caring."

Richard was on his knees, pressing her unresponsive hand to his lips. "Not care? What have I ever done that made you believe I would not care that our precious son is taken from us? And how could I blame you for such a tragic accident? You cannot think I am so unreasonable. Do we not know each other well enough after all this time? Ah, Cis, do not be so proud now. I have ridden without sleep for three days to be with you here—to share my grief with yours. With every league I have begged God to show you that I have had you in my thoughts ever since Piers Taggett gave me the terrible news. Have you not felt my love around you all these hours since Henry's death? It has been with you, I swear, and I cursed the council for holding me to the contract to muster more men that kept me from coming immediately." As his speech gathered speed, Cecily felt his tears on her hand, and something in her heart finally moved.

"Then I am comforted somewhat," she murmured. "But I did not know until I saw you arrive how great my hurt was—aye, I was bitter that you were not with me when I lost another child. Until you know the anguish of being alone as you helplessly watch your child die, I warrant you will not understand my agony." She sat down on the window seat behind her, Richard's hand still in hers. "I cannot deny that I felt abandoned by you—and by God."

"Aye, it would seem He has abandoned us." Richard rose and, letting go of her hand, took a few paces, and turned. "I cannot fathom why, but we have no choice but to accept that Henry's death was His will."

"Then He is a cruel God," she whispered. "Henry was an innocent child. I fear it is you and I that He is punishing."

"Why should He punish us, Cecily? We have done nothing wrong."

"The Bible says our bodies are the temples of the Holy Spirit, who lives in us all. I believe that we have taken too much pleasure in each other and so we are punished."

Richard was astonished by this reasoning, and knew at once that it was her irrational, grief-stricken mind speaking. "We have done nothing immoral, my dearest love. You are mistaken. The teachings of the church also tell us that a husband should not deprive his wife of intimacy, which is her right as a married woman, nor should the wife deprive her husband. We have obeyed those teachings throughout our life together."

"Then why punish us?" Cecily argued. "Nay, Richard, I have lost faith in Him."

Richard came back immediately to sit with her. "Never say so, Cecily. We must always trust in God, no matter what the cost. 'Tis our faith that upholds us daily."

The piteous cries of La Pucelle echoed in Cecily's head. "Jesu, Jesu, have pity," Jeanne had begged, but God had not heard her, even though she died for her faith. What kind of God was He, Cecily asked herself angrily, her heart hardening toward Him in her grief.

"I pray you, let me see your dear face, my love," Richard was saying. Cecily let him remove her veil. She was touched to see the compassion in his eyes. "Ah, Cis, will you forgive me?" he begged, his thumb tracing one of the dark circles under her eyes. "Tell me you forgive me, for I cannot endure this disharmony."

She looked at him soberly. "Aye, Richard, I must forgive you or I fear our life together will be changed forever. It will take some time to recover from our loss, but perhaps we can share our grief in this peaceful place."

Richard nodded. "We will take the time, Cis." He took her face and kissed her gently. "And now, if you can bear it, I would hear how Henry left us."

THE NEXT NIGHT Richard came to Cecily's chamber after Rowena had tended to her mistress and left the room. He and Cecily had spent the best part of the day in prayer, but Richard was not to know how little Cecily trusted in God now. Since losing Henry, she prayed exclusively to the Virgin; surely Mary would understand how it felt to lose a son, she reasoned. After walking in the priory's untidy herb garden, she and Richard had shared quiet conversation at supper together, and Richard thought Cecily would be as ready for them to make love as he was. He was not prepared for her reaction as he pulled her gently toward the bed and tried to untie her flimsy chemise.

"I cannot, my lord!" she cried, backing up to a chair. "How can we ever couple again when I feel this way? Thrice you have got me with child. I give birth while you are gone, and then God takes the child from us. Answer me this: How shall I ever again enjoy making love with you?" Her chin was trembling and her knuckles white as she gripped the arms of the chair. "I do not want to conceive another child and have him taken from me—ever again!"

Richard listened aghast and sank to his knees. "Sweet Mother of God,

Cecily, what can I say to console you?" Almost as quickly he got up, his patience tried. "What about little Anne? God has not taken her from us. She is alive, clever, loving, and healthy, if you would take the time to notice," he snapped and, snatching up his gown, he left the room.

"Aye, but He will take her. You will see, my lord, He will," muttered Cecily, staring with venom at the crucifix on the opposite wall.

The next day Richard sought out Constance in the priory infirmary, where she was grinding up some poppy seeds. She told Richard that she was worried when she had tiptoed past the door during the night and heard Cecily crying. It had been some time after Richard left and so, knocking first, Constance had let herself in and found Cecily wide awake, still seated on the chair with her knees under her chin.

"What can I do, doctor? Is she ill?" Richard asked. "I fear for her mind. She has sunk so low into melancholy."

Constance was taken aback by the duke's familiarity with her, but his urgency and concern touched her. She had had few dealings with him, living as she did in the duchess's apartments. She proceeded carefully. "I cannot tell if she is simply grieving and her humor will pass, or if she is truly ill," she told him. "I have studied the diseases of women from Trotula of Salerno's treatise. It is known some women are afflicted with melancholy following birth, but it most often passes with time, my lord. But although I do not believe it will cure her, I will bleed her, if you so desire."

But Richard was not listening. "What have I done?" he groaned. "I would make amends, but I know not how."

Constance gave him a sympathetic smile. *"Courage, monseigneur. Elle vous adore, vous savez."*

Richard heard her then. "She does? She adores me? Certes, I could not see any semblance of love last night. She looked as though she loathed me."

Constance continued to mash the gray seeds with the pestle as she told him, "I beg of you to be patient, my lord duke. She will recover. The duchess Cecily is as strong a woman as I have ever known."

Her unhurried manner seemed to pacify Richard. Giving a quick bow, he acknowledged her good service to his wife and left. Constance watched him go with sympathy and admiration. Sighing, she again envied Cecily's good fortune in her husband.

15

Normandy, 1441

ichard took Cecily west to Guildford and then south to Portsmouth, and
by the time they left the verdant Hampshire forest of Beare and began
to climb the last hill, they sensed a buzz of excitement in the air. Before their
arrival, many cavalcades and companies of armed men had rolled over the
road and along the coast to gather at the south ports. The ships that had been
ordered to those ports from all over the kingdom the month before had to
be dispersed when the duke had not been ready to leave, but now they were
slowly reassembling.

When the York retinue came over Portsdown Hill, Cecily was not surprised
to see the fields stretched out below them filled with brightly colored tents,
wagons loaded with furnishings and armaments, makeshift pens of horses
and oxen, and clusters of hundreds of soldiers. She was astonished, however,
to see so many ships in the vast harbor, which looked to her more like a bay.
Sunlight was sparkling on its blue-green water. Dover's access to the English
Sea was paltry by comparison, she thought. Beyond the fields, the spire of the
Portsmouth church rose from the town on the headland, and as the York party
wended its way to the port, Richard pointed out the new round tower that
had been built a decade before at the narrow mouth of the harbor to ward off
enemy attacks.

"It bristles with cannon, so I have heard," he said and then grinned. "Why
they built it of wood and not stone, I cannot imagine. One spark and it becomes an inferno."

Cecily learned that they would be joined at Portsmouth by the earls of Eu
and Oxford, Sir James Ormond, and Sir Richard Woodville and their trains.
Indeed, it seemed to Cecily that the whole town was full to bursting with
members of all the noble households. Like Richard, commanders preferred

to commandeer an alderman's or a merchant's house rather than pitch a tent alongside the masses in the fields. Sir William Oldhall was on hand to greet the duke and duchess in front of the modest town hall, and his first words to Cecily were of regret for the loss of little Henry. Touched, Cecily thanked him graciously. He led the way to a large, handsome, half-timbered house that boasted three stories. He looked pleased with himself when Richard complimented him on the choice of accommodations.

"There must have been competition from my brother-in-law, Bourchier," Richard remarked, laughing. "Isabel must be disconsolate, do you not think, my dear?" he asked. Cecily nodded absently. She had met Richard's sister only twice and had not found much in common with her, despite a family likeness to Richard. But Richard held Henry Bourchier, earl of Eu, in high esteem and had requested his presence on this campaign to France. It appeared she would grow to know Isabel Plantagenet better in the coming year.

Before crossing the merchant owner's threshold, Richard whispered to his wife, "The gentleman has reaped the benefits of the wine trade, I suspect," and he indicated the enormous pile of barrels leaning against the side of the house with their telltale stained bungholes. Cecily had to smile when a few moments later she met the said merchant, who bowed and scraped to them as they entered the pleasant hall. Cecily thought his nose might have acted as a beacon on a dark night, and he must be suffering from the gout, she surmised, watching him hobble up the stairs to show them to their accommodations. Cecily extolled the view from the window in her sunny solar to her host, guessing she was looking over the Solent at the distant Isle of Wight.

When Richard saw that she was comfortable, he retired to a room that had been set aside as his headquarters and was relieved to see there was an adequate bed in it. Although aching to make love to Cecily, Richard had kept his promise and refrained from any intimacy for the length of the seven-day journey. He knew he should have left her much sooner on the road to make sure all the troops were mustered, but his concern for her melancholy forced him instead to ride by her side. He was quiet when she wanted it and only engaged her in conversation when she initiated it. He prayed to Monica, the patron saint of wives and mothers, that he might earn Cecily's forgiveness sooner rather than later, as he could hardly bear the schism he had inadvertently caused. Even Richard's squire and gentlemen ushers were fooled into believing her grace the duchess was suffering from a female malady that required the duke to sleep in their tent upon the road. Only Constance knew that Cecily had denied her husband her bed for a far more personal reason. Gossip-prone Rowena occupied herself with Anne and her own two children and hardly noticed anything else.

Little by little, Cecily's heart reopened to Richard, and by the time they reached Portsmouth, she grudgingly admitted to herself that he had demonstrated his contrition and devotion without a hint of reproach or resentment. How I wish I could be as generous, she thought on one occasion during the second day's ride as she watched him engage Anne in a game of Name This while the child enjoyed her lofty perch before him on his saddle. He is a good father, in truth, better than I am a mother, she admitted ruefully. But then her thoughts rushed back to her nightmare of suffering in the Dorking parish church, and she knew she must be capable of great maternal love.

She had studied Richard from under her wide, veiled straw hat that morning and remembered how much she loved his eyes when he smiled. He was smiling then at something Anne was trying to pronounce. Then he had stroked his daughter's dark curls, reminding Cecily how gentle his hands could be when he caressed her own hair, her face, her naked . . . Nay, Cecily! Do not think of such things—not yet. Opening her heart was momentary. It began to close again—but this time she did not slam it shut.

THE TWO PROUD women, the taller in blue and the other in green, eyed each other critically once they had made their reverences, and the guests gathered in the pleasant hall of the wine merchant's house watched with interest. No one else in the room could hold a candle to these beauties: Jacquetta, former duchess of Bedford, and Cecily, duchess of York. Jacquetta was petite and voluptuous, her face heart-shaped with classically symmetrical features, and her hair, fashionably concealed, was said to be lustrous gold. Up close, Cecily could see that Jacquetta's skin had been marred by a pox when she was a child, but she had cleverly concealed its marks with a powder. True, the duchess of York was a year older and there were vestiges of grief still on her face, but Cecily's flawless complexion and brilliant blue eyes attracted attention, and her regal height meant that she wore the fashionable high-waisted, heavily draped, and long-trained gown more elegantly. Jacquetta had chosen to wear the Burgundian headdress of two six-inch silver filigree horns on either side of her temples over which was draped pearl-encrusted lace. Had she not been so lovely, she might have resembled a cow, Cecily thought, vowing never to adopt that absurd style.

But when Jacquetta's husband came to stand next to her, all eyes moved from the Yorks to the perfectly matched Woodvilles. Richard Woodville was, at thirty-five, still a most handsome man with a six-foot frame, broad shoulders, and well-defined legs, which he showed off in parti-color hose beneath the new shorter gown. As pleasant a countenance and neat appearance as the duke of York possessed, he was no match for the elegant Sir Richard.

Cecily, as the superior in rank, spoke first to Jacquetta. "God give you a good day, your grace. I trust your lodging is comfortable."

Jacquetta smiled, causing Cecily to shiver slightly. Jacquetta's eyes reminded Cecily of a cat's—almond-shaped and almost yellow. "Your grace is kind to inquire," she replied in perfect English but with a slight accent. "Sir Richard and I find it adequate but,"—she took in her surroundings, gesturing constantly with her many-ringed fingers—"not as pleasant as this." She sighed. "I miss Grafton already."

Cecily inclined her head, unfamiliar with the Northamptonshire manor owned by the Woodville family. She bristled at the intimation that Jacquetta, who was now after all only the wife of a knight banneret despite her previous title, thought she merited similar quarters to the Yorks'. Some guardian angel made her barb sound innocently sweet. "I pray you have no misgivings about returning to Rouen, madam, with the recent memory of your marriage there with Duke John still fresh."

Cecily felt Richard's arm stiffen in surprise, but she smiled innocently, cocked her head, and enjoyed the other woman's discomfort. Serves her right, Cecily thought. It had been the talk of the court that these two must have begun their affair long before poor John of Bedford was dead. Perhaps Jacquetta had called upon her ancestor Melusine's skills to cause the duke to decline so she could have her knight, Cecily mused. Then she berated herself: You go too far, Cis.

"Aye, I shall be reminded of his final days, 'tis true, your grace," Jacquetta was saying, her own smile mirroring Cecily's. "We plan to have masses said at his tomb as soon as we get to Rouen. Both of us miss him dearly, do we not, Sir Richard?"

Sir Richard Woodville was puzzled by this uncomfortable conversation, and he had the grace to lower his eyes before supporting his wife in her lie. "Ah . . . um . . . why . . . certes, we do, madam," he replied.

Richard extracted Cecily from the situation by bowing to the couple and making his and Cecily's excuses to greet others. "Why the venom, Cis?" he murmured as he led them toward Henry Bourchier and Isabel. "What has she done to you that I am unaware of?"

"Forgive me, Richard, in truth I know not. There was something about her, something untrustworthy that made my skin crawl. I confess I should not have spoken thus, and I beg your pardon. Sir Richard is an affable man, and I enjoyed his company on my way to Calais all those years ago, but she . . ."

She did not finish, for the earl of Eu was walking forward to pay his respects, his diminutive wife, in a rose gown delicately embroidered with the Bourchier knot, on his arm. Cecily glanced back at the Woodvilles still standing in the middle of the room and saw Jacquetta glaring at her. Cecily shivered again.

"Brother-in-law, you are a welcome sight," Henry Bourchier said, grasping Richard's outstretched arm in greeting, his graying moustache twitching over a mouth ever ready to smile. "And Cecily, you grow more beautiful with age, I swear," he declared, kissing her hand. "However, I understand condolences are in order, am I right, Isabel?"

Isabel Plantagenet, Countess of Eu, agreed, her gray eyes, so like Richard's, expressively sad as she detected the ravages of grief on Cecily's lovely face. She had given her husband five sons already and had recently conceived for the sixth time. "My dear brother and sister, it is beyond understanding how one deals with the death of a child. God has been kind to us and allowed our sons to live. I pray He sends you another son soon." For the first time in their limited acquaintance Cecily saw not arrogance but shyness in her sister-in-law's quiet manner and so reached out her hand, gratefully covering Isabel's. Perhaps she understood why Isabel was not often at court but preferred living quietly at Rettendon.

"Let us hope so, my lady," Cecily said simply, cheered at the prospect of forming a bond with this woman in the coming months. "Until He does, I shall look forward to introducing our daughter to you and meeting our nephews very soon. Do any of them accompany you to Rouen?"

NONE OF THE children on the voyage to Harfleur was any the worse for a choppy sea. However, several of the adults took to their bunks and hammocks or hung over buckets or the gunwale. Cecily had discovered on her first crossing to Calais that she was one of the fortunate sailors, and so she spent much of her time during this two-day voyage on deck playing hide-and-go-seek or hoodman blind with the children.

From the poop deck, Richard anxiously watched her. Outwardly she was behaving congenially with him, conversing about their fellow passengers' *mal de mer*, the weather, their plans on arrival in France, and the newly renovated governor's lodgings in Bouvreuil Castle. She had even allowed him to kiss her, and more than once he thought he had detected desire, but Richard could not reach her heart, and more than that, he worried that her faith had been seriously compromised by Henry's loss. However, Richard's chaplain had assured him that the duchess attended services and had made her confession on several occasions during their brief stay in Portsmouth.

"Many of us who are true believers have our faith tested, my lord," Father Lessey had told Richard. "Your lady wife has been sorely tried, but she will feel God's love again, I promise you."

Richard had raised an eyebrow but had said nothing.

Turning now to lean over the side and watch the spray from the bow as it caught the sunlight, he hoped the resulting rainbows were promises of a brighter future with his complicated wife.

The fleet stretched out as far as the eye could see, cogs and caravels transporting not only the noblemen, their families, and their household trappings, but troops, horses, oxen, arms, armor, and cannon.

Richard prayed the news from Lord Talbot, known for his daring in the field, would be good upon their arrival at Harfleur, so that he could settle his family in Rouen before leading his new recruits to reinforce the shrinking English army attempting to rout the French around Paris. He had faith in the stalwart Talbot and intended to make him commander of the army as soon as he had landed and taken the reins of government in Normandy. Would he have to lead those new soldiers, or could he trust Woodville or his brother-in-law to march with them? There was always Oxford or Ormond, but Richard did not trust the latter. Besides, Bourchier had been named captain of Crotoy and would leave almost immediately to help hold that English stronghold on the coast.

His thoughts returned to Cecily. This was exactly the kind of conversation he missed having with her. At Fotheringhay he would throw another log on the fire after they had sent their attendants to bed and they would discuss what was happening with the king and council—Humphrey of Gloucester was losing his power, Cardinal Beaufort had somehow amassed a fortune and loans from him kept even the king afloat—or they would discuss plans for building at one of the York properties. How he loved those late-night talks. He wondered if she missed them too.

Later, as the sun set, Richard approached his wife where she stood on the quarterdeck, determined to try and regain those lost precious times.

"Cis, my mind is crowded with thoughts. If I cannot talk to you, I fear I shall burst. You used to understand my heart and mind. Would you listen to me again, my lady, if we walk together?"

"Certes, Richard," Cecily replied in her new even tone, which told Richard nothing. "Rowena, Constance, you may leave us."

But she had not turned him away, and so he plunged forward. "In truth, I am content to return to France as its governor," he began, after putting his short mantle around her shoulders and linking their arms. "But I worry what happens at home behind my back. Now we are away from shore and only the wind can hear me, I am humbly bound to say the king is not fit to govern by himself, and although Gloucester has his nephew's best interests at heart, no one takes him seriously now, despite the fact he is still heir apparent to the throne. I am thankful I am not an ambitious man or I would have deadly enemies in Suffolk and the Beauforts, but 'tis hard for me to stand by and see those men manipulate Henry so cleverly." He shook his head. "Even your Uncle Beaufort was of less concern in his heyday than these new men."

"But you do have ambition, my lord," Cecily began. "We have talked of your dreams of being a fine soldier and commander, and here you are achieving that goal. But unlike many who surround the king, you also have honor. Soldiering aside, however, I understand you speak now of an ambition concerning your place beside Henry, which I encouraged you to seek but without much success. I had hoped by now you would have achieved an eminent position at court."

Richard was taken aback. "Are you truly so ambitious for me, Cis?"

"'Tis a wife's duty to support her husband, I believe, and wanting him to be the best he can be is part of what a good wife does. If that means I am ambitious, then aye, I suppose I am." She was warming to her subject now, and seeing no argument from Richard, she dared to go further. "Let me remind you that you have the rank and the demonstrated loyalty to influence the king just as much as my Beaufort cousins, and yet they stand closer than you do. Suffolk is unknown to me, except that he is now steward of England, but who is he to wield so much influence? I am certain there are those besides me who wonder why the duke of York is not on the council and making policy."

Richard was not expecting such a well-thought-out answer, and he would have been dismayed to know how openly his astonishment registered on his face.

"Well, why?" Cecily repeated, managing to keep her tone serious. "I trust I am not the only person to see your worth. Certes, 'tis flattering to be governor of France, Richard, but it has occurred to me that perhaps Suffolk and his ilk might feel more secure with you out of the country."

Richard took her hands in his and caressed them with his thumbs. "By Christ's nails, Cecily, you are not simply a pretty face, are you?" he said, teasing her. "Do you think I have not had the same thought?" he added more seriously.

Cecily turned steadfast eyes to his. "Then let us work together to achieve your position in the king's circle, if it is your wish—your ambition."

"My ambition? Much of it is buried in shame for my father's treason. It weighs on me that others might look at me and believe that the sins of the father . . ."

He tailed off upon hearing Cecily's muttered "Pish!" She went on, "Richard, you have more than atoned for your father's folly. No king could know a more loyal subject. As a wife, I can only hope for you what should be *yours by right*. And a strong voice at the king's right hand should be rightfully yours by now. As a woman—albeit one with a pretty face," she teased him back, "I may only encourage, suggest—" She broke off, frowning. "Oh, if only I were a man."

Richard guffawed. "'Tis certain there are many in the king's service—if not the king himself—who are justly relieved you are not a man, my love. The crown itself would not be safe!" He took advantage of her smile and kissed her. "Come, my lady, let us talk no more about my ambitions. My only wish in the last weeks is to console you and make you happy. Am I succeeding?"

Cecily had the grace to look shamefaced. "Aye, my lord. But I believe 'tis also because I am grieving less, thanks be to the Blessed Mother."

"Ah," Richard said, eyes twinkling. "Then you are talking to her again?"

"What can you mean?" she protested. "I have always enjoyed the Virgin's protection. And I pray do not change the subject. My faith is my own concern."

Richard patted her hand and murmured, "Then I shall not speak of it again, my love. Ah, look, your friend Jacquetta and her knight approach."

All parties reverenced each other and passed a few minutes talking of the weather and complaining of the deprivations of life aboard a creaking caravel. Sir Richard's demeanor was deferential to both the duke and the duchess, and he kissed Cecily's hand warmly when they parted. But Jacquetta was quiet, content to let her husband talk while she inspected Cecily surreptitiously from beneath her voluminous hood.

If she thinks I did not notice I was being scrutinized, then she is more addle-pated than I thought, Cecily mused as she allowed Richard to take her below to an unappetizing supper of salted herring and stale bread. She groaned inwardly, knowing that once at Rouen there would be nowhere to hide from the woman.

THE NEWS AWAITING Richard at Harfleur was encouraging. The brilliant English commander, Lord Talbot, was gaining ground in his attempt to relieve besieged Pontoise. He suggested that as soon as Richard could take the reins in Rouen, he should join Talbot in a push to drive King Charles back to the Seine.

"I am sorry, Cis," he said, as they were taking refreshment in Harfleur's small castle, "but you will not have me for long once we reach Rouen. Talbot believes that with these new recruits we can gain the ground lost around Paris. I trust you to establish our household in my absence. I pray the king's council will be prompt with my payments this time. Unhappy men do not make for a dedicated army."

And so, as Richard rode out of Harfleur on the Rouen road ahead of his troops, the barges carrying Cecily, the other noblewomen, and their entourages pushed off from the jetty and turned east on the Seine toward Rouen.

Richard had introduced his wife to a giant of a man called John Blaybourne, captain of a company of archers mustered from the north of England and now in charge of the other men-at-arms for the journey to Rouen. A six-foot-high longbow, which dwarfed most archers, was shorter than Blaybourne and "one of his hands could crush a man's skull," Cecily remarked to Richard following the meeting. But he was gentle of speech and handsome in a way that put Cecily in mind of a Norseman she had seen in Durham once. Aye, he would serve as a fine protector, she told Richard, "as long as Master Taggett does not protest. He will not like being supplanted, in truth."

Cecily's instinct had been right, and a downturned mouth was the result of her gentle dismissal of Piers as her special escort for the rest of the journey. "Master Blaybourne will eventually join the army, Piers, and then you may resume your duty to me. But for now your duty is to the hawks under your care. You must not neglect them, you understand." His obvious disappointment had touched her, but she dismissed him firmly.

The sixty-mile journey up the river to Rouen was marred by several downpours on two of the days, the rain soaking through the canopies and onto the occupants of the large barge, which was sometimes rowed and sometimes pulled along by huge dray horses walking on the tow path. Cecily felt sorry for Richard and his soldiers marching to Rouen, who would spend many a night on soggy ground, whereas the women would be accommodated in abbeys, such as the majestic Jumièges, or at inns along the north bank.

As the barge wended its way to Rouen, Cecily tried to focus on the high chalk cliffs rising on the south bank of the wide river and the rolling Pays de Caux countryside on the other, but in truth she was dreading revisiting that city, which housed memories of the horror of Jeanne's execution and the heartache of her miscarriage. She had hoped never to set foot in the town again, and yet here she was facing five more years of her life there. And so, on the day of celebration for the nativity of John the Baptist, when the many-towered city walls hove into view, she gritted her teeth and took deep calming breaths. Shining in the sun, the bleached walls were at their least threatening, and as she watched the others in her household pointing and smiling in excited anticipation, she determined to throw off her depression and embrace this new chapter in her life.

The ducal barge edged its way to the bustling wharf, where the travel-weary duchess and her party made their final landing. The other vessels docked soon after. Just inside the city gate, a large crowd of cheering spectators had gathered. Cecily knew they must mostly be English. She well remembered the sullen French townsfolk of her last visit.

Cecily declined the waiting litters. "We have sat long enough, do you not think, ladies? The sun is shining at the moment, and so let us proceed on foot." She saw Jacquetta Woodville scowl, but Cecily quickly averted her eyes and waited for the pikemen to form an escort. Lazy woman, she thought, as she watched John Blaybourne marshal his fellow guards into two ranks. She smiled, remembering how easily the man had lifted her off the barge and onto shore one day so that the ladies could stretch their legs and allow the children to run around. He had made her feel like a dainty child, and she had laughed merrily when he told her that she weighed less than thistledown to him. At that moment her melancholy had begun to lift, and the duchess's companions were relieved to hear her laugh once more.

Now Master Blaybourne gave her a shy grin and a quick bow before standing to attention, indicating the escort was ready. As she made her way to the soldiers, Cecily was blissfully unaware that a pair of yellow-green eyes had caught the little exchange between her and the burly captain of her guard.

"I would prefer to avoid the marketplace, if you please, Master Blaybourne,"

Cecily directed him. She did not yet want to be reminded of that day in May when the world went black for her. "I remember 'twas always so crowded," she began, but her lame excuse was cut off by the timely carillon that rang out from the great gothic belfry nearby.

They had gone but a few paces when the sound of hooves attracted everyone's attention. Falling back, the spectators allowed three horsemen to canter through their midst. The leading rider leaped from his saddle and swept his murrey and blue bonnet off his head, making Cecily a graceful bow.

"Your grace!" Cecily cried upon recognizing Richard, genuine pleasure in her voice. "I did not expect you so soon. I am delighted to see you."

Her reception was exactly what the weary Richard had dreamed of. He had ridden ahead of his men, leaving Oxford to command them for the last two days, and hoped he would be in time to meet the barge. It seemed his efforts had paid off, and with Cecily's delight at seeing him, the heaviness in his heart eased. He was sorely tempted to sweep her off her feet and carry her to Bouvreuil, but he had no intention of scandalizing his new subjects before he even had time to meet them. Instead he let his lips linger on her hand as he kissed it. I hope I am forgiven, his eyes tried to say as he looked up at her, turning her ruby betrothal ring under his fingers.

"Aye, my lord," Cecily answered the unspoken question, feeling her heart lift. "I believe you are. 'Twas as much my fault as yours."

CECILY STOOD BY the deep window embrasure in the large room that she and Richard had chosen as their solar and watched her husband inspect the armorer's work on his gleaming bascinet. One of the hinges had been bent during the sea voyage. He had his squire fit it over his head and worked the snout of the visor open and shut, grunting in satisfaction.

"Tell Master Dawes 'tis well done, Roger," he instructed the young man, "and I pray you put it with the rest of my arms. We ride on the morrow."

Roger bowed out of the room, and Richard turned to Cecily. "Forgive the hasty departure, Cis, but I did warn you," he said, putting his arm about her. He hoped that he might share her bed on this last night, but he would not rush her.

Those first few days had been busy for the York household, arranging who would take which of the newly renovated apartments, finding other lodgings for those retainers not among the immediate ducal staff, and Cecily working tirelessly in tandem with Sir William and Sir Henry, chamberlain and steward respectively, to settle the new lieutenant governor into the castle.

Upon the second night's retiring, Richard had sidled into her chamber, hoping that her desire for him might be as great as his for her, but finding her fast asleep curled up in a ball with her hand tucked under her cheek like a child, he had crept away again. And so Richard had bided his time, but now his urge to bed her was a matter of physical torment.

"Would you do me the honor of lying with me tonight, my dear wife?" he finally asked, respectful but desperate. "I yearn to feel you next to me again."

His face was so open and honest and his eyes so full of pleading that Cecily could not forbear to smile and nod. "I fear I have punished you too long, Dickon," she said, and his spirits lifted at the use of his old nickname. "I too have missed you next to me, and I suppose we cannot produce an heir without"—she hesitated—"without intimacy."

Richard was serious for a moment. "Have you reconciled those misgivings that you had at Reigate Priory?"

She took a deep breath and nodded once. Taking his hand and carrying it to her breast, she told him, "I am ready—to put it delicately—to resume our relations, my lord."

Richard grinned. "You mean *fornication?*" he teased, picking her up and carrying her to the bed. "You do mean fornication?"

"I do, I do!" Cecily answered, throwing off her turbaned headdress and letting her hair fall loose. "But you shall not have it all your way, you understand."

"You may have it any way you choose, madam, but it has to be now." And not waiting to undress, Richard pushed her skirts up to her waist and unhooked her tight bodice, and she spread her legs for him. As he untied his hose and codpiece with clumsy fingers, he began kissing the inside of her thighs, relishing the scent of her and the movement of her hips as his mouth moved higher. Freed at last, he thrust into her and almost immediately climaxed with such a cry of pleasure that it might have been heard in the next town, Cecily told him later.

"Christ's nails, Cis," Richard complained. "If you had not made me wait so long . . ."

"Oh, pish, Dickon. I waited just as long," she murmured, snuggled up against him. "In the morning, I shall show you properly what we have been missing. But now . . . now, I'm . . . too . . . tired."

"I love you, Cecily Neville," Richard whispered, her breathing telling him that she was almost asleep. "I always have and I always will." He felt her foot rub his shin and knew she had heard him.

16

Rouen, late Summer 1441

Cecily was disappointed when her courses arrived on their appointed day in early July, a week after Richard had marched out of the Martainville gate on his way to Pontoise with four hundred men-at-arms and a hundred and fifty archers. John Blaybourne was not among them. Richard preferred to leave him and his company behind to protect the duchess. Poor Piers was once again seen sulking when he rode out to exercise the falcons.

"How long before I see you again, Richard?" Cecily had asked, as her husband bade her farewell on the steps of Bouvreuil's inner courtyard. Anne was tucked in the crook of her father's arm, playing with his beard.

"I know not, but I promise to write, and if I can get away, I will. In truth, Pontoise is only three score miles, which should take me not more than, say, a day to cover," he said, laughing at her expression of horror. "Maybe two," he assured her.

Richard had written to her as soon as he had caught up with Talbot. The letter cheered her as she sat idly in her solar, lamenting a woman's lot at this time of the month and especially in this instance. She was kept company by Rowena, Anne, and Sir William's kind-hearted but unimaginative wife, Margaret. Constance had been given permission to return to the convent for the afternoon and visit her old friends there.

> *We are making progress against Charles, and I believe we may*
> *relieve Pontoise in a very short time. I long for news of you and our*
> *little Anne. I was touched by her weeping on my leaving her. She is a*
> *dear child, and I pray that you will find time to let her know a mother's*
> *love.*

Cecily looked up from the letter guiltily. Was her indifference still that obvious to others—to Richard? She believed she had tried of late. Across the room, her daughter was playing pat-a-cake with Rowena on the turkey carpet. A wave of guilt suffused her, and she chewed on her lower lip as she contemplated her child. How foolish I have been, she thought, staring at Richard's words. They had the desired effect, however, for she suddenly called out to her daughter. Anne turned anxious gray eyes to her mother, but when she saw Cecily's smile and outstretched arms, she gave a cry of joy and ran into them, flinging her arms about her mother's neck as if greeting her for the first time after a very long separation. Cecily gasped. What had she been missing all this time? she admonished herself. Why she had denied herself the innocent love of this child, she could not imagine. She gently released Anne's hold and held the girl at arm's length on her lap.

"You are a good girl, Nan, and your mama loves you very much." Then she whispered, "Do you love me too?" and held her breath.

Anne's vigorously nodding curls gave Cecily her answer. The child put her thumb in her mouth and contemplated her beautiful mother. "Pretty," she lisped. "Mama pretty." Then as if at two she had already learned the art of diplomacy, she slipped off Cecily's knee and ran back to Rowena. "Weena pretty, too," she cried, making everyone laugh.

Although she took the time to write to Richard to let him know their night together had not yielded the result they had hoped for, Cecily's disappointment in not having conceived was eased as she rejoiced in getting to know her daughter and learning to be a mother. She even forgot to miss Richard until she received his next letter two weeks after the first. This time the messenger had arrived with some urgency.

> *For some reason the French are quiet, and we believe they are contemplating pulling back. Therefore I am keeping my promise to see you but can leave for no more than two days, and our meeting must be kept secret in case spies let the French know I am no longer at the head of the army. I will have my squire and a groom with me, but no one will know who we are. May I suggest that you tell Sir William you are going on a pilgrimage to Les Andelys, not far from Rouen, to take the water at St. Clothilde's holy spring. The nuns at the abbey will welcome us as pilgrims and perhaps the sacred place will help us conceive a son. Bring Constance or Rowena with you and arrange for John Blaybourne*

*to accompany you but no one else. I will trust you to invent a reason
why you do not want a whole retinue of people, but you may inform Sir
William that it is upon my orders.*

Cecily frowned. Certes, people will be suspicious if I go with only an attendant and one escort, she thought. However, I can understand why Richard
does not want to be observed. She shrugged and read on.

*Meet me on the twentieth day of the month at the abbey and come
clothed as a simple pilgrim, as will I. My dearest love, I can already feel
your sweet body in my arms.*

CECILY HOPED THE dawn departure of a trio of riders from the castle would
go unnoticed by those whose apartments overlooked the courtyard. She
glanced up at the windows of the second floor, where many of the nobles
and their ladies lodged, and was certain she saw a face at one of the windows. Was it the Woodvilles' chamber? she wondered, trying to remember
the position of their apartment. She would have been dismayed to know
that Jacquetta had spent a restless night and was indeed watching the riders
leave that morning. Cecily was glad of her simple gown and her cloak with
its voluminous hood and naively thought that she would be unrecognizable.
But she forgot to mask the legendary ease with which she handled a skittering stallion, and the giant Blaybourne, who had helped Cecily up onto it, was
unmistakable. Blaybourne then effortlessly swept Constance up behind him,
leaving Jacquetta in no doubt that Cecily of York was attempting to leave
Rouen in secret.

A few moments later, the riders passed the royal mews, where Piers Taggett
had spent the night tending to the broken wing of one of his charges. Hearing the muffled hooves on the dirt path that skirted the outside of the eastern
castle wall, he stooped to avoid the low doorway and stood in the shadows
of the mews house to see who was leaving the castle so early. He would have
known Cecily on horseback anywhere and at any time, and his eyes widened
in surprise. Then he saw John Blaybourne's substantial figure on the second
horse, and not wanting to be seen himself, Piers ducked back into the mews.
In his haste he had not seen Constance riding pillion.

A puzzled Piers sat down heavily on a barrel to ponder Cecily's departure. He could not believe his goddess would choose to ride off alone with as lowly a fellow as John Blaybourne. Then he remembered how many times he himself had ridden alone with Cecily. But that was different, he argued, as his anger grew, for, on Christ's holy cross, nothing untoward would ever have occurred with him. Her grace was the purest, kindest, most honorable woman in the world, and he could not imagine himself laying a finger on her noble person. He went with Duke Richard's blessing—indeed, at his bidding, the falconer told himself. There was nothing secret about their rides to the hunt or his lessons in hawking. The whole household knew of them. Sweet Mother of God, what did Blaybourne have in mind? he thought fearfully. Was the duchess in danger? It did seem to Piers that she was riding freely of her own accord, but it was too dark for him to see if the man was holding her rein. Mayhap—he recoiled in horror—Blaybourne had abducted her! Now he was pacing uncomfortably in the low-ceilinged barn, and the birds under his care were beginning to be restless.

"Hush, my beauties. Stay still," he cajoled. "You will break your fast soon enough. But now I needs must think."

BY MIDMORNING, THE riders had reached the eastern bank of the Seine after cantering cross-country from Rouen. Following a tow path flanked by stands of comfrey, campion, and marguerites, they rounded a wide turn in the river affording them a view that took Cecily's breath away. Facing them on another sharp bend a mile away and dominating the spectacular landscape was Château Gaillard. Constance told her mistress that the extraordinary white fortress, whose many towers were lacking slate in their pointed turrets and whose walls were crumbling, had been Richard the Lionheart's pride and joy two centuries earlier.

"In Normandy," she explained in her accented English for the benefit of Blaybourne, "it is known as Coeur de Lion's one-year-old daughter. It has taken *six milles*—how you say? ah, yes—six thousand building-men only one year for finishing. But the English king died the next year, and soon Philip of France he captured it and then he . . . *nom de Dieu*, how you say *abandonné?*"

John let out a slow whistle of awe, but then frowned. "It commands the river from both directions. Why is it still not a stronghold?" he wondered aloud.

Constance chuckled. "I do not understand the ways of men thinking," she replied. "I know only the story."

The little village of Petit Andely hugged the riverbank in the shadow of Gaillard, the ubiquitous chalk cliffs of the Seine rising behind. The travelers were soon walking their horses along the main street leading to the magnificent but not yet completed church of Our Lady with its extensive abbey behind.

Blaybourne used the butt of his dagger to knock on the door of the hostel where pilgrims could lodge, which was run by a small order of Benedictines. They were all that was left of the first Christian convent in France, founded by the sainted Queen Clothilde. A grille in the door snapped open and a white-wimpled, bewhiskered nun peered out.

"We are pilgrims," Blaybourne had been instructed to say in French, and showed his scallop-shell badge. *"Anglais,"* he added, as if the accent had not already given him away.

Constance spoke up. *"Ma maîtresse a besoin de logement, ma soeur,"* she told the woman. "We need lodging for two or three nights, if you would be so kind. My mistress, who is a noble English lady, would like to take the waters and seek help from St. Clothilde."

Hearing her native tongue spoken so fluently, the sister opened the door and beamed at Cecily and Constance. *"Entrez, entrez, mesdames,"* she welcomed them, her smile revealing three missing teeth. "God's greeting to you. Follow me." Blaybourne, leading the two horses, was pointed the way to the stables, where, Cecily had no doubt, he would be sleeping.

Once it was known that Cecily was a noblewoman, she and Constance were ushered into a private room, sparsely furnished, with a small arched window open to the elements and overlooking a cloistered garden, where Cecily could see the object of her pilgrimage. The fountain could be approached by two paths, one for men and one for women, and several of both were slowly making their way toward the bubbling water caught in a room-sized stone basin.

As soon as their guestmistress had left them, informing Cecily that she was invited to the mother superior's table for supper, Cecily asked Constance to do a little exploring while she rested.

"I do not suppose one may request a bath," Cecily remarked, taking in the simple room and laughing. "But in case my husband does arrive early, I will lie down and nap so I do not look so travel-worn."

"I will return in an hour and help you dress for supper, *madame,*" Constance said, hanging a russet wool overgown on a peg. Cecily stepped out of her heavy riding skirt, which Constance shook and slapped to get rid of the dried mud.

Digging into the leather saddlebag, Constance brought out an ivory comb and laid it on the table. "I can at least find rosemary, lemon juice, and a bowl of water in the infirmary with which to cleanse the dust from your hair, your grace. The lemon does lighten it and give it luster."

When Constance had gone, Cecily knelt before the large wooden figure of Christ upon the cross that dominated one wall, the agony carved in excruciating detail upon the crucified man's face. She still could not bring herself to address the Father, Son, or Holy Ghost directly and so squeezed her eyes shut and thought of the Virgin, beseeching her to bless her and Richard's efforts to have a second son. She doubted anyone was heeding her. She suspected her lapse of faith had turned even the Blessed Mother from her. But she persisted, telling her beads and reciting the rote prayers diligently, and she hoped that the visit to the shrine would go a long way to restoring her faith.

As she reached the end of the rosary, something brushed her cheek, startling her, and her eyes instinctively opened. The room was empty. Puzzled, she glanced down at the floor and was astonished to see a white feather at her feet. Then she heard cooing and saw a dove preening upon the windowsill. She gasped, crossing herself.

"You are still with me, Virgin Mother," she whispered, awed. "I promise I shall not stray again."

As soon as she and Constance had attended Mass the next morning, Cecily made her way to the fountain with its statue of a stern Clothilde looking down on the pilgrims as they stepped into the cool water. In front of her a woman held a child with a withered arm, and behind her another woman, whose haggard face betrayed her pain, was quietly praying and clutching her stomach. When it was her turn, Cecily knelt on the grass, her peasant gown giving her freedom of movement, and, cupping her hands, she washed her face in the clear water and let it run down in rivulets between her breasts. She felt it trickle down over her belly and between her legs, and as she gazed intently at the saint's image, she begged Clothilde to make her fertile.

She backed away from the shrine and crossed herself. Glancing idly at the men on the other side, her heart leaped. Richard was in the middle of the queue, barefoot and dressed in a drab green tunic such as an archer might wear. His head was uncovered. He flashed a quick grin before concentrating on his own supplication to the saint. Cecily waited and watched as he immersed himself in the fountain to his knees, cupping his hands and drinking the sacred water.

In a very few minutes they were arm in arm, climbing the chalky footpath to the castle. Cecily could not stop talking. She was too excited to be with Richard on this adventure, where no one knew who they were and thus they were free to act as if they were simply townsfolk from somewhere else come to seek succor from Clothilde.

"And that is why this is called the Lionheart's one-year-old daughter," she finished explaining, as they gazed up at the hulk of white rock that seemed to scrape the clouds. Cecily added to Constance's story only slightly with a fact given her by Mother Agnes at supper. "The English king used to call it his Rock of Andely," the elderly nun had told Cecily.

"I have much admiration for Coeur de Lion, but I could wish I had this fortress at my disposal now," Richard grumbled, "or at least the money it must have taken to build. The council still pinches pennies when it comes to funding my work here, in truth."

Cecily slid her hand through the wide sleeve of his gown and tickled his ribs. "No talk of politics, no talk of war, no talk of money I beg of you, my love. We have more important business to attend to in these two days, do we not?" she teased, loving the surprised gurgle he always emitted when he was tickled. "We have all day to ourselves and no one will know to seek us here."

Unable to break the habit of checking over his shoulder for an attack, Richard had to make sure no one had followed them before he could relinquish himself to Cecily's advances. After walking a few paces back the way they had come and satisfying himself they were indeed alone, he turned around to find that she had disappeared.

"Cis? Cecily, where are you?" he called. She had never ceased to amaze him with her antics, he thought, ever since she was a little girl. "Are you expecting me to search for you?" he said. He was approaching a large unruly bush covered in wild white roses when suddenly Cecily popped up from behind it. He gasped. She was naked, her skin alabaster in the sunlight and her rosy nipples hardened by the cool breeze high above the river. She struck a pose for him. She had let down her glorious tresses and they fell to the curve of her hips. He was reminded of an ancient statue of the goddess Venus he had seen once, but when she stretched out her arms to him, he knew she was no goddess but a nymph, a siren, a naiad, or something so ethereal and yet so alive that he could only throw himself on her mercy and into her seductive embrace.

As though their experience at the fountain had somehow made their coupling sacred, each pleasured the other separately and in silence before they came together many times during that balmy afternoon with only the great white walls of the Rock of Andely as a towering witness.

Pleasantly spent, Richard rolled onto his back and gazed again at the moldering bastion of stone nearby, clasping Cecily's hand between their perspiring bodies. "'Tis strange, Cis, but I feel my ancestors all around me in this place, built as it was by another Richard Plantagenet. A good omen, I believe, for the begetting of another son of our royal house, do you not think?" he asked, turning to nuzzle her cheek.

"Aye, Richard," she agreed, squeezing his hand. She sat up to retrieve her gown and cover them both when a noise high up on the castle ramparts attracted their attention. As if to underscore Richard's pronouncement, one of the huge stones that had come loose over two centuries of neglect toppled at that moment and fell crashing onto the cliff below. Richard chuckled, but Cecily felt a frisson of fear. How odd that they should witness the event, she thought, her mind busy with the coincidence. What if it had a larger and more ominous meaning. What if it were a sign that the house of Plantagenet was crumbling. God's bones, Cis, she asked herself, why so maudlin after such ecstasy? She quickly crossed herself and chose not to bother Richard with her foolish fancy. Snuggling up to him, she closed her eyes and dozed.

ONLY LATER WOULD Cecily receive news from England that made the portent seem not as fanciful. Eleanor Cobham, duchess of Gloucester, long rumored to have dabbled in the dark arts, was denounced on the self-same day at St. Paul's Cross by an astronomer, who, together with a co-conspirator, had been arrested for making a waxen image of King Henry, with Eleanor's consent, and subjecting it to a slow flame. They had all believed that as the wax figure melted, so would Henry's health, and thus Humphrey of Gloucester would become king and Eleanor his queen. Her cohorts were charged with treason, and Eleanor, as an accessory, would have to be tried. The scandal damaged an already diminishing affection between Gloucester and the king, and the duke's influence and power was all but snuffed out like the candle that had melted the little wax doll.

* * *

THE TWO-DAY TRYST was over all too soon, and the journey back to Rouen was taken at a slower pace on Cecily's instructions. She wanted to savor every second of those idyllic days and was in no hurry to return to her routine in Rouen. Her horse found its own path as she sat in the saddle and daydreamed of the secret sojourn. With no one to disturb Richard with affairs of war or state and only Constance to flit silently about the chamber, dressing and undressing her mistress and then disappearing at all the right moments, the duke and duchess of York had known a freedom and tranquility they could not have dreamed possible. If Cecily conceived, she had told Richard upon parting, then she would know they were truly blessed. She determined the nuns of the abbey of St. Clothilde would receive benefices that would astonish them if a child was born of the Yorks' time there.

A loud cry of alarm jolted Cecily from her reverie, causing her horse to rear in fright. Cecily's expert horsemanship prevented her from being thrown, and she calmed the beast quickly. She had fallen behind John and Constance a little way, and now she saw John already on the ground, helping Constance down from their horse. Then Constance was clutching his arm and pointing to a clump of trees off to the left of the path. *"Là bas, monsieur!"* she cried. "I see something moving in the trees there."

"What is it, Master Blaybourne, are you hurt?" Cecily urged her horse alongside him. Then she saw what had startled them and looked about her in fear. An arrow was still quivering in the ground a few feet in front of Blaybourne's mount. "Your grace, you should make for the trees," Blaybourne replied, pointing to two oaks a few paces to their left. His tone was respectful but insistent. "And dismount if you can."

Cecily did as she was bidden, although her legs wobbled like a clump of disturbed frog spawn when her feet touched the ground. If this was an ambush, she thought vaguely, the outlaw was either unskilled with the bow or not very ambitious, for having the advantage of surprise, he had not let fly another arrow or shown himself. John had already unslung his bow and was moving from tree to tree, keeping the area in view where Constance had seen the antagonist.

Suddenly a man leaped down from an overhanging branch and knocked the giant archer to his knees. A fierce fight ensued, terrifying the two women, who peered out from behind a sturdy oak. The stranger, although young, was no stripling and was clothed in a mailed tunic and a hood that concealed his face. Blaybourne, who had drawn his knife, shouted angrily every time he lunged at the man. The younger man was quick on his feet, despite his size, and he too drew a knife. He was less skilled than Blaybourne and missed his quarry several times before achieving a gash on Blaybourne's arm. Blaybourne stepped back to assess his wound for a second, tripped over a broken branch, and fell heavily to the ground.

Before the aggressor could seize the advantage, Cecily had covered the ground between her hiding place and the men and, without thinking, screamed in English, "Stop! Stop this at once!" Immediately the young man put up his knife and started to run, but Blaybourne stuck out his leg and brought his assailant to the ground, and the weapon went flying. Seeing Blaybourne raising his knife to deliver a mortal wound, Cecily ran between them, still shouting, "Stop! Do you hear me, stop!" though now she remembered to use French. Then she saw who the attacker was and she gasped. "Piers? Piers Taggett! Sweet Mother of God, what were you thinking?"

Blaybourne lowered his arm, wincing as he did so, and blinked in amazement when he too recognized Taggett. "You bat-fowling, craven-clotted scoundrel, you might have killed her grace of York. You should be hanged for this!" He dragged Piers to his feet, twisting the falconer's arm painfully behind his back. "'Tis plain as a pikestaff you have not been trained to fight. And your skill with the bow is laughable," he spat.

"Leave him be, Master Blaybourne," Cecily commanded, taking Blaybourne aback, but he obeyed and let go of Piers's arm. "I thank you for your good service, indeed I do, but I would hear an explanation from Master Taggett." She looked at Piers sadly. "You have disappointed me, and I would know why."

Constance, seeing the danger was past, sidled up to Blaybourne and began to check his wound. Piers gawked at her, his eyes starting from his head. "D . . . Doctor LeMaitre." He choked on her name. "I d . . . did not . . . I never saw you. I only saw *him* with you, your gr . . . grace." He jerked his thumb in John's direction. "I thought—I thought my lady, your gr . . . grace had been carried off by . . . by . . ."

A sudden peal of laughter ended his miserable attempt to explain himself, and Cecily took out her kerchief to wipe her eyes. "I am sorry, Piers, I truly am," she apologized between chuckles, "but the idea is too funny. You thought Master Blaybourne was running away with me? Come, Constance, Master Blaybourne, you must see the humor," and she continued to laugh.

Blaybourne, however, was not amused. "You thought what? You ignorant clodpole. You clapper-clawed peasant. That I would abduct the duchess of York? Christ's blood, but you are more of an ass than you look." Picking up Piers's dagger, he appraised it before shoving it into his belt alongside his own knife. "I shall take charge of this. It may be needed as evidence when I give you up to the sheriff."

Piers began to stammer his apologies, and his humiliation was so apparent that Cecily silenced him by holding up her hand. "Let me understand you properly, Piers. How could you have thought Master Blaybourne was running away with me? Of all the ridiculous notions. The duchess and the archer, certes, that would make a good story." She chuckled again, but on seeing Piers's shame, stopped herself from mocking him further. "Let me hear your explanation," she said more gently.

Piers pulled himself together when he sensed the duchess was giving him the benefit of the doubt, and he retold the story of what he had seen at dawn at the mews. "I swear, I did not see Doctor Constance, your grace," he said. "Thus, without a chaperone, I imagined . . . well, you know what I imagined, and I could not let any man defile you!"

Cecily nodded and clucked her tongue as Blaybourne slapped his forehead and groaned, "Clay-brained scut!"

"Poor Piers, I can quite see why you might have misunderstood—" She broke off and frowned. "But how did you know to meet us here?"

"I found out which gate you left by and tried to follow, but I had no way of knowing which road you were taking. I searched a barn or two and even a church, but then I decided to wait to see if you would come back to the same gate, if you would come back at all. I made up my mind to stay one more night and then I would have sounded the alarm for you at the castle."

Cecily could not bring herself to retort that in three days she might have been well and truly used by Blaybourne or even dead. Instead she told him, "If you had but alerted Sir William Oldhall before venturing off to save me, you would have discovered that I was on a short pilgrimage to Les Andelys. Sir William knew where I was. I am sorry for you, Piers, but I trust you have learned a lesson."

He went down on one knee. "I humbly beg your pardon, your grace. I did not intend to kill Master Blaybourne, I swear it. I carefully aimed my arrow into the ground but to warn him, that be all. I hoped to seize him, take him back to the castle, and expose what he had done." He cast his eyes to the ground so that no one would see his tears. "In truth, I resented him for taking my place, and when this happened, I lost my head."

Cecily was touched by such devotion, but she knew she must punish the young man for his attack on Blaybourne. She would not do it publicly, she decided, as the incident was too embarrassing and would only serve to broadcast her absence more widely.

"I forgive you, Master Taggett, but 'tis Master Blaybourne's forgiveness you need to beg. Apologize to him at once," Cecily said sternly. "And come to me on the morrow for your punishment." Piers eased himself on his knees toward John and mumbled an apology. Blaybourne grunted but gave a curt nod, muttering, "Aye, I accept."

Cecily chewed on her lip as she watched the little scene, sorry for Piers but concerned more for Richard's champion archer's future.

"Master Blaybourne," she said finally, watching Constance bandage his arm as Piers rose and stepped out of John's long reach. "I fear your reputation may be sullied through this little adventure of mine, and I am sincerely sorry for it." She suddenly recalled the face she had seen at the window upon their departure and grimaced. Whoever it had been might have come to the same conclusion as Piers. How she wished she had followed her first instinct and had ridden out with a larger retinue, but that was as good as shutting the stable door after the horse had bolted, she decided. "I forbid you to continue your argument with Master Taggett upon our return," she continued, standing tall and gazing sternly at Blaybourne. "Aye, I see the anger in your face, and I cannot blame you for it, but I believe Piers was acting in good faith and tried to protect me. If you love your master, Duke Richard, then as soon as you deliver me safely back to Rouen, I wish you to rejoin him with a message I shall send with you. The fewer people who know about this, the better, and if you are not in Rouen to be talked about, then you can hold your head high. Am I right, Master Blaybourne? Will you do this for me, please?"

She turned those beautiful eyes on her devoted escort and tilted her head, waiting for his response.

"You are too good, your grace," Blaybourne said, going down on one knee and kissing her hand. "And Master Taggett is a fortunate man. You must know I am a devoted servant of your house, and if ever you have need of me . . ."

"I shall call upon you, Master Blaybourne. In the meantime, let us resume our journey. I shall have two escorts and a chaperone now, which might help to curb those wagging tongues."

With Piers leading Cecily's horse and Blaybourne and Constance a length behind, the little group made their way back to Bouvreuil, where the first person to greet them was Jacquetta Woodville with her attendant. Dear God, Cecily thought, she looks as though she is a cat who has caught the bird. She allowed Blaybourne to help her dismount, thanked him perfunctorily, but dismissed him with a curt, "See to the horses, Master Blaybourne," and turned her back on him to face the Woodville woman. She was proud Cis once again, and in control of the situation, she hoped. She must give no one watching any food for gossip.

"We were worried about you, your grace," Jacquetta purred, her eyes flitting over both of Cecily's big, handsome escorts. "Sir William told us you had gone to Les Andelys on a pilgrimage, but we thought you would be back ere now. I trust you are well?"

Cecily gave her a brilliant smile. "I have never felt better in my life, duchess, but 'tis sweet of you to care. Perhaps you too could benefit from the healing power of St. Clothilde."

A MONTH LATER, Richard rode through the Beauvoisine gate at the head of a weary but victorious army after relieving Pontoise. Richard wanted his troops to receive the accolades they deserved by entering Rouen in daylight, and so the army had camped overnight only a short distance away, giving citizens time to line up and cheer and the duke's kitchen staff time to prepare a feast.

Cecily was on the steps of the great hall of Bouvreuil to greet him, the rousing sounds of church bells and cheering crowds floating over the high castle walls. Richard dismounted and ran up to where she was waiting, the long train on her azure gown rippling around her and down the steps. He knelt and kissed her hand.

"My lord, I am overjoyed to see you," she said formally, surrounded as she was by the ladies of the castle and with Sir William at her side. "Praise be to God for returning you to us whole and for your victory."

"Then let us give thanks to Him before we dine, my lady," he said, rising. He turned to Sir William and extended his arm, which the other man grasped in friendship. "I give you God's greeting, sir," Richard said warmly. "I have some good news." Turning to those milling around to welcome him home, he waved his bonnet. "I am pleased to report that our commander of the army, Lord Talbot, has been given the earldom of Shrewsbury for his pains. It could not have been more deserved," he cried, as a cheer went up.

Cecily was only half listening, distracted by the sight of Sir Richard Woodville taking the moment when all eyes were on the duke of York to pull Jacquetta into his arms and kiss her long and hard. Cecily had done this herself many times at Fotheringhay, but there only the servants had witnessed it. Come now, Cecily, admit it, the act irritates you because you dislike the woman, does it not? Chastising herself for her unkind thought, she turned back to Richard in time to overhear Sir William say, "Your grace may not be as happy with a similar recognition by the king for service in France. Edmund Beaufort has lately been raised to earl of Dorset for his relief of Calais."

Richard scowled. "Indeed. I had not known he was even in France." Then he took Cecily's arm and changed the subject. "I trust all is in order here, my lady?" he said, before leading the way into the hall.

After a prayer of thanksgiving had been spoken by Father Lessey, the household and distinguished guests began to take their seats on either side of the trestle tables ranged down the hall. Amid the noise of benches scraping on the flagstones, musicians tuning their instruments, and a general murmur of conversation, Cecily and Richard were finally able to share a moment to talk quietly. Seated by themselves on the dais under a canopy decorated with York's royal coat of arms and hundreds of tiny white roses, Richard whispered that she was as beautiful as he had ever seen her.

Cecily's loving eyes held his as she replied, "Perhaps 'tis because I am carrying your heir, my lord," she murmured, relishing the expression of joy that suffused his weather-beaten face. "Aye, I know it must be a boy. St. Clothilde would not be so unkind."

17

Rouen, 1442 to 1445

*E*dward Plantagenet came noisily into this world on a drizzly day in late April after giving his mother due warning many times during her final trimester that he was impatient to be born.

"Never has my womb endured such a thrashing," Cecily told Richard one night in March before he left on yet another mission, this time to meet and negotiate peace terms with the duchess of Burgundy acting on behalf of her husband. Cecily chuckled. "Either he finds the accommodations too confining or else he is honing his knightly skills. I expect him to arrive early, I have no doubt of that! Conceived in the shadow of Richard the Lionheart's castle, perhaps we should name him for that king—or for you, my love."

"I have thought long about this, Cis, and I decided out there in the marshes of Pontoise that should we be blessed with an heir one day, Edward would be his name—for my grandfather of York and his sire, the third King Edward. We can save Richard for a subsequent son," he told her, winking. "I have an inkling there will be many, unless you lose your looks, my dear." He ducked as she flung her slipper at him, laughing.

Richard made certain to be at this birth, and he was much relieved to hear from Constance that Cecily's labor had been easy. Edward had been in such a hurry to make his entrance that the servants had not even had time to boil water, Constance told him. The next day, when Richard was allowed in to see mother and son, he and Cecily laughed as they watched the infant struggle with his swaddling bands, his chubby face screwed up with the effort. Not unexpectedly, his rage soon erupted in cries that made Richard's greyhound take cover under the bed. Cecily stroked the boy's blond wisps of hair and rocked him gently in her arms.

"Soft, Ned," she cooed, "all in good time you will run around, play, and be king of the castle." Edward stared unblinking at his mother, but her voice and the rocking seemed to calm him, for he stopped wriggling and closed his eyes.

"He looks like your father, Cis, and I am happy he has your yellow hair. Such a contrast to our Anne, who has a look of Isabel about her, I think."

Cecily watched him as he studied his son. She noticed that his face appeared care-worn of late. Not surprising, she thought, with the responsibilities of government on his shoulders and the bad news that the French are gaining ground again. It was bad enough in Normandy—Pontoise had soon been claimed back by the French following the fleeting English victory in August—but King Charles had turned his attention on the long-held English province of Gascony in the southwest, where several nobles had defected from their allegiance to Henry. Richard had no hand in the latter losses, but Normandy was under his jurisdiction. She had witnessed his outbursts of temper against the council in England when he received only five thousand of his promised salary of twenty-thousand pounds to cover the campaign expenses of an army for a full year. How could he meet wages and victualing, let alone arm the troops and maintain military control in the province?

"I am regent, not a miracle-worker," he had shouted to Talbot and the other commanders one evening in the winter, after learning the French had advanced on Crotoy on the northeastern coast and Harfleur and Caen in the southwest of Normandy.

The news from England that a proposal of marriage was being considered by the council between the daughter of the count of Armagnac, the most prominent of the Gascon nobles, and twenty-one-year-old King Henry took Richard by surprise, believing the Beaufort faction was leaning toward peaceful negotiations with France.

"It will anger King Charles, that is certain," Richard explained as a puzzled frown creased Cecily's forehead. "And I wonder what the peace-mongers on the council are thinking. How can it help the cause of peace negotiations with France? Armagnac hates Charles."

Cecily asked what Humphrey of Gloucester, the hawk, might make of it all, guessing that Richard's thoughts were more closely aligned with his. "He is finished, Cis. Whatever influence he had as uncle of the king was buried under the debris of Eleanor Cobham's disgrace. But I believe he would die before he allowed the province to fall.

"But enough of serious talk," Richard said, yawning. He reached over and patted her lovingly. "I am for bed, my love, and you must have your rest. Will you call Rowena?"

Now Cecily sorted through that conversation as she put up her hand to stroke his dark hair. Aye, he has his worries, she mused, while mine seem so mundane.

"Do I have your permission to find a nursemaid, Richard?" she asked, remembering the most important of them. "Anne needs more guidance now that she is almost three. And with Ned joining her, 'tis important to have a constant companion in the nursery."

Richard nodded. "I will have the steward make inquiries, my love," he murmured, careful not to disturb the now peaceful baby. "And speaking of Ned, we should christen him tomorrow, Cis, as I must leave again in a few days. Lady Say and Thomas Scales have agreed to stand as godparents, as we discussed. Though I think we should have asked her grace of Bedford." He chuckled at her look of horror. "I am only half teasing you, my love. Poor Jacquetta, she can do no right, can she?" he continued, and on seeing Cecily's stubborn mouth: "Ah, well, no matter. As for the christening, 'twould be fitting to have the ceremony for our heir in the cathedral, do you not think?"

Cecily made a face. "Oh, do we have to?" It seemed unfair to her that mothers should be forbidden to enter a church after giving birth until a cleansing period had passed, which meant that they always missed their children's baptisms. "I know 'tis not customary for the mother to be there, but if we had it in the chapel here at the castle, I could use the squint and watch unseen. No one would know, and I would not be breaking the church law because I would not be physically in the chapel." She ran a finger down his arm and around the back of his hand. "I did it for your knighting ceremony, remember? Please, Dickon," she entreated, "Constance will not allow me out of bed for long, but 'tis only a few steps to—"

Richard laughed and slid off the bed. "Who am I to stop you, my pampered rose of Raby? The chapel it shall be. I cannot think Edward will care one way or the other." He laughed. "Although wherever 'tis done, he will not take kindly to being dipped in cold water! I do not envy Elizabeth Say her duty."

His greyhound scrabbled out of his hiding place and nuzzled Richard's hand, his tail waving. Just then a flea attacked his neck, and in his attempt to rid himself of the pest with his back paw, his leg thumped loudly on the red and white tiled floor.

Cecily waved them off. "Take yourselves and your fleas away. The wet-nurse will be here anon. Rowena," she called to her attendant, who was seated in the window, sewing, "I pray you, fetch little Anne so she can meet her baby brother. She is confused by the idea that she is no longer the baby of the family. I pray she will not be jealous."

"That is up to you, my love," Richard said, giving her a meaningful look. "Aye, we have an heir, but he was not the first—at least, not in my affections. Henry holds that place." Richard kissed her forehead and straightened his grosgrain short coat. "I think I will take a few hours to hunt, with your permission, my dear." He grinned as Cecily groaned. "You will be back in the saddle ere long, never fear."

There was a knock at the door and Richard went to open it on his way out. Expecting to see Rowena with his daughter, he was caught by delighted surprise to see his sister standing on the threshold.

"Is it convenient for me to see Cecily and your son?" Isabel Plantagenet asked, smiling up at him. She had been shy with him the first few times they had spoken during the stay in Rouen. She could not reconcile the grown man, husband, and father with the little six-year-old boy she had been parted from after their father's execution and attainder. She had been pledged to Thomas Grey before that awful day twenty-seven years ago when they learned of their father's fate, but the Grey family had wanted nothing to do with a traitor's daughter and had annulled the betrothal. Instead, at eight, she was brought up in the household of her Aunt Anne Bourchier and eventually was betrothed and married to that lady's son, Henry. The siblings had only been reunited a little before the departure from England.

"Certes, you may, sister," Richard enthused, kissing her. "The wet-nurse will be here anon, but judging from my son's well-formed lungs, you will know when it is time to leave. God's greeting to you, I will leave you ladies in peace. Cecily," he called back to his wife, "Isabel is here to see you."

Cecily patted the place on the bed that Richard had just vacated and wished her sister-in-law a good day. After Isabel had inquired after Cecily's health and the birthing ordeal, Cecily transferred the sleeping Edward into the crook of his aunt's arm. "God be praised, nephew, what a handsome fellow you are to be sure."

"And how is your own babe, my lady? He is half a year now, I believe. Six boys! How fortunate you are."

Isabel smiled wistfully. "Aye, I suppose I am, but in truth I envy you your daughter."

At that moment, the object of Isabel's envy entered the room, clutching Rowena's hand. Her big gray eyes took in the scene at the bed and, dropping a creditable curtsey to her mother and the countess, she waited to be invited closer. It was then that Cecily saw another child hiding behind Rowena's long dagged sleeves. She frowned, and Rowena propelled the little girl forward, instructing her to curtsey. Cecily was astonished by the child's beauty.

"'Tis Elizabeth Woodville, your grace," Rowena apologized. "She and Anne are inseparable in the nursery, and with her mother also confined . . ."

Cecily cut her off. "Keep her by you, I pray you," she said, and Isabel's eyebrow arched in surprise at the sharp tone. Elizabeth seemed well behaved and passive enough, she thought, and 'twas true that Jacquetta was confined to her quarters awaiting the birth of her fourth child.

Cecily beckoned to Anne, putting her finger to her lips, and the child tip-toed slowly toward the big bed, not once taking her eyes off the white bundle on Isabel's lap.

"He dead?" she whispered, curious. Without warning, she poked her finger in Edward's cheek.

"Nan!" Cecily admonished her, taken aback. "Certes, he is not dead."

"Last baby is dead," Anne said matter-of-factly. "I saw it."

Cecily's heart constricted. She reached down and set the little girl next to her on the feather mattress, throwing off Anne's dainty red slippers and tucking her legs under the coverlet. Anne beamed and snuggled next to her mother. "That was a long time ago, Nan. This is Edward, your new baby brother. You may call him Ned for short. I promise you he will not die." She mentally crossed herself and muttered, "If God has mercy on me."

"Is he not beautiful, Anne?" Isabel covered the prayer to help Cecily. "See how fair his hair is, just like your mama's."

Suitably distracted, Anne had put out her hand to touch the golden head, when Edward suddenly sneezed and opened his eyes. Anne giggled. "Baby ashoo," she said, fascinated. "Can he talk?"

"Nay, he has to wait until he is as big as you before he can talk," Cecily explained. Edward began to fuss and work his mouth. "Perhaps you can teach him, sweeting. He has a loud voice, just you wait and see. He is hungry and will soon let everyone know." She called to Rowena. "Is the wet-nurse ready?"

As Rowena took the baby from Isabel, Anne skipped over to her friend Elizabeth and took her by the hand to show her the baby. Cecily watched as the doll-like face of Jacquetta's daughter bent over Edward and studied him earnestly. "Hush, baby, don't cry," Elizabeth lisped in her high, silvery voice. "All will be well, you shall see."

EDMUND BEAUFORT WAS, like his uncle the cardinal, a tall, haughty man with a prominent nose and piercing blue eyes. But Edmund was half the cardinal's age, blessed with a strong, athletic frame and a winning smile that hid the cruel streak Cecily had witnessed often when they were children. He had ridden into Bouvreuil's courtyard that summer with his retinue wearing the blue and white Beaufort badge to join with Richard in negotiating with the duchess of Burgundy for help in reclaiming English lost lands in the south-west. They would all be leaving in a few days to meet her in Anjou, the lordship of which province Edmund Beaufort had been granted by the crown.

"One day Duke Philip is fighting with us against France and the next day he is negotiating a truce behind our backs," Cecily said to her brother and cousin one evening following a quiet supper in the Yorks' solar. "Where does he stand now? And why do you believe the duchess will be easier to deal with than her husband, cousin?"

The remains of Cecily's favorite sparviter's pie had been cleared away. Richard and Edmund sat on high-backed cushioned chairs at either end of the table. Cecily had chosen a stool on which to perch and was plucking absently at her psaltery, more interested in the men's talk than her music.

Edmund gazed at her. "Still the outspoken Cis I remember," he said, amused. Turning back to Richard, he arched a bushy brow. "Have you not curbed that tongue of hers yet, my lord? I must confess I am unused to being interrupted by a female while I am in serious conversation. I must be fortunate in my dear wife, for I do not believe Eleanor would ever attempt it."

Then Eleanor Beauchamp must be a ninny, Cecily thought, but held her tongue. She was too intrigued to know how Richard would respond.

Richard laid a tender hand on Cecily's shoulder. "Then I am sorry for you, Lord Edmund," he said pleasantly. "I feel fortunate that my dear wife has a mind as good as yours or mine, and I find her questions—and indeed her advice—both insightful and wise." He saw her triumphant smile for a second before she lowered her head modestly to her instrument. "To answer your earlier question, my dear, you have the measure of Burgundy, but, you may remember, his wife Isabella shares the same grandfather as you and Edmund here—John of Gaunt. She is thus a Plantagenet princess, and as Gaunt was also duke of Aquitaine, she has no desire to see it fall into French hands. You see," he said pointedly for Edmund's sake, even though he still addressed his wife, "a woman can be of influence when it comes to politics—as well as being useful for her family ties."

Edmund had the grace to nod. "Touché, cousin," he acquiesced. But he did not care for being patronized, and his next remark had an edge to it that Cecily did not like. "However, it does not mean, dear cousin, that a daughter is as important as a son when it comes to what really matters: inheritance and succession. But I will concede that Duchess Isabella is important to our cause because of her Plantagenet blood."

An awkward silence fell for a moment as his implication tumbled like a smoldering cinder from the fire onto dried rushes. All were surely thinking of Richard's claim to the throne through a female ancestor. Quickly setting aside her psaltery, Cecily rose to fetch more wine.

"Will you hunt on the morrow, my lords?" she asked brightly, doing her best to distract any such thoughts. "I should dearly like to try my new merlin. She is from Turkey, Edmund, and has had to bear with my ill temper while I mourn my sweet Nimuë—my first bird and a precious gift from Richard."

"Certes, I would not say no, madam," Edmund said, relieved at the change of subject and annoyed with himself for putting the Mortimer claim in the Yorks' minds. He had not taken the measure of the younger man yet. His uncle the cardinal had given instructions to watch for any disloyalty to the king or mismanagement in France by the dangerous duke of York.

"Then that is settled, my lord, you shall ride with Richard," Cecily said. "Forgive me, I should have asked sooner, but how does my cousin of Somerset?"

"My brother enjoys high favor with the king and Suffolk," Edmund said. "'Twas not easy for John to return to England and a life of freedom. He brooded upon his eighteen years as a French hostage, and he thought he had been forgotten at court. His marriage greatly improved his humor, although he laments he has not sired a son yet by his wife. He is an ambitious man—as are all Beauforts, I believe, and I include myself in the list," he boasted and then smiled. "Although I am naught but the lowly fourth son with few prospects."

Richard harrumphed. "Despite your lowliness you have not fared ill, my lord. You have the king's ear; you have a powerful uncle; have had an earldom bestowed on you but lately; and, with two of your other brothers being long deceased, I believe you stand next to John in line to inherit the Somerset title, even if you are fourth born."

Again the supercilious arching of the Beaufort brow, which Cecily determined to practice as soon she was alone in front of a mirror. "It seems you are counting my blessings where I am not. The earldom of Somerset does not carry with it one hundredth the wealth of your title, York," he retorted. "And by the way, I do not anticipate my brother's death any time soon. But your zealous interest in my family disturbs me."

Richard began to rise. "Christ's nails, but you are insufferable!"

Cecily banged her cup down hard on the table, startling the two men, who were glaring at each other across the green velvet cloth. "Sweet Jesu! Stop bickering, the two of you. You are behaving like two bullyboys. Next you will be wrestling each other to the floor, and rather than witness that humiliation, I believe I shall retire." She called to Constance and Rowena. "Ladies, pray accompany me to my chamber. Let us leave the boys to squabble."

Both men got to their feet, bowing to the duchess and looking sheepish. "I give you a good night," Cecily said. The quarrel had unnerved her. Her knees felt weak and she needed to gather her thoughts. The tension seemed an inauspicious start to a journey leading to a negotiation, she believed. She hoped she would have a chance to point that out to Richard before the two rode off to Anjou. It was clear to her as a summer sky that Richard of York and Edmund Beaufort would never be friends. Even worse, Edmund might prove to be another wedge between her husband and the king.

By THE TIME Richard returned—without Edmund—the summer was almost over. A month later the golden days of September lent a rosiness to Rouen's white walls and turned the apples in the many orchards a deep ruby red. Cecily could just see the tips of the turning trees as she luxuriated in her copper tub and Constance applied a lemon and chamomile infusion to her hair. She stroked her smooth thighs with a cake of castile soap and smiled to herself.

The last time she had bathed, she had gone with her sister-in-law and their attendants to a spot along the Seine to escape the city heat. Their escorts had erected a small canopy on the riverbank, and they had spent the August afternoon dabbling their feet in the cool water, splashing each other, picking flowers, and dozing in the shade.

"Ho, there!" a familiar voice had called from the rise behind them. The escorts reached for their weapons.

"Richard!" Cecily cried in delight, squeezing water from the bottom of her gown. "'Tis his grace the duke, brave sirs," she had assured the soldiers. "Put away your swords."

Richard kissed her hand and gave her a sly wink. "How now, Cis? I should know why you are breaking my rule about not straying too far from the city. But, in truth, I am too glad to see you to worry." He took Isabel's outstretched hand and kissed it too. "My two favorite family members," he said, and then corrected himself, "two favorite adult family members."

"Pish, Dickon! That is no compliment—we are your only adult family members," Cecily recalled retorting. "Come, sit and take some ale. If I may say so, you look as though you have walked from Angers. I trust your mission bore fruit?"

Richard nodded. "'Tis not over, but we make progress. Edmund has returned to England to report. I was happy to see the back of him, in truth, for he is arrogance incarnate. I suspect he will take all the credit for our dealings with Duchess Isabella. Once again, he will be at the king's side and I shall not."

"Tell me more anon, my lord. For now, forget the road, your worries, and your weariness and sit with us," Cecily had cajoled.

After seeing to his horse and refreshing himself with some ale, Richard removed his sweaty tabard and leather jerkin and sighed with relief to be finally unencumbered. Cecily was offering the horse a handful of grass, so Richard took the opportunity of asking his sister in a whisper if she would mind returning to the city with the escort on her own.

"I will take care of Cecily," he murmured.

Isabel chuckled. "I have no doubt of that, Brother. But do not be long or the tongues will wag," she teased him.

Richard let out a neigh of laughter. The familiar sound had filled Cecily with pleasure.

Aye, life was always sweeter when Richard was there, she thought, feeling around for the slippery soap.

If she remembered rightly, it was not long before she and Richard were alone on the riverbank, and after Richard's nimble fingers had helped her to disrobe, Cecily plunged naked into the shallow water. Richard hurriedly finished undressing himself and then followed her. They soon stood face to face, moving their hands over each other's wet body until their fingers intertwined and their lips met on a whispered "I love you." Richard guided her hand to his prick and let her decide when it was time. I made him wait far too long, she thought, sighing now, as she recalled how she had seductively tongued the water trickling off his torso.

"Ah, cruel Cis," he had moaned. "I fear I must cut your teasing short or—"

He crushed her to him, thrusting into her and crying out in his release. Cecily knew then, with a sly smile, that she had waited exactly long enough.

Cecily let out a little moan in remembered pleasure of that day, and Constance, thinking she had pulled too roughly on a strand of hair, apologized. Suddenly, her mistress sat up, splashing water onto the floor.

"What day is it, Constance?"

"Why, 'tis the feast of the nativity of the Virgin, your grace. We celebrated with a special rosary this morning."

"Aye, I know that, Constance. But has it not been five weeks since my last course? I forget."

Constance knew very well that Cecily was late. A long time ago she had taken over the ritual of preparing her mistress for the monthly confinement. However, it was not her place to badger the duchess into an examination. "You are correct, madame. 'Tis more than five weeks."

Cecily turned a radiant face to her physician. "Then perhaps we had better see if I am with child."

WITH ANOTHER BABE on the way, Ned and Anne healthy and happy in the nursery with the new nursemaid, Anne, who came from the Norman region of Caux, and Richard ensconced at Rouen for a long period, Cecily thought she could not be happier. Yet Jacquetta Woodville was still a thorn in her side.

Throughout the past year, Cecily had tried to define the origin of her dislike for the younger woman but had never been able to put her finger on it. It simply lurked in the shadows to be puzzled over from time to time. A tidbit of information following the tryst at Les Andelys had come to her through Rowena. It had angered Cecily, but as it was mere servants' gossip, she had tried to bury it. Jacquetta was said to have disparaged Constance's skills on more than one occasion, calling the doctor a charlatan. Cecily was well aware that Jacquetta believed she had magical powers—how many times had the woman brought her water-witch ancestress into a conversation—but as Cecily herself was not above believing in magic, she had grudgingly dismissed Jacquetta's distrust of Constance as jealous disbelief in the doctor's more scientific method of healing. It was, however, yet another reason for Cecily's dislike, justified or not.

Cecily could not say when she became resolved to treat Jacquetta with the utmost civility for Richard's sake—especially after both women had given birth to heirs within a month of each other—but she was happy that Richard had noticed the concession. He had commended her on her graciousness more than once, and indeed there was no one who would have guessed the two women did not share the highest regard for each other.

"Your Elizabeth is the most beautiful child I have ever laid eyes on," Cecily had told Jacquetta when they were both in the castle nursery, admiring their respective sons. "And little Anthony here is a bonny boy, as well. But then they have very handsome parents."

Jacquetta had smiled beatifically and in turn had praised Edward's lustiness. "He does not have the look of his father, does he?" she had said, all innocence. "He has the look of a Norseman about him. Was your father a large man?"

Cecily feigned amusement. Lowering her voice, she said conspiratorially, "My dear duchess, if 'twere not such a high-flown idea, I might think you were implying my husband is not Edward's father!" Jacquetta laughed merrily too. "But to answer your question. Aye, my father was broad-shouldered. But you must not forget, madam, that my husband is a Plantagenet. His grandsire King Edward was a giant of a man."

Afterward they had conversed pleasantly of this and that, but deep in her heart Cecily still distrusted the beautiful Jacquetta.

"I AM REGENT of France by *their* appointment," Richard railed at Cecily not long after the birth of their second living son, Edmund. He had entered the sunny solar waving a letter and slapped at it every time he made a point. "Now they are sending Somerset, that braggart who claims to be a military genius, to defend Guyenne behind my back. Somerset!"

Cecily looked up from her needlework. "Soft, my lord," she said sternly, frowning a reminder that they were not alone. Isabel and her attendant, Margaret Oldhall, Rowena, and Constance were all plying their needles diligently, and in a corner Anne was playing quietly with Edward while the nurse looked on. When Anne heard her father's voice, she squealed and ran headlong to embrace his knees. He picked her up and gave her a noisy kiss on the mouth, making the little girl wipe her face and giggle.

"Forgive me, ladies, my temper ran away with me," he apologized with a sheepish grin. "Pay me no heed. I thank you for not repeating my words." He swung his daughter round and round, making her laugh with delight, and the toddler Edward began to take a few halting steps toward them, determined to join in the sport. "*Tiens!* Ned is walking well," Richard cried proudly. "And pray look at that strength of will. He has his mother's stubborn streak, I warrant. Good boy, Ned. You want your turn, eh?"

When he had thrown the delighted Edward up in the air a few times, he carried him back to the nurse, with Anne holding his other hand. *"Madame, je vous rends vos charges,"* he told the plump young woman, who took Edward back onto her lap and gave him a smacking kiss.

"Gramerci, milord," she responded, as little Nan clasped her arms about Nurse Anne's neck.

Richard nodded, satisfied to see how much his children approved of Cecily's choice of nursery attendant. He returned to Cecily. "May we walk together, my lady?"

Cecily put down her sewing and rose. "Constance, pray accompany me." She was pleased at how quickly she had regained her energy since Edmund's birth, and with the salves Constance had prepared, her belly had returned to its smooth flatness albeit with a few more stretch marks. She had been touched by her husband's unbridled pleasure at fathering another son. He had already bestowed his lands in Normandy on the baby and had had him baptized in Rouen's Notre Dame cathedral with great pomp in order to show his goodwill to the English Normans. "He will be a great Norman landowner, while Edward will inherit my lands in England," he explained. "So, it seems wise for us to have him christened in Normandy's most important church."

They descended the newell stair and walked across the courtyard, under the gatehouse, and into the city. It was late in the afternoon, and the farmers were taking their unsold wares back to their fields and farms. Two pikemen followed behind Constance as the duke and duchess made their way down the dirt road between the small houses and garden plots toward the river.

"Now, Richard, tell me why you are so angry," Cecily said, savoring the smell of roasted larks from a cookshop. She was used to Richard's outbursts, but while they never lasted long, they were sometimes ill timed and could be followed by rash deeds.

Richard told her that John Beaufort, duke of Somerset, had been given the title lieutenant and captain-general of Aquitaine and France and put in command of an expedition to secure Gascony. Richard was glowering when he added that the council considered John of Somerset's expedition more worthy of financing than paying Richard's wages or sending more troops for Normandy. "And," he continued, gesticulating wildly with his free arm, "and

he has been made a duke with precedence over all other dukes save Gloucester and me." He had forgotten where he was for a moment and had raised
his voice noticeably. People were stopping to stare at the unusual sight of the
Yorks strolling down the street like any other citizens.

"Forgive me, Cis," he said, lowering his voice when he caught her worried
look. "But did I not finally gain a truce with Duchess Isabella as desired by the
council? Aye, I did. And here I am performing my duty to the king to keep
Normandy safe for him to the best of my ability, even though I lack the promised funds to do so. And the council sees fit to send Somerset with that money
and those troops I have been requesting all these many months to defend
Gascony instead. 'Tis no wonder I am angry. I sent Talbot to put my position
to the council earlier this year, as you know." His voice rose again. "This is their
response, and it is insufferable!"

"Richard, control yourself," Cecily admonished him. "People are watching."
More gently, she said, "It is insufferable that they have placed Somerset above
you. I would dearly love to know what he is planning. He cannot be over you
here in France. You are regent. And I wonder if Edmund knew of any such
plan when he traveled with you?"

Richard turned with Cecily into a church, and Cecily, seeing that being in
private would be best, motioned to Constance to wait outside. He pulled a
letter out of his belt and began to read: "'All the defenses of Normandy must
be on high alert and York must, in addition, give all possible help and comfort
to Somerset,' so says Garter Herald. And Somerset will have authority over
all English lands in France 'where York comes not' is what is writ. By grant-
ing Somerset authority in Maine and Anjou, as well as Gascony, it leaves me
only Normandy." Richard put his head in his hands. "I cannot hold Normandy
without reinforcements, Cis. Talbot at Dieppe is failing to keep the dauphin
at bay, and little by little all that was won by King Harry at Agincourt will be
lost."

Cecily chewed on her lip. It was not fair, she thought. Richard had proved
to be a good and fair governor, so she had gleaned from Constance, who often
brought back tidbits of information from her French friends and relatives.
True, other than at Pontoise, he had not shown himself to be a military man
though she knew he would hate to hear such criticism, but he was not receiving promised support from England, so how could he prove otherwise, in
truth? But to send Somerset! Why, the man had been taken prisoner in Anjou
at seventeen and had spent as many years captive of the French, and now, four

years later, he is thought to have the military experience to command this expedition. Such lack of wisdom! What power the Beauforts must wield. They have hoodwinked the king, Suffolk, and the council. No wonder Richard lost his temper, she mused.

"Oh, I forgot the amusing part of this story," Richard said, with a harsh laugh, glancing down at the letter. "Somerset took an oath he would do nothing to 'York's dis-worship.'" He slapped at the paper again. "Ha! By accepting this command, he has already broken that vow." He reminded her that he had sworn an oath of fealty to King Henry and had a contract with the council to govern English France. To resign that commission would be foolhardy, but to break that oath was treason. "And I have no intention of reminding those already wary of me on account of my past," he declared. "I owe a debt to Henry's father that I was not attainted along with mine." He grimaced. "What can I do, Cis? My hands are tied."

Cecily had no answer, but she was frustrated by her husband's inaction. "Complaining will get us nowhere, my dear. Surely there is someone on the council you can trust to ask for help. Now is the time to assert yourself. You dreamed of being a great commander. Show them that you can be." She sighed, once more wishing she were a man, and then tempered her advice. "But perhaps you could start by asking God's help while we are in His house?" Feeling guilty for her impatience, she resorted to humor. "I, for one, will be on my knees every day praying for Somerset to fall on his bony arse. Come," she said, pulling him toward a colorful statue of the Virgin holding a rather plump Infant Jesus, "let us not waste any time."

A priest poked his head out of a confessional when he heard the unexpected and unusual braying laughter disturbing the quiet sanctity of his church. The priest's presence curtailed Richard's amusement, and taking his wife's hand, he knelt with her on the stone floor.

"Hear me, O Lord, in my quest for patience in my duty to the king," he murmured, "and may my worthiness over my rival not go unnoticed." The rest of his prayer was silent.

Cecily prayed only that her husband might heed her advice and do more to help himself to fulfill his dreams.

RICHARD'S PRAYERS WERE answered in the space of a twelvemonth.

John, duke of Somerset, landed in Cherbourg late in the summer and immediately dealt a crippling blow to relations between the English in

Normandy and their allies the Bretons by ransacking La Guerche, a town in Brittany, for no reason other than to get the elders to bribe him to leave. Infuriated, the Bretons joined with the French that autumn in attacking English shipping along the Norman coast. After these embarrassments and a stern reprimand from the council, Somerset then failed to meet any of the council's goals with regard to confronting the French and defending Gascony. He was immediately recalled for squandering English money and troops, fell into a decline, and died—some said by his own hand—on the twenty-seventh of May, 1444, leaving only a baby girl, Margaret, as his heir.

This might have been better news, Richard told Cecily, if his place—though with the lesser title of earl—had not been taken by his brother and, Richard feared, his enemy Edmund Beaufort.

"We have simply changed one Beaufort brother named Somerset for another," Richard said. "And this Somerset has the brains the other did not. Edmund is a far more dangerous proposition."

"Pish," replied Cecily airily to hide her misgivings.

18

France, 1444 to 1446

*T*hree days before John of Somerset's death, Henry the Sixth of England and France was formally betrothed, with Suffolk standing as proxy, to Margaret, the fourteen-year-old daughter of René, duke of Lorraine, count of Anjou, king of Naples and Sicily. More significantly, Margaret's aunt was queen of France.

Richard and Cecily, who had recently added a daughter, Elizabeth, to their growing family, were surprised by the match. Isolated as they were from the English court, they were not privy to the reasons behind the choice, though they recognized it was surely time for twenty-three-year-old Henry to take a bride.

"I understand why Armagnac's daughter was eventually abandoned," Richard murmured during one of his visits to Cecily and their new baby. "But René of Anjou's daughter? She is not even the elder of his girls and she can have very little in the way of a dowry. What was Suffolk thinking?"

"As part of the terms of his release from the Tower, did not the duc d'Orléans give his word to Suffolk to negotiate a peace between us and France?" Cecily asked, watching while Richard rocked baby Bess in the crook of his arm. "Perhaps he thought this would please the French enough to come to terms, so maybe it was not Suffolk's idea."

Richard grunted. "He backs it, I am certain, because Gloucester opposes it. It still persists—the Gloucester faction against the Beaufort faction. And the king is in the middle."

"Which side would you come down on if you were there?"

"Neither—or the king's, I suppose." Richard kissed the baby's cheek. "We shall find out soon enough why the choice was made. Suffolk will be here anon."

* * *

"MY DEAR YORK, his grace the king is in need of an heir, and we cannot wait until one of King Charles's daughters is of an age to bear a child," William de la Pole, earl of Suffolk, explained. "Aye, a royal French bride would have been desirable, but I regret to say we are not in a good negotiating position. René d'Anjou is Charles's brother-in-law and so Margaret is close enough to be of use, we hope. Before I left, I told Parliament I was merely the messenger doing the council's bidding. 'Twill not be my fault if the arrangement fails."

Richard caught Cecily's fleeting look of surprise. They had both presumed Suffolk was squarely behind the match.

"And peace?" Richard arched an eyebrow. "Is it possible after almost a hundred years of war?"

Suffolk was chagrined. "A truce of twenty-three months was all the French offered." But then he looked Richard straight in the eye and declared, "But the first true one since King Harry died, and I am proud of it. The citizens of Tours themselves were enthusiastic. It was amusing but moving to hear them cry in English, 'Peas, peas' upon the conclusion of the betrothal. And, if you noticed, your people here in Rouen cheered me when I entered the city." He resented having to defend himself to the duke of York, and it showed, Cecily noted.

"But my lord," interjected Cecily, cheerfully intent on lightening the mood, "you must indulge the ladies here who wish to know about our new queen. Is she beautiful?"

"She is perhaps the only woman I have met who might hold a candle to you, your grace," Suffolk said. Then he felt his wife's presence beside him. "I beg your pardon, I forgot to preface that with: besides my wife, Lady Alice, to be sure."

Alice de la Pole smiled, amused. "No need to dissemble, my lord, I know where I stand in your eyes." Suffolk drew her hand to his lips, and Cecily was surprised to see the spark between husband and wife.

Alice's brown eyes swept over Cecily, from the sable-fur-trimmed hem of her blue cloth of silver gown to the translucent gauze floating from her jeweled headdress, and she added sweetly, "Margaret of Anjou is of astonishing beauty, wit, and intelligence, duchess. We all pale beside her." A few quiet gasps could be heard from the assembled company at the slight, and all waited for Proud Cis's response.

Cecily regarded Alice de la Pole, Chaucer's granddaughter, with interest.

So this is the awful stepmother my dear sister-in-law was saddled with once, she mused. She inclined her head imperceptibly. "Is that so, my lady?" she said haughtily. "Then . . ." Richard's elbow pressed hard into her side. "Then I for one cannot wait to be presented," she finished, ruefully resisting a more caustic comment.

Before Suffolk left for England, he had a private word with Richard that was passed along to Cecily in pillow talk.

"What would you think of our proposing to the French king that our Ned be betrothed to one of his daughters? Aye, that was my reaction," he admitted, feeling her turn abruptly in his arms. "'Twas Suffolk's own suggestion, believe it or not. He thinks it might shore up goodwill for a peace."

"A king's daughter for Ned?" Cecily could hardly keep the excitement from her voice. "Do not delay, my love, for fear she is claimed elsewhere first."

WHEN THE EARL of Suffolk left Rouen a week later, he took Sir Richard Woodville and his family with him. Jacquetta had now produced five children, the latest born not long before the Yorks' Elizabeth. With the truce there was little for a soldier of Woodville's experience to do. As well, not being a great lord like Richard, the knight did not have retainers to take care of his estate and business, and he had asked permission of Richard to return to England with Suffolk.

Cecily had come to terms with her unexplained dislike of Jacquetta, and she took the news now with a measure of regret. A bond had formed among all the English ladies, and, as the York and Woodville children grew up side by side in the castle nursery, the two mothers had tried to rub along. Indeed, in April, before Bessie's birth, Richard told Cecily that he would have to ask the widow of his mentor Bedford to stand as godparent to the baby with Lord Talbot, "for we are running out of English noblewomen here in Rouen," he teased. Then more seriously, he said, "I would have you obey me in this, Cecily." He was relieved when she had voiced no objection.

SNOW WAS FALLING lightly on a late February evening the following year when a horseman cantered through the castle gate with a message from the duke of York that he would be returning from his progress to Lisieux in western Normandy earlier than expected.

Sir William brought the message along the dark passageway between his chambers and the duchess's, a page holding a torch to light their way. Christ on his Cross, but it was cold in this castle, he thought for the hundredth time since coming here four years ago with the duke. At least the many towers of the extensive castle were connected by these covered passageways. Going out into the snow with his gouty foot wrapped so heavily was less attractive. The guard outside Cecily's chamber scrambled to his feet and stood to attention when he saw Oldhall coming.

Cecily welcomed him warmly when he was announced. "Sir William, pray come in and enjoy the fire. Rowena, pour us some mulled wine." She plucked Anne from the other chair and waved him to it. "Demoiselle de Caux, if you would be so kind, Nan should go to bed. We shall finish our game in the morning, sweeting," she reassured the disappointed child, moving the draughts board out of harm's way. "Now, come kiss me goodnight."

Rowena handed Oldhall a hanap of spiced wine from a pot suspended over the fire. He cupped his cold hands around it and savored the spicy steam before it cooled enough for him to drink.

"'Tis good of you to see me so late, your grace. But I have received word within the hour that the duke will be returning on the morrow. I thought you should know."

"So soon," Cecily remarked, frowning. "Is there trouble brewing in the province? I thought we still had a truce with France while the marriage negotiations with Margaret are going on. Has the king changed his mind again?" She was remembering Richard's disappointment when the proposed alliance with Armagnac's daughter was abandoned.

Sir William smiled and took a sip of his wine, wincing as he burned his tongue. "Nay. The marriage is going forward, though they have kept Suffolk kicking his heels longer than we had hoped. But now Lord Richard must prepare to meet King Henry's queen in a fortnight at Pontoise and escort her to the coast. We believe the queen and her party plan to spend Easter here before sailing to England from Harfleur."

Cecily made a mental note to talk with her steward about the arrangements she would have to make for the royal visit, but then her thoughts turned to Richard. I wonder if he will want me to go with him, Cecily thought, tapping her finger on the arm of the chair and staring into the flames. She had to confess that she was consumed with curiosity about Margaret of Anjou. She hated the idea of leaving the children. Their well-being consumed most of her time these days, and as soon as her administrative duties of the day were done, she would hurry to the nursery to cuddle Bess, help Edward build something with his colorful blocks of wood—a sweet gift from Piers Taggett, and then watch as Edmund invariably crawled over to knock them down. Edward never cried. He simply balled his fists and shouted, "Bad boy, Eddom," and Edmund would grin and gurgle and knock more down, much to Cecily's amusement. She never tired of watching her brood, as she called them, grow and blossom. Cecily wondered how the news had been received in London that Richard was in communication with King Charles proposing marriage between Edward and one of the French king's two younger daughters.

"Someone has to wed her," Richard had said, when he told her he had approached Charles and that he was entertaining the idea. "It is propitious for us that the girls are too young for Henry. He cannot afford to wait to produce an heir."

Cecily returned her thoughts to Sir William, who was noisily sipping his wine. "Then we must prepare for my husband's return and make everything ready for his speedy departure for Pontoise. I shall prepare to go with him, should he so desire. And you and I must plan for the queen's visit, Sir William." She steepled her fingers and tapped them together lightly. I pray this marriage leads to lasting peace, she mused, but there is bound to be a price.

MAINE AND ANJOU were the price England had to pay for Margaret's hand. Richard's disgust at Suffolk's capitulation in the marriage negotiations manifested itself in a rigorous practice session with short swords with his brother-in-law, Richard Neville, earl of Salisbury, in the martial yard of Pontoise castle in March.

Alice, countess of Salisbury, and Jacquetta Woodville, former duchess of Bedford, were among the noblewomen chosen to accompany Suffolk from England to escort the young queen from Tours to Pontoise. Cecily and Alice were joyfully reunited when the Yorks arrived a day later.

The two sisters-in-law watched the younger, faster Richard thrust and lunge at the older Salisbury, who seemed more amused than assertive in his defensive parries, allowing York to vent his frustration.

"Easy, boy, easy," the veteran soldier advised Richard at one point, putting up his sword and falling back. "Take your time. You are rushing at me like a barbarian. It was not your fault we lost Maine and Anjou. You have done your duty. You still hold Normandy."

Richard scowled under his sallet and ignored Salisbury's counsel. He took up a threatening stance and began to weave around again. "Aye, brother, but for how long?" he growled. "Mark my words, Suffolk will pay dearly for this. Charles has made an excellent bargain and he must be guffawing in his cup of Rhenish. He gave up an insignificant princess with little dowry, agreed to only a temporary peace, and won Maine and Anjou. 'Tis hardly a fair exchange!" In his ranting, he failed to notice Salisbury's move sideways and the next thing he knew, he had Salisbury's blunted sword tip pointing at his heart. "Christ's nails, Neville, how did you manage that?"

Salisbury lifted off his helmet and grinned. "Were you not taught by John Beckwith at Raby never to talk while you are fighting? You took your inner eye off me to focus on your words and the rest was easy."

WHEN CECILY WENT forward to kneel before Margaret of Anjou, she had to admit that the marchioness of Suffolk was right. The fifteen-year-old French-woman was dazzling indeed. Her ripples of golden-red hair were crowned simply with a gold coronet in which were set three large sapphires with in-tervening diamonds. Droplets of pearls the size of pigeon eggs fell from her ears, and the neck, sleeves, and hem of her azure velvet gown were trimmed with ermine. An aggressive energy radiated from the young woman with her pert nose, full mouth, perfect complexion, and purple eyes. Nay, they cannot be purple, Cecily thought, kissing Margaret's outstretched hand, but looking again, she decided they were. She wondered how quiet, saintly Henry would handle his passionate bride.

"Madame la duchesse, je suis contente de vous connaître enfin," Margaret said, raising Cecily to her feet and kissing her on both cheeks. "Your sister-in-law has told me much of you—as has Duchess Jacquetta—and I know you and I will be friends."

Cecily wondered what Jacquetta might have told the queen, but she smiled and assured the young woman of her duty and her friendship. "The duke and I are looking forward to welcoming you to Rouen, your grace, as are the citi-zens," Cecily replied, aware of many pairs of curious eyes watching them.

THE RIVERBANKS WERE lined with cheering spectators as the flotilla of brightly canopied barges wended their way downstream toward Rouen. Within an hour of leaving Pontoise, Margaret had complained of stomach pains and retired to the only section of the boat that could be called a cabin, attended by Alice of Suffolk.

"Poor little thing," Jacquetta sympathized. "What a time to have *mal de mer.*" She was seated in the stern next to Lady Scales and opposite Cecily and Talbot's wife, Eleanor, all wrapped in furs against the chilly March wind. Huddled for warmth in the bow, Alice of Salisbury conversed with Lady Beatrice Talbot and Lady Grey. Cecily was not convinced Margaret's exit had anything to do with seasickness. The Seine is not a roiling ocean, she thought. Alice had told her that Margaret had been distraught upon leaving her family at Nancy and had wept for two days, when she was not snapping at her attendants or demanding attention. Cecily well remembered her own temperament at fifteen and deduced some sulking taking place in the cabin. Aye, it is cold, she thought, and when a drizzle began on the second day as they passed the Lionheart's Rock of Andely, Cecily admitted she, too, would have been happy to spend time in the cabin; nonetheless, the woman was queen and should behave more like one.

Before the voyagers reached Rouen on the third day, they had pulled to shore to take some exercise, and Richard came to see why Margaret was invisible. Suffolk's wife had tried to persuade her mistress to don a more lavish gown for the entry into the city and Margaret had refused, declaring she would not even appear in public.

"What shall we do, Cis?" Richard muttered, hugging his cloak around him. "The people have planned to fete her arrival with a flotilla of dozens of decorated boats and pageants, not to mention she would disappoint hundreds of spectators on the shore. She simply must show herself to them."

Cecily clucked her tongue, frustrated too, but she patted his hand. "You can count on me to think of something to rouse her. She has been friendly toward us all, and I can only think she is homesick, but she must understand her duty as queen."

"Not crowned, my dear. Not yet." And he walked off to some bushes.

As Cecily hurried back to the boat, she pondered how she might have coped with being queen at fifteen. I believe I knew my duty to my family and my servants by then, she told herself, because Mother taught me well. She could recall a few instances of rebellion when in private at that age, but Joan's lessons had been learned. "Never appear weak in public, Cecily, and never forget who you are. Carry your Neville name and Beaufort heritage proudly and let them see it," her mother had told her time and time again. Either Queen Margaret was too stubborn to heed any counsel she may have had or she had received none at all, Cecily decided, and set her jaw in a firm line. Then someone must teach her, she determined.

Alice de la Pole was grateful to be relieved of her vigil when Cecily went aboard. Cecily could tell the marchioness's patience had been tried by the young woman, and she assumed charge of the queen while Alice went ashore.

Cecily knocked on the cabin door. Hearing *"Venez"* from within, she entered, being careful not to knock off her cumbersome headdress on the low doorway. Margaret was reclining on a pile of velvet cushions, stroking a tiny white terrier, which was now baring its teeth at the intruder. Her young maidservant did her best to curtsey to the duchess in the cramped space and then gladly retreated to the deck.

Cecily was dismayed to see the state of Margaret's lovely face, blotched and reddened from crying, her eyelids swollen almost shut. Half a dozen soggy white lawn kerchiefs were scattered around her, and her tangle of red-gold hair had obviously not been brushed that day.

"Your grace, it pains me to see you so unhappy," Cecily began, going down on her knees. "Is there aught I can do to help?"

Margaret's mouth began to tremble and tears welled again. Aye, she is like me, Cecily empathized. It is almost better for someone not to be kind to me when I am upset. For some reason, kindness makes me weepier, and so I must be sympathetic yet stern.

"My mother taught me never to cry in front of our servants, your grace," Cecily said in a gentle tone, sitting on the edge of the bed. "She said it made them question our authority. How can they serve you if they think you are weak? It was a hard lesson to learn, for I was prone to weeping as a child," she lied, hoping God would forgive this small sin in a good cause. "Has one of the English ladies been unkind, *madame?* You must tell me and I shall speak to her."

Margaret shook her head, plucking at the silky hair on her dog's ears. "Nay, Duchess Cecily, everyone has been very good to me. 'Tis simply . . . simply . . ." and the chin began to quiver again. Cecily patted her hand, urging her to continue. "I have never been away from home before, and I miss my family," Margaret said. "Yolande . . . my sister . . . will wed our cousin of Lorraine in a few months and stay in France, close by our mother and father. Why do I have to go so far away?" And the tears flowed again, along with a heaving sob.

"Your grace, stop this!" Cecily snapped, surprising the spoiled young woman into sitting up and snatching a kerchief to blow her nose. "You must learn to behave like a queen. You are no longer just your father's daughter, but a king's wife." Cecily watched Margaret's reaction to these admonitions all the while holding Margaret's hand tight. More gently she said, "I must tell you that King Henry is the kindest of men and speaks beautiful French. He is handsome, too"—to a point, Cecily admitted to herself, adding to the list of little white lies—"and deeply religious. He will count himself fortunate to win a bride as beautiful and intelligent as you are." Careful, Cis, do not condescend, she told herself, but she was pleased with the effect her words were having on the young queen. "I was terrified about wedding—and even more than that," Cecily confided, "of bedding my husband, but I was fraught for no reason, and soon I was laughing at my foolishness. All will be well, I assure you."

Margaret let out a surprised giggle at this shared confidence and gazed at Cecily with gratitude. "Did you like the Lord Richard? Or did it take many years for you to learn to look with love at each other, as I have seen you do?"

Now Cecily was startled. Was it so obvious that she and Richard were so much in love? Joan Beaufort would not have approved, she knew, and the thought made her smile back at the queen.

"I have to confess to you, your grace, that I was more fortunate than you are. I was told Duke Richard would be my husband when I was nine, and as he lived in my father's house as his ward, we became friends before we fell in love. We have loved each other for a long, long time. But love can happen to anyone at any time." Seeing Margaret greatly cheered, she added mischievously, "But you hope it will be with your husband."

Alice of Suffolk was astonished to hear merry laughter emanating from the cabin when she came back. A raised eyebrow at Cecily as they passed was met with a finger to Cecily's lips. "I do not think she is ready to receive Rouen, but her *mal de mer* is passing, my dear marchioness. If the king can have a stand-in for his wedding ceremony, then the queen can surely have one for her *joyeuse entrée!*"

"I COULD NOT possibly do it," the countess of Shrewsbury cried. "Certes, everyone will know. Besides, 'tis disrespectful and I dare say treasonous to impersonate the queen."

Cecily drew herself up to her full height and glowered at Margaret Talbot. "Her grace will show nothing but gratitude, I can assure you, my lady. We cannot disappoint the people of Rouen. They want to welcome the queen. Certes, they want to greet Margaret of Anjou, but how many of them do you suppose have ever laid eyes on her?" She held up her thumb and forefinger in a circle. "Not one! I am begging you, Lady Margaret, do this for England. You are the only one who has the same hair color."

True, Margaret Talbot was certainly no fifteen-year-old, but she was still pretty and owned a magnificent head of golden hair. With Margaret's azure gown, she would look regal enough, Cecily believed, and the voluminous fur hood of her cloak would conceal some of her face.

And so Margaret, countess of Shrewsbury and daughter of the great Richard Beauchamp, earl of Warwick, played queen on the twenty-second day of March, fooling all but a few witnesses in Rouen that day as she processed in a litter, surrounded by her retinue of English noblewomen. Meanwhile the real queen was smuggled into Bouvreuil and went back to bed.

"You are prodigious, my dearest wife," Richard declared late that night, slipping his hand under Cecily's tight bodice. "If Margaret of Anjou proves to be as difficult as this going forward, I do not envy our sovereign lord. Sweet Jesu, she may turn out to be quite a handful." He grinned. "But I am more interested in this handful," he murmured as he leaned forward to kiss her breast.

Baynard's Castle, London

FEBRUARY 9, 1461

$\mathcal{S}$omewhere near the castle, Cecily heard a cock crow.

Sweet Jesu, have I lain awake all night? I will look like something the dog dragged around all day, she thought, gentling her puffy face and damp hair with her fingers. She gave a little snort of derision. Who cares about my looks anymore? Richard is dead these five weeks, and I am getting old, she thought.

But then she chuckled. Well, Cis, it always used to matter, just as it has mattered to the queen these fifteen years. Margaret has always been the more beautiful, she admitted, although I have been the better wife.

Were we always in competition? Were we always enemies? she wondered. Not always, she mused. Her thoughts flew back to Rouen and the day after the new queen and her train of noble men and women had processed to the cathedral to celebrate Christ's resurrection. Margaret had asked Cecily to show her the spot where Jeanne d'Arc had been burned. Dear God, Cecily thought, I remember feeling all the blood drain from my face. Since arriving back in Rouen four years earlier, I had avoided ever setting foot in the marketplace. But I could not refuse the queen, could I? She remembered that she and the queen, accompanied by a contingent of guards in ceremonial livery, had ridden in a canopied litter through the streets and into the market square. Once there, the guards cleared a path for the queen, and vendors, farmers, merchants, and their wives stood respectfully aside as Cecily walked with Margaret to the blackened stake, still rooted in the ground, with its heavy dangling chains awaiting another victim. Cecily was relieved that her emotions stayed in check.

Suddenly the smell of burning wood from a brazier wafted over the gorgeously arrayed women gathered around the queen. They say I screamed, Cecily thought to herself, shuddering, but I do not recall. All she remembered was reliving Jeanne's courageous walk to the stake and the deeply pious young woman's refusal to give up her faith in God. He took her to be with the angels.

Ah, Jeanne, you are with me still, Cecily thought now, and I carry your courage as my inspiration when I am in need.

Did I swoon? Nay, now I remember. Piers Taggett scooped me up just in time and laid me on the cushions in the litter. She recalled his anxious face watching her. She could not forbear to put out her hand and touch his cheek to reassure him. How foolish you were, Cecily, she berated herself now. One never touches a servant, and certainly not a manservant's face. Piers had started, unsure how to react to the unusual gesture from his noble mistress, and Cecily was grateful he had thought quickly and had removed her hand and kissed it. At the time Cecily wondered vaguely if Jacquetta Woodville had noticed. She smiled at her anxiety now, but back then she sent up a prayer to her friend the Virgin to keep Jacquetta focused on the queen.

To give the queen her due, Margaret was aghast when she heard why Cecily had been so affected by the visit to the marketplace, and just as Piers let go of Cecily's hand, the queen hurried to the duchess of York's side. "*Ma très chère duchesse,* I am so sorry. No one told me of your terrible ordeal. Why did you not tell me yourself? I would have excused you with all my heart. You should not have had to endure this. Forgive me."

Cecily thought back on the sincerity of the queen's little speech and the sweetness with which the teenage Margaret treated her for the rest of her Rouen stay. Nay, we were not enemies then.

Nor when Richard was summoned to Parliament in the autumn of 'Forty-five and we returned to England. The queen greeted me warmly enough and even called me her friend. I was carrying Meg, Cecily recalled, sighing now as she thought of her daughter, who she hoped was sleeping more soundly in her chamber after her nightmare.

Nor were we enemies when I named our sweet girl after the beautiful young queen and received a gift from her grace in acknowledgment. Nay, not then. But we certainly are now, she thought grimly, and I hate her even more than I hate Jacquetta of Bedford. But that is another story.

Margaret of Anjou had been feted on her arrival in England in some of the most lavish celebrations London had ever seen. Cecily frowned. All that money spent needlessly on a few days of spectacle with no sign of the thirty-eight thousand pounds owed Richard. Henry had received papal dispensation for the proxy betrothal during Lent, so the formal marriage and coronation went ahead immediately.

And in all the pageants mounted for Margaret's delight she was depicted as a dove. Ha! thought Cecily, what irony. Peace is not a word in Queen Margaret's vocabulary.

The truce brought about by her betrothal to Henry expired the following April, and peace-loving Henry, aching for a final treaty with the French, sent embassy after embassy and received envoy after envoy in the hope of terminating the war. It was not to be. Even when Suffolk proposed to King Charles that England might give up its claim to the French crown in exchange for keeping only Normandy and Gascony, the French balked. Henry offered to meet with Charles in France, expecting Richard, who was still lieutenant and governor, to make the arrangements and accompany him later that year. But 'twas all for naught, Cecily thought. Henry never went, and the war dragged on. Ah, yes, the war that Henry, Suffolk, and Uncle Beaufort wanted to end. What hypocrisy, she scoffed.

But her memories returned to Richard and that first Christmas back in England. Fotheringhay had been decked with holly and trailing ivy, and Anne and Edward had helped bring in the Yule log. At six, Anne was already betrothed to Henry Holland, fifteen-year-old heir of the duke of Exeter and close cousin to the king.

Comfortable in her fourth month of another pregnancy, Cecily looked forward to welcoming Richard home from attending Parliament at Westminster. He had been promised one more year in France, and although Cecily had decided that she would be delivered in England, she was quite prepared to follow him after the birth. Instead, Richard had ridden home through sleet and muddied roads to tell her that he had been accused of mismanagement in Normandy—of rewarding his retainers, men such as Oldhall, with landholdings in France that had not been cleared with the crown.

"I shouted at them then, Cis," Richard had told her, when he burst into her chamber. I don't blame him for being angry, she reasoned now. What else could he pay them with? The council had not sent him money. Cecily shook her head as she remembered the scene, furious that her husband, who had spent vast sums of his own money to pay the king's army, was being falsely accused because of the councillors' own failures. It was intolerable.

Cecily had asked him, "Did you favor your men, Richard?" and he had shrugged and admitted, "Perhaps, but they deserved it. They were hard-working and loyal."

The charges of mismanagement could not be proved, even though the public fashion in which they were brought must have damaged poor Richard's reputation. However, after many months the issue was dropped, and York was promised a large sum of money to compensate him for his previous lack of income. Cecily snorted again. Aye, we never saw much of that amount either, she recalled. And to add to Richard's frustrations, when he knew he would not be sent back as lieutenant of Normandy, he was incensed by the council's choice of successor. She scowled. It was none other than her cousin Edmund Beaufort.

"Somerset!" she said out loud. How did he worm his way into the queen's affections?

"Your grace." The voice of her attendant Beatrice Metcalf penetrated the heavy curtains and her thoughts. "Do you wish to sleep further? I thought I heard you calling."

"I heard the cock crow, Beatrice, but I have not closed my eyes all night," Cecily called. "I pray you make my excuses to Father Lessey. I would rest another hour."

She heard Beatrice and Gresilde whispering as they stoked the fire and gathered up the wine cups from the night before. Soon there was silence in the chamber.

The only good thing that occurred in the whole of that year, Cecily thought, was the birth of Meggie, their seventh child. Whether because Meggie was born in Richard's favorite country residence, Hunsdon, or because the baby had chosen Cecily's own birthday to arrive, when she looked upon Margaret of York, Cecily felt something special touch her heart. She remembered the day clearly.

She had gone into labor on the way to Fotheringhay. "I do not think I can keep this child from being born another hour, let alone another two days or more," she had told Richard, and she had been amused to see his pallor. Sweeping Cecily up into his arms and leaving the rest of the retinue to follow, they left the Ermine Road a few miles north of Hertford in a safe but serious hurry. By the time the midwife arrived at Hunsdon House, the babe was well on her way. Margaret was born with a wise look about her, Cecily recalled, and she had immediately seemed aware of her surroundings. I told Richard that day that Meg would be the most intelligent of our children, and I was right, Cecily thought smugly.

Then she smiled. How Richard had loved this child! The memory of Richard holding Meg moved Cecily to discover that she had still a few more tears to spill. She sniffled into her pillow as she made a promise to make sure this child had an extra share of her love to make up for Richard's absence. He would bounce Margaret on his knee and call her his darling, and she would make him laugh, because she loved the funny way he laughed.

Cecily wiped away the tears and chuckled at that memory. Oh, that laugh of his, she thought. How sweet it was when they discovered Bessie had inherited it. The first time Elizabeth had neighed, Cecily believed the child had simply been imitating her father and had chastised her for her disrespect. But when it became apparent the girl could not laugh in any other way, Cecily had adored her for it.

Her children! How much joy they had given her over the years—and she could even now think equably, though tinged with sadness, on those who did not live to enjoy their childhood. But with the inevitable stab of pain, she had to think of her beloved Edmund, who did survive to be an adult. But to what end, she mourned, cruelly killed at seventeen. Of all her boys, he had been her favorite, if she had been forced to choose under torture. His sense of adventure had reminded her of her own, and when Richard had occasionally punished him for it, she had secretly cheered him on. He had not been big and strong, like Edward, and although he had learned to use a sword with adequate skill, he did not live to fight, as his older brother did. There was a vulnerability about him—dare she say delicacy—that brought out her lioness instincts whenever the other children teased him for being a mother's boy.

And then there was Edward, who had grown daily, it seemed, until he had outstripped his father, and Richard had to make him kneel so that he could box his ears when the rascal had been caught in yet another escapade. How he adores the opposite sex, Cecily said to herself, and made a note to speak to him about his indiscretions. She regretted now that after the Anjou marriage, the king of France had refused the betrothal between his daughter and Ned, and Richard had not had time to find another suitable match for his heir. Perhaps he would now have been married and more circumspect had the match been achieved. Ah, well, Edward would no doubt land on his feet in matrimony, too, just as he did in anything he undertook, she thought. He was born when the stars were perfectly aligned, she believed.

Aye, she and Richard had been blessed indeed with their growing brood, and she tried not to dwell on those she had lost as infants.

After Margaret had come George. She well remembered the cold, damp October day when he had first come into the world and charmed not only his mother but everyone else who knew him. Perhaps because he was born in Ireland, he seemed to Cecily to be an elfin child, frail and pale, with enormous blue eyes and hair the color of moonglow. Ah, yes, Ireland! Those gentle emerald hills that concealed a savage wildness just beyond the Pale. Was that where Richard finally discovered his own power and with that power dared to desire his destiny?

PART FOUR

He knows that of two roads each must take one,
Shunning the second, or the other choosing.
Yet not so absolutely but that things
Might not end otherwise, conceivably,
If by free will a man should choose to act.

ROMAN DE LA ROSE

19

Ireland, 1449 to 1450

*E*xile, more like!" Richard thundered.

He swung around and stared out of the topmost window in the round tower of Wigmore Castle, perched high upon a forested hill a few miles from Ludlow, where the Yorks had come for the harvesting. It was here, where the hawthorn trees and wild rose bushes grew heavy with their red fruits, the Welsh hills rose like dark clouds upon the horizon to the west, and the fertile valley of the Teme and its tributaries stretched to the north, that Richard's ancestor Lionel of Clarence had been laid to rest. Twelve hundred feet below where Richard was standing, the bull badge of Clarence was carved over the castle gate and indeed above every doorway that led to yet more stairs that seemed to climb into the sky. Cecily had remarked on Wigmore's perfect aspect the first time Richard had taken her there. Now it was falling into disrepair, a victim of Richard's financial distress and his decision that nearby Ludlow Castle had to be maintained as the Yorks' primary residence in the Welsh marches, where he had inherited vast estates.

They had ridden out with Piers and another groom, intent on hawking that golden afternoon, when Richard had suggested they visit Wigmore to ascertain whether money should be spent on it. The castle was deserted, and any items of furniture left from Richard's uncle's time were either rotten, broken, or had been stolen.

"Richard, do be reasonable," Cecily cajoled. "I know you wanted to return to France, but that is not to be. Lord lieutenant of Ireland is a most suitable position for you." She did not need to remind him that, as a descendant of the de Clares, he owned the greatest expanse of Anglo-Irish land. "You are a natural choice. And since the events of February, you must know why they do not want you close."

Richard nodded and said nothing. They were both thinking of Humphrey of Gloucester, the heir presumptive and the king's loyal if somewhat irascible and headstrong uncle. Relations between him and the king, and especially with the king's right arm, Suffolk, had deteriorated little by little and month by month while the Yorks were holding court at Rouen, until the king became unnecessarily afraid for his safety at his uncle's hand. Of all the nobles who had surrounded the king since his soldier father had died, Gloucester had tried hardest to hold on to what his brother Harry had won for England at Agincourt. It was this, Richard believed, and nothing else that had set Gloucester against Suffolk and the Beauforts. Besides, his loyalty to his nephew was steadfast. Richard himself was philosophically aligned with Gloucester, although never part of his circle. Even so, Cecily had been frightened to learn of the sixty-year-old duke's ill-fortune and sudden death last February while she was at Fotheringhay, sickly with another pregnancy.

"Poor man was unaware of the danger he was in when summoned to Parliament at Bury St. Edmund's," Richard had told Cecily then, shaking his head. "He was accused of crimes against the crown. Suffolk charged that his adherents were fomenting a revolt to put him on the throne. I regret now that Salisbury and I believed Suffolk's accusations. When I saw Gloucester later, he was in a state of apoplexy, Cis, with veins standing out on his face and neck."

Cecily now stared at Richard's back, his silver-streaked hair curling under at his shoulder, and let out a long breath. Poor Gloucester, he was found dead a few days later, from what cause, no one had yet discovered. Some said it was poison. Some, Richard among them, thought his old heart gave out after such a fit of anger. But Cecily thought it was from a broken heart. All he had worked for on behalf of his brother and then his nephew had been lost. Whatever the reason, the last brother of the great King Harry was gone.

"This means you are next in line for the Plantagenet crown, Richard, and should be named heir presumptive," Cecily had whispered. "This means you could be king—if anything happens to Henry."

"But nothing will happen to Henry, and he and the queen will have an heir soon, no doubt."

In the space of two months that year of 1447, King Henry lost two of his kin who had helped raise and counsel him. As though life was not worth living after his nemesis Gloucester was no longer there to oppose, Henry Beaufort, cardinal, bishop, and councillor, expired on the eleventh day of April and was buried in the marble tomb he had built for himself in his cathedral at Winchester. Cecily had shed no tears for her stern uncle.

"Shall we take the children to Ireland?" Cecily asked after a long pause, the resignation and reasonableness in her voice easing Richard's tension.

He nodded, fidgeting with his dagger hilt. "We shall set up court just as we did in Rouen, I suppose."

"How long this time, Richard?" she murmured, dreading leaving her homeland again, not to mention her favorite castles of Fotheringhay and Ludlow. She went to him and kneaded the knotted muscles in his shoulders.

"You will not like it, Cis. Ten years from December," he answered, relaxing under her fingers. He patted her hand when she gasped in dismay. "But I will take my time about going, I can assure you."

Richard had set some conditions for the appointment and was able to assure Cecily that the king and Suffolk would allow him to recover some of his lost lands from the Irish chieftains and that, should he manage the royal exchequer well, any surpluses would be his. He grunted. "I suppose it was an attempt to make up for the monstrous Rouen debt. But—damn Suffolk all to hell!" he swore, rising abruptly. "'Tis nothing more than banishment. And soon Maine will be back in French hands and, God help them, Somerset will be in charge at Rouen. I was aghast in May to hear Parliament exonerate Suffolk for ceding Maine and Anjou. Christ's nails! He sold us out for the younger daughter of a paltry poet prince." He slammed his fist into his other hand. "It all makes me sick unto death."

Cecily swung Richard round to her and threw her arms about him. "Do not talk of death, my love. What would I do without you, in truth? What would the children do without you? We shall make the best of things in Ireland, and perhaps we shall be touched by the magic of those ancient Gaels."

It was astonishing to Richard how the curve of her body, the silkiness of her skin still aroused him after all these years. She had lost yet another boy child not a month since and named him William for her brother, but it seemed to Richard that she had expended all her grief upon her other losses and had accepted God's will this time with a certain degree of equanimity. He had promised himself not to pressure her back into his arms too soon, but now he could not resist her mouth so close to his and so kissed her passionately. Thoughts of Ireland, Gloucester, and Suffolk were forgotten as Richard reached under her skirt to fondle the most private parts of her, exulting in her moans of passion. Not seeing anywhere to lay her down, Richard moved

Cecily back to the waist-high window embrasure and sat her upon it. Still kissing her, he managed to untie his points, drop his hose, push up her skirts, and thrust himself into her. Cecily spread her legs for him, gripping the edge of the windowsill for leverage. Both found the new position titillating, and not long after finding a rhythm, they climaxed together in a single cry of shared pleasure.

Her legs locked about his waist to hold him in her as long as she could, Cecily whispered, "Such wantonness in an old married pair. 'Tis shameful. But it is as well we left Piers at the bottom of the hill or he might have come to our rescue upon hearing such a cry."

Richard could not bear to let her go. Life always seemed better when Cecily was with him, he mused. And like this, we are as one. Who cares about king, country, or banishment when I have a love such as this and the fruits of that love ever waiting to welcome me home. More pragmatically, he thought, at least in Dublin he would be king of the castle.

Looking over Cecily's shoulder, he saw a pair of magpies fly past the window.

"Two for joy," he murmured, nuzzling her. "They must have heard us."

TWO YEARS LATER, looking back from the stern of their carrack at the dark Welsh hills tumbling into the sea, Cecily took with her images of their journey from Ludlow through the high mountains of Wales, over the treacherous straits of Menai, to Beaumaris on the voyage to Ireland. She had waited the last two years at the rosy-stoned castle of Ludlow, situated on the edge of the seemingly impenetrable land of dragons and Owen Glendower, as Richard prepared for his lieutenancy.

They set off in the middle of June with a mile-long train of carts, pack-horses, riders, and litters that snaked like a gaily colored ribbon along the primitive roads into Wales. They stopped at Richard's castles of Montgomery and Denbigh before inching their way through the forested valleys until suddenly confronted by the barren Snowdon mountains. There the nights were cold, and servants harvested armfuls of heather and bracken to burn, gathering around to sleep on the ground in their cloaks. The green plants made more smoke than fire, Cecily complained one night after a fit of coughing. Richard chided her and reached out to touch her ruby betrothal ring.

"Remember our pact that day of your attack? We must never forget how fortunate we are. We have a tent and fur blankets to keep us warm, Cis. Why begrudge those less fortunate a little comfort—if that is how they see it."

On the gently rocking deck of the two-masted carrack, Cecily smiled at the memory. Richard was a good man and preferred to look for the best in his fellow man. She wished more people knew that side of him, for he showed the world a stiffer bearing. No matter, she decided, because what was most pleasing to her was his kindness to his children. Aye, he had occasionally given both boys a thrashing, but the next day he would take them hawking or fishing. She watched him walking up and down, explaining to the eager Edward and Edmund how the sails worked.

She was hand in hand with Bessie, who was shivering in the cool sea breeze. Nurse Anne, her russet woolen gown billowing out around her, stood by with three-year-old Meggie in her arms. The nurse had grown plump in the Yorks' service, but her devotion to the children and their love for her was worth every flampayne, custard, and sweetmeat the woman consumed, Cecily thought.

Who are you to cast stones, Cis? she asked herself, feeling the swelling belly under her gown. She would have this child in Dublin, and wondered if it would be the first of many born there. She sent a quick prayer heavenward to the Blessed Mother, hoping that this babe would not be taken from her too. Another son of York had entered the world the previous November but had lived only a few weeks into the wicked winter that froze the water in the moat and Cecily's washbasin every morning and mounded snow so high on the roads and fields that food had been scarce and travel impossible. They had chosen to name their ninth child in honor of John of Bedford, but he had none of his namesake's strength and had soon withered. Let this one live, Holy Mary, Cecily pleaded, clutching Bessie's hand so tightly that the child squeaked, "Mama!"

Richard glanced up at the quarterdeck and waved, the pheasant feathers in his cap in danger of being whisked away in the wind. "Papa, papa!" Meg cried. "Do come up here."

The boys scrambled up the steps to join the women, running to the rail to peer precariously over the stern. "If you fall in, we shall not turn back to rescue you," Richard warned. "I shall not hesitate to chain you to a mast for the rest of the voyage if you cannot stay out of mischief. Do I make myself clear?"

Stepping back from the gunwale, both boys nodded sheepishly and rejoined their parents. Edmund slipped his right hand unseen into Cecily's and, as he was wont to do when he felt safe, stuck his left thumb in his mouth.

"Thumbsucker! Mama's boy," seven-year-old Ned taunted him, mimicking his brother and making Meggie laugh. Edmund let go of Cecily's hand and ran full tilt at Edward, knocking him off his feet. A wrestling match ensued, and Richard watched, amused, as the younger, slighter Edmund fought like a scrappy terrier against the stalwart, athletic Edward.

"Do put an end to it, my lord," Cecily begged, casting her eyes heavenward. "You know it will only end in tears."

Too late. Edward had used his fist to thwack Edmund in his belly, and Edmund let out a wail, "Nurse Anne, he hit me. Ned hit me," the predicted tears coming as he kicked and wriggled to get out from under the pummeling. "Get him away from me. He is hurting me," he sobbed, and as Edward raised his arm, threatening to deal the final blow, Edmund begged, "Stop it, Ned! I give in. You win."

"Enough!" Richard bellowed, making several mariners stop what they were doing to stare at the noble family. Edward froze, arm still poised above his blubbering brother. "Never hit an adversary when he is down and pleading for mercy," their father told them. "That is the way of savages. You will learn the civilities of war when you are a little older, but for now, learn this first lesson. Respect your enemy and always follow the rules of chivalry. Now, help your brother to his feet, Ned, and let me see both of you grasp an arm in friendship."

The boys did as they were told, Edward apologizing and throwing his arm about his brother. Edmund wiped his nose on his sleeve and gave Edward a self-deprecating grin. Cecily smiled over their golden heads at her husband.

"Let us hope they will always be friends, Richard," she murmured as he joined her. "'Tis a fearful thing to see brother fight against brother."

Richard grunted. "I was spared any such temptation, my love, but sometimes I wish I had had a brother." He put his arm around her and murmured. "I am hopeful you are carrying a son, and then Edmund will have a younger playmate to lord over."

RICHARD WAS BUSILY occupied from the moment he arrived in Ireland. The Yorks were astonished at the welcome they received. Among the many gifts showered on them before they even arrived in Dublin were four hundred head of cattle and two beautiful Irish horses for Cecily.

Richard had been dismayed that John Talbot, the old veteran, who had preceded him as lord lieutenant, had not proved to be as good a governor as he was a soldier. In fact, he had governed by cruel soldiering, which had not helped matters between the native Irish and those Anglo-Irish who had been living around Dublin since Richard's Plantagenet ancestors had conquered the island almost three hundred years before.

After the first night's banquet, the old earl of Ormond, the leader of the Anglo-Irish in Ireland, who had greeted the Yorks upon their landing at Howarth, told Richard and Cecily, "We have often begged our sovereign lord Henry to send us a prince of the blood fit to rule us and keep the peace beyond the Pale. No one can gainsay that with your royal blood and family ties you are that man, your grace. You are a prince of England and Ireland, and all will bow down before you with true allegiance."

"I hope so, my lord," Richard replied. "I assure you, Ireland is dear to my heart." *As its largest landowner, I am sure it is,* Cecily chuckled to herself, but she did not doubt her husband's sincerity.

Reaching Dublin by boat, the city walls rising from the southern bank of the Liffey reminded Cecily of Rouen's river approach. Once in the Liffey's tributary, the Poddle, which formed the moat for the castle, the small skiff reached the wharf below the Powder Tower, and its royal passengers disembarked. Cecily looked up to see men-at-arms leaning precariously from the ramparts to catch their first glimpse of the new lieutenant. *You have a good man in my husband,* Cecily wanted to assure them.

INDEED, WITHIN A month of their arrival Richard had marched to his earldom of Ulster, and everywhere he went the chieftains gave him fealty, two a little more reluctantly than the others, she recalled. But once those two great chiefs, O'Neill and O'Byrne, had submitted, the rest followed. Henry O'Neill had gone as far as to swear that he would take up arms against anyone who waged war against Duke Richard or his heirs, English or Irish. There was even some civility restored between the two great Anglo-Irish leaders, Ormond and Desmond. Sir William Oldhall had told Cecily that Richard had done in two months what Talbot had failed to do in two years, and Cecily thrilled to his words.

Richard's successes in Ireland were made sweeter when news reached Dublin in August of Edmund of Somerset's ignominious defeats in France after he broke the truce by sacking the Breton city of Fougères. King Charles, allied with Brittany, retaliated, and castle after castle in English Normandy fell to the French armies. Richard was deeply saddened by the events and refused to be cheered by Cecily's point that King Henry had made a mistake in choosing Edmund Beaufort over him to command in Normandy.

"In truth, it is not about an individual—not about me, Cecily. It is about the honor of our country. Somerset has damaged our honorable reputation and lost all that we had gained, and I weep for England," Richard said. Cecily wondered that he did not add, "And all my hard work was for naught," because that was what she was thinking.

At Michaelmas, Richard hosted scores of lords from Meath, Munster, and Ulster both Gaelic and English at the castle in Dublin. It was the first time in living memory that the Irish chieftains had sat down at table together and with a lord lieutenant in his stronghold at Dublin. Before Richard went down to the great hall to receive them, Cecily, heavily pregnant and confined to her chambers, once again reminded her husband that his accomplishments must surely be noticed at Westminster.

"It seems no one has noticed, my dear," her husband told her. "I do not believe Henry cares a ratcatcher's arse about his Irish domain. As long as I keep the peace here, they can forget about Ireland. And once again, the exchequer has failed to send me what I need for next spring's campaign, and hardly enough to recompense me for this summer's. Instead, the council gives Somerset aid for his campaign and rewards Suffolk's favorites with manors and lordships. The king, 'tis said, is bankrupt from all his gifting and the people are taxed out of their homes. Alas, dear lady, they have no thoughts to spare for me and Ireland."

"Then they are all whey-faced idiots," Cecily had remarked as she removed an errant hair from the ermine-trimmed neck of his gown, straightened his heavy jeweled collar, and pecked him on the cheek. "But do not dwell on them today." She fingered the gold ducal coronet that encircled his dark head. "Remember, here you are king." Turning him toward the door, she gave him a little push. "I shall have my spies watching you all and reporting back to me. How I wish I could be down there with you."

"Aye, so do I, my . . . my queen," Richard murmured, his eyes twinkling.

Later Constance and Gresilde Boyvile took turns to describe the scene in the banquet hall from their vantage point near the musicians' gallery.

"'Tis hard to know who are the most colorful—the Irishmen in their plaid wool mantles or the ladies," Gresilde said, one of her many chins wobbling as she spoke. When Richard had retained Sir Richard Boyvile at Fotheringhay a year since, he had asked Cecily if the man's wife might be a suitable attendant to take the place of Rowena, who had asked to return to her sickly husband's side. Cecily had found Gresilde's cheerful henpecking a nice foil for Constance's sharp intelligence, and so had readily agreed.

"Their manners are also colorful," Constance said, when her turn came. "The dogs have never been happier—there are bones and scraps for all. And you will be pleased to hear, your grace, that lords Edward and Edmund are behaving themselves *impeccablement*." She pulled the footstool closer to her mistress, her eyes shining. "When the White Earl made his toast to the duke, madam, and all those wild men stood quietly and bowed down to Lord Richard . . . *Bénit Vierge*, I wish you could see. He was like a king."

Cecily glowed with pride then and later, when Richard opened the first Parliament and within a few hours had waded through a backlog of complaints and grievances brought by landowners and commoners, dealing so fairly with all that his praises were being sung far and wide in the Pale.

But after three days confined to a chair, staring at documents and listening to complaints, he was glad of the chance to get out in the fresh air and ride the thirty miles to Trim to settle a dispute.

Cecily was nearing her time but resisted begging him to stay. Recognizing the plea in her anxious eyes, he kissed her and said, "Never fear, I shall be gone but a day and a half, my love. I defy the child to arrive before my return."

Cecily was loath to see him go but sent him off with a wave from her window.

AT NOON ON the twenty-first day of October, Cecily gave a final push after only two full hours of labor and was delivered of a healthy boy, distinguished by elegant fingers and long feet.

"Mark my words, he will be a handsome man and win many hearts, your grace," Constance told Cecily, administering a potion of boneset and dried ewe's blood to her mistress to help heal her womb. She had known as soon as they were born that neither of the last two boys would survive. They were both too early and both the color of tallow. But she had held her peace and prayed.

Cecily smiled, cradling the sleeping infant in her arms. "You are right, Constance. He has already won this woman's heart."

The doctor raised an eyebrow. "Come now, your grace, we all know it will take a paragon to win Edmund's place in his mother's eyes."

Cecily's eyes twinkled. "Oh, dear, am I that transparent? But, Constance, I truly love them all—certes, for different reasons."

"Aye, your grace." She changed the subject. "What is to be his name?"

"I should like to name him after his father, but I should wait, I suppose." Cecily had been disappointed that her pains had come when Richard had gone that morning to settle a dispute between a chieftain and a member of the Anglo-Irish gentry. She sighed. "I confess this birth was my easiest, and I am only a little tired. He looks like an angel, does he not?" Cecily murmured. "Let us hope he remains thus—for the most part. Angels can be so dull."

"Your grace!" Constance spluttered. "Have a care. There may be some listening who will take offense—those that frequent Satan's realm, I mean."

"Pish," Cecily retorted. "As long as all was left open, as we instructed, there are no evil spirits here to put a curse on this child."

Constance chose not to tell her mistress that Dame Boyvile had forgotten to open the door to the garden at the bottom of the staircase when Cecily's labor had begun. She had already prayed that the omission was not an ill omen.

"Dame Boyvile, I pray you leave word that I would have my husband attend me as soon as he returns. We cannot christen this babe until his father and I agree upon a name," Cecily said, watching the young wet-nurse on the other side of the room unhook her bodice and prepare to satisfy her charge's growing hunger. "I think we should name him Richard after his father, but my lord duke has denied my request thus far, he says, to avoid the confusion of two in the family."

"George," Richard decided, upon holding his son. "He does not look like me, in truth, and reminds me of your brother Latimer."

Cecily smiled, remembering the adoration she had as a child for George Neville, now Lord Latimer. "Very well, my love, then George he shall be. But promise me the next shall be Richard."

"The next, my lady?" Richard swung around, laughing. "How many more do you propose we have?"

"Why, as many as my body will allow," Cecily retorted. "Are you forgetting that until these children grow up, I am the only one who can build the house of York," Cecily replied, reluctantly thinking of the infant sons she had lost. "We must ensure our line is strong."

Richard grunted his assent, making the baby jerk in his sleep. He sat down on the bed, contemplating their child. "He is a fine boy, my dear. We must make plans for him."

"It occurs to me, Richard, that with the birth of this Irish prince, you have a chance to flatter our Irish hosts and throw two antagonists together where they will not squabble. I have been thinking we should ask the White Earl and Desmond to stand as godparents. What think you?"

She had her answer in his respectful approval before he returned little George to his cradle and came back to her side to recount his actions in Parliament. Cecily rejoiced to see her husband's face glowing with the confidence he had gained from governing this volatile province, where the English and Irish still had not come to terms with each other after three hundred years.

BABY GEORGE WAS no more than a week old when Rouen was taken by the French. It did not take long for the shock wave to reach even such an outpost as Dublin.

"All is lost in Normandy, my lady," Richard cried, bursting into Cecily's private office, where she was dictating routine daily instructions to her steward. Cecily rose at once and went to take her husband's hands, moved to find they were trembling. "Charles has taken Rouen—or I should say, Somerset has surrendered Rouen. The rest of Normandy will follow, 'tis certain."

"Taken Rouen?" Cecily whispered. "'Tis not possible. Where was Somerset at the time? Where was the garrison?"

Richard wrenched his hands away and strode to the window, and the steward took the opportunity of slipping away. "He was there, for Christ's sake! At Bouvreuil. With Talbot, your brother William, and Lord Roos, among others. It seems Somerset tried to defend it, but Roussel—you remember the archbishop—begged him to spare the city, and Somerset agreed to negotiate with Charles." He let out a harsh laugh. "He negotiated first his own release along with his family's and Talbot's, but he was forced to leave behind hostages— and I regret your brother William is one."

Cecily covered her mouth with her hand and sent up a prayer to St. George to watch over her sibling. She imagined herself back in the great hall of Bouvreuil, where she and Richard had hosted countless banquets, and pictured the three Beauchamp sisters—Margaret Talbot, Eleanor Beaufort, and her own sister-in-law Elizabeth Latimer—surrounded by their children and wondering what would become of them. She shivered. "What next?" she whispered. "Surely the king—and Suffolk—cannot support Somerset after this?"

"I know not, Cis. I cannot fathom the mind of this king. His opinions and decisions seem to bend like waving wheat—whichever way the wind blows. I have seen him hurry from a discussion clutching his prayer book and muttering that only God can give him guidance. He should have taken orders, in truth, for he cannot give any." He smiled grimly at his witticism. "A king should not have to ask God how to oust Suffolk from his position and reprimand Somerset for his incompetence. I must write to Salisbury and ask for his side of the story."

Richard also wrote to the king and again requested payment for his military needs. But once again, his request was ignored.

HOWEVER, RICHARD NEVILLE, earl of Salisbury, wasted no time with his reply.

Richard took the letter from Sir William Oldhall and, looking around at those gathered in one of the cozier rooms at Lacy Castle, their winter retreat in Trim, broke open the seal, glanced through the first page, and decided to read it aloud.

> *Right worthy brother and most noble duke of York, we greet you*
> *well. It is as you had thought. My lord of Suffolk has been reprimanded*
> *by Parliament, and charges have been brought to bear against him for*
> *disastrous policies and treasonable actions in France. Certes, he appealed*
> *to the king, who dismissed the charges forthwith, calling Suffolk his*
> *good and loyal servant.*

Richard paused. "Misguided Henry bending with the wind again," he muttered, staring up at the casement, where even in March a cold rain spattered the horned window panes. "Would that Somerset had been charged as well," he growled.

Cecily sat watching him patiently. Gresilde sat quietly embroidering, Richard's usher, Roger Ree, occupied the window seat, and Ned and Edmund sat on footstools near their father's chair and tried to look interested. The two little girls were playing with a poppet on the bed, where Nurse Anne kept an eye on them.

Richard straightened the vellum and continued reading.

> *However, not a month later, after a second set of charges was leveled*
> *at him, William de la Pole, duke of Suffolk, was banished from our*
> *shores for a period of five years.*

The listeners gasped, and Richard himself looked up, grim-faced. "Aye, it seems our king has been nurturing a traitor." He looked down again at the letter in his hands.

*Our sovereign lady, Queen Margaret, spoke bravely on his
behalf to her lord, it was told to me, but this time the king could not
gainsay Parliament. In truth, it was Suffolk's agreeing privately
to the marriage terms to cede Maine and Anjou that most angered
the Commons. It did not help Suffolk's cause that no heir has been
forthcoming from the royal union, and people are grumbling that
England has gained nothing from this marriage and yet lost much.*

Richard paused again, and Cecily knew he was thinking of the last time he
had gone before Parliament and tried to point out the mismanagement of the
country and his ideas for reform. The king had been unnerved by the support
York was gaining both in the council and in the country, although he could
not find fault with the duke for his loyalty and duty to his royal person. Giving
Somerset the governorship of Normandy and money to go with it had been
the last straw for Richard, and he had spoken his mind. *A mistake, Richard,*
Cecily thought, watching him now. *You were your own worst enemy that day.
If you had held your peace, you might yet be home in England and acknowledged as heir presumptive. Ah, Cis, should you criticize him when you have
always nudged him to assert himself? Be fair.*

She cleared her throat, reminding Richard that his audience was waiting.
He looked back at the letter, glanced at the second page, and quickly declared,
"'Tis all you need to know." He had decided not to share the rest with anyone
but Cecily, which he did later that evening.

Richard Neville wrote:

*But what of the loss of Normandy? Far dearer to England than
Maine and Anjou, you might agree. I fear it may astonish you to know
that his grace of Somerset has returned and appears still to retain the
favor of the king and, more nearly, of the queen. It makes little sense,
but we are only minions doing the royal bidding. Surely the fall of
English France will be blamed on Lancaster for ever, God help us.*

"But not on York," Cecily interrupted. "York is not to blame."

Richard looked up, as if he were taking in what she had said, but he was
remembering the last time he had been at court. "Perhaps 'tis as well we came
to Ireland when we did, my lady. No one can say I have shirked my duty or
not served my king." He paused and frowned. "Who is now counseling him, I

wonder? I like not that Salisbury views himself a minion when he is one of the older members of the council."

Cecily bit her lip. She never liked hearing criticism of her family, especially not of her eldest brother, but she had noticed he could be milk-and-water sometimes, so she said nothing. She had Meg on her lap engaging Bessie in a game of checkers, and she was delighted to see the younger girl outwit her sister in a move. She kissed the top of the golden head and murmured, "Well played, Meggie." It was as well, she thought, that Elizabeth had a sweet, placid nature, for she would never match the boys or her younger sister in spirit or intelligence.

"Read on, Richard, I beg of you," she said, motioning to Bessie over Meg's head a move whereby the girl could get revenge.

Richard complied:

> *In other news, you must know that our dearly beloved son Richard came into his father-in-law Warwick's title a few months ago through his Beauchamp wife, and having attained his majority is entitled to several estates through her. However, this has put our son in direct competition with our cousin Somerset, married to another Beauchamp daughter, and Somerset claims the land is his. I know not what will come of the conflict, but young Richard is not one to lie down and give up. If you meet him now, you will understand. Tell my sister that he has inherited more of her temperament than mine. Let me assure you that if you are on the same side as the new earl of Warwick, you will have a loyal and brave ally. But woe betide you if you are not.*
>
> *My dear York, it might cheer you to know that your good name is heard often in Parliament and among many of us on the council.*

Richard looked up, and a look of mutual gratification passed between husband and wife. Thank God, Cecily thought. A small step on the path to fulfill his goals. She smiled at him. "Go on."

> *There is lawlessness rife in the country at this time, and Suffolk's downfall has left a void in leadership that cries for a strong reformer. It is a concern that Somerset, as possible heir presumptive, may attempt to fill the void.*
>
> *Alice joins me in sending good wishes to you and your family. Your ever faithful, et cetera.*

Richard slowly sharpened the edges of the folded pages with his finger and thumb and his brow creased. "Somerset again," he muttered. "It seems the man knows no bounds. How can he be considered heir presumptive when he is of bastard stock?"

Cecily could sense Richard's anger rising and stepped in. "Let us not dwell on Edmund tonight, my dear. Let us rejoice in the news that you are not forgotten in London. Besides, it would seem Cousin Edmund has met his match in young Warwick. Come and help Bessie defeat Margaret and me. She is sorely in need of help," Cecily urged, beckoning him. "I am more curious to know why the king and queen have failed to give England an heir, although that is not for me to ponder, knowing how long it took us."

Diverted, Richard winked at her as he took Bessie on his knee. "And now it would seem we know not how to stop!"

SUMMER FINALLY CAME to Dublin, and Cecily insisted that the children be out in the fresh air and sunshine as much as possible.

"All of you look as though you have spent the last few months shut up in a dungeon," she remarked to the four eager faces in front of her. Then she addressed the two little girls: "Hats with brims for you two. Ladies must always guard against getting brown complexions. It makes one look like a peasant."

"What about the boys? Why can they be brown?" Margaret asked. "I hate hats!"

Bessie dug her elbow into her sister's side. She recognized the lift of her mother's chin and narrowing eyes. It meant a reprimand, and she loathed hearing the sharp tone and biting words her mother was capable of uttering. Elizabeth hated conflict of any kind and she avoided doing anything to incite it if at all possible. Her favorite words from either of her parents were "Good girl, Bessie," and she would bask in such praise for hours. She could not fathom why Meg relished an argument—especially with Edmund—and did not seem to be able to anticipate her mother's ire, when it was perfectly obvious to Bessie that it was about to erupt, as it did now. She cringed.

"Margaret! How many times must I tell you not to question your elders? You do as you are told and that is all there is to it. Do you understand?"

Meg hung her head. "Aye, Mother," she muttered, and then was surprised to hear her father's stifled laugh behind her. No one other than Cecily had seen him enter the solar, and he had put his fingers to his lips to warn her not to spoil the surprise. He had been gone for several days to Drogheda, where

Parliament was sitting, and Cecily had not expected him home so soon. But he could not forbear to laugh when he heard Cecily's reprimand and so had revealed himself to his children, who threw themselves at him, clamoring for attention.

Cecily clucked her tongue. "Sweet Jesu, but you do spoil them, Richard," she complained, but her mouth softened as she watched. Her heart had leaped when he had come in, as it always did on her seeing him after a parting. "Margaret is altogether too bold and needs no encouragement."

When the children had run off to play in the castle garden with their nursemaids, Cecily demanded to know why Richard had been laughing. "Someone must discipline them if you will not, my lord," she said, indignant.

Richard drew her into his arms and rocked her from side to side. "I adore you when you are stern. Your back straightens, your chin lifts, and you look at those little faces as though they were billmen in your front line. 'Tis then you more than deserve to be called Proud Cis, and it is then I wish your mother could see you." He held her from him and took her chin in his fingers, noting the persistent mulishness in her face. "I was laughing because I was remembering another little girl who used to speak so boldly to her mother. Why do you think I love Meggie so much?" He lifted an eyebrow. "Aye, because she reminds me of you."

Cecily's resolve to stand her ground dissolved into a sheepish smile, and without losing a beat, she pulled his head to her and kissed him, as through the window from the sunny garden below floated the happy sounds of childish laughter.

LATER, AFTER THEY had supped in private for a change, and Gresilde, Constance, and Richard's ushers of the chamber had excused themselves, Richard led Cecily to the inviting cushions he had placed on the floor of the tiled bedchamber and handed her a cup of her favorite hippocras. For the first time since the previous September, the wood laid in the grate remained unlit, and Cecily's cambric chemise was all she needed for warmth in the balmy night air. She stretched out her long legs on the cushions and sighed with pleasure as Richard set to massaging her feet. It seemed to her that they had not stopped holding court since their arrival in Dublin, and although she enjoyed her role of first lady of Ireland, and felt born to it, she longed for restful moments like this.

Richard broke in on her thoughts. "I have a story to tell you, Cis. 'Tis as strange as any you might read in a romance, and I heard it upon my return this afternoon. It concerns my lord of Suffolk."

Cecily lifted her head to look at him. "Do not say he has been forgiven, Richard."

Her husband shook his head. "If you remember, the punishment was exile for five years. He was supposed to leave England on the first of May, and indeed for more than a month following his release from custody he busied himself with his affairs in Suffolk. On the last day of April he reached Ipswich, where he gathered a crowd and swore on the sacrament that he was innocent of any wrongdoing. The very next day, he set sail with his followers in two ships and a pinnace."

"Where was he going?" Cecily demanded. "To his friend King Charles?"

Richard chuckled. "*Patience, ma belle.* Do you want the story or not?" Seeing her nod vigorously, he went on. "It appears he was making for Calais, but unsure of his welcome there, he sent the pinnace to test the waters. Before it could make land, some pirates came from nowhere and intercepted it. They demanded the sailors take them back to the flotilla." He frowned. "Odd that the pirate ship was named *Nicholas of the Tower,* which is a royal ship, and odd it seemed to know that the pinnace belonged to the duke of Suffolk's little flotilla. No mind, for in the end the duke of Suffolk ended up on the *Nicholas.*"

Cecily's eyes were as big as rose nobles. She sat up, her arms hugging her knees. "So you do not believe they were pirates, do you? It does seem to me they were lying in wait. Sweet Jesu!"

"It was the cry that greeted him when he went aboard that makes me think not, Cis. 'Welcome!' they shouted. 'Welcome, traitor!' Now tell me this. What pirate would care about treason? All are robbers and cutthroats. And their behavior following those cries was even more curious. First they gave him a mock trial and then for a day and a night they allowed the duke to pray and make his confession to almighty God before they put him in a small boat—"

"And cast him alone out to sea? Why, 'tis monstrous!" Cecily cried, but then added, "Albeit well deserved."

"Do stop interrupting me," Richard complained. "They did not cast him out to sea alone but with a murderous little Irishman—who has since returned here and told his story to anyone who would listen at the tavern last night, which included Piers Taggett." He clucked his tongue in disbelief. "I almost cannot think it true."

"What isn't true? The story, Richard, what was the rest of the story?" Cecily urged.

"The man said it took him several strokes of a rusty sword to cut off the duke's head before he rowed back to his ship. From there the pirates sailed for England and supposedly threw the headless body into the shallow water near Dover. I wonder if it has been found."

Cecily grimaced in disgust. "I wonder what they did with the head. Oh, Richard, what a terrible tale. I know Suffolk made your life difficult, but surely he did not need to die so cruelly. Banishment was hard enough."

"You are too kind," Richard said. "I can never forgive him for withholding the support I needed to keep Normandy or for surrendering Maine and Anjou, and certainly not for disposing of my presence by sending me here. Aye, he may not have been an evil man, but I confess I am not unhappy with the outcome, especially if it brings me closer to the king," Richard stated. "However, it pains me more to think that one of Henry's trusted councillors may have designed this hideous act." He shook his head. "One day an all-powerful favorite, the next a headless corpse covered in seaweed. It makes one think."

Cecily suddenly had a vision of her husband's body without a head and she shivered. Thinking she was cold, Richard slid next to her and wrapped her in his arms.

"To THE RIGHT noble Richard, earl of Salisbury, we greet you well," Richard dictated to his clerk a few days later. "I must report that the Irish enemy, MacGeoghegan, with three or four Irish captains and associated with a great fellowship of English rebels, burned down my town of Rathmore as well as villages round about and are now assembling in woods and forts, waiting to do hurt and grievance to the king's subjects. For the which cause I write at this time unto the king's highness and beseech his good grace for to hasten my payment for this land, according to his letters of warrant . . ." He paused. ". . . To the intent I may wage men in sufficient number, for to resist the malice of same enemies and punish them for such wise . . ." Richard paused again, frowning. Then he slammed his fist on the table. "For doubtless, if my payment be not had in all haste, for to have men of war in defense and safeguard of this land, my power cannot stretch to keep it in the king's obedience."

He swiveled around to address his councillor. "Too strong, Sir William? Nay? Then, Master Oram, write on.

"And very necessity will compel me to come into England to live there, upon my poor livelihood, for I had rather be dead than any inconvenience should fall there until my default; for it shall never—underscore 'never,' good clerk—be said, nor remain written anywhere, by the grace of God, that Ireland was lost by my negligence."

He stood looking over John Oram's shoulder, reading what was written in the scribe's meticulous hand, while Sir William hid a satisfied smile. Richard took the proffered quill and scrawled his signature under the date: at Dublin, this fifteenth day of June in the twenty-ninth year of the reign of King Henry.

The bright red wax dripped like hot blood on the parchment. Richard reached for one of his seals and pressed it firmly into the liquid. Sir William noticed at once that the duke had chosen the house of York's white rose cognizance over his personal falcon and fetterlock, and arched a quizzical brow. Richard looked at him, then down at the seal, and gave a sharp laugh.

"I know what you are thinking, Sir William. You are thinking that I am throwing down the gauntlet by brazenly using the white rose." He shook his finger at Sir William playfully. "Look again, my dear Oldhall. All I see is a red rose!"

Cecily walked in to hear the last remark. She waited for Sir William to bow as the clerk scurried out with the letter. "Good day, Sir William. What is this about a red rose?"

Richard smiled as he took her hand and kissed it. "I think Sir William is worried I have gone too far in my letter to Salisbury and the council. What say you, Oldhall?"

Sir William took a deep breath and spoke his mind. "Your grace," he addressed Cecily, "your husband misjudges me. If I may speak my mind plainly, I must confess I am delighted by the strength of his conviction. I have watched Lord Richard stay silent through many months of frustration. He has every right to be angry, and a lesser man would have reached this point years before now, in my humble opinion." He paused, wondering if he had stepped over the line, but seeing rapt attention on both faces, he soldiered on, now addressing Richard. "I believe the time may have come for you to claim what is yours by right, your grace." Cecily gasped. "No one can question your undying loyalty to King Henry, but it is time you took your place as the premier noble in the kingdom." The old councillor had heard it on good authority that the lawlessness and discontent in England was blamed squarely on the ineffectual man on the throne, and he knew many would welcome York as the leading councillor, should Richard be angered sufficiently to return to court. "The country needs you, your grace," Oldhall said to Richard. "It is time to go home."

His piece spoken, he bowed and limped from the room, leaving Richard and Cecily speechless.

"GOING HOME SO soon?" Cecily exclaimed in a hoarse whisper, shooting out from under the bedcovers and her husband's embrace. She thumped on his chest in exasperation. "But Richard, we have only just arrived. The children are about settled in and we were supposed to stay here for ten years. Have you been recalled to London?"

Richard sat up next to her and reached for his shirt. "Forgive me if you are taken by surprise, Cis, but Oldhall was right. I have reached the limit of my patience with the king. You knew I received a visit from William Tyndale this day, did you not?"

"Lancaster King-at-Arms? Aye, I heard." She had seen the herald arrive a little after noon with his small retinue of men-at-arms in the king's livery.

"Henry sent him to assure me that he has not forgotten me," Richard said silkily. "Lancaster spoke long and eloquently of the king's high favor and praise for my loyal service."

Cecily frowned in the darkness. She knew this falsely honeyed tone usually led to a sudden burst of anger on the part of her husband, and she attempted to stem it for fear of waking Gresilde, who slept close by on her truckle bed. "Come now, Richard, you should be flattered that the king sent such an important herald all the way to Dublin, and I . . ."

"'Twas only words, my lady, words!" Richard erupted. "The herald came empty-handed. Not a groat, not a penny, not a noble did the king send me. Just words." He ranted on in a vehement denunciation of King Henry and his council, and Cecily tried to shush him with little success. "I feel betrayed, Cis," he muttered, finally slowing down. "I cannot stay here without funds to put down the MacGeoghegan rebellion once and for all and hold O'Neill loyal. But more than this, I cannot fight for my position at court while I languish in Ireland and allow Henry to lavish favor on others with a lesser claim to privilege than mine. If I could but have a little of the king's ear, he would know I am not his enemy. 'Tis Somerset who poisons the water for me while I am not there to defend myself. 'Tis plain as a pikestaff that with his gifts Henry means to strengthen his Lancaster ties to Somerset and Exeter and so weaken mine. But I am heir presumptive after all, and no one must forget that."

His voice had risen, and Cecily whispered, "Have a care, Richard." Her heart was beating fast. She had not seen Richard so bellicose before.

"'Tis said the crown is bankrupt. Bankrupt!" Richard continued more quietly. "Henry has given away all his lands, grants, and lordships to those covetous men who pretend to serve him. Dear God, what will become of England?"

Cecily put her arms around him then and laid her head on his shoulder. "Soft, Dickon, let us get some rest. We can speak more on it in the morning." In truth, she needed more time to contemplate his words. She was enjoying their life in Ireland, where Richard was king in all but name and she his consort, and she was not ready to see Richard's dreams dashed once again. She knew Edmund Beaufort was a dangerous man, and if he had the ear of both king and queen, then Richard's ambition might be thwarted anew—and at what cost to her growing family. She sighed, coaxed him down under the covers, and turned on her side so that he could cradle her, as he always did before they fell asleep.

"I must go home, Cis. Can you understand and support me in this?"

"Wherever you go I go, my lord. 'Tis not only my duty but my desire," she assured him, although her heart was full of misgiving. Feeling his familiar warmth against her, she made brave to whisper, "I beg of you, though, for the sake of our children, to have a care. You do not want to make an enemy of the king."

AND SO ONCE again the York family packed up its belongings and prepared to move on. Cecily and Richard bade farewell to their Irish hosts at a lavish banquet that Richard could ill afford, leaving as Richard's deputy James Butler, earl of Ormond, to attempt to keep the peace. Richard had made his mark in his short term as lieutenant, and he was assured by the White Earl that he would always have allies in Ireland.

The voyage across the treacherous Irish Sea in late August was not as pleasant as the first one, and Cecily and Constance spent many an hour tending to the seasick children. When they tried to land at Beaumaris, they were met with armed men blocking the watergate entry into the castle.

"What does this mean, Richard?" Cecily asked anxiously when he returned to the quarterdeck and told her they would be sailing on to Denbigh, one of Richard's own townships, instead.

"It seems the king was expecting me, my lady," he snarled, pacing the cramped space, "and it seems he does not want me back. The commander here has instructions to imprison me and my men at Conway in the name of the king if I set foot on Anglesey. Arrested! Christ's nails! 'Tis hard to believe. I suspect the summer incursion by that rebel Cade has made Henry nervous."

Cecily nodded, chewing on her lip. She had listened with dismay when news had reached Dublin in late June of a revolt by commoners and gentry alike from the counties of Kent, Surrey, and Sussex, led by a veteran Irish soldier named Jack Cade. A huge band of rebels had reached the outskirts of London.

"But Cade's followers were not the same sort of rabble who followed Wat Tyler in the second King Richard's time," Richard explained. "These were knights, members of Parliament, sheriffs, and well-known gentlemen along with yeomen and tradesmen. The king and council had to take them seriously."

The rebels' manifesto was reasonable enough, Cecily thought, especially as the first and foremost of the points involved Richard. It stated that the king "has had false counsel, for his lands are lost, his merchandise is lost, his commons destroyed, the sea is lost, France is lost, and himself so poor he cannot pay for his meat," and thus their first demand was for the king to rid himself of "the traitors that be about him." It called for him "to take about his noble person his true blood of his royal realm, that is to say, the high and mighty prince the duke of York, exiled from our sovereign lord's person by the noising of the false traitor, the duke of Suffolk, and his affinity."

When Cecily heard those words, she clapped her hands in delight. "You see, my lord, someone in England does appreciate you," she cried, but was immediately silenced by Richard's glower.

"Soft, my lady, I beg of you. You know not who may be listening. Aye, the words might be flattering, but when I tell you that this Cade fellow put it about that his real name is Mortimer . . ." He nodded as Cecily's hand flew to her mouth and her eyes widened in shock. "Aye, it is falsely put about that he is a kinsman of mine, thus implicating me in this rebellion. Certes, I cannot prove otherwise, for here I sit, helpless and out of earshot!"

"Is Cade still a threat?" Cecily asked, and was relieved to know that eventually all the rebels had returned home, the manifesto had been ignored, and Jack Cade had died trying to defend himself. His body had been quartered, and his head placed atop London Bridge alongside other traitors.

Cade's revolt, however, was only a small part of the widespread discontent up and down the country that year.

20

Ludlow, Autumn 1450

Cecily was never more glad to see the Felton-stone walls and parapets of the York bastion of Ludlow rising from the Corve plain and glowing plum rose in the setting September sun.

"Home," she murmured, her heart singing, as hundreds of townspeople ran out to greet their lord and lady. After the hectic life in Ireland, Cecily was looking forward to being in her own home once more. Bessie and Meg waved at the children who skipped alongside the cumbersome chariot Richard had commandeered for Cecily at Denbigh. Field hands, carrying their scythes and whetstone bags, were wending their way home after a day of harvesting the ripened corn, their faces and necks brown as beechnuts. The men wiped their glistening brows with sweaty kerchiefs and the women untucked their coarse russet skirts from the belts and brushed off the chaff before hurrying to join the cavalcade.

"Look you!" a buxom young laundress cried to her friend, balancing a basket of wet linen on her hip as they climbed the riverbank to the road. She pointed to the two boys riding together on a small palfrey a few paces behind their father on his prancing courser. "'Tis the lords Edward and Edmund. Lord above, how they are grown."

"And handsome," agreed her friend, and Cecily glowed with pride. Ned was sitting tall in his saddle and basking in the attention he was getting from the spectators. He looks older than his eight years, she thought wistfully. Soon it will be time for him and Edmund to have their own household, and we must employ a tutor as soon as we have settled. She was dreading a time when they would not always be with her. She waved and smiled at the enthusiastic townsfolk, pleased with the warm homecoming, which was getting even more boisterous as the procession made its way through the Corve Gate up the hill and into the market square, where the high market cross sat hard by the castle's outer bailey.

Richard chose to dismount at the main gate. He walked back to Cecily. "Shall we go in on foot, my lady?" he coaxed her with a smile, stretching his arms out to his two daughters. Taking each by the hand, he waited for one of his captains to help Cecily from the chariot, and then the ducal family entered the outer bailey with its stables, cookhouses, buttery, and many sheds, where craftsmen joined the scores of servants cheering their return.

"'Tis so good to be home, my lord," Cecily murmured to her husband over Meggie's fair head. "I pray that we may remain here, content, forever."

Richard gave her a wry grin. "I wish it could be so, my dear, and indeed for you and the children, it shall be for as long as you want. But you know we cannot feel safe until I am assured our sovereign lord acknowledges the letters and bills that I have lately sent to him. And I can only do that by going to court."

Cecily's throat constricted. Why can I not feel anything but fear? she asked herself. Have we not wished and dreamed for Richard to take his place all these years? I used to want to be a queen, she remembered, but that was before I became a woman, before I had my children. Joan's words came back to her: "Your duty is to your husband, and you must stand by him always." It is easier said than done, Mother, she thought.

They were at the drawbridge to the high gatehouse tower, and Cecily glanced up at the fetterlock badge sculpted in relief over the portcullis. "You will not stir up trouble, will you?" She touched her daughter's head and looked long at Richard. "These children need their father, and . . ." She paused, biting her lip. "I need my husband."

Richard chuckled as he picked up Meg and carried her through the dark of the archway and to the inner bailey. He kept his tone playful. "What has happened to my ambitious wife, the one who has urged me to take my rightful place at the king's side these many years?"

Cecily took Bessie's clammy hand and hurried to keep up, cursing herself now for having encouraged him to assert his claim. Am I to blame for this? she worried. Sweet Jesu, was I wrong? What is important to me now is my family. Have I jeopardized their safety? "I became a mother," she answered him.

Richard did not hear. He put Meggie down, strode across the courtyard to the round Norman chapel, and knelt before the chaplain to receive a blessing. Cecily gazed after him, tears very close and fear gripping her heart.

* * *

IN THE FOLLOWING week, Richard wrote two open letters to the king, in which he declared his loyalty and willingness to defend himself against false accusations. Receiving no response, he could only conclude that the king had hostile intentions, and so Richard took action to defend himself.

When Cecily stood atop the rampart of the gatehouse tower to watch him go, she could just see the fields to the south of the walled town filled with men-at-arms, foot soldiers, and yeomen from Richard's Welsh and English lordships who had answered his call to form a bodyguard to escort him to London.

Astride his black courser, his white rose banner carried proudly by his faithful captain, Sir Davy Hall, Richard rode out of Ludlow, over the Ludford Bridge and on to London. Cecily did not know whether to feel pride or fear, but she could not scream out to him to turn back. As she descended the winding staircase, looping her long train over her arm and holding tight to the rail, she thought back on their last private exchange when they had broken their fast earlier.

"I will not make the same mistake Gloucester made at Bury," Richard had said. "If I go with a goodly number, it is not likely I shall be set upon by the court party or any enemy. I go in peace, my lady, and I have no intention of threatening London. I simply want to be taken seriously. My dear, I have listened to you, to my own councillors, and to my conscience for long enough, and all have told me to fight for my rightful position. Now I finally hear you. I believe 'tis the time, and if the king will not uphold me, then perhaps God will."

Cecily put down her piece of buttery cheese and wiped her mouth on a snowy napkin. She remained calm, even though she felt the bile rise in her throat. She knew she ought not to show him the fear that gripped her heart, but there was a tremor in her voice. "How do you know you have any support, my lord. Are my brother and his son with you?"

Richard toyed with a piece of cold beef speared on his knife and nodded. "And your sister Katherine's son, Norfolk," he said. "They support my desire for reform, 'tis certain. We must make the king understand that Somerset and his cronies must go."

"But promise me you will not break your sacred oath. You will swear fealty anew to Henry, will you not?" Cecily pleaded, swiftly going down on her knees in front of him and pressing his free hand to her cheek.

Richard put down his knife and drew her onto his lap. "Certes, I will, you silly goose," he assured her. "He may not be a perfect king, but he is the king, and I only wish to help him be a better one." He shook his head. "A kingdom can never afford to be ruled by a bad king, Cis. If only Henry were like his father, good King Harry, then England would not be in this turmoil. But, aye, sweetheart, I will swear fealty, for Henry is still God's anointed. In this, I promise you, I am not my father's son. The people are simply looking for someone of rank to lead reform, and I am he. Come now, Cis, we have been apart before. Have I not always returned?"

Cecily stroked his soft beard and tried to smile. "Aye, but you have never ridden off to confront your sovereign before." She got up and went to the window of the solar, looking down at the steep slope below her. He came to stand behind her, resting his hands on her shoulders.

"Why the glum face, Cis? I cannot ride away with you angry with me."

She weighed her next words carefully, not wanting to alarm him. "I dreamed of La Pucelle's burning again last night," she said softly. "'Tis the first time in a year, and I could not help but think it was an omen."

Richard crossed himself, but if he was unnerved, he did not let her see but instead made light of the dream. "Mother of God, my love, 'tis no wonder you are so lily-livered today. I cannot believe you still dream of her. It was so long ago," he said, putting his arms around her. "No doubt you dreamed of her after listening to Ned frightening Bessie with tales of witches yesterday."

His dismissive tone was too much for her already jangled nerves. Wheeling round to him, Cecily declared, "Jeanne d'Arc was not a witch, my lord. I am sorry I ever confided to you what an impression she made on me. You mock me and her with your insinuations. Mark my words: One day they will revere her in France."

Richard sighed. Anxious to begin his journey to London, he gave in. "That I doubt, my dear, but I promise never to call her witch again. Now let us go and find the children. I wish to make my farewells."

As Cecily reached the courtyard, quiet now after Richard's departure, she hurried to the chapel and was once again comforted by its intimate circular nave. She sat down at her favorite spot opposite one of the sculpted stone corbels that supported the upper floor, clasped her hands together, and closed her eyes. "Blessed Virgin, sweet Mother of God, hear my prayer. I have not begged for your help for a long time, but now I ask that you guard the life of my beloved husband and guide his feet onto the right path. He has become rash and quick to anger of late, and I fear his tongue or his sword may lead him astray"—she lowered her voice to a mere whisper—"or to treason.

Mother of God, in your divine mercy, watch over him and bring him home safely to us."

She did not hear or see the door from the upper floor open, but she suddenly sensed she was not alone, and her eyes opened wide.

"Who is it?" Cecily's hoarse whisper echoed eerily around the walls.

A bright light seemed to float before the chancel door and bathe the chapel, making Cecily put up her hand to shield her eyes. And then it dimmed, and she felt once again alone in the quiet gloom.

"Sweet Jesu," she murmured, falling to her knees on the tiled floor. "Was I dreaming? Or was that a spirit?" She crossed herself and, finding her rosary beads in a leather pouch on her belt, began to pray.

What could it mean? The last time she had seen such a light was in the dungeon at Bouvreuil with Jeanne. She suddenly thought, could it be the same? Had Jeanne visited her in the dream? Was Jeanne's spirit here in the little chapel now? she asked herself, trembling. Mumbling the *aves* one after another as fast as she could, she found the rote prayers calming. "You have always been with me, Virgin Mother, have you not?" she murmured reverently, kissing the golden crucifix on the end of the rosary chain. "It was a sign, I am certain of it."

She smiled. It was then she knew that Richard would come back to her. "Holy Mother, give me strength to do my duty and ask God to keep my family in His care."

GRACIOUS LADY, DUCHESS of York, and right well beloved wife, I greet you well from Fotheringhay, where I have lately arrived from London following a pilgrimage to Our Lady of Walsingham's shrine. Your sister Katherine welcomed me into Norfolk, as did her son and my niece, his wife.

Cecily paused in surprise. Richard had declared his intention of staying close to the king until Parliament opened at the end of November. She read on.

Upon my journey from Ludlow to London, I encountered much discontent in the towns and cities where we passed. You will be right pleased to know that often we were cheered by the people as we went, and some even embraced our cause and joined us on our journey to see the king.

Cecily breathed a sigh of relief for Richard. Despite the force he had taken with him, Richard had confided that he did not know how the people of England viewed him—whether as a rebel, as a threat to the king, or as someone who might take their grievances to Parliament and the king and fight for redress of grievances. It was gratifying that he encountered no ill will, she mused, looking back at John Oram's neat script. She was not to know that there had in fact been several attempts by the court faction to halt his progress to London, and the speaker of the Commons had been murdered on his way to meet secretly with York.

Instead, Richard chose to give Cecily the happier news:

> *Our sovereign lord, King Henry, received me in his presence at Westminster, where I again swore I was his true liegeman and obedient servant. He took me at my word and called me his dear cousin, and it was agreed I should be included in the council, but he would not listen to the need for reform. I went away to stay at my lord Bishop of Salisbury's house, and I drafted yet another bill.*

Cecily drew in a breath. This was the bill, she knew, that would make hard demands on the king. Richard had said he would submit such a bill only if the king had received him kindly and listened to his declaration of loyalty. This bill would demand not only reform but also the dismissal of Somerset. She shook her head. If she could read between the lines, he had submitted it, it had been ignored, and Richard had felt the need to retire to Fotheringhay.

Richard continued:

> *London is no place for women and children now. Since Somerset returned disgraced from France in August, the city is filled with disaffected soldiers—veterans of the endless years of war. They have nowhere to go and no work and have resorted to violence and crime. Even Somerset's life was threatened in the street one day. You will be amused—or not—that I helped rescue him from disaster, and the king had him housed in the Tower for his safety. He is a fortunate man on many counts, in truth.*

Cecily rose from the wooden bench in the knot garden, where she was enjoying some privacy, and began to pace around the neatly clipped privet hedges. Constance, always a constant in her life, was nearby, deadheading roses, and somewhere in the distance she could hear the high-pitched shouts and laughter of her boys playing on the grass along the western wall of the outer bailey. She wanted more information, but upon reading the letter's last paragraph, she knew that, as always, a wife must be patient.

> *Look for me before Martinmas, my dearest wife. I shall answer all your questions—for certes, you must have several—when I next greet you. Commend me to my sons and daughters and tell them I count the days until we are together again. To you I send all honor and love. Your humble and faithful husband, Richard.*

THE COLD, DRIVING November rain pelted the windows, smearing the view of the drab, leafless trees. Ned and Edmund were playing draughts, Edmund slumping further and further on his stool as he watched Ned gleefully amass a large pile of white pieces by jumping Edmund's black pieces on the chequered board. Cuddled on cushions by the crackling fire, Gresilde was telling Bessie and Meg a story, and Constance pored over the writings of Galen, an ancient medical text that was never far from her side.

"The hogs must be good and fat by now, judging by the number of acorns the oaks produced this year," Cecily remarked to Gresilde as she moved the delicate wooden frame around to start on a new corner of her tapestry. "It means 'twill be a hard winter, so they say, but we should have plenty to eat. The steward will order the slaughter to begin in a few days, and I pray my lord will be home for the Martinmas feast." She stopped when she heard the sound of voices in the passageway.

The door was flung wide and a guard outside cried, "His grace—" but was cut off by Richard, who finished the announcement for him. "Duke Richard is come home and desires an audience with his wife, the Duchess Cecily." He had changed out of his soggy traveling clothes and presented himself in a new short gown of saffron velvet trimmed with sable, and a square black bonnet.

"And me!" Meggie squeaked joyfully as she ran headlong into her father's arms.

"By all that is holy, child," Richard exclaimed, pretending to find her heavy as he lifted her. "How you have grown since September." Meg giggled and snuggled her face into the soft fur collar. "And Bess, my good girl. Have you been staying out of trouble?" Richard smiled down at his elder daughter, who had her arms wrapped around his thighs and was nodding her blond curls furiously. "Aye, I am sure that you have."

By now the boys were kneeling for their father's blessing, their earnest faces seeking approval. "God give you welcome, Father," Ned said, his face flushed from the heat of the fire. "We are right glad to see you."

"As am I you, my son. You may rise," Richard told him and kissed Meg on the nose. "I must put you down, sweeting, for I have not yet greeted your mother."

Cecily had risen but had stood back to watch him with the children, her heart rejoicing. Why, Cis, she told herself as she felt the familiar sensual tug in her breasts, you still lust for him after all these years. His face was haggard and he had lost weight. She longed to melt into his arms and soothe away his troubles.

Now Richard was kissing her hand, his slate-gray eyes looking at her with love.

"I trust your journey was safely made, my lord."

"I did not come alone, my lady, and so, aye, it was safely made. We shall be having a few more mouths to feed before I return to London, if my plans bear fruit, so I hope the cattle and sheep are herded in and some are ready for butchering."

Richard sank into a chair close to Cecily's and held his feet up to the fire. "You do not know how I dreamed of this moment on the last leg of the ride from Worcester. God's bones, it was miserable."

Cecily sat down in her cushioned seat, and Edmund sat on the footstool near her and allowed his mother to play with his fair hair. Cecily raised an eyebrow at her husband. "How many people are we expecting? The sheep are penned, and the swineherds will round up the hogs in a day or so."

"I shall instruct the steward to butcher enough animals for a small household this winter. The rest I will take and buy more along the way to feed an army of, I hope, four thousand," he replied. "It must not be said that Richard of York's men pillaged when they came to London—as the retainers of some noble houses are doing."

"Dear God, four thousand?" Cecily exclaimed, dread creeping into her heart. "Are you not merely attending a session of Parliament? You wrote to me that the king received you kindly. What has changed that you need so many retainers?"

Richard shrugged and stared into the flames. "Nothing has changed, and there is the rub. Somerset is still the king's chief councillor, and more than that, he has become the queen's champion. Thus my bills calling for his dismissal are no doubt now residing in the Fleet ditch. I have gained the support of many disaffected citizens and veteran soldiers from Normandy who see Somerset as the reason France is lost. A few nobles may be sympathetic as well, but even so I am not prepared to enter the city without troops at my back." He straightened in his chair and took a sip of wine, averting his eyes from his wife's. "But enough of such disheartening talk. How have the children been behaving? And when may I see George?"

Cecily's face softened at the mention of her youngest. "He chose his first birthday to take his first steps, my dear. He is a beautiful child and a charmer. 'Tis my belief he will get all he desires in life as no one will be able to resist that smile. Our Meggie worships him already, and 'twas she who spent hour upon hour helping him to walk."

Richard grinned and looked over at his favorite daughter. She was sitting close by Bessie, who was busy dressing a poppet, but Margaret's eyes and ears were fixed on her parents. She looked down quickly and fiddled with her own poppet, afraid she might be chastised for eavesdropping.

"George may have all the charm, my love," Richard murmured, "but that child has all the brains. She does not miss a thing."

Despite his weariness, Richard joined Cecily in her high tester bed that night, enjoying its downy luxury.

"I swear to you, my bones cannot tolerate sleeping on the ground or even a straw pallet anymore," he declared, watching Cecily draw the heavy velvet curtains around them, his fingers itching to wind themselves in her still glorious hair.

Cecily chuckled. "Aye, old man, how does it feel to be in your fortieth year?" She playfully touched his prick through his nightshirt, making him jerk his knees up to protect himself. "Does everything still work?" she teased.

Richard grasped her arms and roughly pulled her down on top of him. "Aye, my lady, it does," he replied, laughing. "Let me show you how well." Finally fulfilling his desire, he ran his fingers through the silky tresses that concealed them both from the outside world and whispered, "How I love you, my sweet Cecily," as their lips met. They lost themselves in a lingering kiss. As their passion mounted, Cecily reminded herself to eschew a climax and thus, she believed, conception of a child.

I have had too many babes, she told herself, as she took Richard to pleasurable heights. She was not prepared to bring another child into a world so full of strife and danger for the house of York.

THEIR TIME TOGETHER was all too short. A week later, after more and more men had answered their lord's call and arrived to camp around Ludlow, he was yet again bidding Cecily farewell on the great hall steps.

"If I can, I will be with you for Christmas, my love," he said, dismayed to see her close to tears. "But the longer Parliament is in session, the better for my cause, I believe. If aught goes wrong, I will send you word with Roger Ree. You are safe here, Cis. 'Tis far from London, and I trust the men I am leaving to protect you." He frowned. "You are pale, my dear."

Cecily clutched his arm. "I am afraid. You do not think the king would harm you, Richard, do you?" she asked, breathing hard. She had woken with a toothache, and her whole head was throbbing.

Richard smiled grimly. "With an army at my back? I seriously doubt it. But again, I shall make it known I am his grace's obedient liegeman, so why would he harm me? You worry too much, my dear. Now let us make our farewells."

He knelt and kissed her hand, then rose and mounted his courser, which was fully caparisoned. Richard was magnificent in his murrey and blue tabard, a simple gold coronet upon his dark head. He wanted the finery to inspire the citizens of Ludlow to cheer their lord as he rode out of the city.

Waving to Cecily and his children, he turned and trotted through the gatehouse archway and into the outer bailey. As soon as he was gone, Cecily's hand went to her aching jaw and her face distorted in pain. She climbed the few steps to the children and saw tears streaming down Meggie's face. Ignoring her own distress, she bent down and embraced the little girl.

"He will be home again soon, I promise," she whispered. "Say a prayer for him, sweeting, and the Virgin will protect him. Now dry your tears. You must learn to control your emotions in public, Meggie." She straightened and, grim-faced, walked ahead of them into the hall and went in search of Constance, her own tears forced back into her heart.

RICHARD HAD INSTRUCTED Cecily that he wished Edward and Edmund to witness their first ritual slaughter of a hog at Martinmas. The ceremony marked the beginning of the long process of butchering the livestock and storing food for the winter.

"Not Edmund, Richard," Cecily begged. "He is still so young."

"Stuff and nonsense, Cis," Richard retorted. "Do not protect him so or he will truly grow up to be afraid. He is but a year younger than Ned, and I was even younger when Sir Robert made me watch. It was not practical in Dublin, but here at home we know the butchers. 'Tis something the boys should witness. I regret I cannot be here for it, but I will ask Piers to attend the boys. They trust him, and besides, he is a farmer's son, so he can explain the ritual and prepare them. You need not be present, my dear."

But Cecily could not allow her sons to watch the butchering without her, and since her own father had made her at an early age break a chicken's neck, she knew in her heart that it was considered, at least by men, a necessary part of growing up.

Cecily walked with the boys to the animal pen in a corner of the castle green. The ground was a quagmire from the rain and the many animals penned there, and she was glad of her wooden clogs. Piers had taken both boys by the hand, though Edward soon pulled his away, deeming himself too old for such childishness. Still, he listened carefully as Piers explained what they would see. Edmund stiffened and pulled back, but when he saw that Edward was ready to mock him, the younger boy lifted his chin and walked grimly on. Cecily's heart went out to him.

When they were seated on haycocks outside the small pen, Piers gave the swineherd the signal to send in the first of the hogs. The unsuspecting animal, now fattened from a month of foraging for acorns, waddled in, and giving a few grunts, snuffled at the ground for something to eat. From behind, a farmhand took the beast by surprise and pulled its legs out from under it, and the pig fell over with a squeal of annoyance. Its protests grew louder when the sturdy yeoman knelt upon its bristly brown back and grasped a handful of belly flesh. Edward laughed heartily at the hog's frantic and noisy attempts to unseat the heavy man and dug Edmund in the ribs. But Edmund had seen the second man come forward with a knife in one hand and a long-handled pan in the other, and he began to panic. He looked around desperately for Cecily, who guiltily avoided his terrified eyes. She had no intention of allowing the many yeomen watching to see any weakness in either of her sons.

Piers gently talked Edmund into focusing on what was happening, and Cecily was grateful that the big man put his arm on the little boy's shoulder just as the second man slit the pig's throat. Its hideous death scream still made Cecily, who had heard it many times before, emit a gasp of horror, squeeze her eyes tight, and put her hands over her ears. The pan, positioned to catch the blood, filled rapidly, but the noise, which should have subsided, endured for too long. It was only when Cecily opened her eyes that she realized the scream was coming from Edmund. Jumping from her perch, she unhooked her cloak and flung it over Edmund's shaking body, pulling his head to her bosom and muffling his sobs. She felt all eyes upon them.

"Hush, my child," she soothed him. "You have been a brave boy and your father will be proud of you." She felt his arms fumble for her waist through the mantle, and she tightened hers around him.

At a loss, Edward looked on in dismay, but Piers took charge of him and led him away through the knot of castle workers who had gathered to ogle the initiation. Edward held his head high, and as though he were already a leader of men, he nodded graciously right and left as men twice his size touched their forelocks to him.

Between them, Gresilde and Cecily half carried Edmund back to the castle, Cecily's aloof and inscrutable expression stalling any unkind murmurs that might have arisen to embarrass her son. Inside, her heart was breaking.

That night Edmund had a nightmare, and although the nursery was far from the ducal chambers, his cries awoke Cecily from a sound sleep. Hurrying through the cold passageway that connected the lodgings, Cecily was led by a guard and followed closely by Gresilde.

"'Twas but a bad dream, my son, my sweetheart," Cecily told him as she held his shivering body close. "Mama is here to keep you safe, never fear."

His light blue eyes looked up into his mother's familiar face, and Cecily was dismayed to see the terror in them. "What is it, Edmund? What did you dream?"

"That I . . . I was the h . . . hog an . . . an . . . and a soldier cut my throat and h . . . held his helmet to catch my blood." And he buried his face in her chest.

It was all Cecily could do not to swoon at the image. She lifted Edmund off the bed and onto his knees next to her, crossed herself, and began to calmly recite the *pater noster*. The soft Latin words seemed to comfort the boy, and soon he had joined in, his eyes closed and his hands clasped devoutly before him.

*M*other of God!" Cecily cried aloud from her bed, aghast at her own real- ization. "My sweet Edmund. He foresaw his own death."

She ran to the window and flung the shutters wide, hoping the light would chase away the awful darkness of the nursery scene. I told you he was too young to witness the hog slaughter, Richard, she raged now. Her fists balled as her anger grew for her husband, who had left her a widow and the grieving mother of a most beloved son. I told you, but you did not listen. And I also told you he was too young to fight. But you did not heed me about that, either, did you? Poor little Edmund, I can still see the terror in his face when he told me of his dream. She beat her fists on the wooden shutter and sobbed. "Ah, sweet Jesu, he was too young to die."

She heard a knock on the door and brushed her sleeve over her wet face. Come, Cecily, she chided herself, you must pull yourself together for Margaret, George, and Richard. Besides, how many times had she heard Joan Beaufort tell her never to cry or appear weak in front of the servants. In fact, Cecily's mother had often admonished her never to cry at all. But although she was passing on this wisdom to Meggie, Cecily secretly believed a good weep salved the soul—in moderation, she told herself sternly. One should not burble like a fountain.

"Come," she called, and nodded to the page who slipped in carrying a tray of food. She watched as the boy stoked the fire before thanking him and wav- ing him away. "I pray you leave me and tell Dame Boyvile to attend me in an hour." She yawned and went to inspect the food. She picked up a piece of cheese and nibbled at it.

"Now, where was I?" she muttered.

Wrapping the bedrobe tightly around her, she pulled a chair closer to the hearth. Ah, yes, the end of the twenty-ninth year of the reign of King Henry.

She sighed and shook her head. Poor simple, saintly Henry, who should never have sat upon a throne. It should have been Richard, she mused sadly, and how close he came. He would have been the people's choice had not Queen Margaret and her favorite, Somerset, fought so hard to keep the throne. She frowned, remembering how the queen had accomplished Somerset's swift release from the Tower after Richard had convinced Parliament that the duke and certain others should be removed from the court. The Anjou woman was hell-bent on destroying Richard even then, Cecily mused, but then why did she send me gifts? And kind missives. How puzzling. It was as though she imagined I was married to a different man.

It was during that sitting of Parliament, when Richard's popularity was at its height, that Sir William Oldhall was elected Speaker of the Commons. But the crowing had not lasted long. Somerset was soon at Henry's right hand again, and Oldhall was accused of plotting to kill the king and was forced to seek sanctuary. Absurd, Cecily thought. Even more absurd were the honors heaped on Somerset despite his having managed to lose not only Normandy but Gascony as well by then. The only English stronghold left in France was Calais, and befuddled Henry had given his favorite the prized captaincy of that valuable staple town. What magic had the man woven around the king and queen? Cecily wondered. Had he been a younger man, Cecily might have believed the rumors that Somerset and Margaret were lovers, so many were the favors Henry lavished on the favorite.

"I fear the king will make Somerset his heir presumptive, Cecily, and I cannot stand by and see it happen," Cecily remembered Richard telling her. "He is still a bastard Beaufort and so excluded from the inheritance. If he were a better man, I might accept Henry's choice. But as he is not, it would spell more disaster for England."

Cecily sighed. If only Henry and Margaret had produced a son sooner, the conflict over the heir presumptive would have been avoided.

That was the year, too, when citizens had whispered of Henry's uncharacteristic forcefulness against Jack Cade's rebels of Kent and Sussex, Cecily recalled. "A harvest of heads," she muttered, wincing at the memory of twenty-three gruesome heads atop the drawbridge tower of London Bridge that summer. What had come over Henry, Cecily had asked her brother at the time. Salisbury had shrugged and suggested that perhaps Richard had precipitated the reprisals. "I was present at the council meeting—as was your husband—when a report from the Commons told of a motion made by a member from

Bristol to name York heir presumptive. I have never seen Henry white with anger before." And she could imagine now, as her brother had described, that Richard went equally white—whether from fear or anger she knew not. But apparently he had knelt then and sworn his allegiance to the king with all sincerity.

But had that incident sparked the fire that made Henry finally turn against Richard? Nay, it was probably what happened at Dartford.

"Dartford." Cecily groaned the word as though that village in Kent were the most desolate spot in all the world. "Disastrous Dartford."

She poured herself some ale, cursing when she spilled some on the tap-estried cloth. So many memories, she thought, with so many threads and so many twists. Ah, the fickle wheel of fortune! How she wished Constance were with her now to read the charts for her. But she refused to add to her heart-ache by thinking of Constance.

Instead she forced herself to think on happier times. She remembered Christmas at Ludlow that year. The night after celebrating Christ's birth, she had drunk a little too heartily of her favorite hippocras. Richard had carried her up to their room, and that night she had conceived their twelfth child, named—finally—after his father. How she ached for her husband now. It was hard to believe she would never again feel his body next to hers, never feel his caresses, never hear him gasp with pleasure. Stop it, Cis, she reprimanded her-self. This is not helping.

The news of her conception was the only thing that made Richard smile that January of 1452, she thought grimly, as the road to Dartford had begun on Twelfth Night. Dear Piers was the clumsiest Lord of Misrule I have ever seen, Cecily reminded herself sadly, with his cavorting and hopeless juggling. But he did make us laugh, did he not, Richard?

"Richard! Why are you not here with me and laughing?" she cried, yearning to hear that infectious neigh just one more time.

It was during the festivities that the message from Sir William in sanctuary in London had arrived. "The king made a public statement of his displeasure toward your grace," Oldhall had written to Richard. Sir William! She shook her head when she remembered him now, conjuring up his bewhiskered face and familiar gouty limp. He had stood by Richard no matter what the conse-quences. I warrant he would have rather died at Wakefield alongside Richard than of apoplexy at his town house a mere month before the battle. What a dear old friend he was to us, she mused.

I suppose Richard had no alternative but to sign yet another declaration of allegiance to Henry, she admitted grudgingly, for surely he had more than once demonstrated his fealty. If only Henry had known how much Richard had wanted to avoid civil strife, she mused. But the king's insecurity could not accommodate Richard's growing pride of place, and Richard's determination to follow his path would not allow him to watch while his perfectly valid claim to the throne was continually pushed aside. Ah, how stubborn men can be, Cecily sighed, and how foolish.

She made herself think back again to that winter of 'Fifty-two. By now, she knew, Richard feared for his own safety and that is why he had decided to take action by writing to the king again to reiterate his other vows of loyalty. Granted, 'twas in a less conciliatory tone this time, she remembered, although he had prefaced the missive by swearing that all he had desired since returning from Ireland was to show his fealty to the crown and "to restore good government." Aye, I am certain he used the phrase "good government" or was it "good governance." No matter, Cecily ruefully admitted, for it was then Richard had made a mistake. He should not have written about his personal animosity for Somerset. He had dictated the words with such venom that Cecily had found herself looking at him with a mixture of admiration and fear. What was it he had said? "Somerset laboureth continually about the king's highness for my undoing, and to corrupt my blood, and to disinherit me and my heirs, and such persons as be about me." Aye, my love, those must have been the phrases that turned Henry away from you. Queen Margaret and her Somerset had succeeded, and battle lines between Lancaster and York had been finally drawn.

Cecily swallowed the last of the ale and started to pace in front of the fire. You should have gone to court, my love, she railed at Richard. In truth, you should have told Henry to his face that you were no traitor. Surely he would have seen the truth in your eyes and the sincerity in your voice. Henry had not perceived them before so why this time, would have been your answer, I suppose.

Instead you had remained quietly at Ludlow gathering your retinue. You had not dared approach the king in London without support, but you were equally determined not to appear warlike. That is why you went peacefully to your property at Dartford to set up camp and wait, and not threaten the capital, so you told me.

She chewed aimlessly on a wheatcake and then threw the rest into the fire.

You acted with honor, Cecily told an imaginary Richard. True, you did not obey Henry's summons to attend him in Coventry but went to Kent instead with a goodly number at your back, but only because we looked to your safety. She remembered the prickle of fear that had run up her spine when the last of the company disappeared over Ludford Bridge. She knew Richard had reached the end of his tether, and that end led Richard to rebel. She knew now how foolhardy Richard's march to Dartford had been and his attempt to have Somerset dismissed. She had to admit that Henry had acted swiftly and well for once. He had ordered London to bar Richard's way into the city, and the city obeyed its king. "That was your last straw, was it not, my love," Cecily asked aloud.

Cecily well remembered what she was doing when the messenger had arrived at Ludlow after the confrontation with the king.

She had spent most of the morning wrapped in her fur-lined mantle in the garderobe, enduring the ignominies of early pregnancy. Snappish, she had eventually emerged and spent a pleasant hour talking with Edward in the warmth of the small solar. When the sharp rapping had come on her door, Cecily was jolted from her book. Astonished, she saw it was John Blaybourne, a man she thought had probably been killed in France and whom she had not thought on since Rouen. She rose and gave him a warm smile of welcome as the big man went down on one knee to her. Even in his choice of a bearer of bad tidings Richard showed his love for me, she now thought wistfully. He knew I would trust John Blaybourne and that the faithful archer would be gentle with his words.

It was then that she noticed his sorry appearance. "I see from the mud on your clothes that you have come in haste, Master Blaybourne, and in the York livery, so your visit is official, I presume." Icy fingers were beginning to encircle her delicate stomach, and she was afraid she would be sick again. "What is your news, sir?"

It was then she had learned that Richard and his now-swollen company in Kent had hoped to garner even more support from those who had followed Cade two years before, but the head harvesting of the previous summer had cowed the Kentishmen, and when Henry had arrived with a far larger force only a day later, a standoff at Dartford had occurred.

"My lord of York laid bare the treasons of my lord of Somerset in matters concerning France, demanding that Somerset be imprisoned and answer my lord of York's accusations in a fair trial," Blaybourne had told her, adding that

Salisbury and Warwick had ferried messages back and forth between the two leaders. Henry had eventually agreed to arrest Somerset and set up a hearing on condition that Richard lay down his arms and send his men home.

Blaybourne had deliberately paused then, hadn't he, Cecily recalled, and he could not look her in the eye.

"What then, Master Blaybourne?" She was very close to panic, standing over the still kneeling archer. Dear God, she remembered thinking, they have executed Richard! "Do not dissemble, sir. Is my lord safe? Tell me!" She had cried this out so loud that ten-year-old Edward had run across the solar to protect her.

"Answer her grace at once, sirrah!" Ned had commanded in his boy's soprano, and Cecily smiled now at the memory.

"My lords of York and Devon were received in the king's tent at Blackheath outside London," the archer had continued in a rush. "And they knelt before our sovereign right humbly." Blaybourne lowered his voice. "But they were deceived, my lady."

John Blaybourne told her that the king had broken his promise and that "my lord of Somerset, instead of being in custody, was standing next to the king. Upon seeing him, Duke Richard rose angrily and denounced the deception, whereupon he was seized, disarmed, and escorted into London by none other than Somerset himself."

The scene still sent shivers down her back when she thought of it. Cecily still puzzled over why Henry had not imprisoned her husband there and then, but the king had more humiliation planned for the rebellious duke of York. Richard was made to swear an oath of loyalty in front of a large crowd in St. Paul's church and to publicly lay down his arms. Cecily remembered the order by heart: "The duke of York must never again attempt such a rebellion against the king, and he must always come, humble and obedient, whenever the king commands."

"Aye, like a puppet," she cried to the empty room, wondering if it was then that her heart had begun to harden against the king.

As she poured herself more ale, Cecily pondered why the king had allowed Richard to retire to Ludlow. Strange, she thought, when Henry had no compunction about punishing some of Richard's supporters, whose heads were stuck on London Bridge or bodies hung from gibbets later that same summer. And even their friend the earl of Devon was placed under house arrest. Perhaps Henry had been so unsure of his power that he had not dared harm a royal duke. Cecily rose and went to the window, looking over the cold, gray ribbon of river that flowed beneath the castle walls.

She sighed, recognizing that the whole sorry journey to Dartford had been a colossal blunder. If you had taken London then, my love, you might well be on the throne now, she told his ghost. Instead Richard had returned home, leaving Somerset in high favor at court again, believing himself invincible.

Selfishly Cecily had been ecstatic when Richard returned to her. And thus, safe behind Ludlow's high walls with him that October, she was brought to bed of her eighth son, and her grateful lord granted her wish to name the boy after him. How apt that had been, Cecily smiled now, thinking of her quiet, serious son—at nine, the image of his father—fast asleep with George in his chamber next to Meg's. Delicate though he was in childhood, her little Dickon had hung on to life valiantly through fevers and colds and had gained Richard's admiration for his determination to survive during the few years the boy was to know his father. Poor child, she thought, he will have to rely on Edward to teach him how to be a man now.

As she contemplated the autumn and winter of Dickon's first few months, Cecily remembered it included one of the few bouts of illness she had experienced since her accident in Rouen. It was during those months of severe pain that she learned Queen Margaret had finally conceived.

Queen Margaret! What a thorn she has been in our sides since our return from Ireland. Cecily thought back to their first meeting on the riverboat to Rouen, when the beautiful young woman had confided in her, and on to their unexpected meeting that spring of 'Fifty-three at the shrine of Our Lady in Walsingham, when Margaret had treated her kindly and made Cecily a promise.

Aye, but you did not keep your promise, did you, your grace, and despite all my best efforts to appeal to our former friendship, you could never look on Richard as anything but your enemy. Cecily gritted her teeth, barely hearing the everyday sounds from the Thames and the city floating up to her.

PART FIVE

Know well that no man merits having praise
By virtue of the good in someone else;
Nor does he merit blame for others' sins.
Honor to him to whom the honor's due.

ROMAN DE LA ROSE

21

England, Spring 1453

The March wind roared like a lion outside the new glass windows of the Erber and the rain beat a tattoo upon them. Alice Neville had taken pity on her sister-in-law and invited the Yorks to lodge with her. Richard had been dispossessed of Baynard's Castle, his new London residence, after the Dartford incident.

"I had only stayed there once," Cecily complained to Alice a day after she had arrived at the spacious Erber with her three youngest children. She looked around the familiar solar, remembering sitting on her father's knee by the fire, and noted that little had changed other than the windows and a new balda-chin over the bed that incorporated the Montagu green eagle displayed and the Neville saltire.

Alice has aged, Cecily thought, lifting her eyes from her embroidery to look fondly at her sister-in-law. I wonder if I look as haggard. At forty-six, having borne ten children and become a grandmother, the countess of Salisbury no longer had the youthful energy Cecily had so loved in their younger days. Still, Alice had extended a warm and enthusiastic welcome to her husband's family. Five-month-old Dickon had taken a liking to his aunt immediately and now, propped quietly upon her lap, was gazing earnestly at his mother across the hearth.

"How delicate he is," Alice pronounced, allowing the child to take hold of her little finger. "Nay, Dickon, we do not suck on fingers," she told him gently as he pulled it toward his mouth.

Cecily chuckled. "But I pray you, look at that chin. I have not seen such a determined chin on any other of my children. He will not let go of life with-out a fight, this one. Will you, sweeting," she cooed at him. Dickon gurgled happily, making them both laugh.

How quickly her oldest boys had grown up! Ned and Edmund were now entrusted to a tutor in their own small household at Ludlow. She had cried all the way to Shrewsbury when she had left them earlier that month, knowing that it might be months before she saw them again. If the truth were told, she had not felt well on the journey to London. When she complained to Constance of the lingering ache in her back and lower belly, the doctor had listened carefully and given her tincture of foxglove to make her sleep among the cushions in her carriage. Seeing Richard again and being welcomed into the Salisbury household had cheered her considerably, but now that the men had left for a session of Parliament at Reading, her discomfort seemed more pronounced today.

"What think you of my son Warwick?" Alice asked, pride glowing in her face.

Cecily nodded, beaming. "He has grown into a handsome man, I must say, despite being encumbered by the Beaufort nose." Privately Cecily found the twenty-five-year-old earl a trifle aloof and lacking the kindness of his father. But to be fair, I was only with him for one day, she thought, and perhaps he was intimidated by his father's and Richard's raucous recounting of shared exploits as comrades-in-arms in France. "How does it feel to be a grandam, Alice?" she asked. "Isabel is the child's name, is it not? A pretty name."

"And a pretty child, sister," Alice responded. "But as her mother is reluctant to leave Middleham, I do not see my grandchild much." She frowned. "What of Anne, Cecily? You do not speak of her."

It was true, Cecily thought guiltily, I hardly ever think of Anne. She belongs to her husband's family now and is in the capable hands of Alice's aunt. But such is the lot of a girl born into a family of our rank, she mused. They must leave home at an early age to learn from strangers how to become a lady. How fortunate I was that Richard had no family and he was my father's ward. She well remembered her sister Nan's departure from Raby for Humphrey Stafford's home.

"My Anne is in London at Coldharbour at present, so Richard tells me. The children and I will see her soon. 'Tis hard to believe she will be fourteen in August and will take Henry to husband." Then she laughed. "Do you remember how frightened I was at fourteen, Alice? I must thank you now for your sage advice. You were quite right." She lowered her voice so that Margaret could not hear. "I did learn to enjoy my husband's advances."

They both giggled like children. It was as though the years had melted away and they were back in the tester bed during Alice's confinement reading Master Chaucer's bawdy exploits of the wife of Bath.

"Ah, Alice, how good it is to laugh again. I fear my thoughts have been too morbid these last three years since leaving Ireland. Every time Richard and I are parted, I am terrified it will be for ever."

Alice patted Cecily's hand and counseled her to push her worries aside while she was in London. "We shall ride about together, visit the shops in the Chepe and sail on the river with the children. Parliament will prevail upon the king to include Richard on the council, you shall see. My Richard wants it done, as do many others. The king can dissemble no longer."

Cecily smiled, not wanting to dampen her new-found merriment. She reached out her arms to Dickon and cuddled him against her breast. Bessie was there in a trice, tickling the baby and making him laugh. Odd how the older girl had taken to him like a little mother, whereas Meggie had eyes only for George. Her beautiful children! Her heart lifted, and she found the courage to ask, "What news from court, Alice?"

The only gossip Alice thought worth passing on was that little Margaret Beaufort, Somerset's orphaned niece, had been betrothed to the king's half brother Edmund Tudor, son of the late Queen Catherine, and newly created earl of Richmond. I do not care a fig about Margaret Beaufort, Cecily mused, although she smiled and nodded at Alice. And even less about a Tudor.

If Cecily and Alice had waited a month, they would have had a much more important piece of news to gossip about. Queen Margaret was finally with child.

"Thanks be to God," Richard said, after bringing Cecily the news at Fotheringhay in April. "Let us pray the queen's grace is brought to bed of a healthy boy and heir apparent. We need not worry then about Somerset usurping my rightful claim as heir presumptive. Perhaps—only perhaps—Somerset's ambitions will finally be quashed."

"And yours, my lord?" Cecily wanted to ask but chose not to. Instead she pretended to search for exactly the right color of thread in her needlework basket. Her heart had soared when Richard had made the astonishing pronouncement. After eight years of marriage, many had posited that Margaret was barren, and a few brave souls even whispered that perhaps weak-minded Henry was impotent. Indeed, the few times Cecily had seen the couple, there appeared to be little or no affection between them. And yet she knew

Margaret was desperate to bear a son and had said as much to Cecily the year before when Cecily was heavy with Dickon.

Margaret had greeted her cordially at Westminster, despite the tension between their husbands. "My dear duchess, it has been an age since I saw you. How I envy you your beautiful burden," she murmured, as she eyed Cecily's swollen belly after Cecily had risen awkwardly from her knees. "You cannot know how often I take heart when I think of you and the many years it took for you to conceive. You never despaired, not even after the hideous event in Rouen. Our Lady must truly love you," the queen decided. Then she chuckled. "And now I believe you may soon equal your mother in births. Am I not correct?"

"I am flattered you have uncovered that little-known fact, your grace," Cecily had replied, curtseying again. "And indeed, I am carrying our twelfth child."

"Twelve?" Margaret frowned. "I thought eleven. Or do you count the one you lost in Rouen."

"If I do, then this child is my thirteenth, your grace." She had paused then. It had been a long time since she had thought about little Joan, preferring to have buried the memory in the vault with the infant. She looked Margaret straight in the eye and admitted to herself she could not find the Gorgon there that Margaret had become to her. Why, there is affection for me in her expression, she thought, once again admiring the Frenchwoman's beauty. Surely Richard is wrong about her dislike of him. "I shall pray daily to St. Monica for your own desire to be fulfilled, your grace."

"Still beautiful, I see, cousin." Edmund Beaufort's lazy drawl had interrupted the women's tête-à-tête, and Cecily found herself suppressing a shiver as his sharp features, now stretched into a forced smile, hove into her view. He bowed low to Margaret, taking her ringed fingers to his lips and lingering on them with familiarity. Cecily noticed the genuine pleasure with which the queen gave him a "God's good day, my lord Somerset."

"Good day, my lord," Cecily had responded civilly, giving him her hand to kiss also. His hair was now more silver than fair, and a scar she had not seen before stood out dark on his pale cheek. His eagle eyes alighted on her bulging stomach and he raised one bushy brow.

"Another York seems ready to make an entrance I see, my lady. It would appear his grace, your husband, must spend much of his time at home," he taunted her.

It had taken all Cecily's self-control to keep from telling the arrogant duke exactly what she thought of his despicable treatment of her husband. Instead she had inclined her head and murmured, "Why, Edmund, I do believe you are jealous of Richard." It was a remark full of meaning and yet so flippantly spoken that Somerset could not be certain that she had meant anything more than the simplest jest.

Cecily well remembered Margaret's intense gaze following each speaker as if eagerly anticipating a fight. She was disappointed. Without waiting for a response from her cousin, Cecily had dropped into a low curtsey in front of Margaret and begged to be excused. "The babe weighs heavily on me, your grace," she said, smiling sweetly. "I beg you to allow me to find my husband and retire."

With uncanny timing Richard had appeared at her side. "Your grace," he greeted the queen, bowing graciously. Then he turned to Somerset and barely inclined his head. "My lord," he said curtly.

"Your grace," Somerset replied. "How propitious. I believe Duchess Cecily wishes to retire and thus you must deprive the court of your company."

"You snake," Cecily could not forbear to hiss as she had passed by him, a sweet smile masking her scorn.

"Cis, you have not heard anything I have said, have you?" Richard's voice now broke in on her reverie. He looked anxiously at her scowling face. "Is your pain bad today, my love?"

CECILY AND HER favorite attendant wandered through the fragrant herb garden at Fotheringhay one day in April after a brief shower had left the burgeoning plants sparkling in the intermittent sunshine.

"I am determined to go to Walsingham and seek Our Lady's help to cure whatever this pain may be, Constance." Her hand went instinctively to her lower belly. "I fear it has settled in my womb, but I still have a few good childbearing years left to me and do not want to disappoint Richard. He would dearly love another daughter," Cecily said, unburdening herself as usual to the sympathetic physician.

Constance said nothing. She too had been concerned about Cecily's health since little Dickon's birth, and privately thought twelve births were quite enough for any woman to bear. It seemed that the discomfort became more intense during Cecily's monthly course, but as Constance's skilled fingers could feel no unusual growth in her mistress's belly, she thought seeking a cure at Walsingham a reasonable next step.

"Richard has given me leave to go at the end of the month. We shall take Bess with us. She is old enough for a pilgrimage. Tell me, are you curious to see the shrine?"

Constance nodded. "Aye, your grace. Gresilde has been there and she has told me of the Widow Faverches's vision of the Virgin. I shall be glad to accompany you and the lady Elizabeth. I believe it will be beneficial for her to be away from the nursery. She is an angel and will give you no trouble."

And so, a few days later it was a very excited but dignified Bess who climbed into Cecily's chariot, sat proudly by her mother, and waved farewell to Margaret and George standing either side of Nurse Anne on the steps outside the great hall.

THE GREAT BELL at the Benedictine priory in Walsingham was ringing for nones when Cecily's little retinue reached its destination. Scores of pilgrims straggled along the wide main street, which was flanked by the half-timbered houses of enterprising merchants who had prospered from the influx of visitors to the shrine over the past century. Along the way, Cecily had explained what a pilgrimage was to Bess and why the penitent would trudge the highways and byways and even cross the sea to seek help from Our Lady of Walsingham in the county of Norfolk. Bess's eyes had grown wide with awe when she learned of the vision of the Virgin that had led the Widow Faverches to build a replica of the house in which Mary was visited by the Angel Gabriel.

"'Tis said a little bottle containing drops of the Holy Mother's milk lies within the shrine," Cecily told her daughter. "It is a very sacred place, Bess, and when we begin our walk to it from the little chapel I pointed out to you just now, we must leave our slippers there and go barefoot to the shrine for the last mile to show our penitence."

Bess pondered this last piece of information as the clumsy carriage rolled toward the village, and she eyed the muddy road with misgiving. Piers Taggett helped the ladies from the vehicle and escorted Cecily to the prior's house abutting the impressive abbey, where she hoped to lodge.

A peddler walked boldly to the noblewoman's party and thrust his basket of pilgrims' badges at Constance. "Only a farthing, my lady," he whined, and then caught sight of Bess. "And this 'ere is made specially for a child." Cecily gave Piers leave to buy one for each of her party, and she pinned the tin scallop brooch to Bess's bodice. "There now, Bessie, you are a proper pilgrim," she said, kissing the ecstatic child on the forehead.

The elderly prior greeted her warmly, but he was clearly nervous, wringing his hands within the folds of the voluminous sleeves of his black cassock.

"Your grace, I cannot express my gratitude enough for your visit, and my lord of York has been more than generous, but my poor lodging cannot accommodate both you and our sovereign lady, Queen Margaret, at the same time. I know not—"

"The queen is here? Now?" Cecily broke in, frustration and a tinge of annoyance in her voice. "What should we do? Where can we go?" She saw the fear cross the old man's face and immediately softened her tone. "In truth, 'tis not your fault, father," she reassured him. "But it is late and I have a tired nine-year-old with me as well as several in my retinue who need housing. There must be other suitable lodging."

"Certes, there is, your grace." The prior beamed, mollified by Cecily's kinder tone, and continued, "I have prevailed upon one of our merchant families humbly to honor you with the use of their house in the market square but a stone's throw from here. And the inn is overjoyed to receive your servants and horses." Cecily was amused at his effusive language. "We have never been graced before by two such eminent patrons at the same time. Indeed, her royal majesty was pleased to know that your grace would be here. She graciously begs me to tell you that she will be delighted to grant you an audience at your convenience, and I am bidden to tell her royal majesty if you would be so gracious as to accept."

Cecily bit her lip trying not to chuckle at his pomposity. She smiled at him and accepted the queen's invitation willingly. "You may tell the queen I shall attend her grace as soon as I am refreshed, father." She watched him bow his way from her and then turned to Piers. "Come, Master Taggett, lead the way to our host's house. We should walk, as good pilgrims must."

Despite the lateness of the afternoon, the line of solemn men and veiled women filing into the abbey church housing the shrine still stretched around the priory garden. "We shall join them on the morrow, sweeting," Cecily told Bess. Then she turned to Constance. "If it please God and the Virgin I hope our hosts can arrange a bath for us. I cannot possibly converse with the queen covered as I am with grime."

Bess made a face. "Do I have to as well, Mother?"

"Aye, my girl, you most certainly do."

RELIEVED THAT SHE had insisted Gresilde pack a change of gown, Cecily stepped into the priory's high-ceilinged chapter house feeling refreshed. A dais had been hurriedly erected for the queen's throne, and four of Margaret's gentlemen held a baldachin bearing the royal arms of England and France high above the queen's head. Her retinue stood aside to let the duchess pass, and it was then that Cecily was aware of a familiar pair of eyes on her. As her most trusted attendant, Jacquetta Woodville stood closest to the queen, and Cecily met Jacquetta's cat eyes with her steely blue ones until Jacquetta looked down to curtsey as Cecily passed. Aye, my lady, Cecily thought, you may still be addressed as duchess of Bedford, but now you are a mere baron's wife and no longer above me. She dismissed the woman from her mind as she reached the dais. She took Bess's hand. Mother and daughter humbly knelt.

"God's good evening to you, *madame la duchesse*," Margaret greeted her cordially from her cushioned throne. "This meeting is a coincidence, is it not? And a welcome one, I may say, after so long. I pray you, rise. Tell me, is this your daughter?"

In one practiced, graceful movement, Cecily rocked back on her heels and stood tall in front of the throne, regal in her blue silk brocade. Helping Bess up, she put her arm protectively about the girl's shoulders and replied, "Aye, your grace, I thank you. This is Elizabeth, my second daughter, but we call her Bess, do we not, child?"

Speechless, Bess nodded, her yellow curls dancing up and down and her blue eyes riveted on Margaret's golden majesty. Margaret's early pregnancy was apparent in her radiance, adding to her beauty.

"Forgive her, she is my quiet child," Cecily said, venturing a smile.

"You will share my table, duchess," Margaret announced, and Cecily could only acquiesce with a murmur of thanks. As she walked up the steps and waited for a bench to be set for her and Bess, Cecily caught the look of jealous resentment on Jacquetta's fair face as she turned to whisper something to the ravishing young woman at her side. Cecily recognized the girl who had come to wish Edward well just after his birth in Rouen. Aye, she must be fifteen or sixteen now, she deduced. Such pale loveliness will be bound to attract male attention. Jacquetta would be wise to marry her daughter off as soon as possible.

"Your grace, pray remind me of the dowager duchess's daughter's name," Cecily murmured to Margaret, nodding in Jacquetta's direction. "I met her as a child in Rouen."

Margaret's mouth twitched. "For two ladies who do not see eye to eye, so I have heard, it seems both you and Jacquetta have similar taste in names, duchess." She paused to watch Cecily's consternation. "She is another Elizabeth, and we are pleased to have her at court now that she is wife to Lord Ferrers' heir, Sir John Grey. I have watched many a young man in my household blush and swoon when she comes near. Ah, here is Prior John to give the blessing," she said abruptly as the abbot bustled onto the steps. "I am ready to break my day-long fast."

Jacquetta had obviously spoken enough of Cecily to the queen for Margaret to know there was rivalry between them. Cecily's dislike of the dowager duchess deepened. And she was perplexed. Why, then, was Margaret being so pleasant to her?

Mouth-watering aromas wafted from the fine food the monks placed before the royal party, and Margaret ate heartily. Cecily dearly wished she could comment on the queen's condition, but as it was indelicate to raise the subject before the queen herself did, Cecily picked at her food, wishing the pain in her side would subside.

"You do not eat much, my lady," Margaret noted. "Perhaps the journey has tired you. I made my pilgrimage today and fasted until now, and so, I confess, I am ravenous. *Bien sûr*, I must eat for two," she said coyly, casting her eyes down at her plate.

"May I offer my heartfelt congratulations, your grace. It seems the prayers we offered at our last meeting were heard. Our sovereign lord Henry must be so thankful. May I ask when you expect your child?"

"'Tis thought October, duchess," Margaret said sweetly. Then she looked sideways at Cecily, who was taking a sip of wine, and suddenly, without warning and speaking in French, her voice took on a hard edge. "I will tell you this. My son's birth will put an end to any ambitions others may have of succeeding Henry."

Cecily was forced to use her napkin to cover her surprise. However, without missing a beat, Margaret continued in English with restored childlike innocence and Cecily wondered if she had imagined the extraordinary moment. "You have such a beautiful daughter, my dear duchess, with such pretty manners. Is she yet contracted?"

Margaret's expression was guileless.

Taking a moment to recover, Cecily replied, "'Tis kind of you to ask, your grace, but as yet we have not promised Bess to anyone. I am foolishly attached to my children, I dare say, but they will leave me soon enough."

"I have no doubt I shall be as fiercely possessive of my children. Perhaps because we had to wait for so long for them, duchess," was the queen's benign reply. Her smile showed a genuine warmth again, and she surprised Cecily even more by disclosing, "I came to Walsingham to give thanks for God's gift to Henry and me and to pray for a houseful of babes. What is the purpose of your pilgrimage, if I may ask?"

Having told no one but Constance of her ailment, Cecily was reluctant to reveal to this enigmatic woman the purpose of her journey to the shrine. However, the friendly way with which Margaret tilted her head and searched Cecily's face, waiting to know, unlocked Cecily's tongue. "In truth, I have not felt well since the birth of my little Dickon, your grace. I shall pray the Blessed Virgin will relieve my pain." And her hand found the spot that was now throbbing.

"Then I am sorry for you, my dear duchess, and I shall pray for your comfort on the morrow at mass."

"You are too kind, your grace." Cecily paused. Did she dare speak of Richard, she wondered. Margaret appeared congenial once again, and, despite the veiled threat earlier, she had given Cecily every reason to feel at ease. As if to reinforce this sentiment, Margaret broke a piece of marchpane in two and passed it across Cecily to Bess with a wink and a smile. Aye, I believe she harbors no ill will toward us, Cecily thought, and took a deep breath.

"Much of my pain, I confess, is in my heart, your grace. It comes from knowing that our most noble sovereign lord, your husband, may not hold my dear lord high in his favor of late," she began and saw Margaret's hand freeze for a second before carrying a piece of marchpane to her mouth. "If it please your royal grace, Lord Richard has only had the good of the kingdom and his loyalty to the king in all his thoughts and deeds these past years. I swear to your noble highness on the graves of my dead children, he is the king's loyal liegeman." She knew her cheeks were flushed, and she put her hand up to cool them. Her fingers were trembling. She could see Richard's face in her mind's eye, and it was not smiling. Dear God, she thought, as the silence persisted, have I ventured too far? Did I use too much unction? Or not enough? She lowered her eyes to her plate.

Margaret savored her sweetmeat, her eyes staring straight ahead. Then she wiped her lips with the spotless linen cloth and turned to address Cecily.

"My dear duchess, your love and loyalty to your lord is admirable," the queen began levelly. "And I believe you are sincere. But 'tis not my favor that Duke Richard should seek but my husband's. I do not meddle in affairs of state and live only for the king's comfort and to bear his heirs." Cecily marveled at Margaret's artfulness but was careful not to reveal her disbelief. "I am sorry, Cecily, that your husband would use you to ingratiate himself."

Hearing her first name threw Cecily off balance, and she could not determine whether Margaret was dissembling, but she was quick to defend Richard. "My husband has no inkling I would speak to you, madame."

"Your husband's rebellion last year placed you and your children in grave danger. Pray God, the duke has seen reason." The queen stared at the crucifix on the wall opposite. "'Tis my belief he is not worthy of you."

Cecily lifted her head then and with uncharacteristic restraint replied, "Nay, your grace, if it please you, you are mistaken. 'Tis I who am not worthy of him." She felt herself flush, however, and was dismayed to see Jacquetta of Bedford's eyes riveted on her.

"As you wish, duchess," the queen was saying, "I shall say again, your loyalty is admirable, and for our past friendship, I will do what I can for *you*." Her expression then turned grim as she announced, "When my son is born, things will be different—for all of us."

Later, as Cecily lay back in the merchant's tolerably comfortable bed, Bess snuggled beside her, she pondered the inscrutable Margaret of Anjou.

THE NEXT DAY, hundreds of pilgrims ranged themselves along both sides of the narrow village street to gawk at the queen's procession, which would soon wend its way along the road to Fakenham. Following a mass in the prior's private chapel, Margaret had actually bidden Cecily farewell with a friendly buss to her cheek, then she had climbed into her curtained carriage and hidden herself from the common folk, which had caused some grumbling from those in the queue forming outside the abbey that morning. Cecily could have told Margaret it was a regrettable error in judgment; she knew these people would have dearly loved to see their beautiful queen and might have cheered instead of groused. These were not times to incense them further, she thought.

Cecily, dressed in her plain brown traveling gown and an appropriate veil, had eschewed an offer from the prior to forgo the muddy mile from the slipper chapel and enter the shrine from the chapter house. "I thank you, father, but I wish to worship alongside my fellow pilgrims. I am no different from them in the eyes of God. Today I am Cecily Neville, penitent. But I thank you all the same."

Once inside the abbey church, lit by hundreds of candles, she and Bess gazed up at the brilliantly painted pillars and arches supporting the soaring roof. In a side chapel, gated from the penitents who thronged the nave, a choir of monks chanted quietly as slowly the column of pilgrims reached the wooden house in the middle of the chantry.

"This is the house the widow built, Bess," Cecily whispered. "The Virgin told her in a vision what it looked like. When we go inside, you must be silent and pray very hard for your father and your brothers and sisters."

Bess looked up through the gauze of her veil. "And you, Mam? What about you? And Nurse Anne, and Piers, and . . ."

Cecily smiled. "Aye, you may pray for me and the others too, child. Do not forget Doctor Constance, will you? You would not be here if she had not helped you into this world."

They slipped into the little house and stared about them. The heat from so many candles and warm bodies mingled with the overpowering smell of incense made Cecily feel queasy. Squeezing between two large women, she and Bess knelt in front of the statue of the Virgin, a radiantly golden Virgin, holding the infant Jesus. Other brightly painted and bejeweled statues sat in niches set high in the ornately decorated walls, and Cecily wondered if this was indeed what the Virgin had directed the widow to build. She had imagined something far humbler for a poor woman's house in Judea.

Bess was pointing to the sparkling jewels on a reliquary resting at the Virgin's feet, and Cecily saw the vial inside containing the holy breast milk. She crossed herself again and stared at the object, truly awed for the first time since entering the stifling shrine. She had seen other relics in her life, to be sure, including a piece of the true cross and crown of thorns in the holy chapel in Paris, but to be in the presence of something as precious as the milk that sustained Our Lord touched her own motherhood deeply and brought tears to her eyes. You have been with me always on my journey through life, showing me the way, she told the Holy Mother, but never as close as you are to me now. Praise be to thee and thy beloved Son. I pray you guard my family from harm, keep my dearest husband especially in thy protection, and for myself I ask that my health may be restored to me. If it is a burden I must bear for my sins, then I ask for forbearance. If I am fortunate to grow old in your love, sweet Mary, then I shall devote that time to your service when my children have no more need of me. Lord, give me strength.

She smiled up at the shining face of the Virgin and noticed for the first time that the statue's eyes seemed to be gazing at a point over her head. Turning to look, she followed Mary's gaze and gasped. The lifelike figure of the saint in the niche had the face of La Pucelle. "Jeanne," she whispered. "Is it you?" A beatific smile seemed to curve the mouth of the statue, which appeared bathed in white light, and Cecily began to feel faint as she had all those years ago in the filthy prison. She closed her eyes and crossed herself, but when she looked at the statue again, it was the perfect face of another holy woman martyred for her faith that stared back at her. What can this mean? she wondered. It was Jeanne's face I saw. I know it was. And it was a happy, blessed face. She gazed at the Virgin again and then she knew. She knew with awe and wonder that Jeanne d'Arc had indeed been welcomed into her Savior's company of saints. A warm glow suffused her, and she began to chant out loud, *"Ave Maria, gratia plena."* Her fervor must have moved her fellow pilgrims, for soon they took up the supplication in unison, filling the shrine with prayer. When the chanting ended and Cecily took Bess's hand to rise and let another take their place, she saw the little girl's face was wet with tears.

22

England, Summer 1453

Despite Margaret's offer of help to Cecily, Richard became more and more isolated in the summer of 'Fifty-three. In May he heard that his ten-year lieutenancy in Ireland had been brought to an early conclusion and the son of Richard's old friend the White Earl was appointed in his stead. The young man had been elevated to the earldom of Wiltshire, auspiciously through his father-in-law, Edmund of Somerset.

"Somerset's star continues to rise," Richard complained to Cecily one day in late July as they rode out from Fotheringhay to hunt. The new merlin sat on Cecily's wrist, but though the bird was an excellent hunter, she still missed Nimuë. "The court has moved to Clarendon and still I am not welcome on the council. It would seem my experience in Normandy counts for naught with them—especially since Dartford. I could tell them that it will not be long before Bordeaux falls and Gascony is lost, mark my words, Cis." He gave a harsh laugh. "But who listens to me?"

Cecily watched sadly as Richard's grim face told the story of his ill-treatment at Dartford. She had hoped that he could put his anger behind him, but instead it festered daily. He had sworn the oath never to rebel again, but Cecily feared another humiliation might lead him to break that oath. She tried to turn her mind to this day and their favorite pastime and chose to answer his rhetorical question with: "I always listen to you, Richard, and I heard you promise me a day of sport. Let us not spoil it with politics, I beg of you." She turned her pleading eyes on him and his face softened. "That's better," she murmured.

The sky was cloudless and the light summer breeze fluttered the flowers of the blue-purple flax in the fields. Cecily's wide-brimmed hat kept the sun from spoiling her still porcelain skin and shaded her eyes as she scanned the blue horizon for skylarks. Cecily's bird was trained to hunt small birds but occasionally went after a rabbit. Richard's bigger falcon wove back and forth on its master's glove, hearing noises from its prey in the meadow too faint for human ears. Sensing his bird was eager to fly, Richard loosed the ankle tie, expertly whipped off the embroidered hood, and flung the bird skyward, causing the ankle bell to tinkle in its wake. The riders watched the bird ride the drafts until its wings began to flutter and it hovered over a clump of gorse. A hare sprinted out of the cover, but it was not fast enough for the falcon, which dived like a bolt from a crossbow and felled the animal with its powerful talons in one deadly motion. The sight never failed to awe Cecily. Richard gave a short, sharp whistle, and the bird left the hare's broken body where it had fallen to return to Richard's wrist.

"That's my proud Priam," Richard cooed. "That is how to bring down the weak."

Cecily wondered to whom her husband was really referring but she smiled and also praised the bird.

"Your turn, Cis," Richard said, after securing the tie again. "What thinks Master Taggett of this new bird?"

"She is not as fast as Nimuë, in truth," Cecily replied, stroking her merlin's glossy feathers. "But she is young and her aim is true. Ah, now I hear a larksong." She saw the brown-streaked skylark soaring, hovering, and singing fifty paces from them, and just as expertly as Richard had done, she let her bird loose. "Go, brave Niniane, and find your mark."

"Niniane?" Richard asked, watching the graceful merlin soar high above the unsuspecting trilling skylark.

"'Tis another name for Nimuë, but do not tell her so. She has a very different character," Cecily answered, smiling across at her husband and remembering the day long ago when he had taken her to the mews at Windsor. "My sweet Nimuë was the best of all your gifts to me, Richard, save our children."

The lark was caught and Niniane at once dropped with her prey to the ground. She was recalled by her mistress, while a huntsman ran to inspect the lark. He held it up by its tiny legs and proclaimed it masterfully killed. Cecily stroked the merlin and murmured endearments to it. "We shall need several more like that ere we can make a pie, my dearest."

"I should like to make a pie myself—out of the vultures on the council awaiting my demise," Richard said, and Cecily was relieved to see him neigh heartily at his own joke.

Richard was still laughing with Piers when the sound of galloping hooves caught their attention. Roger Ree came to a well-controlled halt in front of the duke. Bowing in his saddle, he thrust a letter at Richard.

"The messenger told me to deliver it without delay, my lord," he said. "'Tis from my lord of Salisbury."

Richard gave Piers his falcon to hold and tore open the missive.

"Christ's nails! Gascony is lost! Aquitaine is lost! Talbot is killed, as is his son, at Castillon. Bordeaux is threatened and Charles has taken most of Aquitaine for France."

"Talbot killed?" Cecily repeated, half to herself. "Why, the man was eighty if he was a day! 'Tis a wonder he could even carry a sword. Somerset must have sent him again. 'Tis monstrous."

"He was one of our greatest commanders, my lady," Richard corrected her. "If he could not hold Aquitaine, then no one could. But you are right to blame Somerset for this. Perhaps now the king will see reason and impeach him, but I doubt it. All that England has fought to win back in France for more than a hundred years is now lost. And I was powerless to prevent it. God's nails, what a sorry day this is!"

Knowing Richard would have no heart for hunting now, Cecily sighed, turned her horse around, and headed for home. Her first thought was to ask the Virgin for help, certain this news might rouse Richard to more rebellion. She took herself straight to the ducal chapel and spent an hour on her knees thinking on England's losses and recalling the battles her father, her siblings, and her husband had fought in her lifetime. It was all for naught, she mused sadly. All those lives lost, all that land ravaged—and for what? She profoundly regretted the loss of France, but secretly in her heart she rejoiced. Was the conflict in France finally ended? Dear God, let us hope men will see sense and there will be no more war, no more fighting, no more killing. She prayed her own sons would never have to take up arms against others but lead quiet, sober and happy lives on their estates with their families.

"Just as Richard and I can now do," she murmured, dreaming. "With Margaret about to give Henry an heir"—she refused to think it might be a girl—"and no war to wage in France, we can live out our lives in peace."

But she was not naive enough to believe her dream. She had lived through enough turmoil to know that men like Richard and Somerset were never content to rest idle on their estates. Ambition has its price, she thought, and I have learned that to my cost. All I can do is support my husband and protect my children. And, with God's help, we shall prevail.

Sobered by the thought, she rose, bent her knee to the altar, and went in search of Constance.

As CECILY HAD suspected, peace was not to be.

Less than a month later, the lookout on the castle gatehouse peered down in the gathering darkness and called, "Who goes there?"

"The lord Richard, earl of Salisbury. Open the gate!" Richard Neville's herald shouted back.

The winch for the iron portcullis slowly raised the heavy gate, screeching loudly as the chains ground around the wooden wheel. Grooms ran alongside the horsemen ready to help the earl's party as it entered the courtyard.

Richard and Cecily were in the gardens, enjoying a game of hoodman blind with their children in the last of the evening light, when Cecily's brother joined them.

"God's greeting to you all, and I apologize for the intrusion so late in the day, Sister, but I have important, troubling news."

As Nurse Anne herded the children along the path and back to their apartments, Richard grasped Neville's arm and drew Cecily close. "What is it, Brother?" he asked, frowning.

Richard of Salisbury took a deep breath, looking about him to make sure they were alone. "The king has been taken ill. Not of his body but of his mind. It seems Henry has lost his wits. He has succumbed to a fit of apoplexy," he said slowly and deliberately, satisfied with the shocked reaction he was eliciting. "Aye, 'tis true," he assured the gap-mouthed couple. "He knows no one and he says nothing. He simply sits staring vacantly at the wall. My man at court rode hard to inform me of the turn of events. It appears Henry has been this way for a fortnight already."

A worried frown furrowing Richard's pale face, he waved his hand toward the castle. "Come, my lord, let us go inside. The rest can wait until you have had some refreshment."

"WHO KNOWS OF this besides the council?" Richard asked later as Salisbury downed a cup of ale and tackled a haunch of cold venison.

Spearing a choice piece of meat on his knife's point, Salisbury answered, "Only the closest circle and, certes, the queen. Praise be, the court is at Clarendon. If this had happened in Westminster . . ."

"The whole of London would know by now," Richard finished, nodding.

"Aye, the fewer of us who are informed the better. What say the doctors? How long will this last?"

Salisbury shrugged. "They know not, Brother. It came without warning. One moment he was himself, the next his eyes fixed on the wall and his limbs would not move. They must carry him to and from his bed, to the privy—'tis as though he froze like the grasses in winter." He savored the venison, smacking his lips and chewing noisily. "All are in shock."

Richard shook his head, his expression grave. "What does this mean for England?" he murmured almost to himself. "That Somerset rules?"

Richard Neville almost spat his meat out in response. "Never fear, my lord, as long as I am on the council, Somerset will not rule. But it would be imprudent to let the people know the king is indisposed. Their anger against Somerset, whom they blame for the loss of France, would know no bounds. It would not take much to cause rioting."

"Would they think Henry was driven to madness by the loss of France, Richard?" Cecily asked and relished a nod of approval from her elder brother. "Aye, I can see why Somerset might feel threatened now. Perhaps we should spread the word," she said, half joking. "What would be so wrong with that?"

Richard's response was as she expected. "'Tis treason, that is what, Cis," Richard retorted. "Besides it would be wrong for the realm. Aye, it is right no one should know. If God is merciful, the king may recover tomorrow; one can never tell. And what of the queen? She would back Somerset if he moved to take control."

Salisbury grunted. "'Tis as well that she must soon be confined for the birth, where she cannot be of influence. But although Somerset has her ear, he can do nothing without the council's sanction."

"And if this malady drags on?" Cecily asked. "Surely someone must act as regent in the king's place."

She saw her brother flash a surreptitious glance Richard's way, but he said nothing. Pray God you find a voice, Brother, she wanted to remark. Are you firmly for Richard or not?

"All will come clearer when the queen is brought to bed," her husband said. "If Henry has an heir then a regent must be named, and like as not 'twill be between me and Somerset. If it is a girl, then one of us must be made heir apparent. Cast out as I am now, I cannot know the council's mind, Neville. But I tell you this. I will not stand by and allow Somerset to keep me from my rightful place."

Cecily closed her eyes tightly, looked down at her lap, and prayed for Henry's recovery.

"Come with me on the morrow to the council in London, Richard," the earl said, retrieving a stringy piece of meat from between two teeth. "They would know if you are willing to take the reins, should the vote go your way. You do not want them to believe you have no interest."

CECILY WATCHED AS Richard was dressed for the two-day ride to London by two of his gentlemen. The weather had been fine for a week, and the harvest was successfully reaped, the hooded stooks neatly arrayed in rows in the fields to allow the late summer sun to ripen any green grain fully. Soon the harvest helpers would return to their villages, their work done for the season. Later, as summer turned to autumn, the wheat for the castle would be stored in the barns for threshing.

Richard had chosen to wear a plain knee-length, black damask cloak-tunic, albeit trimmed with gold braiding, to mark the serious nature of his meeting with the council. "I wish them to know I am mourning the loss of our sovereign's sanity, Cis."

Cecily affixed one of her brooches to the front of his hat.

"For a safe journey, my lord," she told him, standing back to admire him. She nodded to Richard's gentlemen in approval. "I thank you, sirs." They bowed, leaving the duke and duchess alone.

Richard cocked his head at his wife now, knowing well that she had had a reason for dismissing his servants.

"How now, Cis. Will you chastise me for not coming to you last night? I know I broke with our tradition, but a week in London does not constitute a true parting."

Cecily shook her head. "I lay awake for a time, 'tis true, but it was not to find ways to make you feel guilty. In truth, I could not get the image of Henry's inert state out of my mind. And I began to think back on those times when I was in his presence and how at each one I noticed little instances of odd behavior. Do you remember in Rouen when he suddenly loosed laughter that frightened both of us?" Richard nodded slowly, recalling the incident well. "We remarked upon it afterward, remember? And then I cast my mind back to one of the first occasions I saw him. 'Twas at the banquet after your knighting at Leicester. I saw him stop midway between taking a mouthful—like this—and stare unblinking at nothing in particular. I swear he disappeared into a place that was not in this world. It lasted for all but a moment, but it was curious, nonetheless."

Richard stroked his beard, thinking. "Do you know that Queen Catherine's father went mad? King Charles never recovered, so I heard. They say such a thing may run in a family."

He picked up his silver-hilted dagger and placed it in its sheath, then turned to embrace her. "Come, kiss me, Cecily. If I stay in London longer, I will send for you."

BUT HE WAS gone only a few days.

The lookout on the gatehouse tower alerted the castle to the duke's return, and grooms and pages appeared from nowhere and ran to greet the returning riders. Waving happily, Cecily made her way through the private entrance in the inner ward to greet her husband in the courtyard. Richard kissed her hand briefly before taking her arm in his and leading her up the staircase to their solar. He had barely said two words, but from the grim set of his mouth, Cecily knew something was amiss.

"Somerset attempted to sway the council to deny my attendance, and when I saw that I must flatter and cajole my way into the meeting, I refused to demean myself," he told her, pacing up and down the room, his strong chin leading him and his spurs jangling on the tiled floor. "Have I not been humiliated enough? I left immediately."

Cecily was aghast. "I cannot believe the council would exclude you, Richard. You are the highest ranking duke in the realm. My brother said they must include you in their plans to govern while Henry is indisposed. Has Somerset so much influence? 'Tis hard to believe."

Richard turned, clearly exasperated. "He still has the king's protection, Cis. And he is Margaret's favorite. The council dare not defy him. God's bones, but I thought I had your brother and his whelp Warwick on my side. Together with Norfolk, they should have had enough influence to sway the others and warrant my being accepted, but they wavered."

Cecily was at a loss. She could not defend her brother, and she would have liked to give him a piece of her mind. She watched her husband slump onto a stool and attempt to remove his spurs and boots. She went to his side and knelt down to help him, and then she came to a decision.

"I shall write to the queen," she declared. "And, nay, do not gainsay me this, Richard. I believe she considers me her friend—despite my choice of husband," she joked and stroked his leg. She did not tell him of Margaret's suggestion at Walsingham: I will do what I can for you." She would not raise his hopes. And indeed, she was unsure if the queen even meant what she had said. But it was worth trying. "As I have said before, if women were to run the kingdom, there would be far less fighting and a lot more talking. Let me at least write to her, my love."

Richard cupped her chin in his hand and gave her a reluctant smile. "I feel better already, if that is possible. And if you would write on my behalf, I shall not stop you, although with Margaret so close to birthing, I know not how it will help." He kissed her and stood, stretching. "I swear I thank God for you daily, Cecily Neville."

"Pish, husband!" Cecily retorted, picking up the spurs and carrying them to the chest where Richard kept his finest suit of armor. "'Tis my father you should thank, not God. Now, I will go and find my clerk and you should rest. I will send in the children in an hour to greet you." She kissed his cheek and slapped away the hand that caressed her breast. "Nay, that will have to wait," she said firmly.

"Killjoy," Richard said. He sighed, but fell back gratefully on the soft bed.

Cecily's letter to Margaret took her an hour to compose. The poor clerk started it no fewer than six times before Cecily was satisfied with the greeting alone.

> *Your lowly obedient servant and bedewoman, Cecily, duchess of York, beseeches you with all humbleness and reverence possible that, in the wealth of your good and benign grace, it pleased you to suffer the coming of my simple person . . .*

Cecily halted, loathing herself for the ingratiating language that fell from her lips but knowing it was expected. She was reminded of the pompous prior of Walsingham, and she had the grace to smile. She went on to praise God and the Lady of Walsingham for the child Margaret was carrying, describing the gift in glowing terms: *"the most precious, most joyful and the most comfortable earthly treasure that might come into this land and to our people."*

Then she asked for the queen's intercession with the council on Richard's behalf and shuddered at her own groveling. She prayed it would have the desired effect, however.

When the clerk had finished transcribing, Cecily dismissed him and contemplated her words. She pressed her hand into her side and sighed. The pilgrimage had not cured her infirmity, and indeed she had been in excruciating pain for several weeks following, but she had to admit it had eased over the summer. She truly believed the Virgin had interceded for her as a reward for her pilgrimage. However, Constance had been studying Galen and had learned about stones that lodged in the kidneys and blocked the passage of piss. So she insisted Cecily eat dark leafy vegetables, more nuts, and even the occasional plateful of beetroot, which Cecily detested. "This tincture of goldenrod may also be beneficial," Constance told her, dropping some of the not unpleasant liquid into Cecily's cider. Every day the doctor examined the contents of Cecily's jakes and was certain her mistress's problem was causing their strong odor, corroborating Galen's theory. Constance assured her mistress that her preparations would eliminate her pain. "Then ply me with your remedies, dear Constance, I beg of you," Cecily told the good doctor. But she still prayed daily for divine intervention as well.

She made sure her letter was signed, sealed, and put into the hands of a trusted messenger before she returned to Richard. He was curled up on the bed, snoring gently, and she had not the heart to wake him. She knew he would not be pleased that she had sent the letter before showing it to him, but she wanted the words to be hers—and she had confidence that the queen would recognize Cecily's own voice, despite the overwrought phrases.

She knelt by the bed and put her hands together, observing that sleep took some of the careworn lines from Richard's face. Dear Mother of God, she prayed, let the king recover soon, let my letter please Margaret and thus help Richard, and—Cecily smiled sardonically—let life return to normal.

HENRY'S ILLNESS PERSISTED, and when Queen Margaret gave birth to a son on the thirteenth day of October, the king was oblivious to the event. He never moved a muscle when first shown his heir, causing rumors to fly that little Edouard, as Margaret pronounced his name, was perhaps not Henry's.

"I do not believe it, Cecily," Richard retorted, as they sat before the fire after a supper of pigeon pie. Bess and Margaret played a game of checkers and George pranced around the chamber on a wooden hobby horse under Anne of Caux's watchful eye. "A proud woman like that would not give herself to anyone beneath her rank. Nay, she would never cuckold the king—not even with Somerset. Where did you hear such an evil rumor?"

Cecily was holding one-year-old Dickon's hands while he tried to take a few steps away from her on his unsteady legs, and she marveled at the strength in his fingers and his grim determination. "Gresilde heard it from her husband. I, too, think 'tis absurd. I do not think even Margaret would be foolish enough to have named Somerset little Edward's godfather if he had been her lover. That would be blasphemous, in truth, hypocrisy notwithstanding. Besides, the earl is old enough to be her grandfather."

"Hardly, Cis!" Richard laughed. "And when, pray, has that stopped a man before. He is only five years older than I. And I do not expect to be a grandfather for a while." He got up and took over walking Dickon, praising his youngest at every step.

"It will not be long, my dear. Anne is of age now." Cecily frowned. When Alice and Cecily had visited Anne at Coldharbour, Cecily had remarked upon the dark circles under her daughter's eyes and that her gown hung shapelessly on her. Granted, Anne was still only fourteen, but Cecily remembered her tendency to plumpness as a child and she had imagined the girl would have a few womanly curves by now. The young duchess had been ecstatic at the visit of her mother and aunt—a little too excited, Alice had said upon their return to the Erber. "I pray her husband treats her well," she had remarked. *I must write to her on the morrow,* Cecily thought now and, snapping out of her reverie, she upbraided George for deliberately interfering in Dickon's progress.

"That was not kind, George," Cecily admonished the tow-headed child with the winning smile. "Instead of taunting your brother, come and tell me what you did today."

Cecily had only just signed her name on a letter to Anne the next morning when the sound of horsemen entering the courtyard caught her attention. Leaning out of the window, she saw three strangers, obviously well born, judging by their velvet mantles and the quality of their coursers, dismounting with the help of Fotheringhay pages. Instructing her clerk to hurry with the sealing of her missive, she pressed her signet ring with its falcon insignia into the sticky wax and left the room with Constance to find Richard.

"I did not recognize the men," she told her attendant, "but they appear to have ridden hard."

Richard welcomed her into his privy chamber a few minutes later and presented her to Sir Thomas Tyrell and two other courtiers, who looked askance at the intrusion. However, they had heard about the duchess and were therefore not too surprised when Richard grinned and assured them, "Her grace and I have no secrets from each other, sirs. I pray you, keep us waiting no longer."

Sir Thomas was a big man with iron-gray hair showing under his floppy hat, and he was clearly awed by the ducal couple now standing together. He bowed low again and discharged his mission.

"The king's council has requested your presence at the next meeting, your grace," he began, too intimidated to use the word "summoned" as instructed. "You are requested to proceed from here to London—peaceably and measurably accompanied."

"Peaceably and measurably?" Richard reiterated. "What can that mean, Sir Thomas?"

Sir Thomas inclined his head and looked sheepish. "They did recall the last time you came to London . . . 'tis all, your grace." And he stepped back, waiting for a harsh reprimand for his boldness.

But Richard took pity on the messenger. "Ah, I understand, sir." He turned to Cecily, taking her arm. "Perhaps I had a few too many at my back last time, my lady. What think you?"

"I think you should listen to Sir Thomas, my lord, and hear him out," Cecily said.

Richard nodded. "Is there more, sir?"

"I have to report that the lord chancellor and my lord of Somerset will not be present," Tyrell said quickly, shooting Richard a guarded look. Cecily felt Richard's fingers grip her arm through her sarcenet sleeve, but his expression never changed. "The council seeks to find the right path to take in view of the birth of the prince of Wales. I am instructed to tell you that the council is to meet to set to rest and make union among *all* the lords of this land . . . including your grace and . . ." He stopped, seeing Richard's tacit understanding.

Cecily gulped, for she had realized that with this cryptic message the council was giving Richard permission to bring charges against Somerset. It was a daring move, Cecily thought, longing to discuss it with Richard later, as the duke of Somerset had never been more powerful than he was now, despite the news that Bordeaux had finally surrendered, leaving only Calais and its pale as English possessions in France.

"I shall gladly obey the summons of the council. And I thank you for a message so faithfully tendered," Richard said, acknowledging Tyrell's diplomacy with a nod.

"Sir Thomas, I pray you tell us how fares our sovereign king Henry?" Cecily asked, again astonishing Tyrell with such unaccustomed lack of deference to her husband. Ladies did not usually ask questions with a husband present. He stared at the beautiful duchess with respect. "We have such little news here at Fotheringhay," Cecily continued, "although, certes, we gave thanks for the safe delivery of England's heir. I trust her grace, the queen, and the prince of Wales are in good health."

It was a masterful stroke, Richard recognized proudly, and showed the three men that the duke and duchess of York were not only loyal subjects, full of concern for their sovereign majesties, but also that they recognized Margaret's son as true heir and prince of Wales. Richard could have kissed his wife on the spot.

The king's condition had not changed, Tyrell told them, but the new prince was healthy, as was his mother, who was still confined to her apartments. He also mentioned that Somerset was with the king, who had been moved to Windsor Castle.

Richard let go of Cecily's arm and gave the courtiers a warm smile. "Again we thank you for your good services. Certes, you will all lodge with us, will you not?"

"Somerset is in the Tower at last, Cecily!" Richard told his wife triumphantly one day in November upon returning from a council meeting in Westminster's Star Chamber. They were staying in a house borrowed from the bishop of Salisbury outside the city wall and hard by Fleet Street. "Norfolk accused him of treason for bringing about the loss of our territories in France and demanded he be arrested and imprisoned. Praise be to God, the council agreed."

Cecily felt her knees go weak. This was a momentous decision for the council to make, and she never thought Richard would find enough support to bring the arrest about.

"Who was there, my lord?" she asked. "Surely not the king's men—men like Kemp, Buckingham, Worcester, Tudor?"

Richard rubbed his hands with relish. "Aye, they were and nearly everyone agreed. We have all now taken an oath to uphold Henry's government in his illness. They are allowing Devon to be freed from Wallingford to join the council, and they have granted me leave to bring back my own councillors. Aye, Sir William is among them, you will be pleased to hear."

"Sweet Mother of God," Cecily interjected on a long exhale. She chose her next words carefully. "Are you . . . are you in charge? Someone has to be."

"I know not at this moment, Cis." Richard shrugged and eased himself into his chair, first slapping at a flea on the cushioned seat. "But what I can tell you is that I have been re-granted Baynard's and we can leave this house, send for the children, and celebrate a very festive Christmas there. Does that meet with your approval?"

"Oh, Richard," Cecily cried, rising and draping herself on his lap, "it most assuredly does. Can we have the boys leave Ludlow too?" She nuzzled into his neck as a child might, but the words she now whispered in his ear were those of a confidante and lover.

Richard felt his passion well up as their kiss reminded both of them of their younger bliss. It was as though the tension of the past two years had been miraculously loosed, and for the first time since returning from Ireland, they sent their attendants away and gave themselves up to a night of such carefree lovemaking that they fell asleep, exhausted, just as the cock crowed.

CECILY WAS NEVER happier than at that Yuletide season with all of her children around her and Richard wreathed in smiles as his position on the council became firmer. As Richard promised, they returned to Baynard's Castle. Cecily loved the south-facing apartments that looked out over the Thames. This was one of the few fortified London town residences, and Cecily could not have felt more secure behind its walls.

"You never know what is waiting around the bend," she told Constance a few days after Epiphany, as Meggie practiced on her lute and Gresilde showed Bess a new dance step. "We are safe today, but if the king recovers and releases Somerset, I fear my cousin will think nothing of threatening us."

"You worry too much, your grace," Constance soothed her, and changed the subject. "Have you received news of your sons at Ludlow? I wonder how tall the earl of March is now. *Il sera très beau,*" she said quietly. She did not tell the duchess that she had heard tell Edward was already causing a stir among the girls of Ludlow town.

"Aye, he will be a handsome man," Cecily replied proudly. "I fear he may break many hearts. But not as many as George, perhaps. Just look at those curls and blue eyes."

She was about to speak of her beloved Edmund when a knock on the door interrupted them, and Cecily called, "Come!"

The usher announced: "Her grace, Anne, duchess of Exeter."

The children stared with curiosity at the veiled figure who stepped into the room. The girls had not seen their sister for four years, and George and Richard did not even know her. Anne first curtsied before going to kneel at Cecily's feet for her mother's blessing.

"Dear child," Cecily cried delightedly and raised her eldest to her feet. "We did not expect you." She put out her hand to lift Anne's veil, but Anne neatly stepped away. "Why the mystery, Nan? I pray you, let me look at you." She motioned for the others to gather round. "And see how your brothers and sisters would greet you too."

A tiny sob came from under the heavy gauze. "Mam, I dare not!"

Fear stabbed Cecily's heart as she drew Anne into her reassuring embrace. As soon as she felt the girl's body against her own, she knew Anne was with child, and her first reaction was one of amazement that she was to be a grandmother. Dear God, I am too young, she thought, but then she banished her selfish thought because she could sense Anne's unhappiness.

"What is wrong? I see you are with child, sweeting, so why are you not joyful?" Cecily asked.

Anne stepped away as if ashamed, and Cecily frowned. What was her daughter hiding?

She herded the children together and nodded to Constance. "Children, go with Constance back to the nursery, I pray you. Nan will be there anon, I promise. She has something of a private nature to tell me. Now, run along." Her eyes beseeched Constance to hurry, which the doctor accomplished in a second. "I thank you, Constance. Take them back to Nurse Anne—and," she added with a premonition, "return later, I beg of you."

George took charge and marshaled the others into a line and led them out of the room like soldiers while Constance held the door and then followed.

"Come, my dear," Cecily murmured, ready to hear the worst. Wary as she was, she could not forbear to gentle the trembling young woman onto the settle, plump up the cushion, and ease it behind her back. "When you are ready, tell me what is wrong," she said, attempting now to lift Nan's veil. "You are with child, are you not?"

Anne stayed her mother's hand and, cradling her belly, gave a timid nod.

"Why! That is good news, Nan. I am to be a grandmother, God be praised." Cecily tried to sound cheerful, knowing that she had not heard the whole story. "Exeter must be a happy man." She got no further, for the distraught young woman flung herself down into her mother's lap, sobbing.

"What is it, Nan? Is the child not his?" Cecily hated herself for voicing her suspicion, but she had to know the worst if she was to help her daughter.

Anne sat up abruptly and gasped. "Nay, Mother, certes 'tis his! How can you think otherwise?" Her horror filled Cecily with remorse. Slowly and with trembling fingers Anne drew off her veil, and then it was Cecily's turn to gasp. A welt the size of her palm covered Nan's cheek. Her mouth was swollen and her lip split.

Cecily jumped to her feet. "Dear God in heaven!" she cried. "Who did this to you?" Her eyes widened in horror as Anne hung her head and stared down at her clenched hands. "Oh, do not tell me it was your lord! Your husband? Oh, no, sweet Nan, not him?" Full of rage, she sat down again and cradled her poor, wounded child to her bosom, removing the rest of the headdress and letting Anne's dark curls loose over her bruised face.

"He said 'twas his right to beat me, Mam," Anne whimpered, and Cecily's heart sank. In the eyes of the law, he was correct, she knew, and there was nothing a wife could do to change that male prerogative. Anne told Cecily that this was not the first time. "He is a violent man, in truth. He treats his pages the same way and . . ." She began to weep again. "And he is cruel to his horses and kicks the dogs. I . . . I did n . . . nothing wrong, I promise, except sp . . . spill his wine as I poured."

Cecily stroked Anne's soft hair, murmuring soothing phrases and letting her daughter cry. How cruel fate is, she thought. How could we have known we were sending our sweet child to a monster? John Holland was only fourteen at the time and seemed perfectly respectful. But the deed was done, and they had unwittingly sealed Anne's fate.

She thought quickly and knew Richard must not see his sweet Nan like this. Even though it was clear that clever Meggie was his favorite, he had always had a soft spot in his heart for this eldest daughter, and his fatherly rage could easily endanger his son-in-law's life. Cecily could not let that happen; the consequences would be disastrous.

"There, there, child," she said finally, hearing the sobs lessen. "You are safe here, and here you shall stay. You will sleep with Constance in my apartments. I will send word to Coldharbour that you were taken ill."

"Nay!" Anne was aghast. "He will only punish me when I do go back. Let me return quickly before he knows I was here, I beg of you. I only came . . . I only . . . oh, I do not know why I came." She sighed, her shoulders sagging.

"I was so unhappy, I wanted my family. I told no one where I was going and came with only an attendant and my clerk."

Cecily wanted to cry, but her furious tears would have served no purpose. She remembered the times when she had needed Joan's support and it was her mother's strength that had comforted her. She fetched Anne some wine. "Drink this, my dear, and tell me how your health has been through these first weeks. Have you felt the babe move yet?"

The practical questions brought Anne out of her misery and Cecily was pleased to see a spark of pleasure in her daughter at being with child. When the girl had recovered her composure, Cecily proposed a visit to the nursery to meet her new brothers.

She was determined to keep her daughter close and would find a way to explain Anne's stay to Richard later. *Keeping her confined to my chambers can easily be put down to concern over pregnancy pains that require Anne to keep to her bed,* she decided, *and a letter to Exeter would explain all.*

SHE NEED NOT have worried. Richard was far too preoccupied with what had transpired that day in Parliament to ask his wife about family matters. He paced impatiently in his privy chamber after requesting that Cecily come to him there.

"Now that she is churched and by Henry's side once more, Queen Margaret has presented Parliament and the council with five provisions, the first of which is that she be given the title of regent," Richard seethed, his jaw clenching. "Whoever heard of such a thing? Praise be to whichever saint is responsible for common sense, for Parliament rejected her proposal out of hand. Having a Frenchwoman as regent—and one with Margaret's ambition—would be disastrous for England."

Cecily stared unseeing at her embroidery. "And for your cause, Richard," she said, with no particular inflection in her voice. But her remark incensed Richard.

"What do you mean by 'my cause,' Cis? Are you of the same mind as those men who favor Lancaster and claim that I am only acting out of self-interest?"

Cecily brought her eyes sharply into focus, set aside her needlework carefully, and rose with purpose. "You have not denied that Henry is a weak leader, Richard, and that Somerset has led him by the nose. And the support you have gained from the lords and Parliament of late must have told you that your cause—nay, your claim—is better than any other. Nay, do not interrupt me," Cecily put up her hand. "Aye, Nan's Exeter may be Henry's closest cousin, but he can have no support because he lacks intelligence, cannot curb his violent temper, and more than Margaret, he would be a disaster for England. And Somerset fancies himself next in line, but he was born of the bastard Lancastrian blood. You, my dear Richard, are the true heir to our great-grandsire Edward's crown and should be Regent."

Richard thumped his fist on the mantel and kicked a wayward log back into the flames, causing it to crackle and spit sparks. "But Henry is my anointed king, Cecily. To even think of asserting my claim is treason. Oh, we have gone over and over this again and again, my lady, and I always return to the bitter legacy of my father."

"This is not about claiming the throne, Richard," Cecily said, impatient now. "Henry has an heir, remember? This is about the legitimate Regent, and you are that man."

Richard nodded, finally taking strength from her argument. "You are right, Cecily, but I must wait until I am asked to take the reins, so that history cannot accuse me of acting unlawfully."

"Aye, you must wait," she agreed, and began to massage Richard's tense shoulder muscles.

Cecily's gentle hands began to calm him, and he gave a long, bitter sigh. "But hear this, Cecily. I will fight for my children's rightful place in this kingdom if I am ignored again. 'Tis all I can offer you."

"That is enough, my love," said Cecily, hearing her own words in his vow. "I shall ask no more of you than that. But I will hold you to your promise, if the time ever comes—God willing it does not." She turned him to her and held him close. "There was a time when I thought of little else but asserting your royal claim, in truth. Remember when all I wanted was to be a queen? Foolish girl that I was, although I am a Neville and we are proud stock! Aye, you do remember, and you wanted to be a great commander. But I am a woman now, a wife and a mother, and I can no longer think only of myself but of you and my children's future. As a woman, I am powerless, but your future matters more than ever. I am torn between wanting more for my children and wanting the happiness I would have if you were with me always. I remember my father telling me that those born of noble blood court an early death. 'Tis what I fear the most, Richard, but my duty is to stand by you in building a strong future together. 'Tis a terrible burden on both of us, but we cannot shirk our duty to your family's honor or to our children. But promise me you will keep your family safe."

Richard took her in his arms. "I promise, my proud Cis," he whispered. "I do believe that if I die on the morrow, my children will think well of me and mourn for a spell, but if you were taken from them, they would grieve for ever and a day. With your loving guidance and fierce loyalty, they will make their mark upon the world, I know they will. And with God's help, my way will be made clear."

Cecily smiled into his velvet jacket. "You flatter me, my lord." She looked up and, turning serious again, asked, "What else transpired at Parliament?"

"I voted against the queen today," he muttered, stroking her long yellow hair. "If I did not have her as an enemy before, I surely will now."

"In your own words, she is but a woman, Richard, and a Frenchwoman at that," Cecily reassured him, and Richard found himself chuckling.

"Touché," he whispered, beginning to caress her hips.

"Do be serious, Richard," she scolded him, removing his hands from her. "Do you not suppose that Queen Margaret's motherhood has made her every whit the lioness you have just praised me for being? The king is lost to her, it would seem, and she must protect the babe by herself. Perhaps she believes 'tis better for England to be ruled by a regent queen than watch her husband's and son's kingdom fought over by dukes."

Cecily thought Richard had not been listening, because he continued to stare at the floor. Then slowly he nodded and raised his eyes to the hunting scene woven into a hanging over the mantel.

"You put me to shame, my dear," he murmured. "I have no doubt you would act in a like manner if put in that position. I cannot blame her, I suppose, but her articles of regency will not be acceptable to Parliament or the people, mark my words."

23

England, 1454 to 1455

$\mathcal{R}$ichard's words proved prophetic.

A month later he was asked to exercise his right as the newly named king's lieutenant to open Parliament. He rode into London from Hunsdon on a dreary day in late February with Cecily by his side and made for the comforting bulwark of Baynard's. Cecily noticed the wary and worried looks of the citizens as they hurried about their business in streets that she thought filthier than usual. Crime was rampant, Richard told her, and small bands of armed men stood idling about, ready to take sides if their lords demanded it. Cecily pulled her fur cloak more closely around her and was glad to be riding pillion for once. She felt safe behind Richard's broad back and sword arm and now understood his insistence that she leave the children behind at Hunsdon.

Not long after they arrived, the council issued orders intended to keep the peace in a city where law and order had broken down. The waits were commissioned to entertain on the streets. Torches and beacons lit the wide thoroughfares, crooked lanes, and blind alleys at night. And in an attempt to prevent factions forming for or against one or another political group, no one was permitted to attend upon any lord, alderman, or the mayor until the matter of who was to govern the country had been decided.

"I may be the king's lieutenant now, Cis, but the Commons propose me as protector. However, the Chancellor is a Lancaster man and will not set his seal on it, and so nothing is accomplished," Richard complained. "Chancellor Kemp is an old fool with one foot in the grave, but he is the king's voice for now and holds the Great Seal. So no one will gainsay him."

Richard had joined his wife in her solar after another fruitless day at Parliament in early March. Cecily was attended by Constance and Gresilde and she had been reading some of the writings of St. Brigid to them. Not long after

Countess Joan had bequeathed her daughter that precious book, Cecily had begun to see the wisdom in the saint's words, especially while grieving for her dead infants, and she found the words comforting now as turmoil reigned in London.

"If you are able, I would have you accompany me to Westminster on the morrow," Richard said, swirling the contents of his hanap. "I pray you, dress for an audience with the queen and council. Dame Boyvile may attend you."

When Cecily asked what the occasion was, Richard was close-mouthed. He decided not to trouble her with some of the recent events, including his own controversial act of imprisoning the Speaker of the Commons on dubious trespass charges. The lords had upheld his decision and had invited the lower house to elect a new speaker against their will. All this had not been popular with the Commons. Nay, Cecily did not need to know everything.

Cecily spent two hours the next day readying herself for the unanticipated mile-long journey to Westminster Palace and never probed Richard further. If it was important for him to have her there, she was content to go. She smiled to herself, suddenly recalling Anne of Bedford's reading years ago of the Goodman of Paris's admonishments to his young wife to be dutiful.

Also, she admitted, she was looking forward to breaking her daily routine and showing off her exquisite new gown. She had been away from court for too long, mostly because of her ill health. However, now that her prayers at Walsingham had been answered in Constance's diagnosis and successful treatment of a stone in her kidney, she was back to her old self again and ready to take her place by Richard's side.

Gresilde and Constance slipped the deep blue velvet gown with deep V-neck and lined with white satin over Cecily's pale blue silk underdress. Eschewing some of her newer necklaces, Cecily instructed Constance to clasp her mother's sapphire gift about her throat. She was delighted to have an occasion to wear one of the new high headdresses, a fashion imported from Burgundy in the last year or so. "'Tis called a hennin," she had told Richard the first time she had worn it. More than two feet high, the steeple was crowned with golden gauze that hung down her bare back almost like unbound hair might. Her fingers sparkled with jeweled rings, and drops of pearls fell from her earlobes.

"*Splendide! Comme une reine,*" Constance murmured.

"Ah, but I am not a queen, my dear Constance," Cecily reminded her, turning her reflection this way and that in the mirror, "but I need to show

Margaret that I could be. Besides, she is so beautiful, I have no wish to be put to shame."

"There is none more beautiful than you, aunt," a young man's voice said from the doorway. "May I come in and flatter you some more?"

"My lord of Warwick!" Cecily cried, smiling and holding out her hands. "My dear godson, come and give your old aunt a kiss."

Richard, earl of Warwick, strode forward and bowed over his aunt's hand. His eyes were full of admiration as he gazed at her; then he stepped back and bowed again.

"Your grace, I am sent to escort you to Westminster. My lord of York has been there since early this morning and eagerly awaits your arrival. He told me to tell you he has a surprise for you."

Cecily appraised her nephew in turn. He was not as tall as his father—perhaps influenced by Alice's small stature—but he had Salisbury's high brow and the Neville aquiline nose and thatch of yellow hair. While his brilliant blue eyes were his father's, they did not glow with the same warmth; instead, a steely cynicism made them glitter rather than sparkle.

She took his arm. "A surprise? Then lead on, my lord. I am loath to keep my husband waiting."

Standing on the landing at the top of the wide staircase that led down to Westminster's great hall, Cecily was once again struck by its splendor. The white hart of Richard the Second was carved in a frieze that ran under the many window embrasures, honoring the king who had built the grand meeting place, and colorful ancient banners hung from the magnificent soaring arches of the hammer beam roof.

Cecily saw Richard conversing with a group of men at the bottom of the stairs. She observed he was wearing his ducal coronet, which told her that this was an important occasion. When she and the earl of Warwick had been announced, many in the hall turned to gaze at the elegant duchess of York, including twelve-year-old Edward, earl of March.

"Mother," he exclaimed happily from the middle of the group of councillors, who stepped aside to let him greet Cecily. It was as he went down on one knee beside his father at the foot of the staircase that Cecily first saw him, and it was all she could do not to drop Warwick's arm and run down to embrace her son.

First she let Richard kiss her hand, and after telling him his surprise had pleased her, she gave her attention to Ned. Several people were heard admiring mother and son, for tall as Cecily was, Edward now stood eye to eye with her. His training at Ludlow had prematurely filled out his chest and put muscle on his once spindly legs. He bowed gracefully, aware that all eyes were on them. "God's blessings on you, your grace," he said, his voice teetering on the edge of a baritone. He grinned at her admiring gaze and in his delight dropped the formality. "Aye, my lady Mother, I have become a man since you saw me last."

"A man indeed!" she retorted, knowing she had given herself away. "I wager you and Edmund still wrestle over the last sweetmeat and swing from trees." She turned to Richard, her eyes shining, as the company returned to their conversations. "When did you send for our son, my lord? You know how to hold a secret, to be sure."

Richard drew her arm through his. "Only last week, my lady." He looked over his shoulder at young Richard Neville. "You did well, Warwick, to get her here on time," he said and winked at him. "She is wont to linger over her wardrobe."

Warwick bowed and smiled at Cecily. "It was my pleasure, your grace," he said, and Cecily noted that he was addressing her rather than answering her husband. Then he moved toward a group of nobles, who greeted him with deference. A little arrogant, perhaps, Cecily thought to herself, but a good boy nonetheless and a Neville. She drew Edward's hand through her arm and squeezed it, alarmed at how big it now was. Why, if he grows into it, he will be a giant, she thought.

Richard drew her back to the group he had left. "You are come in good time before the queen is expected. Let me reacquaint you with some of the council," he said, and she thought his tone seemed a little too bright.

"What is this all about? Will you not tell me now, my lord?" she whispered. "You are anxious, I know you are. You cannot fool your wife."

"Bear with me, Cis," he whispered back. "Having you here strengthens my cause." And that was all he would say before they joined the group of councillors.

Cecily recognized her sister Kat's son, John Mowbray, duke of Norfolk, who had been born in the same year as herself. She acknowledged him with a small reverence and he bowed over her hand. "How is your mother, my lord duke? It has been an age since I have seen my sister." Katherine had tragically lost her second husband—her true love—to the wasting sickness and had since married Viscount Beaumont.

"Indeed, she is well, your grace. As you must know, she prefers to spend most of her time in Leicestershire."

Cecily nodded but then, following Richard's lead, she turned her attention to a short, dumpy man with a set of fierce eyebrows and a permanently runny nose. "My lord of Worcester, my dear, the king's treasurer," Richard said, as the formidable John Tiptoft bowed almost double over Cecily's hand. "Our sovereign is fortunate to have such a treasure, is he not?" The others chuckled at his wit, including the subject of the joke, and Cecily was pleased to see they clearly liked Richard. "And you know these two lords, do you not?"

"Lord Bourchier, I am glad to see you again," Cecily said, accepting the viscount's friendly buss across her fingers. "I trust our sister Isabel is here with you. Nay? Then I am truly disappointed."

The handsome, florid man next to Henry Bourchier was ogling her shamelessly, but Cecily extended her hand and smiled. "Your grace, I am glad to see you. Please tell me that my sister Anne is with you. I am beginning to feel like an oddity."

Humphrey Stafford, duke of Buckingham, nodded, and Cecily was glad to see him look a little guilty at the mention of his wife after ogling Cecily so overtly. "She attends the queen, your grace, and will be here shortly. She will be delighted to see you."

Cecily was not so sure, but she acquiesced and asked about both the Bourchier and Stafford children until a fanfare interrupted the proceedings. The courtiers moved away from the staircase as the queen and her considerable retinue processed into the hall.

Magnificent in scarlet cloth of gold, the train of her shimmering gown billowing behind her and the large diamond in her crown catching the sunlight that was streaming through the upper windows, Margaret of Anjou stood regally at the top of the flight of stairs, willing every eye to focus upon her. She waited until her way to the throne in the middle of the great hall was clear before slowly descending the staircase, under a canopy depicting lions and lilies, held aloft by four ushers. Behind her, carrying the infant prince, was Jacquetta Woodville, followed by Cecily's sister and a bevy of other ladies, including the lovely young Elizabeth Woodville, now Dame Grey. Then she saw her own daughter Anne among the ladies, pale but holding her head up high, and the young woman's face brightened when she saw her mother, father, and brother at the foot of the stairs. Good girl, Cecily thought, happy that the few days spent away from Coldharbour receiving her mother's counsel had steeled her resolve to stand up to Henry Holland for the sake of the child she was carrying. Cecily glanced about for Exeter, but she did not see him. 'Tis as well, she decided, or you might embarrass yourself, Cis. The most notable absence of all, Cecily realized thankfully, was Edmund Beaufort, duke of Somerset, who was still where he belonged—in the Tower.

Music followed the queen to her throne. The shawms, trumpets, and sackbuts did not allow for any murmuring between Cecily and Richard. A veritable tableau was created around the dais, with the throne and royal occupant at its center. The queen's household was ranged about her as if to protect her and her prince from outsiders, and Cecily began to feel this was done on purpose. "Them and us," she thought to herself as she watched Jacquetta place the four-month-old Prince Edward on a cushion upon his mother's lap. Margaret held her richly clad son upright for all to see, and the baby squirmed happily in unaccustomed freedom from the swathing bands. All eyes were now riveted on the heir to the throne.

Cecily was puzzled. What is the point of this playacting? she thought, but within a few seconds she knew. It seemed that Richard had requested Margaret's presence, because he now left his wife's side and, stepping to the dais, removed his coronet and went down on both knees. A sudden hush came over the spectators, and Cecily sensed that she was not the only person who did not know why he or she had been summoned. The queen's face was as impassive as a plaster mask. Her gaze held Richard's in cold hauteur, making Cecily shiver.

"Most high and mighty queen of England, Wales, Ireland," Richard began and had to check himself from adding "and France."

"We greet you well, and give you God's welcome in this hallowed hall, home of the king's Parliament. Likewise the lords and I, praising God for blessing you with a safe delivery, welcome our sovereign King Henry's son and heir, Edward of Lancaster"—he paused for effect before stating in a strong, clear voice so that all could hear—"and prince of Wales." The silence in the hall was palpable as Richard continued, "I have sworn allegiance to his father, our sovereign lord King Henry, and now I acknowledge his son and heir as prince of Wales."

Cecily stood next to Henry Bourchier, who had let out a faint sigh of relief, and she glanced up at him, frowning a question. Any remark Bourchier might have made was lost in a rousing shout from every throat in the room. She fell to her knees with the rest as "God bless the prince of Wales" reverberated through the lofty carved rafters. Cecily looked up at the queen then and saw a smile of triumph curl her sensual mouth.

When the echoes died, everyone stood, and Bourchier whispered, "It was imperative that York recognize the prince in public, Cecily. Now we can proceed with the protectorate."

"You mean, Richard will be chosen finally?" Cecily's heart was beating wildly.

Henry Bourchier gave her a curt nod.

"But what about Kemp? I thought he had the final say."

"He does, but too many of us on the council and in the Commons know England must have a regent, and York is the most obvious choice. The chancellor will come around."

"And what about the queen?" Cecily whispered.

"This was a pretty ceremony, my lady, but in the end she is only a woman." And he bowed and moved on before Cecily could frame an apt retort. Turning to Edward, who had most assuredly overheard the tête-à-tête, she gave him a piece of advice instead. "Never underestimate a woman, my son," she said sternly. "You will rue the day that you do, mark my words."

She had been so intent on dispensing her wise counsel that she had failed to notice they were no longer alone and was startled to be face to face with Jacquetta and her beautiful daughter. Jacquetta had grown plump of late but was still pretty, Cecily thought. She turned her gaze on Elizabeth. She was on the arm of a striking young man with chestnut hair and blue eyes, stirring a memory of someone from long ago. Certes, she thought, he must be Jacquetta's oldest boy with her husband Richard Woodville, now Lord Rivers.

Jacquetta and Cecily reverenced each other and Lord Rivers's two offspring were presented. Cecily in her turn presented her son and was disconcerted to see Ned staring boldly at the young beauty in front of him. Cecily pulled furtively on his dangling sleeve, and he immediately turned to Jacquetta and murmured a customary greeting over her outstretched hand. Without any prompting from her mother, Elizabeth put out her hand for the young man, and Cecily was amused to see Ned's own tremble as he took it to his lips. She knows her power already, Cecily thought with a flicker of respect. But then, look who has instructed her!

"Her sovereign highness the queen wishes to talk with you, your grace," Jacquetta purred. "She begs you to attend her in her apartments in the palace as soon as this audience is over. May I convey your acceptance?"

Cecily bowed her head in acquiescence, hopeful that the meeting would dispel her earlier worry that a schism had opened between the Lancastrian queen and the duke of York. She noticed Jacquetta was now giving Ned a furtive appraisal while he responded to a remark of Anthony's, and as the duchess curtsied again to leave, Cecily was astonished to hear her pointed aside to Elizabeth, surely meant for Cecily's ears as well, "Such a big boy for twelve years. And nothing like his father."

Richard returned to her side, visibly relieved that the little ceremony was over. "I am sorry I was secretive, my dear, but I thought it best not to raise your expectations. I very nearly could not bring myself to do it. Seeing you there gave me courage, and having all see that Ned also acknowledged the new heir to the throne might placate a suspicious council."

"Suspicious? But those we spoke with seemed friendly enough, Richard."

"Aye, but will they all support me when I am Protector? I am not so sure."

Cecily leaned forward. "We can talk later at Baynard's. The queen has asked me to attend her in her chambers, so I must go."

Richard's puzzled frown followed her from the room.

CECILY WAS TAKEN aback to see the queen in tears not five minutes after making her reverence in the luxury of the royal solar. She thought of Joan's admonishment, which only recently she had passed along to Meggie when the girl had burst into tears and run off.

"Never cry in front of anyone but your family, my dear. You never want to appear weak."

But it was not her place to remind Queen Margaret. It appeared the queen's ladies, Lady Ismania Scales, Anne of Buckingham, and Jacquetta of Bedford, must be accustomed to such a scene, for they continued to ply their needles and speak among themselves. She knelt quietly and waited for the weeping to subside.

"Forgive me, duchess, but I have suffered much these past few months," Margaret said finally, after blowing her nose into a silk kerchief and motioning to Cecily to rise. "You have not seen my husband since . . . since his illness, I believe?"

"I have not, your grace, but I have heard—"

Margaret cut her off. She lowered her voice, fidgeted with her kerchief, and said bitterly, "He is naught but a vegetable, as weak and wilted as a boiled leek, as pale as a turnip." She leaned over to Cecily and confided in a whisper, "He cannot speak, he cannot walk, he must be carried from place to place, he must be fed like a baby, and he soils himself many times a day. It is unspeakable. And his eyes—those eyes that once looked at me with love—they are dead. Staring and dead. It is terrifying."

Cecily was at once stunned to be taken into the queen's confidence and dismayed to see her display of emotion. Breaking with etiquette, she took the nervous hands into her own. "It is but temporary, your grace," she murmured. "He will recover with the help of his physicians and all our prayers. His subjects pray for him every day. May I lend you my book of the writings of St. Brigid? They have comforted me in my times of distress."

Her kindness seemed to make the younger woman cry more. "He did not even know our son," she whispered, her shoulders heaving. "I thought it would cure him to see his heir, but he did not even know him."

Cecily glanced at the attendants, but only her sister was watching her, the others being engaged in quiet conversation. She sent an imploring look at Anne, who ignored her and only worked her needle more diligently.

Bewildered, Cecily quickly sought to pacify the queen again. "Soft, your grace. You must stay strong for Edouard." She used the French pronunciation that she knew Margaret preferred. "Your son needs you."

Margaret looked up then, wiped her eyes, and shocked Cecily with a sudden change in demeanor. Cecily wondered whether the tears had been a sham.

"If you understand that, my lady, then why does your husband oppose my regency?" the queen asked in a measured voice, slowly but deliberately disengaging her hands from Cecily's. "Now that I know you understand my dilemma, I am counting on your support. Perhaps you can influence him in my favor."

Cecily gulped and stood back. Dear Virgin Mother, help me find the right answer, she pleaded. She realized then how like a fox Queen Margaret was. She had entrapped Cecily and now sat there cold and silent awaiting a response. Cecily hoped Anne might have come to her aid, but it was Jacquetta who came forward to stand next to Margaret's chair, the pair reminding Cecily of a beautiful witch and her familiar.

"I am your grace's loyal subject," Cecily said, her voice faltering in the face of these two intimidating females, "and I assure you I will always work for the good of the realm." She took a breath and, looking Margaret straight in the eye, resorted to the truth. "Your infant son needs his mother, your grace. Surely as Regent, the affairs of state would keep you from his side. I swear I meant no disrespect to your grace in my efforts to console you, and I beg your pardon most humbly." She watched for any softening of the queen's expression, and seeing an almost imperceptible nod of acknowledgment, she was encouraged to finish with a lie. "I cannot speak for my lord, your grace, for I do not know what is on his mind."

After a long silence, in which Cecily was furious to find her knees trembling, Margaret inclined her head graciously. "I believe you are a good woman, duchess, and you speak as a good mother. I pray you are also the king's loyal subject." She turned to where Anne was watching the little scene anxiously. "As loyal as I know your sister is, madame."

Anne fell to her knees. "As God is my witness, your grace," she vowed, crossing herself and avoiding Cecily's gaze.

Then Margaret turned back to Cecily with an enigmatic smile. "It is curious, is it not, how my request of you now is the same one you made of me at Walsingham. How is it you say in England? Favor for favor, *madame?*" Her smile faded and she rose, holding out her hand. "You may leave me, now, duchess Cecily, and I thank you for your . . . your understanding."

Once outside the door, where Gresilde was patiently waiting, Cecily took hold of her attendant's hand and, with her heart still pounding, she propelled Gresilde along the passageway as fast as she could away from the stultifying atmosphere of the queen's apartments. She resolved not to tell Richard the topic of this uncomfortable meeting; he had enough to deal with.

NOT A WEEK later, in his seventy-fifth year, Cardinal Kemp, archbishop of Canterbury and Chancellor of England, died suddenly. The council resolved to send several members to Windsor to inform the king and see for themselves if Henry were recovered enough to take back the reins, choose another chancellor, and appoint a new archbishop of Canterbury.

"Bourchier and Warwick were among them, as was your brother William," Richard told Cecily after the lords had returned. "Henry did not recognize any of them or understand what they were saying. He merely stared. It was pitiful, our nephew told me."

"So what means this, Richard? Someone must appoint a chancellor. Margaret?"

Richard went to the window and polished one of the panes with his sleeve. "It would seem the council is looking to me to begin a protectorate, my love," he said so quietly that Cecily had to approach him to hear. "I shall be Protector and defender of England until Henry recovers his senses or young Edouard is old enough to assume the crown." He sighed. "If I ever had an ambition to be king, I could not have imagined it happening thus. But I shall do my duty by King Henry and my countrymen, as God is my witness, and I shall insist that the responsibility for this decision rests with the lords who appointed me. And for agreeing, I shall expect them to give me their support. It will not be easy, Cis. Many do not like me, but it seems they have no other choice."

"I pray you remember," Cecily said, putting her arms around her husband and laying her head upon his back, "you are not usurping anyone's right to the regency. It is your right and no one else's."

I should rejoice in Richard's success, she thought, but upon recalling her audience with Margaret, she knew for a certainty that his acceptance of the protectorate would make the queen and her adherents hate her husband even more, and she sighed. How long have we imagined this moment? she asked herself. Is this truly what I have worked toward all these years? It did not feel at all like the glorious moment of her dreams.

"I shall pray for your safety and for God to give you the strength and wisdom to perform this sacred duty," was all she could say now. "I am so proud of you."

CECILY WAS IN London when Richard's appointment was made formal on Wednesday, April 3, 1454, and when, a day earlier, her eldest brother, Richard, earl of Salisbury, was appointed Chancellor of England. It was a controversial appointment, Richard told her, proud of his choice. For the past five decades, the Great Seal had been in the hands of churchmen.

Cecily made the decision to move back to Fotheringhay in late May, as soon as she heard that Richard was hurrying north to put down one of the most persistent and violent family feuds that had plagued the country for the past two years. It perturbed her that one faction was her own Neville family, the younger sons of Salisbury, who fought to keep their northern inheritance away from the long-time foes of Neville, the Percys of Northumberland. More disturbing was that Henry Holland, duke of Exeter—Nan's violent husband— had sided with Percy, and riots and uprisings were occurring as far south as York.

"We might as well be comfortable at Fotheringhay," she told Constance, while she engaged in one of her favorite activities—tending to Meg's golden tresses. For some reason the mundane task took her mind off the tedious duties of running the castle in Richard's absence. She dipped the comb in rosemary water before stroking it through the shoulder-length hair. Meg had come down with a case of head lice during the winter, and so Cecily had ordered the beautiful waist-long hair to be cut off so that Meg's young attendant could better remove the pests. Now it was growing back thicker and glossier than before. Cecily appraised her youngest daughter in the polished silver mirror. Young Margaret of York promised to be attractive, and Cecily was glad that the girl's front teeth had recently appeared and were straight. Richard was always quick to point out those large, gray, intelligent eyes that did not miss anything. "'Tis what makes you notice her," he told Cecily. "But I confess, for beauty, none of our daughters can hold a candle to you, my love."

"Oh, pish," Cecily remembered answering, and she smiled over Meg's head into the mirror and resumed her ruminations.

Here it was late June and Richard was still north chasing Nevilles, Percys, and most importantly, Henry Holland, duke of Exeter. Cecily had been horrified to learn of the attempted assassination plot in York against Richard, instigated by Exeter, and her heart was hardened even more against the man who had abused her daughter so violently.

What had Richard written?

The plot came to naught, but it was revealed that Exeter was not merely attempting to oust me from the protectorate, but to place himself upon the throne. It seems his arrogance has no bounds, although his common sense has, for when I succeeded in sending the Percys packing back to Northumberland, his grace of Exeter chose to flee south, where he cannot hide from me, I promise you. If he presumes to cower behind the queen's skirts at Windsor, I think he will be surprised by his lack of welcome. She wishes nothing more to do with him, and I cannot blame her. Moreover, his only friend, Somerset, lies moldering in the Tower, awaiting trial.

I miss you, my sweet lady, and our children. Speaking of whom, I received a report from Ludlow that Edward and Edmund have misbehaved on several occasions, according to their tutor. After I had chastised them in a letter, they wrote me a most humble response full of flourishing phrases about their diligence in their studies and then had the gall to ask me for money for new clothes. I wonder from whom they inherited such impertinence!

Cecily had chuckled when she read this. Now she sighed. She put down the ivory comb, kissed the top of Meg's head, and gestured to the young attendant to ready her mistress for bed. How she missed her two big boys, she thought. Perhaps we can be together again as a family at Yuletide, and yet who knows where Richard might be then.

IT BECAME APPARENT that if Cecily wished to see more of her busy husband, she had to move the family south to Hunsdon. Richard gave his permission for the move, so preparations were made, and the October weather smiled on the cavalcade as it set out from Fotheringhay with the best of the York furnishings and an armed escort of four score men to guard the duchess and her young children. Other than a skirmish with some outlaws upon the second day, the journey was uneventful.

Richard joined his family a few days later following a session of oyer and terminer in Derby.

"A date has been set for Somerset's trial at last," he told Cecily, after they had made love in their big tester bed, around which were drawn Cecily's favorite curtains brought from Fotheringhay. "'Tis later this month, and unless the king recovers suddenly, I cannot believe Somerset will not be attainted and exiled. And with Exeter secure in Pontefract, we should know some peaceful times."

"And the Percys? Are they content to remain on their estates now?"

Richard harrumphed, stroking her back. "Time will tell, Cis. I do not trust your Percy nephew Egremont, I regret to say. He and Exeter were a deadly combination, each egging on the other."

Cecily turned over and looked at him in the guttering candlelight. It was late, she guessed, but she had no sense of time when she was with Richard. He was staring at the canopy overhead, at the white roses mingled with the falcon and fetterlock. "I pray daily for you, Richard," she whispered. "I fear you may have angered God by snatching Exeter from sanctuary to imprison him at Pontefract. I trust you have done penance for the sin."

Richard yawned again. "Over and over, my dear. Over and over. And yet when I heard what the brute had done to our little Nan, a dark cloud settled over me, and I could not emerge from under it until I had punished the whoreson."

"Aye, 'twas as well you had support for his abduction for reasons other than the mistreatment of your daughter. Anne is safe here with us now, and you shall see your granddaughter on the morrow."

"Granddaughter." Richard said the word slowly, a grin breaking across his face, and for the first time in a long time Cecily saw the crinkling around his eyes. "'Tis hard to believe we are grandparents, Cis. Where has the time gone?"

Cecily ran her hand under his nightshirt and caressed his thigh. "I know not, Richard, but when we are together like this, I feel no older than the first time we pleasured each other. Come," she said huskily, "let us forget family feuding for a few precious hours."

DESPITE THE INABILITY of the council to bring Somerset to trial on the prescribed date in October, the York family was in a merry mood at Hunsdon a few days after celebrating the birth of the Savior. Even Anne had come out of her melancholy following the safe delivery of her daughter in the summer and estrangement from Exeter. Cecily was pleased to see her dancing with Ned, who had become his sister's protector once he had left Ludlow and joined his father's household. Cecily had not hidden Anne's troubles from her son, and she discovered that he had also formed an intense dislike of Exeter from his father's accounts of the man's actions in the north. Ned's childhood over, Richard had taken charge of his further education by taking his son to London and acquainting him with those clergy and nobles who made up the council.

"The earl of March has a way with women," Constance whispered to Cecily as they watched the young people go through the paces of a country dance. Cecily had decided a while ago that Ned danced with the precision of a soldier; his style was perfunctory but not without a certain manly charm. "Perhaps he was permitted to read too many romances with his tutor, Master Croft?" Constance added and smiled to herself when she saw Cecily frown. "I am but teasing you, madame. It is just that he is so very handsome, and look at the way he makes even his sister blush and smile."

Cecily decided that she would have a word with Richard about his eldest son's pursuit of the ladies and turned her attention to Edmund, who was gallantly partnering Bess. Now there is a natural-born dancer, she thought, her heart melting as it did every time she studied him. He was not as handsome as his brothers Edward and George, but he had a gentle grace about him. Although he never wavered in his partnering, his eyes had a faraway look as he listened to the lute and recorders strumming and piping the rhythm. Cecily hoped he would gain strength of purpose, for gentleness and grace would not be appreciated by his peers, she knew.

Bess, like Edward, was mentally counting the beats, unlike George and Meggie, who could barely contain their pleasure in the dance. Cecily could see Bess's heart was not in it. 'Tis time we found her a permanent partner, Cecily thought. True, she is only ten, but by now she should know what her future will be after the time she will spend with her Aunt Alice learning to be a lady. It will be hard to let her go, Cecily mused, but Bess was more than ready to turn the corner on childhood.

She mentally scrolled down the list of eligible young lords for her daughter, but unhappily many of them were already contracted or vehement adherents of the Lancaster court. Richard had still not won everyone to his side during these months of his protectorate, and indeed she had been shocked to find out how many councillors had pleaded ill health to avoid many of the meetings. Their absence meant that nothing of note could be accomplished, making Richard look indecisive at best and incompetent at worst. It was unfair to judge him in such a short period, she grumbled to herself, and under such adverse conditions. With Exeter in prison and Egremont captured in a fierce skirmish at Stamford Bridge, the fighting in the north had subsided, and Nevilles and Percys had gone home, thanks to Richard. However, the seeds of hatred had been sown between the two powerful landowners of the north, which would add to Richard's worry. He was learning that doing his duty was fraught with danger, and Cecily was often left with only prayer to sustain her while he held the kingdom's reins.

Without warning, the object of her thoughts came striding into the room, causing the musicians to halt, his children to fall to their knees, and Cecily to rise and go to him anxiously. "What is it, my lord? Your face is paler than ewe's milk."

"There is astonishing news, my lady. I suppose I should be glad of it, but it has come as a shock and I was not prepared." He paused before unleashing the thunderbolt. "The king has recovered his senses."

All gasped and crossed themselves, but little Dickon toddled up to Ned's side and took his hand at Richard's entrance, his face a picture of delight. "Papa," he babbled repeatedly, pointing at Richard and tugging at Ned. "Mama, Papa."

Richard's face softened into a smile, and he picked up his youngest son and tossed him in the air. "Aye, Dickon, your father and mother are here. We will always be here for you." His eyes embraced the other eager faces as he repeated, "We shall always be here for you." The children rose in unison and once again Cecily rejoiced to see Richard's daughters put their arms about their father. They gave him such joy, she knew, as she stood proudly watching the familial scene. Standing in his family's midst, Richard looked at each face in turn as if to take a picture of them with him when he had to leave them again.

"Children," he said, putting Dickon down, his tone turning suddenly serious. "Look around you and take note of your family. Never forget your blood kin, do you hear? The most important people in your lives are right here in this room—not forgetting all those who loyally serve the house of York. Do you understand?" He looked at all his offspring in turn, waiting for a nod of acknowledgment from each. "But hear this. We are also all liegemen of our sovereign King Henry. Let it never be said that York did not serve the king and his country. I beg of you, whatever you may do in your lives, be loyal to your family, loyal to our house, and loyal to your king."

Silence followed this speech. The children stared up at their father and Dickon hid behind Cecily's skirt. Cecily held back tears. What portent had Richard had to cause him to deliver such heady words? She found herself trembling. But then she remembered the reason for Richard's return.

"The king! God be praised for his recovery," Cecily said with as much enthusiasm as she could muster. "We must give thanks immediately. Gresilde, go and find Father Lessey. He must prepare a special mass within the hour." Let it not be said the duke of York did not give thanks for our sovereign's renewed health, she told herself.

As Nurse Anne carried Dickon back to the nursery, the other children stood in a line in silence while the duke and duchess awaited the summons to the chapel.

"What will happen now?" Cecily asked Richard quietly.

"I will tell you what will happen, my dear. Henry will free Somerset, and the queen and her favorite will poison the king against me. I fear the dreadful cycle will begin anew and we shall again be unwelcome at court."

Cecily gripped his hand within the folds of his long, woolen robe so that the children could not see and whispered, "You have more support now, my love, and I think perhaps you may be wrong. You might have snatched the opportunity to take the crown these past nine months, but you have remained true to your oath of allegiance to Henry and to his son. Surely the king will be grateful for your good leadership and want to keep you by his side."

Richard's face was grim. "Not when Margaret of Anjou hates me, Cis. 'Tis as simple as that."

Cecily understood that nothing she said would rouse Richard from his dejection, so she decided to wait for a happier moment to tell him she was again with child.

ALL THAT RICHARD feared in December had come to pass by March, and when the Great Council at Greenwich sanctioned Somerset's release from the Tower, Richard was forced to resign his offices, captaincy of Calais and Protector. The king had also pardoned Exeter; however, the duke failed to attempt a reunion with his wife and infant daughter. Two days following Richard's resignation, Salisbury was forced to resign as Chancellor. Somerset's star was ascendant once again.

After Easter, Richard and Salisbury took their families and retinues back to safe havens in the north. Richard went to Sandal Castle in the south of Yorkshire, and Salisbury saw his family back to his stronghold at Middleham in the dales, taking young Bess with him. Then he and a large retinue joined Richard at well-fortified Sandal to plan their next move. A bond had been forged between the two ousted noblemen, and it was not long before Salisbury's powerful son Warwick, whose lands in the south were still being contested by Somerset and other lands in Wales by the king's Tudor half brothers, Jasper and Edmund, took York's side.

On a bright spring day, the two Richards went to find Cecily, now in the last term of her pregnancy. Richard of York stood facing his wife, while Salisbury took the chair offered and sat contemplating his fingernails.

Richard was bristling with anger. "Somerset has called for a Great Council at Leicester, and Bourchier writes the measle intends to lay out the form of government with him at its head so that he will control the king should he be stricken again. Curse the man! We had no knowledge of that meeting, but we have been summoned to Leicester to profess our fealty to the king. Again! As if I have not sufficiently proved my loyalty to Henry. 'Tis evident, Somerset is determined to keep me from ever having power again, but by Christ's nails, I will be damned in hell before I capitulate to that traitorous whoreson of a bitch!" he cried, his indignation echoing in his jutting chin and clenched jaw.

"My lord! I pray you, remember we are not alone," Cecily exclaimed, glancing at Constance and Gresilde, who pretended they had not heard.

But Richard was so filled with outrage that he hardly heard his wife's admonishment. "We are saddled with a king who is fit only for incarceration in

Bethlehem hospital or, if I am kind, a monastery, and a queen who is . . . who is . . ." He snapped his fingers in rapid succession, searching for exactly the right word for the woman he was beginning to understand was his real enemy. "A she-wolf!" he cried triumphantly.

"An apt description, York, if I may say," Salisbury agreed grimly. "She has become a dangerous adversary, especially now that Somerset is at her beck and call again. Who would have thought that sweet, homesick girl would turn out to be such a termagant. But," he added with a derisive snort, "what can you expect from a Frenchwoman."

"Brother, I beg of you!" Cecily cried, nodding in Constance's direction. "I would trust Doctor LeMaître and Nurse Anne with my life, but . . ."

"But they are Normans, Cecily," Salisbury retorted. "One can hardly call them French, *n'est-ce pas, mon docteur,*" he apologized, as Constance looked up, more amused than offended.

"Pah!" Cecily rejoined.

"Enough, both of you," Richard of York interrupted. "This is hardly a time to discuss the nuances of being French. We must stop Somerset's bid to control the king and the council. God's bones, how I wish I had had enough foresight and support while I was Protector to have put a policy in place to fall back on should the king become ill again. What do you propose we do now?"

The earl shrugged. "I respectfully leave that to you, my dear brother, but I am with you whatever you decide."

Cecily grimaced inwardly, her brother's indecision disappointing her again.

"Perhaps we should make an appeal to the king, swearing fealty but demanding that Somerset be tried as was decided last year," Richard suggested. "What think you?"

Oh, no, Cecily wanted to shout, not again. Petitions have not had any effect upon the king before, so why should one today, and it was the king who had released Somerset from the Tower. She looked from one to the other and once again cursed that she was not a man.

Maybe it was the two pairs of eyes boring into him, or perhaps that he sensed his sister was disappointed in him, but Richard Neville finally spoke his mind. He was now as angry as York and knew they could not afford to waste any more time. "Why not muster a force here and march south?" he said slowly but with conviction. "We will not seek battle but inform the king we must protect ourselves from our enemies at court and let him know they are his enemies too, and that this is in the realm's best interest. Let us gather our northern retainers, summon Warwick with his, and you send to Ludlow for March to come with a body also."

Ned lead an army? Cecily gasped, swallowing her disbelief. But when she saw Richard nod, she burst out, "He is but twelve, my lord!"

Richard waved her objection aside. "Almost thirteen, my dear. I shall see to it he is well protected. I shall send Piers Taggett to alert him. We are not going south to do battle, my dear, simply to parley. Ned will only be the figurehead for our Welshmen to follow." He turned to Salisbury. "I am pleased we see eye to eye, Brother, for your plan accords with my own thoughts."

Cecily had had enough talk of armies. "I pray you, my lords, leave me in peace with my companions while you go and talk mustering matters. But hear me well," Cecily counseled, "if I were the king and I saw a group of thousands led by three disgruntled noblemen advancing upon my capital, I would not think they had merely come to parley."

Salisbury rose and joined Richard at the door. "Cecily has a point, as she usually does," he said, giving his sister a weak smile.

"Perhaps," Richard acknowledged, exiting with grim purpose, "but I have no mind to beat about the bush this time, Neville. The king must know we are serious."

"Sorry, Sister. Your husband seems to have made up his mind," Salisbury said, shrugging when Richard was out of earshot. Then his eyes twinkled. "And to think Alice believes you lead him by the nose."

He scooted out, and the cushion Cecily angrily launched at him hit the closed door. It did not help dispel the apprehension that was knotting her stomach.

IGNORING THE SUMMONS to appear before the council at Leicester, Richard, Salisbury, and Warwick set out for London to petition the king, riding at the head of an impressive army. Cecily had clung to Richard in the privacy of her bedchamber before he went to his own to be attired in his blue and murrey robes.

"Have a care, Richard," she begged him. "Do not do anything rash, I beg of you. Remember Dartford. You must see the king alone, for I believe he wants to trust you."

"It is our intent to speak to Henry, Cecily—if we can get past the queen and Somerset. There are those, like Norfolk and Buckingham, who are ready to be moderate, but we need to know once and for all what support we have on the council." He took her in his arms and smoothed back her tangled hair. "Now hurry with your dressing, Cis. I cannot leave Sandal knowing you are not upon the rampart to wave me farewell."

Before she could caution him further, he kissed her and left the room.

CECILY STOOD WITH Margaret and George on either side of her and Dickon in Meg's arms as the three great lords with their personal retinues rode over the drawbridge and down the hill. Fear crawled up her back and she shivered. Looking down on rank upon rank of mounted gentlemen, bowmen in their Lincoln green, billmen, farmers, townsfolk, and field hands filling entire fields as they waited their turn to follow their lords, she guessed there were more than three thousand men on the march.

Dickon, tired of being held for so long, was squirming in Meg's tight embrace, and so his sister set him on the ground, where he set up a wail.

Her nerves already on edge, Cecily snapped at him, "Hush, Dickon!" startling her son into silence. "What is the matter with you? Do you want your father to hear you crying?"

As though he had indeed heard his youngest's protests, Richard turned in his saddle, shaded his eyes from the sun, and gazed up at the keep. Cecily pulled out a scarf and let it flutter in the wind above her head, and Richard held up a hand in salute. Meg and George waved both arms and jumped up and down, their eyes shining with pride for their magnificent father. His horse was caparisoned in rich damask of York colors and decorated all over with white roses and his royal arms. Behind his immediate escort, his herald carried the banner of the falcon and fetterlock alongside Salisbury's green eagle and Warwick's bear with the ragged staff.

Feeling guilty, Cecily heaved Dickon up onto her hip, enduring a couple of unintentional kicks to her huge belly, and told her son to blow kisses to his father. His tears forgotten, Dickon stared in wonder at the scene below him. "Papa," he gurgled, pointing. "Papa go 'way."

"Aye, sweeting, your father is going a long way away," Cecily whispered, nuzzling the boy's dark head. "But he will be back soon, I promise."

If God is merciful he will, she thought. Blessed Virgin, please keep my husband safe. She felt bereft, as she always did when Richard left, and it seemed her family was dwindling by the day. She missed unsentimental Bess, and she guessed Meg missed her sister even more. How well she remembered that day at Raby when Nan had left for good. Look at her now. She's wife to

Buckingham and at the queen's elbow. "The queen!" she murmured, scowling. Richard should have stayed here, out of her way, out of danger, Cecily thought miserably, staring at the never-ending column of soldiers.

The little group on the keep watched for half an hour until Richard disappeared over the crest of a hill, his army crawling like ants behind him. Cecily turned to go and was startled by two magpies that flew across her path. A slow smile curved her mouth and she sent up an *Ave Maria*.

"Two for joy, Mother!" Meggie cried with excitement, pointing at the birds. "'Tis good luck. Father will have good luck."

THREE WEEKS LATER, Cecily was playing hide and go seek with Meg and George when Steward Heydon sent a page to fetch her down in haste to Sandal's great hall. She flew along the passage from the nursery wing to the spiral stair in the duke's tower and down the few steps into the hall. Richard must have sent a messenger, she surmised, her pulse racing from exertion and nervous anticipation. Sweet Mary, let it be good news!

She held her breath as York Herald knelt before her and began to speak.

"There has been a battle," the burly man announced. Gasps and mutterings from the duchess's household accompanied the announcement. "Duke Richard is alive, your grace, have no fear," he reassured her quickly.

"And my son, the earl of March?" she whispered, horrified to imagine Ned in the thick of battle. "Is he well?"

The herald nodded. "My lords of Salisbury and Warwick also, your grace."

Cecily felt her whole body melt into the high-backed chair. "God be praised," she replied, crossing herself, but then she frowned. "A battle?" Richard had not gone south to fight, he had assured her. How had it come to that? To calm her trembling hands, she gripped the arms of the chair. "Now, sir herald, tell us what has happened."

Given leave, he stood up and took a deep breath. "After he left this castle, my lord of York marched with all speed toward London, hoping to surprise the king and council into listening to his petition. Fearful of the size of our force, the king amassed his own army, not as large as ours, 'tis said, and demanded we repair to Leicester as the lords of York, Salisbury, and Warwick had been ordered to do. The king sent out three mediators to parley with the duke, but instead my lord of York detained them and, saying he would speak to none other but the king, marched them with our force to meet him."

He paused and licked his parched lips. Cecily called out to her steward for ale and the herald drank gratefully. "And did the king meet his grace of York?" she asked.

The man shook his head. "The king would not agree but marched as far as St. Albans and had commandeered the town by the time Duke Richard arrived there. Our forces camped outside the town, which had been hastily fortified with a ditch and some sandbags. St. Albans has no wall, you understand."

Cecily nodded. She had passed by the city on several occasions. "Go on."

"Did I mention my lord of March arrived the day before the battle? His coming enlarged our force by a few hundred Welshmen." He paused, seeing Cecily sit forward, her eyes shining with pride. "Aye, the young Lord Edward was every inch a commander, your grace. You would have rejoiced had you heard the shout of welcome he received," the diplomat cried, warming to his task.

Her pride almost made the news of Edward's arrival—and into harm's way—palatable for Cecily, but she quickly waved the man on.

"The duke sent a written petition with me to read to our sovereign. It begged the king to know him, Salisbury, and Warwick for loyal liegemen and to acknowledge my lord of York as his chief minister. My lord also called for the trial of the duke of Somerset, which had not taken place as the Commons had decreed it should."

Cecily arched a brow. "I expect that did not strike the king favorably." And to herself she added, or the queen.

"You have the measure of it, your grace. The duke of Buckingham had by then been made constable, and the king was counseled that the fair-minded lord might be the only one able to sway his grace of York into retreating. But when my lord of Somerset was not given up to us, I was one of the heralds sent to petition the king again to have the duke removed from the king's council and relinquished to us."

"Was Somerset there when you went?" Cecily asked eagerly. "I would have liked to have been there to see his face. For a moment, he might have been afraid."

The herald, however, by now thoroughly enjoying his mission, refused to be rushed. So he carried on as if Cecily had not spoken.

"The message I took back told that on pain of forfeiture of lands, Duke Richard and his followers must disperse peacefully. Thus rebuffed, my lords of York, Salisbury, Norfolk, and Warwick had no choice but to attempt to see the king through force in order to effect the duke of Somerset's dismissal. 'Twas Warwick's northern retainers who broke down the barrier commanded by Lord Clifford and entered the streets at the back of St. Albans, where all the king's men were taken by surprise."

"Taken by surprise?" Cecily scoffed. "Could they really have thought Duke Richard would have turned tail and run?"

Mutterings of assent and indignation from the onlookers affirmed Cecily's remark.

The herald related the outcome of the fray with relish. "We were fighting hand to hand in and out of houses, down alleys, and even in the taverns. We were prepared to fight, but the king's men had not even donned their armor and many were killed in a short time. Then it was learned the duke of Somerset himself was hiding in a house, and I was one of the soldiers sent by Duke Richard to seek him out. We did better, my lady," he cried, panting with excitement at this point as though he were reenacting the skirmish, and he ran a hand over his perspiring forehead. "We found the traitor and several of us wounded him before one giant finished him off with an axe!" He swung around triumphantly to face the fascinated spectators.

Cecily felt the room spin as she registered the news. Somerset dead? Edmund Beaufort, her ambitious, unscrupulous cousin and Richard's enemy, was dead. It was almost impossible to believe. She grieved that it had come to bloodshed and that one cousin would kill another. That Richard and Somerset despised each other was clear, but she had not imagined it would come to this. Her hands froze on the chair and she must have gone pale, for Constance was at her side in a flash, asking if she were all right. Steward Heydon's face floated in front of her too. She took a deep breath and patted Constance's hand. Focusing on the herald, who was now looking worried, she said sharply, "Why do you stop now, sir? Tell the company who else fell on that day."

"In all, a mere sixty men, duchess. My lord Clifford was among the lords on the king's side, but more important, Henry Percy, earl of Northumberland. My lord of Somerset's heir, young Henry Beaufort, was gravely wounded, as were the sons of Northumberland and my lord of Buckingham."

Cecily sighed heavily. Those last two were her sister's children. Eleanor had lost a husband and almost a son that day, she thought, and Nan had almost lost her son. I pray no one ever brings me such dreadful tidings. But even more horrible was that these Neville grandchildren had been slain by their own kin.

God help us, she thought. She looked back at the herald. "And the king, sir. What of the king?"

"Our bowmen did their worst from outside the barricades, your grace, and it seems our sovereign lord was struck in the neck by an arrow." A gasp of horror made the herald pause. "But he lives, God be praised, and was not badly hurt." He frowned, remembering the sorry scene. "The king's grace was standing alone, talking to himself, his neck bleeding. Those supporters who had not died in the flights of arrows shamefully abandoned him and his banner, which was then crumpled upon the ground and covered in blood. My lord of Warwick, who had led the successful assault on the town, came then and, seeing the king bewildered as he was, fell to his knees and pledged allegiance on the spot. He was joined by his father, Duke Richard, and the duke of Norfolk. It seems the battle was over almost before it had begun, and the duke had captured the king, who was taken to the abbey for his safety."

"You are saying it was a victory for my husband?" Cecily heard herself ask in a perfectly calm voice, although she wanted to shout the words. The wire frame holding up her gauze veil was beginning to dig into her skull, and her head was pounding.

"Aye, your grace," the herald said solemnly. "In three hours, St. Albans was taken and in the abbey all the lords with Duke Richard submitted themselves humbly to the king. On the morrow, the king was escorted to London flanked by my lords of York and Salisbury, with all deference to his majesty, and with the earl of Warwick leading them bearing the sword of state." The herald's face was glowing with pride for his lord when he announced, "In a token ceremony at St. Paul's the very next day, the king received his crown from none other than the duke of York himself."

Cecily looked around the hall. The Yorks' loyal servants were whispering among themselves, nodding and smiling at the news of their victorious lord and fellow retainers. She, too, should be glad, she knew, but deep down in that dark side of her she sensed it boded ill for them all. But she knew she had to suppress her own misgivings, appear as pleased as her servants, and play her part as their triumphant duchess.

She rose, and the company fell silent. "My loyal friends, let us all go to the chapel and give thanks for Duke Richard's victory and the safe delivery of his grace the king. Father Lessey? I pray you ready yourself for a mass and we will follow in a little while." She beckoned the steward. "Sir Henry, reward this noble herald well for his service. I thank you for your honest words, sir,"

she told the kneeling messenger. "Duke Richard is fortunate in his herald."
She was about to make an exit to the chapel when she asked him another
question.

"In my relief at your news, sir, I forgot to ask how many of our men were
lost."

"Only a handful, God be thanked," he replied. "Duke Richard said that
if you asked, one man in particular might be known to you: the archer, John
Blaybourne."

And then memories came flooding back of the gentle giant who had so
ably escorted her to Rouen and later to her romantic tryst with Richard at Les
Andelys. "God have mercy on his soul," she murmured, glancing at Constance,
who crossed herself sadly. "He was a good man and served Duke Richard—
and me—well."

CECILY WAS DETERMINED her child would be born at Fotheringhay, and
despite Constance's remonstrances against supervising a move from Sandal so
close to the birth, the duchess got her wish.

"You are forty years old, your grace, not twenty-five," Constance complained, as they suffered through downpours in early June on their way to
Northamptonshire. The roof of the carriage leaked. Cecily, Meg, and George
huddled in one corner while Constance sought a dry spot at the other end.
Twice the heavy vehicle became stuck in the mud and blocked the road for
hours. Only those on horseback or on foot could pass the duchess and her
entourage.

The high keep of Fotheringhay on the horizon was a welcome sight on the
third day of an arduous journey. All had been made ready for the duchess's arrival. Cecily went at once into her confinement.

She prayed hourly for the safe delivery of her babe, and when the tiny infant girl was born on the twentieth day of July, three months after Cecily's fortieth birthday, she rejoiced in the child's perfection. So grateful to the Virgin
was she that on the day of the child's christening at St. Mary's, Cecily vowed
to dedicate her to the church. She named the baby Ursula for the second-
century virgin martyr.

"THE KING AND Parliament have graciously pardoned all those who fought with me
at St. Albans," Richard wrote to his wife at Fotheringhay in early August after
telling her of his joy at Ursula's birth.

The king can no longer doubt my allegiance and must accept me at his side. My loyalty, thus—as well as your brother's and nephew's— has finally and formally been recognized, God be praised. In the new council, I am Constable of England with our brother-in-law Bourchier as treasurer and his brother, the bishop, as Chancellor. With Somerset dead—again God be praised—I persuaded the king to give the captaincy of Calais to young Warwick.

Cecily let out long sigh of relief, shaking her head in wonder. How suddenly our fortunes have turned around again, she thought. But would it last?

My dearest wife, I am proud to stand at Henry's side. 'Tis my right, and I thank God daily for the small victory at St. Albans. With my new position of influence, I have persuaded Parliament to rescind its former condemnation of that most loyal of dukes, the late Humphrey of Gloucester. I could not rest easy without restoring his reputation. Besides, dearest Cis, the poor man must have endured much at the hands of two most trying wives.

Cecily smiled at Richard's attempt at humor in such a serious letter, but despite Eleanor Cobham's involvement in witchcraft, she had felt a little sorry for Gloucester's widow upon hearing that she had died alone in her prison at Beaumaris Castle three years before.

I would send for you, Cis, and I know you will chastise me for not keeping my promise to you, but tension hangs heavy over the city. It pleases me to know you are safely back at Fotheringhay and I beg your patience for a while longer. There is much to do to reconcile the two sides—for it is now clear to me there are two sides: York and Lancaster—and to facilitate this, I have sent the king, queen, and prince to Windsor, where they are safe. In truth, the battle unnerved the king, and we on the council are fearful for a return of his affliction.

Why are there two sides now, Richard? Cecily wanted to ask him. With Somerset dead and York restored to the council and swearing allegiance to Lancastrian Henry, why should anyone take sides? Unless Queen Margaret had other ideas and was still poisoning Henry against Richard. She grunted.

How wise to send the queen away as well, my lord, she thought. If she is out of sight, perhaps she will not come to mind.

Cecily had wondered how Margaret had taken the news of her friend Somerset's death and then had been surprised to learn how quickly Somerset had been supplanted in the queen's affections by his own son, the new young Duke Henry. Let us hope he is more like his mother, quiet Eleanor Beauchamp, Cecily mused. 'Tis certain he is too young as yet to have influence on the king and queen as his father did.

She read Richard's few final affectionate lines with a smile, marveling that after all this time and the duress of the past year, Richard had not forgotten how to be tender. "And I adore you too, my beloved Dickon," she murmured, using his old nickname for the first time in years and kissing the parchment. I pray you retain King Henry's approbation now and we can settle into a peaceful time again.

Saintly Henry. She conjured up his long, pleasant face and ready smile, his nose almost always in a prayer book, and she shook her head. If only he could be more of a king rather than the ineffectual pious man that he is. How long will others greedy for power stay loyal to him, she wondered, for in our times a king must be able to govern to keep his throne, and he has surely not demonstrated good governance.

She sighed and snuggled down in the tester bed, tucking Richard's letter under the pillow. It was taking her a little longer this time to recover from the delivery, but she was for once enjoying the ministrations of Constance and Gresilde and allowing herself to rest. Richard would be here soon, she hoped.

BUT IT WAS late August before Richard could leave London and see his Ursula. He spent time holding the baby, and Cecily would tiptoe from the room and leave him whispering to his new daughter. She would go and find Meg, whose downturned mouth gave away her jealousy for the newcomer, who had surely stolen her father's love.

"Just wait until she starts screaming, Meggie," George told her one day, much to Cecily's amusement. "Father will come and play with us then. Now let us go and fish. Please?" His liquid blue eyes and sunny smile pried Meg out of her grumps and she ran off happily with her brother, hand in hand. It continued to astonish Cecily how close these two children were.

Cecily walked among the flowers in the well-kept castle garden, admiring the late roses and thinking about all her children. A twinge of sadness marred the reverie. Constance had counseled that, considering Cecily's age, Ursula ought to be the last child.

"You will have to advise Duke Richard of this yourself, Constance," Cecily had retorted, "for I shall not."

A gardener doffed his wide straw hat and bowed to her, and the man was rewarded with a few words from the duchess, who asked about a species of yellow rose that had caught her eye.

"I be calling it Rose of Raby, m'lady. After yourself, m'lady," the leather-faced old man told Cecily, beaming. He cut one of the pale blooms and presented it to her. "Dame Boyvile did tell me 'twas your name once. She said the rose was like the color of your hair, if I may be so bold, m'lady. It did seem fitting."

"I am deeply honored, Master Williams. You should allow me to take a cutting to plant at Ludlow."

Anne and her attendant came skipping down the steps into the garden, giggling together like the young girls they were. Anne waved gaily to her mother, and Cecily saluted her. She observed the spring in her eldest daughter's step and the confident smile of motherhood. Her baby daughter was thriving too, and Richard had granted permission for them to stay on with Cecily. He had no intention of allowing the vicious Exeter anywhere near Anne for the time being, Cecily was happy to know. Besides which, Exeter was the queen's man and thus Richard's foe. The queen's man, she grumbled under her breath. *How many times a day does Margaret of Anjou spring unwanted into my thoughts? Is she truly more powerful than the king?*

"Nan, my dear," Cecily called purposefully. "Come and see this new rose Master Williams has cultivated. He chooses to call it Rose of Raby."

And she pushed the queen from her thoughts.

*T*he queen. Aye, she was our real enemy."

Cecily must have spoken aloud, for the sound jolted her out of a doze on the comfortable cushions a dozen hours after Margaret's nightmare had awakened the castle. How long had she been reminiscing this time? she wondered. Certes, it must be an hour or more, and Gresilde should be returning at any moment, judging by the dying embers of the fire and the angle of the shadows from the wintery sun's rays on the floor.

Stretching her limbs, she got up to look down on the river, its edges rimed from the icy mists that wisped around the boatmen bundled up in warm woolen cloaks. She thought that this must be how the River Styx had been imagined by the ancient Greeks.

But on a finer day the Thames will sparkle, as it did on that Lady Day morning almost three years ago when, Cecily mused, London witnessed one of the most remarkable and yet improbable scenes ever to play out in its colorful history. Cecily frowned as she gazed through the polished horn panes in the window, trying to recall every detail of the Love-day, and how it had come about.

Richard's time in the sun after he had accepted a second protectorate in that autumn of little Ursula's birth was again short-lived. Poor little Ursula. Her time too was short. Her sunny disposition shone in this world for eighteen months until on a day like today her light was extinguished one frigid morning in January here in this castle. Was that before or after Richard had been almost murdered by young Henry Somerset's men? Thank God for the mayor, who by some miracle had been nearby with his escort and had rescued him.

London was seething with armed men, she recalled, and Richard had warned her not to set foot outside Baynard's that winter. He had wanted her to return with the children to Fotheringhay but had given up, she chuckled now, when she refused to be parted from him again.

"You should see yourself, my dear," he had teased her, with his neighing laugh, now heard rarely in these troubled times, "standing proud and tall as though you were the queen herself."

"Sweet Jesu, Richard!" she remembered protesting. "You compare me with that she-wolf? I have not one whit of her malice, let me tell you, but twice her backbone, eight times her offspring, and a hundred times her husband."

Richard had swept her up in his arms then, and they had spent a passionate hour in the warmth of her tester bed. "Proud Cis," he had murmured. "How I love you still."

Cecily found a tear was trickling down her cheek as she relived that scene, whispering, "And how I still adore you, Richard, my one and only love."

She swiftly brushed her hand across her eyes and concentrated on that Lady Day of 1458. It was the only one of Henry's lamentable attempts at reconciling his warring nobles that earned him Cecily's respect. He did try, she thought. But his Love-day, as it had since been dubbed, was a sham.

It should have been simpler to bring about reconciliation on the council once Somerset was dead, she told herself, but Henry could not resist Margaret's spiteful bias against Richard. Henry tried to be fair, she supposed, agreeing to Richard's being named Protector again during a milder attack of his previous malady, but at that time, with Margaret's insistence, he had shown marked favor to the cubs of Richard's enemies: Henry Beaufort, the new, young, and volatile duke of Somerset; the new earl of Northumberland and his brother, the rebellious Lord Egremont; and John, Lord Clifford—all blinded by hatred over the death of their fathers at St. Albans. Others who had declared themselves enemies of the duke of York included the earls of Wiltshire and Shrewsbury and Lord Beaumont, not forgetting Henry's half brothers, Edmund and Jasper Tudor. And eventually Humphrey of Buckingham, who had remained neutral as long as he was able but in the end had sided with the king and queen. It went without saying that Anne's husband, Exeter, would also cling to Lancaster.

And who was with us? Cecily sighed. My brothers, Richard and William, my nephew Warwick, and my sister Kat's son, John of Norfolk. Others would join them, she remembered, but when Warwick had arrived from Calais on St. Valentine's Day, he was greeted with relief by Richard and Salisbury. Surely securing the captaincy of that most vital of garrisons and staple town for

Warwick had been Richard's most important achievement, Cecily thought now. Thanks be to God for Warwick's command of Calais and the seas.

Her brother's son had become a force to be reckoned with, she admitted now. As charismatic and decisive as his father was not, Warwick's exploits as Captain of Calais in the last two years had captured the people of England's imagination. He had garnered a reputation for generosity to those less fortunate, shown himself wily and brave both in politics and on the battlefield, and yet with all the world at his feet, some even wishing he were king, he had remained loyal to Richard. And how Ned looks up to his cousin. But, she now worried, let us hope he remains on our side.

She watched a barge being rowed past Baynard's, its colorful canopy proclaiming its noble owner, but she could not make out the emblems decorating it. It was on such a barge that Henry and Margaret had arrived at Paul's Wharf from Westminster that sunny twenty-fourth day of March for Loveday. A stiff breeze had made the royal pennants and banners stand straight out from the awnings, and Margaret's lithe figure was enveloped in an ermine-lined cloak. Cecily grunted, thinking of the queen processing up Paul's Hill Lane to the great church at the top of it. How beautiful she still was, Cecily reluctantly admitted, though arrogance and anger were beginning to pinch her lovely face.

Hundreds lined the streets that day, but, Cecily grimaced, the spectators were not the usual citizens eager to take time from their busy lives to see their sovereign in full regalia processing among them. These were soldiers, guards, and armed retainers of the lords attending this extraordinary ceremony. One bad word, one false step made by one of the opposing lords, and these men were ready to do battle. Cecily doubted that Henry felt the hostility in the air; he was congratulating himself on a magnificent show of camaraderie and courtliness.

The bells in the soaring spire of St. Paul's began to ring merrily, their carillon echoed by all the churches in London. Cecily remembered she had worn her crimson cloth of silver, her Neville colors, for the occasion. Richard, Edward, and Edmund, however, had all been in various shades of murrey and blue. They had escorted her from Baynard's to the wharf, a stone's throw from the castle, to greet the king and queen as they arrived.

"Never say you heard it from me, Cecily, but today's ceremony is nothing but a foolish spectacle," Richard told her along the way. "I commend his grace's attempt at diplomacy, but I cannot believe so many family feuds or so many offenses—nay, I should say injustices—can be wiped from memory with one ceremonial gesture."

He was right, Cecily admitted grimly now, as she watched the passengers from the barge alight below her. She returned to the scene at St. Paul's heavy oak west door, and the image of it almost made her want to laugh aloud.

First to enter the church was her brother, Richard of Salisbury, holding hands—aye, imagine that, she thought, shaking her head—holding hands with the young duke of Somerset. They had been made to hold hands, these enemies, she remembered. She had stepped away from her sons at that point to get a better view of the leaders of the procession. Henry's chamberlain then bowed to her nephew Warwick, who stepped forward, and he was partnered in this laughable dance of amity with his enemy, the duke of Exeter. Who would think that cherubic face framed in innocent golden curls could hide such a cruel nature, Cecily mused. She was happy that Anne was confined by her courses and did not have to face her vicious husband.

Henry himself came next, eschewing his drab clothes and resplendent for once in a flowing purple velvet robe trimmed in ermine, a jeweled crown upon his head, and genuine pleasure at his brilliant idea shining on his face. How could he not have seen it for the mummery it was? Cecily wondered. He had surprised her by the sincerity of his smile when he noticed her and he had lifted a hand in salute. She dropped a low curtsey where she was standing in the line and could do nothing but return his guileless smile. Dear Mother of God, he does not remember I am not supposed to be his friend, she had thought. When she raised her head again, she saw him gazing vacuously at a point over her head just as he had done all those years ago when he was but a child. His chamberlain steered him toward the church door and it seemed to Cecily that the king had forgotten for a moment where he was or what he was doing there. Once he stepped into the dark doorway, Cecily had heard the organ thundering over a choir singing "Hallelujah!" to welcome their king inside the magnificent church.

Then Richard had stepped forward, his arms held stiffly at his sides, his eyes straight ahead and his determined chin leading. However, when his partner stepped next to him, he turned his head slowly and bowed. Had he known before that moment that he was expected to take the she-wolf's hand? But as he had not said anything to her before they left Baynard's, she believed this must have come as a surprise. He had so slowly taken the tips of the queen's icy fingers in his hand, reluctantly partnering with his greatest enemy in this absurd procession.

And so they all went into St. Paul's to give thanks for this day of loving kindness. She remembered holding young Lord Clifford's hand, grimacing as she thought of the irony now. Aye, he was naught but a boy then, but by the time he arrived at Wakefield, he was well and truly a man.

Once again Edmund's sweet face floated before her, his gentle gaze warm as summer. She shut her eyes tightly to rid herself of any vision of his ghastly end at Clifford's hand. Instead she forced herself to return to that fateful Lady Day.

Aye, Love-day, they called it—and how long did the loving last? A few weeks of festivities had given way to more violence in the streets by June, while Henry and Margaret spent time together at the royal apartments at the Tower and at Humphrey of Gloucester's old palace of Greenwich. She and Richard had stayed away from London, living at Fotheringhay and Ludlow. Richard remained convinced he was in danger from the queen and her minions.

In one disturbing incident in November of that year, Cecily's nephew Warwick had narrowly escaped assassination. He had returned from Calais upon a summons from the council to explain his attack on a Hanseatic salt fleet, and while he was making his report in Westminster's Star Chamber, his waiting retainers were set upon in the great hall. Hearing his servants cry "A Warwick! A Warwick!" the earl had rushed out of the meeting to see what was amiss. Those of the court party and even servants bearing knives from the kitchen attacked him, and the earl barely escaped to his barge with his life, subsequently fleeing back to Calais. I think 'twas then I realized how important it was for Calais to be in Yorkist hands, Cecily thought now. It became pivotal when Richard finally turned his thoughts from standing beside Henry's throne to Henry's throne itself.

A knock on the door startled her. Did she really want to be disturbed yet? After a second's hesitation, she called, "Come," thinking she must make certain Meg was up and feeling better. Oh, and who knows what that pair George and Richard are up to, she mused.

Gresilde and Beatrice bustled in to dress their mistress.

"Did Father Lessey miss me?" Cecily asked as Gresilde rolled one silk stocking up Cecily's calf and tied it above the knee. "Did I miss sext?"

"And lauds, prime, and terce," said Gresilde cheerfully, accepting Cecily's foot for the second stocking. She had been dismayed when she saw her mistress's swollen face but knew better than to question her. "I hope you rested well, your grace. Perhaps a cool compress for your eyes will help," she fussed.

Cecily reached for her robe and shook her head. "Nay, Gresilde, I am suffering from too little sleep, 'tis all. But I must attempt to redeem myself by attending nones or Father Lessey will be despairing of my immortal soul."

An hour later, the duchess of York emerged from her chamber, dressed as elegantly as usual, her high hennin supporting a long veil that floated down her back and shoulders and half hid her face. She was accompanied to the tiny private chapel in the castle, where her dear friend and confessor, Richard Lessey, awaited. After the short service, Cecily begged to be left alone to pray and study her favorite writings of St. Brigid.

She knelt on the tufted hassock decorated with the white rose of York and began to tell her rosary. Father Lessey gave her a benediction and together with her attendants he left the vaulted room. Gresilde would have stayed, concerned for her mistress's melancholy, but Cecily assured her that she would prefer to converse with God alone.

"Dear Lord, I pray you watch over my son Edward in these dangerous times to come," she began. "He is so very young, not even nineteen, and yet he leads an army of thousands who believe in his cause, to uphold his father's birthright. His own birthright, in truth. I cannot ask you to take sides, for it is well known King Henry is as holy as a mortal can be and thus must be in your favor. But Edward is a good boy, and his mother loves him dearly. I beg that you return him to me and his brothers and sisters hale and whole."

Once again, Cecily's thoughts focused on her children. They must be her reason for living now that her husband was gone. *I must be mother and father to them, I suppose,* she reminded herself. *Praise to St. Monica that we found a good husband for Bess,* recalling the sweet betrothal ceremony at Fotheringhay a few weeks before Love-day. John de la Pole was two months older than his bride. The sixteen-year-olds were so shy with each other on that day, she thought back fondly, remembering her own wedding day at Bisham. It had been an odd choice, considering John's father had been the exiled and subsequently decapitated William, duke of Suffolk, Richard's nemesis during the Normandy days. The boy had not been granted his father's title yet, but Richard had believed it would not be long in coming, and thus Bess was well married, lately with child, and back at Wingfield following her visit at Yuletide. And, praise be to God, Anne had found peace in one of Exeter's out-of-the-way manors in Devon with her little daughter.

She gazed up at the crucifixion scene painted on the altarpiece and averted her eyes from the figure on the cross. Instead she focused on the weeping Mary at His feet, understanding more than ever the agony of losing a child in such a barbaric fashion. "Dear Mother of God, comfort me in my losses, I pray, and take into your arms my son Edmund, whose death dare I say was as cruel as your own Son's." She prayed even more fervently for Edward, "my eldest son, whose shoulders are still too young to bear the burdens heaped upon them by his father's death. Give me the wisdom to counsel him well and lead him from conflict, if that be the right way. I fear his parents' ambitions may have set his feet on a bloody path, and I pray he will forgive us. But his fate is in God's hands, and I pray you intercede for me with Him and bring Edward home safely. And finally, dear Blessed Mother, help me to guide my youngest children into God's grace and to give me the strength to protect them always."

Margaret, George, and Richard. Only I can raise them now, she told herself. I alone can protect them.

But you have done that before, Cecily, on that fearful day at Ludlow. She thought back to that summer on the Welsh marches, where she had felt removed from the politics that embroiled Richard in London and where she had spent the last truly idyllic days of her life thus far.

Ah, Ludlow! With its warm, plum-colored stones.

PART SIX

Astonished, shamed and beaten, I did repent
Of what I'd said and done, recalling all
My folly, and perceiving that I had brought
Upon my body martyrdom and grief.

ROMAN DE LA ROSE

24

Ludlow, Autumn 1459

After nones on one brilliant September day at Ludlow, Cecily could not resist the call to the hunt. She called for Constance, but upon discovering the doctor had taken Dickon out to play, Cecily sent for Gresilde and Beatrice to dress her. With Richard and his troops there to defend the town, there was no reason she could not hunt close by, she told the disapproving Gresilde, who clucked her tongue and wagged her finger, making Cecily laugh.

"I shall be perfectly safe, my dear Grizzy," she told the older woman affectionately. "Besides, I can ride faster than any armed soldier. You are naught but an old mother hen. Now hurry with my riding gown."

She and Piers, followed by another falconer, two grooms, and her greyhound, made their way across the Dinham Bridge and directly up Whitcliffe Hill toward the village of Richard's Castle. She watched a red kite soar above them, hearing its distinctive and repetitive *he-he-heea* over the trilling of the Teme far below her. The mild air and the bright blue sky exhilarated her, and she urged her palfrey up the slope. She loved to feel the strength of the horse under her, taking her away from the mundane tasks expected of her every day and allowing her to return to a more innocent time when she had ridden out with her father and had not a care in the world.

Earlier she had watched in amusement as Constance peeked out from behind a blackberry bush where she was hiding from Dickon, who darted up and down the pathways in the castle's kitchen garden as he tried to find her. A quiet, serious little boy of almost seven, he rarely complained and was completely devoted to his big brother George. Most of the time, George tolerated Dickon dogging him from the archery butts to the bowling green or to the stewpond, where he fished, but he could suddenly get impatient with his baby brother and a swift kick or shove would be sternly punished by their mother.

Poor Dickon, Cecily sighed as her horse climbed higher and she thought on the times her son had run away after being bullied, not wishing anyone to see him cry. Then there were the occasions when he would make his mother smile to see his determined chin—just like his father's—thrust forward and his fists balled up ready for a fight with George. She often wished he were more affectionate, but she admired his independent spirit, nonetheless.

"Dickon will follow George almost anywhere," Cecily had told Richard that summer, "but when George flouts Nurse Anne's rules and then denies it, our earnest Dickon draws the line. He does not inform on George, but I can see it distresses him that his brother lies."

"Dickon may not be our most endearing child, Cis, but you cannot doubt his loyalty," Richard had replied, chuckling. "I would far rather have Dickon on my side than George." And Cecily had sighed, knowing he was right, but never wishing to speak ill of any of her children.

Now she crested the hill and took her merlin from Piers, sighing with pleasure as the bird bobbed and wove on her wrist, recognizing its mistress's gentle caress. At this moment the captor and the raptor were as one: the captor waiting for any sign of prey and the raptor knowing it would soon be free. Cecily admitted to herself that it was an experience almost as spiritual as receiving the Host. Both Cecily and Richard visited the mews daily to commune with their falcons, and Richard was wont to have Priam on a perch in his privy chamber while he dictated correspondence to his clerk. Cecily had long ago drawn the line at his bringing the treasured bird into their bedchamber.

"Soft, my sweet Niniane," she murmured, stroking the hawk's glossy plumage. "You shall fly soon, I promise."

Piers was attending to Richard's prize falcon when the greyhound startled a quail from the bracken. The falconer swiftly untied the bird's jesses and unhooded it. Priam saw its prey as soon as Piers launched the magnificent creature into the air, and in a breathtaking display of soaring and plunging, the bird had the unfortunate quail in its talons before it could flit to the safety of the next clump of bracken.

Then a shawm's alarming wail from the watchtower broke the quiet of the Shropshire countryside. Cecily's horse shied briefly and her bird fluttered its wings at the sound. A sudden fear gripped her.

"There, there, my beauty," Cecily soothed the bird and called to a groom. "Take Niniane, I pray you, and Piers," she called out, "I will ride back."

She turned her horse around, anxious to return to the castle and see who it was who came unannounced. An air of tension had gripped the castle and little town ever since June, when its lord had returned with his family after being excluded from a Great Council meeting called by the queen.

"We have heard she means to try and indict us all," Richard had seethed, when he had been apprised of the meeting. "We have sent letters of protest to the king, but it seems he listens to none but her. Salisbury returns to Middleham and Warwick to Calais, and we shall remove to Ludlow."

Cecily had felt a cold frisson at his words. She knew why the three Yorkist lords were returning home. It was clear that they would need to muster forces or they would be vulnerable again, especially as Lancaster-held lands now spread their tentacles around Richard's, Warwick's, and Salisbury's estates in the midlands and Yorkshire. And now the queen was holding court with her young son in Cheshire, north of Ludlow, and Henry was east in Coventry.

Richard had sent word to Salisbury and Warwick that they and whatever forces they had mustered in the last two months should reunite at Ludlow, where they would once again petition the king to refute the allegations against them that the queen and the council had issued in June.

Whistling for Priam to release the quail and return, Piers watched as Cecily took off at a gallop down into the woods that ended at the Dinham Bridge. He grinned and shook his head. "That be our duchess," he said to the groom, starting after her.

After dismounting, her heart still racing, Cecily flew up to the ramparts in time to see the first of hundreds of troops marching toward her and reaching the fields by Ludford Bridge. With a sigh of relief, she recognized the green and yellow banners with the Montagu eagles. Salisbury, she thought, shading her eyes from the sun as she watched the ragged lines of soldiers trudge up to the banks of the Teme. She heard shouts from the inner bailey and ran to the other side of the roof to look down on the melee of yeomen hustling into a neat formation in response to the commands of their captain. This was an honor guard for the earl, she deduced. Needing to don a suitable gown, she picked up her skirts and hurried down the stairs.

"Ah, there you are, doctor," Cecily greeted Constance a few minutes later, as Gresilde struggled with a knot on one of the sleeves of her bodice. "I think we have need of you. It seems my brother is approaching and the duke has requested I attend him."

"Aye, your grace," Constance replied, picking up the discarded riding habit.

"I was told there are hundreds more troops making camp with ours. It is a veritable legion."

Cecily grimaced. For once she wished she had not agreed to stay with Richard at Ludlow, knowing Salisbury and Warwick would come with their armies. I should have taken the children to Fotheringhay for safety, she thought. But now I am here, I must be strong for the children and for our loyal servants. She gazed fondly at her dear Constance, the plump, motherly Griselde, Beatrice, who now attended Margaret as well, and the young local tiring woman who was helping to dress her. Finally, after a critical inspection in her long silvered mirror, Cecily, regal in her scarlet and white gown, proclaimed herself ready to take her place with her husband.

The gallery from her apartments looked down into the great hall, where she saw her husband standing on the dais. A surge of pride overcame her as she saw he was flanked by her two oldest sons. She paused, turning to her attendants and putting her finger to her lips. Half-hidden by an arch, she studied her boys, both in short jackets and parti-colored hose, as though she had not seen them for years.

Ned was seventeen and towered above his father and Edmund, and indeed most of the other men assembled in the hall. She had been astonished by his height when he had arrived at Baynard's before Love-day, but he had grown even more since then and now stood at more than six feet. His red-blond hair framed a handsome face with wide, warm blue eyes, sensual mouth, and her own long, straight nose. Since taking up residence in Ludlow again, Ned had been reprimanded more than once by his father for dallying with some of the young girls in the town. Aye, he is the next for whom we must find a marriage partner, Cecily thought wryly. Standing confidently upon the dais, awaiting his uncle, Edward's eyes roamed the room, giving a nod here and a smile there as he recognized someone. Nearby stood his and Edmund's tutor, Robert Apsall, now arrayed in more soldierly garb, and Edward raised a hand in salute. The proud mother watching her son thought he looked like a king or a god.

On Richard's other side, and plainly less comfortable as a focus of attention, stood her beloved Edmund. His bright blue eyes never wavered from his father's face, as Richard conversed quietly with his sons. Taller than his father but without Edward's stature, Edmund had not yet reached full maturity at sixteen. Cecily saw only the sensitive boy she had always adored, and she shuddered to think of him wielding a sword and doing a man harm, or, even worse, being harmed by another man.

Hearing horses clattering into the courtyard, she hurried along the gallery and down the stairs to join Richard, trying not to imagine where this massing of troops was headed.

As THE MOUNTED retinue clattered through the gatehouse arch and dismounted, it was clear to those waiting in the courtyard that Richard of Salisbury's troops had encountered trouble on their route from the Yorkshire dales.

Striding through the honor guard and taking the great hall steps two at a time, Salisbury was inside the magnificent hall before the steward could announce him. As her brother strode past Cecily standing to the side of the dais with her other children, she gave him an anxious smile. His blood-splattered tabard and shredded chain-mail leggings told of combat. Curious retainers soon surrounded him and his entourage, who were equally disheveled and bloodied. Constance ran forward to one deathly pale young knight whose arm, crudely bandaged, was still bleeding, and hurried him off to the infirmary.

Salisbury wasted no time getting to the dais and informing Richard, "We were forced to do battle on our way here. I would ask, Brother, that you see to our wounded."

Cecily clutched Meggie's hand so tightly that the girl squeaked, "Mam, you are hurting me." Not another battle, Cecily thought, her stomach lurching. Dear God, what is happening?

Richard told the steward to see to the wounded and then turned back to Salisbury. "The king engaged you? But he is still at Coventry, my informants tell me."

"Nay, your grace, 'twas the queen who attempted to cut us off at Blore Heath, but we defeated her, God be praised."

"The queen!" Richard cried. "Who was in command? And how many troops did she have at her disposal? Certes, enough to engage you, to be sure." Salisbury gave an unpleasant bark of laughter. "'Tis said there were more than six thousand of her men there, and we were outnumbered three to one. Thanks to our scouts, who saw Lancaster banners flying over a high hedge on the heath, we were alerted to the possibility of a force in our path concealed behind the hedges not far from Hempmill Brook. I drew up my battle line far enough from whatever archers lurked behind the hedge, and we hurriedly brought up the guns and donned armor. After a fruitless parley, the archers let fly, but their arrows fell short of their mark—as did ours."

The household was now fully attentive, creeping forward to hear better. Salisbury obliged them by turning to address the entire company.

"Our position was less than ideal," he said. "At that point, I had no way of knowing how many men were against us, and so I sought to fool them with a ruse and bring them out of hiding."

Richard arched a brow. "Do let me guess, my lord. You sounded the retreat?"

"You are partly correct, your grace. I sent the middle section of my force fleeing in the opposite direction, and this proved enough to tempt the enemy from their defensive position. But when my center turned around and sur-prised the attackers, we were able to inflict heavy casualties on that first charge. I know not how we staved them off, outnumbered as we were, but our men fought valiantly and some of the queen's soldiers chose to come over to our side." Cecily's ears pricked up at that, for to desert the king and join the rebels meant treason. It told her that many Englishmen must believe in her husband's cause. "God must have been on our side that day," Salisbury was finishing, "for we won the field and chased the stragglers many a mile."

"How many slain, Brother?" Richard asked.

"I did not stay to count, but on the king's side—perhaps four thousand. Our ranks lost close to one thousand, it pains me to say, good and loyal men every one, God have mercy." Then he told Richard, "My two younger sons were taken prisoner, so I have heard, trying to get quarter for some of our wounded. God help them."

Richard put a sympathetic hand on his brother-in-law's arm and murmured an acknowledgment. Observing Cecily over Richard's shoulder, Salisbury quickly descended the few steps from the dais to greet her, apologizing for his disheveled appearance.

"I am sorry for Thomas and John, Richard. We shall pray for their safe de-livery," Cecily told him, imagining that it could have been her own sons. She sighed. "So it has come to this, Brother. York must fight Lancaster?"

He took her hand in his and nodded. "So it seems, Sister. We were set upon, and we needed to defend ourselves. This leaves no doubt that the queen is bent on destroying us."

"Could you not have parleyed further, my lord?"

Richard preempted Salisbury's answer by gently asking Cecily to arrange for refreshment in his privy chamber so that he and her brother could plan their next move.

"And what of my eldest? What of Warwick? Is there word?" Salisbury asked anxiously as Cecily, obeying her husband, gathered her attendants and beckoned to the steward.

"I expect him within the week, my lord," Richard replied. "He has landed from Calais, this I know. But now that you have been intercepted by the queen, I fear he may not arrive here unscathed either."

WARWICK WAS MORE fortunate than his father, although he avoided a skirmish by skirting his own city of Warwick, where the young duke of Somerset was lying in wait.

"It is clear the royal forces are uniting near Worcester," Warwick told his father and uncle, as Cecily sat by the window of the solar and watched the hustle and bustle of soldiers in the inner bailey preparing for combat. Her idyllic summer was indeed over, she knew.

She glanced back at the three lords discussing their next strategy: her brother now at sixty, white-haired and stooped; Richard, with his prominent chin uncharacteristically covered in two days of stubble and his brow permanently furrowed from years of worry; and her somewhat aloof but highly intelligent thirty-year-old nephew, his hawk nose in profile and his mouth in a thin, hard line.

"We have drawn up a new petition," Richard told Warwick, "that will also protest our loyalty. I have sent for the prior at Worcester to submit the bill to the king himself, and I pray the queen stays at home so the king may make up his own mind on this occasion."

Edward suddenly made his presence known to the older men. "Father, may I have the honor of carrying the petition to the holy father?" Richard had been in the habit of inviting his eldest son to any and all conferences with Salisbury, but thus far Edward had been a silent witness.

Cecily half rose in her seat to protest this dangerous mission, for she was now convinced that the king and queen meant her family harm, but Richard forestalled her by answering Edward: "Nay, you may not."

Salisbury gave his nephew a sympathetic grin, and Warwick clapped the young man on the shoulder and chuckled. "Your time will come, Ned, have no fear. You will be asked to do more than carry a petition, believe me."

"I pray not," Cecily piped up from her perch. "Let us hope the king will finally hear reason."

"We have all wished for that before, my love, to no avail," Richard said, going to her and kissing her hand tenderly. "So, O wise one, what would you have us do?"

"Anything that does not involve you all getting killed" was her quick retort. "I hear the bell for terce. I pray you excuse me while I go and ask God's help in that wish."

Three pairs of admiring eyes followed the duchess from the room, and as she turned to bid them a good afternoon, Richard blew her a kiss. With a heavy heart, she dragged herself to the round chapel and to the solace she always found there. But she wondered if even her own Virgin Mary could deter these men from plunging into certain disaster.

A FEW DAYS later, Richard Beauchamp, the bishop of Salisbury and well known to York and his brother-in-law, arrived with an offer of amnesty in response to the Yorkists' manifesto.

"You may tell his grace the king this," Warwick cried, insulted. He had stepped in front of the good bishop before his father or uncle could consult with or stay him. "We thank him for his offer, but we cannot accept. First, we have learned to our distress that a royal pardon has been worth nothing, even one ratified by Parliament. Shall I give you examples?"

The bishop listened patiently as Warwick cited instances, although Cecily could see perspiration on the prelate's high forehead.

"Next, my lord bishop, we three—and there are other lords who are with us—have no trust in those who give the king counsel today. They have disobeyed King Henry's orders, and we have therefore had to muster our forces to defend ourselves from them. Again I can give you examples." Warwick listed several as the bishop shifted uncomfortably from one foot to the other. Cecily was surprised that Richard and Salisbury stood by, seemingly content to let the younger man speak his mind.

When the earl had finished his list, the bishop arched a brow. "Is this all, my lord?"

"No, it is *not* all!" Warwick bellowed, making the bishop's clerk jump as he attempted to transcribe the earl's words on vellum.

"I would have you ask his grace the king whether it is still the law that council members may move freely to and from council meetings. If that is the case, then why was I set upon in Westminster and almost murdered?"

The bishop was at a loss to answer the bellicose earl and stammered a few words of disbelief, though he had been at Westminster at the time and was well aware of the incident. He looked past Warwick at Richard of York and the earl of Salisbury and anticipated yet more reasons for standing firm in rejecting the amnesty.

Richard stepped forward to Warwick's side. "You can see my lord of Warwick's point, I am sure, my lord bishop. What have we done to require the king's pardon, pray? However, we, the lords of York, Salisbury, and Warwick, wish to assure his highness King Henry that we are his liegemen still. Swear you will tell him this."

"Aye, as God is my witness, your grace," the bishop replied, bowing to Richard and ignoring Warwick. "But as a man of the church, I would caution you to pray long and hard for a peaceful end to this impasse. The queen and his grace of Somerset arrived to join the king just prior to my departure from Worcester, and they have gathered a considerable army. I beg of you, do not consider using force, my lord."

Cecily fingered the beads of her rosary in an effort to remain calm. *The whole of the royal army is at Worcester? That is no more than thirty miles from here and but two days' march,* she thought. Glancing up at the gallery above the great hall and seeing the faces of Meg and George peering through the balustrade, she felt a surge of panic. *Her children! Dear God, the children would be in such danger,* she thought. *I was foolish not to have left last month,* she chided herself. *Oh, Richard, I pray you take the pardon,* she willed him.

But Richard was kissing the bishop's ring and bidding the cleric take the Yorkist reply back to Worcester. "As you saw upon your arrival, we too have mustered quite an army," he told Bishop Beauchamp as the man bowed away from him. "Captain Hall, escort the bishop and his retinue back to the Worcester road."

Richard's faithful captain, Davy Hall, strode forward and bowed low, sweeping his arm toward the great hall door for the bishop and his men to precede him.

"There will be fighting, will there not?" Cecily asked Richard fearfully when he came to her bedchamber that night. "How I wish I had gone back to Fotheringhay with the children, but I did not want to leave you, my dearest," she cried, melting into his arms. "It was so selfish of me. I only wanted us all to be together—and happy. I was fortunate to have a happy, carefree childhood, and how I wish my own children could have the same, but I fear . . ."

"Hush, my rose," Richard soothed, rocking her familiar body in his arms and stroking the still golden hair. His face, however, was now turned from her, mirroring his worry and not his words. "It may not come to battle. The king is not looking for a fight. I feel it in my bones. He is a gentle, saintly man as you well know. If I thought you were in danger, I would have sent you away," he assured her, not daring to admit his folly.

Cecily pulled herself away and went to pour wine for them both. She had dismissed Gresilde for the night once her disrobing had been accomplished. Constance had hardly left the makeshift hospital since Warwick's troops had arrived, and Cecily knew the physician preferred to be where she was needed most.

"Aye, 'tis true, but now that he has been joined by Margaret and her other Henry—Somerset I mean, I fear the king will be outmatched. She will be smarting from my brother's victory at Blore, and you must believe she will seek revenge."

Richard sipped his wine, and Cecily settled onto a cushion on the floor and began to knead his feet. He sighed with pleasure. "Ah, Cis, how I wish sometimes we were plain yeoman Dickon and his goodwife Cecily, and we could simply grow old together as comfortably as this, with our children safely around us."

Cecily gave him a wistful smile. "But Goodwife Cecily would still worry about her children and most of all about her husband, because he would have to go off to fight without the benefit of armor and a horse. He might come home horribly maimed and be unable to tend the crops and shear the sheep, or," she whispered, "he might never come home at all." In a trice she was on Richard's lap, her arms wound around his neck. "You will never leave me, will you, my love? I do not care if you come back to me maimed, but promise me you will always come back."

"Silly goose," Richard murmured, though a shiver of prescient fear went through him. "I have the finest Italian armor, a destrier that could trample dozens of men, a sword arm that would rival any in England, and an army of faithful followers. All that will bring me back to you, should we have the need to fight. But I predict the king will not come, but if he does, do not fret about the children. Steward Heydon will see to it that you and the children are taken to safety. Where's my brave Cis? Enough of this melancholy, wife," he chided her in a teasing tone. "Besides, I have hungered for you all night."

Cecily could not help but smile into his cambric shirt. "You still lust for me, Richard, although I am an old hag of nearly forty-five?" she whispered. "Then seduce me again, my love, and help me forget my black humor." She slithered to the floor and began tugging at his points with her teeth. "Let me show you how brave I still am," she murmured. "No simpering miss tonight."

CECILY STOOD WITH Edmund upon the battlements of the tower keep to watch the progress of a fortified trench being dug at the edge of the camp on the other side of the Teme. Richard's prediction that the king would not come had been proven wrong. The royal army was at Leominster and advancing fast.

"We shall have command of the bridges and can fall back into the town if we have to," Richard had explained to a nervous Cecily. "It is safer for us to stay here than to engage the king on the open road."

Cecily stared down at the thousands of troops arrayed in the meadow, the sun glinting on their weapons and armor, their shouts floating up to her on the cool mid-October air, and she reached for Edmund's hand.

"I want you to know how proud I am of you, my son," she began, a catch in her throat. "I have watched you grow all these years and have learned to love your quiet ways."

Edmund turned worried blue-gray eyes on her, and his sweet face reflected what she feared to see most: terror at the prospect of battle and all its horrors. "And my lord father? Is Father proud of me?" he asked, fingering his empty scabbard with his free hand. "The master of henchmen was strict and I learned to fight, 'tis true, but not as well as Ned. It seems I do nothing as well as Ned."

His disconsolate tone tore at her heart, but she stood tall and told him in an even voice what every mother should. "Your father loves you all equally, Edmund. He sees your good qualities just as much as I do. Granted, they are different qualities from Ned's, but in the end you are your own man, and I know which of you I would rather spend time talking to."

"I am afraid of dying, Mother," Edmund suddenly said, staring out at Whitcliffe Hill. "I do not want to die."

Cecily put out her hand to steady herself on the crenel. He had voiced the one thought that she had not dared to contemplate. What should she say? That he should not be so foolish, that of course he was not going to die, that his father would protect him? Help me, sweet Virgin, help me help my son.

"You are a man now, and your training will stand you in good stead, Edmund," she heard herself lecture in a steady tone. "You will have your orders and you will carry them out bravely, because that is how you have been raised. You will be fighting beside your father and your brother, and you know that our cause is just. Your father would not take up arms against his king if he had not been driven to it." She was certain that words made these years of conflict sound too simple, but Edmund was listening intently. "God will watch over you, if you have faith, my son. And," she ended more gently, "there may well be no fighting and you are worrying for naught."

"Have you ever been afraid of anything, Mother? Have you ever had to be brave?"

Cecily was moved that her son would concern himself with her feelings. She thought about the journeys she had made to strange places with Richard, but she had to admit that she had never been afraid—rather, she had been exhilarated by the experiences. But then her mind went back to that terrible day in Rouen, and she decided to tell Edmund of Jeanne d'Arc's bravery and how the Maid had died for her faith. Edmund stood riveted, listening to his mother's description of the execution and how she had lost her first child. When she had finished, he took her in his arms.

"It would seem to me, Mother, that women must be braver than men. They have only their wits to fight with," he declared. He pulled himself away and cocked his head. "Did you believe the Maid was a witch?"

Cecily smiled. "I know she was not, Edmund. I learned last year that the French clergy examined the trial evidence again and pardoned La Pucelle two years ago. She was a martyr, as I had always thought, and one day I have no doubt she will be a saint."

Edmund squeezed her hand. "Thank you for this confidence, my lady. I shall pray to be brave," he said, "and make my lord father proud."

Thanks be to you, Holy Mother, for your guidance, Cecily thought, believing that it had been the Virgin and not she who had chosen the right words. Facing her son, she saw him stiffen as he looked over her shoulder.

"God's bones! Look, Mother, there are soldiers coming over the hill."

Cecily swung around and gasped, fear gripping her gut. The king! The king's army had already come. Running to the stairs, Cecily called to Edmund to alert the castle guards. Then she flew down to the next floor, along the ramparts, and to the ducal lodgings.

Soon trumpets and shawms sounded the alarm and the complicated machinery that managed the portcullis clanked into action, lowering the iron grid halfway. Pealing bells and urgent shouting echoed the warning in Ludlow's narrow lanes. Richard left Salisbury and Warwick in charge of the camp while he and Edward with their captains cantered over Ludford Bridge, under Broadgate, up

Broad Street into the marketplace, ordering the townsfolk to keep to their homes or leave the town. Wagons and handcarts were trundled away, and many women and children fled down the slope of Corve Street and through the back city gate to the relative sanctuary of the northern woods and fields. Those anxious mothers who chose to stay whisked crying children inside their homes and cowered behind bolted doors and shuttered windows. Soon Ludlow's streets were deserted and all was quiet, except for the furious activity inside the castle walls.

At the castle, and taking the stairs two at a time, Richard and Edward with several others in their wake hurried to the roof of the tower keep, where Cecily and Edmund had stood not an hour before. Thousands of men as far as the eye could see were still marching toward Ludlow, the royal banners and pennants flying in the wind. To the west the sun had already set, and Richard knew with relief that there would be no battle that day. It gave him a night to plan his strategy—and make arrangements for Cecily and the children to leave. He cursed himself for not sending them away in daylight. Now it was too late.

Although he could see the king's army advancing on him, he could not really believe Henry wanted civil war. "He has brought this on himself," Richard remarked to Ned, Edmund, and Henry and Isabel Bourchier's sons, who had been in training at Ludlow alongside the York brothers for the past few years. "I hope you learn a lesson from this, Ned. To be king—or duke for that matter—means to be your own man, not the puppet of stronger, unscrupulous ones."

"But should one not repay faithful service, Father," Edward asked, gazing down upon the extraordinary sight in the usually peaceful meadows of the Teme Valley.

"Aye, Son, but one must recompense service judiciously. To give away your inheritance as the king has carelessly done lessens your power and increases another's. It is one thing to be grateful, it is quite another to be beholden."

"It seems to me it must be hard to be a good king," Edward murmured to himself as he followed his father down to the lower solar to plan their strategy.

That evening, servants scurried from the kitchen in the courtyard to the great hall with food and drink for the lords and their allies, including Lord Clinton, Lord Powis, Sir Walter Devereaux, Sir John Wenlock and others, who had rallied to York's cause in the last few days.

Cecily hurried to the nursery tower for her nightly ritual of prayer with her younger children. Compared with the rest of the castle, the cheery nursery chamber was calm, and she was grateful for Anne of Caux's practical common sense, which had kept the tension in the castle from upsetting the youngsters. George was teaching Dickon how to feint a sword thrust, and Meggie was earnestly practicing her lute. Her graceful neck was bent over the instrument, and her yellow hair spread about her like spun gold.

"Tut, tut, children," Cecily said upon entering. "'Tis past your bedtime, I believe. Come, let us gather at the prie-dieu and give thanks to our Savior for this day and to watch over us this night."

"But Mother," Meg began, laying aside her instrument, "what about the king's—"

A warning frown halted thirteen-year-old Margaret's boldness. This was not the time for questions, the girl surmised from her mother's look.

But nothing halted Dickon when he had a question. "Why are all those soldiers in the field, Mam?" the boy asked, tucking his hand in his mother's. "Will there be a battle? Ned says they are come to slay a dragon, but I have not seen dragons hereabouts."

George gave a snort of laughter. "He believes anything anyone tells him, Mother. There's no such thing as dragons, addlepate," he informed Dickon. "The king has come to slay Father, did you not hear?"

Meg cried out in alarm. "Slay him? Say it is not so, Mother. What has Father done?"

"Nay, George! 'Tis you who are the addlepate," Cecily scolded him. "Look how you have frightened your sister and brother. Go with Nurse Anne immediately and wash out your mouth. Use the soap on him, Nurse. Then come and ask God for forgiveness for your cruel words." She knelt down and took the crying Dickon in her arms. "Soft, little one, he knows not what he says. Pay him no heed." Oh, why did we tarry here? she asked herself again. 'Twas the greatest folly.

As George retreated to the washbasin, Meg dared to speak up. "Why must you always punish George, Mother? He is too young to weigh his words."

"Pish!" Cecily retorted, wondering how she was able to conduct such a mundane conversation at such a dangerous moment in their lives. "He knows very well what he is about. Come, let us pray and then get you to bed, Meg." She shivered, but whether it was from fear or mounting anger that she and Richard had put them in such danger, she could not say.

She took comfort in continuing to maintain the children's normal routine. After prayers she tucked the two boys into their big bed and kissed them. "God keep you both this night," she whispered, before leaving Nurse Anne to blow out the candles and stoke the fire. At Meg's door she took a deep breath before entering.

Her daughter was in her bedrobe, sitting on the end of her bed, awaiting her turn for Cecily's goodnight kiss.

"Now we can talk, Margaret," Cecily began, and thirteen-year-old Meg trembled, knowing that when her mother used her full name, it was almost certainly serious. "I fear George may be right and the king is come to do battle. It seems to me the time for parleying is done." She sat down next to the girl and patted her knee. "I shall not explain to you now what has led up to this confrontation with the king and queen, but when we are safe again with your father at Fotheringhay, you shall know. For now, I need you to be sensible, and of all my children, you are the most sensible, the cleverest," she told the blushing Meg. "I am thus counting on you to watch over the boys in case neither your father nor I can do so in the next few days."

Meg's hand flew to her mouth at these fearful words, and her slate-gray eyes grew wide with disbelief. "You would not go anywhere without us, would you, Mam? Are we in danger?"

"Certes, I would not leave you alone, sweet child," Cecily assured her, "but if your father needs me to leave or to go with him, then I must." She could not bear to voice her fear that she might be taken or even killed if Richard were not victorious, and what would become of her children?

She recognized the bitter taste in her mouth was more anger mounting in her. She wanted to accuse Richard for this dangerous predicament, but she knew she was not blameless. Instead she forced herself to focus on Meg's worried face. "That is probably not going to happen, but you are the oldest in the nursery and, in case of need, you must bear some responsibility for your brothers. There are loyal servants here who will take you to Aunt Alice at Middleham or to your sister at Dartington if that becomes necessary. Now, stop looking like a fish searching for food and tell me you understand what I am saying. I am counting on my brave Meg."

Meg drew herself up and clasped her hands neatly on her lap. "I understand, Mother. I will be brave."

"Is there aught I can do for you now, child? I see you have Ambergris under the bed, and you have Beatrice to keep you company."

Meg nodded. "You should tell Ned his dog is here, Mother, and that I will look after him." With a catch in her throat, she asked, "I should like more than anything to wish Father a God's good night. Is it possible?"

Cecily knew the child had avoided the word good-bye and was relieved. She stood up. "I shall tell him to come directly. Goodnight, my dear," and she swept out of the room before Meg could see her tears.

After Richard had said farewell to his favorite daughter, he returned to the great hall, his mood somber. Cecily and Gresilde had joined the lords, who were now draining the dregs from their cups and preparing to ride down the hill to spend the night in the camp with their troops. Richard shook off his melancholy and picked up his leather gauntlets.

"Are we ready, comrades?" With a rousing assent the men exited the hall and hurried down the steps to where their huge destriers were being held by grooms. Richard lagged behind, pulling Cecily behind an oaken aumbry displaying the household silver, and kissed her trembling mouth with a fierceness that troubled her.

"Pray for us, Cis. Pray that the king accepts our petition at the last minute and I shall return here on the morrow without an arrow being loosed. But if we fight and lose, submit yourself to Henry. He will not harm you or the children." And he kissed her again. "Oh, how I have loved you, Cecily Neville," he told her anxious eyes. "For all my life I have loved you. I warrant no others in this realm have loved as deeply as we have. I must return to you—I will return to you."

This time it was Cecily who drew his mouth to hers and stopped it with another urgent kiss. "And I have loved you with every breath, my sweet Richard. Take my heart with you, for if you do not return, I would live without it anyway."

They heard his name called by the mounted knights, and he let her go reluctantly. "Adieu, my proud Cis, my rose of Raby!" he called, striding to the door.

Cecily ran after him. "Not adieu, my lord! But au revoir." She followed him out into the night where the darkness hid her misery and she could stand alone on the steps to watch his torches recede. Then she flew across the courtyard to her sanctuary in the round chapel to pray for his return.

An hour later, still on her knees, it seemed as though her prayers to the Virgin had been answered, for she heard the portcullis rise noisily on its chain, and the thud of hooves told her the lords must be back. Puzzled, she ran to the great hall steps, arriving in time to see Richard emerge first from the passage through the gatehouse.

"How now, my lord?" she cried, as he swung off his mount, his armor clanking. "What is amiss?"

Richard said nothing but grasped her arm and led her inside. They were followed by Salisbury and a furious Warwick.

"That whoreson traitor Trollope!" he cried. "If I ever find him . . ."

Pages and other retainers had begun to settle down on the floor of the hall for the night when the sudden arrival of the lords roused them, adding to the chaos as the knights, their spurs ringing on the black and white stone floor, began unstrapping their armor.

"What happened, Richard?" Cecily asked her husband, helping him unbuckle his sword. She looked around for Roger Ree and spotted him making his way to his master. "Help my lord with this, Master Ree," she commanded, as Richard was too preoccupied with Warwick's ranting.

"Those sons of bitches! My own men of Calais. Pah! Traitors, cowards all! May they be damned in hellfire!" Warwick swore, flinging his gauntlets onto the dais.

"Swearing will not bring them back," his father said, almost as though he were talking to a small boy. "We have no time for whining over what has occurred. We must decide what to do about it."

"Andrew Trollope, a captain under Warwick, has slipped away with many of the Calais men to fight for the king," Richard explained to Cecily. "It was a goodly number that left and he took others of our troops with them. They came willingly enough here, knowing the possible consequences, but in the end, the turncoats claimed they could not bear arms against their king."

"Traitors all!" Ned's voice rose from the group now, and Cecily gasped when she saw her two sons in full armor standing among the others. Dear God, they are indeed men, she thought miserably. Seeing them fully armed shattered the image that she had of them playing together as children on the deck of the ship bound for Ireland, with miniature bows and arrows at the butts, or wrestling on the grass in brotherly sport. But now they were arrayed for real fighting, and her stomach lurched.

The lords and their councillors sat discussing strategy long into the night. Cecily dozed on the steps of the dais.

Finally Richard thumped his fist on the table and rose, knocking over his stool and jolting Cecily awake. "So we are agreed," he cried. "Our cause is lost if we fight with such diminished numbers, and if we surrender we will surely be executed to a man. We should allow our troops to slip away as best they may. Tell me we are agreed."

A resigned "Aye" answered him.

Richard thanked those who had joined him there at Ludlow and advised them to return to their homes. "I thank you all for your good counsel. I shall go north into Wales and then, God willing, to Ireland. Rutland will come with me, and March will go to Calais with Warwick and Salisbury. I fear most of us will be attainted, but if you will bear with us, we can bide our time until the moment is ripe to return. I shall keep you informed as best I can."

A youthful voice caused all heads to turn to the end of the table. It was Edmund, and Cecily glowed when he began to speak.

"I crave your pardon, your grace, but what plans have you made for my lady mother, the duchess, and my brothers and sister? Will they go with us to Ireland?"

The heads swiveled back to Richard, who gave his son a warm smile. "My heartfelt thanks to you, Edmund, for reminding me of my duty to my wife, but I have not forgotten her, I assure you." He turned to Cecily, who he knew was listening. "On the advice tonight of your brother and some of my other councillors, my lady, I shall ask that you remain with the children and throw yourself upon the mercy of the king."

Edmund rose then, his face white. "Upon the mercy of the queen, you mean, my lord!" he shouted. All eyes turned once again to him. "That woman hates us. I would not put it past her to murder our mother and Meggie, George, and Dickon in cold blood! I shall not go with you. I shall stay and defend them with my life."

At that Edward jumped to his feet. "And I shall stay with Edmund, my lord."

Again the heads swiveled to the top of the table. Before Richard could speak, Cecily left her spot on the dais steps and came to stand beside him, looking fondly down the table. "My dear sons, you make me proud," she assured them. "But I must do what my lord and his councillors decide—as must you. What good are you to the house of York if you are dead?" She looked from one face to the other, seeing adoration on one and duty on the other, and she smiled. "Do not be afraid for me, boys. Margaret of Anjou may be a schemer, but I believe King Henry has a fondness for me. He is too saintly a man to harm a woman and her children, and it is a good solution that I request his mercy for us all. If I know King Henry, he will not hesitate to be charitable."

A murmur of assent followed this speech, and Edward sat down promptly, a grin of satisfaction on his face. Edmund, Cecily realized with sadness, was humiliated that she had dismissed his gallantry, but she could not run to him and console him for fear of wounding his pride further. You see you can be brave, my son, she told him with her eyes and was rewarded with a glimmer of a smile.

"To horse then, my lords. Send your captains to inform the troops they may leave their posts and slip quietly away." Richard grunted. "I would very much like to stay and see the queen's and young Somerset's faces when they awake tomorrow facing an empty meadow, but not enough to risk my life and our cause." He took a deep breath and swept his gaze over those seated at the table. "And if there are those of you who believe 'tis best to submit to the king and receive his pardon, then I shall not stand in your way. I thank you from the bottom of my heart for your loyalty and service and wish you God speed, my lords, gentlemen."

The company made their farewells, and one by one made reverences to Cecily, awe, respect, or pity in their eyes. It was still dark two hours before dawn, giving the Yorkist troops plenty of time to gather their belongings and steal away.

Richard embraced his wife quickly and told her he had arranged for a few guards to remain with her, including Piers Taggett, then he left without a backward look, knowing they had said their good-byes earlier. With a supreme effort, Cecily steeled herself for the farewell with her older sons, embracing them both in turn.

"You will write to me from Calais, Ned," she said, still giving him motherly instructions. "And listen to your uncle and cousin."

Her six-feet-three-inch son grinned down at her, shaking his head. "Have you forgotten I am no longer a child, my dear lady mother? I promise I shall write, but I may sometimes keep my own counsel when it comes to my uncle and brother."

Then it was Edmund's turn, and it was all Cecily could do not to throw herself on the floor and beg Richard to leave him with her. Instead she embraced him tenderly.

"I love you for speaking up, Edmund," she whispered. "You see, I knew you had courage, and now your father knows it, too." As he knelt for her blessing, she said simply, "God bless you, my son."

And then her menfolk were gone—her husband, her two sons, her brother, and her nephew and all their retinues, galloping into the Welsh hills, there to go their separate ways. She shivered and only then realized she was cold, but not as cold as when she finally climbed into her empty bed and lay there aching for Richard's familiar warmth.

CECILY COULD NOT sleep. Her mind was a jumble of images from the past days, snatches of conversations, fanciful imaginings, frightening thoughts, and whispered prayers. She wanted to cry, but she could not. When would she see her husband and sons again? Their flight was better than watching their bodies being dragged off the Ludford field, she supposed, trying to take comfort from that.

Despite her despair at her menfolk's departure, and despite the fear for her children's safety, Cecily could not ignore the anger that threatened to overwhelm those first two emotions. Why did Richard not see this coming? Why had he not insisted on her leaving with the children as soon as word came that Henry was on the move toward them? And then, she had to admit that she, too, should have insisted and hadn't, selfishly wanting to stay by her husband's side. Damn, damn, damn! she muttered, what have I done?

She heard the cock crow and that sound brought her to the present and chased the nightmares away. She was thinking clearly now. Throwing on her heavy shawl and her soft leather shoes, she sidled past Gresilde and Constance, asleep on their truckle beds, and slipped out of the door. She ran along the passageway to the gallery of the great hall, not daring to look down and remember the earlier scene. She wanted to feel the fresh air on her face and look across the walls of the town and the Teme to see whether the king was still there. Perhaps he too had slipped away in the night, she thought hopefully. But once on the high ramparts, she knew it had been a false hope.

In the pale dawn, she could see men from the front lines of the king's army hurrying back and forth to the abandoned fortified trench. Then mounted men galloped to it, and she could hear surprised shouting and a trumpet fanfare, waking the rest of the camp. What would happen now? she wondered. Would they just leave? It was quite clear to any clodpoll that there was no one to do battle with. She could see from her perch that the streets of Ludlow were also deserted and the shutters were closed on all the houses. Only the bell of St. Lawrence gave proof that anyone was alive in the town.

It was not long before she saw the first line of soldiers beginning to clamber through the trench and to remove the sacks, carts, and other barricade debris left by the Yorkists. It was then that Cecily realized that once the floodgate was opened to this trickle of trouble, there would be nothing to stop Henry's army from rushing through the breach, crossing the big meadow, and entering the town. Would he, in fact, attack an undefended town? Perhaps not, but she could not take that chance. Her pulse began to race and she ran back down the stairs.

"Arouse the boys and dress them quickly," she ordered Nurse Anne, who simply curtseyed and obeyed without question.

Next she ran to Margaret's chamber and told Beatrice to dress her young mistress and attend her in the great hall as soon as she could. Then it was her turn to have Gresilde and a tiring woman dress her in her magnificent blue gown, quickly braid her hair, and push it under her tallest hennin. Hooking the gold clasp of her purple velvet mantle about her shoulders, Cecily stood back to appraise her appearance in the mirror. "My sapphire necklace, Gresilde. Hurry!" she commanded. Whatever happened to her, she would not go without her mother's precious gift. "And wrap as many of my jewels as you can into bundles for you and the other ladies to carry hidden in your sleeves. If the castle is plundered, we shall not leave them much to gloat over."

Frightened though they were, the attendants took their cue from their indomitable mistress and did her bidding without hesitation.

Already there was pandemonium in the streets of Ludlow when Cecily and her ladies made their way swiftly to the great hall. Shouts and screams could be heard in the distance. The three children were already waiting for her. Dickon was clutching Nurse Anne's skirts.

"Where is Constance?" Cecily barked, looking among the cringing servants for her favorite companion. "Dear God, do not tell me she has already gone to tend the wounded left behind."

Beatrice nodded. "I tried to stop her, your grace, but she said there was one poor lad who was close to death and she wanted to pray with him."

Cecily spotted Piers Taggett calming a whimpering pageboy and called to him. "Master Taggett, be so kind as to go and find Doctor LeMaître. She is somewhere in the lodgings given over to the wounded by the Postern Tower. Go quickly!" Piers, who had armed himself with a sword the night before to protect his beloved duchess, strode from the hall in search of the physician.

Cecily called her boys to her but stayed Margaret. She knelt between them and smiled encouragingly. "Are you ready to embark on an adventure, my sons?"

George smiled back, nodding his head vigorously, but Dickon looked skeptical. "An adventure, Mam? What kind of adventure? I do not like all that yelling and screaming. What is happening? And where is Father—and Ned and Edmund?"

"They have gone on their own adventure, Dickon. They will tell you all about it when next you see them, and you will be able to tell your story. Now, I need you to listen carefully." Seeing Dickon's face relax a little, she told them what she wanted them to do. They listened wide-eyed. "Do you think you can be brave with me?" she finished, and was dismayed to see tears in Dickon's eyes and fear in George's.

"Gresilde, Beatrice, and the other ladies, I pray you take charge of Lady Margaret and walk a few paces behind me. There will be no guards, no men at all about us." As imperiously as she could, she eyed the men and boys who remained, for they must obey her or pay with their lives, she knew. "I pray my actions will have the desired effect, but I give you leave to go—hide yourselves or run. I fear the queen's army will not be merciful to you. I thank you for loyal service to the duke and me, and God be with you all."

"God bless Duchess Cecily!" an old man cried, and suddenly the room was filled with shouts of "A York! A York!" and the hairs on Cecily's neck rose as she took her sons by the hand and started for the door.

Piercing screams and sounds of horsemen and metal on metal were closer now. She gripped the boys more tightly but kept on walking. Seeing that she meant to leave the castle, the two guards manning the portcullis heaved up the grille far enough for the little group to pass under it into the outer bailey before letting it fall behind them. The portcullis might keep out the enemy coming from the town, Cecily realized, but not from the duke's private door in the back of the castle. She could hear from the sound of loud thuds and splintering wood that a group of soldiers had discovered that entry after crossing the Teme by the Dinham Bridge. Just in time the portcullis was lowered behind the duchess as the inner bailey was breached and soon crawling with soldiers looking for valuables to steal and Yorkists to skewer and rape.

With a sinking heart, Cecily saw that the gates to the inner bailey from the town had been flung wide and men were pouring in, intent on plunder. Horses were running wildly to and fro as stable doors were wrenched open by the looting soldiers and firebrands thrown in. The few grooms left were pulled out of their hiding places or those who ran from the flames were caught, and all were stabbed to death in cold blood. Bile rose in her throat, and Cecily wanted to turn and run, but she kept on walking, telling her sons to stare at their feet and never look up. She could hear a couple of the women behind her whimpering and another babbling prayers.

Suddenly a terrible cry reached them from the inner bailey behind the portcullis. Cecily flinched. It was a woman's scream. Who was left? she thought, knowing that she had ordered all the women to follow her. And then she remembered.

"Constance!" She uttered the name as though she had been stabbed. "Oh, no, sweet Virgin, not Constance." The urge to turn back and run to her attendant's aid was overwhelming, but she had to think of her charges—her sons, her daughter, and the other women counting on her. Perhaps it is not she. Perhaps Piers found her in time. But a cold sweat ran down her back as another scream rent the air followed by ribald laughter. Nay, this time she knew she was right. The damnable cowards were violating Constance, her dearest friend, her companion who had asked for nothing but to serve her mistress and her God faithfully, and there was nothing Cecily could do about it. Please, God, let her die quickly was her only prayer, but another shriek of terror rose from the victim, making Meg put her hands over her ears. Then Cecily froze when she heard the last desperate plea, before Constance's voice was finally silenced: *"Mon Dieu, mon dieu, aidez moi. Jésu, Jé—"* In her mind Cecily was suddenly back at the marketplace in Rouen, hearing another such cry to her Savior.

A soldier spat on George. "York's whelp," he sneered. But he did not lay a hand on him. George stared straight ahead and slowly wiped the spittle from his cheek, earning a "Good boy" from his mother. "You are York's *son*. Be proud of it."

She was aware now that Dickon was crying hard, and she squeezed his hand. "Walk on, my sons," she said hoarsely, forcing tears back. Her thoughts were all of Constance. Dear Constance, she grieved. She died giving succor to the wounded. May you wing swiftly to Heaven, *ma fidèle amie,* for you were a saint upon this earth. She called on her heavenly mentor then. Have you forsaken me, Holy Mother? Could you not have protected poor Constance? And Richard, where are you when we need you most?

They were halfway across the wide castle green when Cecily became aware that her daring plan was working, for the soldiers were stopping their pillage to stare at her. She could smell smoke and see flames from at least one house down the hill, and she murmured a prayer for the victims. At once all around her went quiet, and the soldiers fell back to let her pass as she approached the broken main gate. She had hoped to meet one of the king's commanders before now and surrender herself and her women to the king, but the foot soldiers appeared to have no leaders. Yet, now that she had begun this march, she could not turn back.

The men were shoving each other to gawp at the regal woman processing through their midst as if on her way to a coronation and seemingly oblivious of the carnage or the danger around her while clasping the hands of two little boys, one bravely staring at the ground and the other sobbing.

"It be York's duchess," one filthy soldier told a fellow billman. "It be proud Cis, I'll be bound. By all that is holy, she's got pluck." Pluck? Cecily thought, amazed. How can they not see my fear, my faltering steps, the cold sweat running down my back. But the word gave her strength and she walked on.

Others roughly elbowed their way to the front of the mob to get a view of the imposing woman robed in blue velvet, her hennin towering above her. Mostly there was silence, but Cecily did hear one low whistle of admiration and another disgusting sucking sound that chilled her. It was then that she had a curious sensation that she was not alone, that someone else was walking a step ahead of her and parting the menacing soldiers. She blinked twice as her gaze fell on a glowing figure carrying a cross. The brilliant white light upon the vision flooded Cecily, too, making her gasp.

"Jeanne?" she whispered, putting her hand out to touch the light. "Jeanne d'Arc?"

George glanced up at his mother anxiously. "What did you say, Mother?"

As soon as Cecily looked down at her boy's handsome face, the vision vanished, but her courage had returned. With certainty she believed that the Virgin had sent Jeanne to guide her steps. Her head high, she put one foot in front of the other and kept walking out into the marketplace praying someone in authority would arrive. There was such an unearthly aura about the duchess now that none dared touch her. She felt invincible, as though she had heavenly protection, and the trembling left her legs.

She bent to whisper to Dickon, "You are a brave boy." He looked up at her with Richard's eyes and managed a wobbly smile.

With her thoughts still focused on Jeanne d'Arc, Cecily could now understand the Maid's terror on her walk to death. How long could she fend off these bloodthirsty men? she thought, her fear mounting. She had no idea where she was going. And then she saw the market cross and believed Jeanne had led her footsteps there. She prayed that being in its shadow would protect her.

Now that their initial awe had dissipated, the crowd of armed and blood-ied soldiers began taunting the women and closing in on Cecily, who was mounting the steps to the base of the cross. Her ladies and Meg filled the area behind her, facing the crowd. Emulating Cecily's proud carriage, they defied anyone to come near them. It seems they have complete faith in my ability to protect them, Cecily realized with trepidation. But what do I do now? she asked herself, her knees finally beginning to give out. If these ruffians decide to charge us, they will show no mercy. She stared haughtily at the band of filthy men encircling her and noted they were all wearing the swan badge of Prince Edouard. So 'tis the queen who has allowed her men to plunder Ludlow so savagely, she thought angrily. How cruel an enemy she is, but even worse, she has no compassion for her subjects.

The crowd began to shift to allow approaching horsemen to ride into the marketplace, and it was then Cecily saw King Henry. He sat astride a capari-soned destrier far more warlike than its rider, who was not even in armor but was wearing his crown. Perhaps he has been told that his queen had allowed her soldiers to pillage the town, Cecily surmised quickly, and perhaps the peace-loving king had come to try and stop it. He did not approve of punish-ing his own subjects in this way, Richard had told Cecily, and it was partly because of this knowledge that Richard and his council had thought it might be safer that she stay and submit to the king rather than attempt to flee across the country to Fotheringhay alone with three young children. She hoped he had been right for the sake of those with her and the innocent townsfolk, con-demned for living on Yorkist lands.

Reining in his mount, Henry gazed in horror at the scene of devastation in the marketplace. And then he saw Cecily. Holding up his hand for the crowd to stop their whistles and catcalls, he approached the stone cross and looked down at the duchess of York, beautiful still and richly garbed, standing like some ancient goddess courageously facing a hundred armed men as she clutched the hands of her two youngest sons. He bowed in his saddle and put his hand over his heart.

"Duchess Cecily, we greet you well. This meeting is indeed unexpected and most distressing to me. Why are you alone? Have you been hurt?" he asked with concern.

Cecily descended the few steps to the cobblestones and fell to her knees before him. Dickon, not wishing to be parted from his mother for a second, followed her, and George knelt where he stood.

"Your grace, your most noble majesty, I am at your mercy. I am indeed alone, as you can see. My lord of York is gone," Cecily told Henry, her voice faltering, "and thus there is no need for fighting." She felt disloyal in implying that her husband had deserted her, but to protect her family and her women she had no choice. "There are naught but my children and my attendants left here. And one has been cruelly abused and I fear slain by your soldiers. I beg you to spare the rest of us and spare the good people of Ludlow." She raised her luminous eyes to his and found herself shivering. She had no idea how long her walk from the great hall to this place had taken, but it had seemed to her that it might have taken her whole life. A light drizzle had begun to fall, and the wetness on her upturned face, whether rain or tears, moved Henry greatly.

"Rise, duchess. You have nothing to fear from me. I give you my word. I will have you escorted to my pavilion together with your children and your attendants."

He signaled to Humphrey Stafford, duke of Buckingham, to come forward and make the arrangements for Cecily's transport to the royal tent. And then, as if he thought he had done enough, he turned and with his bodyguard trotted back down Broad Street and over Ludford Bridge.

Buckingham dismounted, put Cecily on his own horse, and prepared to lead the party out over Ludford Bridge. No one had given the order to stop the pillaging, and those soldiers left behind in the town took advantage of the inattention to enjoy themselves further at the expense of the people of Ludlow. Houses were looted and then burned and townsfolk raped, killed, or maimed simply for being York's vassals.

As they reached the fine stone bridge over the Teme amid fearful screams, a frantic shout halted Buckingham's group, and Cecily turned back abruptly when she recognized Piers Taggett's voice.

"I tried to stop them, your grace!" he cried, rounding the corner of a lane and attempting to reach his mistress. Frowning, Cecily noticed something was badly wrong with him, and then with a groan of horror she saw that his arm was missing and blood was pouring from his shoulder onto the wet, uneven street. "I swear I tried to stop them," he shouted, clutching the ghastly wound, "but the doctor was the only woman left in the castle when the soldiers broke in. God help me!" He lurched forward then as a well-aimed arrow found its mark in his back behind his heart.

"Piers!" Cecily cried, George's screams ringing in her ears. She leaned down to Buckingham. "My lord! Humphrey! Brother-in-law! I beg of you let me go to the man. He is my loyal servant."

Without hesitation Buckingham swung her off the horse and carried her to the dying Piers. She cradled his head in her lap, wrapping her cloak around his shivering body and hiding the hideous stub of flesh and bone that had been his right arm. He would never again ride to the hunt, never hold his beloved falcons, never more be by her side to protect her.

"Dear Piers, do not leave me now," she sobbed, allowing the grief of the past night and morning to engulf her. "I need you. My children need your protection. Sweet Mary, Mother of God, have mercy on this brave man. He has served me so well." Her tears wet his face as he gazed up at his mistress for the last time. Darkness was closing in on him, but he managed a few final words, wrenching Cecily's heart. "Do not forget your Piers, duchess . . . he loved you well . . . by Jesus, but I am tired." He closed his eyes gratefully, his head rolled to one side, and dark blood trickled from his mouth on his last sighing breath, staining her azure gown.

Buckingham knelt down, gently moved the big falconer, and motioned to his captain to have his men put the body over one of the horses. Cecily sat slumped on the ground, staring at her empty lap. Her eye fell on her ruby ring and a sob caught in her throat; it was the ring that had brought Piers into her life.

"Come, Cecily," Humphrey of Buckingham murmured kindly to his wife's youngest sister. "There is naught you can do for him now. We shall bury him later and I will send my confessor to say a prayer with you at his grave." He led her back to his horse and again lifted her onto the saddle. She was as one dead, he thought sadly. So brave and strong in the marketplace, but now it seemed the life had drained from her. He wondered, as he moved the little procession forward, what would become of her now. "No woman of her noble blood," he muttered to his captain, "should have to suffer such an ordeal. Let us hope this is the end of it." And he silently railed against Richard, duke of York, for abandoning his wife to such cruel scenes of war.

BUCKINGHAM WAS WRONG. Cecily's ordeal that day was not over.

Making their way slowly through the ranks of soldiers now lounging around campfires awaiting orders to disperse or march back to Coventry, Buckingham's charges eyed the king's army with a mixture of suspicion and relief. Cecily's three children, mounted pillion, followed behind the leaders with glum faces, while the stunned attendants stumbled behind the horses with an escort of six guards on either side of them. At the back of the army and set on a knoll was the king's blue and white striped pavilion, royal lions flying. Several men were ranged around the opening, and Cecily recognized two of her husband's friends, Lord Powis and Sir Walter Devereaux, who were both fettered. She presumed they were taking advantage of the king's offer of a pardon on this eve of St. Edward's Day, and she gave them a curt nod.

"The king would see you immediately, your grace," Viscount Beaumont, Henry's chamberlain, told Cecily after Buckingham had helped her to the ground. He bowed low. "If you will follow me."

"And my children?" Cecily asked, watching her offspring slide down into the waiting arms of their riders and making sure they were all safe. "May they accompany me, sir?" She held out her arms and Dickon and George ran to her, followed by tall, solemn Meg, who was doing her best to be stoic.

"I think not at this time, duchess," the chamberlain responded. "The king would give you a private audience. I shall see to it that your children are given some refreshment, and a tent has been assigned to you. They and your attendants may await you there."

Cecily embraced her children and reassured them that she would be with them soon, admonishing the boys to listen to Meg. She watched them move off, then followed her escort into the spacious tent, the back of which was rolled up to let in air and light. It seemed to Cecily that the king had all the accoutrements of a comfortable residence here on the battlefield, including a canopied bed and a small throne. Cecily got down on her knees when Henry entered and took his seat on the throne, and she fixed her gaze firmly on the grassy floor.

"I trust you were treated with dignity, duchess," Henry greeted her.

"Aye, your most gracious highness, and I must thank you for your mercy to me and my children."

"You are fortunate, are you not, *madame,* to have so magnanimous a sovereign?" Margaret of Anjou's voice shocked Cecily into looking up. Had she been there all along? she wondered, her heart pounding. She had not expected to see Margaret here, on the battlefield. Certes! 'Tis why those men with the swan livery were rampaging through Ludlow. They were Prince Edouard's troops, albeit under his mother's command. The queen continued to threaten: "A lesser lord might have been delighted to execute you like the traitor you are!" she spat. "Or thrown you into a dungeon with your brood."

Henry raised his hand. "Soft, my dear lady. We have no quarrel with Duchess Cecily. She is our loyal friend, are you not?"

Cecily was gathering her wits and could only bow her head in a sign of assent. But then she lifted it to gaze directly at Margaret. Cecily's look spoke plainly: I may be your captive, madam, but you have no hold on my spirit despite your threats. And for the first time in their acquaintance, even after all the years of conflict between the queen and Richard, Cecily felt real hatred. She saw it in Margaret's eyes, and she made certain she reflected it back tenfold from her own.

Then the duchess turned to the king. "I submit myself to you, your grace, and to you alone. I beg your indulgence for my attendants, who have served me well. I have nowhere to go save at your highness's pleasure."

Henry cleared his throat as his eyes shifted from Margaret to Cecily. Cecily pitied him for a second, but then found herself impatient with his weakness, boasting to herself that Richard would have known immediately how to act. Her expression, thankfully, did not reflect her scorn.

The few councillors grouped in one corner of the tent watched the scene intently. Henry now looked to them for help, but before Viscount Beaumont could step forward, the queen bent and whispered to her husband. Cecily, still kneeling, could not hear, but she did not like the sneer on Margaret's face. Cecily could feel the dampness in the ground seeping into her knees through her azure gown.

The king's face was now wreathed in smiles. "An excellent idea, my lady," he said to his wife, who smiled sweetly down at Cecily. "Her grace believes you will be well looked after in the bosom of your family, if his grace of Buckingham would find a place in his household for you and your children. Your sister Anne is one of the queen's favored ladies-in-waiting and our dear son's godmother, as you must know." He called to his chamberlain. "Sir Richard, I beg of you, send my lord Buckingham to us."

Cecily knew with a sinking heart that the duke of Buckingham would not refuse his king this order, and she understood perfectly well how Margaret of Anjou had triumphed, even if Henry remained oblivious. To be in Anne's custody would be uncomfortable for Cecily, as the queen would know, being well acquainted with the sisters' mutual animosity, and Anne, in her turn, would be delighted to assert her authority over her youngest sister. But Cecily did not dare demur.

"And now, your grace, is there anything else I may do for you?" Henry was asking her, wanting to end this uncomfortable audience. Cecily blinked at

him, but his words then suddenly conjured up a memory of a scene in Bouvreuil when the boy king had spoken to her, and she wondered if he would
recall it now.

"You are kind, my lord, as I have always known. A long time ago in Rouen,
you promised a very young woman, embarrassed by her poor skill at the
lute, that she might ask a favor of you one day. Do you remember, sire?" She
glanced at Margaret, who was now scowling.

Henry's face lit up. "Forsooth and forsooth, Duchess Cecily, I do remember.
I spilled a cup of wine and you kindly covered my clumsiness. Certes, I will
grant you a favor. I am a man of my word."

Cecily smiled then as Margaret took a step forward warily, wondering of
what nature this favor might be.

"My physician, my constant companion and beloved Constance
LeMaître"—Cecily faltered as she pronounced the name—"was the woman
I mentioned to you in the marketplace who was violated and slain. I would
ask that her body be found and brought to my tent so that my ladies and I can
prepare it for burial. It is all that I ask of you, your grace."

Henry's eyes filled with tears. "Pray accept my deepest sympathies, duchess,
and I shall pray for her soul. Your loss must be great." He sighed. "Ah, war is
a cruel thing, is it not? Lord Beaumont, see to it that the poor lady's body is
recovered."

"I thank you with all my heart," Cecily murmured.

Henry waved her to stand, signaling the audience was ended. "We shall see
what Humphrey Stafford has to say. God be with you, Duchess Cecily."

Somehow she stood tall and straight and then walked slowly by the gloat-
ing courtiers and out onto the hill where only a few days ago she had been
hawking with Piers. She was in a haze of disbelief that in twenty-four hours
her life had so horribly unraveled.

25

England, 1460

"What did you expect, Cecily?" Anne snapped at her sister during Advent, two long months after the rout at Ludford Bridge. "Your husband took up arms against his king. Certes, all knew he would be attainted."

"Enough of your unkindness, Nan," Humphrey Stafford interrupted, easing his large frame into a chair. He had been wounded in the face at St. Albans and was now in the habit of covering the livid scar across his cheek with his hand. He had been touched when Cecily had sympathized with him about it on the ride to Henry's tent. His wife, however, had shrieked in horror when he had first returned to her and kept him from her bed. "I am certain Cecily was fully aware that Parliament would have no choice but to attaint York and the other earls for acting so rashly and wrongly," he told Anne. "Old Sir William Oldhall was also on the list. I was surprised, too, to learn that Salisbury's wife, Alice, had been named."

This made Cecily raise her eyes from her needlework and stare at Humphrey. "Alice? What has she done, my lord? As far as I knew, she stayed at home in Middleham when her lord left to join mine at Ludlow. I did not know you could attaint a woman." She shivered. Poor Alice, where would she go now?

"She was conspiring to raise troops for her husband against the king," Humphrey explained. "As heiress to the Montagu fortune, she will forfeit that now."

Cecily harrumphed. "I suppose Nan and I should be grateful to be younger daughters. We had not a penny from our father when he died."

Humphrey chuckled and Anne gave a small smile. They were sitting in the solar of Maxstoke Castle, not far from the city of Warwick on the Coleshill road. A pleasant moated and fortified manor, the castle was set in the lush

Warwickshire countryside with a large park, where Humphrey had promised Cecily could hunt when the weather was better. Cecily had borne her enforced custody with resignation, though she had endured just about enough of Anne's resentment at her sister's enforced presence in her house and her spiteful insinuations that Richard had abandoned her.

"Have you no compassion, Nan?" Cecily cried, not long after she had taken up residence with the Buckinghams. "I know not if I will ever see my husband or my elder sons again. Try to imagine my misery."

"Have you forgotten that our son was killed by your husband and his friends at St. Albans and that my husband was disfigured?" Anne snapped back, while Humphrey played chess with his daughter. "And you ask for my compassion?" The shrill voice grated on Cecily's nerves, but she bit her tongue. "You are wedded to a traitor, Cecily Neville! What would our mother and father think, if they were still alive? They were loyal Lancastrians, unlike you."

Cecily bristled. "My dear Nan, Mother also taught us about bending to our husband's will and supporting him in all things—as I am sure you do for your lord."

"Check," Humphrey murmured. "Nay, Daughter, I was not speaking to you."

Cecily rose then and, gathering up her needlework, curtsied to both and said, "I see my company distresses you, Nan. I shall go and find my daughter and leave you in peace."

As Anne stared after her sister, Humphrey snapped, "Why must you be so shrewish, my lady? She does not deserve your scorn."

Cecily could not help but overhear his wife's snide reply.

"You do not know my sister as well as I, Husband. Who is to know that she is not planning to murder both of us in our beds? I have seen them together, she and her precious York, as you have not. They are like two peas in a pod—obdurate and proud. Cecily was spoiled and always had her own way, pushing me out of my father's affections. And," she whined, "she turned Richard against me all those years ago. 'Tis insufferable that we have to house her here." She had stamped her foot then, and Humphrey sternly admonished her for behaving like a child in front of their daughter.

"The king holds the duchess in much affection, my lady, or he would not have regranted her so many of her lands or given her a thousand marks for life. It is not wise to voice such angry thoughts abroad about your sister as you do. Now, I beg of you, try to be civil. Come, Daughter, let us enjoy some fresh air."

And he left his wife to her sulks only just after a smug Cecily had slipped out of sight.

Despite the dressing-down, Anne did not alter her tone, and the friction between the two sisters persisted. So it was not surprising that Humphrey rejoiced when he was needed more and more at the king's side. Young Somerset might have the queen's ear, but it was Humphrey of Buckingham and Viscount Beaumont to whom the king turned for counsel. If truth were told, Humphrey had come to respect his sister-in-law's intelligence, engaging her in political discussion and thus adding to Anne's resentment. Cecily found herself liking him, for all he was her husband's enemy, and through conversations with Humphrey, Cecily caught snippets of information about Richard's activities throughout the winter and into spring. Richard had written to her from Wales when he had safely arrived at Denbigh, which letter the king had allowed Cecily to read. It was a letter full of affectionate phrases and concerns for the children, and Lord Beaumont, the disappointed censor, had reluctantly relinquished it to Buckingham to deliver to the duchess of York.

Humphrey told her that Richard had sailed for Ireland after Yuletide, which apparently had taken the court by surprise. Word had reached London in December that only the lords of Salisbury, Warwick, and March had arrived at Calais, and the speculation had been then that the duke of York was biding his time in Wales. Cecily knew now that Richard, safely in Ireland with Edmund, had called for a parliament at Drogheda not long after his arrival there in the new year.

Humphrey said, "Your husband has had the temerity to demand an act be passed that it is treasonable for any person to attempt any action against his life. It astonishes me those Irishmen agreed to such a preposterous thing."

Cecily had given him a glimmer of a smile. "My lord, if you knew how the Irish took Richard to their hearts when he was lord lieutenant, you would understand. He appeased most of the warring chieftains and they love him still," she said.

Not impressed, Humphrey merely frowned.

AND SO THE months passed with only scant information reaching Cecily that cheered her and helped her weather the grief she still felt for Constance and for Piers. Not a waking minute of every day went by without her aching for Richard.

She never cried in front of Gresilde, but the kind attendant felt compassion for her mistress when she would feel the damp pillow of a morning and know Cecily had wept well into the night. Gresilde and Beatrice did their best to minister to their mistress's needs when Cecily had suffered with a bad cold in March, but they knew she missed the skills of her beloved Constance. Humphrey had put his own physician at her disposal, but the man was clumsy, had bad breath, and was so indecisive that Cecily had shooed him away on more than one occasion. And so she settled into melancholy, despairing of ever returning to her previous life with her husband and family together and healthy again.

When the daffodils and crocuses began to bloom, Cecily was cheered considerably by the news of a daring raid in January upon the port of Sandwich by a captain of Warwick's from Calais. Despite his attainder, Warwick had refused to give up his captaincy. He held it by force, and even young Somerset had not been able to enter Calais harbor but had taken over the castle of Guisnes across the marshes, hoping to make a land assault. What brash young Somerset did not know was that more and more men from England, especially Kentishmen, who had developed a fondness for the dashing earl over the years, had found their way to Warwick's stronghold and were building an army for York.

Anne herself told Cecily of the January raid on Sandwich—with a certain amount of relish, Cecily had noted, because the story involved Jacquetta Woodville. The sisters had discovered quite by chance that they did indeed have at least one thing in common: a scornful dislike of the dowager duchess of Bedford.

"It seems our friend Jacquetta's husband, Lord Rivers, and his son—I forget his name—"

"Anthony Woodville," Cecily supplied, remembering the handsome youth she had met at the start of Richard's first protectorate.

"They were readying the king's fleet to attack Calais so Somerset could take up his new captaincy and force Warwick to surrender. Suddenly a ship sailed out of nowhere in the early hours of the morning, and Warwick's men landed at Sandwich unopposed. 'Tis hard to believe, is it not? But what is even harder to believe is that those few men were able to surprise Lord Rivers and Jacquetta in their bed"—and she giggled—"whom they seized along with . . . aye, Anthony, to ferry back to Calais. I hope at least those upstart Woodvilles were able to cover themselves decently."

They both laughed heartily at the thought, and Cecily took advantage of Anne's good humor to find out more.

"And the fleet? Did it not pursue the attackers?"

Anne adjusted her heavy headdress and pretended she had not heard. But Cecily eventually pried the information from her.

"It was disastrous for the king, Humphrey said. As so many of the mariners in the fleet were Kentishmen, Warwick's captain had no trouble turning them to his side. Every ship but one of the king's navy was taken back to Calais." Anne shook her head. Her mood had sobered.

But Cecily's heart soared. Here was proof that all was not lost. Her nephew was holding Calais firm. It was wonderful news.

Later Cecily regaled Meg, George, and Dickon with the story, and then hugged them with excitement. "All is not lost for your father, children. Pray hard for him and your brothers."

"Will Ned be here soon, Mam?" Dickon asked, his earnest little face turned up to his mother, making it impossible for her not to kiss it. "I miss Ned."

"I expect so, little one," she replied, touched by the child's devotion to Edward. It was good to see the bonds uniting her children, she thought, watching as George and Meg now went to finish their game of fox and geese, their golden heads bent over the board in mutual concentration.

This has been my only solace, Cecily mused, stroking Dickon's dark curls as he sat by her knee, whittling a stick: the amount of time I have had to spend with my children. There were times when she worried about their future, fretted that she and Richard should have found suitable mates for them all by now, but mostly she took pride in their growth and accomplishments and thanked God every day that they had not been taken away from her.

"I AM SORRY for you, in truth, but the archbishop is adamant," Humphrey told a stony-faced Cecily not a week later. "It seems he wishes to oversee the education of George and Richard, so I must send them to London." In his letter to Buckingham, Archbishop Bourchier had explained that he was simply honoring an appeal from the boy's elder brother, Edward of March, to continue with their education, and Cecily had seemed to accept the arrangement.

How much more can she endure? Buckingham wondered, watching his sister-in-law's face. Her gaze never wavered from his, and he had to admire the stoicism of this beautiful woman.

"They will be in no danger, Cecily, if that worries you, and when we go to London later in the spring, you will most certainly be able to see them when you wish," Humphrey assured her.

"I thank you for your concern, my lord," Cecily told him quietly. "I shall go and arrange for their departure." She gave him reverence, which he returned, and sedately left the room, followed by an anxious Gresilde. But out of the duke's hearing and out of sight of everyone but her faithful attendant, her reserve broke down. Engulfed in Gresilde's buxom embrace, Cecily let her tears flow.

"Not my boys too, Grizzy. What more can they take from me?" she sobbed.

"There, there, my dear lady," Gresilde cooed in the dim light of a passageway between the ducal apartments and Cecily's own. "They have each other and they are both strong boys. Besides, if none of this had happened, George would already be gone from you to some other household or to Ludlow to learn the knightly arts like his brothers, would he not? And besides, you will still have the Lady Margaret with you. It is not so bad."

By the time George and Dickon were readied for their journey to Southwark, Cecily had recovered from her despondency enough to smile and wave them good-bye from the steps of the castle. She was astonished to feel her sister's fingers find hers in the folds of her gown and give them a sympathetic squeeze.

On the first day of June the duke and duchess of Buckingham, together with their detainees, arrived in London and lodged at their town house on College Hill, a stone's throw from the Erber, lost to the Nevilles now through the attainder. Baynard's had been stripped from Richard once again, and Cecily grew more melancholy that she remained at Henry's mercy. The only bright spot on her horizon was that in London she would be reunited temporarily with George and Dickon. She longed to see how much they had grown.

As they rode past St. Paul's, where Cecily looked wistfully down the narrow street that led to Baynard's, a plump laundress stepped out of a group of women gossiping on the street, squinted to make sure, and pointed at Cecily.

"Look there, good dames, 'tis Richard of York's lady. I saw her at Baynard's once. God bless you, duchess," she called, waving. "All of London is waiting for him and Warwick! When will they invade?"

Astonished, Cecily did not have time to ask a question of her own before Humphrey's men shoved the woman back against the wall of the nearest house.

The woman complained loudly and her friends shook their fists and showered the guards with abuse. Cecily rode on, deep in thought but suddenly hopeful.

"The Devil take you, my lord duke, before York does!" a voice cried from a crowd around the stocks on Chepe as the Buckingham party trotted past. Coarse laughter followed, but Humphrey took no notice and rode on.

Cecily, riding her own horse with Margaret pillion, began to take a keen interest in the bustle of the streets. Past mercers' houses they rode, the shutters on the ground floor propped open to display the wares, and past the great conduit, where children filled their buckets with water piped from outside the city wall. More sullen looks and disgruntled mutterings followed Buckingham. Then Anne cried out as a clod of dirt hit her litter.

Cecily sidled her horse closer to Humphrey. "The citizens appear in an ill humor, my lord."

"They expect an invasion from France, my lady," he said gruffly. "Our old enemies see a weakness in our government here, and with Henry looking over his shoulder for your husband, England is vulnerable." He eyed her scornfully. "I hope you are satisfied that your husband has endangered his country. Now if you will excuse me," and he urged his horse in front of her.

It was as clear as day to Cecily that he, or any king's man, was not popular with the people. Londoners were afraid, she thought now, better understanding the reason for those glowers. But was it an invasion *by* France or *from* France that they anticipated, she did not know.

"MY MOST NOBLE *and beloved duchess and wife, we greet you well from Ireland,"* Richard began, *"where many of your old friends ask after you and our children."*

Cecily's hand trembled as she read her husband's untidy script for the first time in six months. The letter had arrived mysteriously that day tucked into the folds of a newly laundered chemise and discovered by Beatrice. Cecily surmised that it must have been smuggled into the Buckingham residence by someone highly trusted by Richard, because as she read on, she knew Richard could not have afforded that such information reach her host. How she had missed him, she thought, sighing deeply and hugging the letter. But it had not been until she had seen his handwriting that she had known how much.

George and Dickon had been given permission to visit the Buckingham residence for a few days, and she was enjoying time alone with her sons in the garden. The weather had been bad for a week, and she was determined to enjoy the sunshine. She had promised her sons a game of hide and go seek if they diligently studied their Latin. She was grateful that the archbishop had seen to the boys' studies during their time with him, and they appeared quite happy there.

Sending the boys off to scout out good hiding places, she sat on a daisy-covered exedra to read her letter.

I know not when you will receive this, Cis, but I should make you aware that I am not idle here and nor have your brother, nephew, and our son been idle in Calais. You may or may not be aware that Warwick has been with me these last three weeks—she broke off reading to look at the date on the letter: the feast of St. Philip in early May—*and we are near to resolving a plan. We have learned of the discontent with which the people view the king's government and soon our time will be ripe to return. When your nephew sails for Calais again, he will take his mother with him. I know not if you were informed that she came with me to Ireland.*

Alice was in Ireland? Certes, she was doing more than raising children at Middleham, Cecily thought with grim amusement, remembering that Alice had been helping recruit men for Salisbury. And to have fled like that, she must have known she would be implicated with the rest and attainted. She is braver than I, Cecily admitted to herself.

I long to see you and our three youngest. Rest assured Edmund is thriving, away from his elder brother's caustic tongue. He has become a man, and he sends you loving greetings. As for your husband, he begs you to know that you are in his heart every waking moment and he prays daily for the time when you shall be reunited. Your devoted servant, Richard.

A flock of noisy starlings darkened the branches of a beech tree, bringing her back to the garden. She got up from her seat and went to look for George and Dickon, tucking the precious letter into her bodice. She would need to destroy it, she knew, but for a brief time she might hold it close to her heart.

Cecily could not hear her sons' usual boisterous play and frowned. As she wound her way through bushes and shrubs, calling their names, she heard shouting in the street on the other side of the high garden wall. She had been vaguely aware that city noises were reaching her in the peaceful garden, but now she could hear the voices plainly, and there were many of them, coming closer to Bow Lane. Finding a sturdy wooden door slightly ajar at the end of the garden, she tensed, guessing that her sons had slipped through to see what the fuss was about in the street. The stench of dead fish and sewage from the nearby river was overpowering, and she crushed a few rose petals from the blooms over the door's stone arch and held them to her nose.

She discovered her two boys pressed into the archway, watching in fascination as a large group of men surged up from the wharves. Curious herself, Cecily pulled both boys close to her and stood just inside the door, trying to determine the tenor of the crowd. Soon there were other interested men and women hanging from their windows across from Buckingham's house, and Cecily sensed the mood was one of excitement, not anger.

"Sandwich be taken!" a man yelled from within the throng up to those in the windows. "Fauconberg has taken Sandwich. Warwick will follow. It be sure as there be tits on a cow."

George giggled as an adolescent might, and Dickon mimicked him, though Cecily was sure he had no idea what George had found amusing. A cheer went up. "Warwick! Warwick!" And then someone shouted, "Let us get ready to give the good earl a welcome, lads. The ale is on me!" And cheerfully singing a bawdy song, the group swung into Royal Street on its way to the nearest tavern.

Closing the door, Cecily leaned against it to steady herself. Her palms were sweating and her pulse was on fire. Warwick is coming, she repeated to herself in disbelief, and then she recalled what the first man had shouted: Fauconberg had taken Sandwich. William! Her brother, Lord Fauconberg, had obviously distinguished himself, and how proud she felt that yet another Neville had come to Richard's aid.

"Can we play now, Mother?" George said, his ready smile turned full on her. "You promised."

Cecily beamed back. "Aye, I did. Shall I hide first?" As the boys closed their eyes and counted, she ran back to the exedra and ducked behind it. She put her hand on the hidden letter by her heart. Richard would be here soon. She could feel it.

THE LORDS OF Calais, as they styled themselves, were back on English soil soon after, and Gresilde, with a torn parchment in her hand, came hurrying into the children's wing, where she knew Cecily was wont to spend her mornings.

"'Tis said my lord Edward of March is landed with his uncle and cousin, your grace," the out-of-breath attendant told Cecily. "And they came in the company of a papal envoy. Does this mean they have the blessing of the Holy Father? I think so." Her face was pink with excitement. "It must be that my lord of York will follow from Ireland very soon, do you not think?"

She handed the parchment to Cecily, her eyes shining. "I found this nailed on the door of St. Michael Paternoster, my lady."

Cecily read the neatly written poem aloud:

> *Send home, most gracious Lord Jesu benign,*
> *Send home thy true blood unto his proper vein*
> *Richard duke of York, Job thy servant insigne,*
> *Edward earl of March, whose fame the earth shall spread.*
> *Richard earl of Salisbury named prudence*
> *With that noble knight and flower of manhood*
> *Richard, earl of Warwick shield of our defense*
> *Also little Fauconberg, a knight of great reverence.*

She thrilled to the words. When she had finished, she looked at Meggie, who had drawn close and was as enthralled as Gresilde and Beatrice.

"That is our family," Cecily told her daughter. "You should be proud of them—your father, your uncles, your brother, and your cousin. Come, let us pray for them and ask God to let us all go home soon."

CECILY MOVED ASIDE the concealing sheet to allow Beatrice to pour more hot water into the large copper bathtub set in the middle of her bedchamber at Maxstoke in early July. When the bath had been replenished, the attendant retired behind the curtain, and Cecily lay in solitude. She relaxed her body into the delicious warmth, her graying hair floating on top of the water, and eyed her belly. She was always critical of its telltale stretch marks. Then she closed her eyes and sighed. It had been a dismal summer thus far, and this July day was no different. As the rain beat a tattoo upon the diamond window panes, Cecily had decided a warm bath would help to dispel the gloomy weather outside. She knew Anne would grumble when the request was sent, as it meant that several of Anne's busy servants would be needed to haul pails of hot water up the three flights of stairs, and then empty the tub in the same tedious fashion. Cecily didn't care; she needed the tonic.

She cast her mind back to June and the landing of the lords of Calais. The Buckinghams' sojourn in London had been as brief as Warwick's progress toward London had been swift. She had gleaned from gossip brought into the Royal Street residence by the local servants that the populace was tired of the bad governance of the saintly king and his greedy council and prayed the Yorkists would bring about reform. It was King Henry's grasping councillors Londoners loathed and not the king himself. In fact, she had been astonished to discover that people believed he was touched by God not only because of the sacred anointing oil but even more for his holy ways. They wished no harm to Henry, just an end to the lawlessness that the squabbling, unscrupulous men about him had caused.

As one of those men, Buckingham had sent his household back to the safety of Warwickshire. Then he had marched his troops to join the king at Coventry. So Cecily was not in London to witness the triumphant arrival of Edward with his uncle and cousin, but her heart sang when she heard the citizens chanting those lords' names as she had left the city. Immediately upon his landing at Sandwich, Warwick had proclaimed that he had only come to speak with the king and to affirm his loyalty to the crown. Where had she heard that before? Cecily thought, irritated. It was time for a new regime, she had heard a groom say when she had wandered into the stable to see that her horse had been shod, and she agreed.

Aye, Richard, she mused, sponging her body and inhaling the sweet smell of the dried lavender flowers sprinkled on the bathwater, perhaps now it is time to assert your Mortimer claim to Edward the Third's throne—Sweet Jesu, what is that ghastly noise?

It sounded like the hound from hell. She stood up abruptly, convinced that it had come from one of the many children in the nursery. She called out to Beatrice to investigate and grabbed a drying sheet off the stool. Before the attendant could put aside the mending of Cecily's gown, the door burst open and she saw that the dreadful noise issued from the throat of Anne of Buckingham.

"He is slain! Humphrey is slain!" Nan wailed, her thick brown hair tumbling from her coif and her face as white as ewe's milk. She pointed at her sister, wrapped only in the sheet, wet hair straggling down her back. "Your husband has killed my Humphrey! 'Tis all your fault," she screamed. Cecily looked aghast but stepped out of the tub and reached out for Nan, who collapsed into her sister's arms. "Cecily, oh Cis, what shall I do?"

"Come, come, Nan," Cecily soothed, gentling her onto the bed and stroking her face. "Calm yourself, my dear sister, you must calm yourself." Then she whispered, "Remember the servants. I beg of you, pull yourself together."

Anne turned away to bury her face in the pillow, her shoulders heaving, but the noise diminished. Cecily's thoughts were racing. There must have been a battle, she thought, shivering now from cold and fear. And Humphrey's death was the result of men's ambitions—her own husband's included. She clutched the sheet suddenly. Dear God, Ned must have been there. Was it Edward who had killed Humphrey? She prayed with all her might that it had not been her son. And then she thought, is he slain, too?

She had just thrown her shift over her head when two of Anne's attendants hurried in, dropping curtseys to the duchess of York and awaiting orders. Cecily beckoned one to stand close, told the other to fetch some poppy juice, and then allowed Gresilde to help her on with her underdress. Anne still lay facedown on the coverlet, weeping.

"What has happened, mistress?" Cecily asked the first of Anne's ladies, as she sat beside her distraught sister and allowed Beatrice to tie up her wet hair in a towel.

"There has been a battle, your grace," the trembling young woman said, confirming Cecily's fear. "The messenger arrived not half an hour ago with the terrible news." She told them that Salisbury, Warwick, and Edward of March, with upward of twenty thousand men, had gone north and met the king at Northampton. In only an hour they had routed Henry's army and killed the lords Buckingham, Egremont, Beaumont, and Wiltshire.

Cecily could hardly believe her ears: the hated Wiltshire, Egremont, and Beaumont all dead? That was good news, she wanted to shout, and 'twould be even better if Exeter and Somerset were named. She waited for the frightened woman to finish. "Who was slain that was with Warwick?" she demanded and held her breath. Please, God . . .

The attendant shrugged nervously. "It seems no one titled, your grace, but the king was captured in his tent. He knew not what was happening, so the messenger said, and went quietly with my lord of Warwick, God help him."

At that moment another attendant arrived with a corked vial of poppy juice, and Cecily put out her hand for it. Needing to ponder what this news would mean, she thanked the women and dismissed them.

"I shall attend my sister," she assured them, sitting down on the bed. Part of her was reeling with excitement that the Yorkists had been victorious and Henry captured. It might mean Richard and Edmund were on their way from Ireland. But her cautious side was calculating the consequences of such a victory. Aye, Henry had been taken before, at St. Albans, but it had availed Richard nothing. This time, however, Queen Margaret was all-powerful, and Cecily knew the queen would not sit idly by while her husband was in Yorkist hands.

Gentling Anne into a sitting position, she encouraged her sister to swallow a few drops of the sedative, glad to see that Nan had ceased sobbing.

"What shall I do now, Cis?" Nan asked pathetically, as if she had relied on her younger sister to tell her what to do all her life. "You always seem to know."

Cecily gave a rueful smile. If only Nan knew how helpless and rudderless she had felt all these months, but now was not the time to remind her sister of her singular lack of compassion. Nor would she gloat as Nan had, now that the tables were turned. She had seen too many reversals of her own fortune and knew how short-lived they could be.

"I will protect you for as long as you want, dear Nan," she said, noting the poppy juice was having its desired effect. "But for now I shall leave you to sleep while I go and tend to your grandson. He will be frightened." If his grandam's screaming had not terrified the five-year-old Henry Stafford enough, the fact that he would now, by virtue of his father's death at St. Albans, be duke of Buckingham might well accomplish it.

Deep in thought, Cecily closed the curtains about her sister and left the room. Outside, waiting for her, Meg cast anxious eyes at Cecily. "Is Aunt Anne going to be all right, Mother? They told me of the battle. What does it all mean?"

"It means it will not be long now, Meggie," she murmured, squeezing the girl's hand. "Your father will be here soon." She saw her daughter's joy in the lift of her head and spring in her step and, for the first time in a year, Cecily felt optimistic too.

ENGLAND WAS A soggy, mud-mired mess as the summer turned to autumn. The English people struggled through a disastrous harvest, grumbling at the quagmire that the weather and King Henry's government had made of the country.

But for Cecily the sun had come out from behind the clouds of the past nine months and she felt alive again. Edward had come with Warwick. He had sent her word to come to London with Meg to be reunited with George and Dickon and had arranged for her to stay at the late Sir John Falstoff's house in Southwark. Cecily hardly noticed the sodden landscape, for her heart was filled with hope. Anne, still grieving for Humphrey, clung to her sister on the castle steps.

"Will you forgive me for my unkindnesses to you, Cecily?" she had whispered, tears close. "I have to confess I have always been jealous of you, and I am sorry for it. You have been a rock for me these past weeks, and I find myself grateful for your kindness. Say you will forgive me." She wiped her nose on her silk kerchief, her eyes brimming.

Once again Cecily softly chided her elder sister: "No tears, remember? And aye, I forgive you." She patted Anne's hand. "Let us pray that the next time we meet 'twill be in happier circumstances. But now, look to your grandson, Nan. He needs your love before he becomes someone else's ward and has to leave you. Enjoy him while you can."

The road from Maxstoke took Cecily through Coventry, St. Albans, and Barnet. On the third day, the swelling numbers of wagons, riders, and people on foot signaled proximity to London. The mighty spire of St. Paul's soared into view and the cacophony of the capital reached Cecily's ears. The unpleasant city odors caused her to raise a sweet-smelling tussie-mussie to her nose, and Edward's greyhound's bad breath did not help. A dog lover himself, Buckingham had relented and taken Ambergris in with Cecily and her children, and Meg was hoping Ned would be pleased that his little sister had taken such good care of the animal.

Southwark teemed with frequenters of the many taverns and stews, and Meg stared, fascinated, at the streetwalkers, loitering half naked against the sides of houses and ogling potential customers. Cecily was glad when they turned off the High Street and found Falstoff's Place, a comfortable two-story mansion with a walled courtyard and secluded garden.

Standing on the steps, waiting to greet their mother and grinning from ear to ear, were Edward, George, and Dickon. Edward went forward to help Cecily from her carriage, and before he could put out his hand to take hers, Ambergris bounded out, almost knocking him over. Meg scrambled out next, laughing, and ran up the steps to embrace George and then Dickon. Cecily found herself lifted from the vehicle by her giant of a son, and she wrapped her arms around his neck and breathed in the manly scent of leather, horses, and Edward's favorite oil of orris root.

"Put me down, Ned. I may be a year older than when last you saw me, but my legs still work quite well," she said, chuckling.

"God's greeting to you, my lady mother," Edward murmured, setting her down and kissing her hand. "We are all delighted to see you."

George and Dickon eschewed all convention and threw themselves into her arms as she knelt on the step to hug them. "My boys, my dearest boys," she whispered, fighting back tears of real joy. "Meg and I have missed you so."

"Us too," George cried. "But Ned has come to see us every single day, has he not, Dickon?" Dickon nodded vigorously, looking up in awe at his eldest brother.

"Just making certain you stay out of trouble, 'tis all," Edward said with a laugh. "Now, Mother, I hope you will be satisfied with your lodging."

Taking Edward's arm and holding Dickon with her other hand, Cecily went into yet another new home followed by Meg and George cosily arm in arm.

A few days later, Cecily was in her privy chamber writing to her daughter Anne when a servant announced a messenger, whose livery of white and blue embroidered with fetterlocks was thoroughly mudspattered.

"I have a message from his grace, the duke of York, my lady," he began, down on one knee.

With a gasp of excitement Cecily rose abruptly. "From my husband? Are you come from Ireland, sir?"

The man grinned. "Nay, your grace. My lord of York landed at Chester more than a week ago," he said, pulling a letter from his tunic. "He commanded me to give you this."

> *My best beloved Cecily, I am come home and I greet you well. I have tarried at Chester for a few days but will travel to Ludlow soon on my way to London. It would please me if you would meet me at Hereford, for I would see you as soon as you are able. Can you do that, my love? Ask Edward to fit you out with a suitable vehicle, for I know he is in London with you. Until very soon then. In the meantime, I remain your humble servant and devoted husband, R. York.*

Within a day Cecily was back on the road in a magnificent carriage with four pairs of black coursers to pull her swiftly west. While Edward had carried out his father's wish to find the conveyance for her, Cecily prepared herself to see her husband for the first time in a year by bathing in rosewater, lightening her hair with chamomile and lemon juice, and rubbing her body with musk oil. Gresilde accompanied her mistress, and Edward had hired an escort of a dozen armed men to protect his mother. He had told her that Parliament had been summoned to sit and the king was being brought to Westminster for the opening on the seventh day of October. He expected his father would want to be there.

"And what of the queen?" Cecily had asked, always wary of the whereabouts of Richard's nemesis.

"She fled into Wales after Northampton. Our informants have no more news," Edward had told her, playing with a large ruby ring on his forefinger. Every time she saw him Cecily found herself wondering how she and Richard could have borne such a handsome mountain of a man. Even his hands, she noted then, were twice the size of hers.

"I confess, I can hardly wait to see Edmund," he said now, as he handed Cecily into the carriage. "How good it will be to have the whole family together again."

"Aye, it will indeed, my son. But until then, I shall trust you to look after the others like a good boy," she said, and chuckled at his indignation at being called a boy. "Ned, I know you have been in battle, been in exile, and seen much at eighteen, but to me you are still my boy. Now kiss me and be gone. I am in no mind to keep your father waiting."

WHEN CECILY ARRIVED in Hereford, curious bystanders watched the impressive carriage rumble over the stone bridge spanning the Wye, past the square-towered cathedral, and across the drawbridge to the castle.

Cecily could hardly contain her excitement. She hated to have to wait for the captain of her guard to help her out of the vehicle. But as she always did when in the public eye, she walked slowly and confidently on his arm with a pleasant but detached expression on her face as she mounted the steps to the door of the great hall. She had been told that Richard's pet name for her had been taken up by her countrymen. Proud Cis had come to enjoy living up to it.

Broad-shouldered Roger Ree, beaming a smile of welcome, was waiting for her.

"God's good day to you, your grace," he said, bowing low as he kissed her hand and took over escort duties from the captain.

"Good day to you too, Master Ree," Cecily said. "'Tis glad I am to see you again."

"I trust you had an uneventful journey. I am a sorry substitute for your husband, in truth, but he is in conference with some of his Welsh captains and hoped you would forgive him for sending me."

How could she tell this loyal, jovial gentleman that she was disappointed that Richard had not been the first to greet her? She smiled then and assured him she quite understood her husband's responsibilities.

"I am to take you directly to your apartment, duchess. I trust you will find it to your liking."

When the door clicked shut, she gasped as she recognized her husband a split second before his hungry arms pulled her to him, his mouth on hers, and his familiar scent intoxicating her. She melted into his embrace, moaning with pleasure. Every nerve in her body tingled at his touch, and every emotion she had experienced over the year of anxious separation threatened to overwhelm her. She believed she was going to swoon.

"Ah, my precious Cis, how I have ached for you," he murmured, sweeping her off her feet. He carried her to the bed, laid her down as though she were made of the most fragile silk, and carefully removed her elaborate chaperon to free her glorious hair.

Cecily could not speak she was so happy, but she could not take her hands or her eyes off him, caressing his hair now gray at the temples, stroking his face now devoid of beard, and allowing him to remove her shoes and stockings and run his hands up her legs and between her thighs.

"I cannot wait for you, my love," he murmured, and fumbling with his codpiece, he cursed the points that fought his fingers until she gently undid them for him. In his turn Richard was less gentle as he pushed her skirts aside, and like any virginal boy of sixteen, he unleashed twelve months of pent-up desire into her willing body. They both gasped at the intensity of the rush that engulfed them a few moments later, and then, like embarrassed young lovers, giggled over the speed with which they had accomplished their pleasure.

"Richard, my Richard." Cecily whispered his name over and over as though it were a prayer. "I thought never to see you again." It was the truth she had never dared voice during their enforced separation and his exile, and the relief of feeling him next to her now brought that terrible fear out into the open.

"O thou of little faith," Richard chided her, propping his head on his elbow and toying with her hair. "It was knowing you were waiting for me that spurred me on. I cursed myself for not taking you with me that night at Ludlow, my love. But my flight was not comfortable and, in truth, you and the children would have endangered us all."

Cecily nodded. "You were right to go alone, Richard," she said with a sigh. "We have much to talk of, but we have many years ahead of us to tell each other our adventures and misadventures, and no doubt they will keep us amused on long winter evenings when we are in our dotage." She might even tell him of her anger after Ludlow one day, she thought, but not now.

Richard chuckled, kissed her, and then got up to straighten his clothes.

"Must you return to the Welshmen?" Cecily asked.

He feigned surprise. "Welshmen? What Welshmen?"

She laughed. "Certes! It was a ruse that you and Master Ree concocted, I'll be bound. And there was I, cross that you were not waiting on the steps to greet me." She rolled over and pinched his buttock as he bent to pull on his boot. "This was a far nicer greeting, in truth, but I wonder what Gresilde must think."

And then the sound she had missed the most truly told her that Richard had returned. He threw back his head and laughed.

As he was leaving the room, he said, "And when you are properly clothed, my dear, I know there is a certain young man who cannot wait to wrap his arms around his mother."

"Edmund!" Cecily cried, feeling guilty because she had not thought of him once in the past half hour. "My dearest, first find Gresilde for me, and then I will send for him."

"My plan is to take my time going to London," Richard told her as they lay in bed the next morning. "Warwick and I have met, and he has returned to Westminster with a request that the new council issue me a commission to investigate disturbances of the peace in several cities along our way. It will give me a chance to be seen by the populace as a man bent on reform, and if I recruit new followers, I shall not be unhappy."

He was lying on his back, his hands behind his head, staring at the dingy canopy over the bed.

"Let us not talk of politics, my love," Cecily said, running her finger along his chest and around his nipples. She was dismayed to find that it failed to arouse him this time. She stared at his hardened profile. Something had changed, she sensed, and yet he had been overjoyed to greet her yesterday.

"Did I disappoint you last night, my lord?" she asked. "Am I grown old and haggard in a year?"

Richard grinned then. "Far from it, my lusty wife. And you tempt me now, but . . ."

"But what, Richard? There is something you are not telling me, I am certain of it. What is it, my love? We have always been honest with each other, have we not? Or have you been so used to keeping your own confidences while we have been apart that you are out of the habit of sharing?"

Richard responded by getting out of bed, pulling his chemise over his head, and going to the fireplace. Cecily sat up, clasped her knees, and waited anxiously.

"I decided in Ireland that if I returned home I would assert my claim to the throne," Richard muttered. Cecily gasped. "Warwick urged me to do it."

Cecily was out of bed in a flash. Throwing her bedrobe about her, she went down on her knees to him. "I beg of you, do not do this, Richard. For the sake of us all."

Richard's tone softened. "I am sorry, Cis, but it is time. The king has no power over many of his councillors—and they are our enemies. With staunch supporters beside me such as Warwick, Salisbury, and Norfolk, the bishops of Canterbury and London, not to mention Edward, who is distinguishing himself daily, it is time to act. It is time the kingdom had a leader—a real king."

"Sweet Jesu," Cecily whispered. "Do you believe Margaret will sit back and allow her son's right to the throne to be usurped? There will be a bloodbath!"

"Usurped!" Richard cried, angrily. "And what about my right, Cecily? You have always upheld my right. What has changed?"

Cecily rose unsteadily and clutched his arm. "Nothing has changed but you, Richard, and the change frightens me. I have prayed daily for your return, and I had dreams of you standing at the king's right hand again. But I did not dream of being queen."

Richard gave a short bark of laughter. "Oh yes you did, Cis. Many years ago, I'll grant you, but surely you knew after St. Albans that it would come to this?"

Sweet Mother of God, Cecily asked herself guiltily, is this all my fault? Have I created a monster that now threatens to destroy us? Her mind was reeling, but she knew she must keep her head. Perhaps by the time Richard got to London and she had been able to talk to him further, he would see reason.

BY THE TIME they reached Barnet, Richard had close to eight hundred men with him. He had been so busy along the route that Cecily had hardly seen him, let alone conversed with him. As she sat in her carriage at the rear of the cavalcade, ready for the last leg of the journey, she froze when, amid loud fanfares, she saw the new banner carried high over Richard's head. Gone was the falcon and fetterlock, and gone was the white rose of York. This standard bore the arms of Lionel of Clarence, signifying Richard's royal claim as descendant from the second son of a king. It was a direct challenge to the house of Lancaster, descendants of the third son of the same King Edward.

She saw Edmund coming to take his customary place beside her carriage and beckoned him to her. "I must speak with you about your father, Edmund. Do you see his banner? It will surely provoke the queen when she hears of it. Do you know his mind?"

Edmund smiled and Cecily could see he was full of pride for his father. "Indeed, I do, Mother, but surely he has told you too."

Cecily scowled. "Aye, he has, and he knows my reservations." She saw the procession was beginning to move and begged Edmund to ride in the vehicle with her.

"What happened in Ireland, Edmund?" she asked. "Your father seems changed."

Edmund's eyes shone with pride as he told her that in Ireland Richard had been treated as though he were the king. "Both the Anglo-Irish and the chieftains bowed down to him, and I was treated like a king's son. Father took me into his confidence after many a meeting with the lords, and little by little I saw which way the wind was blowing with him. They urged him to return to England and take his rightful place. I knew it for certain after Warwick's secret visit."

Cecily was ashamed to feel a twinge of envy and sadness that Richard had found a new confidante in Edmund. Would it diminish her relationship with her favorite son? She dismissed the thought as petty and returned her attention to Edmund's explanation of Richard's present path.

"My dear Edmund," she argued. "Henry is still the king in Ireland. The people are his subjects, not ours, and your father's rightful place is as chief councillor. Now, I pray you, listen to my words—and not those in your swollen head." She saw Edmund flinch from her rebuke and longed to reassure him of her love, but now was not the time. "Arriving in London under a royal standard will not help Richard's case, I can assure you. I am afraid it will only incite violence, and if you think clearly, you will agree I am right. Now, I beg of you, fetch your father here, for if you will not persuade him to remove those banners, I will."

Edmund opened his mouth to disagree but, recognizing the look of determination on his mother's face, he decided to do her bidding. However, by the time he had mounted his horse, he could see that the army was already on the move and Richard was now unreachable. To her great chagrin, Cecily knew it too, and so all she could do was settle back into the cushions and fume.

THE BELLS OF St. Peter at Westminster were ringing for nones when, on the tenth day of October, Richard of York rode into the courtyard of Westminster Palace, trumpets and clarions blaring, which attracted a crowd. He waited until several of his immediate entourage had also dismounted, including Edmund, and then strode into the great hall.

Arriving behind the first group, Cecily did not wait for someone to hand her down from her carriage but managed with Gresilde's help. The two women hurried inside, Cecily anxious to know Richard's intentions. Being told her husband was on his way to the lords' chamber, she almost ran. The door was wide, and although women did not enter that hallowed hall, she halted on the threshold and gasped when she saw her husband, already at the front of the chamber, with his hand upon the throne. She searched the faces for Richard's enemies, but Lancastrian foes such as Exeter, Devon, and young Somerset had elected to stay away. When Richard turned back, expecting roars of approval from the gathered barons, he faced instead horrified expressions or stony stares. Poor Richard, Cecily thought grimly, 'twas not the reception you expected.

"I am come, my lords!" Richard announced as though the lords were all blind and stupid. "Who will accompany me to the council chamber?"

Cecily's heart sank. She hardly recognized the man on the dais as her husband. Before she could motion to him from the doorway to stop this madness, Richard had run down the steps and was making for the archway at the back of the chamber, followed closely by Edmund. The lords surged after him, but their voices expressed shock and disapproval. The stunned ushers, who had finally gathered their wits, hurriedly closed the great oak doors on Cecily.

At a loss, Cecily moaned. "What shall we do now? Gresilde. We cannot enter the Star Chamber, but I fear the duke is on a path to destruction." Dear God, she thought, he thinks he is the king. Ah, Richard, why must you be so rash now after being so patient all these years? Warwick has smoothed the way for you to get your wish to be Henry's chief councillor, and London is ready for you. What more do you need? Oh, why had he not listened to her?

She looked about her and saw several armed men in the York livery milling about in doorways and so felt safe enough to make her way into the great hall. Gresilde was tut-tutting about the impropriety of their presence in this male bastion when suddenly Roger Ree appeared in front of them and quickly led them up the broad stairs to the royal lodgings.

"My lord duke will be taking over the king's apartments, your grace. Follow me," he said with purpose. The usually affable Master Ree seemed as disapproving of Cecily's presence in these chambers as Gresilde was.

Taking over the king's apartments, Cecily repeated to herself in horror as she mounted the narrow spiral staircase to the second floor, Gresilde puffing behind her. What did Richard intend to do with Henry? She felt sick to her stomach, and she was not sure she could take much more anxiety. Surely he did not plan to kill the king. From the reckless way Richard was acting, she had to wonder how far he would go, and she felt a deep dread.

Cecily could hear Richard's voice floating down from the landing in front of the king's apartments, which he had already reached by the back stair from the Star Chamber. When she arrived on the landing, breathless, she saw Richard's way being barred by two guards.

"Open in the name of Richard, duke of York, sirrahs," Richard commanded. The soldiers wavered momentarily, then held their halberds firmly crossed in front of the portal. It was then Richard saw Cecily. Thunderstruck, he strode to her, that strong chin leading. "My lady, why are you here?"

She recognized the stubborn stance, but held her ground. "I might ask you the same question, my lord," she replied in a low voice. "What are your intentions for the king?" She held his gaze and waited for an answer.

He drew her aside then, his jaw tense. "You know I would no more harm that feeble-minded man than I would one of our daughters, Cecily. But I *will* assert claim now, and no one, not even you, shall stop me." He caught her hand and held it to his heart. "I swear I will not harm him, but I will occupy the royal apartments to show my resolve." He dropped his voice to a whisper, his gray eyes pleading with her. "Please support me now of all times, my love, I beg of you."

Cecily gave a little moan as she saw the desperation in his look. "Oh, Richard, how have we come to this?" Then she bowed her head, resigned. "I am your wife and I must stand with you for better or for worse, in truth. But I fear for us, my lord," she whispered.

He kissed her hand and, tucking it in his arm, commanded the guards to stand aside for the duke and duchess of York. This time the two men put up their weapons and Richard himself flung open the doors to the richly adorned antechamber, where a couple of attendants cowered in the corner.

"Where is his grace the king?" Richard demanded. Their eyes shifted to the door of another room, and following their gaze, he went to it and knocked. Cecily trailed behind at a discreet distance, and when the door opened she could see the king seated on a high-backed chair, his face a picture of bewilderment at this intrusion. She winced visibly at his discomfort, but she was mollified to see Richard at least give Henry due reverence before stating his intentions.

Two of Henry's gentlemen stepped forward, daggers drawn, and tried to protest the duke of York's outrageous demand that the king leave his own apartments and take lodgings in the queen's rooms. Henry held up his hand and smiled sweetly at his champions.

"Forsooth and forsooth, sirs, it is pointless to argue. My lord of York has a stubborn look about him, and we shall have no fighting in here, do you understand?" His expression changed as a sadness fell over him. "Enough of my subjects have lost their lives already," he said with a sincerity that moved Cecily deeply. "Nay, I shall be happy to lodge in the queen's chambers"—he looked past Richard at Cecily in the doorway—"for in my experience a lady knows far more about living comfortably than a man, is that not so, duchess?"

Having forgotten that Cecily would have followed him, Richard swiveled around to see his wife in a deep curtsey. She smiled up at the king past her husband and nodded. "You have the measure of it, my liege. And have no fear, I shall make certain my husband sees to your comfort. After your kindness to me and my children at Ludlow," she said, eyeing Richard purposefully, "it is the very least I can do."

"Ah, well," Henry replied. Richard could only stand and watch as the king rose, passed him by without a trace of rancor, and put out his hand to Cecily.

"You and I go back many years, do we not, duchess? The first time we met, you were not so much in awe of me, I remember. There was some reference to Lot's wife that amused my mother. You made quite an impression on her."

Cecily smiled. "As she did on me, your grace. Your mother was a wise and beautiful woman."

Henry held out his hand. "Come, my dear duchess, why do you not escort me to my new quarters, where we can reminisce. I confess, those were happier times than now, and it would cheer me greatly to talk of them."

Ignoring Richard, the king escorted Cecily out of his own chambers with a calm dignity that left Richard chastened and speechless.

LATER RICHARD AND Cecily sat in the king's solar, each occupied with their separate thoughts, when Roger Ree entered. He related that the earl of Salisbury had hurried from the council chamber after Richard's unannounced arrival, there to report the events at Westminster to his son, Warwick, ensconced in his lodgings at Grey Friars, just inside the city wall. "He took Lord Edward with him," Roger said with a slight hesitation and waited for the expected explosion, but Richard knew enough not to upbraid the messenger and he checked his temper. Cecily was puzzled by Ned's action, but chose to stay silent as her fear increased.

And she said nothing when Richard left her to go to the council chamber the next day, while in his wife's apartments on the other side of the courtyard, God's anointed sat peacefully reading the Scriptures.

Richard was back in the royal lodgings when a barge decorated with the bear and ragged staff docked at the palace wharf. As Cecily was anxiously quizzing Richard on the morning's events, the door burst open and Warwick and Edward strode in. Warwick gave her a quick bow, but he refused to reverence Richard.

"What is the meaning of this?" Richard cried to Warwick, as Edward went down on one knee to receive his father's blessing. "Nephew, why were you not at the meeting today?"

The earl ignored both questions and came straight to the point. "My lord duke, with all due respect, your actions of the past few days are not aiding our cause, and you may be jeopardizing what we have strived for all these years."

"In what way, my lord?" Cecily interrupted, not intimidated by her nephew's piercing eyes and imperious stance. She hoped to temper the anger she saw boiling in Richard and she glared at her husband, willing him to control it.

"Were you aware that his grace took it upon himself to sit on the throne at the meeting today?" Warwick asked.

Cecily gulped as Warwick informed her that Archbishop Bourchier of Canterbury, formerly a staunch supporter, had hurried straight to Grey Friars to tell Warwick, his father, and Edward. "Even Canterbury cannot accept such audacious behavior, your grace," Warwick told Richard. "And we cannot afford to lose his support. And so I made haste to come to you and ask that you reconsider your actions." He watched Richard rise and start pacing the room. Cecily could not help but admire the younger man's forthrightness. "In case you have forgotten, we have sworn to protect the king, not remove him—at least, those of us who were at Northampton did so swear. To all of our supporters you appear to be bent on breaking that oath," he accused Richard haughtily.

Edmund had entered the room just as Warwick ended his tirade. Fists balled and jaw clenched, he advanced on his cousin, and before Richard could address Warwick's accusation, Edmund came to his father's defense.

"How dare you thus impugn my lord father," he shouted. "He has every right to claim the throne, and you know it well, or you and your father would not have supported him all these years." Then he rounded on Edward. "I did not hear you protesting, Brother. Are you with our cousin or with Father?"

"Hold your peace, Edmund," Richard interjected, putting his hand on his son's arm, his anger abating. "We are all on the same side, but it seems we have different objectives."

"You always told me our objective was to rescue the king from his corrupt councillors and bring about reform, my lord," Edward answered, keeping his distance so as not to appear to tower over his father. "We pledged a sacred oath to King Henry and to the people of the realm, and you told me that we returned to England to accomplish that objective. What has changed your mind, if I may be so bold as to ask?"

Cecily recognized the thrust of Richard's chin and the lowering of his brow as a warning sign, and she held her breath. She looked helplessly from one to the other of her family, all in a stance of defensive indignation. She hardly recognized Edmund. What had happened to the frightened, gentle boy who had fled into the night at Ludlow? She feared she must blame Richard. He must have filled the lad's head with dreams of a crown.

"If it had not been for Bolingbroke's usurpation fifty years ago, Edward, I would be on the throne now by right of my ancestor Lionel of Clarence,"

Richard said as if to a schoolboy. "I am tired of being passed by, exiled, shunned, or ignored. The people are weary of the ineffectual king. He has brought nothing but destruction and instability to the realm. They would be better governed by me, I believe, and the time for change has come."

Cecily finally found her voice, and the men all turned to her when she spoke. "Nay, my lord, you are wrong. Not," she hurried on, reassuring her husband, "about your claim to the throne but about your claim that the people can no longer tolerate Henry. While you were abroad, I had time to witness that in truth they love their king for his simplicity, his piety, and his gentleness. To them he is almost a saint, his madness a sign he has been touched by God, and—if you are fair—he himself has done no wrong." She took a deep breath. "And now I must agree with my lord of Warwick that your recent behavior is causing dangerous confusion." She balked at adding the obvious: treason.

Warwick snorted. "Confusion, Aunt? It is coming to open warfare." He turned to Richard. "What would you have me tell the lords and the council, your grace? I will gladly be your envoy, if you will not go to them yourself."

An hour later Warwick was rowed back to the city with a written explanation of Richard's family lineage and a letter asking that his detractors refute it, or if they could not, then to explain why he should not wear the crown.

Sadly, Cecily watched Edward go with him, hating the dissension between father and son. Later, she sat in the chair opposite her husband, who was despondently slumped in his.

"Where did I go wrong, Cis?" he asked so pathetically that Cecily held out her hand to him. She wished she could tell him, but she did not know. Somewhere between Ludlow, Ireland, and London, Richard had lost his way. And she grieved for those simple, long-ago dreams they had both shared.

All through October the lords and bishops deliberated the question of Richard's claim. They thought it was a matter between the king and the duke of York. Henry, in his usual fashion, could not make a decision except to tell his justices to find any objections they could to Richard's written claim. But the justices refused, saying it was a matter for the king and God. Edmund told Cecily that one justice had remarked, "I fear the matter is so high it passes our learning."

"Pah! What an assortment of craven, weak-willed bum-baileys they must be," she had replied angrily.

What will become of this? Cecily wondered, gazing out of the window on that late October day and chewing on her lower lip. For more than a fortnight she had spent many hours trying to persuade Richard to listen to Warwick and take up his role of chief councillor, a role that she assured him would bring him just as much power and satisfaction. But he remained unmoved. He refused even to see the king, though he was lodged so close at the palace. She also spent many more hours on her knees in the royal chapel, which did not afford her the comfort her prayers usually did.

Meg was practicing her psaltery across the room. Cecily was vaguely aware that her daughter was not a gifted player, but the music soothed her anyway. She was idly turning the pages of *The City of Ladies*, in which Christine de Pisan imagined a world run by powerful women, when a rap at the door was followed by the unannounced entry of the man always on her mind.

"Richard?" she questioned, startled but pleased that he should seek her out at this time of day. He had eschewed her bed for more than a week now, and her spirits were very low. Meg abandoned her instrument to go to her father and was rewarded with a kiss.

Cecily was relieved to see Richard smiling, and she approached him with hands outstretched. After only a hint of hesitation, he took them both and kissed each in turn. Then, taking her to the velvet-cushioned settle, he invited her to sit with him. Meg tactfully made her excuses, always embarrassed by her parents' affection for each other, and left them alone.

"What is it, Richard?" Cecily whispered. "You seem . . . well, more at ease" was the only way she could describe the visibly lessened tension in his shoulders and neck. Even the frown that had marred his pleasant features of late was gone.

"I have come to tell you that you and Warwick have won. My quest for the crown was ill-advised. Aye, I see that now, and I shall not pursue it." He saw her face brighten, a reply upon her lips, but he stayed it with a raised hand. "But I have also won, my dear, for I have had my claim acknowledged—my right accepted."

Cecily raised an eyebrow. "How? What can you mean?"

"The lords have come to a decision, and the king has agreed to it," Richard told her, masking his bitter resignation. "It is not the one I had hoped for all those months in Ireland, but it is acceptable to me for the sake of peace in the kingdom. I hope 'tis acceptable to you." He noticed the dark circles under Cecily's eyes and the melancholy evident in them and felt a pang of guilt, guessing he was the cause, but he could not apologize yet for doing what he thought was right. "Before I tell you, Cecily, I must hear from you whether you believe I would have made a good king."

Cecily looked down at her ruby betrothal ring and then up at him. "With all my heart I do, my love. And I have believed in your Mortimer claim from the first time I heard it at my mother's knee from no less a man than my uncle, Cardinal Beaufort. Surely you must know that. Have I not been by your side, counseled you, perhaps pushed you sometimes against your will, and never wavered in my love for you all these years?" She hesitated for a second but knew she must speak what was in her mind. It was the least she owed her beloved husband—her lord. "But I also take as true that Henry is the Lord's anointed and that to depose him would be a sin. But aye, my lord, I do believe you would have made a better king. Does that mean I reject your claim? Nay, it means we have a moral dilemma and one I am overjoyed to hear you say you have resolved." She smiled. "When we were children and I said I should like to be a queen, I was but dreaming. Now I know better. A crown does not afford one happiness. Look at Henry and Margaret. Nay, I am content to be your duchess."

"Or we could add Queen by right to your title." Richard laughed, gazing with love and respect at his remarkable consort. He took a deep breath. "I thank you for your honesty, Cis. First, you will be relieved to know I have relinquished my claim—for now—and have accepted the will of Parliament and Henry." He then murmured an aside: "I pray history will judge me an honorable man." Seeing Cecily impatiently waiting for the crux of his bargain, he hurried on. "It has been agreed by all that Henry shall wear the crown as long as he lives, but on his death, it shall pass to me and to my heirs. I have no doubt our son will be king one day."

Cecily gasped, taking in his words. Her relief was overwhelming. She slipped to her knees and crossed herself. "That is indeed a remarkable resolution, Richard," she said, but then, with hesitant incredulity, she asked, "Am I to understand that Henry is willing to disherit his own son? I fear the queen will not take the news well. Did none of the councillors point this out to his grace?"

Richard scoffed, "I care not what Margaret of Anjou thinks, Cecily. Nor do the people of England. They have turned against her. It does not sit well when a woman attempts to govern and, as I have said before, a Frenchwoman at that. And she has demonstrated willful cruelty to her subjects. Besides, the rumor persists that Edouard is not Henry's child."

"Ah, Richard," Cecily said, and sighed. "I pray you have not stooped to spreading such a lie."

"Nay, Wife, but I will not defend the lady either," he assured her. Joining her on his knees, he took her face in his hands. "Do not concern yourself with Margaret, I beg of you, but simply rejoice in the new turn in our fortunes." He kissed her mouth tenderly. "I bless the day you entered my life, Cecily Neville. A man could not hope to have a better consort."

"Pish, Richard!" Cecily retorted. "I—"

She did not finish, for Richard had stopped her mouth with another kiss—one that would have made Meggie blush.

"I SWEAR TO almighty God and all his saints that I will honor you, Henry, as my sovereign lord until the end of your days and that I shall do nothing to hurt or diminish your reign or royal dignity, nor do anything or consent to anything that might lead to the endangerment or end your natural life. So help me God."

Richard knelt and kissed Henry's ring. The king sat on the very throne that Richard had claimed not twenty days before. Cecily had been given special permission to watch the ceremony from the small gallery of the chamber, and she knew what pride her husband had had to swallow for him to kneel there before the king and his lords and bow his head. *It is for the best, my dearest,* she reminded him silently. *Now, God willing, we can all live in peace.*

It was Edward's turn to give his pledge, and her heart lurched when she saw her magnificent son bend on one knee to the uninspiring monarch enthroned in his monkish garb. Edward's ringing young voice echoed his father's words and with more generosity of spirit. Edmund was barely audible when it came his turn. And then the king rose and in a flat monotone without malice or bitterness spoke his piece.

"I, Henry, by the grace of God king of England and France and Lord of Ireland, do recognize the claim to the throne of Richard, duke of York, and his heirs, which shall be theirs at the time of my death and not before. I charge all persons here to put it abroad that it shall be considered an act of high treason for any person to conspire against the said duke's life. And now, my lords, you must swear to uphold this agreement and all its particulars with the duke, as he must now swear to defend you from those who would object to it. Do you swear?"

With one voice the lords cried, "Aye, we swear." Cecily's skin prickled. She looked down at her husband, standing proudly between his two strapping sons under a huge iron chandelier, and was mesmerized at the sight of so many candles shining brightly down on their heads.

Then below her she heard Henry call to Richard. "My lord, we should hear evensong. Will you accompany me to St. Paul's?"

"'Tis done well, Grizzy, very well," she said to Gresilde as they left, but then she frowned. "However, I know not what Margaret of Anjou will say—or do—when she is told her son has been disinherited. As a mother, I know my claws would be sharp and showing."

Cecily was not the only one pondering the queen's reaction to the new succession, as she learned from Richard later.

"Henry was asked outright to send the proclamation to Margaret skulking in Wales and have her swear to uphold it along with their son," Richard told her, as they knelt on their cushions in front of their little altar to give thanks. "For a moment he glared at us as though he would assert his authority and refuse, but then, much to our astonishment, he threw back his head and laughed. 'My lords, do you really believe the queen listens to anything I say? Nay! I think you will have a fight on your hands, for you have threatened the thing dearest to her heart—her son's future.'" Richard paused as he opened the book of hours to his favorite prayer. "For once I believe Henry was thinking clearly. We dare not dismiss the queen's ambition so lightly."

Cecily resisted saying, "I have been telling you so all along."

THE NEXT DAY, Cecily's assessment of the Londoners' affection for Henry was borne out when the king, appeasing their wish for a formal procession and holiday, sallied forth, and the citizens cheered and chanted "Long Live King Henry!" along the route. Warwick, bearing the sword of state, walked ahead of Henry, who was decked in royal purple with a crown upon his head. Cecily could hear cries of "Warwick! Warwick!," again revealing the strength of her nephew's hold on the capital.

Edward had been given the honor of holding the king's train, and behind him, alone on horseback, rode Richard. The few shouts of "Long live the duke of York!" were drowned out by the others, and Cecily, in a litter with Meg, was saddened that Richard's actions of late had tarnished his reputation with the people. He is a good man, she wanted to shout to them, a good man and true, but instead she sat stoically upright in her litter and stared straight ahead. She took comfort from her children—her daughter by her side, with Edmund, George, and Dickon on foot proudly flanking their mother's vehicle.

"I AM CHARGED by Parliament to ride north and bring order there, Cis," Richard told her in early December. November had passed uneventfully, with new appointments on the council and calm restored to the city. However, news that York's and Salisbury's estates were being pillaged by the northern lords in company with the duke of Exeter was causing concern in the Yorkist government. Those lords had not been present to make their pledges in October, and as long as they, together with those other foes, Somerset and Devon, were out of sight, Richard and his council could not rest easy.

"Aye, it means I will not be with you for Christmas, my love, but Edmund, Salisbury, and I shall keep the season cheerfully enough at Sandal, I don't doubt," he said, stroking her belly as they lay together after making love. "As you requested, Baynard's is being readied for you, though why you would want to leave this luxury for that drafty place, I cannot understand," he teased and, reaching up, snuffed out the candle in its sconce. "God keep you this night, my love. I wish I could ravish you once more, but I cannot stay awake much longer."

It seemed to Cecily that their passion had never been stronger than it was now. Richard's urge to bed her had increased since the difficult October days, and Cecily had become as uninhibited as she had been in those first few years of their marriage. She wanted to believe that the troubles of the past two decades were fading into memory and that she could look forward to middle age and time alone with her husband. She refused to think about Richard and Edmund riding north to quell unrest or about Edward setting out for the Welsh marches to recruit men to aid Richard on his northern mission. After all, Queen Margaret was still in Wales. Warwick, Cecily's nephew, was the most powerful noble in the realm after Richard, Henry was powerless and out of the way at the bishop's palace, and her brother Salisbury was Chancellor of England. As well, the French had changed their minds about invading, and life in London had resumed its normal hustle and bustle, the people seeming contented with the arrangement Parliament had made and with the new Yorkist government.

She turned on her side, closed her eyes, and snuggled against her husband.

Aye, she had naught to worry about except how to keep Christmas without Richard yet with as much gaiety as she could conjure for her children. Perhaps Nan would come from Devonshire with her child and Bess from Suffolk, she thought happily, as she drifted off to sleep.

She dreamed she was a child again astride her favorite jennet in the forest at Raby, with her hair loose and her feet bare, following Richard, who was always a few lengths ahead. Hearing a sound to her left, she reined in her horse and with a cry of surprise came face to face with the white hind. She called out to Richard, but he did not hear her and disappeared from view. She was fascinated by the animal as it stood fearlessly upon the soft green moss and found herself speaking to it as though it might speak back, but it slowly began to move off deeper into the forest, turning back every now and again to make sure she was following. When she got too close and tried to put out her hand to touch the snowy coat, it nimbly leaped away and continued on its path. Unafraid that she was lost deep in the woods, she had faith that the hind would protect her and take her to Richard. She urged her horse on until she could see a clearing and bright light ahead. As the hind stepped forward, it seemed to be absorbed into the light, causing Cecily to rein in and stay in the shadows of the trees. Shading her eyes and searching for her guide, she gradually became aware of other figures floating in the light.

"Richard!" she called, afraid now. "Where are you?" But there was no answering shout, just the eerie, silent, floating figures seemingly searching for something. And then she recognized the serene face of her beloved Constance smiling at her.

"Constance," Cecily whispered, stretching out her hand to the vision, but the doctor faded into the light and the hind took her place. "Mother of God, is this heaven?" Cecily asked the ethereal creature that she was now convinced embodied the Virgin. "Am I in heaven?" But she knew she was not; she was still in the shadow of the earthly trees. And then she panicked, understanding that Richard, too, must have disappeared into that light. "Richard!" she cried. "Where are you, Richard? Blessed Mother, tell me where Richard is."

"I am right here beside you, Cis. Wake up, my love, you are having a bad dream." Richard shook her gently, stroking her thigh. "Tell it to me—and then it cannot come true."

Relief flooded Cecily as she turned into him and pulled his arms around her. "It was nothing, my love," she lied, too frightened to tell him. "I was lost in a forest, 'twas all."

* * *

CECILY HAD TO endure another farewell with Richard. This time she was also giving the traditional wave to her sons from the gatehouse tower of Baynard's Castle.

Richard glanced up at the lithe figure wrapped in a sable-trimmed mantle, the hood sheltering her head from the biting December wind. Cecily took out her miniature version of the white rose banner and waved it in farewell, blowing her husband a kiss. This parting was far less wrenching than their goodbye on that fateful night at Ludlow, and most of their last conversation had been about practical matters for the running of Baynard's in Richard's absence. They had, however, made tender love the night before and talked well into the night about their hopes for the children. Richard promised to make finding a suitable bride for Edward a priority upon his return.

"And when will that be?" Cecily had asked sleepily.

"We shall hold at Sandal, which will afford us ample protection as we muster more men to set the north to rights again. I have given Edward until mid-January to meet with us at Sandal before we launch into any combat. Once we have a large enough force, we shall send Northumberland, Exeter, and their cronies back to their estates once and for all. I cannot say for sure, Cis, but by spring you should see us returned."

"And the queen, my dear? What of her?"

"It appears Margaret has left Wales and is rumored to be over the border in Scotland with her tail between her legs. Our presence in the north will deter any trouble with King James and his wild clansmen. And without him, the queen can do nothing. So do not worry on her account, sweetheart." He had kissed her once more and they settled into sleep.

Cecily was jolted from her reverie now by George and Dickon, who were leaning precariously over the parapet and shouting, "Good-bye Father! Farewell Ned and Edmund!" She watched as Meg hauled them back with a sisterly admonition.

"Spoilsport," George said mulishly, "Go and stick your nose in a book and leave us alone."

Dickon put his hands on his hips and tried to look fierce. "Aye, Meggie, indeed you are a spoilsport."

Cecily sighed, but she was too wrapped up in her own thoughts to chide the children now. She was remembering her last words to Edmund and wishing she could take them back.

"You do not have to ride with your father if you would prefer not to, my son. I will speak to him, if you are reluctant," she had told him after Mass had been said for the success of Richard's mission. She knew that being a soldier was not his calling, and she was willing to speak up for him to Richard if Edmund was averse to joining the northern campaign.

She had not been prepared for his vehement reaction. "I beg of you, my lady, stop treating me like a baby," he sharply complained. "I am every bit as good a knight as Ned, and Father thinks 'tis high time I learned what it is to be on the battlefield. Now leave me be!"

Cecily had paled, and in her anguish at the change that had come over her darling boy, she had stiffened and snapped back, "How dare you speak to me so rudely, Edmund. I am your mother and deserve your respect. Very well, then, go and fight, kill and maim, but do not come crying to me when you have nightmares."

Edmund had kissed her hand quickly then and left in a huff, not even asking for her blessing.

And I was too proud to call him back, Cecily now thought regretfully. She looked down on his light brown head, his murrey and blue cloak draped over the back of his caparisoned horse, and silently begged him to look up at her. Ned had heard the boys' cries and waved cheerily from his huge courser. He then blew a kiss to Cecily before signaling to his retainers to follow him out of the courtyard and through the gate into Thames Street. Then Richard shouted some commands to his meinie, and the horsemen began to make an orderly file behind Richard, Edmund, and Salisbury to trot off and join the bulk of their force waiting outside the city wall at Smithfield.

It was Meg's turn to wedge herself in one of the crenels and wave her kerchief at her father and brother. Richard looked up then and grinned. "Be a good girl, Meggie, and help your mother. God bless you, my child," he called over the noise of skittering hooves on the cobbles and jingling harnesses. Seeing Cecily behind her daughter, Richard blew her another kiss and, unsheathing his sword, touched the hilt to his lips and saluted her.

It was then that Edmund looked up and his face brightened when he saw his mother, brothers, and sister all waving and shouting farewell. His eyes met Cecily's and he put his hand over his heart. "Farewell, Mother," he mouthed, and when he saw her place her hand over her own heart and smile, he bowed his head, knowing he was forgiven.

Farewells had been said and blessings received, and so, with drums beating a steady rhythm, Richard rode out with Edmund by his side ahead of the group of retainers, while Cecily watched them thread their way through the streets, out of the city, and onto the north road. A sudden gust of bitter wind off the river made her shiver, and, tucking her white rose pennon into her sleeve, she marshalled her remaining children indoors with a heavy heart.

CECILY WAS TRUE to her promise to make the Yuletide season a merry one for her children. An early snowfall in the west country kept Anne from traveling to London, but Bess arrived from Suffolk after her young husband, John de la Pole, had ridden off with his men to join Richard. Cecily had forgotten how delightfully prosaic her second daughter could be, and Bess enjoyed her walks and talks with Meg, telling Cecily that her sister had an impressive knowledge of literature already. "I have no time for reading anything but the household accounts, in truth," Bess confided jovially. "I confess I prefer raising good dogs and horses."

After one of the feasts, Cecily paid for mummers to enact the story of St. George and the Dragon especially for Dickon, who hid under the table when the fearsome dragon appeared, belching smoke from its mouth. But peeking from his hideout, he clapped his hands when St. George dealt the fatal blow and released Meg, who played a reluctant damsel in distress.

Cecily doubted that George and Dickon noticed the paucity of fare that year, but Meg and Bess remarked on it. Coming from the country, Bess was only too aware that the farmers had been unable to harvest much after the wettest summer anyone could remember. How Richard would feed his men on the road north worried Cecily.

Too soon for the children, the first days of January meant Epiphany was close and thus the end of the celebrations. Alice had joined in the festivities on Christmas Eve, and on the next day all had attended a solemn Mass at St. Paul's in the presence of King Henry.

Alice brought troubling news from her son, Warwick, that Queen Margaret had crossed the border accompanied by an army of Scots and other mercenaries and was moving south to join the northern lords. Cecily's heart turned over, as it did whenever she heard the She-wolf's name, but this was especially unhappy news.

"My son's informants describe Margaret as a termagant," Alice confided, as they sipped mulled wine and watched more snow fall outside the solar window. "They say her ire at the new order of succession, at Henry, and most of all

at your husband knows no bounds. They have seen her at James's court ranting loudly and without shame, railing against England, which of course her
Scottish hosts must enjoy. God help us if she is not stopped. 'Tis said she even
wears a suit of armor now, though I cannot quite believe it."

Cecily had snorted then. "Well, I can. Even Londoners are calling her She-
wolf."

She prayed that Richard had been able to gather enough men to his banner
and that Edward would soon join him with more. Despite the ill tidings, she
refused to spoil the children's fun, but for surety's sake spent extra time on her
knees, asking the Virgin to protect her husband and two elder sons.

It was while she was at prayer on a snowy day in early January that she
heard a bell tolling and then another and another. When she heard the castle
gate grating open and horsemen enter, she called to Gresilde for her cloak and
hurried along the cold stone passage with her attendant to the nearest open
area to look down on the courtyard. She instantly recognized the cognizance
of the bear and ragged staff.

"A messenger from Warwick," she said. Asking Gresilde to accompany her,
she ran down the spiral staircase and arrived in the great hall in time to see her
nephew stride in, shaking the snow off his voluminous felt hat.

Her heart constricted and she felt sick as she contemplated why Warwick
was come in person. "What news, my lord? Tell me!" she exclaimed, going to
him and receiving his reverence. She could read nothing on his face, but her
legs did not feel part of her, and she would have fallen if her nephew had not
been quick to support her.

"Is it the duke? My husband? Has he been wounded?" she whispered, her
mouth dry. She was vaguely aware that too many pairs of eyes were on her as
she tried to swallow.

Warwick somehow propelled her to the nearest seat. Then, pointing to the
door, his haughty gaze brooking no lagging, he dismissed the curious bystanders without a word.

Cecily was gripping Gresilde's arm as Warwick dropped on one knee to
address her. "Your grace, Aunt, I bring you the worst news," he said in a grim
but gentle voice. "You have guessed it, I have no doubt. There was a battle at
Wakefield, and it pains me to tell you that the duke, your husband, is dead."
He waited as first Cecily stared at him dumbstruck and then uttered a moan
that would have moved even the most stalwart of men.

"Richard! It cannot be! Oh no, please not Richard!" she whispered, searching Warwick's face for a denial while she desperately tried to hold back her tears in front of him. Seeing his nod, her words tumbled forth. "When? How? Where? Oh, sweet Jesu, not Richard! Not my love, my dearest love, my life, my all, my sweet—" She could not continue.

Warwick steeled himself. "Dear Aunt Cecily, you must be brave, for I have more to tell you." He struggled on, much moved by his aunt's grief. "My father—your brother—is also dead, God rest his soul." He knew bringing her the news in person would be difficult, but he had not imagined he too would feel such depth of sorrow upon hearing of his father's death.

Holding her close gave him the strength to finish. "Courage, Aunt," he murmured, "for there is more. It pains me to tell you that your son Edmund was murdered fleeing the scene."

For the second time in Cecily's life, the world went black, and she slid from her nephew's arms to the floor.

EPILOGUE

What can I do? It's not surprising that I
Weep and sigh, with my dear lover dead.
For when I look deeply into my heart and
see how sweetly and without hardship I
lived from my childhood and first youth
with him, I am assailed by such great
pain that I will always weep for his death.

CHRISTINE DE PISAN,
ONE HUNDRED BALLADS

Baynard's Castle, London

*C*ecily awoke with a jolt to find that she had slipped off the kneeler in the little chapel and onto the flagstone floor. She lay there, the cold stone against her cheek, wondering how she had come to be in the chapel. And then she remembered that she had come with Gresilde to attend nones after her sleepless night. How long had she been lying here? Quite some time, she decided, remembering she had sent Gresilde away. With a deep sigh and instead of rising, she chose to prostrate herself, her arms outstretched toward the altar and her face pressed against the rough granite, forcing herself to remember Warwick's dreadful mission. She wished now that she had never woken from her swoon that day.

But she had, and so she made herself think about what had happened after she had been revived that day five weeks ago.

In truth, she had gone through the following few days in a trance, for she could barely remember telling her children that their father and brother had been slain, sending word for the household to assemble in the great hall to give them the tidings of their master's death, ordering her mourning robes to be sewn, sending money to the churches in Baynard's parish for masses to be said for the duke and earl, and indeed how she struggled through forkfuls of food the cook had sent up to tempt her day after day.

She did clearly remember the agonizing sounds of her children's grief as Nurse Anne and Beatrice tried to comfort them in their rooms a passageway from her. After that first day, when she had gathered them to her knee in the solar and explained that Father and Edmund would not be coming back but that they were safe with the angels, she could not bear to be with them for long.

She also remembered the herald arriving soon after Warwick and having to sit through a description of the horror of that fateful day at Sandal and keep control of her emotions.

Richard was taken unawares when the royal army camped but a few miles away at Pontefract just before Christmas. Heralds went back and forth between the leaders, and a Christmas truce was negotiated. As Cecily had feared, food was scarce, and a large group of Richard's men sallied forth one bitterly cold day to forage in the farms and fields around nearby Wakefield. Taking advantage of the diminished numbers at the castle, young Somerset, who was commanding the queen's forces, advanced his army to the plain before the castle, having caught and slain many of the foraging soldiers. And then Richard, incensed by the breaking of the truce, ordered his soldiers to march out of the safety of the castle and face the enemy in the field. He had no idea, so the herald had reported, how large a force the queen had mustered. The Yorkists had been cut to pieces in short order.

Cecily remembered the herald had looked up at her with compassion when he gave her the facts of Richard's death. He was slain among his faithful servants—Roger Ree, Davy Hall—and Warwick's brother, Thomas, and his head struck from his body. When Salisbury had been captured, Somerset declared victory for the Lancastrians. More than two thousand of York's followers had been killed. Cecily groaned now. And what for? she asked herself. Ah, Richard, my love, what was worth losing your life for? Richard . . .

She forced herself to think of his face as it used to be, smiling at her with love, those gray eyes crinkling, or loosing his braying laugh with his children, or concentrating on his devotions, or serious in discussion with his councillors. She could not think of the bloodied, grisly mess of flesh his dear face must have been on that dreadful day. And she refused to accept that Queen Margaret would have so ignominiously treated the head of a royal duke as they said she had, adorning it with a paper crown and making jests about the irony before setting it upon the Micklegate of York. If 'tis true, Cecily muttered to herself, then surely the queen has gone as mad as her husband.

She turned her thoughts from blood-soaked Micklegate to her brother, her sometimes infuriatingly indecisive brother, who, despite their difference in age, in the end had become her husband's closest friend, who had stood with him at Ludlow and fled for his life, and who had fought beside him at St. Albans and Wakefield. The herald said Salisbury had pleaded with Somerset to spare him, even offering the duke money, but in the end he had been dragged from his cell in Pontefract by his own northern vassals and beheaded without trial by Exeter's bastard brother. Cecily felt guilty that she had not seen Alice yet. Alice too had lost her husband. She vowed to visit her without delay.

But now she must grit her teeth and try to reconcile herself to the most difficult of the three deaths that had devastated her family in the space of those twenty-four hours: the cold-blooded murder of Edmund, her beloved second son, the boy who had so endeared himself to his mother with his gentle ways and who had stolen her heart at an early age.

She heard again the herald's harrowing pronouncement. "My lord of Rutland escaped the field with Master Apsall," he had said, reluctant to add to the duchess's woes, and Cecily had been surprised to hear that her sons' tutor had joined Richard. "It was told to me that they took shelter under a bridge, but Lord Clifford had pursued them and his soldiers dragged the earl from his hiding place. Lord Edmund fell to his knees and begged for mercy, for the fighting was over and the battle already won."

Cecily felt her bile rise again now as it had then at such horrifying treatment of her son. Lord Clifford, the man she had held hands with on Loveday, had cut her son's throat himself, may he rot in hell. It was for revenge, the messenger had said, for the death of Clifford's father at St. Albans.

Here, lying on the chapel floor, Cecily's body heaved with dry sobs; her tears were spent, she knew. At least Somerset had buried all three bodies together at Pontefract after sending their heads to York. One day I shall take Richard and Edmund back to bury at Fotheringhay, she promised herself.

A candle guttered and went out. She knew she must have been in the chapel a long time. Gradually raising herself to a kneeling position, she looked again at the Virgin's anguished face. Ah, Virgin Mother, could you not have spared my son? She crossed herself as she gazed up at the crucified Christ and told him, "I know now your mother's agony, Lord. Did she not suffer your death for all mothers? Or must we all lose a son to understand your sacrifice?" She bent her head and whispered a paternoster. A calm had come over her, and when she looked back at Christ, she was filled with compassion and reverence. Over the years Cecily had discovered how much comfort she gained from prayer, and today it had once again brought her strength to go on with her life.

As she got up, brushed the creases from her gown, and straightened her head-covering, she realized for the first time in weeks that she was hungry. She reverenced the altar and slowly left the chapel. Reliving her life with

Richard had given her more solace than she could have dreamed of. Her spirit felt assuaged, and a glimmer of hope for the future without him had crept into her heart. It was as though Richard had released her, though it was possible that her heart might never truly mend. Her other children must fill the void now, she thought, determined to go to the youngest and help them through their loss.

Her legs still did not feel strong, but she walked with new purpose from the chapel. She could not help but ponder what Meg had alluded to the night before after her nightmare. *Do my children look upon me as hard of heart? But, oh, how wrong they are,* she ruefully smiled to herself, thinking back on thirty years of a passion-filled marriage. *Perhaps I should not have hidden my feelings from them. Maybe I should show them how cherished they are and how much I cherished their father,* and so she quickened her steps, longing to hold two of her remaining sons in her arms. *Soon,* she prayed, *she could hold Edward as well.*

Edward. She imagined his horror upon hearing the news from Wakefield. He had been at Shrewsbury, she was told, doing what his father had commanded him to do. But where was he now?

She had arrived at the small solar that the boys shared with Meg during the day and that served as their bedchamber at night. She put her hand on the door and entered just in time to hear Dickon tell his sister, "You aren't even my nursemaid! Leave me be, you . . . you whey-faced wench!"

Cecily gasped, instantly changing from grieving widow to strict mother. "Richard! Where have you learned such talk? Apologize to your sister at once, and then you may go to bed without your supper. I am ashamed of you. To think your father has only been dead these five weeks! You children have lost all discipline." This was not exactly how she had envisaged showing her children her love, but even in grief, she had to maintain order for their sake.

Becoming aware of horsemen in the courtyard, she frowned. George explained that seeing them was the reason for their quarrel and that Meg had rebuked him and Dickon unfairly.

"Come and see, Mother," Meg said quickly, moving back to the window.

Cecily peered down and recognized her son's livery. Her heart began to beat faster. "George, stay here. Margaret, come with me."

"But, Mother, I am a man now. I am the head of the family in Ned's absence. *I* should be by your side," George sulked.

"When you look at me like that, George, all you show me is that you are still naught but a babe. Now do as you are told!"

When Cecily and Meg entered the great hall with their attendants, the herald fell to one knee.

"What news, master herald? Come you from my son?" Cecily went straight to the point.

"Aye, my lady. And I have to report a victory for Lord Edward seven days since!" A cheer rose from the assembled company. "At a place near Ludlow called Mortimer's Cross."

"I know the place," Cecily said eagerly, gripping Margaret's arm. Her heart filled with pride as she imagined her warrior son astride his white destrier, sword raised to the heavens. Mortimer's Cross was a stone's throw from Wigmore Castle, she remembered, and a pang momentarily suffused her as she remembered that afternoon of passion she and Richard had enjoyed there. Aye, 'twas a fitting place for a York to know victory, she thought.

The herald told his tale with flair, thrilling the company, which had grown in number once the news had been circulated that Lord Edward had won his first battle.

"My lord Edward was marching to meet with the earl of Warwick to stop the royal army from reaching London when he heard that a large force was moving from Wales to join the king. Lord Edward turned his army and chose to face this force of Welsh, Bretons, and Irish." It was on the feast of Candlemas, the herald said, adding that some were loath to fight upon such a holy day. "But just before the battle began, a strange happening took place that convinced our troops Edward would be victorious."

Cecily waved him on.

"'Twas close to ten of the clock, and we were chafing at the bit, waiting for the enemy to approach, when we noticed three suns in the sky."

"Three? Do not babble nonsense, man," Cecily snapped. "How can there be three suns?"

"I know not how, my lady. But I saw them with my own eyes. The strange apparition hushed the army, but then my lord Edward turned his horse to us and cried, ''Tis the symbol of the Trinity. God the Father, God the Son, and God the Holy Ghost! It means God is on our side! 'Tis a sign.' And we believed him then. He was so sure and so brave, and the light from the three suns shone bright on his gold-brown head, making him look like . . . like a young god," he cried, his voice filling the hall.

After giving her more details, the herald ended with the news that Edward was now on his way to meet Warwick.

"Let us hope they have now met, herald, for the queen's army is not far from here, I fear. We thank you for your service."

Exultant with the news, Cecily called for wine for the entire company, and her arms prickled when the echoing shout "*À York!*" reached the rafters.

Even so, Cecily recognized the cold grip of fear. Would Edward be in time to unite with Warwick and prevent the queen from marching on London? Despite Edward's victory, and unable to trust fortune to favor York for long, Cecily had good cause to be afraid.

LONDON WAS A city whose nerves had teetered on a knife edge since the news of Wakefield had spread through the lanes, taverns, and wharves in January. For all his popularity, Warwick had not taken charge as the people had anticipated he would after Richard's death. Alice told Cecily she feared he had lost his courage—otherwise why had he not sent out commissions of array to the surrounding counties to protect London from the queen's army. Riders from the north had daily cantered through the city gates to report the atrocities taking place on Margaret's march south. Cecily's heart had wept to hear that Grantham, Peterborough, and Stamford—all formerly under Richard's jurisdiction—had been ravaged by the bloodthirsty mob that traveled with the queen. It was said that nothing was safe in a thirty-mile-wide swath of the oncoming rabble, that the rape and torture of nuns and priests was rampant, the defiling and sacking of churches and abbeys common, and the burning and pillaging of towns and villages unrelenting.

Emerging from her brief period of initial grief, Cecily could only now sense the tension in the streets as people hurried to and from their homes and shops with an eye to the north. Any day they expected to hear the trumpets and church bells sound the alarm. She considered it too dangerous to let the boys go out to play or practice at the butts on those days when it was not pouring with rain or sleeting. Meg, she knew, took comfort in books. Cecily threw herself into the running of the castle, spending hours with Steward Heydon poring over the accounts, settling disputes, and hearing petitions.

She was informed that Warwick had finally gathered a force from the southern counties and together with other Yorkist lords had marched out on the twelfth day of February to prevent Margaret from reaching London. And they took with them as their figurehead that most hapless of monarchs, King Henry the Sixth.

But that was a week ago, Cecily mused now, putting down her book of Christine de Pisan's ballads and removing her spectacles. She shivered and went to throw a log on the fire, the spitting embers disturbing Ambergris. Surely Edward had caught up to Warwick by now. She hoped that their lengthy absence boded well for London's safety.

She watched the boats ply the gray water of the Thames, a wintry sun trying to pierce the leaden cloud that had loosed a few snowflakes onto the cottages and hovels along the south bank of the river. To the east of them she could see the tower of St. Mary Overie.

Being on the water side of the castle, she did not hear the portcullis grind open to let the horsemen enter the courtyard, but shouting did pierce her reverie, as did Ambergris's first growl. The dog rose from his warm spot by the fire and began to bark.

Beatrice came hurrying in, her long face even longer. "The herald has returned with others, your grace, and their mood is grim."

"Where is Lady Margaret, Beatrice? Find her and come down to the hall. Gresilde and I will go there immediately." Cecily gathered up her train and hurried down the spiral staircase through the great hall and onto the steps to the courtyard, where Steward Heydon was conversing with the herald. The man knelt before her, muddied and wet through, and doffed his cap. This time the news was not of victory but of a stunning defeat of the seemingly unassailable earl of Warwick by the queen's army.

"At St. Albans you say?" she asked, annoyed with herself for not controlling the tremor in her voice. "And what of my lord of Warwick? God forbid he is not slain."

"Nay, your grace. The earl and the rest of our force who escaped the slaughter have fled west to find your son, Lord Edward."

"Praise be to the Virgin for that!" Cecily exclaimed, although concerned to hear that Edward had not arrived in time to join the fray and beat back the queen.

"The king was with the earl at the battlefield," the herald continued. "He is with the queen now. Some said they saw him at the edge of the battlefield sitting under a tree, laughing at his enemies."

"Sweet Jesu, the poor man is indeed mad," whispered Cecily, crossing herself. Then she addressed the somber company, looking around the high walls of the inner ward at the servants and attendants hanging over balconies or crowded on stairs and at the soldiers, some wounded, who were thronging the courtyard itself.

"Hear this, loyal friends of York. We are in grave danger." She ordered those who were armed and hale to follow Warwick's trail and join Edward. The wounded must be cared for at Baynard's, and she assured them she would not desert them or the household. "God help us! And may God bless the earl of March!" she ended on a rallying note.

"God bless Lord Edward!" the household echoed, less enthusiastic, and murmured misgivings on their way back to work.

Cecily welcomed the soldiers into the hall, where she took charge, making provision for the wounded, commanding the cook to make food for those leaving to join Edward, and passing through the ranks with a smile of encouragement here and a word of thanks for their duty there. Meg trailed along behind, emulating her mother with nods and quiet words of commiseration or gratitude.

Throughout the procedure Cecily was also desperately trying to think. What if Margaret does enter London? Any loyalty for her royal person or any respect she might have won if she had simply marched south to claim the capital and her husband after her victory at Wakefield had disappeared up in the smoke of every house and field she had burned. Nay, we cannot expect any mercy from Margaret of Anjou. After all—and Cecily saw the irony clearly now—who inherits England now rests between her son and mine.

And it suddenly occurred to Cecily that her younger sons were in danger as well, for they were also heirs to the throne. She must send them away immediately, she decided. But where? To Nan in Devon? You foolish woman, Cis, Exeter would find them there. To Bess in Suffolk? Nay, Bess was too young to take on such responsibility and besides, she was lately with child. They would not be safe anywhere in England, she realized with a jolt. They must go abroad. She racked her brain. Who were Richard's allies in Europe? Oh, if only dear Anne of Bedford were still alive! But that gave her an idea: Anne's brother, Philip of Burgundy. He was an ally, was he not? Aye, after Northampton he had made overtures of friendship to the Yorkist lords. In a split second her mind was made up. There was no time to waste, no time to write letters. The boys must leave at once. Her eye fell on Meg, and she beckoned to her.

"Margaret my dear, I want you to go up to your apartments and tell Nurse

Anne to ready George and Richard for a journey. Tell her to pack their warmest clothes and one fine doublet and bonnet each. I will be there anon."

"Where will they go, Mother?" Meg asked boldly.

Cecily was astonished. "'Tis not your place to question me, Daughter. Pray do as I tell you at once!"

Meg flushed, glancing anxiously around at those standing close, and Cecily felt ashamed for embarrassing her child. "You will know in a little while, my dear," she said more kindly. "I simply do not have time to explain now." With a heavy heart, she watched Meg turn away.

Dickon was on the verge of tears when Cecily found the boys half an hour later.

She clucked her tongue. "Where is your York backbone, Richard!" she admonished him. "You are near ten years old and here you are behaving like a baby. 'Tis not the first time you have been without me."

"But . . . but . . . Meg has always been with us. Why can't she come, too?" Dickon tried to stop his lip quivering, but he did not succeed.

It was his sister who gathered him into her arms and cajoled him out of his fear. "'Twill be an adventure, Dickon!"

This caused Dickon to wail even more loudly. "I did not like the last adventure. I was frightened at Ludlow."

"That's enough, Richard," Cecily admonished him, and then felt another pang of guilt for her sharp words. She should not take out her anxiety on these innocents, she remonstrated with herself. She took pity on her youngest, who looked so pathetic, his thin legs encased in hose far too big for him and his chin trembling, and she held out her arms, taking him gently from Meg. "Hush, child. It will not be for long, I promise, for Ned will come and take London and all will be well."

At Edward's name, Dickon brightened. "You think he will really come, Mother? I would dearly love to see Ned again!" He blinked back his tears and attempted a smile.

Cecily stood up and drew George to her as well. "Now, would you like to know where you are going?"

"Aye, Mother," chorused the boys. "And why?" added George.

"'Tis for your own safety, George. If something should happen to Edward, pray God it does not, then you and Richard are York's heirs and thus are heirs to the crown."

Cecily reminded them to mind their manners, study hard, and write to her often, for they would be guests at the court of the mighty duke of Burgundy. "Aye," she laughed, as their eyes grew round, "and you will have your first voyage on a ship!" She held her thumb between her fingers for luck, as she was taking it on faith that Duke Philip would receive them kindly.

"A ship, Georgie!" Richard enthused, his tears forgotten. "We are going to sea, like the game we played yesterday!"

"Aye, Dickon, and I will protect you, never fear," George told him.

"I am not afraid, George!" Richard exclaimed. "I am a York. And we Yorks are never afraid!"

"There's a brave boy, Richard," Cecily said, much relieved. "I want both of you to remember how brave you were at Ludlow. You can do it again, I know you can. Now, say good-bye to Meg and come with me."

They made their way to the castle quay, where Steward Heydon had commandeered a boat without markings. She saw the boys safely stowed in the stern and then stepped in herself, Heydon taking the bow seat. George's gentleman attendant, holding the boy's luggage, eased himself next to Heydon. Cecily had entrusted the strapping young man with a missive and instructions to take the boys to Philip.

The boatman dipped his heavy oars into the water and pulled away from the pier toward the scores of ships moored in the Pool on the other side of London Bridge. Cecily sat with her black fur-trimmed cloak wrapped around her shivering children as they huddled together for warmth against the damp February evening.

"I will be back with the tide, Meg," Cecily called to the desolate girl on the wharf waving her brothers farewell. "You must take care of everything until I return. You know what to do. You have learned well!"

The boatman rowed from ship to ship, and Cecily and Steward Heydon haggled with their captains to no avail until a sturdy carrack bearing the Flemish name of *Zoete* hove into view. The steward hailed a crew member dumping dirty water over the side. "Your captain, mariner? Where is your captain?" he shouted, and the man nodded and ran off. A few moments later, as the boatman maneuvered the boat alongside and grabbed the rope netting hanging from the gunwale, a burly man with a globe of a face appeared above them.

"*Ja?* I am der captain, Captain Bouwen. Vat you vant?"

Sir Henry stated his business and held up a pouch of coins that Cecily had given him. When the man knew he was in the presence of a noblewoman and that he might be rewarded even more for taking the two boys to Flanders, he nodded and grinned, calling over his shoulder to two of his sailors, who swarmed down the makeshift ladder like monkeys.

There was hardly time to kiss the boys and whisper her love before they were manhandled up the swinging netting and safely onto the deck, their attendant scrambling behind them. Just then a wake from a passing boat caused the boatman to let go of the rope and tend to his oars, and Cecily's hand reached out into the widening space between the vessels, blinking back her tears, as the boys, ashen-faced and crying her name, receded farther and farther from her. Raw panic engulfed her as her eyes focused on the small figures. Would she ever see them again? Was the captain trustworthy? Would they be shipwrecked before they even reached Duke Philip and his duchess? Would Duke Philip take them in? Would Dickon catch cold? Sweet Jesu, what had she done? Had she, too, like Queen Margaret, gone mad?

SHE DID NOT have time to worry about her sons, as London began to shut down in anticipation of the queen's arrival with her horde. But, strangely, Margaret did not come, and a few days after the battle, instead of taking advantage of her victory, she chose to stay where she was at St. Albans and negotiate with the mayor and aldermen of London for the surrender of the city. Back and forth the emissaries rode between the mayor and the queen, Margaret wanting a triumphal entry for herself and Henry and the city's complete surrender. The city fathers even sent three noblewomen to mediate for them with Margaret, knowing that she would treat them well for their past service to her. Cecily was not surprised when she heard that her sister Anne was one, along with Jacquetta of Bedford. They fared a little better. The king and queen agreed to remove the army to Dunstable and that only they and the other leaders would enter the city as victors.

But the mayor and his aldermen hadn't reckoned on the Londoners' hatred of the queen. They bolted their doors, rolled down their shutters, shut up their shops, and even upset carts of food destined for the queen. When Margaret promised that no one would be punished and that London would not be pillaged, the mayor was pleased and petitioned the people to surrender. But instead a riot ensued, the citizens took the keys to the city, and it was clear that London would not submit to the king and queen.

So when the sound of marching feet and fanfares of clarions and trumpets did resound on the eve of the month of March, Cecily knew with pride it was

Edward and not Margaret who was being cheered and feted from Chepeside to Bishopsgate and from Newgate to the Tower. Dressed in her dove-gray mourning gown and her black steepled hennin, with only her precious sapphire around her neck and her ruby betrothal ring for jewelled adornment, she waited on the throne in the great hall for the arrival of her magnificent son.

That day the February rain had finally stopped and the sun was shining on Edward's red-blond hair as he came riding into the courtyard on his white horse, its trappings torn and bloodied, his cuirass dented, and his hand bandaged. To the cheers and shouts of welcome, the grinning young duke dismounted and, standing proudly on the steps of his father's palace, he raised an arm in salute.

Then he strode through the doorway on his long, strong legs, and Sir Henry announced, as Edward's squire had hurriedly instructed him: "His grace the duke of York, earl of March and Ulster, and true heir to the throne of England, France, and Ireland." Edward nodded, pleased with the steward's new styling, and went straight to his mother, where he bent his knee and bowed his head.

"Your grace," he said, his baritone strong and warm. "I humbly ask your blessing."

"You have it, my son," Cecily said, surprised at the hoarseness of her voice. "We give you God's good greeting." Rising, she held out her hands. "Come give your mother a kiss."

"'LET US WALK in a new vineyard, and let us make us a gay garden in the month of March with this fair white rose and herb, the earl of March.'" Meg quoted the words from a parchment one of her attendants had given her. "'Tis what they are saying in the city about you, Ned, although 'fair white rose' is hardly how I would describe you."

"Ha!" Edward replied from his chair, stretching out his long legs lazily. "I suppose you think that fits you, Mistress Nose-in-a-Book."

Irked, Meg shook her head. "I do not, in truth. I am too tall and too plain by far," she retorted and flung the paper on the floor.

Cecily looked up from her needlework and sighed. "Little birds in their nests should agree, my dear children. Meg, allow Ned to finish telling us how the king and queen have run back to York. I do not get tired of hearing you say it, I confess."

Edward frowned. "Aye, it is good news, Mother, but I hear that she continues to plunder her way north. 'Tis no wonder the people hate her." He plucked a flea he saw idling on his left leg and crushed it between his fingers, the wound on his hand still livid. Then he asked Meg to leave so that he could have private consultation with Cecily. He blew his sister a kiss as she left the room. "Even though they make fun of your long neck, Meg, I think you are not unpleasant to look at," for which she rewarded him with a glare and a slammed door.

"You are unkind, Ned," Cecily told him. "Do not let success go to your head. Your father would not wish that." The mention of Richard caused them both to pause for a moment with their own memories. Edward longed to talk to his mother of their loss and his own devastation on learning that his beloved brother had been killed. Although he could not help but notice the ravages of grief on her lovely face, he was not accustomed to speaking with her of such things, and so said nothing until Cecily reminded him of his wish for this private conversation.

"It appears we have two options open to us now that Margaret has gone north," Edward began. "Warwick believes that we must either capitulate and leave England of our own volition or"—he watched his mother's face carefully—"do what Henry Bolingbroke did after he came back from exile: depose the king and take the crown."

Cecily did not bat an eyelash. "Then you must take the crown now, Edward. It is why your father returned from Ireland, it is why he died at Wakefield. Henry is too weak and his queen too strong. Together they are disastrous for England. With Warwick by your side, you will make England whole again. You must depose Henry. It is what your father would have wanted."

She had risen during these pronouncements, causing Edward to get to his feet in filial respect. Then he sank on one knee. "I had hoped for perhaps your reluctant support, Mother. I did not expect to have your royal command." He searched her face for any hesitation. "And what of my conscience? My immortal soul? I swore in front of God and the Parliament not to seek to hurt or diminish Henry's reign nor consent to do anything that would end his natural life. Are you telling me to break that oath?"

Cecily gave him an enigmatic smile. "I also remember the king pledging to treat any action against the duke of York as high treason. I did not see him put those men who attacked and killed your father—during a Christmas truce, no less—on trial for treason. Nay, he honors them, even knighting that traitor Andrew Trollope. An eye for an eye, Edward," Cecily said, astonished by how her heart had hardened. "Besides, you are not seeking to end Henry's life, you are seeking to end his ruinous reign. And if I may point out, my son, you never took an oath to defend the queen, and if the truth be told, 'tis she whose reign it has become, more's the pity for England."

Edward, now imbued with his mother's confidence and approbation, scrambled to his feet. "I have heard Father praise your ability to see things clearly, my lady, but I never noticed until now." He kissed her hand and walked to the door, where he paused to tell her, "It occurs to me that our loss at Wakefield was far worse than I imagined. England lost the chance to have a truly great queen."

"Oh, pish!" Cecily said and put her hand to her face to hide an unexpected blush.

Warwick lost no time in taking advantage of Edward's popularity with the Londoners. He staged a huge rally in St. John's Field outside the city, where Chancellor George Neville, Warwick's younger brother, addressed a crowd that included the lords left in London, the aldermen, and members of Parliament. After a lengthy explanation of Edward's hereditary right to the throne, he read out the points that illustrated King Henry's failure to rule justly and his broken agreement with the duke of York sworn before Parliament a few months before.

Then he shouted, "Is the king fit to rule over us?" And the answer from thousands of throats was "Nay! Nay!"

Two days later, Cecily found herself standing in the great hall at Baynard's listening while a hurriedly called great council ratified the vote of the Londoners. She noted that the lords, bishops, and gentry present were most certainly partisan, but in this time of conflict, she believed what was happening so rapidly would restore good government and peace to the realm.

Edward stood tallest among them, his leadership evident as he greeted one here with a slap on the back or attentive ear and another there with a shared jest or quick word, his smile engaging, his blue eyes sharp but merry. It was then that she knew that even though her husband had commanded the respect of those nobles in his inner circle, he had not Edward's ability to inspire enthusiasm in his followers or his astonishing common touch. How had her son grown so quickly into a man, Cecily wondered, awed. Where was I when this transformation took place? Was I so wrapped up in Edmund that I never looked closely at Ned? How the years had flown by, she mused, and how proud Richard would have been of his beloved eldest son at this moment.

She felt her throat constrict as she imagined him watching from heaven and, perhaps like her, close to tears.

The next day, a proclamation was made summoning the citizens of London to the square outside St. Paul's to witness the formal announcement of Edward's accession. Processing from Baynard's, Edward received the cheering crowds with a serious face and stately wave. He was preceded by Warwick, the orchestrator of this extraordinary event, and the Londoners greeted their favorite earl just as loudly.

In St. Paul's yard, from the steps of the high stone cross, which had been witness to many a historic event down the centuries, George Neville gave a lengthy sermon and then again demanded to know if the people accepted Edward as their king.

A rousing answer of "Yea! Yea!" left no one in doubt that there were now two kings of England.

"Edward cannot sit on the throne knowing the queen and her army are still in the north," Warwick explained to Cecily one night at the Erber, when Alice had asked that her sister-in-law be entertained. "Until Henry is beaten—or exiled—the crown will lie uneasy on Edward's head. Margaret has refused to accept the succession. She means to fight us for the crown. We must march north and confront her."

Cecily sighed but agreed. She looked across at Alice and was again sad to see how thin her dear sister-in-law was. It seemed to her that both of them had aged a decade since Wakefield. Indeed, after her reminiscences at Baynard's on that cold night in February, she had been shocked to see that the color had gone from her hair in the space, it seemed to Cecily, of a few hours.

"How long has my hair been like this, Grizzy?" she had asked Gresilde one night, as her faithful attendant gently stroked the comb through the long tresses. Gresilde had smiled and reassured the duchess that it had gradually been turning white for many months now, but Cecily was certain the older woman was just being kind.

Warwick was telling the small group in the Erber solar that Edward had put out a call to arms and they would all soon be marching north. Alice shook her head. "Then I pray Margaret will take to her heels over the border before an arrow is loosed," she said. "I do not think I can bear to lose any more dear ones."

Warwick leaned over and patted her hand. "Aye, let us hope they will take fright and flee when they hear we are bearing down on them. And now, I promised my daughter a game of merels, did I not, Isabel?" he asked a pretty, pale girl whom Cecily had hardly noticed sitting quietly on a stool near her equally unobtrusive mother, Anne Beauchamp.

"And I must return to Baynard's before dark," Cecily said, rising and going to bestow a kiss on Alice and Anne, "but before I do, Nephew, tell me when can Meg and I expect to be left alone again."

Warwick reverenced his aunt and chuckled. "I think you may enjoy Edward's company for a few more days, your grace."

AND THAT WAS all she did have, for on March the thirteenth the courtyard was once again noisy with horses, armorers, soldiers, cannons, carts full of weapons, and victuals as Edward prepared to leave. He had hoped the proclamation that had been read up and down the country earlier in the month, calling men to his banner and forbidding anyone to help Henry and his adherents, on pain of death, would shore up more support and deter treachery. He also forbade those men who rallied to his flag to rob any church or churchman, deflower any woman, or do violence to any innocent citizen.

With heavy hearts, Cecily and Meg watched him leave, and indeed Edward himself seemed preoccupied as he made last-minute adjustments to his mail and gambeson and checked his destrier's shoes and harness. He had issued his retinue with a new personal cognizance of a golden sunburst in honor of the three suns of Mortimer's Cross, and the caparison on Edward's horse was sewn all over with them.

Cecily watched as Edward lifted Meg in a brotherly hug. "Take care of our mother, little Meggie," he whispered. "Even though she must be easier now that we know of George and Dickon's safe arrival at Bruges, she does not look well."

"Then hurry home, Ned," Meg whispered back, her luminous gray eyes imploring him. "'Tis what will make her happiest. That and when she can see the boys again."

Edward set his sister down and nodded. "As soon as I put Margaret of Anjou to rout," he promised.

BUT THANKS TO her powerful followers, such as Somerset, Northumberland, and Exeter, Margaret had gathered a larger army than Warwick and Edward had anticipated. The two forces met on Palm Sunday on a snow-driven field near Towton in Yorkshire. It was the bloodiest battle ever to be fought on English soil.

Cecily collapsed in her chair when the messenger came with the news of Edward's stunning victory there. Meg sat at her feet as Cecily opened the letter he brought. It was not detailed, but she exclaimed when she saw the numbers. "Near twenty thousand slain? 'Tis pitiable! God rest their poor souls."

The snowy field and a small stream nearby had run with blood, and Edward said he had wept to see the terrible loss of English lives on both sides. "*My lord of Northumberland lost his life for Margaret on that day, as did that traitor Trollope. Later, at York, we executed Devon and Wiltshire, and for that my father is avenged. As for the rest of the Lancastrian army, it is put to flight along with Henry, Margaret, and her puling son, taking those fiends Somerset and Exeter with them. They went north to Scotland,*" he wrote, "*and may they all stay in that barbaric place until hell freezes over.*"

Cecily glanced down at Meg listening intently to the messenger, who was now eyeing the girl with more than passing interest. "Edward will be coming home ere long, Daughter," she rejoiced. "God be praised."

WHERE HAD APRIL and May gone? Cecily wondered. She was sitting on satin cushions in one of the royal barges as it glided along the Thames back to Westminster one warm late June day. She now wished she had not chosen velvet for her coronation gown. This June was turning out to be very different from last, and although she hoped the fine weather would hold for Edward's crowning and for the farmers' crops, she was perspiring uncomfortably.

After the victory of Palm Sunday, her son had remained in the north for a time and then toured other Lancastrian counties, showing himself as king. Peace had come to London, and the streets and shops were bustling again. When spring burst forth, another letter from Edward gave his mother permission to make the royal palace of Shene her own as soon as the London heat became oppressive. Cecily had hoped to return to Fotheringhay, her favorite of the York residences, but Edward was reluctant to allow her there. He had heard of the destruction Margaret of Anjou's army had wreaked in that region, and he wanted to spare his mother any more pain.

Shene had been beautiful in May, Cecily admitted, remembering the placid waters of the Thames flowing past the many-turreted palace set in the green countryside, where herons, swans, coots, and kingfishers all vied for food along the reeded banks. Otters frolicked in and out of the water, and on the other side of the river, pretty little roe came down at dusk to drink.

Cecily soon made her own wishes known for the running of the palace, and she had brightened several of the gloomier rooms by having them freshly whitewashed with lime. Margaret of Anjou had spent summer months here or at Greenwich, and her marguerite cognizance was in evidence in all the royal apartments. Cecily had to admit that the queen had good taste and so chose not to spend more money redecorating. Instead she had her seamstresses make several gray and purple gowns in cooler silk and light worsted as well as the regal cote she wore now. If she was to be in mourning, she insisted on being in fashion.

As the barge drew closer to Westminster, she thought back to that sunny June day when Edward had finally come back south. He had had a triumphant entry into London and then had joined his mother and sister at Shene for some well-deserved merrymaking. The reunion would have been joyful enough if Edward alone had returned to her, but he had brought a surprise.

"George! Dickon!" Meg had been the first to cry out upon seeing the two boys enter the great hall. Cecily could not have described the joy she felt when Dickon ran headlong into her arms.

She looked over at them both now, heads together and pointing at something on shore, and she smiled. They had changed and yet they had not changed, she decided. They had learned some pretty manners from Isabella of Burgundy, but they still fought fiercely with each other and made up again just as before.

She then found Meg seated in front of the boys in the barge with her two pretty young attendants, Jane and Ann, newly sent by Edward as a favor to their fathers. She sighed. Meg was still too outspoken, but Cecily admitted that she would rather have her clever daughter than those two ninnies any day. She settled back on the cushions, feeling happier than she had in a very long time. And in three days, Edward would be crowned king of England. How could life be better? She refused to answer that. She knew the answer in her grieving heart.

The king's barge floated just ahead of them, music and laughter wafting back. Edward was in scarlet cloth of silver, an ostrich feather waving from his bonnet. His head was thrown back in laughter. He had enough character and spirit for two men, she thought, and then winced. Aye, enough for both of her splendid eldest sons. Poor, sweet Edmund, how he would have delighted in his brother's fortune. But with his sensitive nature, perhaps he was better off with the angels, she suddenly thought, then chided herself for such a notion. It was then that she recognized the young man in the barge who had made Edward laugh so heartily. It was Jacquetta of Bedford's son, Anthony Woodville. He and his father had submitted themselves to Edward after the battle at Towton, so Meg had told her. She wondered where Jacquetta was now. She had not come to Shene with her son. Ah, well, good riddance.

It was not long before the towers of Westminster appeared, and the limed walls of the city in the distance reflected the afternoon sun as the barge was eased to the palace wharf. Edward's party had already disembarked, and Edward stood waiting to help his mother off her boat.

Lifting her with ease, he held her aloft for a moment, grinning. "God's bones, my lady, but you are as light as thistledown," he exclaimed. "We shall have to see to it that you have all the delicacies the kitchen can provide at the feast here on Sunday. We cannot have the noblest lady in the land wasting away, can we?"

Cecily would have admonished him soundly but for her preoccupation with Edward's poetic phrase, "light as thistledown." Where had she heard it before? She took his arm and walked toward the entrance to the royal lodgings, searching her memory.

"A penny for your thoughts, Mother," he said, smiling.

"'Tis naught, Edward. Someone else made the same remark about thistledown many years ago, 'tis all, and I was trying to remember who."

"Was it someone other than Father?" he whispered. "Nay, that I will not believe."

Relieved that she chuckled rather than reprimanded him, Edward bowed, making his excuses about a council meeting.

Cecily watched him stride confidently along the wharf arm in arm with Anthony Woodville. "As light as thistledown," she repeated. God's bones! Where else had she heard herself described that way? At that moment Anthony Woodville turned his head to look up at Edward, and the gesture reminded her of Jacquetta. Then she remembered. The image of another figure leaped into her head, one as tall and strong as Edward, also with gold-red hair but bearded. "John Blaybourne!" she cried aloud, making Gresilde turn on the stairs to look at her.

Certes, it was her faithful archer, and she felt guilty because she could not quite remember his face. Traipsing up the staircase, she relived her adventure to Les Andelys and riding out alone with Master Blaybourne, accompanied only by her dear Constance. And poor Piers Taggett had fired an arrow at them, believing Blaybourne had abducted her.

And then in a blinding flash she knew why Jacquetta Woodville had made the odd remark about baby Ned that day in the nursery. "He looks like a Norseman," the woman had said. Dear God! She suspects Ned is Blaybourne's son. Cecily frowned. Surely no one had ever really questioned that Ned was Richard's. Richard had been with her at Rouen a little later in August, she recalled, dismissing the tiny knot of worry in the pit of her stomach, and she could have conceived then and had Edward a little early. Nay, if there had been a rumor, it would have surfaced long before now, she reassured herself, relieved and amused. Cecily was sure Jacquetta would have relished the chance to spread a rumor if she thought she could get away with it, but she had not.

"You are beautiful, my lady," Meg said shyly, watching her mother in violet silk circle her, making sure that every fold of the blue cloth of silver gown was in place, her headdress was straight, the gauze prettily cascading down her back, and every wayward hair plucked from her fashionably high forehead. Meg's attendants stood respectfully at a distance, holding their collective breath, knowing the duchess of York was fastidious when it came to dress.

Cecily smiled her thanks at her daughter in the polished silver mirror and then frowned. "Too many rings, Margaret," she murmured, and removed a large one from quite a collection on her daughter's fingers. "You must learn the value of quality over quantity, my dear."

"How long will the coronation service be?" Meg asked eagerly. "I have been too excited to eat anything today, but perhaps I should, even though we have swans, pheasants, peacocks, subtleties, and marchpane to look forward to."

Cecily clucked her tongue. "Do be sensible, Meg. Certes, you must eat something. We cannot have one of the royal princesses swooning in the abbey. Mistress Herbert, send for some bread, cheese, and ale for your mistress. And when you have eaten, Meg, come and join me in my solar before we walk over to St. Peter's. Thanks be to the Virgin for the glorious day outside. At least we shall not all look like drowned dogs when we enter the abbey."

The female members of Edward's family were to be seated on one side of the choir with the other noblewomen present. Cecily led the way down the nave of the magnificent abbey church at Westminster, with the bishop of

London in front setting the pace. The ladies, clothed in colorful velvets, silks, and satins that shimmered in the glow of hundreds of candles, swayed slowly from side to side in a rhythmic walk to the organ's plangent notes. Hundreds of the lesser nobility, the gentry, and city officials were crammed into the nave cheek by jowl, craning their necks to glimpse the glittering procession in the nave.

Cecily's long train was carried by two very different Margarets: her own fifteen-year-old daughter held up one corner and towered over the only child and heiress of Richard's erstwhile enemy John Beaufort, first duke of Somerset, who held up the other corner. Eighteen-year-old Margaret Beaufort's small, thin frame and long, pained face paled in comparison to Meg's stature and fresh, young beauty. Cecily had felt sorry for the girl when, at only thirteen, she had become pregnant by Henry's half brother Edmund Tudor. The difficult birth of her son not long after she was widowed had almost killed mother and child, and tongues had wagged about Tudor's unconcern for the girl's youth when he had consummated their marriage.

"Despite her Beaufort blood, she is as royal as we are, Mother," Edward had told Cecily upon informing her of the honor he was giving the two young women. "I pray you will be kind to her, for she has done us no harm." And Cecily had acquiesced, unable to resist her son's most entreating smile.

They were now through the intricately carved rood screen, which separated the nave from the choir and chancel and would block the view of the coronation chair to all but an elite few. Cecily found her seat and took pleasure in her surroundings. The soaring arches above her were painted in gold leaf, as were the turrets of the choir stalls behind her. Despite the golds, greens, blues, and reds of the motifs that decorated the stone columns, the dark wood of the choir misericords, and the many colorful banners that hung overhead, there was airiness and light in the magnificent church. Cecily's heart was full of awe for the palpable presence of God all around her and full of wonder at the spirits of those who had worshipped there for hundreds of years before her.

She felt the skin on her arms prickle as the organ crescendoed in a thunderous roar and the choir in the balcony above the great west door sang out an introit. Edward must be approaching, she thought, taking a deep breath and feeling her heart swell with pride. She glanced to her left at her daughters, whispering among themselves, and delighted in them: Nan, her smile brighter now that she was formally estranged from Exeter and accepted under Edward's roof; dear down-to-earth Bess, whose neighing laugh would always remind her of Richard, and who had sadly miscarried in March; and her clever Meggie, who was in need of a husband, if what she had heard about the girl's flirtation with that handsome young herald was true. She was showing signs of being as interested in the opposite sex as her eldest brother was, Cecily sighed.

The lords were now filing through the arch in the rood screen, and she watched as the opposite choir stalls filled with faithful, familiar faces from the past: Richard's brother-in-law, Lord Bourchier; her sister Katherine's son, John of Norfolk; Bess's young husband, John de la Pole, whom Edward had promised to restore as duke of Suffolk; her brother, William, Lord Faucon-berg; and others who bowed their heads in greeting when she caught an eye.

Conspicuously absent, but for reasons known only to him, was her nephew, Richard Neville, earl of Warwick. Alice had said he had chosen to remain in the north to shore up support there for Edward with his brother John, the hero of Carlisle. But Cecily suspected that it was because a small rift had begun to appear in the bond between the two popular cousins, despite Edward's protestations to the contrary. As much as she respected the earl, Cecily was happy that he had left Edward sole recipient of the Londoners' adulation.

She turned her attention from thoughts of Warwick to her own two boys, Dickon and George, now seated across from her and well aware they were being watched. She thought how small they seemed in this vast abbey, despite their noble robes of blue and silver depicting them as new members of the Order of the Bath. What will become of them? she wondered, as she heard the cheering crowds outside the abbey welcoming Edward into the vestry. Edward had given George the dukedom of Clarence, one of the many titles he had awarded to faithful Yorkists in honor of his coronation. Today George was at his sunniest as he grinned across the aisle at Meg, but he would need to curb his temper and his moods before he would be half the man Edward was, Cecily admitted. George had a winning way with him, but she knew how quickly that charm could sour.

Then her gaze fell upon her youngest child, earnestly perusing the pages of a prayer book, and as he felt her watching him, Dickon raised his head and smiled. Cecily's heart turned over. Richard! she wanted to cry out. Those same gray eyes crinkled just like his father's, and his jutting chin and inclination of the head almost made her believe she was seeing Richard all those years ago at Raby. Even though he was perhaps harder to warm to than his brothers, Cecily knew that beneath his quiet facade, Dickon's heart was true and his loyalty unflagging. Richard had taught him well, she thought, as she turned her ruby betrothal ring, taking comfort from its familiarity.

Ah, Richard, was your sacrifice worth it? she asked herself again.

The organ swelled again to accompany Edward down the nave, and, when he appeared from the rood screen, as one the whole of the assembly in the chancel went down on their knees. Hers and Richard's magnificent son! King Edward the Fourth of England. It was hard to believe.

And then he was walking slowly by Cecily, godlike in his purple velvet mantle heavily trimmed with ermine, his face solemn in keeping with the occasion. She glanced up at him and was horrified to see him wink at her. She crossed herself hurriedly. I must have dreamed it, she thought, watching him climb the few steps to the dais on which stood King Edward the Confessor's ancient chair.

The ceremony began with a blessing by Thomas Bourchier, archbishop of Canterbury, and for an hour the congregation remained on its knees. Edward was stripped to the waist and anointed with oil, his broad, muscular back revealing several freshly healed scars from his recent battles. Cecily winced, remembering a few upon Richard's body that she had soothed with salves when they were in Normandy. A sudden twinge of guilt assailed her as she thought of the thousands of lives that had been lost over the years for this day, but she was too intoxicated by the moment to contemplate whether their sacrifice had been too great.

Then it was time to reclothe God's anointed in a robe of cloth of gold and for him to sit upon the great gilded throne to receive the trappings of kingship. First the heavy orb was placed into Edward's right hand. Next the archbishop picked up the silver scepter and the rod from the altar, blessed them, and returned to Edward. "Receive the royal scepter, the ensign of kingly power and justice," he intoned. "Receive the rod of equity and mercy."

The archbishop of York took the jeweled crown on a cushion to Canterbury, who lifted it high to the crucifix upon the altar. "Bless we beseech thee this crown and so sanctify thy servant, Edward, upon whose head this day it will visit as a sign of royal majesty." He turned and again stood before Edward, the crown raised aloft for all to see.

How did we get to this place, Richard? Cecily thought, unabashed tears of joy coursing down her cheeks. If you are watching today, my love, I ask that you send your blessing down upon the head of your son as he is crowned, for there can be no doubt that but for a cruel turn on the wheel of fortune, it would have been you in that chair today. She watched, entranced, as Archbishop Bourchier slowly lowered the golden crown upon Edward's head and cried in a loud voice: "God Save the King!"

At once every man, woman, and child in the abbey and likewise those in the streets outside took up the cry: "God Save the King! God Save King Edward!"

As Edward rose and turned to greet his subjects, Cecily was suddenly reminded of Jeanne d'Arc's long-ago prediction in the cell at Rouen: Cecily of York, you will be the mother of kings, the martyr had told her.

And so I am, she thought, transfixed. Praise be to God.

Author's Note

As a writer passionate about history, I revel in researching the facts, but as a novelist I relish the license to invent when the dramatic possibility is irresistible. And in that spirit, I must come clean about a few of those possibilities that I could not pass up.

The first is Cecily's pregnancy and subsequent miscarriage in Rouen. Why Cecily and Richard did not produce their first living child until 1439, when Cecily was twenty-four, has puzzled historians. We know Cecily and Richard were betrothed in 1424, when they were nine and thirteen respectively. There was nothing to stop them solemnizing a marriage when Cecily reached the legal age of twelve, and there is no reason to suppose they did not marry close to that time, especially as we know that Richard and Cecily were in Countess Joan's household in London in 1428 and that, according to the *Calendar of Papal Registers,* Richard received an indulgence in 1428: "for the duke of York *and his duchess* a portable altar and to choose a confessor . . ." (my italics). So then, why the long wait before starting a family? Once they started, they produced thirteen and possibly fourteen children, so Cecily was certainly not barren. But in most history books you will see 1438 as the date of their marriage, with Anne appearing in 1439. I say "rubbish" to the later date. I had good reason to conjecture that Cecily had miscarried at some point, and I chose for it to happen in Rouen for my story. Thanks to an obstetrician friend, I learned that the damage to the womb might take a long time to heal and resist impregnation following a miscarriage that was the result of a traumatic injury after the first trimester—such as falling from a wobbly scaffold face first onto cobblestones. Further, we know that Richard was absent on many occasions in those seven years and for long periods, which would put a spanner in the works for would-be parents.

I also discovered a couple of genealogy charts that mentioned a Joan as being the Yorks' first child, but she is missing from many of the better-known charts, probably because she died and was buried before proper registration. I chose to include her as she gave me an excuse for shortening the length of time between the miscarriage and the next pregnancy. Also, it was usual to name a daughter for a grandmother, and as Cecily was with her mother for so long, it stands to reason one of Cecily's daughters should have been named Joan.

Little Henry, having been born in February, died at some point before Richard and Cecily arrived in Normandy in 1441. P. A. Johnson (one of Richard's biographers) suggested that perhaps Richard dallied so long before setting sail because of the death of their first son. Richard cited "personal" reasons to the council for the delay. I have no idea where or when Henry died, and so I chose Dorking in Surrey because that is where my family lived when I was growing up. I have taken many walks in the bluebell woods around Box Hill, and writing about it brought back fond memories.

Next I will confess that there is no evidence Cecily and Jeanne d'Arc ever met. However, as I describe, Cecily was in Rouen at the time and was in the same castle where Jeanne was imprisoned. I just could not resist having young, impressionable Cecily be fascinated by this astonishing young woman and find a way to speak to Jeanne. I hope you agree the scene is powerful. What staggered me when I began to research Jeanne's trial is the amount of transcription that still exists. It took me a whole day to read it all. All my descriptions about Jeanne's time at Rouen are accurate except for her meeting with Cecily. I have to confess that as a loyal Englishwoman, I have always looked on Jeanne as a ninny and a nuisance for my countrymen, but by the time I had finished the research and writing of those scenes, I was as convinced as Cecily that she was telling the truth about the voices in her head.

Another dramatic moment that I first learned of from Paul Murray Kendall in his *Richard III*, was the scene with Cecily all alone at the Ludlow market cross with her two little sons. I believe Professor Kendall took license with that scene, but it is not at all implausible, because Cecily was indeed left at Ludlow with her three youngest when Richard fled in the night, and the castle was sacked along with the town. But whether or not she took the walk to the market cross is subject to debate. Again, it was too powerful an image not to include in a novel, and I am convinced the Cecily I got to know over eighteen months of research and writing would have had the courage to do something like that!

I have left the most important of the "did it or did it not happen" instances to last. The rumor that Edward was not Richard's son but the offspring of an archer named Blaybourne or Blackburn in Normandy came back to haunt the York family twice in the twenty-five years following Edward's crowning. The first time was in 1476, when Cecily's son, George, was finally imprisoned by Edward for conspiring to take the crown one too many times, and he put it about that Edward was a bastard and shouldn't be king. Then, in 1483, when Edward died suddenly and his twelve-year-old son was proclaimed king, two counts of bastardy were cited upon the poor boy by the preacher Dr. Shaw, who was defending the right of Richard III (Dickon) to be crowned instead. Shaw told the crowds gathered at Paul's Cross that not only was Edward already married when he had wed his queen, Elizabeth Woodville, but that Edward himself was Cecily's bastard by an archer of Rouen. Ann Wroe in her excellent book *Perkin* or *The Perfect Prince* says: "This seemed preposterous, but George, duke of Clarence, Edward's wayward brother, was also said to have put such a story about; and Charles the Bold of Burgundy (Meg's future husband)* . . . often called Edward *'Blaybourne,'* in fits of rage, long before Dr. Shaw preached his sermon."

And most interesting of all, Cecily herself was said to have flown "into such a frenzy," when she heard of the marriage between her son and Elizabeth Woodville in 1464 "that she offered to submit to a public inquiry, and asserted that Edward was not the offspring of her husband the duke of York, but was conceived in adultery, and therefore in no wise worthy of the honour of kingship." However, these lines are attributed to a visiting Italian in 1483 named Dominic Mancini, who we think was a spy for King Louis of France. He was certainly not hobnobbing with royalty, so could not have heard this from Cecily or her son, Dickon (Richard III), who was about to take the throne. Conjecture has it that his informant was Dr. Argentine, a court physician who had cared for Edward's young sons but who became a trusted servant at Henry Tudor's court. So although the rumor exists, I chose to take it with a large pinch of salt; the Cecily I came to know would have disdained such an affair with an archer, no matter how attractive.

However, Cecily did show her contempt for Elizabeth Woodville by insisting on being styled Cecily, the king's mother, and late wife unto Richard, in right king of England and of France and lord of Ireland. In other words: queen by right.

Jacquetta Woodville was a fascinating character, said to have been involved in magic and witchcraft. She has been accused of using love potions on the young King Edward to help him fall in love with her beautiful widowed daughter Elizabeth. I don't think Edward needed potions; he was a

---

* My parenthesis.

strong-minded young man who loved the opposite sex, and the idea of a secret marriage between him and Elizabeth is perfectly plausible, especially when the story was revealed after his death that he may have been secretly married to another woman before Elizabeth. Jacquetta and Cecily were certainly together in Rouen, and I could not resist the delicious irony of creating friction between these two beautiful and strong-willed women who would one day be in-laws.

I love it when I find out details that can add to the authenticity of my books. England really did have a terrible summer in 1460, with floods, washed-out bridges and ruined crops causing great hardship for the people. "Forsooth and forsooth" and "by St. John" were Henry VI's favorite oaths; and the extant letters between Richard and his teenage sons at Ludlow meant that I had to mention them. It showed me that, in the midst of all the political upheaval, Richard still took the time to parent. I also used actual wording of other letters in some instances, as well as the oath Henry and Richard swore in front of Parliament at Westminster in October 1460.

Cecily of York chose to disappear from public life not long after Edward's disastrous—according to his mother—marriage to Elizabeth, Jacquetta's beautiful daughter, preferring to lead a life of quiet piety with her ladies at her palace of Berkhampsted. She was present, however, at some great occasions during Edward's reign, including a dinner in 1480 given in Meg's honor when she, as duchess of Burgundy, returned to England for the first time following her marriage to Charles the Bold in 1468. Cecily also pleaded with Edward to spare her charming but perfidious son George's life in 1477, to no avail, although it is thought it was Cecily who persuaded Edward to allow George to be executed quietly in his prison cell. She was not there when her youngest son, Dickon, was crowned in 1483 as Richard III, but contrary to some conjecture that she refused to attend because of the slanderous statements of Dr. Shaw, she and Richard exchanged some warm correspondence when he was king, and he visited her to ask her advice on at least one occasion.

Cecily of York lived just past her eightieth birthday to May 31, 1495, long enough to see Jeanne's (fictitious) prediction come true in another generation: her granddaughter, Edward's eldest child Elizabeth of York, married Henry VII, the first Tudor king, and was thus crowned queen of England. Their son was Henry VIII, and his daughter another Queen Elizabeth, and so on down to our own Queen Elizabeth today. Cecily Neville, duchess of York, was the ancestor of them all. Only Meg and Bess outlived their mother, and not by much. Her daughter Anne died in childbirth in 1474, after remarriage to one Thomas St. Leger, a gentleman of no particular distinction except perhaps that Anne finally found love with him. Ned died at 41 and Dickon was killed at age 32 at the Battle of Bosworth on August 22, 1485.

No one has ever questioned the love match that Richard's and Cecily's arranged marriage turned out to be; it was a rare feat in the lives of the nobility in medieval times. It has been my privilege and pleasure to tell their story.

Anne Easter Smith
Newburyport, 2010

Below is a selection of the sources I used in researching *Queen by Right.*

Books

Crawford, Anne. *The Yorkists.* London: Hambledon Continuum, 2007.

Curtis, Edmund. *A History of Medieval Ireland.* London: Methuen & Co. Ltd., 1923.

Gilbert, J. T. *History of the Viceroys of Ireland.* Dublin: James Duffer, 1865.

Green, V. H. H. *The Later Plantagenets.* London: Edward Arnold Ltd., 1955.

Griffiths, Ralph. *Reign of Henry VI.* Berkeley: University of California Press, 1981.

Johnson, P. A. *Richard, Duke of York.* Oxford: Clarendon Press, 1988.

Kendall, Paul Murray. *Richard III.* London: George Allen & Unwin, 1955.

———. *Warwick the Kingmaker.* London: George Allen & Unwin, 1957.

Lowell, Francis Cabot. *Joan of Arc.* New York: Houghton, Mifflin and Co., 1896.

Maurer, Helen. *Margaret of Anjou.* Woodbridge, Suffolk: The Boydell Press, 2003.

Mortimer, Ian. *Time Traveller's Guide to Medieval England.* London: The Bodley Head, 2008.

Norris, Herbert. *Medieval Costume and Fashion.* London: J. M. Dent & Sons Ltd., 1927.

Otway-Ruthven, A. J. *A History of Medieval Ireland.* London: Ernest Benn Ltd., 1968.

Oxford Dictionary of National Biography. London: Oxford University Press.

Ross, Charles. *Edward IV.* London: Methuen, Ltd., 1983.

Scofield, Cora L. *The Life and Reign of Edward IV* (2 vols.). London: Frank Cass & Co. Ltd., 1967.

Shoesmith, Ron, and Andy Johnson. *Ludlow Castle: Its History & Buildings.* Almeley, England: Logaston Press, 2006.

Warkworth, John. *The Chronicles of the White Rose of York.* J. A. Giles, ed. London: James Bohn, 1843.

Articles

Davis, Marion. "Sheep, Cattle and Sword; Some Thoughts About Richard, Duke of York, 1411–1460." *Ricardian Register,* Journal of Richard III Society, American Branch XXXVI, no. 4 (winter 2006).

Griffiths, Ralph. "Richard of York and the Royal Household in Wales 1449–1450." *Welsh History Review* VIII (1976).

Hardcastle, M. S. "The Rose of Raby." *The Monthly Chronicle of North Country Lore and Legend* (January 1890).

Noble, Mark. "Some Observations upon the Life of Cecily, Duchess of York." *Archaeologia* 13, 2nd edition (1807).

Postlethwaite, Ian. "Richard, Third Duke of York." *The Journal of the Yorkshire Branch of the Richard III Society,* Leeds (1974).

Rawcliffe, Carole. "Richard, Duke of York, the King's 'Obeisant Liegeman.'" *The Bulletin of the Institute of Historical Research* 60, no. 142 (June 1987).

Glossary

acton—quilted jacket worn under chainmail.

arras—tapestry or wall hanging.

attainted—imputed with dishonor or treason. Estates of attainted lords are often forfeited to the crown.

aumbrey—cupboard.

avise—to look closely, to study a person.

bailey—outer wall of a castle.

baldachin—a canopy over a throne or held over processing royalty.

bascinet—a helmet.

basse danse—slow, stately dance.

braies—medieval men's underwear, which were not unlike the loin cloths worn in India today. Short ones of fine lawn were worn under hose, and longer, heavier ones were worn by peasants as breeches.

butt—barrel for wine.

butts—archery targets.

caravel—medieval sailing ship.

carol—medieval circle dance.

caul—mesh hair covering, often jeweled or decorated, encasing braids wound on either side of the head.

chaperon—a felt hat.

chausses—tight leggings of mail.

churching—first communion given to a woman following the period of seclusion after giving birth.

claymore—Scottish broadsword.

cog—medieval ship used for transporting soldiers or horses.

cognizance—a badge of a noble house.

coif—scarf tied around the head.

conduit—drinking fountain in a town or city with piped-in water.

cote or *cotehardie*—long gown worn by men and women.

crenellation—indentation at top of battlement wall.

donjon—keep or main tower of a castle.

ewerer—water pourer and holder of hand-washing bowls at table.

exedra—low, grass-covered wall that could be used as a seat in a garden.

fetterlock—a padlock for a shackle; a heraldic device.

fewterer—hunting-dog handler.

flampayne—an egg pie with meat, like a quiche.

fox and geese—medieval board game.

frumenty—soupy mixture of hulled wheat in boiled milk with sugar and spices.

galingale—aromatic root of the ginger family.

garderobe—inside privy where clothes were often stored.

gemshorn—musical instrument of polished, hollowed goat's horn.

gipon—close-fitting padded tunic.

gittern—plucked, gut-stringed instrument similar to a guitar.

gong farmer—man who removes waste from privies and carts it outside city.

groat—silver coin worth about fourpence.

grosgrain—ribbed worsted wool often mixed with silk.

hanap—wine cup.

heir apparent—the next in line to the throne, today often called the crown prince.

heir presumptive—the next in line to the throne in the absence of an immediate heir, but who could be bumped by events.

hennin—tall conical headdress from which hangs a veil. Steepled hennins were as much as two feet high; butterfly hennins sat on the head like wings with the veil draped over a wire frame.

hippocras—a honeyed wine.

hobby horse—fast, light breed of Irish horses said to be the ancestor of Irish racehorses today.

houppelande—full-length or knee-length tunic or gown with full sleeves and train.

jennet—saddle horse often used by women.

jupon—see *gipon*.

kersey—coarse woollen cloth.

kirtle—woman's gown or outer petticoat.

lanner—falcon.

malmsey—kind of wine.

marshalsea—stables of a castle, overseen by the marshal.

meinie—group of attendants on a lord.

merels—game similar to tic-tac-toe.

mess—platter of food shared by a group of people.

motte—artificial mound on which to build the keep of a castle.

murrey—heraldic term for purple-red (plum).

oyer and terminer—commission to act as a circuit judge in the king's name.

The Pale—an area roughly 20 by 30 miles with Dublin at its center controlled by the Anglo-Irish.

palfrey—small saddle horse.

patten—wooden platform strapped to the sole of a shoe.

pavane—slow stately dance.

pibcorn—hornpipe.

pillion—pad placed at the back of a saddle for a second rider.

pinnace—small ship used for communicating between larger vessels.

pipkin—earthenware or metal pot.

plastron—gauzy material tucked for modesty into the bodice of a gown.

points—lacing with silver tips used to attach hose to undershirt or gipon.

poppet—doll.

psaltery—stringed instrument like a dulcimer plucked with a feather.

puling—whining, crying in a high, weak voice.

rebec—three-stringed instrument played with a bow.

rouncy—pack horse used by travelers or men-at-arms.

sackbut—early form of trombone.

saltire—diagonal cross on a coat of arms.

sanctuary—place of protection for fugitives; safe haven (perhaps in an abbey), usually for noblewomen and their children, who pay to stay.

sarcenet—fine, soft silk fabric.

scarlet—high-quality broadcloth usually dyed red with expensive kermes, dried bodies of an insect found on the Kermes oak.

seneschal—steward of a large household.

sennight—a week (seven nights).

settle—high-backed sofa.

shawm—wind instrument that makes a loud, penetrating sound, and was often used on castle battlements.

shout—sailing barge carrying grain, building stone, and timbers common on the Thames.

solar—living room often doubling as a bedroom.

sparviter's pie—two or three partridges, surrounded by a ring of quails, surrounded by a ring of larks cooked in wine sauce (verjuice) in a rough pastry case. A Yorkshire delicacy.

squint—small window in the wall between a room and a chapel. Often women would participate in a service through it.

staple town—center of trade in a specified commodity (e.g., Calais for wool).

stews—brothel district.

stewpond—private pond stocked with fish for household use.

subtlety—dessert made of hard, spun colored sugar formed into objects or scenes.

surcote—loose outer garment of rich material, often worn over armor.

suzerain—feudal overlord.

tabard—short tunic with high-yoked neck, sometimes belted or pleated, and open-sided. A simplified version was often worn over chain mail bearing the coat of arms of a knight.

tabbied—moiré effect on grosgrain taffeta.

tabor—small drum.

tiring woman—noblewoman's dresser or "attirer."

trencher—stale bread used as a plate.

tun—barrel.

tussie-mussie—aromatic pomander.

verjuice—sour fruit juice used for cooking and medicines.

viol—stringed instrument that is the ancestor of the viola da gamba.

voide—final course of a feast, usually hippocras wine and wafers or comfits.

waits—bands of musicians singing and playing instruments in the streets.

worsted—spun from long fleece, a smooth, lightweight wool for summer.

Queen By Right

Anne Easter Smith

Introduction

The Hundred Years War between England and France is still raging when Cecily Neville is born at Raby Castle. Dubbed "the Rose of Raby," Cecily is the twenty-second and youngest child of Ralph Neville, the powerful earl of Westmorland, and also cousin to the King Henry VI. Cecily's fate becomes entwined with the king's when she is betrothed to Richard Plantagenet, the orphaned duke of York, whose claim to the throne is arguably stronger than young Henry's.

Cecily's arranged marriage to Richard develops into a true love match and one of history's greatest love stories. Their growing family lives abroad for many years, as Richard is posted to the English-controlled regions of France and Ireland by Henry's councillors, who fear Richard's proximity to the throne. When King Henry VI becomes unfit to rule due to mental illness, "Proud Cis" must help Richard balance his political ambitions with what is right for their family and the kingdom.

As civil war escalates between the cousins of Lancaster and York, Cecily will suffer the greatest of losses. But in the end, she will witness her oldest son assume his father's place at the head of a victorious army and be crowned King Edward IV.

Topics and Questions for Discussion

1. How would you characterize the initial relationship that develops between Richard Plantagenet and Cecily Neville when Dickon joins the Neville family as a young ward? Why is their betrothal considered a great match for Cecily? How does their formal betrothal ceremony alter the dynamics of their relationship?

2. On a ride through the woods when she is eight, Cecily surprises a white deer and interprets its appearance as a holy sign. Later, at her father's death, she witnesses a white dove, and believes it to be a symbol that her father will be accepted into Heaven. How would you describe the trajectory of Cecily's faith over the course of her life? How does her faith guide her decisions?

3. How does his father's execution during Richard's childhood create a kind of social "guilt by association" that Richard must strive to overcome? How does Richard's behavior at Court bear evidence of his wish to compensate for his family's scandalous past?

4. Given her own station as the noble daughter of an esteemed English family, and the wife of the powerful and well-connected duke of York, why does Cecily Neville feel a special kinship with Jeanne d'Arc, a young French peasant? What aspects of Jeanne's life might Cecily especially admire or envy? How does their encounter in Jeanne's cell change Cecily's life forever?

5. In the scenes involving Jeanne d'Arc, Cecily undergoes moments of intense spiritual awareness, in which she witnesses what she believes is the physical presence of the Holy Spirit. Have you ever felt a similar awareness of a divine presence or spirit? How were those experiences transformative for you? If you've never felt anything of the sort, can you imagine why such an experience might change someone's life and way of thinking? Why or why not?

6. How does the author's strategic use of flashbacks in the novel's narrative enable you as a reader to see Cecily's life through her own memories? Of

the many parts of her life that Cecily's reminiscences reveal, which ones were most powerful or memorable for you, and why? Consider Cecily's childhood, her relationship with her husband, and the births and deaths of her many children.

7. Cecily is surrounded by women who help her navigate her life—her mother, Joan, who informs her morality; her sister-in-law, Alice Montagu, who explains carnal matters with forthrightness; her attendants, Rowena and Gresilde, who take care of all of her daily needs; and her personal physician, Constance LeMaitre, who helps deliver her children and serves as her confidante. What do these relationships reveal about the sphere inhabited by women in this era? Of the many connections Cecily has with women, which seem to influence her most profoundly?

8. How would you describe Cecily's feelings about motherhood? How do the many children she loses in infancy affect her feelings toward her surviving children? How would you characterize her role in her children's development, and how does it compare to her husband's influence?

9. How does Henry VI's mental instability contribute to volatility in the English kingdom and Europe at large? How is the fragility of his mental state foreshadowed in *Queen by Right*? Why does the pregnant Margaret of Anjou, Henry's French-born queen, see Richard's efforts to serve as Regent during Henry's illness as a threat to her child's future? To what extent are Margaret's fears warranted?

10. How does Cecily actively subvert the following advice from her mother: "I suppose you will learn the hard way that women will never be a man's equal in this world. We may lend an ear, we may even counsel our husbands when asked, but we are a man's property from one end of our lives to the other." To what extent does her role in her husband's decision making suggest that her power in their marriage is far greater than meets the eye?

11. What does Cecily's behavior in departing from her embattled castle in Ludlow reveal about her true nature? Why does Henry VI show mercy in sparing her and her young children from execution? Given her frustration with her husband for his absences during other difficult moments in their

life together, were you surprised that Cecily did not bear any resentment toward Richard for putting her in such a dreadful position?

12. How does Richard of York's intense military campaign against Henry VI enable Edward's political rise and eventual crowning as King Edward IV? What does Edward's public reception as a hero and sovereign reveal about the English people's attitudes toward Henry VI? How does Edward's ascent to the English throne impact Cecily Neville personally?

13. If you could relive any periods of Cecily's life, which would you choose to revisit and why? How does Cecily Neville compare to other heroines and historic figures you have encountered in literature?

Enhance Your Book Club

1. To learn more about Anne Easter Smith visit her official website at http://www.anneeastersmith.com/. Be sure to watch the Book TV video segment about Anne's walks through England and about how she keeps historical dates straight while writing. If you're on Facebook, you might also want to visit Anne's Fanpage and share your thoughts about *Queen by Right* at Facebook.com/AnneEasterSmith.

2. In Cecily's life a series of women guide her development from a young and outspoken daughter to the esteemed mother of the English king—first her mother, Joan of Westmorland, then her attendants, Rowena and Gresilde, then her personal physician, Constance LeMaitre. Discuss with your book club the women in your life who have shaped you and helped make you the person you are. What qualities do you recognize in yourself that you feel have been molded by these women? What are the qualities in them you most hope to emulate?

3. Turn your next book club meeting into a movie night! Try watching *Henry VI* with Peter Benson or *Joan of Arc* with Ingrid Bergman, or one of the newer Joan movies, for a full immersion in the world of fifteenth-century England and English Normandy. Discuss how the movie versions compare or contrast to your reading of *Queen by Right*.

A Conversation with Anne Easter Smith

In *Daughter of York*, you explored the life of Margaret of York. At what point in your research for that novel did you realize you might be interested in writing a longer work of fiction about Margaret's mother, Cecily Neville?

I have been intrigued by Cecily Neville since enjoying Sharon Kay Penman's *Sunne in Splendour* almost twenty years ago. She never appeared in my first book, *A Rose for the Crown*, but you could almost imagine her imposing presence every time I mentioned her! Some of my favorite scenes in *Daughter of York* were between Margaret and her mother, and I chose to revisit the beginning scene in *Daughter* in the prologue of *Queen by Right*.

How do historians depict Cecily Neville, and to what extent does your portrait of her agree or disagree with their assessments?

Believe it or not, there is very little written about Cecily that is not incorporated in biographies of the men of the period, but most of those portray her as proud, intelligent, and strong-willed. She was known for her reclusiveness and piety in the last twenty years of her life, and so I have tried to imagine what caused her to shut herself away. True, it was quite common for widows to retire to an abbey (like Elizabeth Woodville), but I chose to use a few life-changing experiences of Cecily's that might have made her turn to God later in her life. I hope I have been true to the information we have about her.

The martyrdom of Joan of Arc, the Maid of Orléans, plays an important part in *Queen by Right*. How did her death at the hands of the English impact Anglo-French relations?

Joan's death probably impacted the English morale most and not English-French relations. In the end, it was what Joan did *before* her death that impacted the relations, especially the crowning of the Dauphin Charles, which coalesced the many French factions under one leader and enabled them to chase the English from France once and for all. It's amusing that today, when a Frenchman and an Englishman argue about who was top dog in their respective conflicts over the centuries, the argument usually comes to an end when the Frenchman accuses the Englishman of burning Joan of Arc. Neither has forgotten that heinous act.

How does Margaret of Anjou's marriage to Henry VI complicate the political future of Richard Plantagenet, duke of York?

The birth of Henry's heir, Edward of Lancaster, was certainly a setback for Richard! As you have read, poor Henry was not a good king—although he was probably a good man—and his bouts of madness might have led to Richard becoming king, but once Margaret had a son to champion, her determination to destroy Richard became an obsession.

How do historians explain Henry VI's state of mental incapacity and his dramatic recovery? Are these episodes attributable to any known malady?

It is believed Henry may have suffered from catatonic schizophrenia or a depressive stupor brought about by a sudden fright (such as the loss of France), which causes the victim to fall into a catatonic trance. His French grandfather also had bouts of madness.

In *Queen by Right*, Cecily Neville's faith sustains her through some of the more difficult periods of her life. What led you to focus on the spiritual dimensions of her character?

I try and stay true to those known facts about a character, and it is known Cecily was quite pious, especially later in life. However, it is fair to say most medieval people of any learning did a lot of praying and were always concerned for their immortal souls. A man might commit murder or order a murder one moment but be at the confessional the next telling his rosary. Religious ritual was a daily part of everyone's life. Because it is a known fact about Cecily, I used the spiritual side of her life as a theme in the book.

Can you describe the kinds of research you do in preparing to write a novel of historical fiction set several hundred years in the past?

Would you like the long or the short answer? Seriously, I never stop researching whether by reading anything I can get my hands on about my period or by visiting and photographing all the locations I write about. For my fifth book, I spent a week in London walking those locations my protagonist would have known, scouring the fifteenth-century chronicles I found at the London Library, and immersing myself in the workings of the medieval guilds. Research is fun, but it is oh-so time consuming!

Is there any historical explanation for the feud you depict between Cecily Neville and Jacquetta Woodville? Why might Cecily Neville find a figure like Jacquetta Woodville less than trustworthy?

You have found me out! There is no evidence for the feud between these two fascinating characters except for the fact we know Cecily strongly disapproved of Edward's marriage to Jacquetta's daughter, Elizabeth (which happens after *Queen by Right* ends). Once I knew that Jacquetta and Cecily were in Rouen at the same time, and that the community of ex-pats would be small, I was certain these two very beautiful and clever women might be in competition and so I grew the rivalry from there.

To what extent is Cecily Neville's betrothal to Richard Plantagenet at age eight atypical of marriage arrangements in that era?

It was not at all atypical among the nobility. In fact, Cecily and Richard were unusual in that they had not betrothed their sons by the time Richard was killed at Wakefield. I think the youngest wedding celebrations I know about were between Richard's grandson and namesake, Richard, also duke of York, and Anne Mowbray, heiress to the Mowbray dukes of Norfolk in 1478. He was four and she was six!

In the course of your research, did you discover where the nicknames "Rose of Raby" and "Proud Cis" originate? How did these monikers enable you to fill in some of the blanks where Cecily Neville's character and person were concerned?

To be honest, I never did find the origin of these nicknames, but they are everywhere in the secondary sources down the centuries. It told me that Cecily must have been very beautiful, and it also told me she was not someone who suffered fools gladly. I have tried to portray her as someone who publicly maintained a cool and aloof exterior, yet had a softer, passionate side when she was with her family.

Why did you decide to tell Cecily's story largely through flashbacks? What advantages did that narrative technique afford you as a novelist?

I would not say the narrative reads as one long flashback. I liked using the "frames," as I call them, to have Cecily reminisce after Richard's death on some years and historical events that did not need to be part of the story. I used them to move the years along. But the story part of the book is chronological and moves forward.

How common was it for noblewomen like Cecily Neville to be attended by personal physicians as part of their retinue?

Fairly common among the royalty. Most noble households would have had a physician, but maybe not all would have one for the husband and one for the wife. Constance is Cecily's foil, and because Cecily was the only girl left at home and then is stuck with her mum for so long, I felt she needed a woman who would be an intellectual equal and more of her own age. I wanted to show that there were women physicians at that time, although they were highly mistrusted by men.

In *Queen by Right*, you characterize Richard and Cecily's relationship as a genuine love match. Is there anything you uncovered in the historical records—other than the existence of their many children—to suggest that they were in fact deeply in love?

No, unfortunately the personal feelings of most of historical people from that time are not recorded anywhere, except in letters. And even those are stilted and formal to our modern ears. However, the fact that Cecily did insist on following Richard around so much instead of staying meekly at home with the children told me that they enjoyed being together. I also thought it was unusual for a wife to plead for her husband to the king on two occasions, which showed me how devoted she was.

If you could somehow travel through time and meet Cecily Neville in person, what would you want to ask her?

Who would you like to see play you in the movie? Seriously, I would like to ask her how, after giving birth to thirteen children without benefit of twenty-first-century hygiene and medical knowledge, her body held up until she was eighty. She had those children in a period of sixteen years, from age twenty-five to forty-one. Our daughters give birth to two or three children these days in their thirties, and we think it's a huge deal! I'd also like to thank her for living such an incredibly dramatic and rich life that lent itself so perfectly to an historical novel.

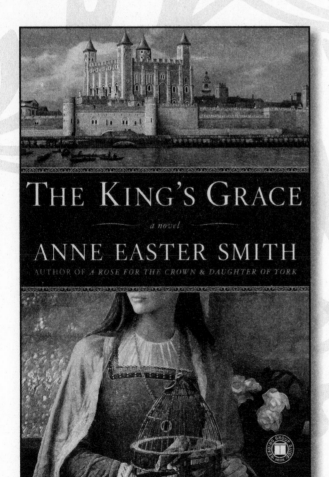